Blood Alley

Goathorn Peninsula

Fursey Island

Green Island

"Othniel" Oyster Farm

Moorings

Brownsea Island looking South

Author – JACK DURHAM
Text copyright ©2017 Alan Turner

Foreword;

The cover of this book shows a very unusual aerial view of Poole Harbour and the Sandbanks Peninsula, especially focussing on Brownsea Island, where the action begins.
To the left side, opposite the large island (Brownsea) is a spit of land jutting into the harbour. This is Goathorn Peninsula where consequences begin to unfold.
"Blood Alley" although not appearing on current maps, is a locally known stretch of water running from the very narrow harbour entrance at the Haven Ferry, all the way past the Southern side of Brownsea Island.
It derives the name from the number of very desperate and bloody battles along this stretch of water during the 18th and 19th centuries, fought by the authorities against the smugglers who frequented Poole Harbour. Many lives were lost during this period. The ochre-coloured sand of the sea-bed caused by the clay found around the harbour, adds to the intriguing name.
This work focuses once again on Alex Vail who has now been made Detective Chief Inspector and his working partner Detective Sergeant Anna Jenkins. With their team, they investigate the discovery of a body on a small beach on Goathorn Peninsula. Events lead to discoveries and action in and around Poole Harbour and along the coast towards Southampton, as well as across the Channel to France.
The places and descriptions are accurate. The reader is invited to check the veracity should they be so inclined.

Any references to characters are purely coincidental and are completely fictitious.

Contents

CHAPTER 1

'What a bloody cockup! Two murders and no arrest. Alex, I thought you would do better than that. What the hell happened?'

'It appears that both the double murderer and the drug dealer drowned in the middle of the Channel. A floating body was spotted by a small freighter roughly on the course between Caen and Christchurch, about halfway across the 150-mile distance.'

'And was a boat found?'

'Only some odd debris; bits and pieces, but nothing that could prove anything.'

Recently promoted DCI Alex Vail was in the office of the Detective Chief Superintendent James Gordon; a sixty-year-old and dour Scot, who had come up through the ranks of police in his home town of Glasgow, many years ago. Although he had been long in the South of England, he had kept his rather gruff and broad Scottish accent. After moving down to London and following a six-year stint there, he had relocated to Bournemouth Police where he was now in charge of all the CID departments with an overview of strategy and operational policy.

Alex knew that he had been in line for a big bollocking over the failure to catch the unknown "George" who they were convinced had killed two people, and then escaped to France with an accomplice. He had been thinking over the course of events leading up to the final dénouement and had come to the realisation that there had been some serious mistakes made in the final processes of the investigation.

DCS Gordon was not at all pleased with the way things had turned out and Alex had not been looking forward at all to this mornings' meeting to explain the lack of finality. He actually thought quite highly of Gordon as he had served his time in the lower ranks and had been promoted through ability and experience, rather than the more recent "fast track" promotions from college or university graduates, who had more experience with exams than what Alex thought of as "proper police work."

'So run through exactly what happened and why no-one was caught. I thought you had surveillance and they were there waiting to be arrested.'

'They were there in the buildings and it looks as though the two of them made a getaway down the river at night in a high-powered boat.'

'Right under your noses, yes?'

'It looks like it.'

'But you were there, so why the hell didn't you see them?'

'It was dark, and we didn't have a good view of the river from where we had the cars.'

'"It was dark." What sort of an excuse is that? Did it not occur to you laddie, that they might make a getaway by boat?'

'Well yes, as they had taken boats before and we think the first body was dumped from a boat taken from the premises, but to be honest, we just didn't have the manpower to cover all the possible places they could have gone.'

'Don't give me that. Let me put you in the picture laddie; you say that they were on the River Stour at Tuckton, is that right?'

'Yes.'

'You must realise that I've been here long enough to know that if they used a boat they would have to go through the harbour entrance, called the 'Run' isn't it at Mudeford? Why the hell didn't you have someone there?'

'We had the RNLI watch officer keeping a lookout, but I guess he doesn't work all night.' Alex knew that this wasn't quite true and he could feel himself reddening, although he hoped like hell that it didn't show. He knew that he should have had a watch put on all the likely places and it would have been simple to ask for a local constable to be on watch overnight, but he was convinced that they would take the suspects at the auction buildings without too much trouble. How wrong he was.

'Okay, so what you're trying to say is that lack of manpower led to this balls-up and you didn't have the foresight to locate a surveillance car on the quay, keeping watch, is that right son?'

'Basically, yes. We had all the information necessary to make the arrest, the drugs connection to France, the circumstantial evidence and the CCTV recordings, but in the end, they just slipped away in the dark.'

'And it didn't occur to you that they might use the river again to get away at some point? Well, I can tell you laddie, that this will not go down well on your record, so you had better tie up the loose ends of this case good and proper. Make them stick, d'you hear?'

'Yes.'

'Do you have all the necessary documentation to follow the other prosecutions through?'

'Yes, we have the evidence relating to the art fraud and the involvement of the gallery owner and her previous husband together with his son. Unfortunately, the son was one of the two lost in the Channel. We believe he was also closely involved in the drugs connection leading to the first murder of his girlfriend but that's going to be a little hard to prove now.'

'A little hard; I'd say it was bloody impossible, wouldn't you?'

'Yes.'

'And how about the lassie in the gallery, did you manage to prosecute her?'

'We did but she only got a suspended sentence due to the lack of hard evidence.'

'And how about the Turkish woman who did the copying?'

It was really obvious to Alex that DCS Gordon had been going through all the details and there were no unchecked corners.

'She was not prosecuted, as what she was doing was not illegal and there was nothing connecting her to the carrying's-on of the others.'

'So, all in all, not something you'd want to do in the same way again, eh?'

'No.'

'Right, now piss off and listen to me, now you've been made up to DCI, you'd better get your next case right, or your promotion won't last long and that's no threat, just reality.'

Alex made a quite disconsolate exit.

*

Alex Vail was the then DI who had been in SIO of the investigation into the torture and death of Yaren Ganim, an art gallery assistant from Turkey whose body was found on a small island in Christchurch Harbour. Following events which included copies of major artworks, having been sold purporting to be originals for very high sums of money, another murder was carried out. It was believed by the killer of Yaren, and to have been that of Jason Chandler who was connected to the dumping of her body in the harbour. It was very likely that he was killed by the man only known as 'George' after that murder had taken place; Jason knew too much and therefore was of no further use to the callous killer. Subsequent investigations had followed his movements and he was traced back to the Marine Auction premises where all the relevant actions had taken place. There was another possible source of information and that was the Italian Mafia 'Don' who had received the copied painting instead of the original. The rest, as they say, is history, although this course of enquiry was thought to be a rather 'lost cause', as getting information from that source was going to prove very difficult, to say the least.

*

Alex went back to his office at Bournemouth Police HQ and called in to see his working partner, DS Anna Jenkins. They had worked closely on the case and now they were both working under a cloud as no arrests had been made even though they had made every effort to bring the case to a satisfactory conclusion.

'How did it go guv?'

'Not well Anna. I think "Rembrandt" is going to watch me like a hawk and he made it clear that my promotion is not watertight.'

'"Rembrandt," is that the Chief Supers' nickname then?'

'That's what the lads call him, but not to his face I'll bet.'

'But why "Rembrandt?"'

'Because his favourite saying is "let me put you in the picture, laddie".'

Anna had to have a little giggle at that. 'I think I'll have to keep that to myself. So what do we have now guv?'

Alex and Anna had a private liaison going on outside work which was kept very quiet and no-one knew that they had been on a few dates and spent a number of evenings at each others' flats, and that's the way they preferred things to stay. They had to be extremely careful and circumspect about their situation and it was difficult in the extreme to keep their private and professional lives emotionally separate.

'We've nothing on at the moment Anna, except the usual run of petty burglaries, break-ins, and larceny, but I dare say that something will happen soon, so be ready to get everything right when the "you know what hits the you know what".'

CHAPTER 2

It was Late August and the weather was warm but not exactly hot, just a very agreeable temperature with little wind. Two National Trust wardens were in a Toyota RAV4 patrolling the beach on the Studland Peninsula. This part of the coast around Poole is particularly beautiful and is a well-protected Nature Reserve, owned by the National Trust. The part of the beach which they were patrolling was on the Poole Harbour side of the peninsula. The driver was named Peter Westlake, and was the National Trust Warden with John Raynes, his colleague, who was new to the job and being "shown the ropes" by Peter. John had joined the Warden Patrol only very recently, although he had been with the National Trust for a number of years.

Peter was in his mid 30's and was around five foot eleven with short brown hair and clean shaven. He had a pleasant personality and a keen sense of humour. In contrast, John wore a black beard and was a slimmer build although around the same height. He also had a thatch of curly black hair and his sense of humour was very dry.

They were making, what was for Peter, a routine trip around the various seemingly inaccessible places where the shoreline was full of complicated little inlets. Because of the proximity of the oil wells which form part of the Wytch Farm Oil Field and the larger and deeper, Sherwood Oilfield stretching some 6 kilometres seaward from Poole, they were tasked to check the roads and access points to the shoreline as a precautionary routine. They had driven along the narrow access road past Goathorn Farm and were making their way to the small beach area on the Goathorn Plantation, where they passed one of the oil wells and would continue on to the Goathorn Pier intending to stop to have a break and a coffee from their thermos. The actual well-heads were almost invisible from the road as they were effectively screened by trees.

'Okay John, we'll just take a little detour and check out the high water line along this part of the beach as it's sandy and we sometimes get bits of driftwood and other stuff that just shouldn't be here.'

'I've seen some of the stuff that just ends up in the most unusual places and it can be very dangerous to the wildlife.'

'You're right mate; at least if we spot it we can do something about it. As you can see from how difficult the access is, stuff can be left here for quite a while where it can do some real harm and very few people get this far into Studland, so it's good that we can at least check some of it. Anyway, it's a bit of fun to drive along the beach for a change.'

'Actually Pete, I'm quite surprised how some of the flotsam gets here because the tidal flow doesn't really get here does it? I mean, it's quite off the beaten track.'

'Surprisingly, sometimes when the tidal flow is quite strong and the wind in a certain direction, you would be amazed at some of the things I've seen. The channels play a big part too, as they twist and turn around the small islands in the bay and these cause weird currents.'

'Does Brownsea Island affect things much then?'

'Oh yes, Brownsea Island being just after the entrance to the harbour makes the tidal flow split and this makes a very complicated flow pattern.'

'How long have you been a Warden, Peter?'

'About six years and I just love the job. I get to see a lot of the Studland Peninsula that most trippers never get to see. Most of them come here for a day out and stay on the seaward side on Studland Bay.'

'Oh, they'll be the nudists then?'

'That's right, and I've seen some amazing sights I can tell you. I have to patrol that section sometimes, especially if there are any problems.'

'What sort of problems do you mean? Surely, there can't be too many of those, I mean everyone is there just to do what comes naturally, aren't they?'

'Exactly, and some of them do too much of what comes naturally if you know what I mean, and that's definitely not allowed. If we get a call from control about someone who has seen something dodgy and reported it, we get tasked to try to locate the "problem" and give advice or warning, whichever is applicable.' Thankfully, we very rarely have to call for police assistance, although it has been known.

'I suppose you must see quite a bit if you're driving along the beach there.'

'One certainly does, but I can't complain. Sometimes the sights are good; but believe me sometimes they are not so good.'

John gave a chuckle and said, 'Seeing some of the tourists, I can believe that.'

'Unless you've actually seen them, you really can't believe it, trust me. There are those who just really don't care how they look, but then, it's up to them and that's how they are, so they just get on with their lives. Fine by me; mind you, there was one funny story recently, which actually happened last summer.'

'Go on then.'

'Well, you know the long path from the main road down to the naturist beach, that sandy track?'

'Yes, it's quite a long hike actually, isn't it?'

'On a hot day, yes, over a mile I think. Well, a couple and their two kids, they would have been around nine or ten years old so, I believe, were making their way to the beach. Hubby was carrying a heavy ice box with all their picnic food, and in his other hand, what was apparently a quite large box with the plates and stuff. On his shoulder, he had two camping chairs and a windbreak in a shoulder sling.'

'Not much gear then?'

'Well, you can imagine what it must have been like as I understand it was a very hot midsummer day, well into the 80's. Anyway, they had got almost to the dunes just behind the beach and the wife saw this bloke walking towards them, stark naked. Well, she screamed and told the kids not to look; but of course, they did.'

'Oops.'

'Yep. The man said to the naturist, "Hey, what's your game mate? I've got me kids here and the wife is very embarrassed. You should be ashamed," and the wife said, "It's disgusting!"'

'They were all very hot, especially the husband who has all this stuff wrapped around him. The naturist says to the man, "Well you do know that there are about two or three hundred other people dressed like me just over the sand dune there, don't you? This is a naturist beach"

'"What!" says the husband, "bugger this, we can't go there, we'll have to go back, Its bloody miles. Come on Mavis, this bloke says the beach is full of people with no clothes on. It's not bloody right, come on kids."'

'And with that, they turned back, kids yelling and not at all happy, to go all the way back. He was sweating under his load to begin with so what he must have been like when he got back to his car is anyone's guess.'

'So was the nudist someone you know then?'

'Yes; it was me.'

They both had a good chuckle.

By this time, they were on the road along Goathorn Plantation and Peter said, we'll just go along the beach here and then we can stop at the jetty right on the point and have a break.'

'Good idea Pete, I could do with a drink.'

'Right, let's get on to the beach,' and he turned the 4x4 onto the sandy beach area. They were just above the high tide mark and the sand was quite soft, but the wide tyres of the vehicle made sure that they did not sink in.

'I understand that the sand is very soft around here Peter?' said John.

'Yes, it can be, but I don't know if you noticed it, but this little baby is fitted with very wide tyres to overcome that, especially as the sand on the dunes is very dry and very soft, but here the sand is wet and can be soft in a different way.'

'Yes, I did think they were wider than usual and I can see why you say the sand on this beach is certainly not like the dune sand,' he said, hanging out of the window and looking down. 'It's very patchy.'

'There are some places that have really soft stuff and you can sink in quite a bit if you're not careful.'

'Is that where the colour changes, does that you give an indication then?'

'Yes, there's some over there, can you see how it is darker than the other parts?'

'Yes.'

'It's all to do with the way the tide brings silt and deposits it at different places like over there towards 'Brands Point'.' He pointed towards the small headland opposite the beach they were on. 'Sometimes the silt is quite black but I don't know why; all I know is that it can be very soft and if you try to walk in it, you'll go up to your knees in soft sticky muck. And there's another place just around the end of Goathorn Point, called "Drove Island," but the local name is "Green Island." The channel runs around the Point and this is what brings the silt on the incoming tide.'

'I suppose we should try to avoid those areas, but I can see that sometimes they're not easy to spot.'

'Yeah, I realised just how nasty this stuff can be when I was over at Rockley Sands a few years ago, with a girlfriend. We'd waded into the water and were going for a swim, but before we had a chance to get deep enough, we both were almost dragged down and we got stuck in this horrible silt. It was like a very sticky mud and we both had a heck of a job to get out and back to the beach. It took ages to clean the stuff off.'

'Sounds nasty,' said John.

As he said this, there was a sort of 'squelchy' feeling as one side of the vehicle seemed to move differently.

'Is that a soft spot then Pete?'

'It could have been, but somehow it didn't seem right to me. I wonder what that was; I must admit I was looking towards Brands Point. I'll just have a look.' Pulling up, he opened the door and got out of the vehicle.

John said, 'I'll take a look as well, so's I know what to look out for.'

They both walked the short way back to where the strange vehicle movement had occurred.

They saw what looked to be a body almost buried in the sand. They had run over this and it was this which had felt so strange and "squelchy," as Peter was to later report.

'Christ Almighty,' said Peter. 'I should have seen that.'

'I'm not surprised you didn't Pete, it's almost invisible, with only his back showing and the shirt is almost a sandy colour. It's obvious now, but it could have been just some flotsam.'

'You say "his back" John. Are we sure it's a bloke?'

'Well, yes, I think so, judging by the size and shape of the shoulders and the short hair.'

'Do you think he has washed up here?'

'I would think that is highly unlikely as the tide rise and fall here is quite low, but as I said before, there can be some strange tide and current combinations, so it is possible, but we'll have to report this as soon as possible and the police will find out more. We can do nothing to help the poor sod but we'll have to stay here until "plod" arrives'.

'Of course; shall I get the coffee out then?'

'I suppose so, but it's a hell of a way to have a break isn't it John?'

Peter called into Control on the radio and made his report giving the location details.

"Warden Westlake to Control."

"Control receiving. Come in Peter"

'Control, we are on the beach on Goathorn Peninsula, We have just run over a body'.

"'What? You've just run somebody over?"

"Sorry, Control, we've just run some-body over! I should have said that it was almost buried in the silt and we were looking towards "Redhorn Point." We just didn't see it and ran over the body.'

"'Bloody Hell, Peter - do you have any idea of sex?"

'It doesn't look like it but I couldn't say if he's had any as he's almost buried,' he said, trying not to grin.

"That's not funny Peter. Just give me your GPS coordinates and I'll pass these to the police."

'Sorry. It looks like a man. We're on the Goathorn Plantation and the small beach about half a mile back from the landing stage at Goathorn Point.' Peter passed the GPS information to Control.

"Received, Warden Westlake. Information is being passed to Bournemouth Police immediately. This message timed at 10.15 a.m. July 15th. I'll call you back with their E.T.A." This was said with a very officious sounding attitude.

"Thanks Control - Westlake out."

Peter turned to John saying, 'I don't think I made a good impression there. Let's just take a look without touching anything to see what we can see, if you get my meaning.'

'Well, we can't really see much can we? I mean he's almost completely buried'

'Believe me John; I had no intention of touching him.'

'I wonder how he died.'

'If, he died?'

'Yeah, maybe it was suicide or worse and if he's been there for a while I'm not surprised that he felt "squelchy."

'Thanks for that John. I don't suppose we can tell anything from what we can see here, so I think we'll just get back in the motor and have a coffee, what do you think?'

'It's better than looking at the body, that's for sure.'

'I'll just pull over to block the road in case someone wants to come and take a look.'

'Like there are queues of cars waiting to come and see.'

'Just following procedure John; all part of your learning curve, you know, doing things the correct way.'

'I know. It's just that you can't get many occurrences like these can you?'

'Too right my lad. This will do me for a while, I can tell you.'

 Peter positioned their vehicle to make sure that no-one could come onto the beach, should they just happen to come along.

CHAPTER 3

Police HQ at Bournemouth, received a call from the National Trust control office at Sandbanks. The information received was routed through various departments and finally, the message arrived at the desk of Detective Chief Inspector Alex Vail. He read the words on the pad and called out to his partner, Detective Sergeant Anna Jenkins.

'Anna, you know I said we should be ready when the "you know what," hits the "you know what?"'

'Yes.'

'Well, it just has. We've got another one.'

Anna was in the office next to his and she called out, 'Another what?'

'Another body.'

'Oh no; I thought we'd finished with that. Our last episode didn't end too well did it? So where's this one then?'

'Over at Goathorn point, but I don't suppose you know that do you?'

'I've never heard of it guv, but I guess it must be on our patch somewhere.'

'It is. I'll show you on a map if you'll come in here and stop shouting to me.'

'Coming guv,' she shouted.

Anna walked into his office and smiled at him. Alex smiled back and said, 'It's always good to see you. I like it better than talking through walls.'

'So come on then where was it found?'

'The story is that two beach wardens were patrolling on the Goathorn Peninsula, that's where some of the oil wells are, and there is a small beach just here, look.' He was pointing to a large map of the area which showed the whole of Bournemouth and Poole, from New Milton in the east to Wareham to the west of Poole and included Poole Harbour.

Pointing at the map, he said, 'This is Goathorn Point and here is a landing stage right at the end. Can you see that just here is a small beach, indicating the sandy strip along the peninsula about half a mile from the landing stage?

'Apparently, they were driving along the beach itself just checking the foreshore as they do, and they said they were both looking over towards Brands Point, and ran over the body that was almost buried in the sand; just didn't see it.'

'I suppose we must go and take a look guv?'

'We must. Are you ready to go now?'

'I've nothing that can't wait so, yes, but how do we get there, it looks to be quite difficult from the map detail.'

'We'll get the Landrover "Defender" from the pool, rather than have to go down the little tracks and get stuck.'

'Okey dokey guv, ready when you are. I quite fancy a trip over to Studland.'

'This is not a fun trip Anna.'

'I know, but it's better than sitting here gawping at a computer screen for hours, 'innit'?'

'Behave yourself.'

''Yes guv.'

'Come on then.'

They made their way down to the parking area where all the pool vehicles were kept and Alex went over to the officer in charge of the various vehicles which were on the strength of the Bournemouth Police. They had a various selection of types of vehicles as their remit covered a very diverse spread of possible terrain and there were many places where a normal car just would not be suitable.

'Hello John', he said to John Metcalfe the OC Car Pool. 'Can we take the Defender? We have to go over to Goathorn Point to check out a body?'

'No problem Alex, there's no claim booked, so it's all yours. Do you have any idea how long you'll be?'

''Nope; we'll have to cross on the ferry at Sandbanks, so how long that's going to take with all the holiday traffic queuing up I can't guess.'

'Why don't you use the "blues and two's?"'

'Now, now John, you know that's not on the cards. This is not an emergency.'

'I would have thought that it could well be as you don't want holidaymakers to go plodding around with a corpse on the beach.'

'I don't think there'll be many people wandering around that beach do you, over at Goathorn?'

'No, I s'pose not.'

'By the way John, can you keep this to yourself, I don't want the "Echo" to get wind of this or those slimy little gits will be out there looking for something to put in tonight's rag.'

'Right'o Alex. No problem. "Mum's the word."'

'It'll get us to the head of the queue at the ferry won't it?' suggested Anna. 'The "Blues and Two's" I mean.'

'I suppose it won't do any harm then, as we're protecting the public from an "'orrible" spectacle.'

'That's my boy,' said John, looking across at Anna with a big smile.

'We'll need all the usual crime scene stuff, won't we guv?'

'Indeed we will Anna. Can you make sure we have wellies, as I happen to know that some of the beach areas have horrible silty stuff and it'll really mess up your shoes?'

'Thanks for the warning. I'll pop down to the stores and get all the stuff I think we'll need. I guess you'll let the others know what and where we're going?'

'Right, I'll tell Tom and Alice what's up and we can get off.'

Alex walked through to the main office where DC's Tom Peterson and Alice Compton were working on their routine investigative tasks. There were other DC's on the team and everyone had day to day tasks and reports to finalise.

'Listen up people. We have a report of a body which has been found almost buried on a beach over on Goathorn Plantation.'

'Isn't that where Wytch Farm oil wells are?' said Tom.

'Yep, but we have no indication at the moment as to any connection with that but its early days. I'll let you know as soon as I have more information.'

Alex went down to the parking area and the Landrover "Defender."

As Alex and Anna left, Tom said to Alice, 'All right for some, gadding off on a "jolly."

'Stop being so grumpy Tom, someone's died, have some respect.'

'Yeah, s'pose you're right.'

Having collected all the equipment for crime scene initial inspection, they got into the Landrover.

Alex said, 'The wardens gave us the GPS coordinates, so I'll just enter these on the SatNav.' He put in the reference details – Latitude 50.675440 – Longitude 1.979908. He looked at Anna saying, 'That should get us right to the spot. I know the area, but this place is quite new to me, so it's as well we have these details, saves us getting lost on Goathorn.'

Setting off, Anna said, 'It's nice to be out with you again Alex, it's been a while since it's been just the two of us and no interference.'

'I know, I was thinking the same thing exactly. Mind you, we're back in the "rut" again, with a murder, or should I say a "suspected murder," as we haven't seen the body yet, so we can't make any assumptions.'

'It does take the edge off things a bit, I have to admit. Still, some time is always welcome, with just the two of us.'

'We'll have to have another date soon; I've been working too hard to make up ground to "Rembrandt" after the fiasco at the Marine Auctions.'

'I know he blames us Alex, but we couldn't have eyes everywhere could we?'

'But I should have covered that point where the boat might have been seen slipping out of the harbour. I really dropped a big one on that.'

'There were so many aspects to that case, what with Mark and his father, Olivia Harrington-Thorpe, Yaren's killer and the other guy, Jason wasn't it? Then there was Marks friend; not to mention all the art 'copy' fraud with the gallery and then the drugs over at Caen. It's hardly surprising that things came a bit unglued at the end.'

'I suppose it was a bit complicated, but we should have seen it coming. Mind you, at least the killer got 'his', didn't he? I mean, two murders and heaven knows how many more he'd done, with his Mafia connections.'

'I don't think we'll ever know will we Alex?'

'I'm sure that's right, but we may get something from the Italian connection, although I very much doubt it, given that he is Mafia. They keep everything very close don't they?'

'That's in the past, so let's get on with this one. Who knows where it's going to lead?'

They drove down the A338 and took a left turn at Westbourne. By taking some of the back roads as a shortcut to Canford Cliffs Road and then via Haven Road they were able to miss most of the holiday traffic as they went down Banks Road and approached the Sandbanks chain ferry which would take them across to Sandbanks Beach and the Studland Peninsula. Passing the Rick Stein seafood restaurant and about to take the left fork to the one-way system, they encountered the traffic queue for the ferry. This was something of a regular problem, especially for the residents in Sandbanks.

Alex said, 'I bet they don't take kindly to people blocking their driveways.'

He was referring to the occupiers of the large and opulent houses on this particular part of the South Coast. Here, the houses would fetch almost unbelievable prices as property values were among the highest in Western Europe and unsurprisingly, these people would expect everything to be the way 'they' wanted it.

'Do you know what Alex, I don't care. Let them wait. I think it's more important that people have a good holiday. These people can afford to go somewhere else and good riddance, they've got too much money already.'

'Did you know that Harry Redknap lived here, but I guess you don't like people like footballers and suchlike, living in these places.'

'Harry Redknap, I'm sorry, but who the hell is he?'

'He's a football manager, quite famous.'

'Huh, footballers. I certainly don't. They're overpaid, they act like they're something special and I think they certainly don't "earn" their money, and they prance about with their stupid haircuts, kissing and hugging each other if a goal is actually scored.'

'Wow, I think I'd better stay clear of that subject, don't you?'

With that, the traffic queue was solid, so Alex said, 'Okay, here we go', and switched on the "blues and two's." The cars were mostly on the left hand side of the road which made things easier for them to make their way along the queue. However, there was a car which was on the right hand lane which was blocking their way. The driver seemed not to have heard the en and just sat there, apparently oblivious. In fact, he was talking on his mobile phone and paid no attention to what was occurring behind him. Alex said, 'Just look at this prat; is he deaf or what?' Pulling right up to the car, he said, 'Give him a blast Anna.' She gave a quick pulse of the siren. Being really close to the car in front, the driver almost jumped out of his seat, turned round and finally saw the police vehicle. He hastily threw his phone down and drove up onto the pavement to make way for the Defender.

'Pillock - I wish I could nick him, but we don't have time.' The police lights made absolutely sure that they went straight to the head of the queue for the ferry. As they got to the ferry slipway, it was evident that they would not have too much of a wait as it was just about to dock and let the traffic disembark.

They waited until the ferry was almost cleared of cars and the deckhand waved them onto the front of the boat, ready to clear the ramp as quickly as possible as soon as they landed at the far slipway.

The ferry soon got under way and Alex and Anna stood at the rail, looking at the craft which was either sailing or under power, entering or leaving the harbour.

'Did you ask the two wardens to stay with their vehicle Alex?'

'Yes, they weren't too pleased, but they understand the situation and that it involves a crime scene.'

As they crossed the fairly narrow channel, Alex said, 'Do you know that the water here is around 60 feet deep?'

'No, but that seems very deep for a narrow bit of water.'

'That's because all the water from Poole Harbour rushes through here as the tides rises and fall and it scours the sea-bed. The current here can be quite fierce and I understand that when the wind and tide are in opposition, the waves can be quite dangerous for small boats.'

'I can see that there are loads of boats whizzing about now. Some of them are quite big and fast aren't they?'

'They are, and sometimes we've had to deal with people who have a damn great cruiser but who don't have qualifications for navigating such boats and very often they seem to rely on electronics. They've more money than sense and when that goes wrong they have no idea what to do and then they yell for help and expect others like the RNLI to come to their rescue. It's all wrong, they should be qualified.'

'Just send them a bill for the rescue services and so on; they'll soon learn their lesson.'
'You don't take prisoners, do you Anna?'

CHAPTER 4

Leaving the ferry, with all the gawping holidaymakers who had been craning their necks to see what the Police vehicle was doing and wondering what was going on, Alex and Anna then drove along the straight section of Ferry Road leading to the Goathorn Peninsula. As the road took a wide turn to the left, Alex said, 'There's a sharp turn back off to the right just up ahead and this leads us to Goathorn. There should be a big five-bar gate with a smaller one beside it. I don't think many people go that way as it is just a sandy track, more for bikers than cars but it takes us to where we have to go.

Going through the smaller gate, they carried on, reaching a group of what looked like farm buildings and then took a left turn and then a right. The sandy track was easy to negotiate in their vehicle and very soon they were on a firmer surface.
'This looks as though it was for heavier traffic,' said Anna.
'Quite right, this would have been made better for the oil-field traffic I think.'
'Well, I know that there are oil-wells on this part of the harbour Alex but I can't see any. Where are they?'
'You won't see them. They're all very well hidden behind specially planted trees. In fact, now it's almost a forest and they really hide any oil-well buildings and pumps. At one time, when they were actually drilling the wells, you could see the derricks but even then they were not obvious. You'd never know just how many well-head sites there are around here.
Now they're simply invisible unless you are flying around up there,' he said pointing to the sky.
'I wish,' Anna said, 'one day I'll go flying again, I hope.'
'So you've been up there then?'
'I went up with a boyfriend once, and the pilot let me take the controls for a while. That was one hell of a 'buzz'. I really enjoyed it and it was a beautiful day and the views just took your breath away. Have you flown Alex?'
'Many, many years ago something happened which I'll never forget. My Mum and Dad were with me - it wasn't long before he died actually, and there were "pleasure flights" in a helicopter over Poole Harbour. My Dad didn't want to go but Mum was really up for it!'
'How old was your mum then?'
'She would have been in her late 60's I guess, because Dad died just 2 years after he retired and they were similar ages. I still miss him terribly after all this time.'
'So your Mum went up in the helicopter. Did you go too?'
'Oh yes. I'd been up a couple of other times before and I just love it.'
'So, did your mum like it then?'
'Let me put it this way; Mum was in one of the rear seats and I was in the front with my camera. The pilot asked me if I wanted to take any special shots as this was his last flight of the day. I told him that I'd a friend who had a new sailing boat moored in the marina, so he said, "This is my last flight of the day, so let's go and take some photos of it."
We flew over the marina and I took some shots of this big new boat and then the pilot said, "I feel like doing something a bit different, I've bored silly flying round and round the harbour all day. Are you game for something a bit special?" 'I said; go for it and I'll never forget what he did next.'
'Go on then, what was it?'
'He said right, hang on tight – and flew to the centre of the harbour, which as you know is quite big, and then he put on full power and bugger me, he did what I am sure was, or at least felt like, a complete "loop" and then dived down quite low to the water. I think my stomach only caught up when we landed and I was so impressed with that. It was only when we got back to level flight, that I suddenly realised that my Mum was in the back that I thought she might have been terrified.'
'And was she?'
'You must be joking! I turned round and looked at her and she had a smile on her face like a bloody "Cheshire Cat!" She absolutely loved it, and she said to the pilot, "can we do that again?" When we landed, my dad told us that he'd watched the whole thing and he'd nearly had a heart attack on the spot. Mum was ecstatic and I had never realised

that she like anything as daring as that. On the way home, she told me that she was always up for the rollercoaster and things like that when she was young, but these days I never get a chance.'

'That sounds like it made her day, that's for sure.'

'Yes, I'll always treasure that experience.'

By this time, they had almost arrived at the point where the SatNav GPS position indicated and Alex slowed down so that they did not miss the partially obscured opening to the beach where Peter and John were waiting with their vehicle.

Their Landrover was actually quite visible as it had been parked at an angle to the beach to deter any possible intrusion to the scene.

Alex pulled up and he and Anna got out and made their way over to where Peter and John were now standing.

'DCI Alex Vail,' he said extending his hand to Peter.

'Peter Westlake. I'm the National Trust Beach Warden and this is my colleague John Raynes.'

Alex then looked over to Anna who took the offered hand of Peter and said, 'DS Anna Jenkins.' John did the same and gave Anna a very long warm look which said volumes to Anna. Alex was watching this exchange and he noticed the look which made him a little uneasy. 'I think I'll keep an eye on this one', he thought.

'So what do we have then chaps, can you tell me exactly what happened?'

Peter then began to explain the series of events leading up to the present situation. 'I'd just decided to take a very small detour onto the beach to check it out for any debris which might have been washed up and would cause a danger to wildlife. I was looking over towards Redhorn Point, that's where loads of clay and chalk was dumped many years ago, so I wasn't looking at where I was driving to be honest, and I felt something weird. I stopped and we both got out as I thought it might have been some of that sticky, silty stuff which we can get around here. That's when we both saw the body.'

'Shall we take a look then?'

They all walked the little way to where the body was almost buried. It was face down, and obviously male.

'I think we can be sure that he's male, don't you think Anna?'

'From the size of his shoulders and what I can see of the body, I think that must be definite Alex.'

'That's what we thought,' said Peter.

'I guess that you two guys are a bit fed up with sitting here twiddling your thumbs waiting for us to turn up, so I think there's not much more we need you for, so if you'd like to go, I'm sure you'd like to get back to your base.'

Peter looked at John and they both nodded. 'Yes, thanks, that would be great. We've seen enough and I'm sure you will take care of everything now.'

'Okay, Peter, John, thanks for taking care of the site. I know you've not gone walking around and spoilt any possible tracks and so on, so thanks again and we'll contact you both later for a formal statement if that's okay.'

'Absolutely; good to meet you both and good luck with the investigation. If there's anything we can tell you or you have any questions, don't hesitate to give us a call via our control. They'll have our locations and contact details.'

'Great stuff, thanks again, 'bi for now.'

Peter and John got back into their vehicle and as they turned their vehicle and were about to leave, Alex went over to the drivers' window. Peter opened this and Alex said, 'Just one other thing. Can you keep this quiet, for now anyway, as we don't want a horde of rubberneckers or even worse, reporters, around here?'

'Of course, we understand.'

'Thanks, 'bye again.'

With that, they drove off.

'Anna asked, shall I get some "crime" tape and put up a cordon around this area?'

'Yes, please, although I don't suppose we'll have to keep crowds at bay, do you?'

'Hardly.' Anna took a roll of crime scene tape from the rear of the Landrover and began to put up a cordon. This was not easy as there were very few places to which she could tie the tape, so she looked around and found a few sticks of the right length to form something to attach the tape to and with a little ingenuity, she was making a good job of enclosing the area.

'I don't know who that is going to stop, but at least we're following "procedure,"' she said.

'I know, it seems a little useless, but if we don't, I'm sure it'll come back to bite me if everything is not done "by the book," Anna.'

While she was finishing off the cordon, Alex was looking carefully at the corpse and making notes about the position and aspect, what clothes he was wearing and any other what he thought were salient points.

Anna came over with a camera and took various photographs to cover all the aspects of the untouched, what they thought might well be a "crime scene."

'I can see some tyre tracks just past the body Alex, should I take shots of them as well?'

'Yes, I think you'd better although I know SOCO will do all this when they get here but just to make sure in case the tide comes in and washes anything away, we're covered aren't we?'

'Alex, have we asked SOCO to attend?'

'Oh shit! No, I should have asked them a while ago and I was so busy telling you my story, I forgot. I'll do it now. Making the call, the response was that they would come over as soon as they could. 'They'll probably have to stay here until after dark and they'll be hopping mad about that. What are your observations about the body so far then Anna?'

She walked over and had a much closer look.

After a few minutes of close scrutiny, she put her thoughts into words. 'For a start I don't think it was a suicide, looking at the stab wounds. I think the body was put here after death and not washed in by the tide. For another thing, I don't think the tide is high enough, looking at the line of weed and the high-water mark, to have brought a body here and positioned him like this. I can see some tyre tracks which aren't those of the National Trust vehicle as it was nowhere near where they'd parked. In fact, it looks as they reversed from where they'd stopped after running over the body, so someone else has been on this little piece of beach with another vehicle.'

'That is bloody impressive Anna. We'll make a detective of you yet.'

'Cheeky sod,' she said, with a grin.

'No, seriously, good work. You are obviously very observant.'

'To look is to know,' she said.

'I like that, Anna.'

'Let's take a look at what we can see without disturbing the body. If we touch anything, SOCO will have our guts for garters.'

Alex bent down and examined, as best he could, the arms and upper torso. It was evident that there were knife wounds on the side of his neck and some bloodstains where it appeared there were slits in the shirt along his sides.

'I reckon he has multiple stab wounds and I'm sure there are more bruises to the torso, but of course as he's face down we can't see those. It's pretty obvious he was murdered but whether he was dead before he was dumped or buried here I can't tell. That's for our "tekkie" lads to tell us.'

'I'm sure we'll know a lot more when George Matthews over at the morgue has had a look at him.

'One thing I'm pretty sure of, like you Anna, and that's the body was put here after death. I think he could have been brought here in a vehicle and someone has made an effort to bury him. Now, either they made a poor job of this, maybe they were disturbed, or if he was only buried very shallow, maybe the tide has just washed the sand and silt away from him, leaving the body uncovered as we see now.'

'Do you think the forensic bods will be able to tell what vehicle it was, from those tracks over there?'

'I don't know if they'll be able to tell us exactly but they'll have a pretty good idea. I've known them come back with some incredible details in the past, so let's hope they can give us some good information sooner rather than later. I'd really like to get things off to a good start here.'

'I suppose you've got some "brownie points" to make up Alex?'

'Yes, I bloody well have,' he said with feeling.

'How about the clothing, surely that will give us some information. I know it looks pretty standard stuff to me, you know, jeans, shirt and so on, but I know forensics can come up with some amazing details.'

'I certainly hope so, because from what I can see, it all looks quite ordinary, though one thing we haven't even mentioned yet Anna, is where did he come from and why was he killed?'

'That's two things. I don't think we have any idea, do we?'

'By the cringe, you're quick,' he said with just a hint of sarcasm.

'So were you,' she said, with a very cheeky smile.

'Will you stop that? You're going to get me going again.'

'Well, I was hoping to, sometime.'

'Anna, behave yourself!'

CHAPTER 5

The SOCO team had arrived in an unmarked white van and Alex asked them to park a little "out of sight" on the road just behind the beach. 'Just in case we have an influx of tourists,' he said with a grin.
A burly man about six foot got out of the van and came over to Alex. 'Hi, I'm Roger Peterson, head of this team. There we have the other two muppets, Rachel Myers,' he said pointing to an attractive woman of about 30. 'She's the good looking one apart from me, and just heaving his body out of the van is Ron Jackson, he's the intelligent one, but for Christ's sake don't tell him.'

Alex introduced himself and Anna to the team. They all struggled to dress themselves in the required paper coveralls and moved over to the body. 'I hope you plods haven't been stomping all over the scene then,' said Roger. 'No, I didn't think you would,' he said without waiting for an answer.

Taking the other two officers to view the body, he asked Alex and Anna to keep back while they made the initial inspection. Just standing and taking a general look at the body, he turned back and said with a straight face, 'He must have fallen from a plane, judging by the "face-plant" he's made!'
This made them all have a chuckle.
Anna said 'Seriously?' keeping as straight-faced as possible.
Rachel said, 'You've got competition in the "irony stakes" there Rog.'
'Touché,' agreed Roger.

The rather "black humour"' tended to be prevalent around murder and death. It was their way of handling bad scenarios and some of the things that the police had to deal with, had caused a number of their colleagues to succumb to problems exacerbated by such occasions.

'Okay, team, let's get to work. The light's going to be fading soon and I for one don't really fancy being stuck out here with all those scary oil-wells pumping away.'
'Do you mean that we won't be out here all night in this place that's like the end of the known world then Fuller, with the strong possibility of an oil leak which would not be something I'd like?'
'Oh shut up, you oaf. Just get your gadgets and get to work. You think too much Ron.'
'Are you always like this with each other then Roger?' asked Anna.
'Pretty much; it keeps reality at bay sometimes.'

They proceeded to carry out their investigation and both Alex and Anna stood watching for a while, eventually saying, 'If you don't need us anymore, we'll scoot off, unless there's anything you can tell us now.'
'Not really, you can see all there is to see right now and anything we find will be in our report tomorrow, but hey, just make sure you arrange for a lowly "plod" to be stationed here until the coroner has collected "Sonny Jim" here. Then we can all go home.'

'Consider it done Roger. Come on Anna, we need some food, I'm starving.'
As they were about to drive off, Roger shouted over, 'Don't forget to call the Duty Doctor to confirm death.'

'Oh bugger,' exclaimed Alex, 'can you believe this Anna, we have to have a doctor attend to confirm the actual death, even though it's pretty obvious he's been here for some time?'
'Do we have to wait for him?'
'I don't think so, as long as SOCO are here.'
" I don't suppose this place has seen so much action for a while.'
'I'm sure you're right sergeant.'

Alex called the station on his mobile and made the necessary arrangements for a Constable to be stationed at the scene for as long as necessary and also contacted the Coroner for the body collection, as well as for the Duty Doctor to attend. 'Maybe he can give us a rough idea of how long "chummy" has been dead and when he might have been dumped here. Probably a "long-shot" though; still, it's worth asking him I suppose.'

'Oh well, we just have to stay here until the local plod gets here and then we can buzz off and get something to eat. I'm famished already.'
'I never thought about how long we might be here or we could have bought some sandwiches or something on the way,' said Anna.
'Can't be helped; we live but never learn, do we?'

Anna and Alex were resigned to the wait for the local constable and watched the SOCO team go about their work. They could see just how meticulous they were, inspecting everything in great detail.
At one point, Ron Jackson called over to them; 'Thought you guys were off, but seeing as how you just can't keep away, this might interest you.'
'What's that Ron,' asked Alex.
'Cigarette butt – unusual - not from the UK,' replied Ron.
Rachel had heard this exchange and looked over to Anna and Alex and said, with a smile, 'Ron's known for his short sentences, but he's clever with it.'
Anna ventured, 'Sounds like he'd make a good criminal then, they like short sentences.'
Rachel appreciated that. 'Nice one, Anna.'
'How do you know that?' asked Alex.
'Because the banding around the filter is not a type I've ever seen before. Not on an English cigarette. We'll have to check the database back at the station. There we've a whole inventory of different brands and their characteristics. That should tell us a lot about whoever was here smoking one of these; bit of DNA if we're lucky.' He was holding up a cigarette end with the filter attached, in his gloved hand, with a pair of forceps about to put it into a small evidence bag.
'That's probably the most he's spoken for weeks,' said Roger.

'Is there anything else that you've found that could give us any clues?' Alex asked this with a degree of hope in his voice.
'Not at the moment, old son,' said Roger. 'We'll let you know.'
'Appreciate that Ron, or we'll go mad sitting here doing nothing, dehydrating.'
'We've got some coffee-making stuff over in the van. You're welcome, help yourselves.'
Why didn't he tell us before, thought Alex?
'You're a very nice SOCO, said Anna. Thanks.'
'We think so,' said Rachel, 'and he's big and cuddly, like a teddy bear.'
'Does he know that you think of him like that?' Alex said quietly.
'I don't know, but he won't mind. He's great to work with.'
Anna replied, 'I know someone like that, but I can't tell him.' She gave Alex a sly but dead-pan look.
Walking over to the SOCO van, they made a couple of cups of very welcome coffee.

As he was quite local, it wasn't long before the Duty Doctor arrived. He very quickly officially confirmed death and he asked the SOCO team if they had finished enough of their work to allow him to move the body for further examination before completing the death certificate.
'Yes, we've done all we can do without looking under the body, so you carry on and we'll have a short break while you do the necessary.'

'Thanks, if I can ask you to give me a hand to turn him over, I can carry on from there.'

Roger and the doctor, with Ron's help, turned the body over.

They all looked at the exposed front of the body and just looked at each other, saying nothing.

The male corpse was wearing a sandy coloured shirt, with the sleeves rolled up to the elbows. The back of the shirt which was on view whilst the body was face-down, was quite unmarked, except for the tyre marks. There were a few bruises visible on the forearms, but as the body was now exposed to the front as he lay on his back, it became obvious as to the cause of death.

'Bloody hell!' exclaimed Alex - 'what do you make of that?'

'Shit!' said Roger, 'Looks like he's been slashed to ribbons, as well as being beaten to a pulp.'

Rachel just looked shocked.

His throat had been cut right round the neck. The bloodstained shirt had been ripped and there were several deep cuts, probably caused by a knife or something bigger, across the chest and stomach area, almost covered by the sliced open shirt.

They all stood and looked at each other, quite lost for words.

'What do you make of that Doctor?' said Alex.

'Apart from the rather obvious cause of death, being the cuts to the neck, slicing the carotid artery, I would say that the large knife wounds were made either just before or just after death. We won't know this until autopsy, but I have to say that it looks like a "frenzied" attack to me.

Anna was looking quite shocked, saying 'I've seen some bad things recently and we can become a little hardened to seeing sights like this, but this is pretty gruesome, I have to say.' In fact, she was feeling quite nauseous, if she were honest, but she was determined not to let it get the better of her.

'Are you okay Anna?' asked Alex, looking quite worried.

'I'm fine guv, thanks but I'll just walk around a little if I may?'

'Of course, just take a walk and get some sea air. It'll make you feel better. It's a bloody awful sight when you realise what someone has done to him.'

Anna turned and walked away for a short distance, grateful that Alex had shown concern for her.

The doctor came over and asked Alex if he was the Senior Investigating Officer on this enquiry.

'I guess I will be when I get back to the station as we were only told that body had been found, so a formal criminal investigation will be confirmed; so I imagine the short answer is 'yes'.

'In that case, I can confirm to you the actual death and the cause of death as severe knife wounds to the neck, torso chest, together with the ancillary heavy bruising to the arms and upper body. The time of death will have to be determined at autopsy and the pathologist will let you know this when he's concluded his examination. However, I would also suggest that the initial cause of death would have been the throat being cut, but also the very deep knife wounds to the lower chest and upper stomach area. I would even suggest from what I have seen is that they could have been caused by a machete type blade.'

'Something like they use in the jungle then?'

'Not necessarily. In fact, I have one myself at home which I use for gardening. It is about two feet long with a slightly curved blade. If this were used against someone, it would inflict a very deep and serious cut; enough to sever some vital organs. Once again, to be verified at post mortem

'Are there any signs of strangulation or maybe blows to the head?'

'No signs apparent on the neck, but again perhaps there was strangulation but without the obvious signs. If the hyoid bone is broken, subcutaneously, then this would confirm strangulation, once again, at autopsy. As for blows to the head, none that are immediately obvious, although as there are some bruise marks on the skull, it is possible that he could have been beaten around the head with something which does not bruise but inflicts damage to the brain. Something like a heavy bar encased in soft rubber.'

'Would that be a possible cause of death?'

'I rather doubt that but it would certainly cause severe damage to the brain and maybe a haematoma of some sort, leading to brain damage and worse, certainly unconsciousness at the time.'

'It sounds as though this poor guy had a pretty rough time at the hands of someone very sadistic, to put it mildly.'

'Indeed.'

'One last thing, doctor, can you give any indication of how long he has been dead?'

'Only as a rough guess from what I have seen and that would be around two to three days. More than that I cannot and will not say.'

'Okay, that's absolutely fine. Thanks, doctor.'

'If that's it, I'll be off then; "had to bloody come, but it's messed up my afternoon now," not too happy but having no choice as the duty doctor.

Alex had seen the coroner arrive in the black van whilst he had been speaking to the doctor.

'We'll carry on here to see the body removed and thanks for your time and observations.'

The doctor left for the return drive to the ferry and back to his normal routine as the coroner walked over to the site.

Anna had returned looking a good deal better for her stroll away from the view of the body with the huge knife wounds to the torso.

'Are you feeling better Anna?'

'Yes, thanks Alex,' she said quietly, grateful for the break. 'The coroner arrived quickly didn't he?'

'I think they must have been local, so they'll have to ferry it back to Bournemouth Morgue.'

The coroner asked the SOCO team if they had finished their work and they asked for another perhaps half an hour to complete their examinations and take all the photographs.

They were also carefully searching the surrounding area, collecting any possible small items that could help either identify the body or lead to whoever brought the body to this location.

Alex said to Anna, 'I think we'll come back tomorrow and have a closer look at the surroundings here. There might be some clues as to how the body was brought here, or who brought it.

There are a couple of buildings right at the end of this road. They're about half a kilometre up nearly on the jetty. Perhaps they might give us some idea of the "comings and goings" around here.'

'Right'o guv. We'll be able to take our time and have a good look around. We need some clues, don't we?'

'We do Anna, we certainly do.'

They returned to the Police Headquarters in Bournemouth.

Completing their work the coroner and his assistant brought a gurney down to the small beach with some difficulty. After placing the corpse in a black body-bag and lifting this to the gurney, they had to actually lift and carry this due to the softness of the sand in the area, eventually managing to move it up to the road where the van was parked.

After the exertion of this, the coroner's assistant said, 'Maybe we should have backed the van down to the beach and this would've been a lot easier.'

'I don't think so sunshine', was the coroner's reply, ''cos I think we'd still be here. Our van isn't equipped for soft sand and we would've probably been stuck.'

'I think you're right,' said Roger, who'd seen the struggles they'd had with the body on the gurney.

'Your van would sink into this stuff, so it's better the way you did it.'

The whole scene was then cleared of any traces of their presence and both the coroner's vehicle and the SOCO Team made their goodbyes and set off back on their respective return trips.

CHAPTER 6

Alex called Anna into his office. 'Hi Anna, just to let you know that DCI Gordon has made me SIO on this one and made it very clear that he wants "no cock-ups."'

'Were you the Senior Investigating Officer on the last case though guv?'

'Yes, but let's face it, I didn't make much of a job of it, did I?'

'But the truth was, we just didn't have the manpower to watch everywhere, did we?'

'DCI Gordon doesn't take excuses, though; so Anna, can you call your friendly pathologist, George Matthews, wasn't it?'

'I suppose you want the autopsy report then?'

'Yes please. I know you've a good rapport with him as I believe you know him from your previous duties.'

'I'll give him a call but I doubt whether he can tell us much yet.'

'Okay, just see what first impressions he can give you then.'

'Right, I'll see what he has to say.'

Anna called George Matthews, the Post Mortem Pathologist who handled the Yaren Ganim murder case. 'Mornin' George; Anna here. How're things down in morgueland?'

'Hello Anna. I'm fine but it's pretty dead down here, as usual.'

Now that's what I call a dry sense of humour, thought Anna. 'Nice to hear from you, how are you?'

'Good thanks George, but we could have done without another murder, especially one like this.'

'I hear your boss didn't get too good a session with DCI Gordon.'

The grapevine was working well, as usual. 'No, he didn't. Things didn't go too well finalising that investigation.'

'So what was the outcome then?'

'Well, it turned out that the main suspect and the murdered girls' boyfriend, who was also involved with the disposal of the body as well as many other things, were both drowned as they tried to get over to France. A load of money was lost as well and the boat they were on sunk.'

'Oh dear not much evidence to go on then?'

'No, so that is why Alex, my boss, wants to get this new investigation nailed down as soon as he can, to get back into his boss's good books. He needs some brownie points.'

'I can understand that Anna, although I don't have much for you at the moment, except for one thing which might help a little.'

'Anything would be appreciated.'

'Well, apart from the very deep knife wounds which most certainly were inflicted by something like a machete or very large knife, it would have been the cut to the throat which would have been the death cut.

'Anything else?'

'Just that the knife used was very sharp. The cut to the neck was very clean and I'd say that it would be been just one swift slicing cut which almost severed the thorax. There is one other thing; that the shirt he was wearing came from somewhere in Poole.'

'What? How the hell do you know that?'

'Because in one of the pockets, there was a receipt, barely legible I have to say, for a shirt paid for about a week ago from a shop in Poole.'

'But that could have been for any shirt couldn't it?'

'Except that this ticket actually had the description which I would think tallies with the shirt he had on. The colour was described and the size, together with the price. I would think it would be quite easy to verify this with one of the shops who would sell this type of shirt in the area.'

'So, no idea of the shop then?'

'No, 'fraid not, that was unreadable but perhaps the boffins could make something more, we'll have to see.'

'We'll get them onto it as soon as possible; it'll move things on for sure. Anyway George, you are a star, thanks. Can you give me a fuller report on the injuries and so on as soon as you can, there's a love?'

'Of course Anna, I'm always pleased to help you, you know that. You are a very pleasant person to deal with.'

'Thanks George, you're my favourite mortician too.'

'Go on, you smoothie. I'll give you as much as I can as soon as I can.'

'Thanks again. See you soon, 'Bye.'

''Bye Anna.'

She went back to see Alex, to give him this little titbit of news. 'It seems that this victim bought the shirt he was wearing, around a week ago from a shop in Poole. The ticket details which George found in a pocket tallies with the shirt as far as he can see and with any luck, we should be able to track the shop down pretty quickly.'

'But doesn't the ticket usually give the shop name?'

'Yes, but in this case, it wasn't readable; but the forensic guys might be able to come up with something in the meantime if we can get it to them.'

'That gives us something to be going on with, I suppose, but it's not much. Still, we never know, it might just lead somewhere. We'll have some photos of his face when it's cleaned up, maybe we can show these round to the shops and someone might remember or even recognise him.'

'One other thing George said is that the knife used to cut the throat was very sharp. Don't fishermen have very sharp knives?' Don't they gut fish and they'd have a very sharp knife? I know whenever I've had to fillet a fish to prepare a meal, the skin is a devil of a job to cut and you have to be very careful.'

'Now that is a very good point Anna, well worth considering, and hereabouts we have plenty of fishermen don't we? Good thinking. All we need is a fisherman. Shouldn't be too hard to find,' he said with just a little possible irony.

'Maybe someone who is just a very experienced fisherman?'

Alex asked his team, consisting of DC's Tom Peterson and Alice Compton to come into his office to join him and Anna for a quick early briefing.

When they were all there, Alex began. 'Okay, what little we have at the moment is this; body found face down on a small beach on the Goathorn Plantation at Studland peninsula, partially buried in the soft sand. He was wearing a "sandy coloured" shirt, sleeves rolled up, and ordinary blue jeans. He had trainers on which looked quite unexceptional. '

'What was the cause of death?' said Tom, 'was it drowning?'

'The actual cause of death is, as yet, unconfirmed, but the throat was cut very deeply, severing the Carotid artery and his thorax as well. There were several very long and deep cuts with a "machete-like" knife. Oh, and he was badly beaten as well.'

'He didn't have a good day then,' said Tom.

This drew a very disgusted look from Alice.

'Right,' Alex continued, 'we know from a ticket found in a pocket, that the shirt he was wearing was bought from a shop in Poole, around a week ago. Unfortunately, the shop name was unreadable. At the moment, that's about all we have and we expect to have a photograph of his face as soon as it's been cleaned up. We can do a quick scan of the likely shops in Poole given that they should have till records. Our only hope at the moment is that someone will or might recognise him from that picture. We need a name, or nationality, age, address, known associates, movements recently and any connections we can make.'

'Struth guv, you don't want much do you?' said Tom.

'You're a detective Tom, so go to it and dig out as much information as you possibly can. I need to know who this chap was, where did he come from, why was he killed and everything we can get.'

'Okay, guv, I understand. We'll do our best and get a good start on this one. With any luck we'll know what he had for breakfast.'

Chuckles from the others.

'Good lad Tom. I'm expecting great things of all of you. We have to make up a lot of ground as I'm sure you're well aware, so do your best please.'

'We will,' ventured Alice. I'll make sure that we both do our best for you.'

'That goes for all of us guv,' said Anna.

'Thanks, guys and gals, let's get to it.'

CHAPTER 7

There was a call from George Matthews with some more results from the autopsy. He was put through to DS Anna Jenkins by the duty sergeant.

'Mornin' Anna. I've got a few more details for you if you're ready for them.'

'Hi George, yes, please. What have you got, anything interesting or stuff that will give us some real information?'

'I don't know just how much this will mean, but I know that a cigarette butt was found which didn't seem to be English, and that's with Forensics I understand, but this chap was not from around here, that's for sure.'

'So what do you think any idea where he might be from?'

'He has fairly dark skin, "olive" complexion I guess, so he could be from Italy or Romania or anywhere in Eastern Europe, it's very hard to be sure until we get some DNA testing done, then we can narrow this down. He was between 40 and 45 years old, quite fit and did some manual work as his hands were quite "work hardened." He weighed 15 stone, so he was well built and quite muscular. I wouldn't like to guess what sort of work he did, but I'm sure that detailed investigation of things like dirt from under fingernails and ingrained "stuff" in his skin will render some clues. He was 5ft11 tall. He was wearing trainers but they look pretty standard to me.

'Before I forget, George, can you clean up his face, you know, get the mud off and pretty him up, so that you can get a decent photo of him that we can show around? We might get lucky and find someone who recognises him, you never know. And while you're at it, perhaps a photo of the trainers, which can help sometimes too.'

'Your wish is my command, oh gorgeous one. I should have a photo within the hour.'

Anna ignored that, but inwardly she liked compliments although preferring them from Alex, who was appreciably younger than George.

'Thanks for that and I suppose you can't hazard a guess at what sort of work George?' asked Anna.

'You'll be asking me for his name soon, my dear. I know I'm good, but I'm not that good – yet.'

'I'm sorry George,' Anna said, with a chuckle, 'it's just that we need all the help we can get right now.'

'I understand, and I'll get a full Post Mortem report to you very soon, I promise. What I can say is that the knife inflicted wounds would have killed him as some of the cuts had severed arteries, and in fact, one had actually cut through bone.'

'That must mean that the cut was administered with quite some force, doesn't it?'

'Indeed, it would have been. I would suggest that whoever did this was either very angry, or very strong.'

'Just a thought George, were there any restraint marks on the body? I mean I don't suppose this guy was just standing there, waiting to be cut down.'

'We're in the middle of checking for those and I think there could well be some restraint marks on the torso, but to be honest, at the moment, there are so many heavy bruises which could easily mask bonding, that it could be a while before we know for sure.'

'Okay George, I totally understand and thanks for this information. I'll pass it on to Alex and we can begin to build up a picture of this man, although we've no idea where he came from or how he got there. '

'One thing's for sure, Anna, he didn't walk there.'

'Christ, you're so cheerful George.'

'I know; it's what keeps me sane love. Better go, I've bodies to cut up.'

'You're a ghoul! 'Bi George.'

'Oh, by the way, we'll have toxicology fairly soon as they're not too busy right now - Bi Anna.'

'Thanks again, 'bye.'

Returning to seek Alex out, she had time to get herself a coffee from the new machine they had "clubbed together" to buy. This was to replace the old and grotty one which appeared to have been in the station "canteen" since Noah was a lad. This one was the type which used the "pod" system and made a really nice cup which actually tasted like coffee and not over-roasted acorns.

Her thinking was that this has improved efficiency and co-operation. The "Feel-Good" factor certainly seemed to have taken a step in the right direction.

Taking a few minutes to herself, she was considering how she might approach Alex about a further "date" and perhaps inviting him to her flat and cook him a meal. Their previous meeting had gone really well when he cooked "Turkey Saltimbocca" for her and made a really good job of it as well; much to her surprise. They had a really pleasant evening and spent the night together - and that part went really, really well. Now she wanted more and had come to realise that Alex was a person she really thought she could become very "close" to. We shall see, she thought. Anyway, I can ask him - I don't think he'll say no.

Alex was finishing up some paperwork relating to other cases which he was working on. These were the mundane jobs, which follow any routine crime investigations; such things as burglaries, car thefts, and similar day-to-day occurrences. These are the "run-of-the-mill" crimes which happen and keep the police of any large town or city fully occupied.

Anna knocked on his door, and he said: 'It's open, come in.'

Anna shut the door before saying, 'A little more info from George, Alex. This man was quite muscular, around 40 to 45 and 5ft 11' – His hands were what George described as "workers hands" as they were quite hardened. He thinks that the knife wounds, which were very deep and in themselves could have caused death, were made by someone who was very angry. Some even sliced through bone and thinks that the blade could be either large butcher's knife or even a garden machete blade. Toxicology shouldn't be too long as they don't seem to be too busy at the moment.'

'One thing's for sure, that there would have been a lot of blood wherever this was done to him.'

'That's for sure I would think. Maybe we'll find somewhere, but later on.'

'This is good Anna; we are making a little headway. We should have the picture soon, shouldn't we?'

'He said within the hour, but knowing George, it'll be here sooner rather than later.'

'Good. And another good thing is that you shut the door behind you, we don't want the troops to hear you calling me "Alex," or they might get suspicious.'

'I'm very aware of that, and I am very careful. While I'm here, can I ask you if you'd like to come over to my place soon; I'll cook us a meal and we can see what happens.'

'Hey, that's terrific, I'd love to come over, in fact, I've been hoping like mad that we could get together again soon if only to put the recent events behind us and have some personal "quiet time."'

'That's great. Just let me know what day would be good for you and I'll do the rest.'

'Will do,' she said giving Alex a very warm smile and went out to do some more investigating.

CHAPTER 8

Some more information was coming through from the Forensics Department. The cigarette butt found at the scene proved to be a Turkish brand. They had taken some DNA from the filter tip which remained and this had shown that the smoker was of Turkish descent. Whether this was the body or possibly someone who had placed the body, was not known at this time. The tyre tracks found near the corpse were from a "quad" bike, but because the tyres were not very specific, they did not reveal anything really interesting. The trainers he was wearing were of a type which would be traceable through the database of trainer soles. This was a very comprehensive list covering almost every trainer made in the world, so identification was almost certain to be possible. Traces of oil were found under the fingernails and these were currently being tested and analysed, the results of which were imminent. More testing was ongoing, but for now, Anna was happy to receive the photograph of the unknown victim. His face had been "cleaned up" and made to look as "normal" as possible. His expression was, of necessity, one of blankness, but it was certainly good enough for someone to recognise him. Good use had been made of "Photoshop" to give him the colour of life rather than the pallor of death. Anna called Tom and Alice to her desk.

'Okay people, this is our man. Both of you can get over to Poole, I suggest starting in the town centre, and show this to any, in fact all shops which sell men's shirts to see if anyone remembers him. He bought the shirt that he was wearing very recently, so there is a fairly good chance that he might have been noticed by a sales assistant.'

'Right,' said Tom, 'we're on it. This photo is quite good and he should be easily recognisable. If only we knew the shop, it would be a great help, but this will give us a good start.'

Alice, who was looking quite "quizzical," said, 'I don't suppose there is anything on the sales slip which has a code or a serial number of some sort?'

'What sort of code do you mean Alice?'

'Well, it might have a special code or reference number on the slip which identifies the machine or shop which printed the slip.'

'That's a very good point Alice. Can you get on to George over at the Mortuary? He'll be conducting the Post Mortem as we speak, so just ask him if this ticket has anything like that on it. That would be magic if it did.'

Phoning George to see if he could just look at the ticket to see what could be made out.

'I know that the name of the shop was unreadable George, but we thought that there might be a "machine code" or something which identifies the shop or credit card machine account.'

'I'll have a look Alice, but I don't hold out much hope. This guy had no wallet on his body, so we can't go back and check his recent transactions. Anyway, I'll have a look and get back to you as soon as I can.'

'Thanks George.'

Alice came back to Anna's desk and said, 'Okay, let's get over to Poole and start looking. George doesn't think they'll be anything, but he'll let me know if there is. There's no point in waiting around here, so we'd better get over there.'

'Thanks Alice, Tom; best of luck. If we get a result, it'll make Alex's day I know.'

'It'll make ours too, to get a good lead so early; fingers crossed,' said Tom.

With that, they both left in a pool car to go over to Poole to begin their "shop to shop" questioning.

Anna popped her head round Alex's door and asked, 'didn't you say something about some buildings just "up the road" from where the body was found? Do you think we should check these out? There may be something there which may help things along, you know, perhaps someone knew him or has seen him around.'

'Good point Anna; I think we should go there 'PDQ' and take a look. Isn't there something about "quad bike" tyre tracks as well?'

'Yes. Perhaps someone up there knows someone, seen someone or even heard someone on a quad bike.'

'Right, let's go over there and take a look at those buildings. Mind you, it's a bit of a "slog" to get there isn't it?'

'It is,' she said with a slight frown, which was, in fact, her being "thoughtful," 'I was thinking about this as we came back from the crime scene the other day. I had a look at the map again and it occurred to me that a quicker way might be to cross the harbour by boat. Could we get to Goathorn Point jetty by boat? Is the water deep enough?'

'I believe so,' said Alex, also looking thoughtful. 'We could check with the Harbour Master, I forget his name now, and he would know if it's possible, I'm sure they most have boats flitting about the harbour.

'But how do we get a boat to take us?' Anna thought that her idea was sinking fast.

'Aha, now, I know that Dorset Police has a Marine Section and it's just recently been "saved" from cutbacks and now it has a link with the Poole Harbour Commissioners. I think they have boats "available" but I've no idea how we go about getting the use of one. I think your idea of crossing to Goathorn is a good one, so perhaps you could get in touch with the Harbourmaster to get some idea of how and when we could use a boat. This would help us to keep our mileage down as well as time saved in an "ongoing murder enquiry." You could stress this point; it may help.'

'I'll give him a ring right away.'

'No, I think a "face to face" might be more productive Anna, especially with your face.'

'Flatterer.' Anna was pleased at this, and she was more than happy to go over to Poole Harbour to garner some help with their possibly "numerous" trips over to Goathorn. They really had no idea how many times they might have to visit the crime scene. Sometimes it could be necessary to visit such places perhaps ten times, over the course of an investigation.

CHAPTER 9

Anna made her way to Poole harbour and sought the Harbour Master's Office. Entering the reception area, she asked, 'Would it be possible to have a short meeting with the Harbour Master please?'

'May I ask who you are and why you'd like to see him?'

'I'm so sorry I should have mentioned that my boss DCI Alex Vail was here before, quite recently in fact.' Showing her warrant card, she said, 'I am DS Anna Jenkins from the Bournemouth Police. I need to seek his help with occasional transport across the harbour, in connection with an on-going investigation.'

'I'm sure that that will be possible DS Jenkins. If you'd like to wait here for a few moments I'll give him a call and see if he's free at the moment.'

'Thank you.' Anna took the chance, while the receptionist was making the call, to look around the office. There were many framed photographs of vessels, some quite large, around the walls. There were also many certificates, relating to officers credentials and similar credits.

Just then, there was a deep voice which seemed to come from a long way down in someone's chest – 'Good morning, DS Jenkins.'

He held out his hand. 'Fuller Masterson; Harbour Master. I do remember a visit from your boss. I was wondering how the investigation which he was working on came out. Did you get the culprits; I heard that they were making a "dash" across the channel apparently?'

'Hello,' replied Anna, taking the offered hand; warm and strong but not squeezing hers. What an interesting name, "Fuller" she thought. 'No, unfortunately for our investigation, the boat which they were on was lost somewhere around the middle of the Channel between Christchurch and Caen. Some floating debris was spotted which confirmed that it had come from the boat they were using but no bodies were found, so we lost both suspects. We've no idea what caused the boat to sink, we can only guess.'

'I suppose there could be a number of explanations as sometimes mysterious things happen to boats out there and without evidence and no boat, as you say, you can only make guesses.'

'Do you think that perhaps their boat had either hit or been hit by another?'

'That is always a possibility and to be honest, if a small boat gets in the way of a much larger one, it is quite possible that it would never be noticed if they had not been spotted. However, how can we help you today, do you have another suspicious death to investigate?'

'Unfortunately, we do. A body was discovered on a small section of beach over at Goathorn Plantation and we have no idea as to how it came to be there, or who may have put it there.'

'I know that you had a strange find over in Christchurch Harbour, something about a 'Blue Moon Island' wasn't it?'

'Indeed, we did. The body was discovered there on a small island which only appears, 'Once in a Blue Moon', according to the locals.'

'I know that happens over there, due to the very unusual tidal conditions in that area, all thanks to the Isle of Wight, which gives four tides a day rather than the usual two. But, I digress; forgive me, you have obviously pressing enquiries to make. How can we help you now?'

Anna was more relaxed now as this man was extremely pleasant and congenial, even though he must have a great responsibility and workload to match. She thought, I'd just better ask him straight out. 'Because our crime scene is right out at the tip of Goathorn Peninsula, our trip time for each visit, plus the inconvenience of crossing over the ferry to Studland, together with the inherent fuel cost, makes our investigation very protracted.'

He broke in, 'So what you're really asking me is for a lift across the harbour to Goathorn when you need to get over there, is that it?'

'Yes, I'm sorry to be asking this, but it would save us a great deal of time and expense and actually really help to move the investigation on; that is of course, if you have any ideas.'

'Hmm, I think we may be able to help you a little, although I don't know how many times we could spare a small boat to take you over there. Would they need to wait for you? I mean, would you be long or would you need to have the boat return at some specified time?'

'I'm sorry to say but at the moment the short answer is, "we don't know." As things stand, the investigation is at a very early stage but we'll have a better idea when the autopsy and forensics are in. We don't even know who the deceased is or where he came from or how he got to where he was found.'

'So all in all, you really don't have a lot do you?'

'We don't, but we are doing all we can to get things moving.'

'I'm sure you are, Anna, may I call you Anna?' He said this with a pleasant smile.

'Of course.' She was really warming to this man who seemed genuinely pleased to help. She just hoped that he would come across with some maritime transport.

'Okay, here's what I can do for you. We have a couple of small boats which are used to "potter about the harbour" doing little jobs, you know, taking things about and doing odds and sods so that I'm sure we can fit in a little trip across the harbour now and again for you.'

'Thank you so much, Mr Masterson that will be most helpful of you and will certainly speed up our initial investigations.'

'I have to warn you though.'

"Oh oh," she thought, here comes the bad news.

'This has two conditions, one is that you call me Fuller; the other is that you keep me informed of your progress with the investigation. It is always good to know about some of the bad things that happen so that we are aware of the "less than appropriate" things that go on around my harbour and that knowledge can sometimes be preventative.'

Inwardly relaxing, she said, 'That's a very "far-sighted" approach, I must say. Of course, we can keep you informed as much as is legally possible and thank you once again for your help, Fuller, it will be most appreciated.'

'Right then, that's settled. All you need to do is give me a call to give the required times and so forth and we can arrange things accordingly. I'm sure my lads won't mind a bit in having a very attractive policewoman to ferry about.'

Anna blushed at this compliment, although secretly very pleased. She was very impressed with Fuller Masterson. He looked about 45 years old or so, had a good physique under his uniform and she already knew he had a very pleasant demeanour as well as being quite attractive.

She said her "goodbyes" and left his office feeling quite "buzzy" after her meeting. She knew that she would be more than happy to see him again. But then she thought, I really must put this out of my head as I know Alex is the one I really want to get to know better and to spend time with, even though this man is very appealing.

She was suddenly in somewhat of a quandary as she travelled back to the Bournemouth Police HQ to report back to Alex the results of her meeting with the Poole Harbourmaster. She was feeling quite "chirpy" after her meeting.

'Hi Anna, how did it go with the Harbourmaster?' asked Alex as she walked back into his office. '

'Super. He is such a lovely man and so helpful.'

'I thought you'd like him. When I saw him before on our "other" case, he gave me some good information and guidance. I learned things I didn't know about boats and tides and stuff like that. Mind you, I think I'll have to keep you away from him, 'cos he's a good looking bloke isn't he?'

'If you say so, I wasn't really thinking about that.'

'Come on, of course you were. You wouldn't be the person you are if you didn't find him attractive.'

'Well, yes, I suppose he is, but he's not for me.' Anna was beginning to blush and she was hoping that it wasn't showing because that might cause problems between her and Alex. She just didn't know if he was the jealous type or not. She was hoping like mad that he wasn't. 'You're my type Alex, as well you know.'

'Don't you worry, Anna, I'm not the jealous type, in case you were worrying, but believe me, I'd fight for you, tooth and nail.'

Now that made her very happy and she gave Alex a really great big smile. 'Thank you Alex.'

'Good, now that's out of the way, can we get some bloody work done?'

'Yes guv,' she said.

CHAPTER 10

'We should arrange a visit as soon as, don't you think?' Alex said, 'Mind you I think I'll give Mr Masterson a call, it's safer that way,' whilst giving Anna a sideways look with a "half-smile" on his face. Anna didn't know if he was serious or not, but she didn't question this.

He called and asked if they could have a boat this afternoon so that they could take a look at the crime scene again and also check on the buildings at the end of the Goathorn jetty.

A boat was arranged to be available at 2pm, so in the meantime, Alex called Tom on his TETRA digital radio to see if there was any progress on locating their victim. This high-tech system gave almost complete coverage and allowed the officers on duty, instant access to high-quality communications, wherever they may be, and they could be in touch whenever help might be needed and in any emergency situation. The TETRA or "Terrestrial Trunked Radio" was a very comprehensive system for communications between officers, such as a "walkie-talkie" as well as a "one-button" emergency call when such an occurrence is needed and operated just like a normal mobile phone for privacy. This meant that all officers when away from their station were able to access and relay information immediately. Alex was hoping that by now, either Tom or Alice had some news but so far, nothing had been received, which did not bode well for the investigation.

Alex put the call through to Tom 'Tom, what have you got? Have you had any luck so far; I've not heard from you? '

'No, nothing yet guv. Alice and I are working from different ends of the shopping area in Poole. It's quite big and takes quite some time to get to talk to the staff sometimes, but we're on it, full-time.'

'Okay then, I'll not bother you and I won't call Alice if you're having trouble in getting round to all the shops and assistants. Don't let them make you wait, just tell them it's an urgent investigation and make them co-operate.'

'Will do guv.'

Alex ended the call and turned to Anna. 'I'm just going to pop down to the canteen for a spot of lunch and then we can get over to Goathorn to see what we can see there, and take a look at the buildings. There may be someone working there who can give us something. Do you want to come with me?'

'No thanks guv, I've some shopping to do, so I'll meet you back here at 1.30 if that's okay, it'll give us time to get over to Poole harbour by 2pm.'

'Right, see you at half one.'

Anna went into the Burlington Arcade to have a look at the delicatessen then to see what there was on offer and to give her inspiration for the forthcoming meal she intended for them, although the date hadn't yet been decided. She thought she would ask him on their way over to Goathorn. She was really looking forward to another night with him after their previously successful evening.

At 1.30 pm Anna and Alex were ready to go to Poole Harbour for their "lift" across the stretch of water to Goathorn Jetty. They drove over to Poole Harbour and made their way to the Harbour Commissioners Office where they asked to see the harbourmaster, again.

'Hello again Alex, Fuller said, shaking hands. Turning to Anna, he said, 'And so nice to see you again Anna. Are you ready for your little trip?'

'We are,' replied Alex, who was keeping a watchful eye on Masterson, hopefully without him being aware of this. He was wrong.

'Okay then, I'll just give you the directions. I'd like to take you down to the slip myself, but unfortunately, there's a bit of a flap on regarding the Condor ferry coming in and I have to see to this.'

'Understandable,' said Alex, rather glad that he didn't have to "keep an eye" on Fuller any longer.

'If you turn left at the roundabout just outside these offices and keep going until you come to some big sheds; they're a horrible olive green colour, then turn right, that'll take you to the harbour marina. When you get there, ask anyone for Jack Sturney. He's as local as they come and you might find his accent a tad difficult, but he's a good chap and he'll stay with you until you're through this afternoon. I guess you won't be all afternoon will you?'

'No, I should think about an hour would be fine for now, if that's okay?'

'I think that'll be fine; old Jack is quite used to "hanging around."

'Thanks.'

They made their way following the directions, to the harbour marina. Asking for Jack Sturney, they were directed to a man who was sitting on a large bollard, smoking something which gave off a very strange aroma. As soon as he saw Alex and Anna walking towards him, he seemingly very quickly threw the cigarette he was smoking, over his shoulder into the water. Anna turned to Alex giving a very "knowing" look and said, 'I think I recognise that smell, don't you Alex? That's not your standard "baccy" I'll bet. It's a horrible smell; it makes me feel quite ill.'

'I think you are spot-on Anna, but let's not "let-on," we need his co-operation. Mind you, I expect he knows we're coppers so no wonder he ditched it quickly.'

They approached and Alex asked; 'Jack Sturney?'

'Aye, that'll be me then, zur. Be you the two police officers what do want to go over to Goat'orn, then? I be told by Mr Masterson that you do want me to take you both over to Goathorn an' wait around 'til you be finished whatever you be wantin' to do.'

'That's right. I don't think it's too far is it, I mean it's only straight across the harbour?'

'Well zur, you might be thinkin' it be straight across yon harbour, but you do 'ave to realise that in the way between here and Goat'orn Jetty, you have Brownsea Island see, then behind that, Furzey Island and just across from there, there be Green Island. All them islands do make it a little tricky for navigatin', if you do see what I means?'

'Why's that?' asked Anna.

'Well now missy, with all them islands, the water b'aint all that deep and we do 'ave to be right careful or we could get stuck on some of that there sand what this 'arbour is so full of.'

'But I'm sure you know all the little channels and turns here, like the back of your hand,' she said, with a disarming smile, thinking, "I know he's having us on, he's bound to know everything perfectly well."

'Since you might say that, I do have to tell 'ee what I do know this here water full well see, as I've been working on and around the 'arbour close on thirty year now, so like as not, I knows most places.'

Alex was thinking, "I'll bet he doesn't miss much that's going on locally. I wonder if he knows things which could help us." 'So you must know all that happens around the harbour then Jack?'

'I don't say that for certin sure, but not much 'appens around local like, what I don't get to know.'

'That knowledge could be very useful,' said Anna.

'Well, just do you ask me an' I'll tell 'ee what I knows 'bout what you do ask me.'

What did he just say, thought Alex, I'd hate to see his letters. 'Right then Jack, that sounds as though it might be very useful to us and when we have a question, we will ask.'

'Right you are zur, ask away when you be ready. Shall we be a'goin' then?'

'Yes, as soon as you are ready.'

'I be always ready to go on the water, mind, 'cos like I did say 'afore, we have to take a little twisty way through between these 'ere islands, so 'as we don't get stuck on the sand, see.'

'We quite understand Jack,' said Anna.

'You be good understandin' missy, thank 'ee.'

Alex was thinking, I guess he doesn't get to talk to many people during his day, so when he gets the chance, he goes into overdrive, this could take longer than we bargained for.

They boarded an "open" day boat. This was a quite large, wooden craft which looked very well used but at the same time extremely well maintained.

'Is this your boat Jack?' asked Alex.

'Aye, 'tis that zur. T'were my dad's afore me, so she's quite a good age now see.'

'I can see you really look after her, she is in good condition,' said Anna.

That pleased Jack and he smiled at Anna, showing a set of teeth that resembled the pilings of an old broken and rotting jetty.

As they motored out of the marina and headed towards Brownsea Island, Alex asked, 'Is she powered by a diesel engine Jack?'

'Aye that she be; tha' can tell by the slow revving and powerful sound, that she be, as well as the smell. There be no mistakin' the smell of a diesel engine. Very powerful and uses but a thimbleful of oil. Very econocomical she be.'

Actually, they were quite enjoying the trip with the motion of the boat causing a breeze of fresh cool air and very soon they had rounded Brownsea. 'Is that Furzey Island then Jack,' asked Anna, pointing to the low tree-filled island ahead.

'That it be little lady, and where be one of them oil-fields. They did find oil under this harbour and way beyond. Tis my understandin' that this here oil-field goes way deeper than what was found earlier and they do call it now the Sherwood oil-field. Tis said that they be pumping oil out for years an' years hence, 'tis my understandin'.'

'Incredible,' said Alex. This was as they were coming round the tip of Brownsea Island and in the channel by Furzey Island. 'Is the channel deep enough here, Jack?' he said.

Alex was wondering about the depth of channels and whether this had a bearing on the deposition of the body which was found in an area where it did not seem to have much depth.

'Aye, I'm thinking that there be enough water for us at the moment, but on the way back we'd best be careful as the tide be runnin', quick as you like, but we should be 'bout okay if'n we b'aint too long awaitin'.

'We'll be as quick as we can, don't worry.' Alex tried to re-assure Jack.

'Tidn't as I'll be a worryin',' Jack replied.

They rounded Furzey and followed the quite convoluted channel system duly arriving at Goathorn Point jetty.

During the approach to the jetty, Alex was looking around the immediate area surrounding the landing point. The trees around were mainly fir and pine and although the wooded area was could not be described as "thick", they did form an effective screen as it was almost impossible to see more than a couple of metres into the wooded area.

CHAPTER 11

As Jack brought the boat gently to the mooring point, there was a man waiting to take the mooring rope, which he expertly tied to a bollard with a "flick of the wrist."

They didn't expect to find anyone at the jetty, but it was going to be a help in trying to get information regarding the movements of people and possibly vehicles around the area.

Alex and Anna left the boat and told Jack that they would be back within the hour, and turned to the man on the jetty.

They introduced themselves and showed their warrant cards to this man, asking his name.

'My name is Bob Chorley,' he said. He was very "stocky" and about 5'6' with a muscular build. He was wearing a blue checked fleece "lumberjack" style shirt-jacket, worn outside his jeans. He had heavy work-boots on and he was clean-shaven with curly brown hair.

'You'll no doubt be aware of the body which was found yesterday, on the small beach about half a kilometre from here.'

'That's right. Strange that, don't know how he got there or who would do it. I work on the oil-field here on Goathorn, on shifts.'

'As you are here, you won't mind us asking you a few questions, as we'll be asking you anyway in the course of our investigations.'

'No, ask away,'

'Do you live here on the Plantation Bob, or do you live "on-shore" as you might say?'

'When I'm on shifts, I stay here in a little cabin on the site, but go home at week-ends.'

'Do you always work shifts Bob?' asked Anna.

'Sometimes we work "turn and turn about" shifts.'

'Can you explain that for me?'

'Yes, there are two of us on shifts as we have to be on "standby" at all times, so rather than being on shift continuously, we change over, usually after about two weeks, so we don't work nights all the time.'

'I see. I don't think I'd like to be stuck out here all night for too long,' said Anna.

'It's very quiet, only the gentle noise of the pumps, otherwise there's nothing to hear.'

'Do you know of anyone who has used or has access to a quad-bike here,' she asked.

Bob did seem to be a little "taken aback" by the sudden change of tack with that question, "I wonder why that caused him to pause?" thought Alex.

'I only know that there is a quad-bike stored in the shed just back there,' he said, indicating the large building about 50 metres from the jetty.

'And do you know who uses that building?' Asked Alex at the same time thinking, "why was he here if he works at the oil-field?"

'I only know that sometimes it's used by people who come to the jetty, and sometimes oil-field supplies are landed here. Perhaps they store stuff here, I don't know.'

Anna was also becoming just a little "uneasy" at Bob's replies. "If he works at the oil-field and they land supplies here, then surely he knows about the building and what's inside it."

'And what is your job on the oil-field Bob,' asked Anna.

'I look after the security and maintenance of the installation and make sure that the spillage bund is kept clear of any obstructions and things like that.'

'"Spillage bund," what is that, can you tell me?'

'Yes; if there should be any spillage or leakage from one of the pumps or for instance if a pipe should rupture, although that is incredibly unlikely, and an "oil-spillage" occurs, there is a ditch or "moat," that's called a "bund", round the complex which would contain any leakage until the well could be capped or shut down. But I should tell you that in all the time the wells have been operating and pumping oil, there has never been a leakage of any sort, but we have to be prepared for any eventuality. I also look after the general state of the pumping station; you know, check and maintain the pumps and machinery.'

'That must keep you quite busy I imagine,' ventured Alex.

'It does, although as everything is so well checked and maintained, quite often there is not much to do, so it's not a hard job although it does carry responsibility.'

'I'm sure it does,' said Anna. 'How long have you been working here?'

'I've been here for about three years now.'

'So you have not seen or heard anything unusual or "out of the ordinary" recently, something which seemed "odd" to you?'

'Nothing really,' and here again he paused slightly as though thinking. 'Although now you mention it, I did hear a motor the other evening. I thought it was a boat coming close to the jetty, but as I was quite a way from there it wasn't loud. I suppose it must have been quite close and not even a boat then because no boats get close to this part of the coast, only the jetty. You see the channel runs past the jetty but anywhere else is very shallow, I think it's too shallow for boats unless they're canoes.'

'So you thought it was a boat, but then you say it was too far away to be a boat. Do you still think it was a boat?'

'Actually, thinking about it, it could have been a quad bike, because they have a similar sound to a big outboard motor, so it could've been that.'

Alex found that very interesting, especially as Bob Chorley had said there was a quad bike kept in the building on the jetty. He turned to Anna with a definite "look" and said, 'Can you give our control a call and ask them who owns this building and who has the key to it?' She nodded her understanding and took out her handset. Alex turned back to Bob and said, 'Unless you know who this might be?'

He looked just a little unsure of himself. 'I can only tell you that I think it is owned by the oil company, but I'm not sure and I certainly don't know who has the keys.' Alex looked back to Anna who was hesitating to make the call. Nodding to her, she put a call to their control room and passed on the request.

'Thanks for your help Mr Chorley; we'll not keep you any longer.' He went off to speak with Jack Sturney, the boatman, whom Bob seemed to know quite well.

"I must ask Jack about Bob Chorley," thought Alex.

Anna had made the call and turned to Alex, saying 'Should we take another look at the crime scene, guv?'

'Good idea. You never know, there might be something which can give us an "overview" of how the body came to be partially buried. That's been bugging me since we first saw him lying there. I mean, why only partly bury him and not cover him completely so that he might not be found. In fact, why bury him at all if you don't care if he is found?'

'Perhaps whoever was burying him, was either interrupted or just changed their mind or maybe they just found it too difficult to dig in that sticky silt?'

'I think you may have just hit the nail on the head there,' exclaimed Alex. 'That muddy stuff must be hard to shovel out and not only that but where did whoever did dig the hole, put the stuff he took out?'

'Let's go and take a look then,' she said.

They both walked back along the road for what Alex estimated to be about a third of a mile, to where the opening onto the small beach was, that the two National Trust Wardens took their Land Rover and discovered the body by driving over it.

Walking onto the beach, they looked at the site which was still cordoned off with "POLICE" tape. The hole which had been dug for the body was evident, which meant that the tides had not been high enough to wash anything away. They both looked carefully at the tyre tracks which had gone beyond the body and Alex said, 'I don't think they are car tyre tracks. 'That's right, those tracks only go one way, so there must be another way off the beach a little further on. I'll just go and take a look.'

'Okay and I'll take a look to see if the "spoil" from digging the hole is evident anywhere.'

As Anna walked on along the beach, Alex was taking a look at the water in front of the burial hole was. As he looked into the shallow water, he could make out that there were slight heaps of silty sand as though this was what had been shovelled out of the beach to make the shallow grave. "That's pretty obvious," he thought, ' but someone must have come here with a shovel of some sort, and I'll bet that it's in that building as well as the quad bike'. As he was thinking this, Anna came walking back along the beach.

'I've found the way off the beach. It's only a gap in the bushes, but enough for a quad bike. Do you think it could be in the building at the jetty?'

'I'm pretty sure it is; in fact, I'd put money on it. Have you had a reply from control about who owns it?'

'Yes, I had a reply a couple of minutes ago. It is owned by the oil company and they have stores and suchlike put in there when they are brought over from the harbour on one of their supply boats.'

'Now that could be a link Anna.'

'I don't know how big their supply boats are, but I'm damn sure they're not particularly small. That means that decent sized boats can get here, at least ones with a shallow draught. We need to know who would come here with a body and how would they get here; in fact why here? Would they bring it by road or by boat?'

'Well guv, I'd say that by boat is a way of not being seen by many people. The road we came along is also pretty quiet and I suppose you could get from anywhere by road and no-one would notice if you had a body in the vehicle; it's not likely to be stopped for any reason over here is it?'

'No, you're right. Either way of bringing the body is a possibility. The problem is that we don't know who he was, his identity, where he came from, who brought him here, and most of all, who killed him.'

'So, all in all, we don't have a lot do we guv?'

'And there's me thinking we almost had the case sewn up Anna,' he said with a dead-pan expression.

There was the sound of an incoming call on the radio. Alex answered the call. It was from one of his DC's.

'Alice; do you have anything for us?'

'I do guv. The shop was in Poole town centre, it was Primark in the Dolphin Centre. It has taken Tom and I ages to not only find these shops and then go round them to find assistants who might help. George came up with a possible store code number which narrowed things down considerably. We went to the ones which had part of this number in their codes and we were able to get the confirmation of the store itself from their reception desk as someone there recognised their style of till receipt.'

'That's very interesting Alice, but is that all you got, just the shop?'

'NO, guv,' she said emphatically, 'I got through to Tom and we both met up in Primark and went to find and talk to all the assistants who were there on the date that was on the ticket.'

'Alice, will you get to the point!'

She was sounding excited and Alex was just beginning to lose his cool, when Alice said, 'We got a positive ID guv! The assistant said that she recognised him because he looked "different."

'Did she say in what way he was "different"?'

'Well, only that he didn't look local – he had a dark complexion and she thought he looked a bit "Eastern European" as her boyfriend is from Cyprus and she said that this chap had similar features to her boyfriend.'

'Okay, good work Alice. However, it doesn't help us much as to his name and where he was from does it?'

'No, but, ah well, you see...'

'What is it Alice? There's something else?'

'Yes, yes.' Alice was excited. 'He was with another man when he bought the shirt. This other man looked to have similar colouring and this girl thought she recognised him, although she wasn't sure.'

'Alice, I really do hope that you have arranged for her to come to the station for questioning. This could be a breakthrough.' Alex was sounding excited and Anna was looking at him very expectantly.

'Yes guv, I asked if she could come as soon as possible. I'm just waiting now for her supervisor to give her permission to come with us straight away.'

'Good girl Alice! Right, well, we're about done over here at Goathorn anyway, except that we were going to have a look inside the shed here but there's no-one here at the moment with keys, so we'll get back to the station and give this girl from the shop a good questioning. If she can give us any clues to the friend, then we have something to go on. See you both back at the nick.'

'On our way guv.'

Alex turned to Anna with an expression which told her that he was very "fired-up."

'Back to the boat,' he said and immediately became full of impatience. He told Anna what Alice had just told him as they walked quickly back to the jetty to take the boat back to Poole Harbour Marina.

Bob Chorley had disappeared by this time, presumably back to work.

'Hello Jack, can you take us back please?'

'Right you are zur, do come aboard an' t'will be my pleasure to ferry you back.'

'We may need to come again, is that all right?'

'Aye, t'will be fine by me, whenever you be ready, I be 'ere awaitin' for ee.'

'That's great, thanks.'

Untying the mooring ropes and jumping back into the boat with surprising agility for someone his age, the boat moved off into the channel and took a course toward Furzey Island and from there to Poole Harbour Marina where their car was parked.

The journey did not take that long but even so; Alex was quite impatient now and said to Jack, 'Can this old tub go a little faster?'

This caused Jack to give Alex a look which would probably have melted the tar caulking on an old wooden ship's decking.

Anna saw this look and said quietly to Alex, 'I think you've offended him by calling it an "old tub," didn't he say that it's been in his family for a very long time?'

'Realising his "gaffe" he quickly said to Jack, 'I didn't mean to be rude Jack, it's just that I'm in a great hurry now to get back as we have some very important information to investigate.'

'I don't pay it no never mind but see here, t'were my dad's 'afore me 'an 'e did look after the old gal with love and many gallons of varnish did my dad, so I do look after 'er similar like, an' to run this ol' diesel engine too fast, do make the bearings wear out quick an' they be precious costly to replace, that's if'n they can be found see, so if'n you don't mind zur, I do keep the speed down to what be reasonable and sensible, 'cordin to these here conditions what we do 'ave today, an' that way you can be certin sure of getting back to where you did come from without no problems, if'n 'ee see what I do mean?'

Both Alex and Anna were quite amazed by this diatribe as it did appear that Jack had said all this, taking what seemed like only a couple of breaths except that when he'd finished his soliloquy, he appeared even more red in the face than normal and about to sink down to the bilges.

Becoming quite concerned for his "well-being", Anna said, 'We understand Jack and we appreciate the care and love which you give this boat which is very obvious.'

She said this at the same time as giving him a "hand" back to the stern thwart where he had been sitting hanging on to the tiller.

"I be thankin' you ma'am, for bein' unnerstannin' an' we'll not be long 'afore we be back in the 'arbour, so don't you go frettin now.'

'Just a thought Jack, I know the water around the Point is not deep, but do you think there are any craft which could get close?'

'Well, 'corse there be them "supply boats" what do come with that stuff for the oil fields, 'an they do 'ave flat bottoms like so that be able to go in very shallow water, an' then there could be one of these 'ere modern boats which have this "Jet Power" and they be able to work in very shallow water, seeing' as they don't have no propellers like.'

'So you think one of these craft could get close to the beach then?'

'I reckons it could, sure enough. These 'ere Jet-Boats go tearing around the 'arbour an' along the parts what other boats would be proper stuck like.'

This gave Alex a frisson of an idea.

They were soon entering the Harbour Marina once again. Jack, again with an apparent lack of effort, made fast to the two bollards and offered his hand to Anna. She accepted this gesture with thanks, at the same time feeling the incredible strength in his grip and roughness of his skin, weathered by the years of being "on the water," she supposed.

Thanking him once again, he said, 'It be my pleasure missy to take you and your boss 'ere if'n you do want to go over to Goat'orn again.'

Saying that they might need his assistance in the near future, they gave their thanks and said their goodbyes, making their way back to the car and drove back to Police HQ.

CHAPTER 12

The shop assistant from Primark in the Dolphin Shopping Centre in Poole was brought back to Bournemouth Police HQ, by Tom and Alice, who had traced her with determined searching of most of the likely shops in the area who would have sold the shirt worn by the victim.

The young woman, who had agreed to attend the interview, was shown into "Interview Room 2." The alternative, "IR1" was often reserved for more difficult and recorded interviews, where possible suspects were often deliberately placed and had far more "downbeat" furnishing and colours. This was purposely designed to put the suspects at a slight disadvantage.
IR2, however, was much friendlier and also designed here for more informality, giving the interviewee a more relaxed feeling, much more conducive to producing positive results during the interview, with information which would hopefully further the investigation.

The woman was seated in one of the "more comfortable chairs" when Alex and Anna both entered the room.
'Good afternoon, I am Detective Chief Inspector Vail and this is,' looking toward Anna, 'Detective Sergeant Jenkins. Thank you very much for agreeing to come here for an interview. I am sure that this is preferable to your colleagues doing their best to eavesdrop if we were to do this at your workplace.'
The woman smiled and nodded. 'Yes, they're a nosy bunch at the best of times. This would make them like a bunch of piranhas.'
Alex looked towards Anna and she took the hint to begin the questioning. They had already decided that Anna was best placed to make the woman feel at ease.
'Firstly, can you give us your name please?'
'My name is Jo Stafford.'
'And how old are you Jo?'
'Thirty two.'
'And are you married?'
'Was.'
'Sorry, don't mean to pry.'
'No, I don't mind. Just didn't work out. I only discovered his habits and friends after the shine wore off.'
Anna looked at Alex and they both understood that there was probably more to be unearthed from that comment, but later.
'And your address, just for our records you understand, nothing more.'
'That's okay, no problem. I live in flat 3, 122 Copers Road in Broadstone.'
'Nice up there isn't it?' said Anna, to further put Jo at her ease.
'It is; peaceful and pretty safe. Better than where I was, back in Upper Parkstone.
Anna knew Broadstone reasonably well and she understood why the mention of "safe" was made. Parts of Poole, being a very maritime oriented port, had some "unsavoury" areas which were better avoided. Broadstone was about 3 miles outside Poole and was quite close to Corfe Mullen, altogether a better area with more quality housing.
'Are you worried about being safe then Jo?'
'I am now, yes.'
Anna could tell that she was being a little reserved and there was something there which would take some uncovering, she thought.
'We'll leave that for now, Jo. Let's get to the man you saw and you say you sold the shirt to. Is that right?'
'Yes, I'm pretty sure it was him. I remembered him because he was obviously not English, if you know what I mean.'
'I think so; can you explain more as to why you thought he was not English?'
'Well, he looked quite a bit like my ex-husband. I mean, my ex was from Cyprus and this guy looked very similar, well his face had the same characteristics, if you know what I mean.'
'Yes, I understand. So you remember him; how about his friend?'

Well, his friend; I'm sure I've seen him before somewhere, but I'm blowed if I can think where.'

Alex now took over and looked very carefully at Jo, trying to judge her response and demeanour. 'Jo, it is extremely important that you try to remember when or where or even who this friend was.'

'Are you looking for either of these men because they have done something bad?' After looking at both Alex and Anna, she answered her own question by saying,' I suppose that must be it or I wouldn't be here would I?' Thankfully she said this with a smile.

'Yes,' said Alex, 'we are looking for a person who can help us with our enquiries over a very serious crime, so anything you can tell us would be extremely helpful in apprehending the person or persons we are looking for. So, this friend, can you think very hard and try to give us some idea of who he might be and where he might be.'

'I'll do my best. I can only tell you that he seems to have been linked to my previous husband in some way, maybe he was a friend of his. I don't think I'd like him too much and I certainly don't want to know him if he's a friend of my ex.' Anna looked across at Alex and gave a meaningful look.

Alex said, 'I really hate to ask this Jo, but I think this is very relevant. You say that that this mystery man could be a friend of your ex-husband, so can I ask you for the address of your ex, so that we can contact him to see if he can give us a direction as to who this "friend" might be. We think that he could be involved with the crime we are investigating.'

She gave the name as Furkan Dimitriou of Granville Road in Upper Parkstone.

Jo gave the name and address of her ex-husband quite willingly and Anna asked her not to divulge to anyone, anything that had been said at this interview.

Anna made a note of the ex-husbands name, which Jo had said was Furkan Dimitriou and as he had changed his first name to Freddie, his nickname had become "Furkin Freddie." He now lived in a small flat in Upper Parkstone. Alex knew that this was a slightly less "salubrious" part of Poole.

Jo asked why she should be so secretive.

Alex said, 'Unfortunately, and I'll be straight with you, the nature of the crime we are investigating means that it could possibly put you in some danger as there seems to be some sort of connection with your ex-husband. This made her become very serious and the way she reacted, prompted Anna to carry on with a question she had not really wanted to ask.

'Jo, I didn't really want to ask this, but now I think I have to; was your ex-husband violent towards you or anyone else?'

Jo went very quiet and looked down at her knees and she began to wring her hands. Eventually, she said in a soft voice, 'Yes, he beat me up a couple of times, when he'd been drinking with his mates. Afterwards, he was always very sorry and promised he'd never do it again, until the next drinking binge with his "friends," and then it would happen again.'

'You say a couple of times; was it more than just a couple of times?'

'Yes, sometimes he would beat me repeatedly, after a bingeing session.'

'But you managed to get away from him?'

'Eventually I did, yes. I took legal advice and my lawyer applied for legal aid for me and I took out an injunction which led to divorce proceedings - thankfully.'

'And, do you have any children, Jo?'

'Thank God, no. I'm so glad that I didn't. To think of a child of mine having the blood of my ex in their veins, sends shivers up my spine.'

Anna had intuitive feelings about Jo's demeanour. 'I get the impression from the way you have said these things to me, that some of the things he did to you, were worse than you have actually said.'

She looked at Alex and then Anna, and then down at her knees again. This time, she looked up with a clear look on her face. 'Yes, they were – I have scars. Do you need to see them?'

'No Jo, that won't be necessary; let's leave it there for now, unless you can think of anything we can use that would lead us to this "friend" you saw with the man who bought the shirt.'

'I can't at the moment, but maybe when I don't try to think about it, it'll come to me.'

Anna said, 'If that happens, promise me you'll call either DCI Vail or me immediately.'

'Of course, I want to help all I can,' she said.

'Thank you so much for coming in. We'll have an unmarked car to take you back to work, and please thank your supervisor for giving you the time, but once again, please say nothing to your workmates. If they ask, which they surely will, just say that you were giving some details about an old school friend who had run into some trouble, but you cannot tell them anything.'

'Okay, I'll do that. Thanks.'

As Jo was about to stand up and get her coat, she turned, stood still for a moment, then said, 'There was something which I've just thought about. This friend of the man who bought the shirt, you know, the one I thought I knew, well, I think he was some sort of fisherman. As far as I remember, he was someone who went out on fishing parties from Poole Harbour, you know, for a day's fishing. Freddie used to go on these trips and I think he may have been one of those. Any more than that, I can't tell you. Mind you, I say for a day's fishing, but sometimes he would be gone for two or three days, but to be honest, I don't know if he was fishing for all that time.'

'But that's great Jo. If only you could just give us a description that would be fantastic.'

'Jo looked a little thoughtful and looked up at the ceiling as though searching for inspiration. 'Yes, he was about six foot, I think, and big, with very dark hair, curly it was, and a heavy dark beard.'

'I don't suppose you know what colour his eyes were?' asked Alex.

'Only that they were very dark, like his hair.'

'Okay, that is absolutely fine Jo, thank you.'

We'll let you get off now   oh sorry, I shouldn't have put it like that.' Alex said, feeling foolish, 'I didn't mean that, I simply meant that we'll get you back to work.'

'That's all right, I understand,' she said.

Alex was thinking, "That confirms it," the photo she had recognised was of the man who was found on the beach. "We have to find this "friend," she has described."

A car was waiting to take her back to the Dolphin Centre.

CHAPTER 13

During the return journey from Goathorn and their inspection of the crime scene, Anna had asked Alex if he had a suitable day for their "dinner date" which she had suggested. He'd replied that the following evening would be more than acceptable and looked forward to it. Her reply was, 'That's a deal then, I have something in mind which I hope you'll like.' Alex's mind was working overtime, considering all the possibilities which that comment had implied. These possibilities were giving him a very warm feeling deep inside as he remembered the previous night they had spent together. He was actually thinking, the meal will be good, but I'm sure the dessert could be even better.

'I'm really looking forward to that Anna. I'm sure whatever you have in mind will give a great deal of satisfaction.'

'Do you mean the meal, Alex?'

'I think you know what I mean, you little minx.'

The feelings between them were becoming very meaningful, and Anna thought that the same went for both of them; at least she thought so.

He'd already made a shuffle through records and made a note of her address and phone number.

'I think we'd better get hold of the keys to that shed on Goathorn and check it out properly.'

'I'll get on to that as soon as we get back Alex. I think I'll start with the oil company, as it seems likely that they have that for storage.'

'Good idea. I've got loads of the usual "guff" to get through, so as soon as you know anything, make a call to the Harbour office and arrange for Old Jack Sturney to give us a lift again. He's a funny old bugger, but he knows this harbour well and I'm pretty sure that he could have information that's useful to us.'

'In the meantime, I'll get Alice to give forensics a "gee-up" They must have something for us by now.'

Anna went through to where Alice was working on her computer, she said 'Hi Alice, could you give Forensics a call and chase them up. We need something positive to work on to do with the body. We need to find out who he was and it would be good to know why he was killed, not to mention who by.'

'Right sarge, I'll give them a bell to see what they've got for us. Have you anything else from the morgue?'

'Not yet but if you can ask Tom to get on to George, he can pass anything on to me. I've got some digging to do to find details of that building over at Goathorn.'

Alice went looking for Tom to pass on Anna's request. She couldn't find him immediately and wondered where he might be. I know, she thought, and went to the door at the rear of the station. She found him having a smoke. She said, 'It's about time you gave up that filthy habit Tom, do you know your clothes stink of cigarette smoke sometimes and it really is a "turn-off," it's no wonder you don't have girl-friend.'

'I do have a girl-friend,' he said, bridling a little at the suggestion, 'well, I had one not long back, but she changed her mind for some reason.'

'And do you wonder why?' said Alice. 'I'll bet your breath smells as well, with all that smoking and it stains your teeth.'

'Okay okay,' said Tom. 'I get the message, mum.'

'It's no good being sarcastic Tom, and in any case, you know you'll get a bollocking from Alex if he catches you having a crafty drag.'

'Yeah, I know. I s'pose I'd better get back. Anyway, what did you want me for, just to give me a hard time?'

'No, you've actually got some work to do. Call George Matthews over at the post mortem and ask what more he can tell us about the body.'

'All right then.'

'And when you've got his report, for Pete's sake take it straight to Anna.'

'Who's Pete then?'

'Go on, you pillock,' she said giving him a shove towards the door.

Tom went off to phone George while Alice called the forensic laboratories over at Ferndown. When she got through to the appropriate department, she was able to give them the reference number of the case they were working on.

The head of the department was Jeffrey Boyd. Alice introduced herself and although she had never met Jeffrey, she had heard of him from other officers who had. He was well thought of and apparently a very helpful and "willing" man, even though he and his colleagues had a very heavy workload. They introduced each other and Alice quickly warmed to Jeffrey and they were soon chatting as though she had known him for a while. "This helps," thought Alice.

He said, 'If you'd like to hang on a moment or two, I'll get the relevant notes appertaining to this case.' Returning to the phone, he said, 'Okay, we have an interim report. The deceased was obviously involved with the sea in some way. We have found traces of fish oil on his skin and under his fingernails.'

'Do you think that this would suggest that he takes part in fishing of some sort?'

'Indeed it does Alice, the traces all show that the fish would be species local to these waters around the Dorset coast. On his clothes, we find residue which suggest that he smoked heavily and this will naturally be borne out by post mortem examination, as I'm sure you realise.' He then changed "tack" somewhat, saying, 'I've heard from other folk that you are very good at your job and a whiz with IT.' He did not say this in a patronising way as could have been the case with some other technical operators had in the past with Alice, and she found Jeffrey most pleasant and the tone of his voice very appealing.

Alice actually blushed when he said this, glad that this was a phone call and not face to face; yet, she thought. 'This man sounds very nice', thought Alice, 'I'd like to meet him'.

It has to be said that Alice was single, although she had had boyfriends but she was quite shy when it came to meeting other men and she was very aware of the fact that she had turned to a certain item of "taste" as a substitute whenever she hadn't the courage to go out on her own. This took the form of cream cakes and she knew only too well the effect they had on her, but they were very nice and made her feel good. Her friends all had boyfriends or husbands and she was beginning to get to feel a bit of a "wallflower" in her mind. However, she now had a private thought that she would try to meet this "Jeffrey" if that were possible. 'I might as well have a try', she thought to herself.

'That's very helpful Mr Boyd.'

'Please call me Jeffrey, Mr Boyd makes me seem unapproachable, and I'm not, I'm quite approachable and you have a very nice voice and I'm told you are a lovely person.'

This time she really blushed, but keeping her control she said, 'This gives us a placing and some kind of location. We need to know what sort of work he might have done and where he might have done it. I don't suppose you can tell us that can you?'

'Oh, but we can Alice. You'd be surprised what we can tell from the smallest pieces of either clothes or hair or fragments.'

'I'm sure you're going to surprise me now aren't you?'

'Would you like to be surprised Alice?'

"Just try me," she thought, her blush gathering intensity, 'Yes please.'

'Well now, we know he was a builder, maybe by trade or perhaps just a "do-it-yourselfer," but from the brick and cement residue we found on his jeans, he certainly came into contact with that sort of material.'

'I'll bet you can't tell where, though can you?'

'As a matter of fact, we can. The sand happens to be a special type which is used in certain "installations", such as bridges or dams, where very stringent conditions of concrete or cement quality are used.'

'Wow, now that is useful. But where would such installations be around here.'

'Ah, now that we can't tell you, because such places exist all over the country, so unless or until we discover something else which can give us more detail, such as travel debris and so on, we will just have to keep on searching.'

'What do you mean by "travel debris"?'

'That means that when someone travels, perhaps regularly, the clothing often picks up minute amounts of dust or particles which come from a particular area. In that way, we can search our databases of what we call "particulates," which can tell us where that stuff comes from. It can narrow down search areas a lot.'

'Yes, I can see that. That's wonderful. I expect you can tell a lot about a person from things like soap or perfume and ....' She stopped herself. She knew she was digging herself a hole and she was beginning to 'lose it', so she paused, and then said, 'I'm sorry, I'm taking up your time, and you must be very busy.'

'I am, but I tell you what, if you're interested, why don't you come over, it's not far to Ferndown, and you can see what we do here. I'm sure you'll find it interesting.'

'I know I would be very interested Jeffrey and I will, thank you. Just tell me when it will be convenient and I'll arrange something so that I can come over.'

'Just give me a call when you can make time and I'll make sure I can show you round. We're actually called the SSD now. That stands for the Scientific Support Department; you know we used to be the CSI.'

'That's very kind of you to take the trouble,' she said.

'Not at all, it'll be my pleasure, and if anything else turns up from our tests, I'll give you a call.'

'I'd like that, I mean, thank you, which would be nice; what I mean is, that is good of you.' She'd "lost it" now.

'Goodbye Alice, hope to see you soon then.'

'You will, 'bi for now.'

By this time she was "fluttering" and had to go to the rest room and run some cold water over her face before she could go to Anna with her news.

The one thing she did not realise was that Jeffrey had been divorced for around three years; he was ready for a new relationship and liked a woman who was not "skinny" and Alice was certainly not skinny - he knew this from questions he'd asked previously.

Alice came back from the rest room, refreshed and calmer. As she was about to find Anna, she had a thought. "Fingerprints;" she must contact the fingerprint section to see if they had any information or matches, thinking to herself, "I'll get onto that straight away."

Whilst all this was going on, Tom had been talking to George over at the Pathology lab.

'So where's the lovely Anna then Tom?' he asked.

'She's busy trying to locate some keys, I believe,' said Tom; 'she's a bit of a "looker" isn't she?'

'You'd better not let your boss hear you say that, he'd go nuts,' said George.

Warning bells were going off in Tom's head. 'Why's that then George, is he keen on her?'

'No, I don't think so, although I don't know so, but I do know that he doesn't think much of "in-work liaisons," so you'd better watch out if you fancy Anna.'

'No, I don't fancy her, just think she's nice, that's all', he lied. 'Anyway, what more do you have for us then?'

'Not a lot actually. We've taken all the organs but no trace of drugs that we can find. However, he was a very heavy smoker as his lungs are like a tar factory. I don't think he'd have had a long life, judging by the state of them. And, the tobacco he smoked, I suppose with an "untipped" or "unfiltered" brand, was of Turkish origin. I think this matches the butt found at the scene doesn't it?'

'Yes, there was one there, but I don't think he was smoking it when he was put there.'

'He'd have had a hell of a job, that's for sure,' offered George.

'So, do you think that the killer smoked these cigarettes as well?'

'I don't know if he did as a regular smoker but we'll only find that out when you find the killer or the person who put the body there. If I might suggest, we know that the victim was a heavy smoker of this brand, but if the other person who left the butt on the beach, was not, then perhaps he just had the one or even took the packet from the victim and smoked them himself. We just have no idea.'

'That's true,' said Tom. 'Is there anything else?'

'The heavy bruising and cuts were caused just prior to death and they are so severe that they could or would have resulted in death in themselves. Some cuts had even gone through bone, so they were inflicted with great force or anger; maybe there was a fight. Also, the bruising was administered again before death. He'd been pretty bashed about. The bruising to the scull could have caused a haematoma which would be very serious in itself.'

'Wow, sounds like a nasty bastard; must have been pretty pissed off with this poor bloke.'

'We're still doing tests, so I'll let you know of anything as and when we have results.'

'Okay, thanks George. Talk to you later.'
'Indeed my boy; Cheerio, and give my regards to Anna.'
'Will do; 'bye George.'

Anna had had some luck in tracking down the key holder to the shed on Goathorn Peninsula. It was indeed owned by Perenco, the current owners running the oil-fields. It was agreed that the keys would be made available to the Police the next day and there would be someone in attendance if they were able to make the crossing again. The name of the person would be John Metcalfe, who works with Bob Chorley at the oil-field.

Anna thought, ''Now Bob Chorley did not mention anything about this guy when we were asking about the key-holder and surely he must have known. Why would he not have mentioned that? Another thing which occurred to her was that Bob Chorley had heard this engine, but why would he hear this – was he ''out and about'' at or near the jetty at a late hour?'' But then she realised that it was so quiet in that area at night, that any sound would probably "carry."

She phoned the harbour office at Poole and arranged for a further trip for herself and Alex the next morning, to Goathorn, to examine the building at the jetty.

CHAPTER 14

Alice came over to Anna when she had finished arranging the trip and said, 'I've got some good info from Jeffrey at SSD Sarge.'

Anna looked at Alice with a little tilt to her head and a quizzical look. 'Jeffrey? SSD?'

Alice blushed immediately. 'Sorry Sarge. SSD is the new name for the Scientific Support Department and Jeffrey Boyd is the head of the section.'

'Oh, I see,' said Anna quite gently, realising exactly what could have happened. She had met Jeffrey Boyd previously and had some knowledge of his background, so she had a fair idea of the scenario which had played out. 'So what little gems did Jeffrey have for us then?'

'He said that they know that he was a very heavy smoker and smoked Turkish cigarettes, unfiltered, judging by the state of his lungs. He was also involved with sea-fishing of some sort as he had fish-oil under his fingernails. He also had traces of a very special type of sand on his jeans. This sand is apparently used on bridges and dams, but he can't be specific, although he said they are looking for "travel debris".'

'Go on, stun me with that one.'

Alice continued, 'Travel debris is the stuff that collects on clothes from travelling to and fro' on a regular basis. They can tell where the person goes from and where they go to, with a bit of luck, so Jeffery says.'

'Let's just hope that he, or they, comes up with the goods pretty soon. So far, we're not getting very close to finding out who this guy was, and even more important who his friend is, although we do have some sort of description.'

'If they can tell us where this sand is used around this area, then perhaps we can get some idea of his movements.'

'I'd rather know more about his friend, to be honest Alice. I know you're good at the "soft" interviews; I wonder if we should get Jo Stafford for another "let's try remember" session.'

'That might pay off Sarge. It has to be worth a try, because if we can find this friend, we'll have a name and place – that'd get things moving, wouldn't it?'

'Okay, can you give her a call and ask her to come in again, when it's convenient for her, but sooner rather than later?'

'Will do, Sarge.'

'By the way Alice, good work over at SSD, perhaps your "Jeffrey" will come up with a more specific placing of this special sand. I have a feeling that this would give us a good starting place for asking questions.'

Alice had only just recovered from her blushing and it happened again at the mention of "your Jeffrey." Am I that transparent, she thought?

While Anna was in Alex's office, she said, 'would tomorrow night be good for you for our 'dinner date?'

'I don't see why not Anna, there's nothing that we can do except wait for all this information to come in and be collated, so, yes, that would be great. I've been looking forward to this ever since you mentioned it. I know you'll be a better cook than me, so I know the food'll be good, but the company even better.'

'Thank you, kind sir; I'm looking forward to our special time together too. We won't get a lot of free time will we, especially when the investigation gets really going?'

'I think that's always going to be a problem Anna, but we'll have to find a way to get some personal time – I'm sure it can be arranged.'

'You're the boss, boss.'

'Not during our personal time - only here. 'Mind you, there is one very important thing for both of us Anna. I am very aware that I have a reputation for actively discouraging in-work relationships and I am being particularly duplicitous, but I'll just have to live with that. What is important is that our personal relationship must never and I repeat, never come into our working relationship. I know I rank above you but I will always respect your judgement and listen to constructive points if they have relevance. We'll have to try very hard to keep the two sides of you and me outside the office and our working time. I really value you as a colleague in the working environment and I would be devastated it that were compromised in any way.'

'Alex, I do realise that if anything were to come out, I would be moved to another station and that is the last thing in the world that I want; so I promise I will do my very best to keep things totally separate. Anyway, I want to apply for promotion soon and take my inspector's exam in the not-too-distant future, so that's another reason for secrecy.'

'I know you'll keep everything under your hat Anna, I trust you completely.'

'Mmm, thank you; oh yes, why I'm here, we have a trip to Goathorn for tomorrow morning with old Jack, at ten. The key-holder will be waiting for us, one John Metcalfe; he works with Bob Chorley at the oil-field.'

'Hang on, how come Chorley didn't mention this when we were questioning him? He said that he didn't know who used the shed or who had the keys.'

'That's right, my thought exactly but to be fair to him, when I contacted Perenco, they just said that there would be a "key-holder" waiting for us at the jetty. They didn't say that he was the usual one. We'll just have to ask him very carefully to explain the situation.'

'Indeed we will. Anyway who the heck is "Parenco"?'

'They're the company who run the oil-fields.'

'I thought that was BP.'

'It was, but that was years ago, and you know how companies change hands these days.'

'Makes me feel a bit of a dinosaur Anna,' he said with a wry grin.

'Don't tempt me! – Of course you're not. In fact I think it's just the opposite.'

'We'll see.'

'Maybe tomorrow night...?'

He went very quiet and the smile left his face and he became very serious and gave her a very hard stare. 'Sergeant Jenkins, unless you have some vital information to impart to your senior officer, please vacate the premises.' He looked at Anna's shocked face but just couldn't hide the smile which came unbidden.

'That's not fair; you nearly had me going there!'

'Okay, I'll leave that for tomorrow night then', he said with a lascivious gleam in his eye.

As Anna turned to leave the office, she said, 'There was something which Alice got from SSD that could be very interesting. There were sand particles found in or on his jeans, the sort that is used on special projects. They suggest that it could be where waterproof and very high specification concrete is used, such things as dams or where water is present.'

'Now that is interesting. Get Tom in here would you and he can get checking around for anywhere they might be building perhaps sea defences, a sea wall or quay.'

'How about a "containment" area like the one that Bob Chorley mentioned, you know the "moat" or "bund" for oil spillage. I would think that has to be pretty waterproof or specialised.'

'Now that's what I call "progressive thinking," Anna. Great; let's get Tom working on that. If we can get where this guy was working, we might have some idea of why he was killed in the way he was, especially if he got into a fight or something. Let's see what Tom can find out – see how good he is. In the meantime, can you get this Jo Stafford back in for a further interview. I'm sure she can tell us more?'

'Already in hand guv, I've asked Alice to interview her as she's so good at the "soft" interview.'

'Brilliant, thanks Anna.'

Tom came to see Alex in response to Anna's request. 'Tom, what do you have from the post mortem chap?'

'Well guv, he said that whoever cut his throat was used to using a sharp knife as, although it wasn't "surgical" it was possibly someone used to cutting fish. He said this because this guy had fish oil under his fingernails, which indicated that he went sea fishing.'

'How do they know it was sea-fishing?'

'Because the oil was from salt-water fish.'

'That could tie in with the information we have that sea-fishing trips were arranged by the "friend" of Jo Stafford, the shop assistant's ex-husband. Okay, Tom, now listen, I want you to search for any special construction sites in as big an area as you can take in at the moment, where special concrete would be used. Use your imagination as to what that might mean, something like a reservoir, a sea-wall or sea defences, things like that. Think ''outside the box'' and we might get a worthwhile lead.'

'Why are we looking for these special sites then guv?'

'Because special sand was found on his clothes which is used in these places, and there might also be particles found which indicate where he might have travelled to.'

'Okay, right, got the idea.'

I won't mention the 'oil containment moat for now, and see if he comes up with that. Oil-field and things linked to that are all around here, so there could be links', thought Alex.

CHAPTER 15

Alex and Anna drove over to Poole Harbour to meet Jack Sturney as arranged at 10am. This time they drove across to the marina and parked up. They walked over to where Jack was waiting; again the cloud of evil-smelling smoke wreathing his head. He looked up and gave them, what might have been a beaming smile, had it not been for the fact that his teeth were not something to be gazed at, however briefly, only "in awe."

In a very ragged voice, Jack said, 'Mornin' Officers,' and gave a very rough and phlegmy cough; turning toward the water he hawked and spat into the harbour.

A feeling of disgust ran through Anna, as Jack said, 'Beggin your pardon missy. Tidn't nice I knows, but this 'baccy what I do smoke be a bit strong.'

'"Strong?"'said Alex, 'I think it's made from tarred rope off an old sailing ship.'

This brought a laugh from Jack which turned into a rough and drawn-out smokers cough.

When he'd recovered from that, he asked, 'Do 'ee know 'ow long 'ee be over at that there jetty, mind, see, I do have to do a little job from someone back at yon 'arbour just about lunch time see?'

Overcoming her earlier revulsion Anna said, as kindly as she could muster, 'We shouldn't be very long today; we only have to take a look inside the big shed just in front of the jetty.'

With Jack casting off, they headed for the other side of the harbour and Goathorn Point.

'Do you know the building over there Jack?'

'Aye, I do knows that be the one what the oil company do own like.'

Why didn't we think of asking Jack that before, thought Alex?

'Do you know the man we are going to meet there, the key-holder, a man called John Metcalfe?'

'Aye, I do know John. 'Ee do work with Bob on them oil-fields.'

"More information that we should have prised out of Jack the first time," thought Alex again, looking sideways at Anna, who knew instantly what he was thinking.

'Do you know what's inside the shed then Jack?' asked Anna.

'For certain shure I knows what's in there. There be one of them 'Beach Buggy' type things, what do they call them'? He mused.

Again, Alex looked over to Anna and said to Jack, 'Do you mean a quad bike?'

'Aye, I'm thinkin' that's what they do call 'em.'

'And is there anything else in the shed that you know?'

'Oh, I do know that there be some oil-field stuff, you knows, pipes and bits of machinery and the like, and then there be the fishin' gear.'

'Fishing gear?' asked Anna.

'Aye, there be fishing gear, kep' in the workshop what be inside yon big shed. For them "sea-fishing" trips what they do make. Takin' groups of fishermen out way off the coast for some sea fishing.'

'But that surely doesn't belong to the oil-company, does it?'

'Oh no, that b'aint belongin' 'o them, 'tis the bloke what comes in his big boat every now and then to take the fishin' trip.'

Anna looked at Alex with a quite incredulous look, the implication of which was that they were learning some really important facts. She said, 'So this man who comes for the fishing gear, does he have the men with him or is he alone?'

'Depends.'

'Depends on what Jack?' asked Alex,

'Depends if'n 'ee be by 'isself or not.' Jack really laughed at this, which brought back the deep-draught cough, which made Anna a little concerned.

Give me strength, thought Alex. 'What I mean is, does he come to collect the fishing gear with other men in the boat with him, or does he come alone?'

'Ah, well, see, sometimes 'ee comes on his own and sometimes 'ee comes with other blokes.'

Anna was quite expecting Alex to throw him over the side of the boat at any moment, but Jack was actually quite enjoying himself, chuckling away as he was.

'Okay Jack, do you know if he comes here regularly or does he come at odd times?'

"Ee do come at times when the tides are right, see, 'cos the water only be deep enough for 'is craft when the tide is up, see.'

'Yes, I understand; can you tell me what sort of boat it is?'

'It be a big boat an' she be a fast'un.

He's definitely going to go for a swim, thought Anna. 'No Jack, what Inspector Vail meant was, can you describe the boat for us, so that we know what to look for? We need to find this man and his boat. We have some questions for him.'

'Why did you not say for me to describe it then? I know this'n right well. 'Tis what they call a "Redbaye Storm-Force 11." See, I's be takin' an interest in boats, so I knows quite a bit about 'em. This'n 'as 2 big inboard diesels with jet drives on the stern and I do know she 'as all them gadgets and gizmos what they do 'ave now, you know, these electronic things like "fish finders" and "depth gauges" and navigation equipment, and she do have radar an' all. Very good sea boat she be, and fast too, they do reckon she'll do about 35 knots or thereabouts.' He was quite enlivened now, talking about boats.

Alex was becoming quite excited. 'Do you know where she is kept?'

'I be not too sure 'bout that, 'cept maybe she do go up to Cobb's Quay, but I'm not certain sure, so don't take that as Gospel, if'n you do see what I means.'

'One final thing Jack, do you know the name of the man who runs these sea-fishing trips?'

'Yes, his name be Martin.'

'Does he have another name? asked Alex.

'I daresay 'e do 'ave another name, you knows, Martin summat or other.'

'But you don't know it Jack?'

'No, or see, if'n I knowed it, I'd 'ave told 'ee, an' no mistake.'

'Okay, thanks Jack, you've been very helpful.'

Alex needed a rest after pulling that information from Jack. He made notes of that information and he was thinking that they had to locate that boat as soon as they could and find the mysterious "Martin."

They were enjoying the trip from Poole Harbour over to Goathorn Peninsular jetty. Anna turned to Alex and said, 'How long have they been taking oil from here Alex?'

'As it happens, I do know a little about it. The British Gas Corporation "as was" discovered the field in 1973 and they started producing oil in quantity in 1979, then BP took it over and recently the new people, you say Perenco I believe; I didn't know them, took over production. What I do know is that they expect to be producing quantities of oil until 2037 or thereabouts.'

'But how does the oil get taken to the refineries, I suppose it goes by tanker?'

'No, it goes by pipeline right over to the other side of Southampton, to the terminal at Hamble where it is loaded to bulk shipping tankers.'

'Wow, that's a long way.'

'I believe it's about 57 miles and it goes right round to the north of the New Forest, round what are called "The Perambulations of the New Forest." There are other pipelines which carry the natural gas; it's quite a complex network I believe.'

'And how big is this oil-field, I mean it can't be like some of the American ones, can it?'

'I don't suppose it's that big, but I understand that it's the largest onshore oil field in Western Europe. The latest discovery was the Sherwood field which they found much deeper than the original discoveries.'

'When you say "deep," I mean how deep do they drill?'

'You are very inquisitive about technical stuff Anna; it's usually blokes who are interested in this sort of information. '

'Knowledge is power isn't it?'

'Quite right; that's me put in my place. Anyway, I know they are drilling down to 5,000 feet and they now drill sideways out under the coast south of Bournemouth for around 10 kilometres.'

'Bloody hell!' said Anna. 'I didn't realise that it was that big.'

'It's enormous for sure, and I do have a story about when they built the pipeline; if you're interested.'

'Yes, go on then.'

'Okay. Well, I have a friend who lived in this area back when they were first beginning to install the pipeline and there were all sorts of protests about disturbing wildlife and birds and so on. There were protest meetings everywhere and my friend went to one where a representative, from BP I think, was answering questions from local residents and people who were against the pipeline, saying it would cause disruption and so on.'

'Well, I can understand that,' said Anna.

'This guy from BP was a diplomat to say the least, and he apparently explained in great detail how they would excavate a trench, and that the pipeline would be buried about six feet below the ground and after this has been laid, the land would be restored. People were saying that whilst it was being dug, the birds and wildlife would all be displaced, but this BP chap said that birds would simply come back and within a month or two it would look as though there was nothing there but forest and woodland.'

'It sounds as though this chap was a "smooth talker," Anna ventured.

'This is the best bit; apparently, there was one old bloke at this meeting who was extremely "vociferous" and kept making silly claims about disturbance, you know, he just wouldn't shut up, making complaints, and he said, "What about the noise from the pipeline when it was running?" The BP man, give him his due, kept his cool, saying, and I quote, "Well sir, I have to be perfectly honest and tell you, that if one were to actually stand beside this large oil pipeline, the top of which will be six feet below the ground, and if the oil was being pumped along it at full pressure, and you were to hold your ear hard against the pipe....."

"Yes?" said this old man, who actually looked triumphant, the BP man said, "You wouldn't hear a thing – all you would hear would be the bird-song. It would be completely silent."

'I'm told that the audience laughed and clapped and the old man walked out of the hall, completely beaten. Of course we know that the pipeline was put in and as he'd said, within a month or so, you didn't even know it was there.'

'Nice one,' said Anna. 'It's just a pity we don't have people like the "diplomatic" BP man in government today.'

'I think I know what you mean, Anna. I have to agree.'

Unfortunately for the others, Jack had heard this story recounted, and was grinning broadly - Not a pretty sight.

By the time Alex had finished this story, they were closing the jetty at Goathorn and there was a man standing there twirling a bunch of keys in his hand.

'That must be John Metcalfe,' said Anna. Jack had thrown a rope to him and Metcalfe expertly tied both the mooring ropes to bollards and offered his hand to Anna to help her off the boat.

'Thank you - Mr Metcalfe?' she asked.

'That's me,' he replied. Looking toward Jack, he said, ''G'day Jack.'

'Good day to you John. 'Tis set fair today an' no mistake.'

'Good to see you too Jack.'

'I see you are the key-holder,' offered Anna.

'That's probably because I'm holding the keys...' was the riposte.

That garnered a smile from Anna and even Alex had to smirk, thinking, everyone's a comedian round here. He turned to Jack and said, 'I don't think we'll be too long Jack.'

Jack replied with another "rotten jetty" smile, 'Don't you be a worryin 'bout that zur, I be here, 'avin' a little smoke, downwind like, so as not to cause any bother to "missy" there.'

'That's good of you Jack; much appreciated.'

'Tis my pleasure zur, us "old-uns" knows 'ow to be polite, us do.' This was followed by another deeply drawn hawking cough.

Walking over, Alex offered his hand to Metcalfe, saying, 'DCI Vail and this is DS Jenkins of Bournemouth Police, and Mr Metcalfe; I understand you work with Bob Chorley, at the oil site.'

'That's right; Bob and I look after the general running and maintenance of the site.'
'Right, let's get a look inside this shed if we may.'

John Metcalfe selected a key from the bunch he was holding and opened the very substantial lock on the large door. All three entered the huge shed and Anna looked over to Alex and they both screwed up their faces at the very pungent smell. 'Oh God, that's awful; what a horrible smell.'
'I suppose it's all the fishing stuff that's kept in that small room,' offered Metcalfe.
'I don't care where it's kept, it's a bloody awful smell, but then I don't know what it should smell like, but I just know that I don't like it.'
'It's pretty disgusting, I have to say.' Looking at Metcalfe, he asked if this was a usual smell.
'I suppose so, but then again, as I've said, I don't get to come in here often, but it is pretty grim isn't it?'

At one side of the building there was a section which was partitioned off to form, what was a "reasonably sized" room, complete with double doors which were heavily locked. There were no windows to this room and it looked very secure. Alex estimated that this room was about 40ft long and 15ft wide.

'I think we need to get a look into this room Anna.'
'Rather someone else then. Maybe SOCO can check it out as it will probably contain items directly concerning our investigation.'
'Give them a call later and arrange this if you will please.'
'Okay guv.'
They took in the very varied items of what must have been oil–field related equipment and parts in the main building. Everything looked extremely heavy and "industrial" as would be expected.
'Do you have keys to this room Mr Metcalfe?'
'The name's John and no, that room is rented to the guy who runs the sea-fishing trips. That's where he keeps all his tackle and stuff like that.'
'Do you know this man's name, by any chance?'
'I only know him as "Martin."'
'But you must see him quite a lot, surely?' asked Anna.
'Not really, because I'm at the site on "watch" for most of the time and as Martin only comes here every so often, I don't get to see him much; and when I do he's usually off on one of his trips, occasionally with a load of blokes on the boat.'
Alex had a question forming, which was related to the conversation relating to the "friend" of the dead man being described as "European" with dark skin. He was wondering if these men were local or from elsewhere.
'John, when you see this "Martin," what sort of people does he have on the boat with him?'
'To be honest, I've only ever seen just him on the boat except once or twice when he had about six men with him.'
'And what did these men look like; I mean can you describe them?'
'They just looked like I imagine blokes going fishing would look like. They all had on anorak type jackets and caps on their heads. I imagine it gets quite cold out there on the water.'
Anna came in here and asked, 'Can you describe what they looked like, and I mean did they look "local?"'
'If you mean were they white, yes, but It was quite dark the days I saw them, so all I can say is that they weren't "black", if that's "PC" now.'
'So, what time of day was this, do you think they were going "night fishing"?'
'I didn't think much about it, but I guess they do go night fishing. It was just about going dark I suppose. I was on night shift and I'd just been up to check on the shed here, as part of my security check.'
'And do you come here to check this building every night?'
'Not every night, but at least once or twice a week. It's not a set routine, if you know what I mean?'
'Okay, that's fine. Tell me, do you know where this "Martin" keeps his boat?'
'I believe it's over at Cobb's Quay.'
'We'll have to get that verified. Do you happen to know what sort of boat this is that "Martin" has?'

'I don't know what it's called but it'll be about 35ft or so, with a quite a large cabin and an open rear deck, for fishing I suppose. I'm sure old Jack will know, he's well up on boats I believe.'

'And does it look seaworthy?'

'Very. It's probably one of the few vessels that can come to this little pier as it has jet-drives and can work in shallow water.'

While this conversation was continuing, Anna was having a look around and she noticed tyre tracks in the dust across the floor, leading to the double doors on the internal room. She waited until Alex had finished talking to Metcalfe and called him over. 'Do you think these tracks could be the same as we saw at the crime scene guv?'

'I think you could be right Anna, and do you know what, I think they are from a quad bike or certainly something similar, just look at the width of the imprint.'

He turned to Metcalfe, and said, 'John, do you know if there might be a quad bike in this room?'

'I think there could be, as I sometimes hear what must be a quad bike, running around, although not often. I can't say for sure as I have never actually see this room open. I suppose it only gets opened when they go fishing.'

Alex was thinking that there was nothing much else that John Metcalfe could tell them, so he told John that they had finished their "look around."

'Okay, we're all finished here; thank you for taking the trouble to let us take a look. You can take the keys back now. Who do you take them to?'

'We keep them in the field office.'

'You mean in the oil-field site office?'

'That's right.'

Again, Alex wondered why no mention of this was made by Bob Chorley during their initial meeting. There's something not quite right here, he was thinking. Also, why would Chorley say that he didn't know who owned the shed?

They parted company, with John Metcalfe walking away towards the oil-field site and Anna and Alex to the jetty, to take the boat back to Poole. Alex turned to Anna and asked, 'What did you make of that?'

'Do you mean, why did Metcalfe have the keys, which are kept at the field site office and yet Bob Chorley said he didn't know who owned the building or who had the keys, is that about it?'

'Exactly.'

'Something we have to check up on, although I can't think of any reason he wants to keep that knowledge to himself, when he knows his colleague has access to the keys and is fully aware of who owns the building. 'Weird, to say the least, guv. And another thing, didn't Bob Chorley say that he had heard what he thought was a boat and then changed his mind to a quad bike?'

'Yes, I think he did. Curiouser and curiouser, methinks.'

'I wonder how Alice is getting on with asking the shop assistant to come in for another "chat," and Tom with his search for "special" concrete stuff.'

'We'll have to check when we get back. I want to have a briefing as soon as we can because there are a few things which need to be brought together to give us a clearer idea of where we are heading.'

'I suppose we have a good direction with this "fishing boat" don't we guv?'

'Yes, Anna, I think we could have something which is much bigger than we could have imagined.'

Anna looked a little puzzled at that comment. 'I don't know quite what you mean guv.'

'The way I'm thinking is perhaps just a little "far-fetched" at the moment, but what would you say to the suggestion that this boat is being used for "people-smuggling"?'

'I know the suggestion was that there were illegal workers but I hadn't thought of that; but now you mention it, I suppose it could be a possibility. Would that boat have the ability to cross the Channel and bring a number of men back?'

'You heard John Metcalfe say it looked very seaworthy and I think these boats are built to be out in quite "heavy-weather," much like trawlers, although obviously not for severely bad weather. Perhaps you could ask your Harbour Master friend about that sort of boat?'

'I will.'

I thought you would, thought Alex, mindful of Fuller Masterson's possible attraction to Anna. Then he said, by way of changing the direction of her possible thoughts, 'We have a date tonight, don't we? I'm really looking forward to it; it's been on my mind for a while now, ever since you suggested it.'

'Maybe not as much as me, Alex.' she said, looking at Alex with a very warm smile.

CHAPTER 16

They had left the "guv" and "sarge" axioms behind and now they were Anna and Alex. He arrived at Anna's flat as arranged and as he rang the doorbell he was feeling just a little apprehensive. Not in the least about the meal that Anna was going to cook, but simply because he wanted everything to go as well as had previously been the case on their previous date. That evening and night had gone so well and they'd both been so "high" on feelings, that he simply wanted things to go the same way. He really was falling for Anna and he sincerely hoped that she was feeling the same way. He could look to the future and he was thinking that he could put the past, the tragic consequences and ensuing turmoil and sadness, behind him and now find happiness. Sometimes, he had thought that he might never find happiness and love such as he had felt for his wife and that the gap which had opened up following her death would never be healed.

She had been killed when a drunken driver, in the country for only a few weeks, from where they drove on the right; had gone through a red light and hit the car his wife was driving, full on the side. Alex had always recriminated himself for not insisting that her car had side impact airbags, but the truth was that they were much more expensive then, so they'd had to settle for a cheaper model. But for the lack of this side airbag, she would probably still be alive.

But now, Alex had finally managed to put the hurt and self-recriminations aside and allow himself to be taken to a different place. A place where the hurt and pain had been put behind him, and now he was coming to realise that had it been him that had been killed and she been left, he would have wanted his wife to find someone else to love and cherish and to have deep feelings for. Now that Anna had come into his life, he realised that things could and would be different. He would find that "healing" that had been so elusive.

With these thoughts circling in his head, the door was opened and Anna welcomed him with a huge smile and the waft of something very special in the air. This time it wasn't just her perfume, but a something very inviting in the food line.
'Hi Alex, spot on time. I knew you would be.' He said nothing but put down the bottle of wine he'd been holding, on to the table in the hallway and reached out to her. Putting his arms around her, he pulled her to him, holding her very firmly. She reached up and put her arms around his neck and they kissed. A long kiss, a hard, passionate kiss, as though they had been building up to this moment; which in fact they had. For days, they'd had to restrain themselves, in the knowledge that their "out of work" environment must stay completely divorced from their work lives. They both knew that should they be considered "a couple" in the "together" sense, then they would be made to work in different stations at the very least. That was becoming unthinkable.
'Hey, tiger, I can't breathe', she said, when they finally broke apart. 'I hope you're hungry.'
'Yes, but I'd like some food as well,' he said.
'Oh, so that's the way it is; I see. Never mind the meal I've been slaving over for hours, to tempt you and impress you, all you want is nookie. That's all you blokes have on your mind isn't it?'
'Now that's not fair. You want me just as much as I want you, go on and admit it.'
'Well...yes...but we've been busy all day, and we've had to put up with Jack and his boat trips. It's given me an appetite, all that sea air.'
'Me too, but I'd like to eat as well. But to be truthful and to be absolutely fair, just to keep things on an even keel, since you mention boating, and given that we missed lunch due to your nattering to your "fancy man" aka Fuller "Harbour" Masterson, I'm absolutely starving!'
'Bastard,' she said, giving him a quite firm punch on the shoulder, 'he's not my "fancy man," he's just a very nice person, polite and gentlemanly.'
'And I'm not?'
'Don't be daft, you're all that and nice and cuddly too.'
'That's all right then, as long as you got what you wanted from him; information that is.'

'I certainly did, but that's for tomorrow back at work. Tonight's for us, isn't it?'

'Sure is.'

Alex looked at her, up and down, feasting his eyes. 'You look terrific Anna.'

She was dressed in a long, silky, "burnt orange" colour skirt and a simple black halter neck top in a similar lightweight fabric. This clung to her figure and as she turned toward the kitchen, it became obvious as her breasts were accentuated. This observation had a more or less immediate effect.

'Thank you, one tries you know,' she said with a little mock curtsy.

'That combination really accentuates your slim figure, as if it needed accentuating, which is doesn't; it's really sexy.'

'Right, now, if you can peel your eyes off me, are you staying? If you are, you can put your coat in the hall cupboard and then perhaps you would like to pour us some drinks, all right?'

'Your command is my wish, oh gorgeous one.'

'Right, and don't you forget it,' she said in a very serious tone.

Alex hung up his coat, and took a look around the flat, as he'd not been to Anna's before. Inspecting the room, he took in the quite extensive bookshelves. He noticed many books which indicated her depth of interest in other than "pulp fiction" which he had quite wrongly expected. The room was furnished mostly with what he recognised as IKEA furniture. Not expensive but very comfortable and stylish. Going over to the kitchen area, there was an open high "counter." Placing the glasses and bottle, Anna handed him an opener and he deftly uncorked the bottle with a satisfying "pop."

'My kind of sound,' said Anna.

He poured two glasses, handing one to Anna.

"You approve of my living style then?"

'I certainly do; very nice and very "you."

Taking a sip she said, 'Mmm, that's nice.' She was doing something with lots of pots and pans and spice jars; something which smelled extremely appetising, not to mention "oriental."

'Hey, that's smells really good.'

'Oh, shit! I didn't think to ask – I hope you like Chinese?'

'You must be joking, I love it.'

'Thank heavens for that. I've made a simple "Sweet and Sour Chicken" dish with rice and a sauce. I hope you like it. It's simple but tasty.'

'If it tastes anywhere near how it smells, it'll be fantastic. I can't wait.'

'Well, you'll have to; but at least the food won't be long,' Anna said looking back over her shoulder with a very cheeky smile on her face. They were both looking forward to their time together and Anna was determined that it would be memorable.

'Would you like to put a CD on, whatever you can see in the rack that you like?'

'Good idea.' Going over to the CD rack he looked at her collection. As they had discussed on their previous dates, they had fairly similar tastes in music, so he chose an Enya album, "Storms in Africa," and put it in her player. 'I hope you like this one Anna,' he called over to her.

'Anything relaxing and melodic, you know what I like. It's nearly ready. If you'd like to set the table, you know, the usual things; you'll find everything in the sideboard unit just over there,' she said, pointing to the cabinet opposite the kitchen.

As Alex was setting the cutlery and table mats and napkins, he said, 'I like your flat Anna, everything is really nicely decorated and not "over-fussy," if you know what I mean. Your taste in furniture is great, I really like it.'

'Thanks, I like it to be "uncluttered" and with simple stuff, you know most of it is IKEA, as I'm sure you can tell.'

'Whatever, it doesn't have to be expensive to be in good taste and design.'

'That's true, and anyway it's easy to achieve a good look as their stuff is always well designed. I especially love those chairs over there,' she said indicating a particular style which Alex recognised. 'I find that chair is so comfortable and relaxing. Are you ready to eat?'

'I certainly am.'

'Then, if you'd like to take these plates over, I'll bring the wine.'

They sat opposite each other so that they could have all the meaningful "eye contact" that played such an integral part in their burgeoning relationship.

Alex raised his glass to Anna and said, 'Anna, thank you so much for coming into my life after so long "in the wilderness", you have given me back the feelings which I was coming to think had been locked away, but now they are back to life, thank you.'

'Thank you Alex. Our relationship has taken on a very strong meaning for me as well; a toast,' she said raising her glass also, "to us."

They touched glasses and Anna said, 'Bon appétit'.

'Toi aussi, mademoiselle.'

'You've been learning French, I can tell,' she said.

'Now you're taking the piss, Anna.'

'Not at all, I just wish I could learn it – I only know a smattering, but I like France and maybe we could go there for perhaps "Le Weekend" as they call it, one day; that would be nice.'

'It would be rather great, wouldn't it? We'll have to try to arrange a weekend off together and organise something.'

'I'd really like that, something else to look forward to.'

'Why, what's the "something else" you're looking forward to?'

'Can't you guess?'

'Oh... but I think I can.'

'Just get on with your meal and stop grinning.'

'I've got to say one thing Anna.'

'Oh yes, and what's that then?'

'This meal is bloody delicious, thanks so much. It makes my cooking very "second rate."'

'Nonsense, your Turkey meal was great.'

'It was "alright," but yours is better. The ginger gives it a great "punch" and the sweet and sour sauce superb, just a hint of sesame, and the very thinly shredded carrot and the sliced red pepper gave it a whole new dimension.'

'I'm impressed that you have the palate to appreciate the little "extras," most blokes wouldn't have a clue when it comes to taste.'

'I suppose it comes from living on one's own and having to rustle up meals which are not full of stodge, or preparing something that ends in "ding".'

'Whatever, I'm still impressed,'

'Thanks "hon."' Alex wasn't sure if that soubriquet was received well or not; so he left it for the time being.

They continued enjoying their meal and when they had finished, Anna served up the dessert of fried Cox's apples with cinnamon sugar and crème fraiche.

This was received with obvious satisfaction by Alex and a big smile from Anna.

'Would you like some cheese Alex?'

'No thanks, I'm absolutely satisfied, thanks.'

'Oh, well, in that case you can go if you want', she said, "deadpan."

'No! You muppet. You know bloody well what I mean. I know you're not satisfied; anyway, not yet.'

They looked at each other, saying nothing, except with their eyes.

They moved to sit together on the sofa and listened to music, talking about various things and quite soon, they were cuddling up and getting very intimate. They kissed, long and gently, their feelings growing surely and swiftly.

He reached up to her face and very softly and gently stroked her cheek. This provoked a look of intense warmth from her.

He felt her slender form through the soft halter neck top she was wearing and his hands moved up to feel her softly firm and naked breasts. This was making his blood pressure rise - as well as other parts of his body.

Anna was responding to his touch and slid her hands down his chest. She was caressing him with a similar touch to his, and this was also making her very aroused.

He stood up and gently pulled her up to him. They were standing, holding each other very close, with their bodies touching in all the good places. He slid his hands down to her buttocks and pulled her to him, feeling the warmth of her body, especially the heat transferring from her pubic area to his. Alex slid his hands down her hips and began to slide her skirt up, feeling the smooth naked skin of her thighs.

She was making similar moves down to his crotch and began to caress him with gentle moves which were making his stimulation very evident.

He felt her smooth skin and moved his hands round to caress her buttocks, realising that she had no panties on. This, for some inexplicable reason, probably only known to men, had an immediate and further effect on his person.

Everything was expanding, to the point where he asked Anna, 'Shall we go somewhere softer?'

'I think that's the best idea I've heard tonight.'

Anna led the way to her bedroom. This room was very "gently" decorated with soft colours. The decor was not fussy but elegant, whilst at the same time, being very comfortable. She had a double bed which pleased Alex. The thought of making love in a single bed was not the most appealing.

They continued their petting and began to undress each other. Alex was appreciating her body with a sense of wonderment, if he were honest. She had a slimness that was not in the least skinny, but she was firm from her fitness regime. Although she kept fit by going to the gym on a "regular" basis, it was not in any way obsessive, simply that she kept very much "in trim." This is what Alex was so enthralled by.

Her skirt dropped to the floor and as Alex took in her exciting body, he looked down and was absolutely smitten.

'You've gone Brazilian!' he exclaimed in wonderment and extreme pleasure.

'I guessed you'd like that,' she said, smiling.

Alex had a grin a mile wide on his face. 'Oh – my – God!' he said, 'That is wonderful. Thank you.'

He moved his hands down to caress her pubis where the skin was so soft and smooth. He moved his head and laid his cheek against her to feel the warmth. His fingers played with her lips, gently caressing them. She responded by running her hands down his body which was also very firm, and she ran her hands down his thighs and continued caressing his, by now, very hard penis.

They sank down to the bed where they continued to caress and touch and feel each other.

She was gently but firmly stroking him, then, moving down his body, she took him into her mouth, kissing him and using her tongue to great effect.

Moving her body, she gave him a very tender look, moving her legs to straddle him. She was kneeling above him and began to move gently, sliding along his rigid penis, slowly back and forth, savouring the feeling of his length moving gently along her vagina, without penetration.

Soon, he was becoming so close to a climax that he had to slow things down a little. He gently rolled her over on to her back on the bed and moved his head lower down her body, where he began to kiss the soft skin of her pubis. He began to gently rub his cheek again on her soft, smooth skin – he took in the musky aroma of her sex; he gently kissed her lips, his tongue probing deeper, licking and playing with her clitoris. She was giving gentle moans of pleasure. He was ecstatic at the incredibly sensuous feeling of her naked and hairless vagina. So beautifully erotic, he thought.

Anna could feel an orgasm rising within her and she gently took hold of his shoulders and drew him back to look at his face.

'Take me Alex, give me all that you have, I want you so much.'

'I want you Anna, I need you. I want to be deep inside you, I want to be "as one" with you.'

'Come inside me darling, I need to feel you deep within me too,' Anna said with feeling.

His thrusting and her movements became synchronised and their lovemaking was, if anything, more intense than their previous night together. They both felt their passions well up into a fountain of eroticism.

Their movements increased, their bodies became melded together and they finally climaxed, together, in a very intense and powerfully shared orgasm.

They both lay, pleasantly exhausted, continuing to caress and kiss each other.

'That was wonderful Alex, thank you.'

'You don't have to thank me; don't ever thank me, it took me so high I thought I was going on a space flight. It's me who should thank you, but we don't need to say that. We just need to keep these feelings and let them grow for both us equally. I simply have this wish, that what we have now will go on getting better and better, so that we can share each other in every way possible.'

'What a lovely sentiment. I agree with you and I feel exactly the same way. I'm sure that something has started between us that's worth really working harder and harder to keep improving, to keep loving thoughts and loving feelings for each other. Does that sound a bit "gooey?" 'No! Of course not; we have something really very special. I'll be honest and say that it's happening really "by chance," as I never really gave it much of a thought until I began to realise just how good you are at being "you," and anyway, there's nothing wrong with being a bit "gooey", as long as it's private.'

Anna responded by looking a little serious. 'Yes, that's what's going to be the hardest part, I hope you realise. Now that things are getting or rather got, serious, we have to be extra especially careful at work. We have to keep our feelings really "buttoned up" – or in your case, "zipped up,"' she said with a huge grin.

Alex gave her a gentle shove and she fell back onto the bed, giggling.

And everything started over again.

They finally managed to drift off and they both slept deeply, holding each other in a tender embrace, with complete satisfaction, and their urges "sated"; for the time being anyway.

In the morning, Anna woke a little before Alex and she slipped out of bed quietly, to go into the kitchen and make some coffee. She was standing at the worktop, waiting for the kettle to boil and, silently, Alex appeared by her side. He was wearing only "boxer" shorts, whilst Anna had a very long and baggy "T" shirt which came below her knees. She was just a little startled. 'Oh, you sneak,' she said, 'I was going to surprise you.'

'If you want a surprise, come here', he said, and pulled her to him in a gentle but firm embrace. Their bodies were touching in all the right places again. Alex could feel her warmth and he said, 'I can feel your warm and very beautiful pussy and it's making me very horny, I'll have you know.'

'Do you think I can't tell,' she said, smiling. With that she lifted her 'T' shirt up above her thighs, saying, 'What a lovely way to say "good morning"? It's a good job you've got baggy boxers on,' she reached down and took hold of his penis, guiding it with unerring accuracy, into her.

'Fuck me darling,' she said with intense feeling. 'Fuck me with all of you.'

Their lovemaking couldn't wait for the coffee........ that came to the boil just a little after they did.

CHAPTER 17

Whilst Alex and Anna were over at Goathorn, Alice had managed to encourage Jo Stafford, the shop assistant where the murder victim had purchased a shirt, to come in for another interview.
Alice had taken her again to the more "well-appointed" interview room, IR2.

'Thanks for coming in again Jo, I realise that it must be inconvenient, but I have to stress again that it is most important that we find the "friend" who was with this man who bought the shirt. Now, you said before that you thought you recognised him, but couldn't place him. I really hope that you've searched your memory and found more details. This man could lead us to clues which help to solve a very serious crime. So far, you are the best link we have and I'm hoping that your memory has not deserted you. Have you had any further thoughts on who he is?'
'I think so, but I'm not sure.'
'Don't worry; just do the best you can, Jo.'
'Actually, I think I do know him, or at least, well, I don't actually know him, but I think I know where you might look for him.'
Alice's heart rate jumped slightly.
'Okay, you saw him with the man who bought the shirt who you've identified him from the photo we showed you. His "friend," is he someone you have seen before or know who he might be?'
'I think he might be someone who used to go on fishing trips with my ex-husband.'
'And these fishing trips, did they go out to sea or just along the coast?'
'I think, and don't quote me on this, that they used to go out to sea but I don't know how far.'
'And how long did they go for, just at night or were they out for longer?'
'Sometimes they would go out early evening and come back the next morning, you know, "night fishing" and sometimes they would stay out for a couple of days.'
'And do you think when they stayed out for a couple of days, that they went very far out to sea?'
'I've no idea, sorry, my ex didn't talk about it much. He was a secretive person. Things weren't too good between us, if you know what I mean.'
'I've not been married before, so I don't really know, but I think I can guess what you mean. So do you have a name for this friend?'
'I'm sorry, I can only remember hearing the name which sounded like "Markus or Mehmet," although I doubt that was his real name.'
'Why do you say that Jo?'
'Because he had very dark olive skin, like my husband. He could have been from Cyprus, so I think his name would be changed to something more 'English', like 'Marlon'. See, my husband's Cypriot name was "Furkan" and he got loads of stick for that, so he changed that to "Freddie," pretty soon. Mind you, that was a mistake as he was then called "Ferkin Freddie," and that made him mad as well.
'I can see why,' said Alice. Can you describe this "Markus"?
'He had black curly hair, quite like the man in your photo and his skin, as I said, was "olive", like most Cypriot men, although he was not as "swarthy" looking compared to my husband; in fact he looked a lot more attractive and "polished", if you know what I mean. He also had a heavy black beard.'
'And do you know where this man and your husband went to join the boat for their fishing trips?'
'I've no idea, sorry, only that he went down to Poole. He just said something like, "I'm going fishing tonight, and I'll see you later." Sometimes, as I say, he'd be gone for one night, sometimes for two or three. I never knew and he never told me. He'd just come back.'
'And did he tell you where he'd been?'
'No, never. He was very, what I would call, "uncommunicative."'
'And you didn't worry, I mean when he was gone for a couple of days.'

'Do you know what, by the time he was going on these trips, I didn't really care if he came back or not. Sometimes, I'm afraid I rather hoped he'd not come back. It would have saved me a lot of bad things. I know it's not a nice thing to say, but sometimes I wish he'd had an "accident" when he was diving, that would have solved the problem.'

'So he went diving then?'

'I think he used to go diving when he was back in what he said was his home town, called "Karpaz Gate Marina" on the northern coast of Cyprus; at least that's where he said he lived. Perhaps he just worked at the marina, but that's where he used to go diving. He may even have been an instructor there.'

'That's interesting, thought Alice. 'And when he came back from his fishing trips, is that when the abuse happened?'

'Usually, yes. He'd either been drinking or would go out again and get drunk. When he came back, it would all start. The hitting and worse.'

She didn't pursue the "worse" part of Jo's reply, just let the thought sink in. 'As you've given us the address of your ex, we can contact him to take our investigation further.' Alice was feeling very sorry for this young woman, who was not that far from her own age. 'Okay, Jo, I won't ask you any more about that, I can see it hurts and I think I understand, although thankfully it has never happened to me. All I can say is that now you are divorced, maybe you can get your life back together.'

'Yes, I'm trying, I have a new boyfriend and he is very nice, a local lad who is good to me and he really cares.'

'I'm so glad for you Jo; you seem a really nice girl. I wish you all the best of luck for the future.'

'Thanks, and I hope I've been able to help.'

'You certainly have thanks again. We'll get you back to your home. If you'll just wait here, I'll arrange a car for you.'

'Thanks.'

'All the best Jo.' Alice went out of the interview room and went to the desk sergeant. 'Can you get a car to take Jo Stafford home please, she's been very helpful?'

'Okay Alice love, will do. Just be a mo', I'll give her a call when it's here, is she in IR1 or 2?'

'IR 2.'

'Done.'

'Thanks Bob.'

That was Bob Thomas, the Desk Sergeant.

CHAPTER 18

After Anna and Alex had parted, she left her flat before him, to "stagger" their arrival at the station. Anna was talking to Alice as Alex walked in. He said a quite light-hearted "good morning" to his team and instantly, Alice's "radar scanner" was receiving signals from his demeanour which served once again to re-inforce her thought that he was "seeing" someone, although she had absolutely no idea who. 'Anyway, I'm happy for him', she thought. To be fair, Alice was herself quite smitten by Jeffrey Boyd, the head of forensics at the Ferndown facility of SSD. She had taken a short trip after her shift had finished the day before to pay a visit to the department, after calling him to make sure that he would be there and they could meet. Their meeting went very well and they seemed to hit it off. They were similar in age and as Jeffrey had a good idea of her looks from his enquiries, he was able to be very calm and collected when she walked in and he was very complimentary, which put her instantly at ease. He could see that she was quite nervous at meeting someone with whom she'd had only contact on the phone, but he made her feel comfortable and their meeting turned into a very "extended" one. The final result of which was that they would see each other outside work to continue their quest for learning about each other. Alice was very happy to be in this situation as she was beginning to think that life was "passing her by." Her private thought was that she would have to cut down on her cream cakes, which had become quite an irresistible diversion in the absence of another "distraction," but hopefully, that was to change.

'Okay, people, let's have a briefing. Is Tom here?' asked Alex.
'Yes,' said Alice, 'he was in the canteen just now, shall I go and fetch him?'
'If you wouldn't mind Alice, thanks. Just tell him that I expect him to be in the office by this time of the morning and not swilling coffee and chatting up the female constables.'
'I'll pass on your message guv,' she said with a grin, 'that'll put a fire under him.'
Alice walked down the two flights of stairs to the canteen to give Tom his "gee-up", and while she was gone, Anna went into Alex's office wearing a very wide smile. She quickly checked behind her through the door, looking down the corridor. 'What a lovely night, I'm not sure that I've come down to earth yet. That gets a great big "Wow" from me.'
'Not only a "wow" night for me but a 3 star meal as well, that was so nice, and I have to say that I don't think I've ever had a better night, ever, what with all the "extras" as well.'
'Extras?'
'You know what I mean, that smooth little creature of yours.'
'Oh that, I know you mentioned a little while ago, that you preferred "considered baldness"; did you like it?'
'Like it - I absolutely love it '– he paused – 'and you.'
'Do you mean that?'
He looked her straight in the eye. 'Yes, unequivocally, yes.'
'I do like that.' - She turned. 'Oh oh, I can hear footsteps...then she said in a louder voice, 'Okay, guv, briefing now, yes?'
'Yes, Anna, can you get Alice and Tom and we'll all go into the main office.'
'Okay guv.'
Anna went into the corridor as Alice and Tom were coming back. Anna looked at them both, turned back and gesturing with her thumb toward the main room, said firmly and without preamble, 'Briefing – now - main office.'
They all trooped to the large office on the second floor which was the CID department of the Bournemouth Police. Their working office had an open aspect and a number of desks where the more mundane tasks were carried out, such as writing statements or general paperwork carried out by the other staff working in the CID section. Whilst the various desks and computer stations were usually occupied, there were specialised sections where more detailed searches on computer were made, one of which was where Alice usually spent her time, as she was recognised as the team "IT specialist". The other desks were where the constables and other ranks carried out their tasks. However, at the far end was the larger Incident Room, where the special events, in this case, the murder

investigation, where laid out. There was a large whiteboard on one wall and here the important facts and related information, photographs and links were itemised and displayed. All information, as it came in, was collated and transposed to this board, so that everyone could see instantly, the state of the investigation.

Alex walked in and said 'Okay, we have a second briefing, to bring together all the information and facts that we now have. First, Tom, please. What do you have?'

'Right guv, I got on to the sand companies and got quite a bit of information regarding the special sands that are used in certain types of installation and I thought as this seemed to be concerning the oil-field over at Goathorn, there might be a link to oil installations. I discovered that over at Swanage, there's a place called "California Quarry", where they've been building a special drilling site. When I got on to the office controlling the site, I enquired what sort of concrete they were using. I was told that when building certain parts of the site, very dense concrete has to be used, for instance when the pipes are buried.'
'Who are "they", Tom?'
'Sorry guv, "Perenco", the company who runs the oil-fields now.'
'Right, now we know who "they" are. Carry on.'
'Now, Alice has told me that she's had a word with Forensics;' At this point, Tom looked over to Alice and gave her a surreptitious wink to show that he knew she'd been there, ostensibly to see Jeffrey Boyd and that he'd keep that to himself. 'So I think I'll let her tell you about this in a moment, if that's okay?'
'Fine, carry on Tom.'
Anna interrupted. 'I had a thought on that point. If, as we think is possible, illegal workers are being brought over from France or wherever, they wouldn't be very welcome at the oil company. They would be inspected by all sorts of departments and I really don't think they would be using illegal workers.'
'That's a very good point Anna. We'll keep that in mind, but I think you're right.'
Alex pointed back to Tom.
'I've also been on to Cobbs Quay office to ask if they know about this boat called a "Redbaye Storm-Force", or something like that but they seemed a little bit cagey and told me that they can't be sure, but I also asked about a "Martin" and they said they'd got a load of "Martins" with boats, and suggested that I go over there and have a look. I had a look on Google at their website and from the photos; they've got hundreds of boats there.'
'Maybe you should get a photograph of this "Task Force" type of boat, if there is one, and take that over to Cobbs Quay and have a look round to see if you can see this boat. That way, you can find out who owns it.'
'Okay guv, will do.'

'Alice, what do you have from Forensics then?'
Alice was doing her best not to blush, as her visit to Ferndown was most enjoyable for her and, apparently, for him. They got on well together and had agreed to meet again, outside their respective offices. Gathering herself, she said, 'This, "sand" which was found, was not sand at all. It turned out to be "magnetite".'
'What the heck is magnetite then? I've never heard of it - has anyone here heard of it?' asked Alex, looking around at them all.
Anna answered, 'I've heard of "magnesite", but it could have been "magnetite", but I don't know which spelling is correct and in any case I've no idea what it is.'
Alex apologised, 'Sorry Alice, do carry on.'
'Magnetite, spelt with a "t" is a mineral, the most strongly magnetic mineral found in nature; It's a common iron oxide. It's also called "lodestone" and was probably related to iron and is actually magnetic. It was probably used to make the very first magnetic compasses. Apparently, it was first used in China around 300 BC.'
'Well, we live and learn,' said Tom. 'I can see that you've been reading up on it Alice.'
'It's called 'knowledge, Tom,' she retorted, giving him a sideways look, but actually feeling rather pleased with herself. 'But, apart from all that, magnetite, as well as among other things, is used as an abrasive additive in "waterjet" cutting.'

'Alice, I appreciate your new role as the "font of all knowing" but can you please get to the point about this stuff found on the body?'

'Sorry, guv -the main thing is that magnetite is also used as an additive to concrete to make it about 60% more dense than normal concrete and that it is used especially in oil-field installations for things like supporting and encasing pipes and other bits of things around the oil-field site, which need extra-strong material. It's also used on high-density and strength installations like sea defences and harbour walls.'

'Now we are getting to the "nub." Good stuff Alice. So this guy had this magnetite in or on his clothing. I think it fair to say that this all ties in and puts him in the frame for some sort of construction work, do we all agree?'

There was a small chorus of agreement from the assembled multitude of three.

'And Tom, you said that there was an "on-going" oil drilling installation over at Swanage, you said "California Quarry"? Is that right?'

'Yes, guv.'

'I've never heard of that place, have you Anna, Alice?'

Tom ventured, 'I think it's quite near Swanage, or at least, near a big caravan park, you know holiday homes and the such-like.'

'And there's an oil drilling site there?'

'From what I can find out, yes and it's not too far from the coast.'

Looking around at them all he said, 'I think after Anna's thoughts on the wisdom of using illegal workers, perhaps we should leave the oil company connection for the time being and perhaps look to sea-defence work where that sort of material would be used. So let's, just for a moment, try to follow a "plot-line". If this dead guy was involved in some way with working on some sort of marine project, and I don't know at the moment how we can confirm this, as he was not English, but from what seems to be a Cypriot or Turkish derivation, this suggests to me that either, he is completely "legit", and we have to confirm this somehow, or he is working "on the black" so to speak. Now, my suspicious mind says that if he's not "kosher", then he could be an "illegal immigrant", brought over to work for low wages. Now, the thing that I need to know is, is the work being done over at this "California Quarry," being done by the parent company, "Parenco" I believe, or is it a sub-contract outfit who might employ "dubious" people? Tom, I leave that to you to find out the facts, although now somehow I doubt this.'

'Okay guv, I'll get onto that.'

'One thing, Tom, make bloody sure that you have your facts right, or we'll be in big trouble if we go and start accusing the big company of something they either don't know about or are doing completely correctly, so get it right.'

'Yes, boss.'

'Now, Anna and I went over to Goathorn, as you know, for another look around the building there. We found, or rather Anna found, tyre-marks in the dust of the building, which looked very like a quad-bike tyres. We couldn't find one because it would be stored in the internal room within the building. I'm requesting a search warrant so that SOCO can take a look. It has a disgustingly strong small but maybe it's all the fishing gear that would be stored there. It had no windows and had some very secure locks. We have found out that it was leased from Perenco to a guy called "Martin", who has a 35ft and powerful fishing boat, which we think might be moored at Cobbs Quay, where Tom is going to try to find this boat. He stores all his fishing-gear in this shed, but no-one has ever seen inside it. My thought process leads me to suspect that a possible scenario might be to pick up would-be immigrants from France, bring them over during the night and either keep them hidden or take them over to Swanage to work on this oil installation, or maybe some other place along the coast. How does that sound to you all - plausible?'

Alice said, 'Yes, it does.' What Alice was actually thinking was, why did it take two people to go and look at a shed? – Hmm. 'But surely, if he was bringing in people to this shed, wouldn't they have been either seen or heard by someone over there?'

'That is a very good point Alice and certainly worth checking into. As you say, if they were landing people there, there's a very good chance that they would be spotted, so that tells me that should this be happening, then they would be landed somewhere else. Good; moving on.'

Anna then said, 'Jo Stafford has been brought in for another interview. How did it go Alice?'
Alex looked at Anna, just a little sideways, which told her that he was just a tiny bit put-out by her stepping in, so she looked suitably sheepish, which seemed to be accepted.

Alice looked extremely smug saying, 'I got a result. Jo Stafford told me that her ex-husband not only abused her after his drinking sessions, but that he often would go out on what he told here were "fishing trips", which sometimes lasted not just overnight, but up to three days. When he came home he was always tired, probably drunk and very uncommunicative. She told me that this friend who he goes with was called just "Marlon or Markus" but that he'd probably changed his name as he was also from Cyprus, like her ex-husband. He had black curly hair and had a dark complexion with a heavy beard, but that he looked a lot more sophisticated than her ex. The ex-husband," Ferkin Freddie" as he was nicknamed, would go down to Poole Harbour to meet the fishing boat for their "trips".' Alice stopped there as Alex held his hand up, 'Hang on, Marlon or Markus, could that be Martin?'
'Could be,' said Alice.
'Ferkin Freddie, now there's a name for you,' said Tom. 'Where did that come from?'
'Apparently his name is "Furkan" and he changed it to "Freddie." The rest I'll leave up to you Tom.'
'Alice, very well done with your interview. We now have a name to the frame. We have the ex-husband's address, so I think we'll have to go and see him. If Tom can find this "Martin" and get a surname for him, that would be great. The other information we need, and most importantly, is who killed this guy, who is he, and who planted him on the beach? Actually, this would seem to tie in to the theory of this boat going over to France to collect individuals and bring them back here. For what purpose exactly, we've yet to establish.
'Perhaps the dead guy was the friend of "Martin," if that is the one who we think it is, and why kill him and then dump the body there?' asked Anna. 'That's another burning question to which we'll have to get answers to.'
Alex called his superior officer, Superintendent Alison Beavers to ask for the issue of a search warrant for the internal room in the shed at Goathorn.
 'Can this not wait until you find the owner of the shed Alex?'
'I don't think it can ma'am.'
'Why not; surely it can only have items that apply to the fishing operation?'
'To be honest, when we were looking inside the large shed, the smell I got was really overpowering and although I don't know much about fishing, there was something about the smell which made me think there was something else in there; what, I don't know, except that it did smell to me like something putrefying, although that could well be fish but I would really like to take a look before we ask the owner. If we ask his permission, by the time we find him, it might have given him time to clear out anything incriminating.'
'I see what you mean Alex. The problem is that we don't have a really good reason to issue a search warrant and I have to say that I'm reluctant. However, do you think that SOCO could get into this room without breaking the locks, so that it won't be obvious that we've had a look? But, we're not having this conversation are we?'
'No ma'am but I'm sure it's possible; they're pretty good with the technical stuff these days and I'm sure there are "ways."'
'Okay, if SOCO can give me an assurance that they can do this, then I will issue a preliminary warrant and if you find anything really incriminating, I can implement the full warrant. Let me know as soon as you can.'
'Will do ma'am, thanks.'

CHAPTER 19

Tom drove over to the other side of Poole, across the new internationally award-winning "twin sails" lifting bridge, linking Poole and Hamworthy. He was rather hoping to see the bridge lift, but that wasn't to be. It was supposed to be quite a sight when both "sails" were lifted to the top allowing boats with tall masts to pass through to the boatyards further up Holes Bay.

Passing various huge sheds belonging to Sunseeker Powerboats which seemed to have taken up much of the area surrounding the quay in Poole, he was making his way to the marina at Cobb's Quay. Sunseeker made the most expensive and lavish powerboats for people with huge amounts of money and, according to some, dubious amounts of taste. However, they provided much needed employment for skilled boat-builders and craftsmen and women of all categories from the manufacture of the hulls to the final fitting-out of the extremely luxurious interiors, not to mention the engine and power-plant installations. Whether the profits from these expensive "toys" stayed in the UK or went back to the owners of the company in China, was perhaps unknown to most, but it provided important employment for a substantial number of skilled men and women.

Tom made his way through the many varied industrial and commercial buildings which made up Hamworthy and came to Cobbs Quay Marina. There he parked up and went in search of the marina office. He was remembering the previous investigation where he had to visit the Lymington Yacht Haven and where he'd had a rather deflating encounter with one of the office staff. The very attractive receptionist, whom he really had considered approaching, turned out to be of a "different persuasion." He was sincerely hoping that this time, a similar occurrence wouldn't happen; although he did rather hope there might be someone there who took his fancy.' 'One never knows, he thought.

Locating the offices he walked into reception. There were a number of people at the desk and they were being attended to by the reception staff. As he waited for the desk to become free, he walked around the large room. This area had a vast array of photographs lining the walls with pictures of boats for sale of all types and sizes. Looking at an aerial photograph, Tom was amazed at just how big this marina was and how many boats were berthed there. It was evident that the majority of these craft were power, with not so many sailing boats. He was thinking that it could be a strong possibility that it is because it's not too easy if you have to wait for bridges to open before you can get your yacht up here.

He approached the reception desk, which had now become free. He found himself looking at a stunningly attractive girl with blonde hair and a deep tan, who gave him a big white smile with perfect teeth. Trying hard to overcome the lump in his throat, he managed to croak, 'Could I speak to someone who can tell me about one of the boats here and the owner?' Tom was instantly smitten by this beautiful girl and he was on "high alert," although he knew that this lady was way out of his league. She asked him to wait and she would find someone who could help.

'Who shall I say is asking?'

'Sorry,' he said trying to unglue his eyes from her, and fumbling out his warrant card to show her, 'I'm Detective Constable Tom Peterson from Bournemouth Police.'

'I hope you've not come to arrest me, officer,' she said with another huge smile.' Tom was finding it really hard to concentrate. He couldn't help himself and he said, 'It depends on how naughty you've been, madam.' 'Miss,' she replied. 'I'll have to confess later, I'm afraid,' she said with a giggle, 'I have to attend to some other things, but if you'd like to wait for just a moment, I'll get our yard manager to try to help. His name is Roger Whitehorn, I'm sure he'll be able to help you.'

'Thank you - Miss?'

'Geraldine Dobson, but my friends call me 'Genny Dobbs', that's Genny with a 'G''

'Thank you, 'Genny with a 'G'.'

She gave him another brilliant smile at this and she turned away, Tom was still floating just a little off the ground when a man walked over, wearing a thick navy coloured sweater and jeans, with folded down blue sailing boots. He had a mop of curly brown hair and he also wore a dark tan. He held out his hand and said in a distinctive local "burr", 'G'day zur. Can I help you?'

Tom introduced himself to Roger and asked if he could tell him if he knew either the owner or the location of the boat they were searching for. Tom had taken the trouble to search the internet for a photograph of the Redbay Stormforce 11. He pulled this photo from his pocket and offered it to Roger. 'This is the type of boat we are looking for and we believe it is owned by a man called "Martin," do you know this craft?'

'I do indeed, Detective Constable. She's a beautiful boat, very well equipped and fast too. Very seaworthy and very safe.'

'Would you say she could cross the Channel?'

'I reckons she could cross the bloomin' Atlantic, if'n that were needed. She's a great sea boat, all sorts of safety gear on board. Even got them "suspension" seats for the crew for when the sea do get rough. You don't get many boats with that sort of equipment, an' she's got twin turbo diesel engines. A real beauty.'

'How many people would she take then?'

'I'd say about 12 as a maximum, plus two crew. I know that Martin takes them fishin' "parties" way out to sea. Sometimes they be gone two or three days.'

Toms' ears pricked up at "Martin." 'Thanks for your information, so do you have a surname and address for this "Martin"?'

'I don't actually know his surname, but I'm sure that little lady over there can tell you. His details will be on her computer thingy.' He gestured toward "Genny." 'She's moored out on pontoon number 4, right at the end.'

'Thanks, Mr Whitehorn.'

'Oh, call me Roger, everyone 'ere does. See you, 'bi.'

He walked back to the reception desk and he repeated what Roger had told him. She gave Tom another flashing smile which was turning his knee joints to something between soft and softer. "Genny Dobbs" checked on her computer files for the location which Roger Whitehorn had mentioned. She soon located the details and said, 'Here it is. The boat is on pontoon number 4 and almost at the very end. It's quite a big boat, so that's where the larger craft are berthed. The owner's name is Martin Goodyear.'

'Could I go and take a look at this boat?'

'I don't think that'll be a problem but I'll just ask Roger if that is okay.'

'Thanks. In the meantime, do you have an address for him, Martin Goodyear, I mean?'

'We do indeed.' Genny gave him this address, which was in Corfe Mullen.

'Just one personal question, does he pay his bills on time or does he have anything outstanding?'

'I don't know if that would be allowed as we do have a confidentiality program here, but I'll just check.'

'I am Police, he said, I think that should prove sufficient.'

Genny was looking down at her computer screen and raised her head slightly, giving him a slow look from under hooded eyes which sent a definite shiver up his spine.

She went into the back office for a few minutes and came back with the information.

'Everything seems in order now.'

'Does that mean that it was not always right?'

'There was a problem, but that has been put right.'

'I don't suppose you could tell me what sort of problem that was?'

'I'm afraid that information like that would be very confidential unless there was an official reason for asking,' she said, again with a beautiful smile. This completely disarmed Tom.

'Okay, thanks.' Tom thought that this might need a little further "digging" and could be relevant. 'You've been a great help, Genny Dobbs with a "G"; I may be back if I have any further questions if you don't mind.'

'I don't mind at all, Detective Constable Tom Peterson. I'll come quietly if I've done anything wrong.'

Tom had a very personal thought; I'll bet you don't come quietly, but he said, 'I'll make sure I bring my handcuffs then.'

Genny just looked him straight in the eye, with a gaze which spoke volumes and said, 'That would be interesting,' with the merest hint of a smile. Tom looked back also with a direct look, also saying nothing but gave a very slight nod and then went out to the pontoons to find the boat.

He couldn't believe what had just taken place. Was she coming on to him? Has my luck changed? Nothing ventured, nothing gained, he thought.

He made his way up the long pontoon number 4, carefully stepping over the many ropes which moored the boats. This pontoon was about 200 yards long and walking out he was amazed at the various boats of different sizes and quality. They were mainly sport boats with outboard motors, but some were bigger and much more expensive cruisers. Some had "fly-bridges" and some had cabins. Nearly all of the smaller boats had covers over the exposed sections of the craft. It was obvious that the owners took great care to maintain their boats and Tom supposed that with, what must have been high cost of berthing a boat in such a marina, they would be very keen to keep the craft in tip-top condition, ready for action whenever the need or opportunity arose, not to mention the re-sale value. Nearly at the end of this pontoon, Tom saw the very boat he was looking for. As his information told him, she was about 40ft long and had a quite high and sharply raked bow. There was a cabin which took up about one third of the overall length of the craft. He looked in through the window next to the helm position and he could see the various electronic equipment consoles set out close to the wheel. He could make out what he took to be a radar set, and a GPS screen, similar to a car one he supposed, although probably more accurate, given the need to navigate close to the coast. There were two similar screens with one being angled toward the position he guessed a navigator would use. He was not sure what these were, but again he supposed they were some sort of navigation screen, to show their position and where they were headed. There were other items of electronics which Tom took to be "high-end" nautical equipment. He thought to himself, I'm not surprised he goes well out to sea in this beauty, with all this equipment. Taking a look further back in the cabin, he saw the special forward facing seats, but they looked very complicated having at the base, what seemed to be either hydraulic or pneumatic tubes. He imagined that they must be the special seats for when they are going fast and they have straps so they can be strapped in if things get really rough; the one's Roger Whitehorn had mentioned. Wow, I'll bet it's something else to be in this baby, he imagined. As the boat was moored along the pontoon he was able to see the name on the stern, "Predator."

The description of this type of craft was that of a "fast patrol boat," suitable for high speed interception work. A very apt name, thought Tom, I'll bet that could mean intercepting pirates.

Less than reluctantly, he walked back to the reception desk, going over to Genny, who was looking down at some paperwork. As he approached, she looked up and gave Tom a big smile. Tom's insides did a small "loop the loop" again. He said, 'If I won the lottery, I'd have one like that. She's a beauty – just like you,' he added, instantly feeling that he'd gone a little too far.'

'That's lovely of you, thank you Detective Tom.'

'I might be back, Genny Dobbs, with a G,' he said.

'I look forward to it.' This was said with a final flashing smile.

As he was about to walk out of the reception area, which was now empty, she called to him. 'Don't forget your handcuffs, Detective Tom.'

He couldn't think of anything to say and even if he did, his throat was too constricted, so he just raised his hand in salute and walked out feeling about two feet off the ground; driving back to HQ in a cloud of anticipation.

Back at the CID office, Tom went directly to see Alex.

'We have a name and the boat guv.'

'Great. So what's this chap's name?'

'His name is Martin Goodyear and he lives in Corfe Mullen. I've had a look at the boat and it is certainly very capable of crossing the channel according to the Head of the Marina. It's about 40ft long and has quite a big cabin. Apparently it can carry up to 14 people.'

'Okay Tom, Good work. "Did you get a description of this bloke?"'

Tom realised with a jolt that he'd not asked Genny for this, and covered up by saying, 'my informant hasn't actually met him; so, no.'

I think it's time we had a chat with this Martin Goodyear and the ex-husband of Jo Stafford. I think they are both involved in this "whatever-it-is" and therefore the murder, since we know that the body was of someone from a different country and that there could be a definite connection with this boat. My thoughts are becoming more towards people-smuggling and perhaps even worse would be the prospect of the sale of "organs".

'Bloody hell. Do we know which country guv?'

'We think its Northern Cyprus.'

Anna had come into the office as the door was open and she heard the final part of this exchange. She said, 'Excuse me, sorry to butt in, but aren't Cypriots allowed legal entry to the UK, they wouldn't be illegal?'

'Hi, Anna; no, in fact they're not. I've checked up; their passports are only TRNC passports; that's Turkish Republic of Northern Cyprus, and they're not recognised by the UK, so if anyone tries to come here to work, they are strictly speaking, illegal and would be deported, immediately, supposedly.'

'And we know how long it takes to get deported don't we guv? I believe there are literally thousands waiting for deportation but nothing seems to be done about it.'

'Thankfully, that's not for us to worry about Anna.'

Tom spoke, 'So if this boat, or Martin Goodyear and this other guy, who could be "Ferkin Freddie," were bringing them in, they'd want to keep it very quiet wouldn't they?'

'I'd say that's a 'no-brainer' Tom.'

'But would bringing in a few illegal's be worth all the aggro guv?' asked Anna.

'I don't really know how much the illegal's pay to get to the UK, do you, but I'm sure it must be thousands.'

'I don't reckon doing fishing trips would pay for the fuel and running costs for that bloody great boat,' suggested Tom.

'Have you seen the boat then Tom?' asked Alice, who had been walking past and heard the last part of this conversation.

Tom turned to Alice to answer her question. 'I'll say I bloody have. I went over to Cobbs Quay and they told me where she was berthed and I had a look at her. She's a big 40ft boat with a large cabin and can take about 14 people. It's got masses of electronic gizmos and it must cost a bomb to run.'

'I think I agree with Tom, guv. Surely fishing trips can't make a great deal of money. Do you think we should check around to see if we can find out just how many times he takes this boat out and how long he goes for?'

'I think that's a very good idea, Alice. Tom, I'll task you for that. I'm sure Cobbs Quay will know information like that because surely he re-fuels there I imagine.'

Tom was instantly very keen to go back to Cobbs where he would not only gather that information but he would hopefully see the lovely Genny with a 'G' again.

'I'll go over there and ask them guv.'

'You could just give them a phone call, which would be easier surely?'

Tom was felt thwarted; then he said, 'but I do have a good contact there and I'm sure,' here he paused slightly, 'that they can give me a better overview of the movements with a "person to person" conversation, and I might think of other things when I'm actually in the "boaty" environment. What do you think guv? I might find somebody who can give me a description.'

'Okay, maybe you're right. This time I want all the information and everything relevant. The last time there were gaps and holes in our reports and I think this led to the cock-up.'

'Right guv, I'll make sure that I get everything I can.' You can be sure of that, he thought.

'Okay, go and see what you can dig up for us.' Tom was more than happy to go back to have a chat with his "contact."

After Tom left the office and Alice had returned to her desk and computer, Alex turned to Anna.

'I'd like your assessment of this scenario. Illegal workers picked up from France, brought back to Goathorn, or somewhere in the area, where they are kept, overnight, maybe in that internal shed in the large building, to work "on the black".'

'So far, I'm with you guv, but what about the murder?'

'I'm coming to that. Let's suppose that there's an argument or a fight and this victim is killed, they then have to get rid of the body.'

'Hang on guv; surely it would be the easiest thing just to chuck it overboard. It would probably be washed up somewhere and there would be no clues.'

'If this murder happened at sea, I'd agree with you, but let's suppose it took place on-shore somewhere, even at the oil-site. They wouldn't want the body to be found there or there would be links. Someone would know about how the workers got there and even if they'd keep quiet about working "on the black" they'd not want anything to do with a murder, surely?'

'Unless perhaps they're trying to put us "off the scent," so to speak.

'I guess you're right. I can see that a body would be hard to disguise in that case, so it might make sense to "cloud the issue."

'Unless there are other ways of disposing a body over there?'

'Do you mean that there could be others?'

'Why not, we know nothing at the moment do we?

'We still do not have a full autopsy report do we?'

'That's true, we don't. I'll get on to George and chase him up, see what he has to say.

'Another thing which kind of bothers me is why the body was only "half-buried"? Didn't Bob Chorley say something about hearing a boat or maybe a quad bike?' This makes me wonder if he did hear a boat and that boat was actually something to do with the dumping of the body.'

'For me, guv, I have to wonder why the body was actually dumped on that small bit of beach and not even buried properly, you know, why not just dump it in the sea as was suggested earlier?'

'That's something we have to fathom out Anna. I don't know at this stage and until we can get some better information regarding the trips out on this boat, we'll have that unanswered question. My gut feeling is that perhaps this Bob Chorley heard something, went to investigate and they either saw or heard him coming and legged it. There must be a good reason and maybe we should have a "brain-storming" session now to get some ideas together.'

'That does sound a possibility, but I'd have thought that if they'd been seen, Bob Chorley is a lucky man.'

'Yep, does sound a bit "iffy," but all we can do at the moment is chuck ideas about.'

'Oh, you mean run it up the flagpole and see which way it blows?'

'Will you get out of here Anna!?'

CHAPTER 20

Three days previously.

It was dark, very dark, and the boat was making its way by GPS and depth gauge to find the Goathorn Jetty. Quietly, keeping the engine revs low and moving slowly around the harbour channels very carefully, the boat approached the jetty and made fast the mooring lines to the bollards. The engines were put in neutral but left running on "tick-over," making very little noise except for a gentle "burble".

A body was passed over the side onto the jetty planking, wrapped in a polythene sheet. Two men left the boat with shovels strapped across their backs, and picked up the body. Carrying the body with not a little difficulty, they made their way a short distance along the southern beach of the Goathorn Peninsula. They found a small patch of sand which formed the beach and "unrolled" the polythene sheeting. The body rolled out onto the sand. They took the shovels began to dig a grave for the body in the silty sand.

'This is fucking difficult', said one man. 'This stuff isn't sand; it's more like sticky bloody mud.'

'Just shut up and dig, for Christ's sake, we don't have much time. If that tide gets any lower we'll be stuck here with a body and then we'll be in the shit and no mistake, so just dig will you?'

'But why here in this stuff?'

'Because it won't get washed out by the tide and it'll stay buried.'

'I don't know why we didn't just chuck it over the side, rather than piss around doing this.'

If the stupid fucker hadn't started the argument with the others when he did, we'd have been in the channel and we could've done, but doing it here in the harbour, we're stuffed or the body would be found somewhere here in the harbour and all hell would break loose.'

'Yeah, s'pose you're right Martin.'

'Right, so stop yakking and get digging.'

They hadn't been shovelling the very sticky and heavy "sand" for long, when they heard a voice.

'Is anyone there?' said the voice.

The two men stopped digging and kept very quiet.

'Hello, is anyone there?' again.

They still said nothing. An indistinct figure appeared at a distance through a gap in the hedging which bordered the little beach.

One of the two men, who had stopped digging, whispered, 'what do we do now?'

'Nothing,' was the whispered reply, 'you go back to the boat and get ready to cast off, but just hold her with both lines in your hand, we may have to get under way quickly, but I'm going to sort this bloke out if I can.'

'But he'll see what we are doing. Shouldn't we "take care of him"?

'Don't be fucking stupid, he's probably one of the oil-field workers and if we "sort him out" as you call it, there'll be police here bloody quickly, if that's what you want.'

'Okay, you're the boss, I'll get back to the boat, but don't be too long or as you've said, we don't want to be stuck here.'

'Right, so shut up and piss off back to the boat.'

As the first man ducked behind the hedge bordering the small beach and ran off back to the boat, the figure took shape, became more distinct and approached.

The figure spoke. 'Hoi, what are you doing here at this time of night, you've no business being here, I don't know what you're up to, but it's bound to be something dodgy.'

It's all right; I'm just getting some of my stuff from the shed back there.' He pointed in the direction of the large shed on the end of the Jetty.

'Oh, are you that fishing bloke then, that takes the parties out for fishing trips?'

'That's right, so there's nothing to worry about.'

'It's a bit late innit, but why are you here, I thought you said you were getting stuff from the shed?'
'I know, I forgot to get some gear earlier and it's too important to leave.' He thought quickly and said, 'and I'm just digging for some bait, so why don't you just piss off and leave me alone?'

As the figure came closer, he became more visible. The voice said, 'I work on the oil-site, who are you?'
'That doesn't matter, let's just say I'm the "fishing trip man" and leave it at that.'
By this time Bob Chorley was close enough to see that there was a half-buried body lying on the sand.
He saw that this dark-skinned man, who had curly hair and a heavy beard, was wearing a cap which didn't really contain all the hair. He couldn't see the face too well but he didn't look "English." 'Bloody hell, what's that then?' he said, pointing to the body. 'What are you doing?"
'What does it look like? I'm digging for bait, but never you mind, just forget you've seen anything'
Having seen exactly what was going on, he said, 'Digging in this stuff is pretty difficult and I can see what you were trying to do.'
'What made you come out here now, at this time of night?'
'I heard what I thought was a quad bike, 'cos I know that there is one that comes from that shed, but now I know it was your boat I heard, and that's why I came to investigate.'
'Well, if you just forget that you've seen anything, I'll be on my way.'
'But you can't leave that "thing" here, can you? I mean, I'll have to report it.' Bob was looking very "cagey" now.
'What's your name?'
'Bob.'
'What could I do to make you "forget" things, Bob, apart from making you join him, then,' he said pointing down to the body and looking at Bob with a very hard and menacing stare.
That caused Bob to worry as it dawned on him that this was a body and therefore someone had killed him. He actually thought; I suppose this bloke's done him in and now he's trying to bury him. Regaining his bravado, he said, 'I'm sure you can think of something to make me lose my memory.'
With that, a wedge of banknotes was offered, and a hand extended to take the cash, but before the notes were released, the hand was snatched back.
Bob growled, 'What's your game then?'
'Let's just say this, if anyone comes sniffing around asking questions about me and they are told anything about this,' he said, gesturing to the body, 'you will suffer the same fate. Do you believe me? Take a good look at him and don't forget, I know who you are.'
Taking a closer look at the body, the wounds and blood were all too evident. Bob Chorley was then told in no uncertain terms, and graphically, exactly what would happen to him if he called the police or told anyone what he had seen tonight. There was a description of a large "fish knife" which was around 18" long and extremely sharp, as well as a "boning knife" were two of the items which would be used and the sort of injuries that they would inflict, were carefully outlined. Although it was so dark, some of the knife wounds on the back of the body and the blood staining on the shirt were more than obvious.

This caused Bob to be seriously worried and he decided there and then that it would actually be easier and safer to comply with the conditions mentioned.
Bob was actually now very frightened and decided to go along with the "agreement," to the point where the body was left in the "half-buried" state and he decided to withdraw quickly.

The cash was exchanged and the man with the dark curly hair watched Chorley disappear rapidly into the night in the opposite direction to the jetty and he ran back to the remaining man on the boat. The boat engine note rose and it immediately left and disappeared into the night.

Once again, using the electronic navigation aids, way was made through the harbour making its way back under the "Twin Sails" bridge, returning to a berth at Cobb's Quay in the early hours of the morning. It appeared that no-one saw their return.

Bob Chorley had never seen the boat which had brought the body and consequently had no idea who the owner or skipper was except that he now knew his voice and accent and that he was the person who made "fishing trips." Although he saw his face, it was so dark that he wouldn't be able to describe him in any detail. He could only say that the man he spoke to had dark curly hair and beard and had what seemed like a dark complexion. He didn't know his name or where the boat went and now he really didn't want to be mixed up in what was obviously a dead body and he was now content to keep very quiet about everything, the money helping as well as the very clear warning he'd received regarding his silence. Having seen the body, he was quite sure that it would be very wise to heed this warning.

Having reached their berth at Cobb's Quay Marina, the boat was moored and the two men left quietly, walking along the pontoon. The skipper of the boat said, 'We have to be careful because they have CCTV cameras all over this place, so keep your head down but don't make it too obvious. Just keep it slow so we don't draw attention to ourselves. Just make sure you see the cameras and avoid them because I don't want to be seen.'
'Okay, do you know where they are then?'
'Yes, you can see them quite easily; the casings all look the same.'
'Right, yes, I can see one there look,' he said pointing to a camera high up on the side of a building.
'Don't look at it you fucking idiot; the point is we shouldn't be seen. Just keep out of the direct line of sight and we should be okay.'
Moving quietly to their car, they left the marina as silently as possible

CHAPTER 21

After Alex had asked Tom to go back to Cobb's Quay Marina to get more details about Martin Goodyear and his boat, he'd had a thought. Perhaps if I can kill two birds with one stone, so to speak, I can get some good information which would please the boss.

He intended to get to know Genny Dobbs a little better and if he could do this, then perhaps she could "keep an eye" on this Goodyear and his movements. His task was to track his "comings and goings" as much as possible and this would give a good indication of when he made his trips and also maybe he could be tracked.

After making his way back to Cobb's Quay, he felt a little apprehensive about what he now intended. Outside the reception office, he hesitated slightly, out of sight, and took a few deep breaths. He opened the door and saw at once that Genny was behind the counter, with no-one waiting. "Phew, thank goodness for that anyway"' he thought. As soon as Genny saw him, she treated him to another brilliant smile, and "Hello Detective Tom."

This made his heart rate increase considerably. He was about to say something, but his tongue had suddenly become glued to the roof of his mouth. He finally managed to gabble something resembling "hello" and lapsed into silence while she looked at him with a very pleasant countenance, saying, 'You're back again and so soon; you must find something interesting here.'

He was regaining his composure somewhat and that allowed him to duck behind his "official" reason for being here. 'I'm afraid that I'm here on official enquiries, Genny Dobbs with a "G,"' he said. This made her smile again and he nearly lost his composure again at the response he was getting from what he considered a gorgeously attractive girl. He thought, "Why me"? As well he might.

Then she threw him into a flat spin when she said, 'I find it incredibly attractive to have a real-life detective here, am I involved?'

'In what way do you find it attractive?'

'I mean, it makes me go all "fuzzy" when I think I might be taken to a police station and interrogated.'

'We don't actually "interrogate" people, we "question" them.'

'Would you take me into a cell and question me, then?'

'Only if you had done something worth investigating, then we would have to question you.'

'And would you like to question me, Detective Tom?'

'I think I'd find that extremely pleasant Genny, so tell me what you've done so that I can question you over it.'

'I haven't done it yet, but I'm sure I can think of something.' She said this accompanied by another smile and a very meaningful and direct look from her dark green eyes. 'Or maybe you can you think of anything that would make you arrest me?'

Tom returned her look, now that he was regaining his "balance" as it were. 'I can think of a number of things, but maybe this is not the time or the place to discuss the possibilities of your misdemeanours. Perhaps we could do this somewhere else, do you think that would be a good idea?'

'I think that would be a very good idea. Where would you like to take me to discuss my wrongdoing?'

No, I daren't say that, he thought, and instead, 'Maybe I could meet you in a local pub and I could arrest you later for being "drunk in charge."

'Oh, "drunk in charge" of what?'

'Me, if you like,' said Tom, with his insides going slightly crazy.

'Okay then, perhaps we should make a time and place for this crime to be committed?'

'There must be a local pub which is your favourite or maybe one which I go to?'

'I'd prefer one away from here because a lot of people know me and you know how gossip can get around.'

'I certainly do Genny. Okay, there's a pub/restaurant I know over in Branksome; it's called the "Crown and Sixpence." Would that be good for you, and I can pick you up from here tomorrow night, if that's okay, at around 8?'

'No, I tell you what, I know the pub, so I'll meet you there. It's a bit early for you to come to my place, so this time, shall we do that?'

Tom was just a little "taken aback" by this, but he said, 'Of course, I completely understand, and I'm so pleased; no, delighted that you've agreed to this, thank you.'

'Okay, that's a date then. Now, what was your "official" business?'

He'd completely lost the track following this result, and he couldn't quite get over the nagging feeling that he had been "propositioned" and it was her giving him the "come-on" rather than the other way round. What the hell; she's absolutely stunning and maybe my luck has changed, he thought.

'Oh yes, the "official business," well, as you know from yesterday, we are gathering information about Martin Goodyear. We need to know his movements, and possibly the times he comes and goes, and who he meets or who goes with him, things like that.'

'Oh, I see, you want me to spy on him, is that it? Has he done something wrong?'

'I can't tell you that, but not really to spy, just to let me know what you can find out so that we can put a picture together about him. Our problem is that no-one seems to see him or know him. Have you met him?'

'No, in fact, I don't think many people have seen him as he is "just a name." Is he in some sort of trouble then?'

'I'm sorry Genny, but I can't say anything at the moment as our enquiry is in the very early stages.'

'Okay, but this is fun; I mean to be part of an investigation. It's quite a turn-on.'

Tom had the thought, hold that until tomorrow night and we'll see how much of a "turn-on" it really is.

He realised that there was nothing more he could do today, but with the prospect of an "insider" to gather information, he was sure this would go down well with his boss.

He had said goodbye and was about to leave, when Genny, who was looking down at some papers, raised her head slightly and looked at him from under hooded eyes, saying again, 'and don't forget your handcuffs, Detective Tom.' He almost floated back to the station.

CHAPTER 22

Alex and Anna drove over to Corfe Mullen to find the address they had been given for Martin Goodyear, the owner of the fast boat which was the centre of the enquiries regarding the death of the victim found on the small beach at Goathorn Peninsula.

They easily found Henbury Park Road and parked a little way from where they thought the property was.
It was not obvious which of the large houses belonged to or was occupied by Martin Goodyear. There were a number of very large detached houses stretching down the hill from where they parked. 'Why can't they put numbers on these houses?' asked Anna. 'It would be much easier than a fancy name board.'
'I suppose if you can afford a bloody great house like this, you don't want anything as common as a number,' Alex suggested. 'Oh well, we'll just have to walk down there until we find it, I suppose.'
'Never mind, the walk might do you good,' said Anna.
'You cheeky little Sergeant Minx,' he said.
Anna just chuckled as they walked down the fairly steep hill, checking the name plates as they went, looking for a house named "Waypoint," which was the name of the given address.
When they had walked almost to the bottom of the hill, they went round a curve in the road and the house they were looking for was right there. They stood and looked at each other for a moment.
'Bloody hell, Anna, this guy must have some money to afford a place like this.' It was a very large detached house with a double garage. The drive to the house was quite long and had a number of lights on high posts lining it. On the large paved area in front of the garage was a boat on a trailer. This boat Alex knew was called a "Boston Whaler" and had a very wide flared bow. It was about 8 metres long and sitting on a 6 wheel trailer. On the stern was a large Mercury 300 outboard motor. 'Take a photo of that Anna, if you would. I want to get some details of that craft and how much it would cost.'
'It can't be cheap can it?' she said, whilst holding up her camera phone and taking a shot of it. 'It looks fast though, doesn't it?'
'How the rich have all these play things,' said Alex. 'But I really don't suppose this guy plays, not if he has this bloody great fast boat which we know he uses. This one must be cheap in comparison to that one. What I want to know is how he makes this sort of money by taking out "fishing trips."
'Hmm, there does seem to be a little disparity, doesn't there?'
'I think there's a thumping great disparity Anna and I intend to find out just what this guy does. Come on, let's see if he's in - or maybe he's out fishing for his supper.'

They went to the door and pushed the button to hear a muted and "far-off" ringing sound.
No answer.
'Let's just go round the back, he might be in his large pool which of course he will have.'
'Probably stocked with enormous sharks or tuna fish he's caught on one of his fishing trips,' said Anna.
There was indeed a large pool, but it was empty and deserted.
'Oh well, we'll just have to make an appointment to see him, I'm sure Alice can get his number somehow and in the meantime, we can find out just what this house has cost and how much this boat is worth. We'll have some idea of the amounts of money we are dealing with, or at least finding out where this money has come from.'
'I'm damn sure he won't be too forthcoming with the truth about the source of his income, do you think Alex?'
'I think you're dead right. Let's get back to the office and see what's come in, if anything.'

Returning through Poole, Alex and Anna had a little more time to be "personal" and they managed to discuss their burgeoning relationship. They had shared a few nights together and now tended to alternate between their respective flats. Alex lived in a quite small flat in the Boscombe area of Bournemouth, where he had moved to following the death of his wife a few years previously. He had recounted the events previously to Anna, that the driver had been well over the drink drive limit, but he had only received a light sentence for "dangerous driving" due to his defence that he was not used to traffic lights or driving on the left.

This did not sit well with Alex and it had taken him a considerable time to come to terms with her sudden death. When he and Anna had talked about this, he had preferred that she'd died instantly rather than been left severely injured and had to endure what would have been many years of pain and probably disability. Thankfully, they had never had children, although Alex would still be open to the idea.

While they were discussing their current relationship, it had become obvious to him that he was now completely over her death and had moved on, although he still had fond memories. He was also sure that his wife would have been happy to see that he had found a new direction and purpose in life and this was becoming more and more evident that the person was Anna.

The only problem which both Alex and Anna now had was that of keeping quiet about their relationship to work colleagues and their "higher ups," as should this become known, it would have meant that they would have to then work in different stations, which was not what they wanted. They were a good team and worked very well together as they had great respect for each other.

They returned to the station, rather empty handed after their abortive attempt in finding Martin Goodyear at home, but at least they had seen where he lived and the sort of house he lived in. This in itself had given them an insight of some sort and reason to delve more carefully. They really needed to speak to him quite urgently now, to get some answers to questions that were central to their investigation.

As he walked towards his office, Alex called to Alice and Tom to join him with Anna in his office for a quick update.

'Okay, we tried to get to see this Martin Goodyear who has the boat in Cobb's Quay Marina but we only found his house, but no-one at home. However, he has this bloody great detached house in Corfe Mullen and there was a boat in the drive. Anna, could you show them the boat please?'

Anna quickly linked her phone into a computer and brought up the picture of the Boston Whaler sitting on a six-wheel trailer on the drive, to the large screen.

Tom looked at the photograph and said, 'Christ, I wouldn't mind a boat like that to bomb around the harbour, would you guv? I wonder how much that would have cost.'

'That's what I want you to find out Tom and also just where he bought the big boat which you saw at Cobb's Quay and how much he paid, if you can. I know you already have a picture of the big one.

Tom replied, 'I'm going to meet my informant tonight guv, so I'll get that info looked into then.'

'Tonight; I haven't authorised overtime?'

'Yes, guv; I thought it would be easier to talk to them away from their office as they might be overheard or be seen to be looking into files and stuff that they shouldn't; it might jeopardise their job.'

'Right, yes, you're quite right, good lad. If he can get those figures it will give us a clearer picture of what sort of money he has to have or obtain, to finance these "trips." Good to see that you are conscientious after hours, so to speak.'

'Alice, we need to speak to this Martin Goodyear and quickly, so can you please dig out a contact number for and any other information you can find, especially about his finances.'

'I see there is a number on that boat guv; doesn't that give us something to check up on, I mean there must be a register somewhere of these boats?'

'Absolutely Alice, good thinking. I'll leave that to you.'

The meeting broke up and they all went to their respective tasks. Tom was looking forward to his date with his "informant" and hoped that he would have good results in several directions, some to bring back to his boss. He was sure that there were some "brownie points" to be made tonight.

After leaving work, Tom had gone home and was sprucing himself up for the forthcoming date with the receptionist from Cobb's Quay Marina and he was due to meet her at 8pm at the "Crown and Sixpence" pub in Branksome. He made a real effort and told himself not to be too "pushy" tonight and let things take their time. He was going to play things softly because he wanted to get some information about Martin Goodyear and his movements, so he decided to ask about those things quite early on to get them out of the way and leave things clear for him to "chat up" this girl whom he fancied incredibly.

He finished his preparations after showering and a really close shave, followed by some, not too powerful after-shave. Thinking, I don't want to overpower her; he dressed in a clean shirt left open-necked, chinos, slip-on loafers, and a casual but classy jacket. Looking at himself in the mirror, he was finally satisfied that he would make a decent impression, and set off for the pub.

Arriving at about a quarter to eight to be sure of a good table, he sat so that he could see when she arrived. He got himself a small beer and sat waiting, hoping that she would actually turn up. There was always a chance that she would stand him up and as 8pm came and went he became more and more to thinking that she was actually not going to turn up.

At about 8.15, she came into the pub and looked around. Tom had seen her as soon as the door opened and he noticed, as was his normal observational habit, that looking around a number of other men in the pub had noticed her entering. Their heads turned in unison to look at this stunning girl, walking in. She quickly scanned the room and saw Tom who had stood up and was looking in her direction. As soon as she saw him, she flashed a brilliant smile and Tom had what felt like a jolt of electricity run through him.

She wore black jeans which were very tight-fitting and showed her shapely legs to good advantage. She had a dark green silky looking top which hung very loosely on her shoulders; the material cleverly accentuating her breasts, without hugging them, which Tom found extremely attractive.

Oh – my – God, she looks stunning, Tom was thinking.

Walking casually over to Tom, she just said, 'Hi Detective Tom,' still smiling.

He tried to return the greeting, but for some reason his tongue had become stuck to the roof of his mouth again and his mouth felt as dry as a sand dune. Licking his lips to enable coherent speech, he managed to croak, 'Hi, Genny Dobbs with a "G."

'Oh, you remembered. That's so cool.'

'How could I forget? But can I say something Genny.'

'Of course, Detective Tom,' she replied slowly, giving him a steady gaze; what would you like to say?'

'What I want to say is that you look absolutely fantastic, I mean you look gorgeous.' But what he had actually meant to say was that she looked incredibly sexy, but just managed to stop himself in time. Keep it cool, he'd said to himself, yet again.

'Thank you Detective Tom, that's very nice of you.'

'I mean it, you look sensational and the truth is that I'm amazed that someone like you would agree to a date with someone like me.'

'But why are you amazed Detective Tom?'

'Well, I'm just an ordinary bloke and you must meet so many extremely "well-off" men who have loads of money where you work, all those boats and so on, and yet you have agreed to meet me tonight, I mean, I'm surprised; very, very pleased, but surprised.'

'You might be surprised at some of these well-off people Tom; they can be quite rude and self-obsessed sometimes; quite unpleasant in fact, sometimes very egotistical. You seem different to me, much more pleasant.'

This pleased Tom. 'Thank you for that. Anyway, what would you like to drink, Genny with a "G"?'

'I'd like a gin and tonic if that's all right. I know it's a bit old-fashioned, but it really is a nice refreshing drink.'

'Of course, that's absolutely fine. I'll just get it for you. Please don't go away.'

'Do you think I might then?' she asked, looking surprised and quite concerned.

'It has been known in the past,' he said, 'I'm just very wary now.'

'Don't worry; I'll not be walking out on you. I think I told you when you first came to the Marina that I was turned on by policemen, and you are a good-looking policeman, so it just seemed to be a natural thing to agree to a date. We'll have to see what happens, won't we?' She was wearing another of her enticing smiles.

'Well, yes, but I have to say one thing to you and it's actually very important, or at least it could be.'

She became very attentive, and leaned towards him slightly. The very loose top she was wearing didn't have a particularly low neckline, but as she leaned, it presented Tom with an extremely tempting view of her very, enticing breasts.

'And what's that then Detective Tom?' she said, watching his eyes taking in the view which was holding his attention. He reluctantly pulled his gaze back to her face and said, 'You have to stop calling me Detective Tom, just Tom is good.'

'Oh, why's that Detective Tom,' she said with a giggle.

'It's because I'm off duty and in a place like this, it's really not a good idea for people to hear that I'm Police. Some folk take a great dislike to that fact and it could, and has in the past, caused a good deal of trouble.'

'Oh, God, I'm sorry, I didn't realise that it would cause you problems, but what else can I call you then?'

'Can't it be just Tom?' He went off to get the drinks.

When he came back, she gave him another "hooded eyes" look and said, 'But I find "Detective Tom" is quite sexy, but if you insist, it'll have to be just Tom.'

'Okay, just in here then, Tom, anywhere else you can call me what you like.'

'Oh, I will,' she said with a very wicked grin. Then she looked quite serious and said, 'but I know you want some information as a result of my spying for you, don't you?'

'I'm sorry, but yes, I could do with some information to get me some brownie points with my boss after my last "cock-up" on a previous case.

The phrase "cock-up" caused her to raise one eyebrow. 'A "cock-up," what on earth did you do then?' As she said this, there was another hint of a sneaky smile.

'I had to get some information but I missed getting some obvious CCTV data and I had to go all the long way back to get it. My guv wasn't too complimentary about my status as a detective, to say the least.'

'Oh dear, perhaps I can help a little in that direction.'

Tom's working ears pricked up at that. 'How do you mean Genny?'

'Well, I asked around to see if anyone knew when Martin Goodyear had brought his boat in recently, and apparently he was seen a few nights ago, well not seen exactly. You see the CCTV cameras are on 24 hours a day and when they were scanned, as they routinely are, his boat was spotted mooring up in the early hours of the morning and two men left the boat. It would seem that they tried to avoid being spotted on the cameras.'

'How do you mean; could you actually see them clearly?'

'The chap who checks the CCTV results was doing a quick scan and when he passed the time when usually there's nothing to see, he saw a movement and went back to check it. That's when he saw the boat being tied up and these two men leaving the yard, but I don't think he could see their faces.'

'You say that they appeared to try to avoid being seen; obviously not very successfully.'

'They were ducking around trying to avoid the cameras but apparently hadn't seen the camera that's specially hidden.'

'That's a smart move by your people. I'd like to see this footage. Would that be possible?'

'Yes, of course. You can come in your "official capacity" whenever you like. I can introduce you to our security chap who checks the camera results.'

'That's great Genny, thanks. That's going to help us a lot. I wonder why they were out so late.'

'We don't often get people coming in to the marina after dark, but maybe they were out fishing, I don't know. Do you want me to keep a check on when they come and go?'

'That would be a fantastic help to our investigation Genny, but won't that get you into trouble?'

'No, I don't think so. It'll be quite easy to do that as we often get people asking for all sorts of information.'

'Do you have facilities for fuelling at the marina?'

'Oh yes, we have all the servicing needs catered for at Cobb's.'

I'll bet you do, thought Tom, and not just the boats. 'Then, perhaps you can let me know how much fuel he takes on board and when he comes and goes, if that's not too much trouble.'

'I'll see what I can do for you Tom, but you'll have to do something for me in return.'

Tom had a little frisson of unease at that comment, but he said with bravado, 'I'll do whatever I can Genny with a "G."

She smiled one of her brilliant smiles and just looked calmly and steadily at him. 'I'll tell you what I'd like you to do.' Very quietly, she told him. – His temperature, amongst other things, climbed alarmingly.

They continued their evening date and enjoyed each other's company, with Tom following her instructions to the letter; to the point where Tom had plucked up enough courage to suggest that they continue at his flat. He had actually spent quite a while tidying up and making the place respectable, just in case, he'd thought, I might as well; you never know your luck. He was now beginning to think that it might have been a very good idea that he'd taken the trouble.

Tom had actually found Genny to be very intelligent and interesting; something he'd not actually expected. He had the very unworthy thought that she might have been a bit of an "air-head" but he was thinking now that it was completely the opposite. He said, 'Genny, I know you're probably going to blow me out for saying this, but I would really like to carry on getting to know you as I find you a very interesting person, not to mention completely gorgeous.'

'Why would I "blow you out Tom?"

'Well, I know this is our first date and you did say that you would meet me here as you thought it was too early to go to your place, and I completely agree. But maybe you'd like to come to mine, but if you'd rather not, I understand.'

'Actually Tom, I'd like that. Where do you live, is it near here?'

'I have a flat in Northbourne. It's not very big, but I like it, and it's quite modern.'

'I think, if you've asked me there, I get the impression that you've tidied it up. I mean, most blokes I've known seem to live in a permanent state of untidy.' Genny said this with a hint of irony.

'I must admit, I've had a clean-up, but I have to tell you that usually I'm quite a tidy person.'

'That's good to hear Tom. How about I follow you to yours and then if I feel like running out on you, I can just drive away. I'm sure that as a policeman, you are quite trustworthy.'

'The last thing I want is for you to feel the need to run out and I promise you I won't do anything to upset you. After what you told me that you'd like me to do, I think you might just want to hang around a little longer.'

Genny had mentioned a few things that really "turned her on," and Tom was more than ready to oblige.

'Okay, let's go. I won't drive too fast so you won't lose me.'

'I think it'll be hard to lose me, Tom,' she said with a final smile before they left in their respective cars, 'especially if you have to arrest me and put me in handcuffs.'

Tom had some very vivid and arresting thoughts himself, at this remark.

They had a very engaging and energetic evening, to say the least and Tom was more than pleased with progress; in fact it could be said that he was "over the moon" with his new girlfriend, or informant. And to cap it all, he found an extremely interesting use for his handcuffs, definitely not in the Police Officers Operations Manual.

CHAPTER 23

Alice had managed to find a phone number for Martin Goodyear, even though it was unlisted. She had "ways and means" that baffled most of her colleagues, but they had to admit it was incredibly useful to have her IT skills on hand.

Anna was given the task of contacting Goodyear and suggested that she and her DCI could arrange a visit to ask some questions.

In the meantime, Alex asked Tom about the prices which had been paid for the boats which Goodyear possessed. 'What did you find out Tom?'

'I got some more info from my contact at Cobb's Quay. It seems that the Redbay 'Sentinel' Stormforce 11 which is called "Predator" and usually berthed at Cobb's quay was bought second-hand and priced at £190,000. This boat has a range of around 400 Nautical Miles and had a top speed of some 40 knots.'

'That would make a trip to France a very easy and relatively quick I should think.'

'How about the boat on his drive?'

'From the photograph which Anna took, and the serial numbers, Alice found out that it is a "Boston Whaler," a 230 "Vantage" and it is 8 metres long. It's valued boat at £140,000.'

'Bloody hell, this guy has some money; I just wonder where it came from. Together with that damn great house of his, he must either be in banking or some other financial set-up, or if I'm very suspicious, another way of making a shed-load of money, but I'm damn sure it doesn't come from bloody fishing. Okay Tom, well done. It seems that your contact is coming up with some interesting information.'

'There's more to come; as they've said that they'll try to keep tabs on how much fuel he takes and when he comes and goes. Oh, and there's more, the other night, they apparently came back very late, in fact in the early hours of the morning, and two men left the boat and they went out of the marina trying to hide from the cameras.'

'I guess from what you're saying Tom, is that they didn't hide very well.'

'That's right guv, there's a camera which is virtually hidden from view and unless you know it exists, it can't be spotted, so they were seen.'

'So we have some facial shots then?'

'Unfortunately, no, they kept their heads down but at least we know that there were two of them and we can have a good estimate of their height and build from the shots, I believe.'

'So you haven't seen the footage yet then?'

'No guv but I can get access to it at any time, and I've made sure that it's been kept and not deleted.'

'Good. If you've nothing else more important on at the moment, you can get over there and take a look at the footage and if you can, get a copy of the best images.'

Tom was more than pleased to get another chance to see Genny.

'That gives us a good starting point Anna. I think we can get round to asking him a few questions about his fishing trips.'

'And who he takes with him; perhaps he has regular people who help him do whatever it is that he does.'

'I think that we need more information on the times that he goes out and how long he is away from the marina,'

'But if we only ask him some seemingly innocuous questions, that shouldn't alert him, should it?'

'Maybe not Anna, but why are we asking him these questions? He might realise that it isn't just a routine enquiry.'

'I have an idea that might just work guv. How about we say that it's in connection with possibly patrolling this part of the coast as his boat is listed as a "Fast Patrol Boat," and maybe he could help us with looking for illegal economic migrants crossing the channel. You know, we are understaffed and need all the help we can get at the moment.'

'I don't know if that'll work, Anna but it's an interesting avenue. Mind you, he wouldn't be very keen to help us if we were able to keep a close watch on him all the time, which would be the case if he were "with us" so to speak.'

'Yes, he'd hardly be too pleased if he had to provide his location at all times; that would be a "given," I would suggest. Mind you, if he's actually involved with bringing in illegals, it would make him avoid the idea with a vengeance.'

'I think you've made a very good suggestion Anna, and I think we should at least have a little "chat" with Goodyear to see what his reaction is.

'The only thing I can think of against this is why the police would be involved with illegal immigrants, surely that's for the Border Control to be patrolling.'

'But we know that they are severely stretched with the usual crossing routes where the channel is narrower and they can get over in rubber dinghies. Surely they wouldn't be patrolling this part of the coast where the distance to France is around 75 miles?

'That's true, it would necessitate using larger and more seaworthy boats wouldn't it? I think you're right guv, they just wouldn't have the resources for this. Maybe this type of questioning of Goodyear will just "rattle his cage," and we can ask about his fishing trips and get some names.'

'Let's do it Anna. Give him a call would you and we can arrange for a little visit?'

Anna called Goodyear's number and she was mildly surprised when a woman answered the call.

'Hello, this is the Goodyear residence.' The voice was in well-spoken English.

Anna assumed that this would be a maid or perhaps an au pair. 'Good morning, this is Sergeant Jenkins of the Bournemouth Police. Would it be possible to speak to Mr Goodyear please?'

Anna had realised that to say that she was a detective, would give the game away instantly, so she just gave her name and rank.

'I'm afraid that Mr Goodyear is out at the moment.'

'When will he be back please, we would like to speak to him.'

'What do you need to speak to him about?'

'That is between Mr Goodyear and us, madam; if you could just tell me when he'll be back please.'

'Oh, very well.' This was said with a hint of petulance. 'He should be back tomorrow morning. He has been out on a fishing trip. That's what he does, he runs fishing trips right out in the Channel, and they stay out for up to 3 days.'

That was more information than she had expected and wondered why it was necessary to give that explanation. Perhaps she had been told to say that, should anyone enquire.

'Can I ask who you are?' she asked.

'I'm just a friend of Martin, I mean Mr Goodyear.'

'Very well,' Anna continued, wondering what sort of "friend" she might be, 'would you please ask him to call me as soon as he returns?' Agreeing, Anna gave her the number to call.

Going back to Alex's office, she said, 'There was a woman who said she was a "friend" of Goodyear's, and that he was away on a fishing trip but due back tomorrow, so she'll ask him to call me. She did tell me that he usually goes on these trips for three days at a time, but I felt that this information was something she'd been told to say. I did say that I was "Sergeant Jenkins" and not "Detective Sergeant." I thought it best to keep it to that as he'd probably wonder why a detective was calling him.'

'Now that's very good thinking Anna. Do you know, I think your suggestion could well work and anyway it won't hurt to make him aware that we know about him, at least in some way?'

Tom had returned to the marina at Cobb's quay and walked in to reception, expecting to see Genny Dobbs, but he was more than a little surprised when he saw a different face behind the desk.

'Good morning, can I help you?' said the new face. She was a very pleasant young woman, but she wasn't Genny.

'Yes, I was rather hoping to speak to Genny Dobbs, is she here today?'

'No, she called in this morning, feeling unwell, so she is taking the day off and hopefully she'll be back tomorrow.'

"Damn!" thought Tom, "I should have phoned first." 'Not to worry, I'll come back tomorrow, but I'll phone first.'

'Can I help you with anything?'

'No thanks, it's a personal matter and I need to speak to her. I hope she's not too unwell.'

'I really don't know; she went out last night, and I think she's feeling a little "under the weather."'

'Okay, well, wish her well for me.'

'I will; who shall I say called for her?'

'Oh, I'm just a friend of hers. Just tell her I'll hopefully see her tomorrow.' The receptionist had realised that this chap was probably the one Genny had seen last night. The one who'd made her so tired that she needed a day off. She also knew to not ask any more questions as he'd obviously not wanted to give his name.

Tom was thinking, I'm not surprised that she's in no fit state to come into work today, after last night. That was some session! I wish I had her number and I could give her a call, but that information had somehow been overlooked during their evening and night.

On his return to the station, he had to tell Alex that his trip had been abortive but that he would go back tomorrow. Alex was not best pleased that he'd had a wasted journey and said to him, 'Didn't you think to check that your informant was there Tom? Obviously not,' he said answering his own question. 'Clever.' He said this accompanied by a quite hard stare.

'Sorry guv, I should have checked first.'

'Yes, you should Tom. Get your checking head on next time; we can't waste precious time running about with no results.'

'Yes, guv.'

'As you're here, you can get on to the pathologist and see what else they have come up with about the body, you know, anything more that can give us a more definitive picture of who he was and where he came from.'

With that, Tom went off with his tail between his legs again, and called the mortuary, asking for George Matthews the pathologist. His intention was also to call the Forensics department but then he realised that Alice was very friendly with the boss there, Jeffrey Boyd, so he went and asked her to get in touch for any further information. She was only too pleased to have the reason to call him.

When George Matthews answered, he said, 'This is DC Tom Peterson from Bournemouth Police.'

'Hello Tom, I suppose you'll be wanting whatever else we got from the corpse.'

'That's about it, yes please, anything you can give us.'

'Okay, well, apart from what you know already, that he was about six foot in height, very muscular with a heavy black beard and curly hair, the only other thing really is that the blow to the head which caused the subcutaneous damage, almost certainly would have led to his death, although perhaps not immediately. Quite when the throat was cut, either post or anti mortem, I can't say, except that it was very severe and as you know already, the thorax was severed. The heavy and extensive bruising was caused prior to death, meaning that he was pretty severely beaten. I think the damage to his lungs from smoking those horrible cigarettes which he seemed addicted to from our tests, would have killed him soon anyway.'

'So do you think that as he'd been so badly beaten, that this was done in a sort of "fit of rage", or something like that?'

'I think that could well be a reason Tom.'

'Okay George, thanks for that. I'll get some more info from forensics; maybe they can tell me more about this bloke.'

'I'm sure they will. Give my regards to the lovely Anna for me would you?'

'Yep, 'course. Thanks again, 'bye George.'

Alex was given the information that George had passed on regarding the severe beating details.

'It would seem like the killer or killers are a really nasty group who are quite prepared to dish out some heavy punishment.'

'It sure does guv,' agreed Tom.

'What about the forensics, anything from them?'

'I thought Alice might get more from them, you know how reluctant they are to get their fingers out, and she seems to be very friendly with the boss there, so I asked her to call him.'

'Okay Tom, fair enough, I'll see what she has to say.'

CHAPTER 24

There was a phone call mid-morning which was taken by the Desk Sergeant, who called Alex and told him that there was a call from a Mr Goodyear. 'Put it through please Bob.'
Bob Thomas had been warned that he might call and that he was not to make it known to Goodyear that Alex was a Detective.
The phone on Alex's desk rang and he picked up the receiver. 'Here's that call for you,' said Bob. I didn't mention detectives, just as you said.'
'Thanks Bob, best to keep this guy in the dark for now.'
Bob Thomas was the sort of desk sergeant that every station would hope for. He was meticulous and always ready to defuse a potential situation when someone came in to the front desk and was very angry or irate, perhaps drunk and abusive. Bob would usually be able to turn the situation round and calm things down so that information was forthcoming and the appropriate action taken.

Taking the call, Alex said, 'Good morning Mr Goodyear, this is Chief Inspector Vail. Thank you for returning our call. We would like to meet you to ask for your assistance.'
'How can I help the police Chief Inspector?'
'It is possibly a rather strange request, but I think it best if we actually meet. Could we come to see you soon?'
'As you probably know from your previous call, I've just returned from a fishing trip after some three days, so I'm a little tired right now, but you could call maybe tomorrow morning; is that convenient?'
'Yes, that would be fine, shall we say about 11?'
'Okay, that's good; I should be awake by then.'
'I'll be there with my sergeant Jenkins, so until then, and thank you.'

Alex called for Anna and said, we need another chat with Bob Chorley, so can you please arrange a trip with Jack and get Bob Chorley to be available for interview. No excuses from him though.'
'Sure thing, guv. I would imagine it will be this afternoon, is that okay with you?'
'Yes, and I don't care if he is not "on-shift," we need to get to see him.'

Anna was pleased to speak again to Fuller Masterson the harbour master and arranged for Jack Sturney to take them over to the oil site at Goathorn Plantation that afternoon. She thought that Masterson was a thoroughly agreeable person to deal with. She also called the Perenco management office that dealt with the site at Goathorn and asked that Bob Chorley be available that afternoon, to help with "Police Enquiries." The person who took that call from Anna asked what the problem with as the police were making enquiries of one of their employees. 'We are not at liberty to divulge any details of our ongoing enquiries, but I will just say that we wish to interview a witness and that is all I can or will tell you.'
'We would like to be kept appraised of any involvement with the police with one of our employees,' said the voice with just a hint of haughtiness.
'I'm afraid that as I said, we are not able to discuss matters with you, but what I will say is that we just need to clear up some details with him and he is not in any sort of trouble.'
'Very well, the message will be passed to the site at Goathorn and Mr Chorley will be available at the time you request;' was the officious sounding reply, obviously miffed that they were being kept in the dark.

That afternoon, Alex and Anna duly arrived again at the Poole Marina to find Jack waiting near his boat. As usual, he was sitting on a large mooring bollard, wreathed in his "pungent" smoke.
As they approached, he treated them to one of his smiles but unfortunately, they were both a little too late to look the other way. He flicked his so-called cigarette into the water, gave a phlegmy cough, hawked and spat into the already fairly polluted water of the harbour.
This did nothing to endear either of them to Jack, but said a friendly "hello."

'I be sorry 'bout that, but t'was needed, though it be good to see both of 'ee agen, an' no mistake; 'specially you missy, with you bein' so good lookin.'

'Thank you Jack, that's very nice of you.'

'Well, I do likes a good lookin' lady, that's for sure, but 'tis a long time since that my good lady wife went to see Davy, an' I do still miss 'er, truth be telled.'

'I'm sorry, "went to see Davy?" Did she run off with someone?'

'No, no, Davy Jones, missy. You know, "Davy Jones' Locker." 'Tis where people do go when they die in the ocean. See, she were drownded some fifteen year ago, terrible accident it were; she bein' on a sailing boat what did come into collision with the Sandbanks Chain Ferry. It were in May of 2001, terrible it were, terrible.'

'I'm so sorry Jack. What happened; surely the ferry can't collide with anything; it runs on chains, doesn't it?'

'It do run on chains Missy, but see, the sailing boat what she were on were tackin' the wrong way and what with the tide ebbin' so quick, the current pushed the yacht alongside the ferry and the fierce current did push the boat right under the ferry which were 'alf way 'cross the channel there. Pushed the yacht right on 'er side it did and she were sucked under. 'Er body was washed right out along that there "training bank" by the current and she were finally found over on Studland, on the beach she were, washed up by the tide.'

'Oh that is so terribly sad. I gather from what you said that she was "buried at sea?"'

'Aye that she were. The ol' gal loved the sea she did, an' we did lots of sailing in them days. Seemed fittin' to 'ave 'er go that way.'

The conversation had taken a sad turn and Jack handed Anna into the boat and quietly removed the mooring ropes and was strangely quiet for the remainder of the trip across to Goathorn. Meanwhile, Alex and Anna enjoyed the cool breeze and sea smells coming from across the harbour.

Leaving Jack in a respectful silence, Anna lowered her voice a little and said to Alex, 'It certainly is a beautiful place, the views across to Sandbanks and Brownsea are just stunning, and you say that the sunsets seen from Evening Hill are something else?'

'They certainly are. I used to take a lot of photographs around here, and going back quite a few years, I was in a local camera club. Many of the members would show their pictures and I entered a few of some really spectacular sunsets taken from there.'

'That's interesting, a little more about your "life and times" Alex. What were your favourite subjects, people, places, what sort of stuff did you take?'

'Stuff, stuff? I'll have you know that I had a couple of "firsts" in the competitions.'

'I'm impressed now; sorry to have presumed the wrong thing there.'

'Don't worry Anna; I won't hold it against you.'

'You did the other morning, and look what happened...' The look which passed between them spoke volumes, swiftly followed by smiles.

'Returning to the subject,' he said, 'my favourite topic was, quite naturally, the harbour, as I spent so much time here. I used to go windsurfing and later when I had various boats, I would go out with a friend of mine, Gary, who was a very experienced boating chap, to take photos of the racing powerboats.'

'Wow, I bet that was quite exciting. Did you get close to them to take "action shots?"'

'I certainly did; in fact one time we got almost too close and if it weren't for that friend I mentioned, we could well have been in a very serious accident; in fact I think I would probably have been killed.'

Anna looked quite shocked. 'Why, what happened?'

'I was in a small speedboat which I had at the time and we had positioned ourselves, or should I say I, positioned the boat, close to the racing line which was indicated by the buoys. You have to understand that these buoys are quite a way apart and the racing line is taken as a sight from one buoy to the next. Well, I thought, wrongly, that I was in the right place but I think that as we hadn't dropped an anchor, I'd inadvertently drifted into the racing line. I had a friend who was actually taking part in the race and I wanted to get a close-up of him. A little too close, it has to be said. As his boat which weighed about 4 tons and was approaching us at over 60 knots, that's nearly 70 miles an hour to you landlubbers, they were coming in a straight line towards us. I had the camera lined up to take the shot and my friend shouted, "Look out, we're too close." Luckily the engine was still running but in neutral. He reached over and put it into gear and slammed the throttle full ahead. I was looking through the viewfinder to get the close-up and as I pressed the shutter, our little boat accelerated very quickly and Gary put the wheel hard over and we just about got out of the way. I fell over as he'd turned so fast and as the race-boat passed us we were actually drenched by the bow wave which broke right over us.'

'That sounds as though it was a little too close for comfort Alex.'

'It was far too close for comfort, to put it mildly. The next time we tried to take photos, I used a telephoto lens and kept well out of the way. That scared the pants off me.'

'Sounds like a good idea; maybe I should scare you sometime then?' said Anna.

He just looked at her with a silly grin.

As they arrived at the jetty Jack said, 'If'n you don't mind, I'll just 'ave a little smoke as 'ow you said you wouldn't be over long, but just you take as long as you've a mind, 'an don't worry about 'ow long you might be a takin', as I be a sittin' 'ere, quiet like, mebbe thinkin back to them times when the ol' gal an me would go sailing, sometimes on them great big old sailing ships what were still about and we would be out on the water for days, sometimes mebbe's a week on them longer trips and we would go right along the coast for miles and miles, and do you know, once upon a time, we even got as far as Penzance and back, an' that were a right good sail, to be sure, what with a fair wind and good sea, an' we did right enjoy that there trip, that we did.'

Alex was actually thinking did he draw breath? After this diatribe he seemed to have an occasional propensity for elongated monologues, and he's just been sitting on the boat for about half an hour without saying a word and then, that.

'You must have enjoyed those days Jack,' said Anna.

'Tha' can be certin sure of that Missy, but hold hard now, you'll be wantin' to see this chap Bob what I do know, so don't let me be a holdin' you up now.'

Alex was thinking that although Jack was entertaining, he had a job to do. 'We'll be back quite soon Jack. Thanks for waiting.'

'That be no trouble zur, no trouble whatever. I be glad to be doin' a service for you both."

'Let's go Anna,' we don't have all day, like some people,' with a meaningful look in Jack's direction.

As they walked off, Anna said, I don't suppose he gets to talk to many people and he's glad to have the company.'

'You may think this Anna, I couldn't possibly comment,' he said drily. He stopped abruptly and turning back to Jack, Alex said, 'Jack, just one thing you might be able to help us with; do you know of any other boats which come over to this jetty here at Goathorn?'

'I b'aint be too certin sure zur, but I do think I did see one of them very quick fibyglass boats what are called "Boston Whalers" a while back. I weren't actually 'ere, so to speak, but I were out on the 'arbour and did see this 'ere boat wizzin' past me back from what looked like this 'ere Jetty like, if you do catch my meanin' zur.'

From their previous trips, they both understood that Jack knew a great deal about boats and boating, so Alex had no reason to question Jacks' knowledge of the "Boston Whaler."

'And when was that Jack, do you remember?'

'I do think t'was two or three nights back, but you're to understand what my ol' mind b'aint be too good these days, if'n you be pardonin' me zur.'

'So you saw it coming away from here and do you know where it was heading?'

'I do think she might 'ave been 'eadin' t'wards Sandbanks and out to sea, but I can't be too sure 'cos I didn't pay it no never mind see.'

'And you say this was late in the evening?'

'Yezzur'.'

'But if this were late in the evening; surely it would be very dark?'

''T'would be that zur, but see, I do knows all them buoys in the 'arbour, so's I do knows where I be goin' like, and I could see this white boat clear enough.'

'And where were you going then Jack?'

'That be a little "private," if'n you knows what I mean zur.'

Realising that Jack was not involved in the investigation, and he may have some private things to take care of, so I'll just leave this, Alex thought. Jack seemingly knew nothing more about the visit the boat had paid to the jetty, but it was very useful information, none the less.

Leaving Jack to his obnoxious smoking concoction, they walked along the track to the entrance of the oil site where they had instructed Bob Chorley to be available. The track was bordered by quite thickly grown pine trees, forming a quite impenetrable screen to the actual oil pumping site. Finding the entrance they quickly made their way to the cabin which was the office and storeroom of the site. One the side of the cabin bore the logo "Perenco," who were the site owners and operators. As they approached the office, the door opened and Bob Chorley came out to meet them.

They shook hands and Bob said, 'Come inside, take a seat.'

The cabin was quite spacious and Anna thought, remarkably tidy for a "site office."

Alex began, 'Mr Chorley, we are interested in some of the answers which you gave to questions during our previous encounter. We know that you were on duty the night that you said you heard what you thought was an outboard motor running and then changed this to what could have been a quad bike. We did ask you think about this and now wonder if you've had any further thoughts about what you actually heard.'

'As I said before, I wasn't sure of what it was; it could have been one or the other.'

'So you didn't see anything other than what you heard?'

'No.'

As he said this, Anna noticed the shift of eyes and the look which instantly alerted her. Following her training in interview techniques, she had been on too many interviews and asked too many pertinent questions of various types of people not to have become very aware of the facial expressions which sometimes give away lies or evasions of truth. This was one of those times and Chorley's expression said to her that he was not telling the whole truth.

'So you didn't go out to find out the cause of the noise then; your job is security of the site I believe?'

'No.'

Alex came back with, 'Why didn't you go and check because surely a noise at that time of night would have given you cause for further investigation?'

Now Chorley was quite uncomfortable it seemed to both the Detectives that he was looking a little nervous. There was a slight sheen on his forehead which didn't seem attributable to the heat in the cabin, but which they both noticed.

'I didn't think it was worth checking.'

'I don't think your Company would be too pleased if they thought that something so unusual for that time of night was not being investigated, do you?'

'Probably not, no,' Chorley replied, looking even more uncomfortable.

'Then perhaps you could tell us the truth then,' said Anna with a very direct and unerring look at Chorley.

'That is the truth,' said Chorley, his tongue flicking round his lips which were drying rapidly.

'I don't think so,' she said. 'I think you did go out and see what was the cause of the noise and I also think you saw something else, which you don't seem to want to tell us about. Isn't that right?'

Chorley was decidedly uncomfortable now and his forehead now had beads of sweat. He kept trying to moisten his lips but that didn't seem to work and his voice was now becoming quite 'dry' sounding.

Alex decided to go in hard. 'Do you know what I think Mr Chorley, I think that you heard this noise, which you recognised as a boat, and you went to have a look, but as someone at that time of night is more than likely to be up to "no good," you went to have a sneaky look. Did you see something which gave you cause for concern?'

'No.'

Neither Alex nor Anna took this to be a truthful response, as he was looking so uncomfortable. In their experience, when someone looks like this and their body language is shouting at them, it had become the time to "put the pressure on."

Alex looked hard at Chorley, saying nothing for a few moments to let the import of the gaze and the silence sink in. This had the effect of putting Chorley even more ill at ease and he looked at both the officers, one then the other and back again. The sheen of moisture on his forehead had visibly increased.

Alex then said, 'Let me put a possible scenario to you Bob; you heard this noise, which you recognised as a boat engine, which had presumably tied up at the jetty, or you would have said you heard a boat going away. I've done enough boating to know that a boat leaving would sound totally different to one coming alongside a jetty. Hearing the noise, you went out to have a look at what was going on. Maybe you came across the person or persons beginning to bury the body which was found here as you well know.'

Anna was studying Bob's face as Alex was saying this, and she was completely convinced that something similar to what Alex was suggesting, had actually taken place. He was very nervous, looking "shifty" in the true sense of the word, in that his eyes were looking this way and that, flicking from side to side as if to look for a way out.

'I think from your silence that we can take it that you did see a body being buried?'

Anna asked a direct question following Chorley's silence, 'Did you know the person they were trying to bury, Bob?'

'No, I couldn't see who it was…' He clamped his mouth firmly shut, realising that he'd "put his foot in it."

'So you did see the body? I also think you knew the person Bob,' said Alex.

'No, he was face down.'

'That confirms that you did see him, doesn't it?'

There was a palpable silence, while Bob chased thoughts around his mind trying to find a way out of the hole he'd dug himself. He was also very mindful of what had been said to him by the person "digging," by way of a very illustrative warning, should he divulge the very details which were being "dragged" out of him now. It's not my fault, he was thinking, I didn't say anything, it was them who suggested it. However close to the truth it was, he was trying to convince himself that knowing he hadn't volunteered the information, exonerated him; but the result would be the same.

He was trying to do what he called "thinking hard," but nothing seemed to gel at the moment in his state of mind. His brain seemed to have turned into a soggy lump.

'I didn't really see him,' Bob said, 'cos it were dark.'

But you saw the person who was digging?'

'Well, sort of.'

'How do you mean, "sort of?"'

'Well, he was wearin' a cap pulled down over his eyes.'

'But you could see the colour of his skin?'

'It wasn't black but it was dark, but that's all I could see.'

'Could you make out the colour of his eyes,' asked Anna.

'No, but they were very dark – black I'd say.'

'So, you saw this man, or were there men?'

'I only saw one man, but I heard someone running back towards the jetty.'

'What happened then?'

'I asked him what he was doing and he said, "What does it look like; I'm digging for bait," then he told me to mind my own business. I could see he wasn't digging for bait, even though it was dark, I could see the body.'

'Okay, so you saw him digging what was obviously going to be a grave, so what did you do then?"

'I got bloody scared, that's what I did.'

'So the man who was digging, what did he do?'

'He told me to "forget what I'd seen."'

'And you said?'

'I said it would be hard to forget what I'd just seen; you know a dead body lying face down in the sand, half-buried.'

'So what did you do then?'

'I said I needed something to help me forget what I'd seen.'

'So you wanted money I presume.'

'Yes. I've not got a lot of money and it was the first thing I could think of.'

'So what happened then?'

'He held out a wad of notes but when I went to take them, he held on to them and told me exactly what he'd do if I told anyone what I'd seen.'

Anna then said, 'So what did he say he'd do; do you remember'

'Remember? I'll say I remember. He said that he'd find me, 'cos he knew where I worked, and where I lived and I'd get the same treatment as the bloke lying face down in the sand. He explained that there had been a fight and this bloke had done something which upset the "others." I don't know who he meant, but that this bloke had been beaten and cut with knives and stuff like that, before he'd croaked.'

'And did you believe him?'

'With a body lying in front of me and seeing all the cuts and bloodstains and everything, yes I did bloody believe him, in fact I was shitting myself and I don't know why I'm telling you all this now 'cos it means that I'm in some real danger, doesn't it?'

Chorley was now really scaring himself, and with good reason, Alex was thinking.

'Did he have an accent?'

'Well, not really, I think it may have been slightly foreign but I don't know where; you know I couldn't place where he came from, but I don't think he was English, although he spoke good English, it wasn't an English accent that's for sure.'

Looking quite calmly at Chorley, Anna said gently, 'I think that basically you are a good man and what you have seen must have been very disconcerting, so you quite sensibly said, I think, that you would say nothing after his threats, but you have readily told us all these facts, which you feel will put you in danger, and this makes me think that you have a good heart.'

This seemed to calm Chorley somewhat and looking between both Alex and Anna, he said, 'I didn't want to tell you and I didn't say anything; that was until you said that because of my silence you knew what had happened.'

It was Alex who then decided the course of action and giving Chorley the benefit of a stern look, said 'we didn't know for sure, but we are both experienced police detectives and we know when someone is lying. It is good that you have given us this information as will help our enquiries. We could in fact, prosecute you as an accomplice as you have taken money and not reported to the police what happened, but I think for the time being we'll leave that aside Mr Chorley.'

'But won't I be in danger now? He said he knew where I worked and where I lived and he'd come and find me. I work here on my own and now that you know things, you're bound to follow things up aren't you, and that means that he'll be looking for me.'

Alex then sought to calm the man down as he had become very agitated as he realised the enormity of what might happen to him. He said, 'Yes, you are in some danger but we will make arrangements to keep you safe. We will be keeping a very close eye on things here from now on, and I'll call the Perenco office to make sure that you will be kept under observation for the time being until we can make a better situation for you.'

Looking toward Anna, Alex said, 'I think we'll have to move Mr Chorley to a safer place as soon as we can, seeing as he has helped us.'

'I'll get onto that as soon as we get back guv.'

'Okay. Bob, is there anything else which you can tell us about this chap who was doing the burying, do you know him or the other man?'

'I only know that he is the bloke who takes fishing parties now and then and he gets his gear from the shed at the end.'

'The one you said you didn't know who owned it or who had the keys?'

'Yes.' Bob looked down at his feet at this.

'Why didn't you say you knew at the time Bob?'

'I was trying to keep my head down after what I'd seen and what I'd been told.'

'I suppose that's fair enough Bob,' said Alex. 'Now have you seen any other boats come to this jetty recently?'

'The only boats I've seen are the ones which bring the oil site stuff over from Poole Quay, and I know those blokes. It doesn't come much at all as the site is simply a pumping station now and all the big stuff and equipment have gone. It's all just maintenance gear now.'

'And you don't have a name for this man?'

'No.'

'But how come you know who he is and that he collects fishing gear from the shed and yet you've never seen him?'

'I only know from what Jack has told me; you see Jack sometimes comes over this way and he'll stop for a chat and a cup of tea in our office if he's got the time. He knows a lot of what goes on in the harbour, so maybe he knows this bloke's name.'

He may not know the name, but the police had already established that the man involved with the fishing trips, Alex thought, and that was Martin Goodyear.

CHAPTER 25

Alex and Anna made the trip back to Poole Harbour Marina, thankfully without having to suffer any more of Jack's extended and breath-defying speeches. This time he was quite deep in thought it seemed, probably after the recollections of his wife. This time they were able to enjoy the quiet throbbing of the diesel engine and the gentle hiss of the water from the bow of the boat. The clean sea air and the breeze was very enervating and the views around the harbour of the many boats making their way either out to the open sea or returning to their moorings were delightful, to say the least. Turning to Alex, she said, 'This is so much better than being in amongst the traffic and the pollution we have to suffer on a regular basis. It must be so nice to be out on a boat and enjoying the open air and sea breeze.'

'It certainly is, and maybe one day I'll get another boat. I used to enjoy just being on the water regardless of whatever boat I had.'

'Have you had many boats then?'

'I've had quite a few over the years, usually just small boats. I progressed from windsurfing to small speedboats, sometimes quite fast ones, and eventually ended up with a quite large cruiser, but I found that was just too expensive to maintain and to run; it was built of wood and had a very big engine. It would cost an arm and a leg just to start the engine and to go anywhere worthwhile would be so expensive, so I sold it and then events took a turn which meant that it ended my flirting with the sea.'

'But you enjoyed it while you have the time with the boats?' Anna choosing to not pursue the "events taking a turn."

'Oh yes, loved it and the one thing which I think I learned overall was a very great respect for the sea. I didn't have any serious problems, but now and again something happened which made me realise that when things go wrong at sea, unless you are completely prepared and have really good knowledge, then it can become suddenly very serious and very dangerous.'

Anna was having a few thoughts about being with Alex on their "time off" and maybe having a boat to take on trips along the coast to places she had not been, places which might be "off the beaten track" so to speak, for private time. Her thoughts were brought to an end when they bumped into the dock in the marina and they were literally back on dry land and back to work.'

'Thanks Jack, for all your help, it's been a pleasure to have these little trips and it's saved us a great deal of time and trouble in getting over to Goathorn. We'd have to done a load of waiting in queues in traffic to cross by the ferry.'

Anna was being nice to Jack and deliberately overlooking his less than attractive smile and phlegmy cough, not to mention that unmentionable tobacco he smoked.

'Thank 'ee missy, 'tis my pleasure to take you two good officers across my 'arbour, 'tis no trouble at all. Any time you need to go agen, just you tell Mr Masterson and I knows 'e'll be only too pleased to 'elp; 'im bein' such a nice boss.

'We will Jack, and we may see you again,' said Alex. 'By the way, as you know so much about the harbour, perhaps we could ask you some more questions a little later on, should that become necessary?'

'That'd be my pleasure zur. Just you be askin' away, and I be right glad to tell 'ee what I do knows, 'bout what you be askin'.'

As they made their way back to the car, they were just going over the situation as things stood at the moment. 'I think we should have a briefing first thing tomorrow morning before we have the 11 am meeting with Goodyear over at Corfe Mullen, Anna.'

'Good idea; we really need to bring everything together as at the moment we just have a few facts and no clear idea as to why this guy was killed and what the bigger picture is, do we?'

'You're right. Shall we have a quiet drink this evening, somewhere away from the office?'

'I think that's a great idea; we'll see what happens after that shall we?'

'Who knows?'

'I think I do,' she said, treating him to one of her private smiles.

The next morning, the team participating in the investigation which was now code named "Goathorn" were called into the main office for a briefing. Present were Tom, Alice, a couple of DC's drafted in from another section to add to the numbers who could do the more mundane tasks, together with Alex and Anna. Also due was their superintendent, Alison Beavers.

They were all assembled in the main incident room and there was a general hum of conversation before proceedings began. The whiteboard at one end of the room had the usual photographs of the corpse, taken from various angles and with degrees of detail which were extremely explicit. The known facts such as the Turkish cigarette butt found at the scene, the photos of the tyre tracks and other salient facts were written up so that everyone could see the evidence so far.

The main door opened and Superintendent Beavers strode in. She was a woman in her late forties and had been promoted following her previous experience with the Met in London. She was one of the "Fast Track" promotions and most thought her university graduation would have played a large part in this. However, she was generally well thought of and she was prepared to listen to all arguments and opinions before giving her verdict on operations generally. This went down well with the lower ranks as sometimes the higher echelons could be quite intransigent, which did cause some ill feelings.

'Morning ma'am,' said Alex, as she came in saying a general "good morning" to everyone. 'Please carry on Alex,' she said.

'Okay, this is what we know so far. Body found on Goathorn Peninsula beach, not far from the oil pumping site about half a kilometre from the jetty at Goathorn. The body had been badly beaten and bearing severe and deep knife wounds, probably caused by a large knife or machete type blade. Post mortem shows that these wounds were more than likely made pre-mortem during the beating and what appears to be torture of the victim. Several of these wounds would or could have caused death due to their severity, but the main cause of death has to be either the neck being so deeply cut or the heavy wound to the head. Whether the neck was cut first is probably immaterial at this stage. Currently we have no ideas as to why this would have been done. Also, why this victim was tortured has yet to be established. All we do know is that there was possibly a fight. Again, whether this was on board a boat or on shore somewhere, we don't know. We also think that the body was carried to the site by a boat called a '"Boston Whaler." If this fight and subsequent murder took place on a boat, then we would expect to find some DNA corroboration, when we find this boat.'

'The person who was burying the body was discovered by Bob Chorley who works at the pumping station. He says that this person was dark-skinned but not black. He had curly dark hair and beard, also dark eyes. This information is not really relevant as it was late at night and very dark. However, his command of English was good but his accent was not particularly strong but possibly slightly foreign, although not English.
The suspect was wearing a cap pulled down over his face.
Chorley was warned off and paid not to mention this to the police, but on questioning yesterday, he confessed that he saw and spoke to this person. There was another person, we presume a man, who was heard running away towards the jetty. This was presumably to the boat which had carried the body and ready for a getaway.'
Tom interrupted here, asking, 'Why was the body only half buried guv?'
'That we don't know Tom, or why it was being buried at that particular place but I think the presumption has to be that the sand at that point is so heavy and sticky that it was taking too long. Perhaps the tide was not high enough to give time, so they had to get away. Once they were seen, there was no point in hanging around and they took off in their boat. We also think now that the person who was doing the digging was probably Martin Goodyear, the one who apparently runs the "extended" fishing trips and who has the large, fast boat moored at Cobbs Quay. This we know from Tom's contact and the fact that he has seen this boat.'
'So you don't think this big boat was used to dump the body then guv?' said Tom.
'From what I know about boats, if it had been, the engine noise would have been louder and Chorley said he thought that what he had heard was an outboard motor or a quad bike. This large boat would sound completely different as

it has twin diesel engines which have a noticeably different sound. 'No, I think it very likely that it was the Boston Whaler and very possibly the boat which Goodyear has or had on his drive when we first saw his house. We have a meeting set for 11am today with Martin Goodyear and, now this is strictly for our ears only, I want no hint of what I'm going to tell you to get outside this room, is that clear?'

They all nodded their assent.

'We are going to ask him for his help in "policing" the English Channel for illegal immigrants using his fast boat, as facilities in that direction are so limited. Tom's information tells us that this craft has a top speed of some 40 knots and a range of about 400 miles, so it would be entirely possible for him to "help us" to protect the borders. We know this is not strictly what would or could happen, but as we now think that he is actually involved in people smuggling or bringing in illegal workers, and therefore is more than likely to refuse to help and give us some excuse or other. It is our intention, if he gives us some unreasonable excuse, to make arrangements to follow his next "trip" to see just where he goes and what he does. Should this indeed be the suspected transportation of illegal immigrants, we need to know just where he gets them from and where he takes them to.'

Alice held up her hand to ask a question. 'Yes Alice?'

'If this means paying for fuel to cross the channel and go chasing around after him, won't our budget be a little stretched guv?' Here, he looked across at Superintendent Beavers, who gave a slight nod, but said nothing.

'It'll be a lot stretched Alice, but we have to find some other way of keeping a check on what he does. However, I don't really see him agreeing to this unless he is extremely altruistic.'

Looking across to Beavers, she gave him another nod, indicating for him to continue.

'I'm hoping that it rattles his cage, just enough to make him take some action which gives us some answers to questions that we just know how to ask at the moment, if that makes sense.'

Superintendent Beavers then spoke. 'I'll sanction a certain amount for this little charade, but if it doesn't produce results quickly, then I'll pull it, as it's not strictly by the book but I can see how it might just make him make a rash move. Do you understand this? Please don't make it entrapment.'

'Yes ma'am,' said Alex, 'understood.'

'Good, what else do you have?'

'The post mortem shows that he didn't have any drugs in his system, but that he was severely beaten around the body and head. The pathologist has said that several of the blows and cuts could have been fatal but it was certainly the blow to the head which caused the death, officially. He had a bad lung condition from smoking unfiltered strong tobacco and would not have lived many more years.'

'And do you have a name for the deceased?'

'Well, according to the shop assistant who recognised the photo of the victim, her ex-husband used to go on these fishing trips with a chap named "Gary," whom we haven't been able to contact as yet, so we can't identify him. We need to speak to this ex-husband as soon as we can track him down.'

'Track him down? How long have you known about him from the shop assistant?'

'For about three days ma'am.'

'Then perhaps I could suggest that you make it a priority to contact him to get some good information; or is that asking too much?'

Alex was stung by this seeming rebuke and felt himself reddening, much to his annoyance. He knew that she was right, and he should have made that a priority but he had more than enough loose ends at the moment. He made a mental note to put this into practice immediately.'

'No ma'am, this is next on our list of follow-ups.'

'Good. Please keep me informed of progress.'

'Yes ma'am.'

She left the office with a gentle swirl of perfume.

There was a slightly uncomfortable silence in the room. Alex said, 'That told me then. Right, so the next thing is to get back to this Jo Stafford shop assistant woman and get the address of the ex-husband, go to see him and get as much information about these bloody "fishing trips" as you can.'

'We have his address guv,' said Alice. 'Jo Stafford gave it to us when we first interviewed her I believe.'

'Shit, we should have followed this up by now! This is bloody ridiculous, why wasn't this done?' He knew that the answer to that question was on his own doorstep and he realised that perhaps all the trips to Goathorn were over the top. Right, you and Tom, go and see this guy and get as much information and names, together with times and dates and so on. I think it better that you both go as you could then do the "hard guy, soft guy" routine which might help. We have a meeting with Goodyear at 11 this morning, so let's get to it people.'

Tom spoke up. 'Before you go, guv, I've got some figures for you about the movements of the "predator."'

'Good, make it quick as we have to get over to Corfe Mullen.'

'Well guv, "Predator" goes away for a few days at a time, and I have a list of the recent dates of him leaving and returning, together with the amount of fuel he has taken on board. A piece of information I think you'll like is that he also takes his Boston Whaler boat to Cobbs and fuels up there and sometimes he has it berthed there, although he usually takes it away on the trailer. I have those dates as well for you.'

'Great stuff Tom, you've done well, or at least your contact has. He sounds very useful and it seems you have a good rapport with him.'

I think you could say that, thought Tom. 'Yes guv and I think I'll have to keep this contact sweet because you never know when we might need more information regarding boats. It does look at though a very large number of boats are kept up at Cobbs Quay and I'm sure that this contact will come in handy in the future.'

'Yes, look after him.'

'I will guv, don't you worry about that.' Inwardly, Tom was determined to keep a good rapport with his contact. So far, his rapport had been more than good.

CHAPTER 26

They had met once again at the office, arriving at differing times for the sake of prudence as they'd spent another very enjoyable night together which further improved their feelings for one another. Both Alex and Anna were managing to keep their assignations as well as their feelings completely separate from their colleagues. It was difficult but they both realised that their respective futures would be in the balance should their personal situation become known to their bosses.

After driving across town and through Poole towards Corfe Mullen where Martin Goodyear had a very large and expensive house, they were passing through Broadstone when Anna turned to Alex with a concerned look as she remarked that Jo Stafford lived there.

'Yes, and I hope she's safe because I'm getting the feeling that her ex-husband may be more deeply involved than we thought. If that's the case, then he is going to be very careful as to what he does at the moment.'

'Do you think we should give her some protection guv?'

'I think we should consider it, certainly, but not just at the moment. Let's just wait and see what Alice and Tom get when they meet him. I think that'll be quite illuminating, to be honest.'

'Okay guv, but I have to say that I'm quite concerned for her safety.'

'Noted, Anna. I'll take a decision as soon as we hear from Alice and Tom.'

Climbing up the gently rising road from Broadstone up to Corfe Mullen, they came to the summit and as the road levelled off, they soon came to the turning down Henbury View Road where the house of Martin Goodyear was that they had found on their previously wasted journey.

Coasting down the hill, they passed the high quality houses of the area, all of which had a really good view of the fields locally. These had numerous horses in paddocks and the trees were mature and mainly of oak and chestnut.

They turned the quite sharp bend to the left and pulled up at Goodyear's house. This time, the Boston Whaler boat which had been parked on a large trailer on the driveway the last time they had called, was absent.

'I won't say which of us should take which part this time, let's just see what happens and you just go with the general drift and do whatever you think is appropriate, okay?'

'Got it guv; we'll see what happens and I'll keep an eye on his reactions to your suggestions.'

'Yes, you did well with Bob Chorley and I'm sure that when you put him on the spot, he just gave in and admitted everything. That was great Anna.'

'Thanks guv; I'll keep watching this one as he seems to be the main suspect doesn't he?'

Walking to the door, they produced their warrants ready for inspection. Alex was going to knock on the door, but changed his mind and pressed the bell. The door was answered by a woman who looked to be in her early thirties. She was very attractive with blonde hair and a good tan, which accentuated her brilliant smile. 'Good morning, I believe you're here to see Mr Goodyear, is that correct?' He recognised her voice as the one who had answered the phone previously.

'It is indeed, and if you could let him know that we're here, we'd appreciate it.'

The woman gestured for them to enter and they moved into the very spacious reception area. She disappeared into the further reaches of the house and whilst she was gone Alex and Anna had a chance to take a good look round to the furnishings of the house, such as they were able from where they waited.

The decor was tasteful in the extreme, with the elegance of someone who knew the meaning of taste, unlike some of the wealthy people Alex had dealt with in the past. Sometimes, he'd had to talk to or interview wealthy people and when their homes had been visited, the shock of the sight of some of their pieces of gilded everything and mismatched but obviously overly expensive furniture had left him quite appalled.

Martin Goodyear appeared from the rear of the house. He was dressed in white chinos, sockless boat shoes and a polo shirt top with the obligatory small logo. He was, simply stylish and very obviously expensively dressed. Anna was realising yet again, that when someone has good taste, they do not have to be ostentatious, simple but classy, and it shows.

On the other hand, Alex was thinking about how this man had made his money, as the large boat he had moored at Cobbs Quay and the Boston Whaler, together with this house, amounted to a very large pile of money indeed. Questions which I am sure he won't want to answer.

'Good morning Mr Goodyear. It's very good of you to see us.'

'Good morning Inspector,' and turning toward Anna, gave her a rather longer gaze than he had given Alex, and gave an almost imperceptible nod, saying simply, 'Sergeant.' Anna realised that his look was not just a "cursory" glance but carried more meaning. This did not sit well with her, but she remained collected and unmoved.

'I believe you rather want my help in some way, is that right?'

'Yes , we have had a rather unusual request from the Border Control in that due to their only having a small number of craft available for policing this part of the Channel, they have asked us to suggest likely owners of suitable craft to keep a watchful eye on possible illegal immigrants along this part of the coast.'

'Why me, Inspector, I mean, I only take fishing parties out as I think you well know?'

'Yes, we are aware of your fishing interests from our enquiries and we do know that your boat, called "Predator" I believe, which is moored at Cobbs Quay Marina, is probably one of the most suitable boats in the area.'

He said nothing, but was quiet for a few long seconds, looking at them both. Eventually he said rather slowly, 'I realise that you have been making enquiries.' He was silent for several seconds, and then, 'Yes, the boat would be eminently suitable as you say as it is actually very seaworthy. But and here is the rub, even if I were to agree to your suggestion, to take time away from my regular bookings would cause me a great deal of problems.'

'Your loss of income and fuel expenses would of course, be covered, and you would be doing the country a great service.'

Anna was watching is face and body language closely, and she was getting a distinct vibe that he was not at all pleased with this suggestion.

'Do you know what,' Goodyear said, 'I don't really care about doing the country a great service, as you can see, I'm not from here and I have no allegiance, except to myself and my income.'

Alex and Anna had both realised that Goodyear was obviously not born in England as his skin had this olive complexion and together with his dark curly hair and heavy beard, which put his extraction as more "Eastern Europe." At first, Anna had thought that he'd had a really dark tan from being at sea a lot, but she'd realised that it wasn't just that. Now he'd just told them he was not from England, she'd already made a mental note to do some deep digging about him. She was now convinced that his name was not Martin Goodyear at all, but an assumed name. She would find out, notwithstanding that his English was almost perfect. He had a slight accent, but very slight.

'You say you have no allegiance Mr Goodyear, but surely it would be in the national interest to take some action which would prevent the influx of illegal immigrants when we all know just how much of a problem it is when people who have no rights to be here, do whatever they can to get into the UK?'

'As I say, I don't really care and if they want to risk their lives to get here, then I think they deserve a chance, because they have to be desperate to take that sort of risk, don't you think?'

Anna had picked up that he was being quite inflexible and Alex said in a conciliatory tone, 'That's not for me to say sir; I'm just acting on instructions.'

'Yes, of course, I understand.'

It was quite hard to get his facial expressions during this conversation as his eyes were so dark as to be unfathomable.

'I don't think it would interfere too much with your fishing interests surely, and you can't be making much money from just taking fishing parties out?'

'What I make from my fishing interests, is no concern of yours inspector.'

Anna was silent, keeping a careful watch on Goodyear, and now she was more convinced than ever that he was beginning to lose his temper.

Alex continued, 'I have to say, I was wondering how you managed to afford the two boats which you have; Predator must be a very expensive boat and the Boston Whaler is a new boat I believe.'

'Why have you been checking up on me? I know you're police and you say you're here on behalf of the Border Agency, but I'm beginning to doubt that somehow. How dare you question my wealth and how much my boats cost? In fact, how do you know that I have a Boston Whaler?'

'We know about the Whaler from our last visit, when it was on the driveway.'

'And how do you know that it didn't belong to a friend; you are making assumptions and I really don't like your questions inspector. I think it's about time to bring this meeting to a close. You know my answer and I will not move on this as I'm sure you realise.'

'From my professional point of view, I would really like to know how you can afford this house and its' furnishings together with the expensive boats. Would you like to tell me your profession before you became a fisherman?'

Anna thought that Alex had just taken a "step too far" this time.

Goodyear exploded. 'Now, I take great exception to this inspector. Firstly, I am not a "fisherman." I take parties out to sea in a very seaworthy craft and it is my responsibility to make sure of their safety in such dangerous waters. Secondly, how dare you come here and ask for my help and then turn it into what I think amounts to a police enquiry. How I made my money is of no concern of yours and had it not been for your digging into my personal life, I may well have told you, but now, I am saying nothing. I want you to leave.'

Anna spoke, trying to calm the situation, 'Mr Goodyear, we didn't mean to pry into your personal affairs, maybe it's because we are professional police that we automatically ask these questions, but personally, I have to say that I am very surprised that someone who professes to be so responsible, can be so dismissive of the safety of people who are risking their lives to seek a better life, even though it's illegal, and yet you are not prepared to give a little of your time to protect them.'

Turning to address Anna, he gave her a look which implied that he thought of a woman as someone slightly lower in the scheme of things than a cockroach, and said; 'Sergeant Jenkins - I believe it is sergeant isn't it, - I really have far better things to do than to spend a great deal of time running around the English Channel in the off-chance of finding a very small boatload of potentially illegal immigrants. Do you actually have any idea of just how big the Channel is between here and France and how slender the chance of actually spotting a small boat would be? ; No, I thought not,' he said without waiting for a response.

That made Anna really angry. 'Yes, it is Sergeant - yes I am a policewoman with all that entails - and yes, I do know how big the Channel is, as I am actually educated, for your information, and not just some dumb female as you seem to be insinuating. My point is, that you have shown your attitude towards your adopted country is certainly not what we might expect or perhaps where you come from, the expectation of assistance with important issues does not have the same place in the queue as here in Britain.'

Alex had made the decision to terminate the interview and said to Anna, 'I think we had better leave Mr Goodyear to his fishing trips.'

With a look towards Goodyear which could cause a rug to roll itself up, Anna strode off in the direction of the main door, passing the expensive and elegant furniture. Seeing this again made her more than ever determined to discover exactly who and what Goodyear is and what his real name was as well as where he came from. Maybe there was a connection with the nationality of the victim? Another thought crossed her mind as she opened the door to the empty driveway, that the description that Jo Stafford had made of the "friend" of the man in the picture who was actually the victim, almost exactly fitted Goodyear.

It was left to Alex to remain courteous or as courteous as he could be towards Goodyear and he said 'Thank you for your time. I will pass on your comments and reaction to the appropriate department. Good afternoon Mr, er, Goodyear.'

The pause was not lost on Goodyear.

CHAPTER 27

Tom and Alice had made their way to Upper Parkstone whilst Alex and Anna were conducting their "interview" with Martin Goodyear.

'What do you think we'll find Alice? Do you think he's mixed up in this murder in some way?'

'From what we know so far and the descriptions that Jo Stafford has given us, I'm bloody sure of it.'

Alice looked very concerned and looked hard at Tom. 'Just make sure that you don't call him 'Fuckin' Freddie,' that's all, or it'll make him mad.'

'Of course not; the thought ever entered my head, did it?'

'Yeah, well knowing you, I wouldn't be surprised; you can be a bit of a dickhead sometimes Tom.'

'I realise that this is now way beyond a joke, so I'll stick to what we know, okay?'

'You'd better,' she said giving him another very stern look.

'It's a bit grotty up here isn't it Alice, compared with down the other side of Parkstone?'

Yes, I've a friend who lives near the golf club at Parkstone and she has a flat there, it was very expensive and it's a lovely area.'

'Would that be Parkstone Golf Club then?'

'You're pretty bright, do you know that Tom?'

'Yeah, well, I don't know about golf do I?'

'Neither do I, but "golf club" and "Parkstone," didn't that give you a clue?'

'Okay, smarty-pants, let's hope you're as clever when we get to talk to Fuckin' Freddie Dimitriou.'

'Actually, I don't know quite what to expect, especially when Jo says he was violent.'

'Let's just hope that it was only when he was drunk, but maybe we should be on our guard, what do you think?'

'I think we should take all the sensible precautions, like keeping our radios within reach, just in case.'

'Are you worried then Alice?'

'Not with you around Tom; you can be the "strong one" and I'll try to keep it "softly softly."

They'd taken a right turn about half-way along Ashley road into Granville Road and were in the more artisan housing area of Upper Parkstone. Here, some of the larger Victorian houses appeared to have been converted to flats. Some of these had been well cared for, but it was evident that some hadn't from the general clutter of toys and old bits and pieces that could be seen littering the fronts of some of the houses. They passed some newly purpose-built flats and could see that almost the entire roofs of the four or five blocks were covered in photo-voltaic panels.

'That's the way all houses should be built,' said Tom 'all making use of the free energy from the sun'.

'Couldn't agree more Tom, it's just that we don't seem to get that much sun, do we?'

'I know, but I was reading somewhere recently that it doesn't take all that much actual sunlight to make electricity.'

'You actually read - that's a revelation.'

'Oi, watch it, or I'll nick your "Danish" next time I see you with one.'

Alice had a rather pleasing notion that since she had been "meeting" her Forensic Department head, Jeffrey Boyd, she'd been very carefully checking her "Danish" intake.

'Shut up you, or I'll tell the guv about your "contact" at Cobbs Quay'.

Tom was about to say something, but he clammed up and simply said, 'What about my contact, he's very valuable and a good source.'

'I'm sure she is a good source, and not just of information Tom.'

That took the wind right out of his sails. He was wondering how the hell she knew that.

'Never mind all that, we're here. That's the place isn't it?'

They'd arrived at the address that Jo had given them. Exiting the car, Alice asked, 'Do you think we should check the back to see if there's a way out, just in case he might make a run for it?'

'You've been watching too many cop dramas on telly, Alice. Why should he make a run for it?'

'I don't know, but it does seem as though in every case where a suspect is questioned, they never seem to think that they might make a dash and get away from the back entrance.'

'I suppose it wouldn't hurt to just have a look for future reference, would it?'

'You never know, the information might come in handy later on, and we do know that he was violent towards his wife. Who knows what he might do if he's that sort of bloke.

'Okay, let's just have a quick look round the back.'

They noticed that the main door had four different bell pushes with names beside them. Some of the names were illegible but one distinctly looked like it started with "Dimi" something, but the writing had faded as had most of the other names. Walking round to the back, it was evident that the house had been converted from an old two-storey Victorian house into what were obviously now, four flats. At the back of the house was a metal fire escape. It was clear that this was not part of the original house but gave access to the flats on both floors. The garden, the overgrown area behind the house quite unjustifiably called a garden, had a couple of undernourished trees, best described as bushes, a very untended flowerbed and various items of unused and broken garden implements as well as old pots.

'They don't seem to have green fingers do they?' said Alice.

'No, but let's see if this bloke is in, shall we?'

At the moment they had no idea as to which flat was occupied by Dimitriou, but walking back to the main door at the front of the house, Tom pushed the button beside the label which they presumed was for Dimi and heard a very distant buzzing coming from above. 'We know that his flat is upstairs then,' said Tom.

'I can tell you're a detective Tom,' said Alice.

'If you were a bloke, I'd thump you.'

'If I were a bloke, I'd thump you back,' Alice said with a laugh.

They heard footsteps clumping down the stairs. 'No carpet on the stairs then,' said Alice.

Tom just had time to look at Alice and say, "Sleuth," when the door was opened by man with a sullen look on his face. His appearance was "swarthy" to say the least, his hair was cut very close to the head and he had a few days growth of beard. His face would be described as "olive complexioned" and his stained 'T' shirt and jeans completed the look of a person that Alice would not like to spend time with.

'Mr Dimitriou?' asked Alice, holding up her warrant card in front of his face, with Tom doing the same.

'Yeah, who wants to know?'

'We are from Bournemouth Police and we're making enquiries concerning people who have been on fishing trips recently from Poole.'

'What's it got to me with me?' was the very surly response. Alice detected a certainly "non-English" accent. I wonder where he's from, she thought, although he seemed to have a good command of the language, suggesting that he'd been in the country for quite some years.

'We understand that you have been on a fishing trip quite recently together with other people and that you stayed out on the water for about three days.'

Dimitriou now looked a little less surly but his eyebrows rose to give him a "questioning" countenance. 'Why are you asking me, what's it got to do with me?'

'Because we understand that you were on one of these trips and we need to ask the people concerned a few questions.'

'What questions. What's this all about?'

'Perhaps if we could come in, we can talk in your flat.'

'I don't want police in my place, do I?'

'In that case, perhaps we can just stand here where everyone can see that you are being questioned by two rather obvious police officers and they will draw their own conclusions, Mr Dimitriou.'

'I s'pose you'd better come in then,' was the grumbled response. 'I don't want anyone poking around asking me what's going on.'

'Thank you.' Tom followed Dimitriou up the uncarpeted stairs, with Alice bringing up the rear. As they moved up the staircase, Alice was taking full notice of the state of the interior of the building. It was obvious to her that the occupants had varying degrees of care spent on the landings. The downstairs "front" doors were quite well painted and cared for, with a mat outside. What the interior was like was only a guess, but they were certainly better than the upper two flat entrances, which were, to say the least, unkempt.

So far, Tom had said nothing, leaving everything to Alice and she seemed to like it that way, so he kept his own counsel, for the time being, although he too, was being observant.

Dimitriou opened the door and went inside ahead of Alice. Hmm, needs lessons in manners, she thought to herself.

Tom closed the door behind him, but surreptitiously engaged the catch which held the door lock from latching. He was being "sensible," in his mind.

'So, what's this about then?'

'We have information which leads us to believe that you have a friend who you go on fishing trips with, who perhaps comes from the same part of the world as yourself. Is that correct?'

'What information, what friend?'

'Just information from someone who saw you with another man recently. This man had very dark curly hair and beard and was about six foot or so. He had a similar complexion to you and our information is that you have a friend and that all three of you go out on these fishing trips.'

Dimitriou's expression had darkened. 'Where did you get this information, who gave it to you?'

'All we can say is that we are investigating a criminal matter and we are simply following information which we have been given to try to find links and to make sense of what we've been told.'

'What criminal matter is that then?'

'We are not at liberty to say at the moment. Can you just confirm that you were with the man I have described to you, in Poole approximately three days ago?'

'What if I was?'

Tom came in here with, 'Can you just answer the question, yes or no?'

Dimitriou scowled at Tom. 'Yes, I've nothing to hide, anyway, what about it, is he in trouble?' Dimitriou was now becoming very wary and his demeanour was speaking volumes to Alice. If he knew that this "Gary" was dead, then he would have to be very careful in what answers he gave.

'Again, we can't say, I'm afraid.'

Tom said, 'You could say he was in trouble – he's dead – how much trouble do you want?'

This made Dimitriou look from one to the other, but to Alice, he did not seem to react as would be expected when hearing that a friend was dead. Instead, he just looked almost uninterested.

'And his name?'

'Gary.'

'Gary what?'

'Don't know, just Gary.'

'And where was Gary from.'

'Around here somewhere. We just met him when we go fishing.'

'And you don't know where he lived?'

'No.'

'What did he do for a living?'

'Don't know.'

Tom became the "hard" one saying, 'You mean to say that you are with someone for three days and you know nothing about him?'

'Yeah, well, he didn't talk much and anyway, we're fishing.'

Alice thought that there was no point in pursuing this matter further. Perhaps this was better left for a further questioning when the time was right and with someone who was better at extracting information. Someone like Alex.

'I actually also need to know the name of your friend who you also go with on these fishing trips.'

'If you must know, his name is Martin, not that that means anything.'

'Is he the skipper of the boat?'

'Yeah.'

'And how often do you go with Martin?'

'From time to time, why?'

Tom again said quite harshly, 'It would help our enquiries if you would just answer the questions as accurately as you can.'

Once again, the sullen response. 'It varies; sometimes we can go once a week or other times it may be two weeks before we go.'

'And how long do you go for, just the day?'

Dimitriou was beginning to look quite a lot more "cagey" now and he wasn't quite so quick to answer with a question.

'No, we often go for two or three days, depends on how good the fishing is.'

'And where do you go?' asked Alice.

He gave a sly grin and looked at Tom in a way which said that he thought Alice was soft in the head. 'Where do you think? – out to sea, where the fish are.' The sarcasm was intense.

'Thank you for that piece of information, I didn't realise that that was where you went fishing.' The reciprocal irony was suitably barbed. 'What I meant was, how far out to sea do you go or how far can you go in the boat you're in?'

'Depends, sometimes its' a few miles, sometimes it's a long way. I don't decide where to go.'

Tom thought that was interesting. Did Martin decide? That was pretty obvious, especially if this was actually the Martin Goodyear whose boat he was on. He asked, 'Does the boat belong to Martin?'

'Yes, it's his.'

'If you go quite a long way out to sea, then this boat must be very seaworthy,' said Tom.

'Yeah, it's a beauty, go all the electronic gizmos and it's even got seats with pneumatic suspension so that when she's going fast, it's not uncomfortable.'

'And do you often go fast?"

'Yeah, sometimes.' This was said with a much lighter tone and less surliness. Now Tom was thinking, if they go fast, is that because they are rushing to get to or from a fishing area or is there another reason, but on the other hand, you don't go belting around using up fuel unnecessarily.

'How far do you go when you're looking for fish?'

'The Channel is very wide at this part, so we could go anywhere.'

'How many people go or is it just the three of you?'

'Sometimes there are more, it just depends.'

'Depends on what?' said Alice.

Now Dimitriou was becoming a little more "cocksure" of himself, and he said with a supercilious and arrogant smile 'Depends on how many of us there are.'

'When did you last see your friend Gary?' asked Tom, choosing to ignore that riposte.

'A couple of days ago, why?'

Does that mean two or more?'

'Dunno two, three, I've forgotten.'

'Perhaps you'd try to remember as it may be quite important.'

'Why would it be important?'

Mr Dimitriou, or should I call you "Freddie," which is an Anglicised version of your name "Furkan"; we will ask the questions. Please try to be more accurate and tell me when you last saw Gary.'

He tried to look as though he was thinking hard, but not convincing either Tom or Alice. 'Three.'

At the mention of his nickname, Dimitriou had become much more cautious as he came to the conclusion that they knew a great deal more about him than he'd realised.

'Who told you my nickname? I'll bet it was that bitch that I was married to.'

'Would that be the one who you regularly beat up when you were drunk then, Freddie?' asked Tom in a tone of voice which put Freddie on his guard.

Alice gave Tom a very hard glare which said to him, "you shouldn't have said that." With Tom's last remark, Alice was thinking that they had asked enough questions to "rattle his cage" and maybe cause him to take some action which would lead to a further direction in their investigation, and now perhaps Tom had said rather too much.

'Well, she had it coming to her, didn't she?'

'Why was that then? Perhaps you couldn't control yourself, was that it?' Tom seemed to be getting in a little too deep and the whole idea of this initial meeting was to "sound him out," not to make him become suspicious. Dimitriou was angry now and began to look very threatening. His face had darkened and his hands had formed fists as though he were ready for a fight.

'What's that bitch been saying, I'll bet she's been slagging me off hasn't she?'

Alice sought to pour some oil onto the troubled waters. 'She hasn't been "slagging you off" as you so succinctly put it, Mr Dimitriou, but since it was Jo Stafford who identified a person to us when shown a photograph; we automatically check and make inquiries. The connection to you was purely due to the fishing trips which had been made by yourself and your ex-wife told us the basics and we just followed up the enquiries.'

That seemed to placate him somewhat, and Alice took back the enquiry by saying, 'I think we'll leave things at that Mr Dimitriou,' and she again gave Tom a look which told him that he'd overstepped the mark. 'Thanks for your time. I'm sure we will have some more questions in due course.'

'I don't know what all the fuss is about,' Freddie said, in a very surly manner.

'I think that perhaps you do, Mr Dimitriou,' said Tom.

'What's that supposed to mean then?' Dimitriou said aggressively.

'Nothing really,' said Tom rather lamely.

'I think you'd better piss off then, and leave me alone. I've done nothing wrong or you'd say so.'

Alice almost got hold of Tom's shoulder as he turned away, but she let him move towards the door and followed him, saying, 'Thank you for your time Mr Dimitriou, we are going now.'

Tom and Alice exited the flat and as they were going down the stairs, Alice was behind Tom and said quietly to him, 'Don't you say a word until we're in the car.'

They walked across the road and both got into their car. Tom started the engine and looking behind him in the wing mirror, moved off. Alice then exploded. 'What the hell do you think you were doing, by saying that he'd regularly beaten his wife?'

'Well, he got me riled, with his attitude. We know that he knew this Gary and that his was the body and I'll bet that he knows exactly what happened to him.'

'That's what we'll leave to Alex and Anna but you've probably made him more likely to keep things to himself. That was really stupid.'

'Yeah, well, if he knows how and why this "Gary" was killed and where he came from, I'm sure the guv will get it out of him.'

'No thanks to you then, Tom.'

They drove back to Bournemouth Central Police station in silence.

CHAPTER 28

Arriving back at the station, they went directly to Alex's office to give their report of the meeting with Dimitriou. Both Alex and Anna had returned from their trip to interview Martin Goodyear which had ended as they rightly expected; that Goodyear refused to help them in their spurious invitation to act as civilian Border Patrol in the English Channel.

They'd not expected him to agree and made the bid simply to give him a little "push" to do something which might lead to him showing his hand. They suspected him of possible "people trafficking" by going over to France to collect illegal immigrants and bringing them back to the UK in his fast boat. Their thesis was that if this were the case, then the murdered man was probably either an illegal or someone who was known to the boat owner as well as possibly others who were involved. It was more than obvious that some sort of argument had resulted in a particularly vicious attack leading to the violent death of the victim.

Alice knocked on Alex's door.

'Come in Alice.'

She'd been seen walking from the car with Tom.

She and Tom filed into the office and Alex said, 'So how did it go with "Ferkin' Freddie" then? What was your impression of him?'

This question was directed at Alice as Alex rightly presumed that she would have been the one to mainly conduct the questioning.

'My first impression was that he was living in quite a low quality flat in a block of four. The lower flats weren't too bad, but the upper two were a bit shabby.'

'What was his flat like then, I mean inside?'

'Very ordinary, not too clean, shabby furniture but could have been worse I suppose.'

'Okay, so what did you get from him then?'

'He eventually agreed that the man who he went fishing with was named Martin and he had a very fast boat. Also, that they went out for two or three days sometimes and when I asked where, he was evasive and just said wherever the fish were, but that could be anywhere. He just said that the Channel was very wide from this coastline.'

'Did he say how many people went on these trips?'

'He said two or three, sometimes more but he was very cagey and wouldn't give clear answers. He did say that the third man was named Gary and this must be the victim I think. There was no way we could bring that into the conversation as I thought that this was something which you or Anna would prise out of him later on. He was very wary when we said that we knew his nickname and he asked where we'd got that from.'

'And what did you tell him?'

'We said that we'd found someone who had recognised a man in the photograph as one she'd seen him with when he'd gone fishing and we'd simply followed up on that information.'

'I don't think he was very pleased at that was he?'

'He wasn't but he hadn't caught on to the fact that Jo had never seen him with either Martin or Gary. Mind you, he guessed that it was his wife who had supplied the information and he accused her of "slagging him off" and he was very nasty about her. He seemed to forget that he was the violent one. Anyway, he said that the boat would often go very fast and I didn't follow that up as he would just have said again that they were going to wherever the fish were.'

Tom was standing quietly listening to the exchange between Alex and Alice, hoping that she would not mention his comment to Dimitriou that he used to beat her up, which made him lose his temper.

'So what are your conclusions Alice, what are your feelings about Dimitriou?'

'I think he's a thoroughly nasty man who has a temper, which we know already, and I wouldn't be surprised if he was involved in the death of this "Gary" person. All three people are from what Jo would suggest, seem to be Turkey or Cyprus or that area of the Mediterranean, including this "Martin" who has the fast boat. If there was a fight of some sort, someone had the ability to savagely beat another man and kill him.'

'I do think that there has to be a link between these three people and if these so-called "fishing trips" means that they're actually crossing the channel to ferry illegals to this country, then we will have to find a way of keeping a very close check on where they go and what they do.'

Tom finally spoke as he had managed to breathe a little easier now that Alice had not exposed his gaffe. 'So how can we do that guv?'

'I know it's going to be very difficult, so I'm open to suggestions, but I guess we have to somehow keep a watch on his boat and when it leaves the marina and from there we have to find some way of keeping tabs on it.'

'Isn't there some type of electronic system for keeping tabs on boats; that's if this boat is involved guv?'

'Indeed, and we have to find out, so perhaps your contact at Cobbs can give us the nod when he next goes out, so we can keep a check.'

'I'll get onto them to see if they'll do that, but I don't want to officially involve them if we can help it.'

'Okay, I understand, but it shouldn't take much to just give us a call when he leaves the marina.'

'Unless it's late at night, guv.'

'That's true. There must be another way to track this boat because we can't go around following it, it would be too obvious and we don't have any craft available anyway.'

Alice then said, 'I wonder. Could we put some sort of tracking device onto the boat, you know, without him knowing, so that it could be tracked with GPS or something?'

'Now that's a very good suggestion Alice and I don't know if that's possible or whether we could do it, but I'll get Anna to look into it. Maybe she could check with the Harbourmaster at Poole, he might have some ideas. Tom, can you get on to your contact and ask for their co-operation?'

'Sure thing guv.' He was only too pleased to have another reason to see Genny Dobbs, and he was very keen to keep her gender a secret, to let Alex think that she was a "he"; although Alice seemed to know and he just hoped that she would keep that to herself.

Alice, could you get Anna to pop in please, I don't know what she's doing at the moment.'

She went out and looked into various offices to try to locate Anna. She found her in the small room they used as a canteen and was standing by the relatively new coffee machine which they had all clubbed together to buy, enjoying a creamy cappuccino. 'Hi Anna, the guv would like to see you, I think he's got a little job for you which you might like.'

'Oh, what's that then?' she said, her interest roused.

'I think he wants you to go and see someone you like.'

'Okay, sounds interesting, I'd better leave my lovely coffee and see what our lord and master wants. What are you on at the moment then Alice?'

'I'm looking into Martin Goodyear's finances and all I can get on him and his background.'

'Good luck with that.'

The door to Alex's office was open and Anna walked in. 'Alice says you want me for a little job guv.'

'Yes please Anna. I'd like you to go over to Poole Harbour and speak to the Harbourmaster. I know you'll like that, even though I think it's asking for trouble.' As he said this, he gave Anna a look which she couldn't quite be sure of. It might have been a touch of jealousy or it might not; she didn't know, but secretly she hoped it was the former. That would mean that Alex really meant what he'd said the last time they'd had a night together.

'What do I need to know then, is it to do with this investigation?'

'Yes, Alice has made a suggestion which I think is quite a possibility, but I need to know some facts. We need to find out if this high-speed boat belonging to Martin Goodyear, or whatever is his real name, is doing and where it is going. Her suggestion is that the boat is tracked by GPS and I think that's a real possibility, and I'm sure there are devices already in existence used for that, but I think Masterson would be able to give you more info on that.'

'Okay guv, I've nothing on that's urgent at the moment and I know we need to get things moving ahead on this case, so I'll go over right now. I'm sure he'll be there.'

'I'm sure he will, Anna.' This was said with a strong hint of irony combined with a quite "steely" look which spoke volumes to her.

'Don't worry, I'll behave.'

'Get out of here.'

CHAPTER 29

Anna had the forethought to phone Poole Harbourmaster's office first and made sure that Fuller Masterson was there. She asked if he would be able to see her shortly and he was only too pleased to invite her over once again. To confuse matters, she had become aware that he had a soft spot for her.

She'd spent another night with Alex at his flat, where he once again had cooked a very nice meal for them and they'd spent a very enjoyable evening, relaxing and talking to one another; getting to know each other better. They'd also spent a very passionate night, with extremely fulfilling sex. Their relationship was going from strength to strength and they were both managing very well to keep the fact that they were seeing each other outside of work, a total secret. Or so they thought. Alice, being a very astute woman and recently having formed a relationship of her own after a long period alone, was now becoming very aware of the little looks and body language that sometimes occurred between Alex and Anna, even though they were extremely careful. She was not sure, but she felt that something might be shared between them, apart from just the working relationship. However, the secret was totally safe with her as she liked both of them enormously and was only too aware of what might happen should it become common knowledge, especially to higher authority, who took a very stern line on inter-departmental relationships. For their part, Alex and Anna were very careful and almost obsessional about keeping their private lives completely separate from the workplace, both working hard to keep the secret safe, albeit all too often very difficult and stressful.

Anna arrived once again at the offices of the Poole Harbour Master, Fuller Masterson. She had been there a few times now, thanks to the previous case which had come to such an inconclusive ending. She'd had to speak to Fuller about the various aspects of Poole Harbour relating to the tide times and the movements of vessels. His information was very helpful and she found him to be a most agreeable and helpful man and more than a little attractive. His manner was charming and he was apparently a "gentle man" from the times she had had occasion to talk with him before.

She was waiting only a few minutes whilst he finished a phone call. His office door opened and she was met with his face lighting up with a brilliant smile. 'Anna, how nice to see you again. Do you need Jack again, I'm sure he'll be only too pleased to help. I only wish it were me taking you over to Goathorn.'

'Hello Fuller, it is nice to see you too. I know it's only been a short while since I was here last; time seems to rush by, doesn't it.'

Anna didn't even know if he were married or not and she was inwardly berating herself for not finding out. However, she realised that it was immaterial as however attractive she found him she now had a very serious relationship with Alex. I should put him out of my mind, she thought to herself quickly.

'No, although Jack has been enormously helpful, I need to ask you some questions.'

'Of course Anna, any help I can offer will be my pleasure. What would you like to know, am I married or do I have any kids, things like that?'

Anna was completely taken aback, as he'd said this with a wide smile and she felt herself blushing and she could do nothing to stop it. She felt her face redden and she almost had to fight for breath for a moment. With a degree of self-control, she had to pause and collect herself. In the brief silence, he then said, 'I am so sorry, I shouldn't have thrown that one on you but I thought I'd save you the embarrassment of asking because I think you might have just been about to put the question. Am I right?'

'How did you know that Fuller?'

'Because I find you very attractive and I thought it would save possible problems, but not blushes, as I can see now. I thought it would be a good idea to tell you that I am not married, now at least, and I don't have any kids, although that was not my choice.'

Whoa, she thought. More information than I need at the moment. What am I supposed to say now?

'That has answered a question I may have got round to Fuller, but I do have to tell you that I am currently in a relationship and even though I do find you extremely attractive, I cannot and will not change my situation, much as it is difficult.'

'Now that is a shame, but I'm happy for you, even though it's quite a blow, but I guess I'll just have to live with it, wont I?' He did indeed find her very attractive with her dark hair and slim and athletic figure. His private thoughts had to be kept to himself for the time being, although he really wished that he could make them known, but now was not the time.

'I don't think you'll be without someone for very long, as someone like you will have the ladies crawling over hot coals for you, I should think.'

'I'd never be that conceited Anna, but thank you for the compliment. Perhaps we should get to talking about more serious things, like work; maybe that'll cool things down.'

'If you say so Fuller, it may for you...'

'Okay, what is your official reason for your very welcome presence?'

'Right, ahem,' pulling herself together, she went on, 'we are working on a case as you know from our previous visits to Goathorn, and we now think that the person who takes fishing parties out for two to three days at a time, is actually visiting France and bringing back illegal immigrants. We don't know this for sure, but so far the body which was found was from Turkey or Northern Cyprus and another one of the three people we are interested in was also from the same region. The boat owner is possibly from that area also, but we don't know for sure at the moment. What I need to know is how can we track the fast boat which he has and uses for the supposed fishing trips, without him knowing?'

'Do you know what sort of boat it is?'

'Yes, it's called a "Redbaye Stormforce 11" and it is a fast boat.'

'I know the craft you mean. It can carry around 12-14 people and it will do around 40 knots. That's very fast for an offshore boat and very seaworthy. She's probably got an array of electronic equipment and a boat like that would probably have AIS or Automatic Identification System. This is what tracks all the shipping around the world via GPS. Having said that, I doubt that many small craft have this equipment fitted but as I say, this craft could probably have it amongst all the other safety equipment on board.'

'So it would be easy to track this boat then, by GPS software I take it?'

'Yes, GPS would be the actual tracking method. However, if, as you suspect, this craft is being used for something other than legal fishing, then I would suggest that the owner or skipper would have the AIS unit disabled in some way, so that they can't be tracked.'

'And radar couldn't keep tabs on them in the Channel?'

'Unfortunately not, because radar, although it's very good, cannot reach right over the Channel as it's around 130 miles wide between here and say Caen. That's why GPS is so good now.'

So how could we keep tabs on them if they've disabled their equipment?'

'I'd say that perhaps the only way is to put a GPS tracking device on board without them knowing it and somewhere it cannot be tampered with. That way, you'll always know exactly when and where they are.'

'That sounds too easy, Fuller.'

'I don't think it would be too difficult, especially as you're the Police, although I dare say you need some sort of authorisation to plant such a device for surveillance, but I'm sure it's "do-able" for you guys.'

'Wow, it does sound possible. Doesn't it? I'll have to check with our office which deals with that sort of thing and maybe get some permission sorted out. I'll bet our tech boys will have the necessary bits and pieces.'

'I'm sure they will, although it's not too difficult as they have these trackers for cars don't they?'

Smacking her hand to her forehead she said, 'Of course, of course they do.'

'One thing though; I think you'd need a Satellite Modem Unit as then it will communicate by satellite even when there is no other link, like a phone signal, so wherever it is, it can be picked up.'

'Thank you so much for this, Fuller, you've been a great help, as ever.'

'It has been my pleasure yet again and please don't think too badly of me for saying what I did.'

'Of course not, I just hope we understand each other.'

'We do, and I still look forward to your next visit, whatever the reason.'

'Thanks Fuller, as ever, it's been a pleasure.' She was about to go to the door and she turned. With a half-smile on her face, she said, 'can I ask a personal question?'

'Of course, ask away,'

'Can I just ask about your name, "Fuller," it's so unusual; I mean where does it come from?'

'Well, from what I understand, as my family seems to go back for quite a long time, the name is derived from the time when fleeces were made into felt.'

She was looking very puzzled. 'Fleeces into felt?'

'Yes, back in mediaeval times, apparently it was necessary to bash the wool, repeatedly for hours, to make the fibres dense and matt together to make the felt. I've done a little research and it seems that until a wooden machine was made to do this, hammering the fibres was done by women. It was a very hard life and the invention of the machine released them from a terribly hard life.'

'Do you mean that they enjoyed themselves more then, and didn't have a hard life anymore?'

'No,' he said laughing, 'of course they had a very hard life anyway, what I meant was that they could get on with better jobs.'

'Okay, I understand the bit about bashing the fibres, where does the "Fuller" come in?'

'Well, the process of bashing was called "Fulling", and from what I can understand from my ancestry, the person in charge of this operation was called the "Fulling Master" so I can only presume that somewhere along the lineage, there was a son who became the "Masterson", which became the family name and my parents probably were interested in history and I became "Fuller."'

'Now that is very interesting and must give you pleasure to know that your ancestor was appreciated by the ladies of the village or town.'

'If you put it like that, I'm sure they did.'

'And now, I appreciate you as you are in charge of something very important.'

'Oh, stop it; you'll make me all cocky.'

Now that remark made her think that now was the time to go before she embarrassed herself.

She gave him a smile and he opened the door for her. As he was quite a bit taller than her, he put a very gentle hand on her shoulder as he said goodbye. She felt the firm strength in that hand. A strong "frisson" ran through her. She turned and gave him another big smile, which he returned. She did have more than a mild feeling of "regret" as she went down the stairs and through the main doors into the fresh sea air, where she took in a few deep breaths to bring her heart rate back down to normal.

Driving back to the police station in a sort of dream, she went over what had been said in the harbourmaster's office. She felt slightly guilty but at the same time she was secretly thrilled that someone of Fuller's character and standing would be attracted to her. It was a sincere compliment she thought and relished the feeling that it gave her, not to mention the confidence. However, she was sure that Alex was the one for her and tried to push any further thoughts in that direction to the back of her mind.

When she arrived, she saw Alice working at her desk. She was staring intently at her computer screen until she realised that Anna was there. Looking up, Alice simply said, 'I see you've had a nice time over at Poole then.' Again Anna blushed as she realised that her face had given away the very pleasant feelings she had.

'It's just hot in the car Alice.'

'Yes, of course.' This was accompanied by a certain look, which was not missed.

What have you got on Martin Goodyear then Alice?'

'Not too much at the moment, although I did find that he comes from Turkey and he was involved in some sort of 'Import and Export' business, but that can cover all sorts of activities, can't it?'

'So do you have any names of this business that we can check into through Europol?'

'That's what I'm working on at the moment. I should have some results before too long.'

'Is his name actually Martin Goodyear, because that doesn't sound Turkish to me?'

'No, I don't think it is, so I'm taking a different approach to trace his name, through British Passport Records and Immigration control, people like that. It all takes a load of time.'

'I know, but if anyone can get the "nitty gritty" you can Alice. Just let me know when you something interesting.'

'Sure will guv.' She looked up at Anna again and smiled sweetly, 'enjoy your day.'

Anna mumbled, 'you too,' and turned swiftly away to regain her composure.

As Anna almost disappeared into the corridor, Alice called back, 'Anna, I've just got something!'

She went back to find Alice beaming as she turned away from her screen. 'What've you got Alice, anything good?'

'I think so. It's Martin Goodyear's real name. Europol came through with the goods rather sooner that I'd expected.'

'Go on then, spill the beans.'

'Okay, well Martin Goodyear was originally from a place called Mersin, on the southern coast of Turkey, fairly opposite to Cyprus. His name was 'Metin Denizci. I looked up Denizci and it means 'Sailor' in Turkish. Well, Metin isn't far from Martin, is it, so I can see why that came about. It also seems that he changed his name by deed poll at some point.

'I can see how he would change the name into that, well done Alice. Do we have anything else from Europol?'

'Not at the moment, but they're working on 'Furkan Dimitriou,' you know Jo Stafford's ex-husband, but nothing so far.'

'Okay, great stuff Alice. I can go and give something for Alex to chew on now. I think we might be able to shake a few trees if we can get authorisation.'

'Authorisation for what?'

'Can't tell you yet, or I'd have to put you in IR1 for a while.'

'Oh no! Not IR1, that's gruesome.'

'I know,' Anna said, moving off to see Alex.

CHAPTER 30

Anna knocked on Alex's door. A disinterested sounding voice said, 'come in.'

As the door opened and he saw who it was, his eyes lit up and he gave a big smile. 'Hi Anna, good to see you back.'

'Why, didn't you think I would then?' she said.

'I never know when you go to see Mr Gorgeous Harbourmaster. He might have carried you off somewhere for all I know.'

'Don't be daft, as I keep saying, he's just a very nice gentleman.'

Anna was fighting within herself to stop another blush creeping up her face.

'You may think that, but let me tell you, I know he's got the hots for you; I've seen it in his eyes when he looks at you, not that I blame him in the least.'

'No, don't be silly, he was just very helpful and did whatever he could to give me what I wanted.'

'I'll bet he wanted to give you more than that, the git.'

At that, the blush rose unbidden, but Alex was actually looking down at some paperwork which had caught his attention. Anna was very thankful and walked over to the window which was slightly open, took a breath of fresh air and turned back, saying, 'He told me about AIS and what it could do.'

'That sounds like some kind of nasty disease, what's AIS for heaven's sake?'

'No, you numpty, AIS is the Automatic Identification System used to keep track of all the shipping in the Channel and across the world actually.'

'I know I've done a fair bit of boating, way back, but it was only in small boats, so how am I supposed to know what AIS is then?'

'I just presumed that as our "font of all knowledge," you'd know.'

'Nice of you to think that, but I couldn't possibly comment. Anyway, this fast boat would have this surely, if it goes out to sea?'

'Well, possibly Fuller said, but he also pointed out that if this boat skipper character is up to no good and wants to keep out of sight and not be seen, then he would more than likely disable it.'

'He's probably right; shit.'

Anna was looking hard at Alex and then she realised; he'd known about AIS all along. 'You knew about AIS didn't you?'

He then had to let the smile burst on his lips.

'If we weren't here I'd make you suffer for that.'

'Ooh goody, I'd like that.'

'Alex, we're at work!'

'I know – sorry. There's a but?'

'Yes, there's a but. Fuller says if a GPS tracker were to be planted on the boat, and one which has a "Satellite Embedded Modem," then this would enable real-time tracking directly to a computer via a satellite as there would be no continuous cellphone coverage at sea.'

'Now that is some good news.' Excitement of some degree was rising in Alex. 'This means that we could keep tabs on him wherever he goes and although we won't know what he's actually doing, I guess that where he goes could be very indicative of his motives.'

'But we'd more than likely need some sort of authority for this, you know, "invasion of privacy" and all that tosh, but I'm sure we could get it.'

'I'm sure you're right my girl. So your trip was worth it then?'

Again, Anna's heart gave a little "hiccup," and she said, 'It certainly was. And that's not all; I've just seen Alice and she's got some information through Europol about our skipper of the fishing boat. His real name is "METIN DENİZCI." Apropos of nothing, Denizci means 'sailor' apparently. He comes from Southern Turkey, a place called Mersin, in Mersin Province. You can see where the "Martin" comes from. No information so far about his finances but he was involved in "Import/Export" activity and we know what that means.'

'We do, almost anything dodgy can be hidden by that description.'

'Guv, on the way back, I was doing some thinking.'

'That's not unusual for you, now is it?'

'You know what I mean. Well, you know Jo Stafford had told me that "Ferkin' Freddie Dimitriou had done some diving back in his home town in Northern Cyprus, but that wasn't covered when Alice and Tom interviewed him?'

'Yes; what's your point?'

'Well, I had a look at a map just now and where Metin Denizci, alias Martin Goodyear comes from, is not that far across the water to Cyprus, and if Dimitriou comes from somewhere along the coast, it's just possible that Martin met Freddie, and they began their games there. Maybe they became involved with drugs and made money from that. Goodyear has to have made a shedload of money from somewhere to afford those two boats, hasn't he? What do you think?'

'I think it's well worth checking further Anna. I think I'll get on to our Tech guys and see what they can give us in the way of a tracking device suitable for our needs. If you can check out this Dimitriou's origins that would be a great help in pulling some strings together.'

'Right'o, I'll give Jo Stafford a call, maybe she can give me some detail and we won't have to tell Dimitriou that we are checking into him further.'

'Smart girl, Anna. While you're here, do you happen to know what Tom's up to at the moment?'

'I think he's gone over to see his contact at Cobbs Quay.'

'Okay, see you later.'

Tom was actually very nearly at Cobbs Quay Marina, having phoned this time to make sure that his "contact" was available. He was pleased that she would be there and he was looking forward to pressing her - for information as well. Arriving at the Marina, he parked his car and walked into the reception area where he spotted Genny who was attending to a couple of people, giving them her usual courtesy and charm. Maybe they were going to buy a boat or just asking about one they had in the marina. No matter, Tom was quite happy to wait and feast his eyes on Genny. After a few minutes, Genny spotted Tom and she gave a visible "start" and for a moment, she was put off her stride, but soon returned to her two customers. Finishing their enquiry, they left, obviously more than satisfied. Genny turned and looked toward Tom and gave him a great big smile which made him more than pleased. He walked over to the reception desk and said, 'Hi Genny, good to see you.'

'Hi Tom, I'm so glad you came. Are you here officially?

'Yes, actually, but as you are my official contact, and they think you are a bloke, I have to keep that a secret, but at the same time I have to give them the information they require. If they knew who you were and what you looked like, I wouldn't get a minutes peace.'

'And what do I look like, Tom?' Genny said, putting her head on one side and giving him an innocent look.

'Abso-bloody-lutely gorgeous, and that's putting it mildly, not to mention, stunning, incredibly sexy and most important of all, a beautiful person.'

Tom had said the right things, and she rewarded him by giving him the most incredibly sexy look which made his knees go weak.

'After the other night, I needed a day off to get over it, did you know?'

'I didn't realise until I came over to see you but they said you weren't well and had the day off sick.'

'After the night we had, I needed a rest.'

'Yes, I seem to remember we were a little tied up; or at least you were.'

'More like shackled, I seem to think,' she said with a giggle.

Again, a picture formed in Tom's mind. 'Genny, can I see you again?'

'Yes please Tom, I'd like that.' She gave him another of her "special" looks.

'Okay, if you let me have your number, I'll give you a call tonight and we can arrange a date. At the moment, we have a lot on and I'm not too sure of my work schedule.'

'Why, is there something special happening?'

'We're working on something which might involve keeping a close eye on Mr Goodyear's boat and its movements.'

'Ooh, that's great, I mean this is real detective work isn't it, you know keeping a close eye on someone without their knowing.'

'I suppose so, but please keep this to yourself; we don't want to spook him until we know more details.'

'Of course.'

'How about the Red Lion, over on the main road?'

'Great, I'll look forward to that.' She wrote down her number and handed him the note, 'this is my mobile number,' which Tom carefully put into his wallet.

Tom was thinking once again, why me? Of all the people she sees here who must find her as attractive as I do, and yet she seems to like me; my gain, he said to himself.

'Now,' said Tom, 'to official business. If you are able to give me some times and dates of when Goodyear took "Predator" out and when he came back, that would be enormously helpful.' He really didn't know Genny that well and just supposing she actually knew Martin Goodyear; she might just let something slip, so he kept quiet.

'I do have a couple of times for you. He took the boat out about three days ago and you have the video copy of when he came back. He took it out again yesterday, but came back the same day. He usually goes out for two or three days at a time, but I think you know that.'

'Great. The next time he loads up with fuel, can you give me a call or send me an email, with the time and how much fuel he takes on board, you know that sort of thing. I need to know if he's going to make a longer trip.'

'Okay, Detective Tom, I can do that. I do know that when he goes on a longer trip he takes on quite a huge amount of fuel, but I suppose if he's out fishing, he needs more fuel.'

Again, Tom said nothing about their suspicion that he was going over to France for purposes "other than fishing."

'While I'm here, I think I'll just take a look around to see if there is anything that might give me some more information; you know, talk to a few people, it's surprising what some folk will tell you about other folk. That's how we get quite a bit of our local knowledge.'

'Right'o, but be careful out on the pontoons, we don't want to see a soggy cop coming back in here; one who's tripped over a mooring rope or something and taken a dive into the water, it's happened before.'

'I'll be careful; I don't look too good when I'm wet.'

'Oh, but you did after that shower we had,' she said, with a very meaningful look.

Another very pleasing and highly charged picture flashed through Tom's mind at that moment, as he went out to the pontoons, wearing a very stupid grin on his face.

CHAPTER 31

Alex called the technical services department and asked to speak to Peter Tomlinson, who was the head of department and an old friend.

'Tomlinson here, how can I help?'

'Hello Peter, it's been a long time. Alex Vail.'

'Alex; hello. It's great to hear from you. Yes it has been a long time hasn't it. I hear on the grapevine that you are at Bournemouth now and a DCI is that right?'

'Yes, for my sins. I've been here for a while now.'

'I seem to remember that you were getting over your tragic loss. Are things better now?'

'Yes thanks Peter, much better, in fact, I'm just starting a new relationship which I think and hope is going well. We'll see what happens, but so far it's looking good, if I'm careful.'

'How do you mean careful, I don't think you'll blow it, if I know how you were with Sandra.'

'No, it's not that, but I can't say any more, or I'll have to kill you. Anyway, how are things with you; how's your health these days?' knowing that Peter had had a minor heart attack some time previously. Are the stents still working well?'

'Yes, they seem to be, no problems and a big glass of red each night on doctor's orders; not too bad really and I shouldn't complain.' Peter was considerably older than Alex and their friendship went back many years. 'Still being told what to do by "'er indoors," but ours is not to ask why, just do... or take the consequences - or words to that effect,' he said with a chuckle.

'Oh, it sounds like she's still giving orders and managing you.'

'You could put it that way Alex; anyway, what can I do for you? I'm sure you didn't just call for a chat. You have something you need help with?'

'Yes Peter. We are involved with a murder which has "nautical" connections and we have to follow the movements of a boat, ostensibly being used for long-distance fishing from Poole Harbour, but we suspect it's being used for other things and we need to track it.'

'Ah, you'll be needing something like a tracking device, methinks, as if chummy is engaged on dodgy stuff, he won't be using AIS.'

'You know about AIS then?'

'Oh yes, we get to know about most of the electronic gizmos these days,' he said without even a hint of sarcasm. I've been advised by Poole Harbourmaster that we would need something called a "Satellite Modem Unit. Do you have them?'

'We don't have them here but I can get one arranged quite quickly once you have the authority. This can link directly to a computer so that it can be monitored in real time and you'll always know exactly where they are, although it won't tell you what they are doing.'

'That sounds exactly what we need Pete, great.'

'One thing though Alex. You are presumably going to plant this "covert" device where it can't be seen or hopefully found, is that right?'

'For sure, we'll have someone put it on board well out of sight, but is there a problem?'

'The only thing I would warn you about is that whoever plants this device, and it's not very big, but it should be placed a distance from anything magnetic or the signal may be corrupted and the compass would surely be affected and that, I would imagine, would cause problems.'

'Thanks for that Peter. I'll make sure that it is put in a safe area.'

'Okay then, shall I give you a bell when I have it ready?'

'Yes please and I'll get the authorisation signed off right now.'

'Right-o then, and don't leave it so long next time, we'll have to meet when you can and we can have a proper '"catch-up."

'Will do and give my regards to your Doris.'

'And you look after your new lady; let me know how you are getting on, I could do with some "juicy bits" at my time of life.'

'Go on, you dirty old bugger, cheers.'

Alex hung up and dialled the office of DCS Gordon for authorisation of the tracker.

When he got put through, a very gruff voice said, 'Vail, how are things down there; are you doing any better? I understand you have another murder?' The word "murder" was pronounced with a very strong "murrrda."

'Yes sir, everything is in hand and I'm calling to ask for authorisation for the placement of a covert GPS tracking device on a boat we want to follow closely.'

'And where will this boat be going and what will it be doing?'

'We think that it might be involved with either drug-smuggling or illegal immigrants or maybe both, from France and back to the harbour at Poole.'

'And you think that by tracking it, you will be able to prove something, although surely all you will know is where it is.'

'Yes , but if they don't do what they tell us they normally do, which is fishing, then by the time that they go where they go and the speed they use, we can gain some very interesting information with which to question them on.'

'And this will solve your murder then?'

'It will go a very long way to giving us a motive and MO.'

'Okay then, I'll authorise this. Get your people to collect is as soon as you like '

'Thank you sir; I'll have a courier collect it.'

'Alex.'

'Yes?'

'Don't fuck this one up laddie, d'you hear me?'

'No sir.'

Alex called for Tom who had returned from his trip back to Cobbs Quay Marina.

'So Tom, what information did you get from your contact?'

'Only that "Predator" had gone out a few days ago and they came back at night, and we have the CCTV data on that which we've seen. Yesterday they went out but came back quite quickly later that afternoon. They also take on board a great deal of fuel, more than usual, when they go out for a three day trip.'

'Anything else?'

'Well guv, I went out to have another look at the boat and one thing did strike me was that this boat didn't look like a fishing boat to me. I mean the open deck at the stern was not that big and I'm sure all the deep-sea fishing boats I've seen on You Tube seem to have a big area and long rods sticking out, although I don't know what they are for, but this boat is very narrow and sleek and just doesn't seem like a fishing boat to me.'

'I see what you mean. Do you have a picture of this boat to hand?'

'Yes, I'll just get it, hold on.' Tom went to his desk and got the photo of the Redbaye Stormforce 11, returned to Alex and held out the picture.

Looking at the photo, Alex looked up at Tom and said, 'Well observed Tom, I think you're right. This boat is not one I'd like to be on in the middle of the Channel, rocking about while blokes were fishing, and this is not a trawler so it would be simply drifting if they were fishing. It's very narrow as you say and it looks more like a boat built for speed in rough conditions. I guess that's where the name "Stormforce 11" comes from, or am I being stupid?'

'You've done a bit of boating haven't you guv, in the past I mean?'

'Yes, and every boat I've either had or been on, has rocked about if it's not moving. A narrow hull will have a particularly violent movement and I reckon this boat would make anyone throw up in minutes even if they could stand upright, which I doubt. This fact gives me even more reason to think that these guys are absolutely *not* fishing and I'm now more than ever convinced that they are doing something very dodgy. We just have to find out what. I've arranged for a GPS tracking device to be planted on the boat so that we can track their movements, directly on our computer here.'

'I'd better keep that information to myself when I see my contact over at Cobbs then.'

'Yes, absolutely. I know you've seen the boat, is there any way that you could get entry to it so that we could plant this device? Did you take a good look at it?'

'Yes guv. I know the cabin is locked up tight, but the stern deck is open, and I saw some lockers around that area although I don't think they have locks, in fact I'm sure, so maybe there is somewhere there that could be a good place to plant this thing. How big is it?'

'I've no idea yet, but we'll have it quite soon and then we'll have to find a way of getting it put on board so that no-one sees it being done. That could be quite difficult I'd imagine as there are always people about in a place like that.'

'I'll ask my contact what time the boat will be unattended and when would be the best time to get to it without being seen.'

'But don't, for Christ's sake, tell him why we're doing this.'

'Yeah, I've realised that Goodyear may be known to them, so I've said nothing that will give things away, although they do know that the police have an interest in Goodyear, so maybe they'll keep things quiet.'

'If they don't they could blow this whole operation to bits, so impress on this contact to keep everything to themselves or they could be included as an "accessory" should things go tits-up.'

'Okay guv, will do. I'll have a good one-to-one with them and make them understand exactly the situation.'

'Good, do that.'

'Should I go over there maybe after my shift and have a look at the boat at the same time. I might be able to spot a likely place to hide the tracker?'

'If you want, but I can't sanction overtime for that, it'll have to be on your own time, but wait until we get the device because we don't know how big it might be yet.'

'I don't mind guv, I quite like going to the marina. I've been thinking that perhaps I'd like a small boat to mess around in.'

'I know I've had a load of fun when I had boats.'

'Why did you stop then guv?'

'To be honest, it became too expensive, especially when I had a 30ft cruiser with a bloody great engine. Another reason was that I realised that I didn't have the expertise or training to go right out to sea. I had a few quite scary events which made me decide that I was a danger to myself and others, so I took to windsurfing instead. That gave me all the adrenaline rush I needed.'

'And this was before you became a copper then guv?'

'Yep, back in the days when I had a life and time to enjoy stuff like that. As you well know, this job takes up about everything you have.'

'I know guv, but it's addictive isn't it? I mean I love the job.'

'I'm very glad to hear that Tom. You're doing well here in CID, so keep it up.'

'Yes guv, thanks.'

'Now get out of here and do some work, I'm busy.'

Tom exited, feeling quite good about his work, his situation and prospects, both in the job and his private life.

CHAPTER 32

Hmm, now that is very interesting. Anna was musing over some information which she had managed to uncover from the Turkish Embassy in London and their enquiries relayed to Ankara and the appropriate authorities there. She had asked if the name Denitczi had any links with the police or drug enforcement agencies. She was quite amazed to find that this name had several links to investigations into the suspected movement of cocaine from the country. She had further asked if there was a known exit point from where the cocaine could have been exported. It was suspected that several consignments had been moved from Mersin, a small coastal port on the southern part of Turkey. How they had been transported was not known as no actual drugs were found despite several attempts to find shipments. However, there were suspicions of shipments being taken by fast boat to a place on the Cyprus coast called Karpaz where there was a modern marina and dive centre. When Anna had heard dive centre, she had put in a further request directed to Nicosia regarding the name Dimitriou and any relation to that dive centre. Wonder of wonders, there had been a link although not strong. There was no proof but the fact that there were recorded "suspicions" made her think.

She had sat quietly and thought about the possibility of drugs being shipped from Mersin to Karpaz as both names, Dimitriou and Denitczi had links to these towns. Furthermore, it was known by the authorities that shipments had been made but no knowledge of how they were smuggled and by what methods, across the water. She went in to see Alex to share the information she had gleaned so far and to put her thoughts to him.

She went first to the coffee machine and made two cups of cappuccino, taking them both into Alex's office. The smell preceded her and he looked up as she came in holding the two mugs. 'An angel has just landed,' he said, giving her a big smile. Returning the smile she said, 'I've got something which I think is very interesting. I've had some good results from Turkey via their Embassy in London regarding drug shipments from Denitczi's home town of Mersin to a place on the northern tip of Cyprus called Karpaz where Dimitriou worked as a diving instructor.'

'Go on, this sounds interesting, but how do we know that Dimitriou was involved?'

Jo Stafford did mention something about diving during our interview, but it didn't seem that important at the time, but maybe Alice could give her a call to get some further details. We don't know that he was involved, but if there is a link, it could give us a better idea of how these two are linked, maybe financial. The authorities say there is no evidence of how the shipments were transported or by which means. They only know that they were made, but can't prove anything. Well, I got to thinking that as they are both seemingly involved, or at least linked, however tenuously, there has to be a way of transporting these drugs without them being discovered.'

'Yes, and what did your devious mind come up with, may I ask?'

'How about this - to make shipment without sniffer dogs, which, I presume they have over there, they have to hide the smell of the cocaine, for that is what they knew was being moved. I thought of ways of hiding the stuff especially when connected or linked to diving.'

'You're going to tell me that they took it underwater aren't you?'

'Unless they had a bloody submarine, no; but just supposing the cocaine was put into diving air tanks, would they be checked out, as the gear is pretty substantial and usually very tightly shut up, you know, with the pressure in? I would think it highly unlikely that authorities would expect anyone with air tanks to de-pressurise them and undo all the special equipment, just to have a look inside.'

Alex looked thoughtful for a moment, and then said, 'Bloody hell, I think you've hit on a pretty serious possibility there Anna. Do you want to get in touch with a diving outfit here and ask if what you say is likely or even possible?'

'I think it might prove or disprove my idea, so yes, let's do that.'

'You really surprise me sometimes Anna, I mean this is something I wouldn't have thought a girl would think of.'

'And why not, we do have brains you know?' She was bridling just a little at this assumption that she should not think of something technical.

'I'm sorry it's just that it's so unusual for a woman to think along technical lines like that. I didn't mean to be patronising in the least.'

'Well that's all right then, I just thought for a moment that you considered that only men could think outside the box. Anyway, women go diving and they would have an understanding of equipment wouldn't they?'

'Yes, of course, but you don't know about diving do you?'

'I did go out with a guy for a while who used to dive, so I did learn a little about the equipment.'

'But it didn't last?'

'Obviously.'

Alex thought it best to let the matter drop after that stone-wall riposte.

She went out to her desk and looked up the number of a diving equipment supplier which she recalled was somewhere in Bournemouth. Finding the number she was looking for, she saw that their premises were not far away, so she decided to go over to see them and ask for their technical advice rather than trying to describe it over the phone.

It was a fine and dry summer afternoon and there was little wind. It was the time of year she liked the best, not too hot. She was very happy that her relationship with Alex seemed to be progressing well and they were gently but firmly establishing their feelings for one another. She had been without a meaningful relationship for a considerable time and she was now very hopeful that the feelings between her and Alex would grow further. She was quite confident that things were going in the right direction and she felt good. Her career had taken off with her being promoted to sergeant and she was hopeful of taking that further and putting in for her inspector's exam in the not too distant future. This would depend on Alex's recommendation to a large extent, so she was always mindful of this. It actually put a little strain on her side of the relationship sometimes as she realised that should things go wrong, it could probably affect her chances of promotion, but for now, things were looking good.

Arriving at the Diving company's premises, she pushed open the door and walked into a room filled, what looked like capacity with all manner of wetsuits, air tanks, harnesses, flippers, masks and all the multitude of equipment which scuba divers used. Walking over to the main desk, she showed her warrant card to the chap serving.

'I am Detective Sergeant Jenkins from Bournemouth Police.'

He said, 'I expect you want someone to go and get a body from the sea somewhere then?'

'Not this time sunshine. We have our own unit for that sort of thing.' She had a sudden thought; why didn't I think of calling them I'm not thinking straight? Oh well, I'm here now and I can still ask the questions. 'Can I speak to a technical person who knows about all the equipment and so on please?'

'Sure, I'll get Marcus; he's our top mechanic around here and knows all the equipment.'

The assistant went to the rear of the shop and called through a door, 'Hey Marcus, the police are here for you.'

Marcus came through the door looking quite worried and walked through the main showroom. He was very bronzed and had a physique which was obviously due to quite some time in the gym as well as swimming. He had short blond hair and was clean shaven. He was wearing a 'T' shirt bearing the logo of the company with a white silhouette of a diver with scuba gear on a black background. Cut-off jeans and sandals completed his look. He walked up to Anna and greeted her with, 'G'day.'

She said, 'don't look so worried, I'm not here to arrest you.'

'Damn,' he said with a big grin and a flashing smile from a set of very even teeth, 'and there I was hoping that you'd drag me off screaming into a cell with you. Now that would have been interesting, to have been dragged off by someone as dinkum as you constable.'

'Sergeant actually,' Anna said, with mock seriousness.

'Bugger, that would've been even better.'

Anna realised that despite the Australian accent, she had to put a stop to this, however flattering his attention might be. 'Come on, let's get this straight, I have a serious investigation ongoing and I need your expert help.'

'Absolutely my pleasure sergeant, what do you need to know?'

'Okay, this may be strange but supposing I had to move some cocaine without the smell being detected by some means or other, would it be possible to do it inside an air-tank? I mean, would the authorities, if they were suspicious, ask you to open the tanks so they could check them?'

'Wow, that's a hell of a suggestion. It's a new one on me. I hope you're not going to do the smuggling,' he said with another flashing grin. 'Let me think a mo.' He was silent for a few moments and then said, 'I would just say that yes, it would be possible to put some cocaine inside an empty air-tank if it was rolled really small and went through the opening at the top of the tank. The valve used is about 25mm so they would have to be probably linked on a string to get them out, a bit like sausages but how you'd be able to find the string is another matter. However, if the authorities were suspicious, as you say, then they would see that the tank was nearly empty by the pressure gauge and then they could have this removed to check.'

'Could the tank be re-pressurised?'

'Well, yes, I suppose so.'

'But if this gauge was "doctored" in some way so as to look full, would they still ask to check.'

'Sergeant, when an air-tank is full it has in the region of 4,000 lbs of pressure and to vent that is a very specialised and quite dangerous thing to do. I really don't think they'd be very popular, especially with the divers whose tanks had been filled, if they had to empty them and get them all refilled. It just wouldn't be the thing to do and would cause a lot of bad feeling and bad tempers. In any case, even when a tank gauge shows "empty," there is still some air pressure there. This is done to make sure that no contaminants can get into the tank as the air pressure will be greater than the ambient air pressure, so that's another reason for not taking a gauge off. It would actually make the tank unusable and that would really piss people off, believe me.'

'But could a pressure gauge be made to look "full" and would that stop any further examination?'

'Yes, it could be done I suppose.'

'And it would not look "rigged"?'

'Not if it was done properly.'

'Thanks, that's all I need to know.'

'But hey, if they were using the tank to transport coke, they couldn't then use them for diving.'

'Oh, why's that?'

'Because once the tank has been contaminated, it would be useless, not to mention dangerous to use if for breathing, I mean it could lead to all sorts of problems if you were down say about 50 metres and you start to feel a bit groggy.'

'Yes, I can see that.'

'Mind you, why would you want to have a false gauge, I mean it could just be sealed up and pressurised. Then there would be nothing to see.'

'But could "sniffer dogs" detect any smell then?'

'Do you know, I don't think that a valve that holds over 4,000 pounds of pressure would actually leak any smell, do you?'

'No, I s'pose not.'

There was a pause as Marcus looked thoughtful. 'There is one thing that might be a give-away; I mean that might lead to a discovery of smuggled drugs.'

Anna wondered if this revelation might bring her idea crumbling down. 'What's that then Marcus don't tell me my idea has just been trashed.'

'You haven't said where these drugs are coming from and where they are going but perhaps the port authorities where these tanks would leave from have X-ray machines.'

'X-ray, can they X-ray steel tanks then?'

'Oh yeah, no problem.'

'And do you think that packets of cocaine would show up on the X-ray?'

'To be honest, I don't know.'

Anna thought swiftly about this and then realised that the small port of Mersin would probably not have any such hi-tech equipment, but she would check later. 'Thanks for that, I'll have to make some more enquiries about that.'

'Sorry to maybe have chucked a spanner into the works sergeant,' he said with a grin which didn't quite work too well.

'Maybe not, but it's a possibility.'

'I hope not, because not many places would have that sort of equipment, so maybe you could be okay.'

'Well, thanks Marcus, you have given me the information I need to do some more investigation, so I'll get off now.'

'If you're sure; there's nothing else I can help you with?' he said this with a hint of a leer which really put her off, and he was really trying to be nice.

'One other thing - If we asked you to put these facts in writing, should it be necessary for evidence, could you do that?'

'Yeah, I don't see why not. It's not as if it's illegal to put the possibility in writing, as long as we don't actually do anything like that. It could be very life-threatening if a rigged gauge was wrongly fitted and someone put on some scuba gear to dive. It could kill them.'

'But surely, don't they check that so that they can breathe before going under the water?'

'You're not daft are you sergeant?'

'I don't think so. Thanks for your help.' She turned away, looked back and said over her shoulder, I have to get back with your information. 'Bye'.

'Anytime sergeant, come back again if you need anything.'

Unlikely, she thought, and made her way back to the office.

CHAPTER 33

Alice put a call through to Jo Stafford, but she only got a recorded message asking her to leave her details. She left a message asking Jo to get back in touch as soon as she could. Then Alice called the shop where she worked and asked if it would be possible to speak to Jo, if she was there. After a short pause, a voice called out, "Jo, there's a call for you - no, I don't know who it is." The phone was passed to Jo who said, 'Hello, who is this?'

'Hello Jo, this is DS Alice Compton from Bournemouth CID. Is it okay to have a word?'

'Yes, is it important? Has anything happened?'

'No, nothing has actually happened, but I need to ask you for some more information about your ex-husband's scuba diving activity and what you know about it.'

'What can I tell you?'

'Do you know when he was involved with this diving?'

'I only know that before I met him and he was living in Cyprus, he was a diving instructor in a place called Karpaz, I think it was. It was on the northern coast of Cyprus, right up near the end of the island.'

'Did he make a lot of money when he was there do you know?'

'He didn't like to talk about it and when I asked him, he would become very unresponsive. I do know from some of the things he did say, that he had made quite a bit, but I think he became involved in gambling and lost a lot.'

'Do you think he made this money from his diving?'

'I don't think he could have done, because there's not that much in diving training is there, certainly not the sort of money that Freddie would have liked.'

'So do you think he was involved in something else to make money?'

'I don't know, but I wouldn't be at all surprised because when he's been drunk he's said some things which made me think he was involved in some other activity which he wouldn't talk about, and when I asked him something, he'd become very abusive and tell me to mind my own business.'

'And would this be the time that he began to be violent towards you?'

'Round about that time, yes.'

'Do you think that he could have been involved with drugs, would that be a possibility?'

'Again, from some of the things which he did say; not say exactly, but in a roundabout way sort of refer to, I would say that it was more than likely. I know once he did mention someone called '"Mertin" he knew in Turkey, but other than that I couldn't say, I'm sorry.'

'Do you happen to know where this Mertin came from?'

'I'm sorry, only that it was somewhere on the coast. I can only think that Dimitriou would have known him from the diving connection.'

'Jo, you have been very helpful. This may have just given us some links which we need, thank you. Let me just say this; if Freddie happens to get in touch with you, do not under any circumstances let him know that you have said anything about a drugs connection or that you have even mentioned a Turkish connection. Is that clear?'

'Absolutely; I won't mention anything and I just hope that he doesn't contact me anyway.'

'Okay, that's fine and thanks again. Keep yourself safe Jo.'

'I will, 'bye.'

Alice relayed this information to Alex who was pleased that a more definite connection was being suggested between Denitczi and Dimitriou. They now needed to get more confirmation of the dealings between the two or at least a confirmation that the two had met there, possibility through the diving connection. If it could be proven that the two were working together, it may give an indication of a possible drug trade between Turkey and Cyprus. This would have made the sort of money which Denitczi would need to fund the boat he had at the moment as well as the house he lived in.

Alex called a brief meeting of the team on this investigation. Anna, Alice and Tom together with a couple of DC's who were assisting with the more routine enquiries, filed into the incident room.

'Brief going-over where we are at the moment people,' said Alex. 'We have the body but we have no idea why he was killed and who actually killed him. We know that the "fishing trips" are more than likely not those at all, thanks to Tom who has pointed out an obvious point, which we should have spotted earlier I have to say. 'That is that this boat, the "Stormforce 11" is not a fishing boat at all, more a fast sea-going patrol boat. As he pointed out, fishing boats usually have a wide open deck at the stern for the fishermen to stand around with their rods and stuff. This boat doesn't have that. Furthermore, fishing boats usually have quite a wide beam so that they don't rock about too much when they are drifting. This boat is very narrow and I know from my own experience that it would rock about so much on a choppy sea that fishing would be almost impossible, I would think. Well done Tom, for that observation. I think that we now can be certain that this Martin Goodyear, or as we know his real name is or was Mertin Denitczi, is running trips, possibly to France for either drugs or illegals, or both. We don't know this for certain and I have arranged for a "Satellite Modem Unit" GPS tracking device which we will plant on board this craft. This will enable us to track his movements and exact position in real-time directly on our computers here. We won't know what he is doing but we'll know where he's doing it. From this date we can get a pretty good picture of what he's really up to.'

'Do we know of any drug connection guv?' asked Alice.

'Not yet, at least nothing conclusive, but Anna has suggested, what I think is a very possible method of taking drugs between Turkey and Cyprus, which is where Dimitriou was a diving instructor. Anna, would you like to explain your theory?'

She took over and looking just a little pleased with herself, said, 'I went to a Diving specialist in Bournemouth and spoke to a technician. I asked if it would be possible to insert cannabis or heroin into a scuba air-tank. He said it was quite possible, difficult, but do-able, although not cannabis as that would be too bulky.

Tom said, 'bloody hell, it would have to be a very small tubular shape to go into a tank as it would have to go through the pressure gauge hole wouldn't it?'

'Yes, it would Tom, but the technician said it might be possible if they were tightly rolled and on a string so that they could be removed. This might be a way that a drugs trade was carried out between these two back in Turkey, but we can't prove this at this stage. However, it must be a strong possibility for raising money for his boat, don't you think?' They all nodded assent at this possibility. 'And, if this method were proven to be possible, just think how much could be put into one of these tanks – they are bloody heavy.'

There were quite a lot of "nods" around the group.

Alex said, 'All credit to Anna for thinking of this as a possibility, it's a new one on me, but I think it could be a strong possibility.'

Alice then said, this is all very well, but we still know nothing about the murder, why it took place and why the body was dumped there, do we?'

'Thanks for pointing that out Alice but yes, you're right, we don't know. I've received authorisation for this tracking device and it'll be here this afternoon and I think Tom, as you are already known over at Cobbs Quay Marina, you should be the one to place it on the boat. I know you've had a good look round at it haven't you? Have you found any likely place it can be hidden, away from anything magnetic?'

'I think so guv. There's the open section behind the main cabin and there are a couple of hatch covers which didn't seem to be locked, so with a bit of luck, I can put this gizmo inside there. Perhaps it might be an idea to have a sticky back on it, so that I can just put it up on the underside of the locker, or whatever is there, so that it wouldn't be seen unless someone was feeling all around.'

'That seems good thinking to me Tom, but how will you do this without anyone seeing you?'

'I don't know yet guv, but maybe I can get a little help from my contact. They probably know a good time to go out there, the boat is moored right at the end of one of the pontoons, so there won't be many boaty types right out there, unless I'm very unlucky.'

'Okay, I'll leave that to you then, but be bloody careful; the last thing we want is this Goodyear character getting wind of what we're doing.'

'Right'o guv, I'll make sure that it's done properly.'

'Right, anything else we should know about while we're here; any further information or ideas from anyone?'

'All that I have managed to find regarding the finances at the moment is that the authorities know of a drugs link between this place called Mersin and the marina in northern Cyprus called Karpaz,' said Anna.

Alice raised her hand and Alex nodded to her. 'I had a word with Jo Stafford and she has confirmed that her ex, we now know as 'Freddie' Dimitriou was a diving instructor in Karpaz, so it isn't too far a stretch of the imagination that he and Denitczi had some kind of connection.'

'That's certainly food for thought Alice, so you can follow that through.'

'There is one other thing that I was thinking guv,' said Anna, 'do you think we should have that shed checked over by SOCO, I mean, if he had some bodies, I mean illegals kept in there for some reason, there would be traces surely?'

'I think that would be a very good idea. We were going to do that anyway but I'll get on to that right away and get them over there. Can you get the keys made available to them and tell them that they may have to "find their own way into the internal shed, as the keys have been "lost."'

'I'm on it guv.'

CHAPTER 34

The tracking device arrived by courier from the Technical Department and Alex called Tom in to his office. 'Here it is Tom; there's a note here that says it should be good for a number of days. All we need to know is where and when he goes and comes back. If we know when he's on his way back from what we think might be France, we can keep a very close eye on him and see who he has on board.'

'And if they're really fishermen guv.'

'Exactly, because if they tell us that they are fishing but actually over somewhere on the coast of France, we know that they are giving us bullshit; now can you get on to your contact and get their advice on the best time to fit this?'

'I've already done that guv and they say that late evening would be a good time, when most boaty types have brought their craft back and when it's dark, there are very few around anyway. I was thinking as well that it might be a good idea to ask Cobbs Quay officially to turn off their CCTV while I do this, so that there would be no evidence which could be seen "inadvertently"?'

'I don't see why not, but I think I'd better have a word with their top man so that there is no "leak."'

'Okay guv, just let me know when you've done that and I'll arrange to go over there and fit it.'

'Right, what's the boss's name, do you know?'

'I know the Yard Manager is Roger Whitehorn, but I don't know the big boss's name, although I can find out quickly.'

'Okay, do that and let me know.'

Making sure that he was not overheard, Tom phoned his "contact," Genny Dobbs. When she came to the phone, checking around him he said, 'Hi Genny with a "G," this is Tom.'

'Hello detective Tom, so nice to hear from you. Are you going to arrange our date?'

'I will in a moment, but first, I need to ask you the name of the top man in your marina as my boss wants a word with him.'

'Is it about the investigation which you are on at the moment, then?'

'Yes, actually, but this must be kept very quiet as it's now become very important and we need to keep secrecy, do you understand?'

'Of course; what are you going to do; you know that I'll keep everything quiet, don't you? Our Marina Master is David Cunningham. Now then, how about that date?'

'Well, I have to come over to your place, I mean Cobbs, late one evening for a special assignment, so when I know which evening that'll be, can I give you a call and if you're free, maybe we could make a night of it. What do you say?'

'I say yes, Tom. We could maybe go for a drink or a meal or something.'

'How about all three?'

She gave a sexy giggle, 'That sounds even better. I'll wait for your call then. I'd better go as I have a lot of people here who want some attention.'

'I know how they feel Genny. Call you later okay?'

'Sure, 'bye for now.'

Tom gave Alex the name of the Marina Master and a call was made asking to be put through to the head of the Marina.

'Cunningham here, how can I help?'

'Mr Cunningham, this is DCI Alex Vail of Bournemouth Police. We have an ongoing investigation which, among other things, involves a boat which is moored in your marina. We have received formal authorisation to place a covert tracking device on this boat so that we may know when and where it goes. More than that at this stage, I cannot say, but I am officially asking for your permission to allow one of my officers to place this device, covertly, without the owner's knowledge of course.'

'When would this take place Inspector?'

'Quite late one evening, if that's possible.'

There was a short pause, while this request was considered. 'I don't think that would be too much of a problem Inspector, providing the boat was not in any way damaged or put in peril, and of course, you have correct authorisation.'

'Of course; this device is extremely small and is simply a GPS tracker which will feed data back to our Head Office in real time so that we know exactly its whereabouts.'

'And what will you do with this knowledge inspector?'

'As you would imagine, we keep it to ourselves and we would ask that you do exactly that as well; as I say, this investigation is extremely serious and could become more so. It is our intention to make sure that we keep everything completely safe and bring this matter to a proper conclusion.'

'Of course, I understand. Is there anything I can do to help?'

'One thing which would be most useful is that an agreed time and day is arranged for this work to be carried out. It will only take a few minutes, but we would like your CCTV recording to be turned off for that short period, for the sake of secrecy.'

'I think that can be arranged without too much trouble. Just let me know your intentions and I will organise this. I take it that you would like the fewer number of people who know about this, the better.'

'Indeed, I think that's a given, including your staff; I'll let you know our intended time then. Thanks for your help Mr Cunningham.'

'Glad to help inspector. In fact, I think I should really be the one to carry this out to guarantee secrecy. We'll talk again soon. Call me on this number,' he said giving his mobile number.'

'Goodbye.'

Alex called for Tom who was not far away.

'Guv?'

'Tom, I've had clearance from the Marina Master to carry out our "clandestine" operation, so you can choose the best time from your informant, to carry this out and let me know.'

'Okay guv. I'll suggest tomorrow evening, somewhere around 10 or 11 pm, when the place is pretty deserted.'

'Right, that sounds good to me. I've got go-ahead to have the CCTV recording to be turned off for the time it'll take you to put it in place. I don't think it should take too long should it?'

'I reckon about 10 minutes, to get to the end of the pontoon, stick it in place and then back again.'

'And without being seen?'

'My contact will give me the word about the best time.'

'Good. We'll have to co-ordinate this with the Marina Master as it will have to be only him who knows about turning off the CCTV.'

'Okay guv, I'll get this sorted right now.'

Tom went off to phone his contact at Cobbs Quay Marina, once again.

'Can I speak to Genny please?' asked Tom when the call was answered. She came on the line. 'Hi Genny, it's Tom again. I have to do something which will take only about ten minutes, during which I need to "not be seen doing it" out on the pontoons. Can you tell me the best time when no-one would be around; you know when the place is very quiet?'

'What day Tom?'

'Tomorrow evening.'

'Okay, hmm, let me think.' She paused for a few moments. 'I reckon about half ten would be the best time; most if not all the boats are back by then and the owners would probably be in the bar anyway, so it should be very quiet out there. I don't know what you'll be doing but you'd be seen by the cameras though.'

'That's been taken care of by our boss, so don't worry about that. As soon as I've done what I have to do, we can meet and I'll take you for a meal. Is the Red Lion up on Blandford Road okay with you, do you fancy a bite there and we can do whatever you'd like after that?'

She gave a little giggle and said, 'I fancy more than a bite, as you well know, and you know very well what I like after that, detective Tom.'

Tom was getting a warm glow spreading from somewhere around the groin region once again. She had this effect on him, and with good reason. They'd had a number of dates now and they generally ended up with the both having amazing sex. Genny had insisted a couple of times that Tom had used his handcuffs to keep her well "attached" to the bed-frame; while he did what she insisted on - which wasn't too much of a problem for him.

'Okay, I'll be there at around 10.15 then and I think your boss will be waiting for me. As soon as I've finished, I'll give you a quick bell and see you in the Red Lion. Is that okay with you?'

'Great Tom, I'll get myself ready.'

'I'm ready already,' he said. 'See you tomorrow, Gen.'

'Don't forget the "you-know-what's'" detective Tom.'

Tom put the phone down and sashayed back to his desk.

'Have you got a time yet Tom?' was the shouted question from Alex.

'Sorry guv, I was just making a note of it on my pad.' No I wasn't, if I'm honest, he thought. 'It's okay for tomorrow night about 10.30. Can you get the boss there to have the CCTV turned off for about 10 minutes or so, and I can run up there and fix this thing?'

Alex nodded and reached for his phone. Dialling the number for David Cunningham, the call was answered quite quickly.

'Mr Cunningham, DCI Vail again. The time we have arranged for is tomorrow evening at 10.30. If you could have the CCTV turned off for 15 minutes at that time, we will carry out the work.'

'Very good, I'll make the necessary arrangements and be assured that only I will know that the cameras will not be recording. If by some chance the operative who checks the tapes does actually spot a missing 15 minutes, he will be given some excuse or other to indicate a malfunction; but don't worry, I don't think it will be spotted anyway.'

'That's great, thank you for your help. Believe me; this will help our investigation enormously. I'll keep you informed.'

'Very well inspector, good-night and good luck.'

CHAPTER 35

The next day, after many enquiries had been made to various international departments regarding the possible trade in drugs between Turkey and Cyprus, it had been revealed that there was a considerable and very lucrative trade between the two countries; much as between other countries, as the drugs trade was so far wide-spread.

The other possibility which was becoming quite clear was that there was a large movement of migrants from countries such as Syria, Afghanistan, Iran and Iraq through Turkey and, usually by sea crossing to Greece and then Italy, who made their way over enormous distances to their goal of France and then hopefully to England. Here they were convinced that their chances of work and a new life would lie. The large numbers of economic migrants who were not EU citizens and therefore could not enter the UK under the normal regulations, together with refugees who were mostly fleeing from a seriously war-torn and completely damaged region, were desperate to find a new home. Some would stay in Germany, who had an "open door" policy to migrants and refugees, and some would seek to stay in Italy or France, but this was not an easy option. So many would try to reach the shores of the UK where they thought their destiny lay, but there were so many obstacles and for so many, the only way was to try to enter the UK without the authorities knowing. They had escaped their countries with money but no possessions, and all they could do, would be to fall prey to the "people traffickers" who would take them across waters which separated their countries from their vision of safety and security. They would pay huge amounts of money for doing so, taken by the completely unscrupulous traffickers, in heavily overcrowded and unsafe boats. Too many times these boats would either sink or be so overloaded as to capsize and dump them in the sea to drown. It had become a humanitarian disaster of enormous proportions. They had nothing except their desire to find a new a better life, but had virtually everything stripped from them, including their dignity along with their passports and identity. The result of this was that they arrived, if they were lucky enough to have survived the incredible journeys and hardships along the way, with no means of legal entry into a new country. This is why there was such a frenzied and determined move to gain access to the UK via either the Channel Tunnel or by stowing away on a truck bringing goods across the channel on the ferries. Once there, they were convinced that there was a way to gain a better life.

This is why, perhaps, that "Predator" was about to cross, once again, to the French coast, to collect a number of migrants who had paid far over the normal excessive amount to an "agent." They would be either skilled professionals or qualified people who had the misfortune to come from a country where their passports were not recognised by the UK, in this case, northern Turkey. Having made their way to a pre-arranged part of the coast in France, there to be collected and taken to the UK on a safe and fast passage. They would be in a boat which would not sink and be guaranteed a way to be taken to the UK coast where they could "disappear." There would be transport arranged to take them to a large city whereby they could be "integrated" into the area where there would also be a good number of similar cultures and help from their own people, to "meld" into the population.

This "network" had been set up and was working well. It was kept to a small number of migrants who had paid a very high price and were of a good education and therefore stood a good chance of integration with little problem, except that of identity. Even this was taken care of, which is why their "fare" was so high. It was lucrative in that the authorities were not looking for this problem in the area in which "Predator" was working and all its movements were, on the surface, legitimate.

The money gained from this trade was enhanced by the further shipment of drugs. It was during one of these voyages that drugs became a real problem and a vicious fight ensued which resulted in a death. A body was "dumped" at Goathorn after being badly beaten and cut during the fight. The boat had to be cleaned quickly and the body disposed of. It was thought that the best way was to do this in a "known" place and perhaps obviously not the place a body would have been expected to be.

So it was that "Predator" had made her way once again across to France, to a small and pre-arranged collection point at "Le Pointe des Grouins" on the Cherbourg Peninsula where there was a sufficiently deep water access point. As there were no houses in the vicinity and with a small beach, it was ideally situated and secluded where the passengers could be embarked away from prying eyes. A small road gave access to this part of the tip of the Cherbourg Peninsula. How the passengers had made their way to this point, was part of the detailed planning which constituted the money-making organisation which was taking place and had been working surprisingly smoothly for a considerable time.

This boarding point had been chosen due to an almost direct line from there to Poole Harbour and probably the shortest distance from France to England at that part of the Southern coast apart from the Dover/Calais route.

CHAPTER 36

The placing of the tracking device was agreed at the top level with the Marina Master, David Cunningham. It was now about 10.15 pm and Tom had prepared the device, ready for attachment. He had asked the Technical Department who had supplied this unit, to put a special pad on the back of the unit, with a matching and locking pad which would adhere to the material of the hull.

After making a confirmation phone call to the Cunningham, Tom entered the now quiet reception area. He quietly waited and after a short while, Cunningham appeared at the top of the staircase leading to his office on the first floor. Tom held up his warrant card for Cunningham to inspect. 'Good evening officer,' he said, shaking hands with Tom. 'Is everything ready?'

'Yes, all set. I just need to get to the boat without being seen.'

'The CCTV cameras are on, but no data is being stored. This way, I can keep an eye on you. In fact, I have some "walkie-talkie" radios which I thought might be useful. If I spot someone who might see you on the pontoon, I can give you warning and you can keep out of sight until it's clear again.' He handed Tom one of the radios.

'That's a great idea Mr Cunningham, thanks.'

'Here is a covert earpiece, so that there will be no sound to carry, especially as it is so quiet tonight.'

'That's good thinking.'

'Indeed, and if you'd like to wait here for a moment, I'll go to the office and the CCTV screens. Wait for me to call you.'

'Okay.' Tom clipped on his earpiece.

Cunningham went back up to the office and shortly, there was a radio call. "Tom - radio check."

Tom returned the check. "Receiving."

"Okay Tom, It's clear to go, the pontoon's empty at the moment."

"On my way."

Tom went through the exit to the pontoons and made his way out where "Predator" was currently moored. The night was partly cloudy and the moon was only in the first quarter, consequently it was quite dark. However, Tom had not realised that there was subtle lighting along the pontoons. This was probably to ensure that boat crews and owners to make their way along the pontoons with a degree of safety. However, it did make him quite visible, so he was very alert and kept checking around. He saw no-one but moved quite stealthily. He was nearly at the target boat, when there was a radio call in his earpiece. "Tom, take cover, there is a person on the parallel pontoon to you. He is walking slowly at about the same rate as you, but a little behind where you are. I don't think he's seen you. Just keep down and I'll keep you informed."

"Received - will do."

Ducking down behind the hull of a boat which was just high enough to hide him he looked across the other pontoon and saw the figure Cunningham had seen. He couldn't make out if the other figure was actually going to a boat, although he could see by the movement that it was a male. "Why would he be following me?" he thought, "no-one knows that I'm here and what I'm doing, do they?" so he dismissed the thought. He radioed to Cunningham, "Can you see what that man is doing?"

The answer came back, "I think he is just going to his own boat. Hold on – he's stopped and he's getting on board a craft. Yes, he's bending down and doing something. He's out of sight. I think you can carry on."

Tom stood up and carried on to the end of the pontoon, to the moored boat. He could make out the name "Predator" on the stern. "This is the one," he said quietly to himself. Moving to the stern of the boat, he climbed over the substantial guard rail and dropped onto the deck. He moved right to the back of the section of open decking. Here was the locker he had spotted on a previous visit. It had a recessed brass ring-pull, but no lock. Opening this quietly, he felt inside. There were a few items such as small buoys, some unidentified things. Tom had no interest in knowing their use but he found what he really wanted - space. He felt upward to the top of the locker area. This was actually under the moulded seating at the stern of the boat. Feeling around he found a recess which suited his purposes. Taking the tracker from his pocket, he carefully removed the backing paper covering the adhesive on the self-locking pads which the technical unit had added to the pads. These pads were the same material used to fit most of the interior panelling in modern aircraft. Using this material meant that the tracker could be removed when necessary, but had an incredibly strong bond when the two parts were pressed together. The adhesive on these pads was also of very high "industrial" quality and strength.

Reaching up under the moulding, he pushed the unit as hard as he could to attach the tracker to the fibreglass material. The strength of the locking pads would hold the tracker in place regardless of all the relentless pounding a long sea voyage at high speed would give it. Alex had spoken to the Technical Unit head Peter Tomlinson, about the positioning of the unit and the likelihood of it being dislodged. He had been given an assurance that it would be no problem, especially as the stern of a boat would probably receive the least amount of excessive movement.

"Job done," he said to himself. "Let's get out of here." Standing up, he took a look around, and finding the area clear, he vaulted over the guard rail and began to walk smartly down the pontoon, back to the main building.

Cunningham's voice in his earpiece then said, "The figure on the other pontoon has returned and out of my view, otherwise no-one around. Have you finished?"

Tom keyed his radio transmit button. "Affirmative; on my way back."

"Okay, I'll re-activate the CCTV data collection computer in a couple of minutes, once you're back."

Walking back down the long pontoon, he kept checking around him. Seeing no-one, he was nearly at the main door, when he heard a slight noise behind him. Turning round, he just had time to see a male figure, large and well-built, jump at him. He was later to say that all he saw was a man, dressed all in black, with dark curly hair and a black beard. When the man jumped at Tom, he was knocked over and fell to the ground. Without a sound, his assailant smashed Tom in the face and punched him repeatedly on the body. He was dealing heavy blows to the torso and kidneys, as well as to the head. He had some sort of "cosh" which he used to beat Tom around the chest, breaking some ribs. The pain was incredible and Tom was losing consciousness as he heard a door open, and Cunningham shouting, "Hey, what are you doing?"

This was of course, a useless question, as the man leaped up from Tom and ran around the side of the building. He was very fast and as he seemed much younger than Cunningham, who had opened the door. It has to be said that he was not slightly built. The dark figure made his getaway and soon disappeared in the darkness of the side of the building.

Tom was lying on the ground, groaning with pain. His ribs hurt like hell and his face felt like it was like a piece of raw meat.

'Are you alright?'

Through the pain, what Tom actually thought was; "What a fucking stupid thing to ask, of course I'm not alright."

'NO, I'm in bloody agony, I think I've been hit by a lorry or something. Who the hell was that?'

Tom managed to sit up with help from Cunningham, who said, 'I didn't see him, he must have been waiting just out of camera view. I was coming to make sure you got back so I could lock the doors, when I saw him jump on you.'

Reaching for his Police Radio, Tom pressed the emergency button and the call was instantly answered; "Control."

'DC Peterson. I've been attacked. Intruder at Cobbs Quay Marina. Tall man - six foot plus - dark or black curly hair - black beard. Dressed all in black - Last seen running towards Blandford Road.'

"Received, DC Peterson. Are you hurt?"

'Affirmative; I have facial bruising, possibly cuts, can't see, some blood and maybe broken ribs, don't know.'

"Ambulance on the way DC Peterson. ETA ten minutes. Mobiles alerted."

'Roger that Control, thanks. Standing by.'

Tom was now sitting against the building wall, feeling the excruciating pain in his chest as he wiped some blood from his face, with his sleeve. Cunningham had run into the main area and returned with some paper towel to clean up and stop the bleeding from the cuts and abrasions to his head.

'It's a bloody good job you came out when you did or the bastard might have done a lot worse, thanks.'

'I'm only sorry I didn't see him sooner, or maybe he wouldn't have attacked you at all.'

'Maybe; but what I want to know is who the hell is he and why did he attack me? No-one knew what I was doing or why I was here. Or did anyone else know of tonight's mission?'

'I told no-one, not even the person who checks the CCTV data. I simply turned off the computer and turned it back on again when you said you were nearly back. As I said before, it's highly unlikely that the short time gap in the recording would be noticed as they don't sit and look at hours of nothing happening. They simply quickly scan things unless there is a very good reason to check closely, but no-one knew about your mission.'

'Well someone seemed to bloody know, or why would they jump me if I was just someone coming back from a boat I'd moored?'

'I'm sorry, I have no idea; I wish I could help.'

An unmarked police car pulled up, closely followed by an ambulance. A uniformed officer approached Tom at about the same time as two paramedics came trotting over to Tom, who was sitting propped against the wall of the marina building.

'Hi Tom,' it was one of the local Poole lads who Tom knew reasonably well. 'Seems like someone didn't like you too much old son.'

'You could say that, but who the hell it was, I've no bloody idea.'

'I'll take some notes after these two have had a look at you, okay?'

'Yeah, I'm not going to run away.'

The paramedics led Tom carefully over to the ambulance and checked him over. They cleaned the cuts on his face and when they opened his shirt, the livid bruises were more than obvious. Carefully feeling his ribs, they confirmed that at least two, maybe three were possibly fractured. 'We should take you to Poole General for check-up; you may have concussion or a fracture to your face, but we can't tell here.'

'Okay, but I'll have to file a report first, all right?'

'Yeah, sure. We'll wait here; you won't be long will you?'

'No, not much to tell but I have to do it, procedure and all that.'

His police friend came over. 'Okay Tom, do you want to give me a report or do you want to do it back at your station?'

'I'd better give you the short version. Just call it a mugging for now, because this is part of a larger investigation we're working on, and I'd better keep it simple, if that's okay with you John.'

'Sure mate, you must be hurting. I saw the bruising and stuff. You're going to be sore in the morning.'

'Do me a favour John, will you?'

'Sure Tom, what's that?'

'I had a date tonight and now it's not going to happen, so can you just nip into the Red Lion and see if there's a very tasty looking blonde girl, sitting by herself and tell her that Tom can't make it. I don't want to ruin a good relationship that's only really just started.'

'That's tough shit Tom. You'll be telling me that you've got a date with the gorgeous Genny Dobbs next.'

That caused Tom to stiffen up which brought a sudden wave of pain and he looked up at John with a look of disbelief. 'How the hell do you know that?'

'You must have hit lucky mate, there's a queue a mile long for Genny.'

Tom was having a rush of mixed feelings and after a pause, he said, 'no, don't worry, I'll give her a ring, I just hope she understands.'

'Don't worry, I can pop in tomorrow and confirm that you got cold feet.'

'You bastard.'

'Only kidding mate. Don't worry, just get yourself strapped up and give me a call in a day or so, to let me know how you are.'

'Will do, thanks John.'

John went back to his car and drove off, while Tom made a call on his mobile to Genny.

The call was answered after a couple of rings. 'Hello.'

'Hi Genny with a "G," it's Tom.'

'Hi Detective Tom; I'm here waiting for you.' This was said in a low, husky voice.

That didn't help his pain one little bit. 'Genny, I'm sorry; I'm not going to make it tonight. I know it's late and you're there, but something's happened and I can't get to you.'

'Why Tom, what's happened?'

I've been attacked and I have to go to hospital for a check-up.'

'Oh my God!' she said. Who attacked you, did you see him; do you know him?'

'No, just jumped on me, I didn't see it coming.'

'Are you hurt, I mean what did he do, he didn't stab you or anything?'

'No, but I think I've got some broken ribs. Look, they're taking me to Poole General, so I'll give you a ring tomorrow if that's all right?'

'Yes, of course, is there anything I can do, it must be painful?'

'It is, but nothing you can do that wouldn't make it hurt more, but thanks for asking Gen.'

'Okay then, don't worry about tonight. I'll speak to you tomorrow.'

'Yeah, 'night Gen.'

'Goodnight, take care.'

He was thinking; "I was taking bloody care but some bastard knew." There was something nagging him but he didn't know what it was. Maybe it's just the pain making me woozy, he thought, and dismissed it.

'Come on mate, let's get you to the hospital, we can't wait here all night while you have a love chat.'

Tom was taken to A & E at Poole Hospital, where he was checked over and pronounced fit to go. The doctor told him that there was nothing really to be done for broken ribs, except rest and be careful. He prescribed painkillers and told him to take it easy. Tom phoned a local taxi company to get him back to the Marina and his car. This will go on expenses that's for sure, he thought.

The drive back home was extremely painful.

CHAPTER 37

Tom had a painful night, even after taking a few Tramadol tablets to make things more comfortable. He was going over the events of the previous evening and preparing to make his report to Alex when he got to work.

Driving to the station, taking things very carefully he arrived just after nine in the morning. He went along the corridor and made his way directly to the coffee machine, where he pressed the appropriate buttons for a large Cappuccino. Leaning carefully against the worktop while he waited for the mechanics to whirr into action, he caught sight of Anna walking past.

'Glad you could grace us with your presence then Tom.' Anna walked in and pressed the buttons for a coffee also, without looking at him.

'No hint of sarcasm then DS Jenkins?'

'No Tom, you're late. How did last night go? As she looked up, she saw the cuts and bruises on Tom's face then. 'Oh my God! What happened to your face?

'That's why I'm late – I placed the tracker, but after I got back to the yard, I was attacked.'

'Hell! - Sorry Tom. I didn't know. What happened?'

'After placing the tracker, I was almost back to...' - Anna interrupted him. 'Come on, Tom, Alex's office now, I'll bring your coffee.'

They both went to Alex's office, Tom walking in obvious pain. Knocking on the door, a voice shouted, 'YES?'

They both went in and Anna motioned Tom to sit down and said to Alex, 'Tom was attacked last night.'

Tom sat down very carefully.

'What!?' Alex looked up from his paperwork and saw Tom's face.

'Jesus Christ Tom, tell us what happened. Are you hurt? I mean, I can see your face but there are other things?'

'Yes, guv, I'd fitted the tracker all right and I was almost back at the marina building and a big bloke jumped on my back. We went down and he punched me several times on the face and head and then he must have had some sort of cosh, because he broke three of my ribs.'

'Oh bloody hell, Tom. This shouldn't have happened. You were supposed to be there incognito, right?'

'Yes guv, that's what I thought. Only Cunningham, the marina master was there and he'd disabled the CCTV date record as promised. He'd given me a radio so that we could communicate while I was on the pontoon. He called me up to say that there was a man on a parallel pontoon to me, but he seemed to be no problem. Then he said that the bloke had apparently gone back to the marina building while I was placing the tracker, so I went back when I'd finished but saw no-one. It wasn't until I got back to the main door, that he came out of nowhere.'

And did Cunningham see him?'

'No guv, he said that this bloke must have been close to the wall so that the cameras wouldn't see him while he waited for me. He'd put the CCTV data back on but it probably won't show anything.'

'Did you see him; I mean can you give a description?'

'No guv, like I said, he jumped me from behind. All I can say is that I only got a very quick look. I phoned it in to the local plod control and they sent out a mobile, but let's face it, by the time they got their arses into gear, chummy would have been long gone.'

'Unfortunately, I think you're right lad. What description do you have?'

'As I said, only a very quick look and it was dark but tall, well built, black curly hair, black beard, dressed in black.'

'Hang on Tom. Black hair - beard. Who does that remind you of, Anna?'

'Of course! Martin Goodyear. He has a dark beard and black curly hair.'

'Right, got it in one.'

'Is there anything else you can tell us Tom?'

'There is something; I'm not sure if it is important, and I was thinking about this last night. Something happened later on. See, I was going on a date, so I phoned her to say I couldn't make it. When I said I'd been attacked, the first thing she said was, "did you see him; do you know him?" I mean, how did she know it was a "him?" or was it just supposition?'

'And you hadn't said anything before she said that?' asked Anna.

'Nope, nothing.'

'I'd say that was very questionable Tom, I think you're right to be suspicious. Who was this girl, someone you've been seeing before?'

'Yes guv. I have to tell you, she is my "contact" at the marina. She's the receptionist.'

'Okay, understood Tom. How many times have you seen her?'

'I've had about three dates with her up to now, but she's seemed more than helpful. I really don't want to think that she's involved. It'd make me look a complete prat.'

'No Tom, don't think like that. Plenty of people have been used in a similar way. They get your confidence, and then they stab you in the back. I think we have to delve into this young woman's background, don't you?'

'I think I'll have to go with you on that one guv. Oh, there was one other thing, I was speaking with a mate from Poole station and when I told him I had a date with a blonde girl, he asked me if it was Genny Dobbs, from the Marina. When I said yes, he said that there was a queue for her apparently. Now I wonder just who she knows and who else she goes out with.'

Anna spoke, 'Doesn't that suggest that she knows Goodyear and has passed on information?'

'Absolutely. Okay, give me her details and we can get Poole CID to do a check on her, is that all right with you Tom?'

He gave Alex her contact details and then asked, 'Will they be discreet or will they let her know that we're checking her?'

'I'll make sure they keep you out of it. I just want a background check to see who she knows and who she might have spoken to. I take it she knew about your intended mission last night?'

'No way guv; I just told her that I was on a job and I'd see her later on, you know about 10.30. I was to meet her in the Red Lion on Blandford Road.'

Anna said, 'It does seem very strange that the person you describe as your assailant, bears a strong resemblance to Martin Goodyear, and it was his boat you were placing the tracker on. It would look as though he knew and was waiting for you, doesn't it?'

'Yes sarge, it seems likely, but I wish it didn't, because it looks as though Genny may have told him.'

'Okay Tom, let's get some details and take it from there. In the meantime, you get yourself home. You shouldn't have come in, but you've done a good job and I'm sorry about the consequences.'

'Thanks guv, but before I go, can we check the tracker to see if it works. I'd hate to think I've wasted my time and got busted ribs for my trouble.'

'Yes, of course – Alice, could you fire up the software for the tracker please?'

Alice had come in half-way through the conversation with Tom and she was looking very sympathetically at him. 'Of course, it won't take a minute. I'm so sorry that you've been hurt Tom, I hope you get some rest and get better soon.'

'Thanks Alice, I know the ribs are going to hurt for some time, but there's not much that can be done except wait and take painkillers.'

Alice went over to her desk and opened the program which took the tracker details. They walked slowly with Tom, over to her desk.

'Here it is guv,' she said, pointing to the screen which was showing a map. The exact location of the tracker was clearly placing it in Cobbs Quay Marina, at the end of pontoon no.4.

'Okay, we know where it is now, but how do we know when it moves, Alice, can it tell us that?'

'I think so guv, the software seems to have all these things covered, but I've set an alarm to tell us when it moves, so if we're not here or the office is not manned, we'll know that it's on the way somewhere.'

'Will this be recorded if no-one is here?'

'Yes, I've set auto-record on this program.'

'Great, all we need now is to see that it's on the way over to France and we can get things moving to intercept it when it returns. Then we'll see what's going on, with any luck.'

'I can have the GPS location linked to my Smart Phone, if that's any help and I can record the movements.'

'Brilliant, that means we'll know in good time. Thanks Alice, good stuff. Right, now Tom, get yourself home and leave us to get on with this while you do some healing. Keep in touch, okay?'

'Will do guv thanks; see you all later.'

Tom got up slowly and obviously painfully from the chair and was about to go to his car when Alex said, hang on Tom, I'll get one of the traffic cars to give you a lift, driving must be bloody painful.'

'It is guv, thanks.'

'Right, take a couple of days and we'll get you picked up. Your car should be safe here,' he said looking at Anna with a grin.

'I'll see to that,' she said, thinking, that was a nice gesture.

CHAPTER 38

Anna had called the SOCO team of Roger Peterson, Rachel Myers and Ron Jackson and arranged for them to take a look at the "lock-up" inside the main building at the end of the Goathorn Peninsula, owned by the oil company, Perenco.

'Roger, this office or whatever you call it is inside the main shed and has no windows and only one large door. We need to know what is inside this room. We know it is used by a Martin Goodyear although that is his English name. He is Turkish, but that's of no matter. We are told that he keeps fishing gear there, but we suspect that he doesn't go fishing but far more sinister activities. Can you take a good look round and see if there is anything incriminating or whatever in there?'

'Do you have keys for it Anna, although we don't actually need them but they would be handy?'

'No, but I am in the process of obtaining authorisation for a search warrant. Do you need that, actually?'

'Actually, yes, sorry. If we go barging in without permission, we could leave ourselves wide open for litigation, as I'm sure you realise.'

'Of course, sorry Roger. I'll get the okay from our people first and give you a ring. It shouldn't take long, but perhaps you could arrange transport or whatever you have to do, to save time?'

'Will do; just give me a bell when you have it.'

'Okay, 'bye Roger.'

Alex had called his superintendent, Alison Beavers, to get clearance for the SOCO team to have access to the interior locked room used by Martin Goodyear.

'Why do you need to look in there Alex, what do you think might be incriminating in that store?'

'At the moment, we have no idea, but there might be some DNA or something that gives us a link to the body which would then give us a real tie-up with Goodyear. They might find something else, but nothing will be removed unless it is completely obviously linking things up.'

'Okay, it sounds reasonable, but don't forget that if nothing is found and it is discovered that they've been in there without good reason, we could be sued or whatever. I guess that someone with the money that this guy has, he would have a very competent and expensive lawyer on hand.'

'I agree ma'am, but I really would like to know what's in there.'

'Very well, I will sign a temporary warrant, which can be revoked should there be nothing found. If anything should turn up, it can be confirmed.'

'Thanks ma'am. I'll get things moving.' He picked up a phone and called the SOCO office.

'Hello, SOCO,' was the curt answer.

'Hi, this is DCI Vail, is Roger there?'

'Yes.'

'Can I speak to him?'

'I expect so.'

'Is he busy?'

'I expect so.'

Alex was becoming a little riled. 'Am I talking to Ron Jackson?'

'Yes.'

'I thought so. Do you think you could put Roger on please?

'I expect so.' There was a pause for quite a few seconds and then there was a clatter as the phone was dropped on to a table or something. Then, 'Hello, Peterson here, is that Alex?'

At last, thought Alex. 'Yes, I guessed that was Ron, the man of short sentences; I ought to give him one,'

'That brought a slight chuckle from Peterson. 'What can we do for you Alex, oh and by the way, congratulations on your promotion; I've not spoken to you for a while?'

'Thanks Roger. As you know, we have that body found over at Goathorn. There is a large shed there and inside this there is a sealed room which we need to have searched for any clues which might bring a number of lines of our enquiry together.'

'Do you have keys for this room Alex as I guess it's locked?'

'No, and yes.'

'Sorry?'

'I mean no, we don't have keys and yes, it's locked. We think it better not to tell Perenco that we are going there, just in case it's leaked and someone says something.'

'So you want us to do a 'ghost' entry then, you know pass through the doors so that no-one knows we've been there?'

'That's about it, yes.'

'Okay, I think we could manage that. When would you like this done?'

'As soon as you can please, but I warn you, the stink inside the shed is bloody awful. Christ knows what this bloke stores in there, it's supposed to be fishing gear, but I've a suspicion that it's more than that. We've a temporary search warrant until we find something, or not, as the case may be.'

'Okay, we'll go over this afternoon, will that be good for you, I mean will you be there?'

'I think we should, so shall we say about 2pm and we'll meet you there?'

'Right'o, see you there then, I'll bring the team.'

Alex called Anna and asked her to arrange for Jack to take them over to Goathorn. After making the call, she went back to Alex and said that it would be impossible as Jack was on another assignment and he would be tied up all the afternoon.

'Damn. Isn't there anyone else who could give us a lift?'

'Apparently not.'

'That's a bloody nuisance, but we'll just have to go by road again, so can you arrange the Defender again?'

'No problem guv.' She went down to the motor pool to arrange this. It was now about 10.30 so she thought to get some sandwiches and a flask made up in the canteen as the trip to Goathorn could take quite a while if the traffic was quite heavy and the ferry was busy and this time they would probably not use the blues and two's as it was not officially urgent. She also checked with SOCO that they were ready to go. Returning to Alex, she told him that she'd arranged a packed lunch and drinks for their trip in case they were held up for a while.

'That's good thinking Anna, thanks. I remember last time we were there, we were famished and if it weren't for Rachel on the SOCO team; we could have died of thirst. We'd better get off pretty soon.'

'Okay, I'm ready when you are guv, so are SOCO.

Collecting the Land Rover Defender, they set off in convoy with the SOCO van.

The trip over the ferry at Sandbanks was uneventful though the sight of two Police vehicles crossing to Studland was creating not a little speculation with the holidaymakers.

Pretty soon, the two vehicles were approaching the Goathorn Peninsula and then on to the end of the spur where the building in question was situated.

They pulled up close to the large wooden shed. Alex got out and walked over to Roger. 'Do you think it might be a good idea if we parked somewhere out of sight, just in case we are seen; I mean, we are quite obvious and if we're seen, we could be reported and that would raise some awkward questions.'

'Yep, I think you're right Alex. This is supposed to be quite "covert" isn't it, so yes; maybe we should park both vehicles just over there in that parking area behind those trees. If we can do this without being interrupted, the better it will be.'

With that, Anna and Ron Jackson drove the vehicles to park out of sight.

They all gathered at the entrance doors to the shed and Ron said, 'Maybe you guys shouldn't watch me do this or I could be nicked.'

'Bloody hell, Ron, that's the longest sentence you've come out with for a while,' said Rachel.

'Cheeky wench,' he said.

They stood back while he rather expertly opened the main doors, and they all walked inside. The smaller sealed room was on the left hand side of the large space and the double doors were sealed with two very substantial padlocks.

Once again, Ron took his tools to the locks and after a few minutes of fiddling, the details of which they couldn't see, the padlocks were opened.

One door opened and they all collectively took a step back, covering their faces with their hands.

'Christ all bloody mighty!' said Roger. Rachel looked stunned. Anna had taken an inadvertent intake of breath and immediately wished she hadn't. The stench that emanated from the room was incredibly powerful.

Roger said immediately – 'Dead body.'

'What!?' said Alex.

'No question, can't mistake that smell. Not fresh either.'

'Oh Christ, this we don't need,' groaned Alex.

'We'd better take a closer look, but I suggest you guys keep back for a while; it's not going to be pretty.' He was looking at Alex and Anna as he said this. Turning to Rachel and Ron, he said 'Okay, team, let's get suited and booted to take a good look.'

Anna and Alex were more than happy to step back outside the shed and into the fresh air.

'What the hell is going on guv?' was Anna's first comment.

'It looks like there's been some real trouble here and if the first body was the result of a fight, then perhaps someone else was involved and they're here.'

'But why here and not dumped somewhere else?'

'Who knows Anna? Let's just see what they find in there, but I have to say that I'm not looking forward to whatever they do find, it's not going to be pleasant with that smell.'

CHAPTER 39

The SOCO team quickly found the source of the smell. There were two bodies wrapped separately in polythene sheets and loosely tied up. They were not hidden, but simply put in a corner of the internal shed, close together. Ron asked, 'Should we take a look inside guv?'

'I think we should, if only to know the sex and condition. We're supposed to do this so that whoever owns this room doesn't suspect that we've been here.'

They were all wearing masks in an effort to block the smell, but they were not very effective.

Ron said, 'Better masks guv?'

'Good idea mate. This is some of the worst and I don't want to throw up just yet. Can you get those 3M 6000 series masks; you know the ones with the activated charcoal filters. They'll be more comfortable. Just make sure that the filters are new.'

'Will do.' He went back to their van and returned with three masks which they were glad to change over.

'Rachel, can you take some photos so that we can tie them back in the same way?'

'Okay guv, I've got the camera in my bag, I'll just nip out and get it.'

'Good, Ron and I will wait until you've taken the shots before we untie the ropes.'

Roger took a look around at the heaps of what appeared to be fishing gear, rods, nets and other items. They were not stored in any sort of order, just haphazardly around the perimeter. There was also a quad bike in one corner. Roger took a closer look at the tyres and said, 'I reckon this has to be the one which left tyre tracks near the first body. There's sand in the tyre treads.'

'Agree with that,' said Ron.

Rachel returned with her camera and began taking close-up shots of the wrapped bodies and the knots used.

They all turned their attention to the two loosely wrapped bodies and carefully untied the knots.

Roger gently pulled aside the polythene sheet on the first body, turning his head away as the sheet revealed the putrefying corpse. The corpse was male and the skin, although waxy had a darker colouring. 'I reckon this man was from a similar place as the first victim. Look at his face colour.'

They looked and nodded their agreement. He was dressed in a checked shirt which had obvious tears or cuts and was heavily bloodstained. 'I reckon there are stab or cut marks under there. We can't take off the shirt for obvious reasons, but it looks like it.'

'I don't think we can do more than take a cursory look guv, do you? I mean, I can see there are cuts and contusions to his face which could indicate a fight, but if we move too much, it might be discovered that someone has taken a look and I gather that the investigation needs to keep that to very quiet at this stage.'

'Quite right Rachel; let's just take a look at number two shall we?'

They moved to the second body and removed the knotted rope in the same careful way. There was another male corpse with similar skin colour, or perhaps lack of it. He had black curly hair and similar facial evidence of bruising and cuts. He was wearing what looked like a fleece sweatshirt which was also heavily bloodstained and had many slash marks.

'We'd better get Starsky and Hutch to take a look then,' said Roger, with an unseen grin. Give them a shout please Rachel, and for Christ's sake give them masks or they'll be chucking up all over the place.'

Smiling to herself, she went out and motioned to Anna and Alex to come in. 'You'd better put these on,' she said handing them two of the special charcoal filtered masks, 'or you wouldn't last more than a couple of breaths.'

'Thanks, I know we've smelt death before, but that smell was beyond the pale,' said Anna.

'It's pretty bad, that's for sure.'

When their masks were in place, they went with Rachel back into the room and looked at the bodies.

'Oh fuck,' exclaimed Alex, 'there are two of them. This is a nightmare.'

'Pretty bad aren't they?' said Roger looking from one to the other. 'They both seem to be of a similar extraction to the other one and they've been beaten and slashed in the same way it would appear, although we can't take anything off them.'

'No, that would make it obvious to anyone who would move them, if they wanted to move them that is.'

'How long do you think they've been dead Roger?' asked Anna.

'Hard to tell without taking a good look, but from the smell, I'd guess about three days. Putrefaction has started as they've begun to swell; you can see from their stomach size and the power of the smell means that the bacteria in the gut have been working hard at decomposition. The two main chemicals at work are Pentmethylenediamine and Butandimine, and that's what produces all the odours.'

'Easy for you to say Roger,' said Alex.

'The gruesome facts are that the intestines are packed with millions of micro-organisms that don't die with the person. Therefore these organisms start the job of decomposition immediately by breaking down the dead cells of the intestines. As the bacteria starts to eat through the gut the first sign is usually a greenish patch on the lower right belly which also blisters. Then special bacteria called clostridia and coliforms start to invade other parts of the body and putrefaction spreads across the stomach before travelling down the thighs and across the chest. This rotting produces foul-smelling matter which includes the gases hydrogen sulphide. This is what you smell, like rotting eggs, as well as methane. These internal gases push the intestines out through the rectum, the tongue may protrude and fluid from the lungs oozes out of the mouth and nostrils.'

'STOP Roger please,' yelled Anna, 'You're enjoying this aren't you?'

'It's a good job that they aren't a couple of days older or "Black Putrefaction" will be taking place,' added Roger ,'when the tissues collapses and all the gases escape, and everything else with it.'

'Oh God,' exclaimed Anna, 'You are evil; I don't even want to think about that, it's utterly disgusting.'

'Facts of life, and death,' he offered.

'So what do you reckon then Roger, cause of death as far as you can tell?' asked Alex.

'Only a wild guess, but from the look of the slash and cut marks on the shirts, they could have been stabbed to death but the marks and contusions to the faces and heads, could point to a bad fight or something like that.'

Alex looked over to Anna and said, the fight angle would fit in with the first victim, wouldn't it?'

'Yes, I think that's a strong possibility, but until George has had a look at these two over at Pathology, we won't know for certain, will we?'

'Okay, let's get these two wrapped up again and can you have a good look round just to see if there's anything like a weapon or something which might give us some clues?'

'Will do Alex, but we'll have to be careful not to leave footprints or it'll be too obvious.'

'I see what you mean; the floor is quite dusty, so maybe for now, just a quick look around and some photos, what do you think?'

'I think that's probably the best way. We'll do that and make a careful retreat; we'll make sure that the padlocks are in the right place too.'

Roger then made sure that the ropes and knots were replaced exactly as shown in the photographs.

'I think it's all back as it was. We matched the placing of the ropes and knots very carefully, so I don't think anyone will be suspicious.'

'Great stuff; thanks Roger, and looking towards Rachel and Ron, 'and you guys.'

The SOCO team retreated after re-tying the polythene wrapping very and after closing the doors, the padlocks were re-locked carefully and they went back to their van, loading all their equipment.

Alex and Anna also returned to the Discovery. 'I'm thinking that there could be a strong possibility that all three murders could be either linked or happened at the same time. One was buried, or at least they were tried to be buried and these are the other two.'

'That would fit in but we'll have to see what the forensics have to tell us Alex. They'll be able to tell us if all three were killed at the same time – hopefully.'

She then changed tack saying, 'Do you know what Alex, I'm bloody glad we had those sandwiches and coffee before we got here, or I don't think I could face anything now.'

'Absolutely, that had to be the most disgusting smell I've ever smelt. What concerns me now, however is, when were the bodies going to be dumped or disposed of and where?'

'Well, surely they couldn't be left there much longer could they?'

'Not without turning to liquid I should think; in fact I wondered why they hadn't been dumped before this.'
 'Oh, that's more information than I need thank you.'
'Sorry; we'd better get back and write this up, and get hold of Goodyear pretty damned quickly. He's got some explaining to do I'd say.'
'I'd suggest that he would be trying to move the bodies very soon although why he hasn't yet is very worrying, isn't it?'
'Yes, you'd think that moving them was a first priority. There must be some other reason why they are still there.'

Driving back to their station, they were both understandably very quiet, having just been through that experience. On the way, Alex's phone warbled some strange ring-tone, which made Anna chuckle. 'What on earth is that?'
'Oh, I don't know, just one of those damned tones that seem to just embed themselves into the phone without any rhyme or reason. I'll have to change it, that's really dumb.'
'You may say that Alex, I couldn't possibly comment.'
'Okay, smarty-pants, I suppose you have something very clever and avant-garde?'
'Nope, just a telephone ringing; as this is just what it is. Shall I answer it, seeing as you're driving?'
'Good idea partner.' Anna liked that.
She took the call. 'DCI Vail's phone.'
'Sarge, this is Alice. He's on the move!'
'Do you mean Goodyear?'
'Yes, we had the computer setup to give an alarm whenever the boat was moved and it gave an indication about 5 minutes ago.'
 'Guv, Alice says the boat has moved, about 5 minutes ago.'
'Right, try to find out where it's headed and we'll have to get it followed, if possible. I don't quite know how we'll do it yet, but we must keep tabs on him, at all costs.'
'Alice, do you have any indication as to where he might be going?'
'Not at the moment sarge, he's only going towards the harbour, just about the "Twin Sails Bridge," so Tom says.'
'Hang on Alice, I'll just pass this on to – um, the guv,' I'll have to be more careful, she thought, that's the second time.
'If this is Goodyear, he's just about at the bridge at Hamworthy.'
'Okay, tell her to keep a log of where he goes and keep watching. We'll be back in about 45 minutes, tell her.'
This was passed to Alice and then Alex said, 'I wonder if this is Goodyear or maybe it's that other bloke, Dimitriou, or maybe both; we'll have to find out. Maybe we could have the boat stopped before it leaves the harbour?'
'Well, won't we be going over on the ferry Alex, perhaps we'll see him or them going through the Haven if we can't stop them? I don't know how quickly they'll get to the ferry crossing.'
'There's a good chance of that, as I don't think we can stop a boat unless we can get the marine section to scramble a boat in time. Get back to Tom and get him to call the Police Marine Section and see if there's a possibility?'
'If not, at least I have a pair of binoculars in my kit, so perhaps we could at least see who is driving the boat, even spot anyone else on board.'
'Good thinking Anna.'
They were about ten minutes from the chain ferry at Sandbanks, but had to wait for it to be at their side of the slipway. They had no way of knowing which side of the Haven it would be on, but with binoculars, they could possibly get a clear view of "Predator" passing.

'We know that Goodyear is heavily involved in something big and with three bodies now linked to him, he has to be our main suspect, doesn't he?'
'Yes, he'll have a devil of a job to explain not only the one body on Goathorn beach but two more in the shed; but what does make me wonder, is why did he or they, dump the body on the beach where it was bound to be found?'
Alex frowned; 'That's been puzzling me as well, but just maybe they were going to bury the first body deep enough not to have been found, it was only sand after all and it should have been easy to dig.'
'But was it though? When I spoke to Roger on the SOCO team, he did say to me that the sand was very "sticky" as it was probably a mixture of "Ferruginous" sand mixed with "Agglestone" sandstone and the dumped clay and slate

from Redhorn which is opposite the little beach where "Gary" was found face down. I asked him about digging a grave in that stuff and he said it would have probably been very hard going.'

'Agglestone, Ferruginous," it just looked like dirty old mud to me. I know "Agglestone Rock" over on Studland. Have you ever been there?'

'No, but I have heard of it, what's it like?'

'It's weird, just a bloody great lump of what looks like sandstone, perched on a small conical hill. It's about a mile from Studland village and it really looks as though it has no place there at all, as all around is nothing but scrub and sand. I was told once by an old local chap that the legend is that the devil threw the rock from the Needles on the Isle of Wight, with the intention of hitting either Corfe Castle or Salisbury Cathedral, but he was a lousy shot and it landed in the middle of the Studland peninsula. I don't know if it's true, though, but I do know that the word "Aggle" was taken into the old Dorset dialect to mean "to wobble," probably because it sits at a strange angle and looks like it's about to topple over.'

'It could be true, couldn't it Alex?' Anna asked with a sideways look and her head to one side.

'Taking the piss again, sergeant?' he said with a chuckle. 'If I weren't driving I'd give you a good slapping.'

'Promises,' she said.

They were driving along the Studland peninsula and were approaching the ferry landing as Anna ventured, 'Another bit of local knowledge for me; all very interesting, but for now I just hope we can either catch Goodyear or at least confirm his whereabouts.'

'Yes, and I'd like to think that he's the one who clobbered Tom and we can charge him with that as well.'

'I wonder how Tom is, you know, how his ribs are mending.'

'I'd think they're still bloody painful. I know that when I had a couple of broken ribs, it was all I could do to turn over in bed.'

To get a further insight into Alex's past, she asked how that had occurred.

'Have you got time for this, the ferry's here?'

'Yes, I'd really like to know about your bad times, so that you can appreciate our good times, anyway, it'll take about fifteen minutes to get across.'

'Now that's a different way of looking at things Anna, I like that.'

The ferry disgorged it's cargo of cars and tourists on foot and they were soon being directed towards the front of the ferry. When the vehicle was secured, they got out and went to the upper section and stood by the railing, looking at the very interesting view of that part of Poole Harbour entrance.

'So go on then, do tell, you have me intrigued by your eventful past. We can keep a lookout for Goodyear's boat from here, we have a good view.'

'Okay, well, it happened here in Poole, on the quayside actually. On a Tuesday evening, they used to have an impromptu motorcycle meeting and there could be literally hundreds of bikes all lined up along the quayside. It'd become quite a tourist attraction. I was into bikes in those days and this particular evening, it was around dusk I think, I was standing on a small roundabout which was just where the old Poole Pottery factory was situated. Around this roundabout there were, I suppose, about a hundred people watching two or three bikers showing off, doing "wheelies" down the quayside and finishing at this roundabout. Are you with me?'

'Yes, I'm intrigued.'

'One of the lads doing this began his run and built up speed and then "pulled a wheelie." As he was about halfway down his "run," a car pulled out from the ones parked along that part of the quayside. Well, this made him drop the wheelie to avoid the car. The problem was that he then tried to pull his bike up again, which he did, but too late, he realised that he was too close to the roundabout at the end of his run; he braked too hard and skidded. He dropped the bike on its side. The bike slid straight into the crowd standing around the roundabout - I was one of those people in the crowd.'

'Oh no, did he hit you? – well I suppose he did or you wouldn't be telling me this.'

'He certainly did, although I was actually standing behind a poor girl who was injured more than I was. The bike ran over her leg.'

'Oh God, that's awful.'

'I was directly behind a cast iron bollard, you know the ones which look like a cannon, and they're all down the quayside.'

'Yes, I've seen them, very chunky looking.'

'They may look chunky, but this bike actually smashed the one I was behind and the bike must have reared up as it hit me in the chest and shoulder.'

'Ouch!'

'And to make matters worse, as I was lying there, on my side, some bloody idiot next to me, chucked his cigarette end on the ground and tried to stamp it out.'

'Was that problem then?'

'Only if you understand that the bike's tank had punctured and there was petrol running down the gutter.'

'Oh shit!'

'Absolutely; but no fire thankfully, and then the rider who had slid off the bike, uninjured apparently, jumped up and ran across the road and straight into the nearest pub, the Lord Nelson, so I'm told. As we subsequently found out, he phoned a taxi to take him home. I understand that when he got there, he told his girlfriend what had happened, after phoning the police to say that his bike had been stolen that evening. While he was having a shower, his girlfriend, give her her due, as soon as she knew that he'd run away, phoned the police and blew the whistle on him.'

'Good girl - and did they get him?'

'They certainly did, and prosecuted him for dangerous driving and leaving the scene of an accident. He got four years for that, points and a fine.'

'Good, he deserved it. What happened to you though, you say you had broken ribs?'

'Yes and a suspected fractured collar bone, but like Tom, there isn't much you can do for those sorts of injuries except rest and wait.'

'Sounds very painful.'

'It was, and I still have a spot of back trouble from time to time. But while I was in the hospital being checked over, I saw the girl who had been hit and I found out that she had lost one foot.'

'Christ, that's terrible; the cowardly bastard should've got a longer sentence for that stupidity.'

'I agree. The funny thing is that a little later, I was back at the quayside and I saw the broken bollard laying in the council yard. I asked if I could have it, and I took it home as a reminder of how lucky I was not to have been more injured. I really think that thing saved me from a much worse injury.'

'Well, I'm very glad that you seem to be in one piece now, at least everything was working the other night, was it?' She was looking at him with a very satisfied look on her face.

Alex's phone, gave the strange ring again.

CHAPTER 40

This time Alex took the call. 'Hello?'

'Guv, it's Predator,' Alice sounded very excited. 'It's heading for Goathorn, at least we think so, it's a bit hard to tell but it looks that way rather than going out to sea. Tom tried to get the Marine Section to do a quick launch but they said it wasn't possible in the time and their boat is not a fast one.'

'Shit! I bet he's going to pick up the bodies.'

'Bodies, what bodies' guv?'

'We have two more in the lock-up on Goathorn Alice; we'll fill you in later, but we have to try to get back there pretty damn quick. Keep me informed on the boats' whereabouts.'

'Will do guv.' The call ended. Alex turned to Anna. 'You heard that?'

'Yes, can we make it back there in time?'

'Bollocks! We'll have to wait until we get offloaded and then turn round and belt back there. I wonder where SOCO have got to.'

'I think they'll be across and well on their way back to station Alex, they were a few minutes ahead of us and must have got the previous ferry.'

'Damn, damn, damn! We'll have to use the blues and two's and try to make it back there as quickly as we can. If he's going to pick up the bodies, we'll have no evidence and heaven knows where he'll take them.'

'At least we can track where he goes, can't we?'

'Yes; can you get on to Masterson and ask him if there's a way of stopping the craft? Meanwhile I'll get this truck turned round as quickly as I can, we have to get there to have any chance of an arrest.'

Anna called the Poole Harbourmasters office and asked to speak to him. 'Who is calling please?' asked the receptionist.

'DS Anna Jenkins from Bournemouth Police.'

'Very well, one moment please, I'll call him.'

There was a slight delay until the resonant voice of Fuller Masterson came on the line. 'This must be the delightful Anna, how are you?'

'Hello Mr Masterson, I'm fine thanks, but I have an urgent problem.'

'From that I gather that you have someone with you, your boss perhaps? How can I help?'

My boss DCI Vail and I are on the ferry at Sandbanks and we have just found out that the boat we have under surveillance is heading towards Goathorn which we have just left. We need to get there to somehow apprehend the boat crew but it seems impossible to get back there in time. Is there anything you could do to stop this boat, please?'

'One moment Anna, let me think about this for a few seconds. I don't know if there is anything I can do in such short a time.' The line went quiet as he thought through the possibilities. 'Anna, I am truly sorry, but there is nothing I can really do with this short notice. I don't think Jack would be much use as his boat, as you well know, is about as quick as a slow boat to China, and we have nothing which would get there in such a short time. More to the point, we would have no way of apprehending him, would we, even if we could get there?'

Anna was thinking, even if we do get there, this man has killed or been involved with the death of at least three people and who knows what he is capable of?

'That's okay Mr Masterson, I appreciate your honesty and I understand your reasoning. We are actually tracking this boat, so we know where he will be. Hopefully, we'll be able to do something if we miss him here. Thanks again.'

'Anytime, Anna, you are always welcome, you know that.'

'Yes, thanks; goodbye.'

By this time, they had disembarked the ferry and Alex put on the blue strobe light, while Anna held the traffic up to allow Alex to turn the vehicle round quickly and drive back on to the ferry. This was happening much to the interest and excitement of the tourists waiting to board the ferry. The intrigue was palpable and they were chattering and trying to guess what was happening.

'Look at all these grockles Anna, they don't have a clue as to what this is, but it won't stop their conjecture. I just hope there are no bloody journalists in one of these cars or they'll be tailing us back to the shed and we just don't have the bodies to keep them away right now.'

'And the body we do have isn't much help either, is it guv?'

'Now who's being ghoulish?'

'Sorry guv, black humour.'

Having finally boarded the ferry and made the return crossing, they were driving "hell for leather" back along the Studland road. "Predator" was crossing Poole Harbour at a speed which was somewhat faster than the regulations would allow, but Goodyear and "Freddie" Dimitriou who were both on board, were not concerned with that. All they wanted was to get to the shed at Goathorn as quickly as possible. When Goodyear had spotted Tom at the Marina and attacked him, he had realised that the police were looking for him, and suspected that Tom had done something to the boat, but didn't know what. He had intended taking Tom somewhere and make him give information as to what he'd been doing. This would have worked except that he wasn't aware that the marina master David Cunningham had been in the office watching the CCTV cameras. His arrival had thwarted Goodyear and put a stop to that plan.

He had known that Tom was a detective from his "friendship" with Genny Dobbs, who had told him that Tom was "doing something" that evening. This had led to Goodyear waiting to see what was going to happen. The next day, he'd been to the boat and searched everywhere, looking for anything suspicious, but found nothing, despite looking in every possible place. The one place he'd not looked was "up" as the tracking device was attached to the most inaccessible corner of the underside of a locker. Undetectable, as it actually had been.

As "Predator" approached the jetty at Goathorn, Goodyear said, 'just get the flat-bed truck that's inside the shed and put them on there. We'll bring them back here and take them out to sea to dump them.'

'We should've done that before, you know, why did we bring them back here to rot in that shed?' asked Dimitriou.

'How was I to know that there'd be another quick shipment to bring over, don't be such a prick.'

'Yeah, well, if we hadn't had those immigrants to bring back we could've sorted this out by now.'

'Do you think I don't realise that, you fuckwit. We have people over there and they have to pay us. The people we really don't want to get the wrong side of or our operation goes tits up are our agents. They get the punters who pay; to give you the money you need so badly for your stupid gambling habit, or would you rather give that up and get caught?'

'Yeah, all right, so we have two stinking bodies to get rid of. Where are you going to do that?'

'I don't know right now; I haven't thought it through. Knowing the police are looking at this boat means that they are on to something. We have to get away from here for now to give me time to think.'

'I'll bet that they got on to us because of that bloke we didn't bury. I told you we should have dumped him somewhere else.'

'Do you know what, if you say any more about that, I'm going to personally do to you what I did to him and I won't be trying to bury you afterwards?'

Dimitriou was becoming a little scared; he knew the temper possibilities of Goodyear and took his words seriously. Predator was close to the jetty and approaching quite quickly. Goodyear throttled back and then put the twin jet thrust in reverse and increased the engines. This had the effect of bringing the boat to a standstill very quickly right alongside the jetty. Dimitriou jumped over the side to take the mooring line, which he quickly tied to a bollard.

'Here, take the stern rope while I go and open the shed doors and get up there as quickly as you can. We have to get out of here bloody quickly.'

He threw the stern rope to Dimitriou, jumped over the rail and ran up the jetty to the shed which was about one hundred yards from the jetty. Out of breath from the hundred yard dash, he took the keys and unlocked the padlock, throwing the large door open and rushing inside. Again, he unlocked the heavy padlock to his small room within the large shed and as he opened the door to this, he was almost overcome by the appalling smell which hit him.

A few moments later, as he was about to enter the room, Dimitriou ran in behind him and stopped suddenly.

'Fucking hell! That's the worst thing I've ever smelt. We can't take them, they're just too bad, I'm not going in there and lifting them, they're rotting.'

'Yes you fucking are, you rat. Just shut up and get them both on that,' he said pointing to the flat-bed truck in the far corner of the shed. Fire up the quad bike and we can tow it quicker than we can pull it. DO IT!'

Freddie ran over to the truck and jumped on to the quad bike and turned the key. The starter motor growled and turned over quite sluggishly. 'Oh shit!'

'Try again, 'shouted Goodyear.

He tried once more and again the engine turned over slowly.

'That's all we fucking need,' said Goodyear and went over to the quad bike. 'Let me try.' He pushed Dimitriou aside and jumped on to the saddle turning the key once more. This time, the engine coughed once and then the engine started. 'Thank fuck for that,' he said and ran back to the bodies.

Dimitriou hitched the flat-bed to the quad bike and quickly turned it round and took it the short distance to the first body.

'Take his feet,' said Goodyear.

'I'm going to throw up in a minute,' said Dimitriou, looking very green, 'I just hope I don't pull his feet off.'

'Just breathe through your mouth; maybe the smell will stop you from saying anything.'

With great difficulty, due to the slippery nature of the contents of the polythene sheeting, they lifted the rotting corpse and almost threw it on to the flat-bed.

'Now for the other one.' Once again, they lifted the now very slimy body with its attendant intensely disgusting smell of death, dumping the slippery package on to the trailer.

'Right, take it outside and I'll lock up here.'

Dimitriou turned the quad bike and trailer, exiting the small room and out through the main doors, where he waited. 'Thank God for the fresh air,' he said, 'I can't wait to get rid of these two.'

He was joined by Goodyear who jumped on to the pillion seat. Freddie pulled away and began to gather speed. 'Keep it down you bleeding idiot!' yelled Goodyear.

'Yeah, okay,' replied Dimitriou, over his shoulder. They were about half way back to the boat, when he drove over a rather deep pothole. The resulting bounce of the trailer simply caused the body closest to the rear, to roll off onto the ground.

Neither of them saw this until Goodyear turned round to check. 'STOP! - you fucking idiot,' he shouted.

Freddie stamped on the brakes so hard that the inertia made the other body slide sideways on trailer. With no sides to stop it, the second body slid gently off, the ropes becoming loose and allowing the body to ooze partly out of the sheeting.

'I do not fucking believe this,' Goodyear groaned.

CHAPTER 41

On the way back to the building on the Jetty, Anna phoned the office again. 'Where are they Alice?'

'They appear to be at the jetty at Goathorn sarge.'

'Shit, we're on our way back there. I tried to get the Harbour office to help but they can't get anyone at such short notice.'

'I tried our Marine Section sarge, but they don't have a boat spare at the moment and the only one they had is a small inflatable dinghy and that's out on a job. In any case, and they said that wouldn't be any good at all.'

'Looks like we're on our own then. Just keep tabs on where they go if we don't get back there in time.'

'Will do sarge. We'll watch them all the way. Do you want me to alert the firearms section, especially as we suspect him of at least one murder?'

'I'd think that would be a good idea Alice, but I don't think he'll be there when we get back and anyway, by the time any Rapid Response Unit could get there it'll be far too late.'

'It's not going too well is it sarge?'

'Thanks for that Alice. Keep me posted.'

'Okay.' Anna cleared the call

'What did she say?' asked Alex.

'She said that they were at Goathorn jetty and she didn't think it was going too well.'

'She's bloody right about that.'

'Let's just hope that we get there in time to catch them.'

Alex was driving as fast as the road would allow. Thankfully the traffic was very light but he still had to be careful.

'Should we put the siren on guv?'

'No – if they hear that it'll just make them move a lot faster.'

'Yes, of course. Just be careful, we don't want to take out any tourists.'

Whilst they were leaving the ferry landing, Goodyear and Dimitriou had managed, with extreme difficulty, not to mention distaste, to lift both bodies back on to the flat-bed trailer and reached "Predator." They literally threw the two bodies onto the stern deck. Goodyear said, 'There's a gap in the trees about 30 yards back. Just dump the trailer and bike there, we don't have time to waste. We can come back and do that later.' Then Goodyear started the engines of "Predator" and Dimitriou loosened the mooring ropes, jumping over the stern rail just as the boat was pulling away, just about managing to landing in a sprawl on the deck. Goodyear pushed the throttles full ahead and the boat surged powerfully away from the jetty.

But the boat was headed towards the Haven before he intended to turn back to the harbour. This was a big mistake. As the boat gathered speed, he'd not had time to switch on and look at the depth gauge. This would have shown him that there was not enough depth of water to the right hand side of the jetty; only a sandbar. As "Predator" reached about 15 knots, she grounded on the sandbank with a "whump" and came to a sudden and complete stop, as the bow reared up appreciably, with the twin jets doing their best to push the boat forward. The channel he'd followed on the way in to the jetty was over to the left. This would have been deep enough, but being in such a hurry, was the cause of being apparently stuck on the sandbank.

'SHIT, SHIT, SHIT!' yelled Goodyear.

'Oh fuck, now what?' shouted Dimitriou.

'Don't worry; we'll just suck our way out of this. Hang on.' With that; having throttled the twin 240hp turbo diesel engines back to idle, he engaged the downward reverse thrusters and pushed the throttles fully forward. The engines roared to full power and the enormous pressure of water was actually blasting the sand away from under the stern section. At first the craft stayed firmly held by the sand as the boat had pushed to almost half its length onto the sandbar.

'She's not moving!' shouted Dimitriou.

'She will,' was Goodyear's retort, and quite soon, the powerful thrust of the jets actually scouring the seabed, had the result that the sand was actually releasing the grip on the hull and the boat began moving back. She gathered speed as she slipped back off the sandbank and Goodyear throttled back to allow the boat to be re-aligned to the right direction. 'Thank our gods for that. Any more of that sand being blown into the intakes and it would have damaged the internal props.'

Once turned toward the left side of the jetty, Dimitriou said, 'We can go straight across the harbour now.'

'Don't be even more stupid than you are, you dickhead, if we take a straight course, we'll end up stuck again. We'll have to take a course back to port of Green Island and then cross round the back of Brownsea.'

'But why are we going back to the harbour then, I thought we were going to take these things,' he said pointing back over his shoulder, 'and dump them at sea.'

'Change of plan. I'm going to get to my "Boston Whaler" and put them in there. I reckon that boat is less visible than this one, don't you?'

'Yeah, right, good idea; it's going to be tricky changing them over, but yeah, I see what you mean.'

Giving the engines three-quarter throttle, Goodyear kept the speed to around 30 knots and at this speed he could keep a closer watch for more sandbanks. As he made a sharp turn around the back of Green Island, the boat heeled sharply, and then slowed down considerably. 'Now what the fuck is happening,' yelled Goodyear, 'we've lost power.' As the boat slowed, it dawned upon him that the intakes had been fouled by something, and this caused the lack of thrust.'

'What's the problem Martin,' yelled Dimitriou.

'I think the intakes are blocked, that's what's happened. After everything else, it's all going to shit.'

'How do you mean, the intakes are blocked, what intakes?'

As the craft slowed to a standstill, he said bitterly, 'Of course, you don't know about jet boats, do you? Well under the boat and just in front of the jet units, there are two intakes for the water which the jets blast out of the stern, get it?'

'Yeah, by why are they blocked if they're under the boat and we're not stuck on a sandbank are we?'

'No, but you've heard of "Japanese Seaweed" I take it, everybody has?'

'Yeah, what about it?'

'Well, this fucking stuff is so dense and invasive and great long strands of it grow at a fantastic rate and you can bet your life that it's what's been sucked up into the intakes.'

'So now what do we do?'

'It's not "we," it's "you."'

'Me?'

'You heard. You're the diver, you'll have to go under the boat and rip out this sodding seaweed.'

'But we've no SCUBA gear.'

'But we've got some plastic tubing, just get some and I'll tie it to the guardrail and you can stick the end in your mouth and breathe while you're under there.'

'You WHAT?'

'You heard me.'

'You know diving Martin, so you'll know that you can't breathe air through a tube below about 2 feet of water, your lungs don't have the strength.'

'We only draw about two feet, so you won't have any problem then, will you? So get moving and stop bellyaching.'

Dimitriou resigned himself that arguing was absolutely of no use, so after Goodyear had found the plastic tubing and tied the end to the stern rail, he passed the other open end to Dimitriou, who was stripped to the waist. He then went over the side and pushed himself with great difficulty, under the hull of the boat. He was fighting his natural buoyancy, but steadying his breathing, he managed to clamber right to the centre of the hull where he could see the great fronds of weed hanging down. Pulling this repeatedly, he eventually managed to clear the metal grid and after about ten minutes of struggling, he had cleared as much as he could and went back to the surface.

He was actually quite drained by the exertion of having to keep himself from floating back up and he was very glad to be helped back up onto the boat by taking Goodyear's hand.

'It's all gone Martin, it's as clear as I can get it.'

'Good, that's probably the most useful you've been all week. Now let's get going, we've wasted enough time.'

Pointing the boat across Ramshorn Lake they skirted Brownsea Island, toward the far side of the Harbour, now reducing speed to lessen the chance of being spotted at the illegal high speed.

By this time, he had switched on the GPS unit to locate his other boat, a "Boston Whaler," which was moored to a buoy close to the centre of the harbour.

Alex and Anna arrived at the jetty just about five minutes after they had left in "Predator."

Seeing the empty jetty, they both realised that they had literally "missed the boat."

'Damn, damn, damn,' said Alex.'

'We had to try though guv.'

'I know Anna, but let's just have a look round to see if they have left any clues. Let's have a walk back to the shed; there might be something to see.'

They walked slowly, if a little dejectedly, back along the short stretch of road leading back to the large shed. After about thirty yards, Anna spotted the little trailer in a gap and almost hidden by the trees. 'That wasn't here before guv,' she said.

'You're right. It does look as though it's just been dumped. Look, it's been pushed right into the undergrowth. Let's take a closer look.'

They moved over to the trailer. 'Just look at that Anna, that's the quad bike isn't it?'

'Yep, and judging by the mess on the trailer, which is still wet, it's been used recently.'

As they moved closer, the smell became more than obvious.

'Oh Christ, it's the same smell as before. They must have moved the bodies on this. They've used the trailer to take them to the boat and made a dash for it. Where the hell have they gone, that's what we have to find out?'

Get on to Alice can you, see where they are now?' Anna called the office, where the call was taken by Tom. 'Tom, what are you doing in work, you should be resting?'

'I couldn't just sit around sarge, I was going mad, and anyway, there's too much happening and I need to know why I was attacked. Someone has given information away.'

'We'll have to sort that out later Tom, is Alice there?'

'She's just gone to the canteen or the loo, but she shouldn't be long.'

'Is the tracker display on?'

'Yes, it shows the boat moving across Poole Harbour, just to the west of Brownsea Island.'

'Hold on Tom, I'll just pass this info on to Al... the guv.'

She put her hand across the microphone on the handset and said, '"Predator" is just passing Brownsea Island across the harbour,' Alex.

'Okay, just keep us in the picture tell him.'

'Both you and Alice keep a close watch on them; we'll finish up checking around here and get back as soon as we can.'

"Predator" was coming close to the Boston Whaler and Goodyear said, 'take that mooring hook and do exactly as I tell you, right?'

'Okay, what do I do?'

'I'll bring her to a stop just before the buoy and you reach under it to catch the mooring rope. When you've got it, lift the buoy and put the rope on the bow cleat. Then we can leave the "cargo" here and take "Predator" back to Cobbs. No-one will come and check the Whaler. We can sort that out later.'

'Why don't we just dump the bodies and let them either sink or float away?'

'Because if we do, and if they don't sink, the bodies are bound to be found somewhere and they can be identified as foreigners. That would make the police suspicious and because the police have been to see you about the fishing trips and they also came to me with some crazy scheme for me to travel around the Channel looking for boatloads of immigrants.'

'Is that why that bloke was looking at "Predator" the other night, you know the one you tried to get?'

'I don't know for sure, but I was tipped off that the police were doing something that night. It could've been him, but I gave him a good beating before some other bloke came and intervened.'

'But what did he do to the boat, do you know?'

'I don't think he did anything, he just got on board and looked around, but there was no damage, so I just think he was snooping. Anyway, let's just get these two tucked away out of sight and get back so that we can keep our heads down. They have no idea where we've just been have they?'

Obviously unknown to either Goodyear or Dimitriou, the police knew exactly where they'd been and probably why they'd been there, although proving this would be awkward unless a full search warrant could be issued for the lock-up within the shed. Unfortunately, there was no actual suspicion which could be attributed to either Goodyear or Dimitriou at this stage. There had to be some sort of link or grounds which would enable a search warrant to be issued, other than the temporary one which had been authorised. They would probably have better luck once they had returned to the station and seen the Superintendent with the discovery of the two bodies.

'Right, we'll have to go back and see where they've gone. There's nothing else we can do here I don't think.'

'I don't suppose either of the guys from the oil site would have heard or seen anything. Do you think it's worth checking as we're here?'

'Actually, that might be a good idea Anna. Let's go and see who's there.'

Turning the Defender round, they drove the short distance to the oil site gate. Pressing the intercom button a voice answered. 'Yes, can I help?'

'This is DCI Vail from Bournemouth Police. Can we have a quick word?'

The gate lock buzzed and they entered the site and walked over to the cabin, where the door opened and John Metcalfe greeted them.

Alex asked if he had seen or heard anything in the short period before their arrival.

'Yes, I did hear that quad bike moving about a while ago. I guessed it was the fishing guy moving some stuff around.'

'But you didn't see anything?'

'No, I just heard the bike. By the way, just after you came the last time, Bob was moved to another site. Why was that, was it anything to do with your visit?'

'No, it must have been coincidence I suppose,' Alex lied.' He didn't want to divulge that Bob Chorley had given them the information about the person or persons involved in the attempted burial of the body and the description he gave them. This made him very vulnerable and he was now under police surveillance for the duration of this investigation, with arrangements being made for him to move to a different address.

'I did wonder at the time, because Bob was very touchy for some reason around the time when that body was found. He said nothing to me and he was very reserved, to say the least.'

'Maybe he was affected by what happened; it's not every day that a corpse is found so close to where you work.'

'Maybe,' said Metcalfe. 'Anyway, we have a new bloke now, he's alright.'

'So you saw nothing then?' asked Anna.

'Nope, sorry.'

'Okay, thanks anyway. We'll leave you in peace.'

They made their way back to the Central Police station in Bournemouth.

CHAPTER 42

After an uneventful return journey back to the station, Alex and Anna went straight up to their office to find Alice and Tom poring intently over the computer screen.

As they walked into the room, Alice and Tom turned round. They had what can only be described as an "excited" look on their faces.

'So, where is the boat now, Alice?' asked Alex.

'They are back at the mooring guv. They got back about half an hour ago.'

'What the hell are they playing at?' said Anna, 'surely they can't have taken the bodies back there?'

'That's if they've taken them at all,' suggested Alex, 'although I can't think of what else they would've done. I just hope they haven't just dumped them in the harbour.'

'Surely not,' suggested Anna, 'they can't have been that stupid; they are bound to be found.'

Alice intervened, 'I don't know if it's significant guv, but on the way back to Cobbs Quay, they seemed to stop in the middle of the harbour, close to Brownsea Island. They were stopped for about 20 minutes and then went on again, back to where they are now.'

'Okay Alice, can you possibly get a GPS location fix on where they stopped and then get Google maps to see where they stopped. Maybe that will give us an idea as to why.'

'Good idea guv. Hang on, while I get the latitude and longitude figures from the plot we took.' Alice's fingers flew across the keys and very soon, she had the precise location of where "Predator" had stopped for that short time.

Putting up on the screen the Google map, she entered the GPS location and it showed the spot where they stopped as among a line of boats, moored in the harbour, just off the main channel.

'Fantastic,' said Alex, 'it looks like they either stopped beside a boat or tied up to it. Can we see exactly which boat?'

Taking a closer look at the zoomed image, Anna said, I don't think it's that clear, but we can count the boats along the line of the one's which are moored; that way we can find it if we go out there.'

'What do you think they did there guv?' asked Tom.

'I'll give you three guesses Tom,' said Alex, looking around all three standing by the computer screen.

'Do you mean they've put the bodies on to a boat in the middle of the harbour and legged it back to Cobbs?'

'I reckon that's about it Tom. Right, Alice, I want you to keep a constant check on where that boat is, while Tom and I go out to take a look at the boat we think they stopped at. Is that okay with you Tom?'

'I think so guv, I don't get seasick.'

Anna looked a little concerned. 'I don't know how choppy it is out there today guv; I'm only thinking about Tom's broken ribs. I'm sure they must be painful, aren't they Tom?'

'If I'm honest, yes they are and maybe if it's a bit rough, well, I don't know.'

'No, you're quite right Anna, it did look a bit rough as we came back, now you mention it, so forget that Tom. You keep where you can't move around too much. In fact, I forgot, you should really be off sick, shouldn't you?'

'I know guv, but like I said before, I'd far rather be doing something useful that sat watching daytime TV.'

'I can agree with you there, for sure,' said Alex. 'Okay, I'll take Anna. Can you get on to our friendly harbour master and see if we can get Jack to take us out there. Meanwhile we can check out how many boats are moored out there.'

'Just one thing guv,' said Alice. 'There might be a slight problem. Google Earth take these photos only every so often, so I don't suppose the boats shown on this picture,' and here she leaned closer to the screen, 'taken in 2015, are still in the same position.'

'Damn, that could be a problem for sure.'

'Not only that guv, but when you look closer at the picture , you know zoom right in, the boats seem to be in different positions, almost as though three photos had been taken, one after the other, when the tides and currents were different, look.'

They all peered closer as she zoomed in. 'You're right, that's a problem.'

Tom had an idea. 'How about checking the relative length of the boats shown on that photo and then when you get close to them, you could estimate which one it was?'

Anna then said, 'Hang on a sec, exactly where did they stop Alice, can you show me?'

'It was around the front of Brownsea Island, quite near that funny looking building which is just off the shoreline of Brownsea Island, I don't know what that is.'

'Show me please.' Alice entered the co-ordinates 50.698043 – 1.973967 and the cursor moved to a point just to one side of the building Alice had mentioned.

Pointing to the building, Anna said 'That's "Othniel." They farm oysters there. The mooring buoys are quite distinct there and your co-ordinates show a mooring buoy; look, the third one to the right from "Othniel."

Tom said, 'But it's empty, there's no boat there.'

'Maybe not then, but perhaps today there is a Boston Whaler, belonging to Goodyear or Metin Denizci to give him his proper name, moored there. If we can get Jack organised, we can soon find out.'

Alex then said, 'Let me add a word of caution. We have to make sure that the boat we think it is actually belongs to Goodyear, before we go breaking into it. Don't boats have to be registered or something? Didn't you take a photo of the Boston Whaler which was on Goodyear's drive?'

'Yes, I did. It's still in my phone, I haven't deleted it.' She took out her phone and found the picture of the boat on his drive. 'Yes, I thought I noticed it before.'

'Noticed what, Anna?'

'On the side of the boat near the back, there's what looks like a serial number, with "SSR43375," that's the Small Ships Register, if I'm not mistaken. That will give us all the information we need, complete history, owner and all that sort of thing. All we have to do is search on the UK.GOV website small ships register and hey presto.'

'Brilliant; nice one Anna.' Let's just hope we can get Jack again.'

'Can't wait guv.' This was said with heavy irony. 'I'll see what I can arrange.'

'In the meantime, Tom, can you search the register with that number and verify that it is the one we want?'

'I'm on it guv,' said Tom.

Anna phoned her friendly Harbour Master and he soon came on the line.

'Hello Sergeant Anna,' he said. His deep mellifluous voice sent a little tingle down her back. 'How nice to hear from you again, I'm hoping you need my help again.'

'I'm afraid so, Fuller.' Anna had taken the precaution of closing her office door while she made the call, just in case anyone else overheard.

'Please don't be afraid, I'm always very glad to be of service to our local force, as you well know.' This last phrase was spoken with a very slight chuckle, which did nothing to quell the frisson which ran through her.

'Okay then, we need someone to take us over to the edge of Brownsea, close to the "Othniel" oyster farm to check on a boat which is moored there. We suspect that it is linked to our investigation.'

'That's no problem at all. In fact I think Jack is as taken with you as I have to admit I am, although perhaps I shouldn't say that should I, but then I like oysters, and you know what they say about them don't you?'

'No, you shouldn't and yes, I do, but I think perhaps it's best left at that, don't you? Mind you, I think I can count Jack out to be honest, but thank you for the compliment. Yes, we need to take a look at this boat as a matter of urgency.'

'Okay Anna, leave it with me and I'll get something organised as soon as I can and get back to you quickly. I'm afraid that although I would love to stay chatting with you, I do have something which I have to attend to right now, but you know, as always, you are welcome any time. Just let me know when you are coming and I'll try to make time.'

Anna was more than a little warm around the neckline after this verbal encounter. I think I'll have to cool things around here, she thought. She went to the canteen area and made herself a drink of fruit juice to regain her composure. As she returned to her office, her phone rang. 'DS Jenkins,' she answered.

'Anna, it's Fuller, I've arranged for Jack as soon as you are ready. Will you be coming over right away?'

'As soon as DCI Vail and I are ready, thank you.'

'I deduce from your response, that you are not alone.'

'That's correct Mr Masterson; we'll be there very shortly.' She was not alone, but thought it better to reply this way and thankful as she'd left her door open.

'What a pity that I won't see you alone, but I do have a previous appointment, so that's not too big a disappointment Anna, maybe another time.'

'Of course, thank you once again for your help.'

Going into Alex's office, she said, 'All arranged – we can go over to the harbour as soon as we like and Jack will be ready.'

'Okay, got your hat and coat?'

'You know me, always ready.'

'I certainly hope so...'

'Steady tiger, walls have ears.'

'You're right, sorry. Let's go.' As they passed Alice apparently gazing into her computer, Alex said, 'We're off to your GPS co-ordinates Alice; let's see what we can find there. When you get any information on that registration number, give me a call.'

'Will do and good luck guv, let's hope you find something.'

'Thanks, but it's the "something" that worries me.'

CHAPTER 43

Anna was driving as fast as was legally possible, to Poole harbour to meet Jack again for a trip to try to verify that the Boston whaler they suspected was possibly "visited" by "Predator" on the way back from Goathorn. The traffic was always a problem between Bournemouth and Poole at the time of day they were making the trip, so Anna was given permission to use the "Blues & Two's" to speed their trip. Timing was important, so that could check on the suspected boat as soon as possible. A call came on Alex's phone. Looking at the display he said, 'Alice, what do you have?'

'We've checked on the SSR registration number guv, and it is a Boston Whaler registered to a Martin Goodyear of Corfe Mullen, Dorset. The boat was bought two years ago and the details show the price and dates of acquisition and all that stuff which I'm sure you don't need at the moment, guv.'

'Okay Alice, thanks, that's fine. We just needed to know that that boat was or is actually his, so that we're not making any more cock-ups, we've enough of those at the moment.'

After ending the call, he said to Anna, 'Yes, it's his boat, so if we can take a quick look at it, we may see something which we can use for prosecution.'

'If he's dumped the bodies in the boat, I don't think we'll need any close searching, do you Alex?'

'No, I think you're right.'

They made the journey to the Harbour very quickly and went straight to the quayside where Jack was in his usual position of sitting on a mooring bollard, wreathed in a cloud of his foul-smelling smoke.

As he saw them approach, he stood up and flicked the brown-stained cigarette stump over his shoulder, hawked and spat into the water, gave a rough cough and then treated them to a smile which they had, by now, come to dread.

'Aah, a good day to 'ee both,' he growled in a voice which rather resembled a boat being dragged over gravel. 'It be good to see 'um agen, 'tas been awhile.'

'We've missed you too Jack,' said Anna, not really meaning it wholeheartedly, but to make him feel appreciated.

'Thank'ee, that be right nice of you missy,' said Jack. 'If'n you be ready, I be ready to take you both over to wherever you do want to be taken to, an' no mistake. It be my pleasure agen to be of service to you nice folk.'

Here we go again, thought Alex. He's like an old clockwork toy; once you set him going, you can't stop him until he's unwound. 'That's great Jack, can we get going as we're in quite a hurry today. We just want to go over to Brownsea to check that a particular boat is where we think it is?'

They boarded the old day-boat of Jack's and set off across the harbour, which was rather choppy this time and not the smooth and gentle crossing they'd made previously.

'Don't be a' feared if'n you do get a bit of spray comin' over the bow coamin' today; there be just a little chop on, see, so mebbe you do want to sit up alongside me, here on the stern see, where it be a little drier?'

This was directed at Anna, accompanied by another rather sly grin from Jack. 'I'll be alright Jack, thanks, it's not too bad.' The thought of actually sitting beside the old sea-dog reminded her that in her experience, dogs had a less than pleasant smell, and this could be one of them, nice though he was; never mind his real reason for asking her to sit beside her. Mind you, "coaming" was a new one on her. Anyway, her softer side suggested that he was lonely since losing his wife in such tragic circumstances.

'Okay missy, wherever you be happy, t'will make me happy too; now tell me where you do want to go to.'

'The boat we want to check out is close to the "Othniel" oyster farm. Do you know it?' said Alex.

'Oh, I do know it like, 'tis quite new I know, not been there that long to my mind, but them oysters is not for me. I tried one once upon a time and it felt and tasted just like what I do spit into yon 'arbour, see.'

Too much information, thought Anna. She had no problem with seasickness, but that didn't help at all.

They made good time for the relatively short trip and soon they were getting close to the structure called "Othniel." It was a strange building, on stilts, sitting not far from the shore on the southern side of Brownsea Island.

Alex said, as they passed the rather odd looking building, 'I don't know much about oysters, but I would imagine that this harbour is a great place to grow them. I once went to Arcachon near Bordeaux where they have enormous oyster beds and a huge oyster industry and it strikes me that this is a similar sort of area, you know, fairly shallow and frequent tidal movements, is that right Jack?'

'I don't know no "Carcrashon" as you call it, but I do knows that they grow nearly 500 tons of oysters a year hereabouts an' they do even sell 'em to France.'

'I wonder how that'll work after "Brexit"?' said Anna looking at Alex.

'I can see a price change on the cards there, for sure.'

'That's their problem. Right now, ours is to look for this boat. It should be just over there,' she said pointing toward the harbour entrance. They were getting close to the building and looking beyond it they saw two empty mooring buoys and on the third, there was a white boat. It was about 200 yards beyond the building and although they could see that it wasn't a yacht, like most of the other boats moored around there, they could see that it was a sports boat. 'What do you think Anna, is it the one we're looking for?'

'Hard to tell, but we'll soon find out guv.'

As they became closer, they could make out a name on the bow. When it became readable, Alex said, 'Yes, "Boston Whaler," that's it. Let's take a closer look. Can we pull alongside please Jack? We'd like to take a look at this boat.'

'That be no problem zur, I'll just pull alongside 'er, and p'raps you could take our bow painter and make fast to 'er stern cleat while I do put over a couple of fenders?'

Anna was thinking, "bow painter, make fast, stern cleat, fenders," what the heck is he talking about? But I guess he means tie us to it. However, Alex seemed to know what he meant, as he took a rope from the bow of Jack's boat and tied it to the stern of the Boston Whaler. 'Can you see the registration number on the rear of the hull Anna?'

'Yes, it's SSR43375 – that's the one all right.'

'Okay then, let's take a look under the canopy. I'll just release a part so we can just look, I don't want to do anything which may alert him that someone's been looking.'

'I don't think that just by taking the cover back a little will be obvious guv.'

'You never know Anna, with someone like him; I wouldn't be surprised if he'd rigged up some sort of booby trap.'

'Maybe you're right guv.'

Alex then twisted a couple of "turn-buttons" which held the canopy in place and lifted the corner of the canopy. The immediate uprush of stench which assailed his nostrils, made him jump backwards and he almost lost his balance as the boat rocked violently. 'Oh my God,' he said, 'He's only put the bodies on this one.'

'Why the hell's he done that? He must realise that we're after him. I wonder why he's taken Predator back to Cobbs Quay in that case.'

'Do you think he'll have got there by now?'

'I'm afraid he will have, after all the time it's taken for us to get here. I'm sure he'll be long gone by now. Perhaps he's gone back to get supplies on board for a longer trip. Maybe I should have had him arrested him as he got back to the mooring over there?'

'Arrested him for what guv?' said Anna. We have no proof that he's done anything wrong, only the two bodies and if we'd arrested him after finding two bodies, even though we suspect him of being involved in the first one, he'd only say that it was nothing to do with him, wouldn't he?'

'Yes, but if we had him in custody, we could at least given him a good questioning. We'd have him for 24 hours.'

'But then he wouldn't have moved the bodies and now that he's put them in a boat which belongs to him and we know from the tracker details, that it was him, as we have his movements plotted, we can build a case, surely?'

'I think we can rely on the information we have to at least make the arrest. We have the photographic evidence from SOCO which is incontrovertible and I would certainly think that there is some sort of DNA links to be found. We must put this boat under surveillance as soon as we can, so that we'll know who and when the bodies are removed. Surely they can't be left here. In fact, I really don't know why they were left and not dumped somewhere else before now, but there has to be a reason somewhere.'

'So in the meantime, do we go to Cobb's quay marina and make the arrest, guv?'

Let's make sure that he's there first. I don't want to make another cock-up. We have to have a strong evidential link between him and the bodies we found.'

'Okay, shall I arrange the surveillance then? Should it be done from Brownsea or somewhere else?'

'Yes, maybe someone could be based on "Othniel," they'll be out of sight but with good coverage of this boat.'

All this dialogue was being carried on out of earshot of Jack, who was sitting quietly in the stern, holding the tiller, and now smoking one of his evil smelling cigarettes, and thankfully the wind was taking the smoke away from Anna and Alex.

Anna made the call to headquarters. 'Alice, can you contact "Othniel" and get their permission for a constable to be stationed on their building just off Brownsea, so that he can keep watch on the boat we are beside at the moment. It's the Boston Whaler belonging to Goodyear as we suspected. There are two bodies on board, probably the one's we found over at Goathorn and we think he's moved them here, although we have no idea why.'

'Maybe Tom wouldn't mind doing that sarge; it'll keep him quiet and give him some time to mend.'

'Good idea Alice, don't ask him, just say that it's my order. I don't know how long it will be, but I really can't see it being for too long, given the state that we know the bodies are in. You'd better arrange for a second DC to cover in case it's overnight. I'll leave Tom to sort out how he'll get there.'

'I'm sure the oyster people will have a boat for their staff, so I'll get him to check on that and arrange things.'

'Okay, I'll leave it to you and Tom to sort out. In the meantime, where is Predator right now?'

She's stationary at Cobbs Marina guv.'

'Okay, great, we are going to try to get over there to make an arrest, so please keep a constant check.

'Will do sarge.'

Alex had heard this exchange and nodded his agreement regarding stationing Tom on "Othniel." At least we'll have good warning and if Tom takes a camera, we can get some shots of them doing whatever they do, although if they're going to move the bodies, I think that's going to be difficult. Can you tell Tom to take a telephoto lens with him as it's about 200 yards away from the oyster building?'

'I'll pass it on.'

Turning to Jack, Alex said, Jack, we're finished here for now, so can you take us back to the harbour as quickly as you can please?'

'Roit you are zur, I'll be takin' you back as quick as this ol' gal will tak' us; but she'll only go 'bout 10 knots flat out, 'an as'n I did say back afore now, 'tis not good to be runnin' this ol' diesel engine too fast, for tidn't goin' t'do any good to them bearin's, what are so terrible costly to replace, if'n you knows what I do mean?'

'I understand Jack, but please do your best; this is now very urgent.'

'I will zur, I will, I do unnerstan' what you be needin' to get back, soon as is possible, so I be doin' my best, you can be certin sure of that.'

'Good man, Jack.'

Jack pushed the old boat as hard as he dared, and a little more if the truth be told, and they made good time across the choppy harbour, back to the quayside. Once back on shore, Anna gave Jack a hug and said a big "thank you" for his trouble. This brought a big smile to the old man's' face, which Anna thought was worth holding her indrawn breath for, whilst the hug lasted, which was not long at all; but slightly beyond long enough.

As they walked back to their car Alex said, 'that was a little beyond the call of duty Anna, but well done anyway.'

'Thanks Alex. Not something I'd like to make a habit.'

'Right, we have to get over to Cobbs marina quickly now, to see if they are around still.'

As Anna drove, a call was made to Alice back at headquarters. 'Alice, any movement on the boat, can you see?'

'Guv, the only thing that has happened since they got back to the moorings, is that the boat has moved around the Marina to another spot, where it was for about half an hour, now it's back on the original mooring; apart from that, nothing.'

'Okay, thanks. Keep looking; I'm expecting something to happen soon, although I don't know what yet, but I'll keep you posted.'

'Right-o guv. By the way, I've passed on to Tom your instructions about surveillance at "Othniel" oyster farm building and he's not too pleased about being stuck out there on the water. I told him it would be an "experience" for him to be on a little island in the middle of the sea and he should enjoy it.'

'And what did he say to that then?'

'His exact words were; "So now I'm Robinson bloody Crusoe then."

Alex passed this exchange on to Anna and they had a little chuckle at that.

'Tell him it'll do him good to get some "sea-time" in, and we expect some action sooner rather than later.'
'Okay guv, will do,' ending the call.

CHAPTER 44

Goodyear and Dimitriou on board "Predator" had returned to Cobbs Quay Marina after having great difficulties moving the slippery packaged bodies into the Boston Whaler. They had moved "Predator" round to the fuelling berth, where they took on a capacity load of diesel.

'Why did we dump those bodies on the Whaler, Martin?' asked Dimitriou.

'Because we couldn't leave them in the shed in case they were found by one of the oilfield workers and called the police.'

'Why would they find them, they were in your locked shed.'

'Is that shed airtight then?'

'I don't suppose so, why?'

'Because, you idiot, the smell would be a giveaway wouldn't it, it was bloody awful.'

'Yeah, that stink would be noticed, I suppose.'

'Noticed - you could hardly ignore that, even if you were only passing the building, so they had to be moved, and to put them on the Whaler means that the smell won't be noticed in the open air.'

'Oh, yeah, right. But what are we going to do now, with the bodies I mean?'

'We couldn't have them on board here could we, or the smell would pollute the whole marina, so as we can pick them up on the way as we've a collection to make over the Channel, so we'll dump them right out in the middle between here and France. That way, the current will probably take them right along the coast, that's if they don't sink, so there'll be no connection whatever with us.'

'That seems a good idea. If only they hadn't started that fight on the way back the last time, none of this would have happened.'

'I know, but you should know that when a Turk loses his temper, he goes "all out" and there's no stopping him. You of all people should know that after what you've done to your wife.'

'Yeah, well, she asked for it, didn't she?'

'I doubt that, knowing you. You're a mean bastard when you're drunk.'

'But you'd have thought that those blokes you were bringing back and heading for a better life, would have been more thankful and not started arguing.'

'How the hell should I have known that they'd start all that?' Anyway, I had no idea that the bloke that I finally stopped would have those knives on him, did I? If he hadn't started the trouble as we were nearly back here, maybe something could've been done about it.'

'What was that fight about anyway, you know the one where you finished him off? You were in a hell of a temper.'

'I'm not surprised; all that way back over here, only to start on the other blokes, telling them that the whole thing was a scam and to demand their money back. I couldn't let him put all the others off now could I?'

'What I don't understand is why he didn't say anything before we left France.'

'Because, you nutter, if they'd got here and demanded their money back for some reason, then they'd have had a free ride.'

'Silly fucker, if only he'd known more about you, he'd never had taken the chance. Trying to face up to you was the worst thing he could have done. Still, it must have been a bit scary when he pulled those knives.'

'That's where a bit of "hand to hand" combat training comes in handy, isn't it?'

'So you were in the army then?'

'Not the army, but let's just say that I had the training, and leave it at that.'

Dimitriou knew Goodyear well enough not to ask any more about that subject. 'He found out the hard way, not to mess with you, didn't he, I mean, you beat the shit out of him and then used his own knives on him and that's after he'd killed the other punter in the argument and you certainly made sure of him, but we should have buried him better surely?'

'I didn't realise that the sand was so bloody sticky and hard to dig, we'd have been there all night and then that bloke came from the oil pumping station. Maybe I should have sorted him as well, there and then.'

'But you say you made sure that he wouldn't mention anything to the police. Do you think he did?'

'Oh, I doubt it; see, I called his employers and got his address, and paid him a visit. He didn't know who I was, because it was so dark that night he came out when we were digging, that he couldn't see me, but when I reminded him, he nearly shat himself. He couldn't stop shaking; he couldn't even talk.'

'So he won't say anything?'

'I doubt it, seeing as how I did a little surgery on him.'

'Bloody hell, but hang on, I know the first one is the bloke we tried to bury but are the other two the ones who had the fight on the boat?'

'Yes, now shut up.'

'That makes three. People don't mess with you, do they?'

'No, and anyway, the police haven't found us have they, and if we get a move on this evening, we'll be well out of the way and they'll have nothing on us. They won't know where we are or where we go, so stop worrying and just go and get the food for the trip, but be quick about it. We'll put on our wet-weather fishing gear to make the transfer of the bodies. It's going to be a little messy I should think. While you're gone, I'll check that everything is ready here.'

Dimitriou went off in search of the necessary provisions for their trip and the return journey with what they expected was a full complement of immigrants, who were to pay a great deal of money for the chance of entry to Britain. When they were landed at the pre-arranged point along the coast, transport had been arranged that would take them to local stations, where they would then make their way to destinations which had been carefully arranged, for them to "blend in" to that area. They were separated at the landing points so that suspicions wouldn't be aroused by a number of obviously "Eastern European men" all turning up together.

This trip had been made a number of times and when they had returned, it seemed that it was simply another fishing trip. However, had anyone actually seen any fish or could it be verified that fish had been caught?

Dimitriou came back with the necessary provisions for the trip they would take later that evening. Goodyear said, 'We'll take Predator over to Ridge Wharf and wait for the tides to be right for when we get back. Then we'll go over to get the two bodies on our way and get over to France to pick up our shipment.'

'Why Ridge Wharf then, it's quite a long way isn't it?'

'Well, not all the way to Ridge Wharf, but in the River Frome there are some moorings which are hardly ever used and we can use one of those for a while, until we're ready. It's better to wait over there where it's quiet rather than being stuck here where we are known. I just don't want anyone to know where we are.'

'Is everything ready for when we get back, you know the "onward transport" for those blokes?'

'Yep, as usual; we'll make the drops as before, at "Milford on Sea," I've checked the tide times and we'll just about have enough water if we get the timings right.'

'Didn't we have a spot of trouble dropping those blokes off at Keyhaven the last time?'

'Yeah, I shouldn't have gone past Hurst Castle where the ferry runs. We were unlucky to be seen, but I don't think it's caused any trouble; but this time I'll land them by Milford. There's a bank of stones on the beach just there. It's a good point of reference as there's a small road called Saltgrass Lane which runs really close to the beach. I'll make sure we get the van as close as possible so that all we have to do is put our bow to the beach and let the blokes jump off. At least with jet drive, we can get close in to the shore but if they get their feet wet, so what, they'll dry and it'll be much quicker for us to get off the coast and back and up to Cobbs; job done!'

A little later Dimitriou, having returned with all the provisions, said to Goodyear, 'I've got all the stuff skipper.'

'Right, if everything's aboard, let's get off and over to Ridge, or at least the entrance to the harbour on the River Frome.' Dimitriou cast off the bow line and the stern rope had already been removed, so they moved into Upton Lake and towards the "Twin Sails" lifting bridge at Hamworthy. As they were not "overheight" it was unnecessary for the bridge to be lifted and they motored gently into Poole Harbour, turning to starboard past the ferry terminal and headed across the tip of Arne Peninsula and using their depth gauge, followed the channel into the mouth of the River Frome. As they entered this, they saw, just ahead of them, an RNLI inflatable with two crew on board.

'Shit!' said Goodyear. 'We didn't need this.'

One of the crewmen on the RIB waved to signal them to stop. Goodyear had no choice as to have ignored this would have certainly have alerted them that something was wrong, so he throttled back and selected neutral as the boat hove to. The RNLI RIB pulled alongside, and Goodyear said, 'Hello is there a problem?'

'Not at all, it's just that we would warn you of the lack of depth further up, but I'm sure you know that, with a beautiful boat like that. Anyway, you'll have all the electronics on board won't you?'

'Thanks for the warning, but yes, we do have all the gadgets and we are aware of the tide times, so we should be okay.'

Are you going up to Ridge Wharf then?'

'Yes, we're meeting some friends at "The Granary" for an evening meal. We'll probably overnight there and come back tomorrow.'

As the RNLI RIB drifted gently back, the stern of "Predator" came into view.

'I see you've got twin jet drives, so you won't have to worry about fouling the bottom. The Granary sounds like a good idea, nice food. Mind you, you're going to attract some attention from the grockles with that beast.'

He said this looking at "Predator" with a very appreciative eye. 'I'll bet she's fast. What engines does she have?'

'Yes, she's fast; about 35 knots tops, but then she does have twin 250 Yamaha diesels.'

'Wow, with a shape like she has, she'll take any sea, I should think.'

'She certainly does, but if you'll excuse us, we'd better get up there or we'll be stuck on a mudbank.'

'Of course, sorry to have held you up. Thanks for the info and have a good evening.'

'You too, g'night.' With that, the two RNLI crewmen opened their throttle and they sped off back to their base in Poole.

'You were uncommonly polite there,' said Dimitriou.

'If I'd been aggressive, they would have been suspicious, and I hope by saying that we were going to the restaurant, if asked by anyone, they'll tell them that. Not that we've anything to worry about, but I just want to keep out of the way for now and I don't think they'll be back tonight.'

'Sure, I understand,' said Dimitriou.

That'll be a first, thought Goodyear.

After a short run further up the river, they spotted a secluded mooring buoy and quickly made fast to this after turning the craft round. Which was a difficult manoeuvre due to the length of the boat and the narrowness of the channel; but with the use of the twin jet drives, this was accomplished quite easily. They ran lines to the buoys fore and aft and back to make fast to the cleats on the boat. This would make sure that the boat did not swing with the change of tide and they would be ready to move without any further manoeuvring, simply slipping the ropes off the cleats.

'Now we wait for dark. It may be that the tide times aren't quite right and we have to wait until tomorrow. I'll just check the tides and the run-time to France. We should be able to get our two friends aboard quite quickly shouldn't we?'

'If you say so, but I'm really not looking forward to it.'

'Just make sure we have all the waterproof gear ready, we don't want to get any stains from those two, do we?'

CHAPTER 45

On their way over to Cobbs Quay in an attempt to question Goodyear, there was a call from "the office" as headquarters was known. It was Alice. Anna was driving, so Alex took the call.

'Hi Alice, what's new?'

'Weeell, you know that I said they were back at Cobbs Quay Marina guv?'

Alex had a dread feeling from the way Alice had begun. 'Don't tell me they've moved again; you said they were back at their moorings.'

'They were, but now I can't get a reading. They've disappeared. I can't trace them.'

'Bollocks. What's happened Alice, you had them on screen? Why have they disappeared?'

'The only thing I can think of is that the battery has died. How long did the tekkie bods say that it would last?'

'They said it should last "for a number of days" if my memory serves me. How long has it been installed?'

'It's been about three days now guv. Surely it should have lasted longer than that? Or do you think they've found it and "disposed" of it?'

'Oh, I bloody hope not. If they've found it, it means that they know that we're on to them. I just hope that it is only a battery failure, but that's bad enough. I'm going to give those tech blokes a piece of my mind when I get back.'

'Maybe the tracker had been used before they gave it to us and the battery wasn't fully charged.'

'I tell you what, they'll be "fully charged" when I get to them, but let's be practical. There's nothing that we can do except try to find out where they are. Is Tom briefed about keeping watch tonight?'

'He's already there guv, he seemed keen to get himself set up. He really wants to catch them in the act and get an arrest.'

'There's only one problem with making an arrest out there as he's stuck on a platform and they'll be in a boat. We'll have to find a way of stopping them in the act. Leave it to me Alice, Anna and I will talk it over on our way back; we'll go to the marina anyway for a word with their boss.'

'Okay guv,' and ended the call.

He turned to Anna. She'd guessed much of what had been said from the call. 'That's all we need; now we've lost them. But someone must have seen them, I mean with a boat like that, people would notice wouldn't they?'

'I'd say that's a definite guv. But who would see them; are there any boats which patrol the harbour?'

'There's the harbour Patrol which is run by Dorset Police. I believe they have routine runs which cover much of the harbour, so with any luck, they might have seen this boat. I'll give them a call, but maybe there are other sightings. Who else would be in and around the harbour?'

'How about the RNLI guv? They have their big base just past Sunseeker's boatbuilding sheds, maybe one of their boats were out and about. Perhaps we should give them a call as well.'

'Good idea Anna. I'll do that as well.'

Alex put in a call to Dorset Police Marine Section via his TETRA radiophone. Asking to speak to the Poole Harbour section leader, he was put through quickly to the Harbour Office. 'This is DCI Vail from Bournemouth and I'm making enquires to find out if a particular boat has been seen today in or around the harbour.'

'Hello Inspector, I would really like to say we can help, but to be honest, I think it highly unlikely as our boat has been out along the coast for much of today and is due back soon, but as far as seeing a particular boat in the harbour, I think it very doubtful. What boat is it that you are looking for particularly?'

'It is a "Redbay Stormforce 11" to be precise. It is currently under investigation with regard to possible criminal activities.'

'I actually know the one you mean; it's a very distinctive boat. What are these criminal activities then?'

'I'd rather not say at the moment, except that we need to have a long talk with the owner as soon as possible.'

'Okay, we'll keep an eye out for it and give you a bell if we see it. I'll ask around the lads when they get back, I mean the ones who have been out and about.'

'Great, thanks; we did have a tracker on board, but it seems to have packed up and that's a bloody nuisance.'

'I can understand that; anyway, we'll keep a weather eye open for you, good luck.'

'Thanks again,' Alex said as he ended the call.

Then, he called the RNLI headquarters and spoke to the duty officer. After introducing himself, he asked if there were any chance of a sighting of the vessel named "Predator" which he described.

'I don't know if any of our lads would have sighted this vessel, but there have been a few RIB's out on training exercises today and I could ask around those who've returned, if they may have seen it.'

'That would be very helpful, as we seem to have lost contact with it.'

'If you know the owner, you could always call them on their VHF radio, as you know their name. You could call them on the general frequency.'

'That is a possibility, but as we are conducting an investigation and this vessel is part of that, so perhaps that wouldn't be such a good idea.'

'Oh yes, I see what you mean. Anyway, let me ask around the station and see what I get. If we have any sightings, I'll call you right away. Let me have your number then please.'

Alex passed this on and thanked the officer for his help.

'I don't think there's much more we can do at this stage Anna, do you?'

'Not without making everything far too public, no, but we do have to do something about them possibly collecting the bodies from the Whaler, maybe tonight. We have Tom out there watching, but what can we do about arresting them?'

'Maybe another call to the Marine Section to see if they can give any assistance in that direction, I'm sure they could assign their fast boat to help, if it's available.'

'Give them a call; I'm sure they'll help when they know it's a murder investigation.'

'I will, but I'll have to make it very clear that the information has to be kept quiet. The last thing we need is a leak to the press at this stage. If the "Echo" gets to hear of it, they'll be all over us like a rash.'

'Yep, especially that little rat-faced reporter Bert Metcalf. Do you remember him at the other investigation?'

'Do you mean the investigation that we don't mention?'

'Yes, you know the one. He was so pushy and just kept on and on trying to get information.'

'It's his job.'

'I know, but I found him totally objectionable to be honest.'

'Not the person to have as a friend, I'll grant you.'

'Bloody good reason to keep things quiet, don't you think?'

'It's a "given" guv.'

They were pulling up at Cobbs Quay Marina and after parking, went into reception, asking to see David Cunningham, the Marina Master. The receptionist, unknown to either Alex or Anna, was Genny Dobbs, who was talking with two people who were making enquiries. They had no idea that she was in fact Tom's "informant." She also happened to be the one who had told Goodyear that the police were making enquiries about him. Also unknown to them was the fact that Genny Dobbs was more than just a friend to Goodyear.

As they were waiting for Cunningham, Anna gently pulled Alex's arm and moved him away from the reception counter.

'Alex,' she said softly, 'I think I recognise her voice. She was the one I spoke to when I called Goodyear's house and a woman answered. I'm sure this is the same voice. It has a certain "huskiness" to it which is quite distinctive.'

'That would seem to be very possible Anna, especially as she works here; she's bound to have met Goodyear. Tom came here and maybe he mentioned that the police were making enquiries about Goodyear and she could have passed this on.'

'You don't think that she was Tom's "informant" do you?'

'With this connection, yes I do and what's more, if that's the case, then now we know why Tom was attacked. She'd have passed on the time that Tom was going to place the tracker.'

'In that case, Alex, it's a damned good thing that Cunningham was keeping watch on Tom whilst he was out there fitting the tracker. If he hadn't been watching, Tom could have been killed. We know this guy's a killer. If Cunningham hadn't stepped in, who knows what could have happened?'

'Christ Almighty! You're right. We'll have to ask Tom to give us the name and description of this "informant," so that we're sure.'

David Cunningham came through the inner door and the receptionist pointed Alex and Anna out to him. He moved over to them.

'David Cunningham,' he said extending his hand, 'I'm the Haven Master. Firstly, may I ask how the young detective Tom is, after his beating? I didn't see him after the paramedics had taken him, but he looked very shaken and in quite some pain.' Alex motioned for them to pass to a more private part of the reception area.

'Thanks for asking, Mr Cunningham; he's on the mend I'm happy to say. He suffered a couple of broken ribs and some heavy bruising. In fact, from what we know now, we think he's rather lucky not to have suffered much worse and thanks to your intervention, he was spared that, so on his behalf, very many thanks for your timely action.'

'I'm very glad to her that I was of some help. But you're here for something else, so how can I help you now?'

'We need to know where "Predator" is now, you know the Redbay Stormforce 11 belonging to Martin Goodyear. We were tracking him, as you probably gathered, but now for some reason our tracker is not functioning. Whether he's found this or perhaps it is just the battery which is down, we don't know. Either way, we need to know where he is, so any help or clue you can give will help enormously.'

'I'll see what I can do, certainly, but if he's left here, he could be anywhere, either in the harbour or even up a little creek somewhere; there are loads of places a boat can be out of sight, that's if he is in the harbour and not gone out to sea.'

'We don't think he's gone out to sea as we have observers watching, so we're trying to locate him within the harbour area.'

'Just hold on a moment and I'll check to see if he's been here or maybe we know something about his movements. I'll ask reception.'

He went over to the reception desk and spoke to Genny Dobbs. Alex and Anna watched her facial expression and body language very carefully whilst Cunningham was talking to her.

'What do you think Alex, does she look guilty or suspicious to you?'

'Nothing; she seems as cool as a cucumber. Maybe we're on the wrong track.'

'I don't think so, I'm sure about her voice and she's in a perfect position to keep Goodyear informed isn't she?'

'I trust your instincts Anna. I know how good you are with understanding body language and things like that. You've understood mine extremely well, several times in fact, haven't you?'

She looked at him from under hooded eyes and with a very sensual expression which said volumes to him.'

'But I was right, wasn't I?'

'You certainly were, I'm glad to say,' he was giving her a gentle smile as he said this.

Cunningham moved back to them and said, 'Goodyear moved "Predator" to the fuelling station a while ago and filled his tanks. Apparently he has larger than normal fuel tanks and this can only mean that he's going to make a longer trip, although I do believe he goes out for maybe three days at a time on fishing trips, so who knows where he gets to?'

'And do you know where he took the boat to after that?'

'I'm afraid that we have no idea, except that our other receptionist said that the other man with him had been shopping for food, as he came back loaded with bags of food and drink. "Enough for an army," she said. '"They must be going to do a lot of eating and drinking and not much fishing with all that stuff."

Anna turned to Alex saying, 'Now that is interesting.'

'My thoughts exactly.' Turning back to Cunningham, Alex held out his hand and said, 'Once again, our thanks to you Mr Cunningham for your actions, on behalf of Tom and for your help and information. I would ask, however, that you keep our enquiries and interest very much to yourself at this stage. This investigation has become much more involved than we at first thought and has now turned very serious.'

'Of course, it goes without saying that I will mention nothing.'

'Not even to your staff, please.'

'Naturally; my lips are sealed, you may be sure of that.'

'Thank you.'

After Cunningham had left, Alex and Anna went outside to their car. While they sat there pondering on what had taken place inside, Anna asked if she should call Tom to see if he'd seen anything yet, seeing as how he'd been on "observation" for some time.

'Good idea, he may've seen something. Give him a bell.'

Anna called Tom's mobile and he answered quickly.

'DC Peterson.'

'Hi Tom, its DS Jenkins. How're things over there on Oyster Island?'

'Hi Sarge, things are not too bad; in fact, it's bloody interesting, the way they grow the oysters from seed. I didn't know they had so many oysters growing around here.'

'I'm sure it is, but that's not what you're there for, certainly not scoffing freebies; what, if anything, is happening?

'Nothing at the moment Sarge, but I've got a great view from here, so if they show up, I could get some good shots of them.'

'What about later on when it's dark, do you think you could still get photographs?'

'I think so, with this camera, it's surprising just how good low-light shots can be.'

'Okay, let's just hope that we can get something which could be used as evidence.'

'Do you know when they're likely to come then Sarge?'

'We don't know where they are at the moment, but we'll keep you informed.'

'I thought you had a tracker on board, how come you've lost them?'

'That's a good question Tom. It seems like the battery has died just when we needed it.'

'That's tough; we need a break don't we?'

'We certainly do; anyway keep your eyes open, I'm afraid this could be a long wait.'

'No problem, it's quite nice sitting here watching the goings-on in the harbour and I think the rest is doing me good.'

'That's good Tom, get yourself right again and back in the saddle again soon.'

'Will do Sarge,' he said, and went back to his protracted observation.

Back in the car, and turning to Alex, she posed the question, 'If they have a load of provisions and a full fuel tank, surely that can only mean that they are about to take a long trip; maybe across the Channel again?'

'I think you are exactly right Anna. What bothers me though is how can we stop them if they decide to make a dash for it? We just don't have the resources to intercept them on the water and they can be really fast. I mean, we just don't have any craft that could keep up with them do we?'

'Unless they stop at the Whaler over by "Othniel," that could be pretty difficult, I can see that.'

Why wouldn't they stop to pick up the bodies though, surely that is a "given"; they can't leave them there for Christ's sake, they'll turn into liquid?'

'Ugh, that is so gruesome but do you think they know that we know about the bodies then Alex?'

'I don't think they do; at least I hope not. I don't see how they would know as they don't seem to know that we've been over to the shed on Goathorn.'

'Do you think we should have left someone there to keep watch for them?'

There was an incoming call which Alex took. 'Hello, DCI Vail.'

'Inspector Vail, this is the duty officer at the RNLI Poole. You asked us if any of our chaps had seen the Redbay Stormforce 11 boat, anywhere around the harbour today.'

'Yes, did you have any luck?'

'We did.'

Alex looked quickly over to Anna and gave the "thumbs-up," accompanied by a smile. He switched his phone to "speaker" so that Anna could hear the conversation.

'A couple of our chaps in an "Inshore Rescue RIB" were on a training run and they came across "Predator" around the entrance to the River Frome. I think they stopped her just to admire the boat; it's not every day that one sees such a craft around.'

'And do you think the boat was going after that?'

'The two men on the boat, that they saw anyway, said they were going up to "The Granary" restaurant at Ridge Wharf to meet some friends for a meal.'

'And do you think that's possible, I mean, I know that the Frome isn't a deep river and that boat must have quite a draught?'

'You're quite right, it is quite shallow, but I guess that such a craft would have electronic depth finders on board, and they have jet drives so that they can manoeuvre in very shallow water, although one would think that they'd checked the tide times before attempting a run up there.'

Anna raised a finger to Alex for him to pause the call. 'Just a moment, if you would,' he said to the officer.'

'Do you really think that they've gone up to Ridge Wharf,' asked Anna, 'I mean why would they, with a full load of fuel and provisions? Wouldn't they just moor up and wait for night so that they could make a dash across the Channel?'

Alex nodded and spoke to the duty officer again. 'Would there be a place for this boat to moor up for a while, say until dark?'

'Oh yes, I'd say there were a number of unused mooring buoys up there, especially at this time of year with so many yachts out on the water, so yes, they could easily moor up and wait for a while.'

'Right, many thanks for your information, it's been very helpful. We need to know what this boat and its crew are up to, so we're keeping our eyes open. If you hear or see any more of this boat, perhaps you could let us know at once.'

'Of course, glad to be of help.'

'Oh, one other thing you might be able to help us with; is it possible to track the movements of all boats in the English Channel?'

'Certainly, using the AIS system.'

'And that is?'

'That's the Automatic Identification System used on board all vessels. It enables GPS tracking with full details of position, speed and all the information necessary to keep track of a vessel.'

'And this "Predator" would have this on board?'

'I would certainly think so, but if they don't want themselves tracked, then they wouldn't have the AIS box working and they would be invisible to the system. That would make them vulnerable though, for sure, as the Channel is such a busy shipping lane, with so many ships. They would have to have something to warn them of other vessels I would think, maybe they have radar.'

'Thanks again for all this information. We will have to think of a way of keeping tabs on them.'

'No problem, good luck.'

Finishing the call, Alex turned to Anna and said, 'we're on a hiding to nothing here. Even if these guys do have this AIS system that this RNLI chap mentioned, I really doubt whether they would use it so that they keep literally "under the radar." What do you think?'

'I agree. Unless we could get the Coastguard to chase them, we don't have a way of stopping them getting out of the harbour, do we?'

'I don't think so. I do know that the Coastguard only have quite large "cutters" and they are not particularly fast, certainly not fast enough to catch these guys. I think our only way is to either catch them as they collect the bodies, if that's what they're going to do, or wait until they come back.'

'If they go over to France, and we think to collect illegals, or drugs, or whatever, then they'll come back won't they?'

'Well, yes, but will they bring them back here or take them somewhere else? If they land them on another part of the coast, we'll never find them. How the hell do we keep tabs on them without the tracker?'

'Damn those tech blokes, Alex said, 'they said it would last and now it's given us a whole load of extra problems, just when we thought we were getting somewhere. I'm going to have someone's balls for this.'

'We must get another tracker on to the boat somehow. I don't know how, but there must be a way.'

'Just a thought,' said Anna. 'How about if we can find them wherever they've moored up in the River Frome, could we get one of the Dorset Police Maritime Section to have a diver get to the boat, unnoticed if it's dark, and put a new tracker on the boat somewhere?'

'That's a bit of a "James Bond" type operation, but just perhaps, just maybe, it could be a possibility Anna; hell, let's give it a try. At least if it is possible and we can do it, we'll know where they are, as we hoped in the first place and we can keep tabs on them.

Alex placed a call to the technical section of the Dorset Police and spoke to his old friend Peter Tomlinson.
'Hi Peter, Alex Vail here, I need a word with you.'
'Oh, hi Alex, what can I do for you?'
'It's about that tracker you supplied for our tagging a particular boat here in Poole Harbour, do you remember?'
'Yes, I know we had to put some fixing material to the back, so it could be put on to fibreglass, if I remember correctly.'
'Yes, that's right, and that bit worked, but the problem is that you said the battery would last for a few days, but it actually failed after only two days and now we've lost track of the boat; well almost anyway, and it's put our plans in jeopardy, to say the least.'
'Oh Christ, I'm sorry Alex, I really thought that the battery would last. I'll check into it; I can only assume that it had been partly used and not re-charged properly, or the battery would not hold a charge; but that's no help to you is it?'
'Not really, but we do have a window of opportunity if you can help now.'
'Sure, whatever I can do.'
'We think we might know where the boat is right now, waiting for the tide and darkness to make a dash for it. I won't go into full details, just to say that we need to get a tracker; that works; onto the boat somehow without the two on board noticing.'
'We can certainly supply another one quickly, but will whoever fits this, be able to get on board or will they have to put it on the outside of the boat?'
'Well, I'm thinking that we might be able to get a diver to approach the boat in the darkness, underwater, and get to the boat, but I doubt very much if he would be also to actually get on board, so I think we have to find a way of fixing it outside, where it won't be dislodged by high speed on the water. This boat does something like 35 knots.'
'Bloody hell, that's fast and the tracker would have to be fixed pretty well to stand that sort of force.'
'I know, that's our major problem as I see it. Do you have any ideas, I mean, you're the specialists, I'm only a plod with this clever stuff.'
'Let me give it some thought Alex, I'll get something organised and let you know just as soon as I can.'
'Okay Peter, thanks. In the meantime I'll get on to the Underwater Section and see if they have someone who could pull this off, and I don't mean pull off the tracker.'
'I didn't really think you did,' said Peter with a chuckle.'

Alex then called the Underwater Section to see if they could help. After explaining the particular problem to their head of operations, he was told that they could indeed supply a diver who could approach the boat and fix the device, providing that the fixing could be achieved.
Anna, who was, of course listening to this conversation and how it was transpiring, motioned again to Alex that she had a question.
Alex asked the section head to hang on for a moment and turning to Anna he raised his eyebrows in query. She then said, 'what about the bubbles from the diver, wouldn't they be seen if they happened to look out over the river?'
'That's a very good point; I'll ask him about that.'
Speaking again to the section officer, he said, 'I've just been advised that the bubbles from the divers' Scuba gear might give the game away. Is there anything that could be done about that?'
There was a chuckle from the other end, 'Well yes, if the water was still, the bubbles would not only show but they'd make some sort of noise as well, and I don't think our diver could hold his breath long enough for a clandestine approach...but there is a way I think. The way I would suggest is by using a "re-breather unit." This emits no bubbles at all, and they are used for underwater photography mainly where bubbles cause a lot of problems. The only trouble is that we don't have any at this station.'
'Damn, that's going to be a problem then, isn't it? Do you have any suggestions?'

'I'd think the best thing you can do is to approach a Scuba diving centre, we have one here in Bournemouth, I don't know if you know of it?'

Alex looked over to Anna and asked, 'Didn't you go to that diving centre to ask about air tanks or something?'

'Yes, I did; maybe they can help?'

'Yes, we do know of them. I'll give them a call right away, and thanks for your help.' He ended the call and turned to Anna. 'Give them a call would you and if necessary, go over there and chat 'em up. I'm sure you can get their help.'

Anna called the dive centre in Bournemouth which she had visited before. The call was answered by an Australian accented voice. 'Hello, this is Marcus at the Dive Centre; do you want to go diving today?'

'Hello Marcus. Not today thanks, but who knows, one day maybe; but you can help. I did come to see you guys before about air tanks and you were very helpful. By the way, this is DS Jenkins from Bournemouth Police.'

'Oh yeah, g'day; I remember you; very tasty for a copper.'

Oh dear, thought Anna, I'll have to go through this again, but all in the line of duty.

'Thanks for the compliment, but I'm in a real hurry as we have an urgent problem which I think you may be able to help us with.'

'Glad to be of help to our local force. What can I do?'

'Okay, firstly, can you assure me of your confidentiality, as we are working on a very serious case and we need to keep total secrecy at the moment?'

'Yeah, sure, no problem, mum's the word and all that.'

'Good. We need to get a small unit fixed to a boat which has two men aboard, without them being aware of anything. What I mean is we need to have someone approach the boat completely unseen.'

'I guess your Police Underwater Unit could do that, couldn't they?'

'Yes, they could, but we think the bubbles would be spotted and that would compromise the whole operation.'

'Gotcha; yeah, that would be a bummer, so I guess you need a re-breather unit which releases no bubbles.'

'That's exactly what we think we need and our lads don't have any, so my question is, do you have such a unit?'

'We surely do. We have a "KISS®" re-breather unit; it's a beaut.'

'And does that mean that a diver can approach without being seen?'

'Absolutely, unless the water is crystal clear and that won't be anywhere around here will it?'

'I don't think so; do you have someone who could do this for us, very quickly, as we need to get this done right away?'

'They have to be trained and I suppose the only one who's available at the moment, is me; will I do?'

Anna remembered him as a muscular, very bronzed man with dazzling white teeth. She put this thought right away and said, 'That would be great, thanks. Can I get back to you when we have the item we need fixing.'

'Sure, no worries; just let me know where and when and I can get kitted up.'

'Great Marcus, I'll get right back to you.'

'Reckon that'll do. G'day Anna.'

Anna ended the call and turned back to Alex. 'Yes, they have a re-breather unit and Marcus, the boss there says he can do the job for us. He just needs to know where and when and he'll be ready. Do we have another tracker then?'

'I'm waiting for a call back from Peter Tomlinson of the tech department. As he said this, his phone emitted his usual bleeping, indicating an incoming call.

'DCI Vail.'

'Hi Alex, Peter from the technical department, or as you say, "Pete the Tec."'

'Hello Pete, what do you have?'

'We have another and this time more powerful tracker. Same procedure as last time, direct link back to the office computer, and this time with a fully charged and new battery, so it should give you at least four days of continuous use, if not more.'

'That's good news. How about fixing it to the boat?'

'Well, I thought about that and what bothers me is that we can't use magnets for obvious reasons, not only because that would affect the tracker, but magnets don't really stick well to fibreglass do they?'

'Shit, you're right, so what can we do?'

'The only thing I can suggest is that you use an underwater adhesive, something that is used for swimming pool repairs. I do know of one such called "Underwater Magic™" and that's supposed to be pretty good. I would think that if that's used and the tracker put on the stern, it would take the least punishment from the turbulence at speed.'

'Do you have any?'

'Nope, but I'm sure that you can soon track some down.'

'Okay, we'll get on to it. I'll have a car come to collect the tracker as quickly as I can. Thanks Pete. Let's just hope that this time it works and we get a chance of keeping tabs on these bastards.'

'Right'o mate, good luck.'

Anna had heard this exchange and she said, 'I'll get back on to the dive centre, they're bound to have something.' Without waiting for an answer, she called the dive centre again. Once again Marcus answered, and she didn't wait for introductions. 'Marcus, it's Anna Jenkins again; do you have any underwater adhesive that we can use to fix a small unit to a fibreglass hull?'

'Yeah, we use that stuff all the time, its bloody great. Called "Underwater Magic®" and it's a one-pack polymer which is pretty well instant. The only problem is that it has to be squirted on to the unit or fabric if you're going to use that, with one of those "sealing guns" that they use for, you know, sealing round bathtubs with silicone. But that shouldn't be too much of a problem to be honest. We have those things, so all I need to know is what is going to be stuck and how big it is.'

'As far as I know it's about 50 millimetres across and quite thin, so maybe a piece of fabric would cover this and give you better adhesive area make a good bond.'

'You seem to know what you are talking about; I'm impressed. Not many girls would have a clue.'

'Thanks for the compliment, but we do have a fair share of brains in our department.'

'Don't mean to be patronising; so, sorry.'

'As you would say, "no worries."'

'Gotcha,' he said, 'fair dinkum; you're speaking ozzie just like a native. Just get back to me with the time and we're off.'

'Great, thanks Marcus. Just let me have your invoice when the job's done and we'll settle up. This goes on our expenses, so not too expensive please.'

'Okay, so costing no big bikkies then?'

'Sorry, and I thought French was difficult?'

'That's Oz for not too expensive, but I could be paid in other ways, if you know what I mean.' He'd said this with a very "knowing" sound to his voice.

'I'm sorry; I don't know what you mean,' she said in a very stern voice. 'I have to go, sorry.'

'Okay, right, see ya later.'

'Bye.'

Back with Alex; 'Do we have the tracker guv?'

'We have a car on the way to pick it up, so let's find out exactly where to take the diver so he can get into the river without being seen.'

'But we don't know where "Predator" is yet, do we guv?'

'No, but if we get someone to go up the river in a small boat with an outboard motor, we can spot it without raising any suspicions I would think. Do we know anyone with a small boat, by any chance?' He said this with no real expectation of a good response. He was wrong.

'I have a friend whose boyfriend has a little runabout, maybe she could ask him. I know he works from home so he should be free. I'll give her a call.'

'That would be great and it'll save the diver from having so swim halfway up the river looking for it. If you can give your friend a ring, I'll get Alice to look on Google Earth for a suitable spot for the diver.'

'Will do, but perhaps we ought to tell Marcus what sort of boat to look out for, it should be easy to spot as it's so unusual isn't it?'

'Good idea. Yes, we don't want him swimming up and down just on the off-chance of spotting it.'

Alex went over to where Alice was working on other enquiries, which were all part of the everyday working of a CID office. 'Alice, can you pull up a picture of the area around the River Frome; we're looking for a suitable spot to get a car close to the river so that we can get a diver into the water unseen.'

'Sure thing guv. Can I ask why we have a diver and what's he going to do?'

'Sorry, there's been a lot going on, but briefly, we have to get another tracker fixed to "Predator" and we think it's moored somewhere in the river, waiting for nightfall so they can make a getaway unseen. If we can get a properly working tracker on board, we can keep it monitored. We've a new and working one being collected and we have a diver waiting for instructions, ready to go, so we need directions and location for him.'

'Understood; I'll get the location and check it out. I'll give you a shout when I have something.'

'Good girl; thanks Alice,' and she entered the appropriate details for the map of the area.

Finding the river Frome she checked out all the possible roads which might give access to a place where a diver could enter unseen. There were very few roads and in fact no roads to where it was easy, but she did find one possibility; in fact, probably the only one. Knocking on Alex's office door, which was partly open, she looked in. 'Come in Alice, have you found something?'

'Yes, guv, there aren't many places where you can approach the river from a road and I think the only place that would be suitable is just outside Wareham. There's a bed and breakfast place I've found on the map and I think there might be a track down to where a boat is docked in what looks like a private mooring. I'd think that a 4x4 would get there without any problem.'

'Super; could you see any mooring possibilities for this "Predator" boat there?'

'Yes guv, I could see a number of empty buoys, although they could be used now, but I'd think there's a very good chance that our boat has moored at the first one they came to, if they're going to make a run for it, don't you?'

'I'd say that's a given, Alice; good work. If you can give me the GPS co-ordinates, I can get the "4x4 Defender" from the car pool again and pick up our diver. I think we have someone who has a small boat who will be able to take a run down the river to see if they can spot "Predator." That would save a great deal of time and trouble.'

'Right,' agreed Alice, 'and if you tell the diver and this chap who will go in his boat that the first moorings begin after the first big bend in the river after you leave the harbour. I'm sure that's where "Predator" is likely to be moored. Just come and take a look at my screen, I have the satellite picture up at the moment and you can see exactly what I mean.'

'Okay, just hang on while I get Anna to take a look, because she's the one who will take Marcus over there. Can you take a print-out for her?'

'Absolutely.'

As she was doing this Anna joined them and they all looked at the computer screen which showed the location of the mooring buoys which may be used by "Predator."

Anna said that she'd talked to her friend and her boyfriend was more than happy to be involved in a police investigation and he was ready to go down to Evening Hill in Poole Harbour where his little speedboat was kept. I said we'd reimburse him for his time and trouble. Is that okay guv?'

'Of course; we don't have the resources for this, so whatever it takes, I'm not going to let these bastards slip through our fingers.'

'Not like the last time eh guv?'

'Thanks for reminding me Anna,' he said with heavy irony. 'Right, give him a description of the boat and tell him to get "under way" as soon as he possibly can and to give us a call the moment he spots it.'

Anna made the call and things began to move quickly.

'Anna, can you get the defender from the car pool, get over to the Dive Centre and pick up this Marcus character and get yourselves over to the place that Alice has indicated on the Google Map?'

'Do I have to go alone guv?'

'You're a big girl now; you don't need me to hold your hand.'

"I'd like you to," she thought, but said, 'It's not that; it's just that this Marcus is pretty "pushy" and I don't want to have to fight him off. I think he might try something, even though we're police. I really don't want to take the risk, if you follow me?'

'Has he said anything then?'

'Let's just say that he's just a little too forward for my liking, shall we?'

Alex thought this over for a couple of seconds and realised that once again, he had the problem of another male who realised that Anna was very attractive and his mild jealousy came bubbling up. In an attempt to keep this under control, he agreed to accompany Anna on this, very important journey. It was their chance to regain the upper hand in keeping this boat in view and possibly catching the murderers with cast–iron evidence in the form of the two bodies currently left on board the Boston Whaler, moored in Poole Harbour.

'Okay, it might be better if there were two of us, just in case extra pair of hands are necessary.' He was actually thinking that it would only be his hands that were the extra ones needed.

Alex phoned down to the car pool and spoke to Philip Mason the head of the section.

'Hi Philip, DCI Vail here. I need a "Defender" quickly please; I just hope you have one available. We need to get a diver over to Wareham as quickly as possible.'

'It just so happens that you're in luck. One has just come back. Just let me get it checked over and it's yours. Just get the paperwork sorted and it'll be ready.'

'Nice one Philip; thanks. I'll let you know as soon as we're ready this end.'

'Okay.'

'Anna, I think we've just got time to grab some lunch before your friend's boyfriend makes his trip over to the river and let's just hope that he spots "Predator".'

Okay guv, I'll just let the others know our movements and I'll be with you.'

Anna went over to Alice who was at her computer. 'Alice, Alex and I will be taking the diver over to Wareham right after we've had a spot of lunch. We'll go over and pick him and his gear up and then take him to where we hope my specially recruited "boatspotter" will find "Predator."'

'Is this "boatspotter" one of ours then?'

'No, he's a friend of a friend who happens to have a small boat and he's going to dash over to the River Frome to see if he can see "Predator," without raising suspicion. We think they're waiting for dark to make a dash for it.'

'So what's the diver for then?'

'He's going to fix the new GPS tracker to "Predator" without being seen. He's going to use special SCUBA gear that doesn't make any bubbles so that he can approach completely unseen.'

'Let's just hope this one works better than the last one. It seems that Tom got beaten up with no real result doesn't it?'

"Fraid so,' said Anna.

'Have a good lunch, you two,' she said with slightly longer look and a "knowing" glance with very slightly raised eyebrows, which made Anna's pulse stop for a couple of seconds.

Quickly regaining her composure, Anna retorted offhandedly, 'It'll only be a quick burger.' Alice was actually thinking rather ironically, "of course," but Alice being Alice, she said nothing more, except, 'have a good lunch.'

CHAPTER 46

The car which had collected the new GPS tracker from the technical department had arrived back at the station. 'Great,' said Alex, 'we're all set now. All we need is word from our "boatspotter" that he's found "Predator" and we're good to go. Shall we grab a quick burger?'

They were outside the station and as they crossed to the car park, Alex said, I think we'd better just nip to that place on Lansdowne Crescent, if we're lucky there might be a parking space just outside.'

'No time for a gourmet three star meal then guv?'

'No, you muppet, that's to come later I hope.'

'That would be nice, we've not had much chance lately have we?'

They had a short drive to the burger bar in Lansdowne Crescent and as luck would have it, there was a vacant parking space right outside. On the short drive, Alex said, 'We must have another night together very soon; I miss you with all this going on.'

'I look forward to that more than you realise, I think. It's been too long. It is so hard keeping a low profile to the others and I have a sneaking suspicion that Alice knows something.'

'Has she said anything?'

'No, but she gave me a look just now which made me think she had some inkling, but if I know Alice, she won't say anything to anyone.'

'Just make it known to her that we know about her friendship with the head of Forensics; that should keep her head down.'

'That's mean, Alex.'

'Maybe, but effective, I should think.'

Alex had just taken a large mouthful of his "delicious" burger when there was an incoming call, but it proved to be Anna's phone. It was her friend Paula, to say that she'd had a call from her boyfriend on his boat.

'Has he found the boat Paula?'

'I think so; do you want his number so you can talk to him directly?'

'Yes, please.' Paula passed the number directly, saying 'I'll get off the line so you can get on to him. Good luck.'

'Thanks Paula.'

Quickly calling the new number, it was answered directly. 'Hi, this is Jim, is that Paula's friend Sergeant Jenkins?'

'Yes, hi Jim, I understand that you've found "Predator"?'

'I sure have. She's moored up just round the first bend as you go into the river, on the second mooring buoy. She's also facing out of the river, so they must have turned her round before mooring; not too easy with a boat of her size I'd have thought, but they're moored fore and aft to buoys to keep the boat steady on a rising tide.'

'That's absolutely fantastic Jim, you've been extremely helpful and we really appreciate this. It'll enable us to carry on with our plans now and it's saved us a shedload of work, believe me. Finally, just let us have a bill for your time and trouble and I'll make sure it's handled quickly.'

'Okay, thanks, no hurry.'

'Right, thanks again, must go and get moving now.'

She turned to Alex and told him the news, which made him quite excited. 'Yes! We can get these bastards tracked again and this time we make no mistakes.' He was chewing his burger with renewed enthusiasm, as that was what was actually needed.

Anna cleared the call and immediately called the dive centre to speak to Marcus.

'Marcus, DS Vail, Dorset Police.'

'G'day Anna, have you found the boat then?'

'We have.'

'Bonzer, I'm ready to go when you are.'

'Right, we'll be there to collect you and your gear in about 20 minutes, is that okay with you?'

'Sure is, I'm all togged up and ready to go with me squirter in me hand.'

This gave Anna a very fleeting and most unseemly vision, which she very quickly dismissed by saying, 'Pardon?'

'I mean I have my special adhesive gun ready to go.'

Thank heavens for that, she thought, 'Oh, right, good. We'll see you shortly, 'bye.'

'Right, let's go,' said Alex, taking a final slurp on his drink; they went back to the car pool to get the keys for the Defender. Making their way as quickly as possible to the Dive Centre at West Howe. As soon as they pulled up, Marcus was waiting at the door, already dressed in his wetsuit.

'G'day Anna, 'he said, and looking past her, he spotted Alex getting out of the vehicle on the other side. His face fell briefly, but recovered to say, 'Hi, you must be Anna's boss then.'

'Yes, Detective Chief Inspector Vail,' and held out his hand, saying, 'this is very good of you to help us out. Our Marine Section doesn't have this sort of specialised equipment and we think that this could play a very special role in our investigation.'

'Not a problem mate, glad to help out. Let's get going if you're ready.'

'Okay, do you need a hand with your gear?'

'No thanks, if you don't mind, I'll handle the re-breather unit. I like to handle the stuff that's going to keep me alive and then it's only me that's to blame if I don't come back up.'

'Don't put it like that Marcus,' said Anna in alarm.

'Don't worry, she'll be right.'

'Who, is there someone else coming with us?'

'No, sorry, it's me Aussie slang again; it means "everything's going to be alright."

'Okay mate, gotcha,' said Anna, pointing her finger like a gun, at Marcus.

This evoked a big grin from Marcus causing a flash of his brilliant white teeth highlighted by his bronzed face.

'Okay DCI Vail, if you'd like to plant yer foot Anna, we can get this show on the road.'

'I think he means, "drive quickly" guv,' said Anna.

As they all got into the Defender, Marcus carefully placed his special unit in the rear and slammed the door. Jumping in, he said, 'D'ya know I think this sheila's getting the hang of a new language.'

'This "Sheila" is actually a police sergeant I'll have you know Marcus,' said Anna huffily, although she only said this for Alex's benefit, if she were truthful.

'Sorry sarge, I'll mind me manners.'

Alex was quite amused by all this banter, but he said, 'Shall we just get there?'

Anna was once again driving and this gave Alex time to talk to Tom who was sitting on his thumbs and waiting for something to happen.

'Tom, how're things over there, I know you won't have seen them yet as we've discovered that they are holed up in the River Frome and we think they're waiting for nightfall to make their move.'

Alex heard a rather exasperated sigh from Tom. 'Sorry that you're stuck on that place, but we simply have to keep track of them; if they do go to the Whaler and move the "you know what", we have to be ready for them."

'If you know where they are now guv, how will you keep tabs on them when they move?'

'Ah, well, we have a new tracker and this time we have to fix it onto the boat without them seeing this taking place.'

'How the hell will you do that?'

'I won't, but we have someone who will. We have a diver with SCUBA gear that doesn't give out bubbles and he's going to approach the boat unseen and stick the new tracker with underwater glue.'

'Sounds good; just hope it works, but supposing they spot the diver near the boat?'

'Is the water that clear?'

'No, I suppose not, well not here anyway.'

'It has to work this time. We'll keep a close eye on them and as soon as they move, we'll know.'

'Yeah guv, but how are we going to catch them on the water, I mean if they come to the Whaler and I spot them?'

'That's our next problem. I'm going to contact our Marine section; I know they have a RIB with twin outboards. I think they'll be able to help in that direction. I'll keep you in touch Tom, stick with it. How're the ribs by the way, any better?'

'Yes, thanks guv, with this rest it's helping, although I'm getting stir crazy, but at least there are things to look at. There are a few boats with some good looking girls going by.'

'I'd have thought that you'd have had enough of good looking girls for a while, Tom.'

'When I'm back on duty properly, I'm going to have a word with Genny Dobbs.'

'I think you'd better hang fire on that lad, because there's a very good chance that she'll be charged with being an "accessory" because she knows Goodyear and she probably has been feeding him information; something we'll have to find out.'

'Right guv; actually, I'd like to wring her neck.'

'I didn't hear that.'

'No guv.'

'Okay, it shouldn't be too long to wait now, so keep your eyes peeled.

'Eyes peeled guv.'

Alex then placed a call to the Marine Section Duty Officer Paul Rickson.

'Sergeant Rickson, Marine Unit,' was the response to the call.

Hello Sergeant, this is DCI Vail of Madeira Road. I wonder if I can ask for your help on a case which has come to a rather quick head and we need some marine assistance.'

'Okay, DCI Vail let me have some details and I'll see what we can do.'

'Right, thanks; I'll be as brief as I can. We have a murder case which has spiralled into two more which we know about, possibly more. We have one body but the following two are still on board a boat which is moored in the harbour, close to Brownsea Island. We have one of our chaps keeping watch on this boat, a Boston Whaler, moored close to the "Othniel" oyster farm island. He can give us immediate sight of the boat which we think will come to collect the two bodies. What will be done with them is a matter of guesswork at this moment.'

'So I guess you will need some bodies to stop this other boat and catch them in the act of transfer, if I have the right idea?'

'Exactly; the boat we are waiting for is actually moored up in the River Frome and we are about to have a tracker covertly fixed to the boat so we'll know their precise movements. '

'If they're keeping their heads down, they won't have their AIS active, that's for sure, and they won't be contactable by radio, I'd imagine.'

'I think that's a given. Do you have any boats available at short notice that can give us a hand?'

'As you probably know, we have two fast boats, one is a RIB and she has two big outboards, so has the speed for a chase, and the other is the big Police boat which has more muscle but isn't so fast. I know we can get the RIB on stand-by, but I'll have to check on the big boy. Can I come back to you on that?'

'Okay, fine, but you'll understand that we have to get things ready for some quick action as soon as we know they're on the move.'

'I appreciate that and I'll get on to it immediately.'

'Thanks Sergeant,' Alex said, ending the call.

Anna asked if the Marine Unit could help and Alex said, 'Yes, they can help with a RIB but they're not sure about the big boat. We should know pretty soon.

Alex turned round and said, 'Marcus, I think you understand that what you hear is extremely confidential, especially at the moment as no arrests have been made and should any of this information get to be public, it could compromise our actions at the court stages.'

'Sure Inspector, understood. No worries, she'll be right, there'll be no yabber from me; I'll keep all this to meself.'

Anna had entered the GPS co-ordinates which Alice had given her, of the bed and breakfast premises close to where the suspected boat was moored. They were soon turning left and just out of Wareham.' Where the hell are we Anna, I can't see any sign of the river?'

'We're in Bestwall Road guv and we take the track where there's a sharp left in the road before we get to the guest house. If we take that track, it leads us down to the river where we can get Marcus in without being seen by anyone.'

'How do you know he won't be seen, are we going to be a long way from "Predator"?'

'Actually, no guv; from the satellite picture I saw with Alice, there is a private mooring with a big white cruiser there; perhaps it's gone, but it does give us a great place well out of sight of where we now know "Predator" is.'

'Okay, fine, let's just hope you're right.'

CHAPTER 47

Reaching the sharp left turn, they turned onto the track which would lead to the private mooring. On this last leg of their trip, Alex took a phone call. This was from the Marine Unit Duty Officer.

'Hello, is that DCI Vail?'

'Yes, I hope you're Sergeant Rickson.'

'Yes. I've got some good news and some not so good news.'

Alex was thinking, "Oh shit, now what's going wrong?" 'Okay, give me the good news first then.'

'We can get the RIB out to your Whaler, or at least on standby somewhere out of sight, ready for instructions, but the bad news is that we can't get the big boy as she's out on Border Patrol along the coast and won't be back until late tonight.'

'I suppose the RIB is better than nothing, although maybe I should have mentioned that the boat we are tracking is a "Redbay Stormforce 11," does that mean anything to you?'

'Indeed it does, I know that boat, I've seen her quite a few times, a real beauty, and I know she's very fast.'

'Well, that's the rub. If she gets away, we've nothing that will catch her have we?'

'That's very true, so maybe we should make sure that we can make the arrest at the right time, to make sure that they don't do a runner. Is the suspect aboard now?'

'Yes, but there are two and we don't know at this stage if they are armed. With three murders so far, I don't think they'll have much to lose if they put up a fight.'

'Do you think we should have armed response on standby?'

'I think if I can get things organised quickly enough, that's a good idea.'

'As they would be on our boat, should I contact AR and arrange this?'

'That would be helpful Rickson, thanks. I'll leave it to you to sort out but please keep me informed.'

'Yes, will do.'

They were bumping down the track and after about 300 yards, came to the small but very private mooring where there was a landing stage but no boat tied up. 'This is it,' said Anna, parking just behind some bushes.' Alex took a look around, 'This looks ideal. We can't see the river, so they can't see us. From what Alice said "Predator" should be just beyond this cut and to the right. Are you ready to go Marcus?' he asked, turning round to check.

'Sure thing cobber, let's get this thing fixed. Do you have any preference as to where it should go?'

'I suppose it should be where there will be least disturbance, so maybe on the stern?'

'Sounds bonzer, do you want it below the waterline or above?'

What's all this "cobber" and "bonzer" stuff; I suppose its ozzie slang, thought Alex.

'I think it'd be better out of the water as there will be lots of turbulence, and I don't want this thing ripped off.'

'Right'o chief, I've got the gun and patch ready, so all I need is the tracker; switched on mind, and we can do it.'

Alex took the tracker from the package and following instructions from the technical department, activated the unit and passed it to Marcus. 'Hang on, I think we'd better check that it's working; I'll just contact Alice back at base to see if she's receiving.'

Anna had already been dialling the number as Alex had said this. Alice answered almost immediately and the phone was passed to Alex, who responded with a nod and expression which showed his appreciation.

'Alice, DCI Vail here, can you check to see if you have a signal as I've just activated the unit.'

'I was ahead of you guv, I saw the "blip" come up just as you must have done that. A good clear signal and it's just a little way from where we think "Predator" is moored. Can you see it?'

'No, we're parked just out of view of the river but Marcus is just about to go into the water and fix the unit. Keep a close watch on this now as we expect it to move sometime just after dark.'

'Will do guv.'

'Okay Marcus, whenever you're ready.'

He already had the re-breather set fitted on his back and taking hold of the huge flippers in one hand, and his mask in the other, he said, 'Can one of you bring the adhesive gun and the tracker with that patch of fabric which I'll use to give a good seal?'

Anna said,' I'll take that guv.'

They walked the few yards to the timber landing stage and Marcus sat on the edge while he fitted his flippers.

He said, 'Before I test the set to make sure everything is working, I'll just glue the tracker to the patch. He used the adhesive gun and ran a small amount on to the patch and then pushed the tracker into the mound which had formed. 'That'll do the trick; she shouldn't come off, this stuff's stickier than a gecko's toes.'

That made Anna laugh out loud.

Alex was thinking of a more 'English' expression.

'Hey girl, you've got a lovely laugh, y'know, real sexy.'

'Enough, you've got things to do.'

'Yeah, and I've got to stick this thing as well,' he said with a brilliant but cheeky grin.

Fitting his mask and mouthpiece, he slipped into the water and disappeared below the surface. After a few moments and no sign of any bubbles, he re-appeared. Holding out his hand, she passed him the gun and the patch.

He disappeared beneath the water with barely a ripple and all she could see was the gentle movement of the large fins disappearing into the murky water.

Moving into the river, he turned to the right and very soon he saw the shape of a boat above him. Slowing his movements, he approached the stern of the boat and although it was blurry, he was able to make out the name, but it wasn't "Predator." Sinking down to the river bed, he moved further until another shape appeared in the murk above him. He did the same thing and rose nearer the surface. This time, it was the bow of a boat and he remembered that someone had said that "Predator" had been moored facing downriver, so perhaps this was the one. Making his way to the stern of the boat, he repeated the manoeuvre and looked up at the name which was quite visible as it was in quite large lettering. "Predator."

Okay, here goes, he thought. Tucking himself well under the boat, he held the patch with the tracker now firmly adhered to it, against the hull while he used the gun to run some more lines of adhesive to the material. When he was satisfied that there was sufficient, he let go of the gun and let it hang by the cord which he'd put round his neck. Moving gently, he very carefully raised his head just above the water line and looked up. There was nobody looking over the stern, so he pressed the patch as firmly as he could, just above the water level. That should do it, he thought. This blighter won't come off, not with all that stuff, it's as sticky as a swagman's shirt in summer.

Alex and Anna were both waiting on the landing stage. She said, 'Can we make a date while we're waiting? I'd love to have another night together, it's been too long.'

'Yes, can we make it sometime next week, so that by then, hopefully, this mess will be behind us and we can relax a bit?'

'Okay, that sounds good. I'll check our movements when we get back.'

'I know the movements that you'll like Anna; well you did the last time.' He was looking at her with a very meaningful expression.

'I've got some others planned,' she said with her head slightly lowered, looking at him from under hooded eyes.

'Look out, he's back.'

Satisfied with his placing and its adhesion, and sinking back down into the relatively murky water, Marcus had made his way back to the landing stage.

A hand appeared above the water holding up the glue gun, swiftly followed by a mask, which was summarily pulled off together with the breathing gear.

'How did it go?'

'Great, no worries, she was the second boat along. Your bloke who spotted her was right; she was moored with the current, not the usual way facing upriver. I guess they did that so that they could make a quick move when the time was right.'

'That was our thinking too. You've done a great job Marcus and we appreciate your efforts.'

'I guess that was probably the only way to get the tracker on to the boat. Couldn't you have done that before when it was moored up at Cobbs Quay?'

'How do you know it was moored up there Marcus?' asked Anna.

'We get to know quite a bit about the various boats, especially unusual ones and even more so when the bloke who owns it is a diver.'

'For a start, we did fit a tracker to it up there, and one of our chaps was assaulted and quite badly injured when he did that; but that's another story. That tracker failed which is why we've had to do it this way, thanks to your special breathing gear. Anyway, what's the connection with the owner being a diver then, how do you get that connection?'

'We hear a lot of things about people in the diving community and we just heard that this guy who is supposed to go on fishing trips on this boat, has diving experience.'

'That information ties in with some of the details which had been mentioned about Furkan Dimitriou, or "Freddie" as he is known locally,' said Anna. 'He was a diver at Karpaz Gate Marina in Cyprus, if I remember correctly.'

'You say "supposed" Marcus?'

'Yeah, I guess that this boat is not really suited for fishing, although I don't know much about deep-sea fishing, but all the ones I've seen have a large rear open section for the fishermen to stand to be able to cast, and this boat only has a small stern section and a quite large cabin with seats in. It's more like a fast patrol boat as far as I can see.'

Turning toward Anna, Alex said 'I think you remembered correctly and this also corroborates what we've said before about being a fishing boat. Have you met anyone from this boat then Marcus?'

'No; in fact I've only heard the odd things to be honest. I've actually seen the boat once or twice as she's been either going or coming. Nothing unusual there I suppose.'

'And were there any people on board when you saw it?'

'No just the two of them as when I've seen the boat before.'

'But you've not met either of them off the boat or know anything more about them?'

'No sorry, nothing.'

'Okay, right, I think we're done here so let's get Marcus back to his work.'

Anna phoned through to Alice to tell her that they were leaving and now it was up to her to keep watch on any movement of the boat.

This time, Alex drove the Defender and after dropping Marcus back at the Dive Centre and once again thanking him for his efforts, they returned to their station at Madeira Road. During this short drive, Alex and Anna had arranged for a meal at a local restaurant which they both liked, followed by a nightcap at her flat. They were both looking forward immensely to that with things finally looking like closure to the case; but then they weren't to know what was about to happen.

Arriving back at their station, they both walked up to the first floor where their CID offices were and went directly to see Alice. She was at one of her two computers and one was showing the map of the area where the boat was moored with the new tracker on and working.

'Hi guv, sarge,' she said with a definite note of expectation in her voice.

Alice was a very likeable person and since she and the head of the Forensics department of their force had become "an item," she was much more lively and ebullient. Previously she had felt very much a "wallflower" and was beginning to doubt if she would ever find a life partner. However, since her involvement with Jefffrey, she had actually cut down her intake of Danish Pastries considerably, although she had been asked not to lose too much weight as Jeffrey liked her to be "cuddly" as he put it. "I've got the best of both worlds," she had said to herself, "I've not got to stop my Danish and he's such a nice man, I'm really lucky to have found him." She still didn't realise that it was probably the other way round, as he'd been intending to seek an introduction to her for some time, but he was actually quite shy. In the end, it was their work which proved the matchmaker.

'How's it going Alice?'

'Good guv. We've got a working trace on the boat so all we need now is for it to get moving and go over to the boat where Tom is on watch.'

'I think poor old Tom is probably bored shitless; I know I would be after all this time. Still, if it keeps him from moving about too much, that's more time to get over his injuries, I suppose.'

'As long as he stays awake when the time comes and "Predator" gets there to collect the bodies, if that's what they're going to do that is, which is the main thing.' This was Anna being just a little "righteous" and perhaps being a little hard on Tom, who after all, didn't have to be back on duty although it did help to have someone on protracted watch.

'So all we can do now is to wait for action. I'll call the Marine Section again and see if they're okay with the RIB. If they have a problem, then we have a bigger one. We have to find some way of stopping that bloody boat when they get to the Whaler with the bodies.'

'Are you going to sanction the AR section guv?'

'I think to have some real muscle around when they turn up will be advisable rather than strictly necessary, although we don't know if they're armed or not. I don't want to take that chance, so yes, I've arranged to have some guns on board.'

He then called the Marine Section and spoke again to Paul Rickson. 'Have you managed to sort anything out for me Paul; can we have that RIB?'

'Yes, I've arranged for it to be on standby and from what you said, we should have some action by the time light begins to fade.'

'That's about right. We expect them to make their move when it gets dark enough so that they won't be seen when they make their transfer.'

'Transfer, what are they going to transfer, you didn't mention that before, I don't think?'

'Sorry, I thought I'd told you. We know that there are two bodies which have been left on a Boston Whaler, moored near Brownsea and close to Othniel Oysters unit. We have one of our team on constant watch there and he'll be able to take photos and keep us informed. We think the two on board this boat called "Predator" which we are tracking, will come and pick up the bodies to be dumped, probably somewhere in the channel.'

'And how long have they been on the Whaler?'

'We think for about two days now, although we don't actually know how long they've been dead.'

'Jesus Christ, they're not going to be nice to handle by now then; I wouldn't be surprised if we could smell them from where we are at Poole Quay.'

'Yep, I reckon they're going to be a bit ripe, that's for sure.'

'You said that these guys on "Predator" are armed'

'No idea, but I don't want to take chances; so if possible, I'd like the AR team to be ready.'

'All done and arranged,' said Paul.

'Great, thanks. Just tell them to keep themselves at readiness and I'll keep you informed of any movement. By the time they leave the Frome, we'll have enough warning I'd think.'

CHAPTER 48

Having arranged for an early meal in a local restaurant, Alex and Anna were about to enjoy a relaxing and romantic evening. Alex had driven them to a restaurant not too far from Anna's flat.

'I just hope we're doing the right thing since we have this ongoing case.'

'I think we need to unwind some, don't you Alex?'

'Maybe you're right; I just hope everything is ready and we don't get any more failures. I thought we could walk back to yours afterwards and then I don't have to worry about drinking too much.'

'Good idea Alex, I know you like your wine.'

'I'm not that bad am I?' he said.

'No, not at all, in fact I like my wine of an evening just as much as you. I think walking back is a good idea anyway; we can walk off all that food. If I'm too full, it affects other things, I don't know about you.'

'If you mean what I think you mean then, yes; that, my darling, is absolutely the last thing I want.'

They exchanged highly charged glances, which showed that they were both more than ready for an intimate encounter.

They had agreed that a starter was unnecessary so they went straight to the main course.

They both liked sea-food and Anna had Moules Mariniere and Alex opted for pan-fried trout with sautéed potatoes and roasted baby tomatoes. Alex had ordered a Gewurztraminer from Alsace for Anna, which was her preference when having seafood, and Alex had gone for a French Moelleux from Bordeaux.

'I've not had that before Alex, is it nice?'

He offered her his glass; 'Have a taste, I think you might like it. I think this one is a blend of Sauvignon and Sémillon, but I could be wrong, I'm not too up in wine but I do know what I like.

She took a sip and having tasted the gently sweet feel, she said, umm, that's nice, just sweet enough but very soft; a bit like you in fact.'

'Oh, go on, you're just saying that to get me into bed; anyway, I won't be for long.'

'Huh, I don't need to say anything really, do I?'

'That's true. Would you like a dessert?'

'I don't think so, thanks, maybe just a coffee; the coffee is nice here I know.'

Their waitress came over and Alex simply asked for two coffees with the bill to follow in about 15 minutes.

After their meal, they were walking the fairly short distance to Anna's flat. 'I really enjoyed that, and I know that you did, thank you. Will your car be okay in the car park?'

'I think so; they have CCTV there and I do know that they keep it well maintained, so there should be no problem if some "scrote" tries something. I can nip back for it in the morning and still be in the office on time.'

'Do I deduce from that, that you're inveigling your way into my bed for the night?'

'I think you deduce correctly madam.'

'Oh, in that case, enveigle away,' she said with an impish grin, whilst hooking her arm in his.

'It's a bloody good job that we're not near the office or we might be spotted by one of the local lads, and that would definitely not be a good thing.'

She quickly removed her arm, but he pulled it back into position. 'Do you know what, I don't care? It would only be seen as a gesture and nothing could be proved.'

'True, but once seen, the balloon would go up and we'd be sunk, wouldn't we? I mean, we take enormous trouble not to be known as a "pair," so I think I'd better be more careful,' and once again she took her arm away.

'As ever, you are right. I'll have to leave the more physical stuff till later then.'

'That's my boy,' she said with a giggle. 'Anyway, we're nearly there.'

Anna opened the door to her flat and as previously, Alex could smell the clean, fragrance of her home and of her. It always had a very calming and pleasant effect on him. 'I love the smell of your flat Anna, mine is musty compared with this.'

'Your place is fine, it's just that it has a "male" smell to it, which I like; in fact it probably has the same effect on me as mine does for you.'

'That's okay then. Shall I put some music on?'

'Yes please, whatever you like, I know you'll choose something appropriate. But before that, can you come here please?'

He looked over to her and saw that she was standing with her arms crossed. Her voice had had quite a sharp edge to it, which immediately worried him. As he approached, she couldn't keep her stern look and broke into a smile. 'What?'

'You haven't kissed me.'

'I'm sorry, I was about to smother you with them, but maybe this will keep you quiet for a bit.' He took her in his arms and held her very tightly, whilst at the same time kissing her very passionately. She responded with a similar greedy kiss, which seemed to go on for a long time. When they finally broke apart, she was breathless.

'It's all right for you, you can hold your breath but I can't.'

'Maybe you can hold something else then?'

'Mmm, let me think about that, while I get some glasses and some wine.'

'Sounds like a good idea to me.' He moved over to the sound system and chose a suitable CD with a gentle instrumental from Toumani Diabaté on the Kora.

She came back with two glasses and a bottle of red. Pouring two glasses, she said, 'shall we sit on the sofa and just listen. I find this music incredibly relaxing.'

'Me too,' responded Alex, I really don't know why there isn't more of this music played as background music on some of these TV programmes.'

'I've heard this sometimes, I must be honest. It is so gentle that unless one is listening to it, I don't think it can be really appreciated.'

'I was reading the other day that Toumani's family spans some 72 generations and they all were musicians who played the Kora. In fact one track which I listened to recently, had him speaking about this and he said that the music he was actually playing was never written down, but passed down from father to son, father to son, right down the generations, for hundreds of years.'

'I'd say that was pretty impressive, and it's beautiful music, I just love it.'

They sat together in a very relaxed atmosphere and talked about this and that, but not about the case they were involved in at the moment; that was by mutual agreement, to be kept at work and their two lives as separate as possible. Things were getting very cosy and Anna said, I think I want to take you somewhere.'

'You always take me somewhere darling, whenever we are together and in private, I go to a place I never thought possible. I mean, I had a good relationship with "you know who," but what we have is so much better, and I don't mean to belittle my time with her, but you have taken me by storm, so to speak. You take me to heights I have never known. You could say that you "blow my mind,"' as well as other things, he thought.

'I'm so glad that you feel this way because the more time we spend like this, the more I think I know what direction I want my life to take Alex.' As she was saying this, she was looking at Alex in a way which made his stomach tighten. Does she mean what I think she means?

'Do you mean that you'd like to take things further Anna?'

'I think that's a distinct possibility, but for now, let's just take things as they come. I'm more than happy to spend all my spare time with you and I look forward to the time when we can do more and not have to be so circumspect. I know that we have to keep things very quiet for the sake of both our jobs.'

'Yes, I know,' he said with a sigh, 'but we're stuck with the regulations and the last things on earth that I want, is for us to be separated and work in different places.'

'You can bet any money you like that if that happened, they'd make us work a long way apart, so let's just keep things ticking over for now shall we, and enjoy our time together.'

'Agreed; anyway, where's this place you wanted to take me to?'

'Well, I'll give you a clue; it's not a million miles from here.'

'Umm sorry, no idea.'

She gave him a playful punch and took his hand to pull him up. When he seemed reluctant to move, she turned and pulled him through to her bedroom.

'Ah, now why didn't I think of that?' he said.

Laughing, they both fell on to the bed and indulged in some passionate kissing and fondling. Things were becoming very heated and they undressed each other with indecent haste. Both naked, they caressed each other and succeeded in making each other very aroused. Anna moved to straddle Alex and he was more than ready for some sexual progression.

There was the ringtone of an incoming call.

'Leave it,' said Anna, who was at an erotic highpoint, 'I can't wait.'

'It's from the office.'

'How do you know that?' she said in exasperation.

'Because I told Alice to only call me if there was an emergency.' He reached to the bedside table where he'd left the phone and looking at the display, he saw that it was indeed from Alice.

'Hi Alice, is there a problem?' Anna was playfully touching parts of his anatomy that had nothing to do with work. He tried swatting her hands away, to no avail. She kept on playing with his penis, which was more than ready for further action; except that as his attention was diverted by what Alice was saying, then so was a certain amount of blood supply, causing a definite decrease in the libido department.

Alice sounded very excited, 'Guv, we've lost the signal from the tracker. It was fine and it just disappeared about two minutes ago. I thought I'd better let you know straight away.'

Sitting bolt upright, he exploded; 'Shit, shit, shit! What's happening, what the hell is going on?'

Anna had stopped making movements in the sexual direction and had become very concerned. Alex looked at her while talking to Alice as the significance of her call had become apparent. She mouthed, "What's happened?"

Alex was just about to tell her when he stopped himself, just in time.

The pause from Alex gave Alice time to say 'I don't know what happened, but it does occur to me that they could be on the move and we have no way of knowing where they are or where they're going.'

'Alice, give me a moment to think about what to do and I'll call you right back. Just check your screen again to make sure it isn't some computer glitch.'

'Okay guv, I'll check it but I really don't think it's our end.'

He cleared the call and turned to Anna. 'I'm sorry darling, but our bloody tracker has gone again and now they could be on the move and we don't have any bloody idea what is happening.'

'Oh Christ Alex, not again! We could lose them. What should we do now, call out the Marine Unit with the AR team?'

'If we do that and it's a false alarm, we're going to look complete idiots and bang goes any future co-operation, but if they are on the move and we don't call them out, we'll miss them and they'll destroy the evidence we need.' I'll have to go to the office to co-ordinate things, sorry.'

'Of course you will and I'll come too, but hang on, don't forget Tom is there at the Whaler and he can tell us what's happening if they turn up there.'

'That's all very well, but by the time he sees them, they'll do what they have to do and be away again. We needed to know that they were on the way to give us time to get the Marine Unit and AR boys close, so that we could make the arrest.'

'You get dressed; I'll call Tom to see if anything is happening over there. You can tell Alice that you called me and that'll explain my turning up at the office at this time of night.'

'Okay, good; just ask him what he can see out there, if there's any movement.'

Anna put in a call to Tom and he answered almost immediately.

'Sarge, I was going to call you; Alice has just told me what has happened. She said to be ready as they might be on the way.'

'That's right Tom, it's all going to pot again; it seems that our attempt to put the tracker on board may have gone pear-shaped'

'Sarge, sarge, that's not the problem now, to be honest; well it is.'

'What do you mean?'

He sounded very agitated as he said, 'The real problem is that I can't see a bloody thing. It's so dark that all I can see are the lights right across the harbour; anything close to me is absolutely invisible.'

'But you have a camera which takes shots in low-light conditions, don't you?'

'In low-light yes, but there's NO light, nothing, no moon, everything's black; maybe I could hear something close but that's all, I wouldn't be able to see them. I asked one of the staff chaps here and he said that tonight is a "Dark Moon", whatever that's supposed to mean, except that he said it's the time just before the New Moon which means there's no bloody light at all.'

'Oh Christ, I'd better let Alex, I mean the guv, know.' She slapped her thigh as she realised that she'd said "Alex," but that was the least of their worries. 'Just keep in position Tom; I'll let you know what's happening as soon as I can.'

'Right-o sarge.'

Anna relayed to Alex what Tom had said. 'What, no moon, there must be some light surely? We never thought to check that?'

'Short of giving Tom a bloody great spotlight, nothing; so what do we do Alex, I mean should we alert the Marine and AR Unit, you know, to have them on stand-by?'

'We can't have them stooging around the harbour on the off-chance of something happening.'

He was dressed by now and Anna nearly, 'So, Anna, I'll dash over to the office and you follow shortly. I'll tell everyone that I'd phoned you immediately, so there'll be no misunderstandings about why you've turned up.'

'Okay, I'll be about five minutes behind you.'

As he was about to scoop up his car keys, realisation struck him that his car wasn't there, but in the restaurant car park. 'Bollocks; Anna, you'll have to take me to the restaurant, I've left the car there and I can't run all the way, it's too far.'

'Okay, hang on; I'll only be a couple of minutes. You'd better tell Alice what is going to happen.'

'I will when I can bloodywell decide what to do. Well, that's our evening fucked up; or not,' he said with a very wry smile.

'You could say that,' said Anna looking very downhearted.

He called Alice again. 'I'll be there in about twenty minutes Alice, in the meantime, can you call the Marine Unit and ask the duty officer what their state of readiness is and explain our problem?'

'Will do guv; are we going to call them out?'

'Half of me wants to, and other half says not, in case it's a false alarm.'

'But if we don't try to catch them at it, we'll miss our opportunity.'

'Quite right; do nothing until I get there and I'll think it through on my way. Have you checked our computer again?'

'Yes, and everything is running properly; we just lost the signal. Do you think they found the tracker?'

'I'm beginning to think it highly likely, as it would have been just visible if someone had looked over the stern, although why they should've done that, I've no idea, but it does seem to be most likely scenario.'

'Perhaps they were just checking their ropes and stuff,' offered Alice.

'See, there again, women so often get right to the heart of things; I think you could have hit the nail on the head. Anyway, I'll be there soon.'

'Okay guv, I'll keep in touch with Tom.'

Anna drove Alex to his car at the restaurant car park and they both set off for the office. 'I'll go a little slower, to arrive just after you Alex.'

'Okay, but don't worry too much about it, we have too much at stake now to worry about turning up together; in any case, I phoned you and you would've set out straight away and we have similar distances to travel, so just get there safely.'

They kissed briefly and drove quickly but separately to their office, arriving at similar times and went up to the second floor office where Alice had been on duty for hours. 'Have you been here all the time Alice?' asked Anna. 'Yes sarge, I wanted to keep a close eye on what they were doing; I didn't want to let them give us the slip again.' 'You should have had one of the other "plods" cover while you had some time off.'

Anna realised that she had used a rather derogatory word, calling the other ranks "plods," but Alice didn't mind, as they used the term quite frequently. 'Very conscientious of you Alice and much appreciated.'

Alex came over to where Anna and Alice were talking. 'Alice has been here the entire time guv.'

'Quite beyond the call of duty I'd say,' said Alex, 'You're a brick Alice.'

I've been called better things, she thought, but took it as a compliment. 'So what's the plan then guv?'

Alex had given the situation some thought as he'd raced over to the station. 'I'm sure that they had got their supply of fuel on board with the intention of going over to the Whaler to remove the two bodies on board. I don't know if they know that we know they have them there, but we must assume that they're not going to leave them there to decompose any more than they are already and they'll want to get rid of them to remove the evidence. So, I really think that they're going to make the attempt tonight, and with all that fuel on board it seems likely that they'll be going over to France, so I will call out the Marine Unit and have them standing by.'

'But how will they know, or more to the point, how will we know, when they're coming out of the river and heading towards Brownsea Island?' This was Anna asking the burning question.

'That is the question. With no moon, it's going to be bloody difficult to see them, but surely there must be some way of checking the movement of boats.'

'Roger,' said Anna.

Alice looked up and Alex said, 'Ah, Fuller, good old Fuller.' After the extremely sudden and disappointing conclusion to that night's events, the last thing Alex needed was to be reminded of Fuller, the Poole Harbourmaster, to whom he thought Anna was quite attracted. The old green eyed monster was rearing its head again.

'Yes, Fuller, he's the one with radar surveillance of the harbour. He told me once that they tracked the movements of boats by radar all the time. I wonder if they do this 24/7?'

'Can you call them and find out?'

'Of course; I would think that they'll have someone on duty who would keep watch. I'll call the Harbour Office.'

She dialled the number which she actually knew by heart, but made a show of looking up this detail on-line so that Alex wouldn't be aware of this. It wouldn't have gone down well, of that she was sure.

'Harbour Office, Duty Officer, how can I help?' was the response as the call was answered.

'Hello, this is Detective Sergeant Jenkins from Bournemouth police. Can I speak to Fuller Masterson please?'

'I'm sorry sergeant, but he's off duty now. We only have the Harbour Control Officer on duty now; the Harbourmaster goes off duty at six.'

Anna tried hard not to be disappointed by this news; she'd been looking forward to hearing his voice again. "Stop it," she thought, "I mustn't think like this, especially after what was going to happen tonight." 'Oh, that's fine, could I speak to the Control Officer then please, I have an enquiry about radar coverage of the harbour.'

'Can I help in that direction, as you are speaking to him?'

Caught a little off-guard, Anna quickly regained her composure and said, 'Oh, great, thanks, er, can you tell me if you have radar coverage of the harbour at this late hour?'

'Sergeant, we have radar coverage 24 /7, so the answer to your question is, yes. You obviously have a reason to ask, so how can I help you?'

'Well, we have surveillance on a craft which we think is involved in a very serious crime and we need to know its movements tonight especially, given that we cannot see this boat as it is a "Dark Moon" night, so we rather need your radar.'

'Okay, I can see that; even though you can't,' he said, smiling to himself on his wit. 'So do you know where this craft is at the moment or where it is going?'

'We know that it is, or was until very recently, moored up just into the River Frome and we think it will make a run to Brownsea Island to a point close to the "Othniel" oyster farm building.'

'And what do you think will happen when and if they get there?'

'That's what we need to know. We have the Marine Unit and AR squad on standby to possibly make an arrest when we know their movements.'

'Okay, just let me have a look at our radar plot and see if this craft is showing up, although I don't think we cover that far across the harbour.'

'Damn, that makes things more difficult then.'

'Just hold on love, we might be able to help.'

'That's "sergeant," to you,' she said in a much clipped tone, absolutely hating to be called "love."

'Sorry, I'm sure "sergeant,"' he said. 'I think we can help; if this boat moves, we'll pick it up as soon as it enters the Wareham Channel.'

'And can you keep watch and let us know exactly when it moves?'

'We can if someone sits here and watches the screen.'

This guy was beginning to really "get" to Anna. 'So are you saying that you don't watch the screens all the time?'

'We can't just sit here watching the screens all night, can we?'

'I would have thought that the term "24/7 surveillance" would indicate that someone would be keeping a close eye on the shipping movements.'

'Sergeant, with all due respect, this is sleepy little Poole Harbour, not Rotterdam; just a little place with almost everything happening during the daytime, except for a few ferry movements, so no, we don't sit here glued to the screens, however much you'd like us to.'

'I accept that, but I say again, this is a very serious crime which we're investigating and it would be enormously helpful if, in this instance, someone could keep a very close eye on the screen and let us know exactly when a boat or "craft" as you call it, actually leaves the area of the River Frome and heads across the harbour. I think this "craft" will be travelling quickly as this "craft" is capable of forty knots, so I would imagine that it would feature rather highly in your picture of a sleepy little harbour. Do you think this is possible? Actually I imagine Mr Masterson would be less than pleased if he knew your lack of enthusiasm.'

This seemed to put the guy in his place and his voice became much more attentive and official, not so "laid back" as with his previous tone. 'Of course, we'll have someone to keep a close eye on this area and as soon as we spot something happening like you've said, I will personally call you, if you give me your contact number.'

This Anna gave, and was quite glad to end the call.

Alex had been listening to this on the speaker and he was giving a small smile at the exchange which had taken place.

'He really pulled your chain, didn't he?'

'He shouldn't have called me "love."'

'That wasn't his best move, but at least he's going to help and let us know when it comes on to their screen.'

'I'll get the Marine Unit updated and ready then.'

'Good idea guv. I'll get some coffees, I'm sure Alice would like one wouldn't you?' she said calling over to her.

'Oh, yes please, I'm spitting feathers here. I didn't dare taking my eyes off the screen and since the trace went, I've been a bit of a dither.'

Anna was just about to go along the corridor to the coffee machine, when there was an incoming call on her phone. 'DI Jenkins.'

'Hello sergeant, this is the Control Officer at Poole Harbour. As soon as we looked at the area you indicated, we saw a moving craft and plotted its course. It appeared to have come from the direction of the River Frome and seems to be heading towards Brownsea Island, although they could also be heading for Blood Alley.'

'I'm sorry, "Blood Alley?"'

'That's the area of water to the South of Brownsea Island, known to be where some of the bloodiest battles took place between smugglers and Government forces a few centuries ago. Also the red streaks in the sand added to the intrigue.'

'Thanks for that history lesson; very interesting, but how fast are they travelling, can you tell?'

'Sergeant, we can tell exactly and it was 20 knots, although they have now slowed down. As you may or may not know, there is a speed limit in the harbour and this was way, way over that, so they are in trouble already. If you're going to have your Marine Unit get out to them, they're going to have a heck of a job, because as I think I'm right in saying, they are based at Poole Quay, and to...'

'Hold on, hold on!' she said, and motioned to Alex. Putting her hand over the mouthpiece, she said to him, 'They're on the way. They've left the Frome and headed towards Brownsea or maybe Blood Alley.'

Speaking again to the duty officer, she said, 'Do you know where they are at the moment?'

'As I said, they've slowed right down through the moored craft. They must have their own radar or they'd plough straight through them. Oh, hold on...It looks to me that now they could be heading towards the main channel.'

Anna turned back to Alex, and told him their position.

'Bloody hell, that's where "Othniel" is, I'll call the Marine Unit.' Pulling out his phone, he called their number which he'd logged in a while back.

The call was answered immediately. "Marine Unit, duty officer speaking."

'Hi, this is DCI Vail, Bournemouth Police.'

'Yes, we are on standby, waiting for your instructions.'

'They are on the move and moving towards the target area we discussed, close to "Othniel." They're on their way, so you'll have your work cut out to get there in time.'

'Okay, hold the line.' Turning to his boat coxswain, he shouted "It's Go Go Go lads. Fast as you can."

Returning to the phone call, 'It's going to be bloody difficult to race around in this dark, y'know, with no moon and virtually no visibility.'

'I'm aware of that, although I didn't realise it was a "Dark Moon" tonight and I realise that makes things more dangerous. All I can ask is that you do your best to catch these killers, but take care, we are presuming that they are going to transfer two bodies, but we don't know if they have guns, although it's a strong possibility.'

'Understood; things are underway as we speak. I'll do my best to keep you informed.'

'Okay, thanks.'

Alex then phoned Tom.

'Tom, just to put you in the picture, our target is on the way towards you, although we can't track them, they are on Poole Harbour radar, so they're doing it on their radar. They were doing around 20 knots and from what I know, although they seem to have slowed down. We understand that they are about half-way across, in fact they must be quite close by now, so keep looking.'

'Okay guv, will do, but like I said, I can't see a bloody thing; all I can do is hear them. Will the Marine Unit be able to get here?'

'Dunno son, I just bloody well hope so. It's going to be very dangerous for them in a RIB without on-board radar and they have to look out for moored boats.'

'Maybe they've got a bloody great searchlight, which would help.'

'Actually, I think they have, and by Christ, they're going to need it. Let's just hope they can get to you in time Tom.'

'What if they don't come here then guv, what are they going to do?'

'I wish I knew mate, I wish I knew.'

CHAPTER 49

Previously, on board "Predator," both Goodyear and "Freddie" Furkan were ready to make a dash across the harbour after dark to collect the two bodies from the "Whaler."

They had provisions for their intended crossing to France where there were a number of specially selected organised people were waiting to be collected.

Goodyear turned to Freddie and said, I've got to make some calls to arrange for the drop-off people to be ready for when we get back. They have to be absolutely ready to make a quick pick-up and we need to get them out of the area as soon as possible. We can't have odd-looking blokes being seen in a mini-van; that's going to arouse suspicion and we really don't need that with what we have to sort out at the moment.'

'No Martin, I know what you mean. We've got enough on our plates haven't we, what with that bloke who you sorted and then the other two. What a fucking mess that was, I mean why the hell he came on board with bloody great knives in the first place, beats me.'

'It's my fault, I should have checked him when they first boarded. I'll be bloody careful this time I can tell you. Anyway, while I'm making these calls, I want you to make sure that the pressure pump and hose is working properly. We're going to need that to clear up the mess from the two bodies when we get them aboard.'

'Yeah, I'll bet they stink to high heaven by now and they're going to be bloody difficult to handle; I mean they were a bit slimy the other day when we moved them before.'

'Don't remind me. Oh, and when you've done that, just check the mooring lines. I don't know if you realise this, but tonight is a "Dark Moon" and it's going to be as dark as the inside of a whale's belly tonight.'

'Who said that then, some clever bloke I'll bet?'

'As clever as you maybe Freddie?' Goodyear said with heavy sarcasm.

'Yeah, well, I never said I was clever did I? Anyway, what's a "Dark Moon," is that when you can't see it?' he said with a snigger.'

'And you said you weren't clever - but that's it exactly; as far as I know, when the moon is in the shadow of the earth, no light falls on it and the New Moon hasn't appeared, there's a time when it's invisible and no light – and as it just so happens to be tonight, we'll have total darkness to do what we have to do.'

'It's a bloody good job that we've got radar then, innit?'

'Go on, piss off and do what you have to do, and while you're there, check the stern jets and the deflector plates, just in case that bloody Japanese sea-weed has wrapped itself round them; we don't need that right now.'

'Right; I bloody well hope not as I don't fancy going under again, do I?'

Goodyear made his phone calls while Freddie went out to the stern to prepare the pressure pump. This was a hose which had been installed to clean up the rear deck after the "fishing" parties. There was always some mess to be cleared after their spurious "fishing trips" because they actually did some fishing, just to make things authentic, should they ever be challenged; which so far they hadn't, but Goodyear didn't take chances.

Freddie arranged the hose and started one engine to provide the power for the pump. When the engine was running at low revs this provided sufficient power to the pump to give a very forceful jet of water which was taken directly from the river via an inlet below the waterline.'

The light was beginning to fade as he finished testing the pump and turned off the engine. Everything was working as it should and he thought, I'll just check the moorings. Going to the bow, he looked over to the mooring buoy, where the rope had been passed through the mooring buoys eye and back to the cleat on the gunwale of the boat, where it was tied off, ready to be slipped quickly and easily in the dark. "That should be easy enough, I reckon." He made his way to the stern and looked over to do the same as before with the mooring rope. This time, he made a quick check down to check the jets, to make sure it was free of weed.

As he looked down, he caught sight of a patch of blue, just on the water-line. I don't remember Martin mentioning that; still, suppose he knows about it, thought Freddie. Satisfied that all was well with the moorings, he went back to the cabin where Martin was finishing his calls.

'Just make sure that you're there and waiting. I'll call you when I know my arrival time. The GPS will give me a very accurate timing, so I should be able to tell you well in advance so that you don't have to wait around. You can wait somewhere else and then get to the pick-up point quickly. It's going to be very dark tomorrow when we get back, so you won't be seen. Are all the arrangements for their onward trip in hand?'

'Yes,' came the reply.

'Good, now piss off and wait for my call tomorrow.' He ended the call without further comment.

Freddie came back into the cabin. 'Is everything okay then?'

'Yeah, both mooring ropes are easily slipped. I'll just have to whip it off the cleats and pull the ropes in and we're good to go.'

'Why the fuck are you trying to sound like an American; you're a Cypriot, and don't you forget it. I think you've been over here for too long.'

'Well, you speak like a Brit; you'd never know where you're from.

'I know, and I've had to bloody work on it like you won't believe.'

'One thing; you didn't mention that you'd had a little bit of work done on the stern.'

'What are you talking about, I've had nothing done to the stern, what d'you mean?'

'There's a blue patch about 150 mill square just on the water line. I thought you'd had some work done and they'd covered it up while whatever had been used was setting or whatever.'

He looked very concerned. 'What the fuck is this; I'm going to have a look.'

He moved through the cabin to the stern and leaning over the rail, he looked down to see the patch, just visible now in the gathering gloom. 'Shit, what the hell is that?' he said angrily. 'Is this some kind of joke? Have you put that there, you dickhead?'

'Me, no, why would I do that? Don't be daft, do you think I'd mess about with your boat, you'd kill me.'

'You're right there, but if you've not done it then someone has put it there; I don't know when, but I know it wasn't there when we took on fuel, because I checked over the stern as I always do. That means that it's just been put there. How the hell has that happened?' With that, Martin leaned over the stern to try to reach the patch. He couldn't; so he said to Freddie, 'Here, hold my legs so I can reach this thing, and for fuck's sake don't let go or it'll be your legs that go into the river.'

Freddie held the legs while Martin reached right down to the waterline to reach the patch. He tried to lift the corner, but it was too well fixed and he couldn't lift it.

'Shit, it won't move, what the hell is that fixed with? Lift me up.'

Freddie pulled him back on board. Martin was extremely angry now and he was quickly thinking of how this patch could be removed. 'There was something under the patch I think, I could feel a small bump; what the hell could that be?' he mused. Then a thought occurred to him. 'I'll bet it's a bloody tracker; some bastard has been here and fixed that while we've been moored up, because there's no way it could have been done while we were on the move and all we've done is come from Cobbs where we loaded fuel and came straight here. How come we didn't see or hear anything?'

'Whoever it was didn't come on foot or in a car, there's no road over here and we would've noticed if someone was walking around here,' said Freddie, 'then how the hell was it done?'

Martin said, 'If it was someone with SCUBA gear we'd have seen them, or at least their bubbles, we were always keeping a watch.'

For once, Freddie had a thought; with his diving experience, he realised how it could have been done. 'How about if they had a re-breather set, something like a Kiss® set-up, we'd never see a diver and he could have used that special adhesive, which is why you can't get it off.'

'Just for once, I think you could actually be right; nice one.' That made Freddie just a little smug, for once.

'All I have to do is to get that patch off and see what's under it. Do we have a chisel on board Fred?'

I must be in his good books, thought Freddie, as Martin had never called him "Fred" before. 'As it happens, yes, because I put my toolbox on board the other day and I know I've a couple of chisels in there.'

'Right, can you get me one so that I can get this bloody patch off. It's obvious that "they" know where we are, so we'll have to be ready to move quickly when it's dark and get over to the "Whaler" under cover of the "Dark Moon." With no light, we'll be virtually invisible and if I can disable this tracker, if that's what it is, they won't know where we are. A quick transfer and we can be off to France, unseen and untraced.'

Freddie went below to fetch his toolbox and while he was gone for those few seconds, Martin had a good look around to see if there was anyone or anything around, like a vehicle, but he could see nothing and the area around where they were moored was flat, so any car would have been easy to spot. As Goodyear did not know the area, he'd not noticed the raised bank behind the gulley which runs alongside the river, made when the gulley had been first dug. This had been high enough to screen the Defender from view when they drove there.

Freddie returned with the chisel and Martin told him to hold his legs again, while he tried to prise the patch off the hull. It was extremely difficult to reach down, and he made repeated attempts, with no success.

'No, pull me up, this is ridiculous. You'll have to go down and try it from the water.'

'Me, why should I go down again?' he whined.

'Because you're the diver and I said so.'

Freddie realised that it was useless to argue with Goodyear, so he got ready to get into the water. He was used to cold water, but even so, it was not the best way to spend his time, but this was no place to defy his boss, so when he was in the river, he swam round to the stern and reached up to take the chisel which Martin was holding out to him. He began to try to open up an edge of the blue plastic material which was so firmly stuck to the fibreglass hull. As he ran his fingers over the area of the patch, he too could feel a lump in the centre. 'Yeah, I can feel this thing as well, Martin,' he said.

'Never mind feeling the bloody thing, just get that patch off and we can take a look at it.'

'Okay, it's not easy trading water and trying to get this sodding thing off.'

'Will you stop bellyaching and chisel it off?'

'Okay, okay, I'm trying but it's stuck worse than a limpet.'

'Just keep at it, it can't have been on that long and I'm sure that adhesive takes a while to set, so it should come off, just keep at it.'

Freddie kept pushing at the corners of the patch and gradually, a part became free and he tried to pull the corner but to no avail. 'It's not moving!' His legs were aching from the constant paddling to keep afloat and his arms were the same from the constant attack on the patch. Gradually, he managed to free a corner and as more and more of the fabric came clear, he was able to pull harder and eventually, the patch was almost free.

'What can you see Freddie?' said Martin.

'I can see a metal thing in the middle.'

'Pass it up to me.' Freddie passed the metal object up to Martin, who was leaning over the stern rail.

'Just pull the rest of the panel off and get back up here.' As he said this, Freddie called out to him; 'How do I get back up, can you put the ladder over?'

'In a minute, I'm just going to look at this thing.'

'For fuck's sake Martin, I'm freezing my bollocks off here.'

Somewhat grudgingly, he put the stainless steel ladder which clipped to the stern rail, over the side. Freddie climbed back on board, rubbing his legs and arms in an effort to get warm. 'That was bloody near impossible, you know, to get that patch off. I don't know what glue they used, but it's amazing stuff.'

'Never mind all that, this thing's a bloody tracker; I thought so, so they do know where we are, but not for long.' He said, I expect you've got a hammer in that tool box of yours, haven't you?'

'Yes, it's in the box over there.' Martin moved over to the tool box and rummaged around to find a hammer. He went closed the toolbox lid and placed the tracker on it. With a vicious blow, he smashed the tracker. He hit it again and again, obviously in anger.

'Now let the fuckers find us, once we're back in the harbour tonight,' he said.

CHAPTER 50

Earlier that day, Goodyear had realised that information had been passed on to the police which can only have come from Bob Chorley. He had to find him to see just how much he'd told them. Thinking of how he could find Chorley, he'd realised that the people who were bound to know his address, were his employers, Perenco.

He'd made a call to their local offices. "Good morning, Perenco, how can I help you?" was the response when the call was answered.

'Hello. I am trying to find the address of a cousin of mine who works for you over at the oil-field on Goathorn Peninsula.'

'Oh yes, the one in Poole Harbour. We have a number of oil-fields in this area as perhaps you know. I must tell you that it is company policy not to give out addresses of our employees as a matter of privacy, so I'm afraid that I can't help you.'

'Oh, that's a pity as he is a cousin, as I said, but we've not been in touch for quite a while and I know he lives in this area, but I don't know exactly where. My problem is that there has been a death in the family and I happen to know that he's not been informed and we cannot find a phone number for him. We need to contact him as you can understand and I really need to go and see him to break the news personally rather than by telephone and there are legal issues as well.'

Oh, I am sorry to hear that, but I really don't think I can give you that information, but if you'd like to hold for a moment, I will check with my office manager to see if we can help in this instance as there seem to be special circumstances.'

'Thank you that would be most helpful; of course I'll hold.'

There was a pause of about 30 seconds and the receptionist came back on the line. 'I've checked with my manager and she says in this instance it would be in order for me to give you his address, although we do understand that he is due to move to another address and location which we do not have, in the very near future, if he hasn't already.'

'Not to worry, if you can give me the current one, I can call to see if he's still there. Perhaps if not, his neighbour might know where he is moving to. Does he have a phone number so I could check first?'

'I thought you didn't want to call him by phone but to see him in person.'

'Yes, you're quite right, but I could simply call him to see if he answers the phone, I'll know that he's there. I won't have to say anything, will I?'

This seemed just a little strange to the receptionist, who paused for a few seconds then said, 'Very well, I'll just look up the details for you, please hold on a moment.'

Goodyear waited for a few more moments before she came back on the line. 'I have his address, but we have already deleted his phone number as we have been advised to do, so all I can give you is his current address, but I will repeat that he may have already moved; we don't know.'

'You say you have been "advised" to delete his number; can I ask who advised this?'

'I'm sorry, I don't know those details. All I know is we have been told and I'm taking a risk with my job even by doing this, so please don't ask me anything more.'

'Okay; just his address then please.'

She passed on the details and Goodyear thanked her and ended the call.

Very late that night, armed with the address, he drove quickly to the address he'd been given. He realised it was not too far from where he lived in Corfe Mullen. Chorley's flat was just north of Broadstone and was easy to find. As he arrived, he took a look at the front of the building. He saw from the panels on the bell-push that Chorley was on the first floor. He pressed the button and waited. Looking around, he saw that there were three cars parked along the pavement. He had no idea which one would belong to Chorley, but memorised the three models for perhaps future reference, not knowing if that information would be useful, but one never knew.

He pushed the button again, a little longer this time. Goodyear had realised that if he was moving to another "unknown" location, that there was a very good chance that he was being moved by the police after giving incriminating evidence, which would make him a target. "You certainly are matey," thought Goodyear.

There was the sound of steps on the stairs and then the sound of a voice behind the door. 'Who's there?'

'It's the police. Open the door Mr Chorley.'

'Have you come to move me to the new location then?'

'Yes, just open the door so we can come in away from view.'

'Oh, okay; good idea.' The door opened slightly and a face appeared round the edge of the door. As soon as he saw Goodyear, he recognised him as the man who had been trying to bury the body on Goathorn.

'Oh fuck, it's you,' he shouted, and tried to shut the door. But Goodyear had pushed hard against it with all his weight as soon as it had opened a little. This caught Chorley off-guard. The door now was pushed back together with Chorley, who fell into the hallway and landed heavily at the foot of the staircase. Goodyear slammed the door shut behind him and reached out for Chorley, grabbing him by the neck. He gripped very tightly and Chorley, who was by no means slightly built, was so terrified that he only struggled slightly. He knew that this man was capable of murder and he was trying to think of what to do to help his situation.

Goodyear had pulled a long, thin knife from a scabbard under his coat and now waved this very close to Chorley's face.

'Up,' he said, pointing up the stairs. Chorley resisted slightly and Goodyear swiped the blade across the other man's cheek. This made a long and quite deep cut and the blood began to well up.

'Move or I'll do that again.'

This time Chorley moved up the stairs, holding his cheek, trying to stem the blood, without much success as the blood was now running down his neck and seeping into his shirt.

'What do you want?' said Chorley.

'To make sure you don't tell the police any more than you have already, which is far too much. We had a deal to keep quiet, if you remember. You took the money but told them anyway and that really pissed me off, so I'm going to make you pay for your big mouth.'

As they reached the top of the stairs, Goodyear pushed Chorley into the open door to his flat. Again, holding him by the throat, he gripped tightly and as he reached the main room, kicking the door closed behind him, he saw a chair and reached out with his free hand to move the chair to the centre of the room. He pushed Chorley down on to the chair and holding the knife across his throat, reached behind him where a hank of slim rope was hanging from his belt. 'Where are your car keys and which one is it in the road?'

Thinking that this thug wanted to take his car, he thought maybe that would satisfy him. 'They're on the table over there,' he said pointing.

'And which one is it?'

'It's the Ford.'

Chorley was thinking furiously about trying to make a run for it, but with the knife held firmly against the side of his neck, his options were seriously compromised. Preferring to wait for an opportune moment to perhaps try to slip off the chair and run to the open door to the flat, he remained as still as possible.

Unfortunately, this gave Goodyear all the time he needed to run a quick loop around the torso and very soon he had Chorley very securely trussed. Goodyear had looped the thin rope in a special way which climbers used to shorten a long rope, but which allowed the loops to be pulled free very quickly. With the extra length, he made absolutely sure that Chorley would be completely unable to free himself, and because the chair was positioned in the centre of the room, it would be highly unlikely that it would be possible to access anything which could be reached to cut the rope. Besides this, because of the military training which Goodyear had undergone in the so-called "Special" Forces back in Turkey, the binding was more than sufficient to hold his body extremely securely. He also tied Chorley's legs apart, off the floor to the chair legs.

'What are you going to do?' said Chorley.

'Kill you, what else did you expect?'

'I won't say anything, I swear.'

'You've already said too much. I'm just here to give you what you deserve.'

The way in which Goodyear had said this, with no emotion and no expression, made Chorley very, very afraid.
'Just so that you know what is happening, I'll explain it to you, I'm in no rush. Firstly, I'll cut your shirt collar open on one side of your neck. This will expose your shoulder muscle. Then I will use this knife,' and he held the long and extremely sharp knife close to Chorley's face for a moment, 'to make an incision down to just below our clavicle and just before your first rib, is an artery. This is called the subclavian artery. When this artery is cut, the bleeding is almost impossible to stop unless there is some serious medical intervention. In your case, there will be no medical intervention.'

By this time, Chorley was feeling ice-cold in terror. The way in which this information had been delivered, made him realise that he was about to die. 'Why do you have to do this, I won't be telling the police anything, I promise. You've scared me enough, I won't give anything away, I won't tell them that you came here.'

At this, Goodyear actually smiled. 'You won't be able to, so don't worry yourself about giving anything away, you've already done that, so I'm just going to practise what I learned in my specialist military training, things like how to make people talk, how to torture and how to kill. I could have killed you quickly, but I think you deserve to die slowly, so when I cut this artery, it will take anything up to one hour for you to die.'

'You bastard,' Chorley said through clenched teeth, 'you fucking bastard.'

'I know, but there are some things that you have to do. I can't say I'm sorry, because I'm not, but nobody who does this to me, gets away with it, believe me.'

He did.

"I can shout for help as soon as he's gone," thought Chorley. He knew that his downstairs neighbour would be back from work in less than half an hour, so he could yell and yell and with any luck, help would be available. He was unable to move any part of his body as it was so tightly wrapped. He couldn't move his legs or feet as they were also bound to the chair legs, off the floor. So there was no chance of banging his feet on the floor to attract attention, but at least he could shout.

The next thing that Goodyear did was to hold Chorley by the throat again, but this time with his thumb on one side of his neck and his fingers on the other. He had placed them in a position which made Chorley 'gag' and fight for breath. He very nearly blacked out and he had to open his mouth wide to try to suck air in to his lungs.

He was choking and his vision blurred to the point where he had no control over what Goodyear was about to do. As his mouth opened and his tongue protruded from the 'gagging' sensation, Goodyear quickly caught hold of the tongue and held the knife ready to slice off his tongue.

To say that Chorley was terrified, is a complete understatement. He simply lost control of his bladder and his trousers began to colour with the liquid which was coursing down his leg.

'No, I won't do that, because you'd die too quickly.' Reaching into a side pocket of his leather jacket, Goodyear pulled a roll of industrial adhesive tape. Pulling off a length, he began to wind this around Chorley's head about five times. 'That should keep you quiet for a while,' he said. 'Now to the main job.'

Goodyear then sliced open the bloodstained collar of Chorley's shirt. The cut on his cheek had actually almost stopped bleeding. The shoulder was exposed right across the large muscle and with the sharply pointed blade, he began to probe deep into the tissue. Chorley was making some animalistic sounds as the knife probed deeper. It hit a bone and Goodyear had to twist and turn the blade to probe deeper. He said, 'I think this is the one,' and gave a little smile of self-congratulation. 'I've not forgotten everything although it's been a long time since my training,' he said. Locating the artery and with a determined pressure, pushed the very sharp blade into the deep vein. 'These knives are great for gutting fish, that's for sure.'

The pain of the cutting was intense and very soon, the feeling of the blood loss was causing very deep distress as Chorley knew that he was going to bleed to death and there was absolutely nothing he could do about it.

Blood was now gently coursing down his chest, soaking the shirt and running down onto his trousers. It was not actually flowing, but just continuously seeping.

Goodyear took one last look to satisfy himself that everything was secure and with a slight wave of his hand, turned and went out of the flat, closing the door firmly behind him. As he went down the stairs he took some paper tissue out of another pocket and wiped the blade clean. Then he slid this back into the scabbard inside his jacket. Then he took off the gloves he'd been wearing and went out to the street. Looking around and seeing no-one walking or driving up in a car, he walked to where he'd left his vehicle.

He drove off, content that he had achieved revenge.

CHAPTER 51

The RIB with the crew from the Police Marine Unit and the AR team were taking great risks on a moonless night, travelling at speed in the harbour. The number of boats moored out on the "trots" as the lines of moorings were called, were a great hindrance as the only way of spotting these was with their high powered searchlight. The coxswain of the boat shouted to his colleague, over the noise of the twin outboard motors, 'It's all very well having this light, but having to dodge about spotting one moored craft and then another is bloody dangerous. If we hit one of these at the speed we're doing it's going to be a right mess, and no mistake, so just keep flitting about from side to side and we've more chance of spotting them.'

'Okay skipper.'

Meanwhile, "Predator" with the two suspected murderers aboard, was almost at Brownsea Island. Dimitriou had been looking around, trying to see in the incredibly dark harbour. He saw the flashing of the RIB searchlight way in the distance across the harbour and yelled to Martin, 'We're being followed. I think they're chasing us; there's a boat with a searchlight belting up behind us. They keep swinging it from side to side.'

'If that's a police boat, then they use an RIB and that won't have radar or GPS so they're probably relying on the searchlight. I know we've radar, but at the speed we're doing, it's going to be fucking dangerous to get to the "Whaler" this way.'

'So what can we do, slow down a bit?'

'No way, dickhead, do you want them to catch us?'

'No, but if we don't slow down we could run slap into a small boat which our radar doesn't pick up.'

'For once, you're right; so I'm going to approach the "Whaler" from the other end of Brownsea. If we turn off to starboard and go round the back of Brownsea, we can come back along the channel close to the island where there is plenty of water and inside the line of the moored boats.'

'That's clever that is Martin.'

'It's also why I'm driving this and not you.'

Martin then actually slowed the boat and reaching over to the controls on the helm position, switched on their navigation lights briefly and then off again. He repeated this action again and then said 'Hold on.'

He then swung the helm over and they made a sharply heeling turn to starboard to go round the back of Brownsea. Carefully checking their depth finder electronic display, they were able to keep to the narrow but deeper channel.

'This is called "Blood Alley," yelled Martin.

'Why did you put the lights on then?'

'So that they could see where we were. They would presume that we're heading out towards the Haven, but now we've turned, and they can't see us, we can go round the back of the island, out of sight. While they're chasing to where they think we are, it'll give us time to get back to the "Whaler" and do what we have to do. With any luck, while they're looking for us, we can make a getaway.

'Seems like it'll be good place to dump our bodies out in the Channel but I'm not looking forward to trying to get them out of the "Whaler", they were slippery enough when they were in the shed back at Goathorn, so fuck knows what they'll be like now.'

'Why do you think I said to put on our wet-weather gear? So that we can clean up afterwards. The main thing is to get rid of them. Mind you, now you mention it, dumping them in Blood Alley might be a good idea, because the tidal flow is very peculiar here and they could be washed out to sea on an outgoing tide, like we have tonight. I think we'll do that. That way, they'll have no idea where they've come from. What's the situation with the boat following, have we lost them?'

'It looks like it; I can't see any searchlight now. If they didn't see us turn, then they won't know where the hell we are.'

'Yeah, not only that, but if we are being tracked by the Port Radar, then we'll have disappeared behind the island. If we can get to the "Whaler" and chuck the bodies in, we can slip back into Blood Alley, dump them over the side and be straight out through the Haven Run and into the Channel and away to France. That way, we still get our main job done and there'll be no evidence.'

'We're going to have to be damned quick then, you know, getting the two bodies over.'

'I know, so as soon as I pull alongside, run a loop to the bow cleat of the "Whaler", and I'll run one to the stern, that should hold us close and we can both jump over and we'll just throw the bodies on board, slip the loops and we can be on our way in a couple of minutes. Got that?'

'Yep.'

They were moving at nearly 40 mph and very soon they were at the far end of Brownsea Island and turning hard to port, were heading back towards Poole Quay in the narrow channel between the Island and the line of moored boats. Martin had checked on his radar plotter, the number of boats actually moored and knew the exact position of the "Whaler." This enabled him to race towards this at full speed and only slowed down when he was within a short distance. As the boat slowed, he was able to just make out the ghostly white hull of the "Whaler." Slowing down, he cautiously moved the craft alongside the other boat and put the jet-drives into reverse, with a very brief burst to bring the craft to a stop exactly alongside. Martin was expert at boat-handling as his craft was a very advanced and highly equipped vessel and he was well practised in manoeuvring it in confined spaces. His many incursions into unusual locations had given him much experience. Now the two craft were alongside, Freddie quickly looped the bow line to the cleat on the port bow quarter of the "Whaler" and Martin ran to the stern and did the same with the stern rope.

Freddie reached over and unlocked the boat cover for a large enough section to give them access. He leaped over the side onto the "Whaler" and quickly located the first body, wrapped in polythene sheeting. Although it was tied with rope, it was still almost impossible to lift. The smell coming from the corpse was virtually indescribable and he yelled to Martin, "I can't lift it on my own; it's so bloody slippery, you'll have to help me."

'Oh shit,' said Martin, and he had no choice but to quickly jump over to help Freddie lift the body and literally throw it on to the stern of "Predator." 'Christ, the stink is worse than I expected; it's worse than a four day old dogfish that's been left in the sun.'

'I know, I can hardly breathe; just thank fuck that we're not in the shed again, at least the open air means that the smell will go when we move.'

They began to lift the second body, but as they got it into a position where they could heft it over to "Predator," the body began to slide out of the polythene cover. It flopped onto the deck in a slimy drool and fell with a gentle slurping sound, leaving them holding the empty cover. The smell then really got to them and they both began to feel nauseous. Parts of the torso actually split open and innards and intestines actually oozed out and onto the deck.

'Oh, fucking hell Martin, that is really disgusting. I think I'm going to throw up now.'

'For Christ's sake wait until we get whatever we can over to "Predator." We'll just have to come back here some other time and clean up. Now, we have to get away before the others catch us. They must be looking all round the island for us and we have to go. Come on, get this bundle of slime over, we don't have time.'

They gathered up what they could of the cadaver and heaved it over to the other craft. It fell to the deck with a "slurping" sound and slid across to the far side of the open cockpit. They were now covered in a slimy, smelly and gelatinous, not to mention extremely odorous layer of decomposing flesh and other body contents.

While this was going on, Tom, who had been sitting on "Othniel" for most of the day, watching for what was actually happening now, had seen and heard nothing in the gathering gloom and now that there was absolutely no light whatever, he could only hear the gently purring of the pumps on the oyster farm building. As they were actually about six feet above the water, he could also hear the gently lapping water around the pilings the building was sitting on. But now, he could hear something else. There was a gentle roar which he could hear was getting closer. He thought that it was just another boat coming through the harbour. Now, the roar had subsided and then gently rose in pitch again for a few moments, then died away to the gentle throb of idling diesel engines. He instantly realised that this would be the boat he had been waiting so patiently for, all day. He reached for his phone and called the number he'd programmed into his phone for this very purpose.

His call was answered immediately.

'DCI Vail.'

'Guv, they're here. They've just arrived. They must have come from the far end of the island because they didn't come past me. I heard them rev the engines to stop and they must be alongside now.'

'Bugger, we expected them to come from behind you, but they've been too clever. Can you see what they're doing Tom?'

'Can't see a bloody thing guv, like I said before. It's inky black here. I can only hear the engines ticking over. Is the RIB coming?'

'Yes, they should be very close to you now Tom. They'll be coming from the other side of where you are at the moment, so you probably won't be able to see them yet but they have a searchlight so that they should be able to see other boats moored. They can't move too fast as it's so dangerous, but if those two chummies are doing what I think they're doing, we should be able to catch them "at it."'

'If they're just moving two bodies, they shouldn't be long and they'll probably make a quick dash for it.'

'Just keep your fingers crossed that the RIB full of police and AR boys can get here in time.'

Just then, Tom saw a flash of light way off to his left, and the light was moving across the water. 'I think I can see our boys' guv. I can see a light, must be their searchlight. Can't see the boat yet but I can hear an outboard.' Then Tom saw the RIB, or at least the searchlight which was on the bow, flicking from side to side. 'Yes, it's them; they're just beyond the line of moored boats.'

'How many moored boats are there, do you know?'

'I counted about twenty before it got dark and I don't think there are any more arrivals since then.'

So is the RIB coming through them or round them?'

'I can't quite see, but it does look as though they're coming through the line of moored ones.'

The helmsman of the RIB was taking a big risk and he had been made aware of the urgency of what they were about to attempt, which was making him push so hard. As the searchlight had been swinging from side to side, he'd seen the white hulls of the moored boats and was steering a line between them. What he hadn't seen was a 40ft cruiser which had a very dark blue hull and the upper-works were covered in a matching tonneau cover. This made the boat virtually invisible even when the searchlight crossed past it. Unfortunately, it was in a direct line with their path.

Their RIB was travelling at around 25 knots and with 8 crew on board, the overall weight was nearly two and a half tons. The searchlight swung once again across the various moored boats, and this time, the dark blue hull was spotted.

The helmsman threw the wheel over to starboard as hard and as quickly as he could, but it was not quick enough to avoid the impact. Although somewhat softened by the inflatable collar surrounding the fibreglass hull, it did not stop the inertial force exerted by the boat, the twin large outboard engines at the stern and the combined weight of the crew, from bursting into the side of the cruiser bow. Everyone on board was either thrown into the sea or into each other. There was total confusion and the searchlight was the first thing to suffer. Almost complete darkness completed the disaster. The engines were still running at almost full throttle, which was compounding matters. The engines were stopped by the helmsman and the sea was filled with shouts. One of the Marine Unit was able to contact their base on his radio.

"Do you have casualties?"

"Unknown at present, we are recovering all personnel from the water. Will advise when we have a head count."

There were various splashing bodies with lights on their lifejackets and soon they were all alongside the RIB, which although damaged, was still afloat. A couple of officers were injured, suffering broken arms and cracked ribs where they had been thrown against the cockpit section. They were helped on board by those who had managed to pull themselves aboard using the ropes strung around the outer inflatable section of the craft.

"Understood, Marine Unit, standing by," said the officer on the radio. He advised that help would be on the way immediately, in the form of the Harbour Police Launch.

Tom had seen their approach and heard the impact. All that he could see were the small emergency lights on the various floating crews' lifejackets.

He was still through to Alex on his mobile phone and actually shouted as the collision occurred. 'Oh SHIT! – Guv, I can't believe what I've just seen.'

His shout had almost deafened Alex. 'What's happened Tom?'

'The RIB's just run smack into a big cruiser and everyone seems to have been thrown into the water. I saw them coming towards me with their searchlight and then suddenly, there was that great big dark blue cruiser right in front of them. They must have seen it too late and they went smack into it.'

'Oh Christ, we don't fucking need this - Is there any sign of the "Predator," or can't you see anything still?'

'No, I can't see what's happening except that they seem to be getting back into the RIB, but I don't think it's going to go anywhere, it seems to be stuck into the bow of the cruiser, from what little I can make out, which is bugger all, to be honest – wait a minute, they've turned off the outboards on the RIB but I can still hear diesel engines idling, so they must still be there.'

On board "Predator," they had heard the approach of the RIB in the distance and seen the searchlight. They had been just about to release the bow and stern lines and Martin had engaged the drive and was about to push the throttles ahead, when he heard the collision. He had seen the searchlight pick out the large cruiser in silhouette and shouted, 'They're going to hit it, look, and I'll bet they can't see it as it's so dark.' At the moment he'd said that, there was a large "whump" as the RIB hit the cruiser.

'That's one up for us then Freddie. That'll keep them busy for a while, let's get out of here.'

'Lucky for us then Martin, bit of a bugger for them,' he said laughing.

'Right, let's get back around to Blood Alley and dump these two slimy things over the side. We can clean up once we're out in the Channel. Let's just hope they either sink or float out on the tide.'

'It'll be fun for some of the passengers on the ferry if they spot them floating out on the morning flow, won't it.'

'If you say so, you ghoulish bastard.'

'Hark who's talking,' said Freddie.

CHAPTER 52

"Predator," having made the escape to the Channel, after dumping the two decomposing bodies into the harbour in Blood Alley, was making good progress to France. There they would collect their cargo of illegal migrants coming from Northern Turkey, with the intention of bringing them back to the UK and delivering them to a remote location along the coast of Southern Britain.

Soon after they were clear of the coast, they took it in turns to hose themselves down to wash away the gore and slime which was coating them after their recovery and subsequent dumping of the two bodies in the area behind Brownsea Island in Poole Harbour.

'Thank fuck for that,' said Freddie, as he climbed out of his heavy wet-weather gear. 'I'm bloody glad to be out of that stinking gear. I thought smelly fish were bad but that was something else, I've never smelt anything like it, ever.'

'I have Freddie, like after you've been to the heads.'

'Heads, what the fuck are the "heads?"

'The toilet you bird-brain.'

'Oh. Yeah, well, it's not my fault.'

'It's nobody else's, is it?'

'Well, can't help it, it's the curry.'

'Enough, just get out on the stern deck and give it a bloody good hosing down, we don't want any residue of those two, no trace whatever.'

'Right, I'm on it.'

Back in the harbour, the police launch had arrived at the scene of the collision with the cruiser. The SO in charge of the Police section was taking details of the casualties and informing the ambulance crews back on Poole Quay of their injuries. All the paperwork concerning the collision and the damage report would have to wait until the morning light. He turned to the coxswain of the RIB and asked if the damage to the cruiser would cause it to sink.

'I don't think so, as our bow was quite high up above the waterline and the hole in the bow is about three feet above that, so unless there's a storm, we should be okay. Mind you, I don't think the owner's going to be too chuffed about it.'

'I don't suppose so; it looks like it's going to be an expensive repair.'

'You could say that; I'd say bloody expensive, personally.'

'Let's just hope they don't have you for driving without due care and attention then.'

'That, my friend, is just not funny.'

Tom had called Alex again and asked if he could get the Police Launch to collect him from "Othniel" as it was there anyway and bring him back to the quay so that he could go home.

'Of course, Tom, you must have had a boring time, with nothing happening all day and then this.'

'The bang and the noise made it all worthwhile though; but I don't suppose it's done our job much good, as we haven't caught them, have we guv?'

'You can say that again, all our efforts have once again been fucked up. Back to the drawing board, I suppose. Can you come in to the office tomorrow, are you fit enough?'

'Yes, sure thing guv. All this sitting down and not moving about has given me a chance to keep the ribs from grinding together and I feel fine.'

'Good man, see you tomorrow at 8 then.'

'G'night guv.'

Alex turned to Anna, who had been with Alex during all this period of waiting and hoping. He said, 'Well, that it. We're back to square one now. They'll have made their escape and we've nothing to show and now the chances are that they've disposed of the two other bodies so there's no evidence.'

'I don't know about that guv; how about the DNA on the boat. There's bound to be something however much they may have cleaned up.'

'I hope you're right Anna, I hope you're right.'

'And anyway, they have to come back don't they, I mean he's not going to leave the boat somewhere and if he thinks that we don't have evidence, then he's probably so egotistical that he believes he's bombproof.'

'I certainly hope you're right,' he said rather disconsolately.

'Tell you what guv, why don't we call it a night and you come back to my place? I'll see what I can do to cheer you up; I mean there's nothing we can do until they get back. Maybe we could ask the coastguard to keep a radar check if that comes within their area?'

'That's a good thought Anna; I'll get on to that tomorrow. And what would you do to cheer me up, may I ask?'

'I don't know, but perhaps I'll think of something,' she said with a twinkle in her eye.

She did in fact, think of something, and that something did more than cheer Alex up. In reality it made him feel rather more than cheerful, it made him downright ecstatic, but then it seemed to do the same for Anna.

The next morning, Tom appeared, much more mobile than he'd been previously and his forced immobility seemed to have been the boost he needed. Talking with Alex about the happenings of last night, he had moved to the subject of Genny Dobbs, his "contact" at Cobbs Quay Marina. He was still smarting at the way he had been obviously taken in by her charms; not that he'd not enjoyed them, far from it, but he was suffering from being used by her, rather than her giving him the information which he'd hoped for of Martin Goodyear.

'Do you think she knew Goodyear then guv?' Tom said.

'I think she more than knew him, Tom, I think she may have even lived with him, or at least been very close to him. Anna seems to think that she recognised her voice from the time she first phoned Goodyear. Let's just suggest that she and Goodyear were an "item," and you turned up asking questions about him, she told him and he then got her to give you the "come-on," which she seemed to do, then it would follow that he knew everything and that's why you were beaten up.'

'Now you put it that way guv, it does sound as though I was "had."

'Don't worry Tom; you wouldn't be the first to have been caught in the "honey-trap."

'Guv, guv.' Alice came running in to Alex's office without knocking. She was highly excited.

'What is it Alice, don't get your knickers in a twist.'

'Another body guv, they've found another body and we know who it is.'

'Oh Christ, we don't need this. Go on then, who is it?'

'Bob Chorley; he's been found in his flat and he's been there for some time apparently.'

'Why the hell haven't we checked him before now, we knew he was in some kind of danger which is why we moved him right back at the beginning of this case – didn't we?'

'I know he was supposed to be moved, but from what information I can get, his move hadn't taken place.'

'Oh, for Christ's sake, how come everything goes wrong? I suppose because we hadn't heard from him and we thought that "no news was good news," that we didn't think to check.'

'We shouldn't have left it to chance, but with so much going on so quickly, we didn't get round to it,' Anna said.

'How was he killed, Alice, do we know?'

'It looks as though his throat was cut but in a different way.'

'How do you mean "a different way? That's just like the others. This killer seems to like cutting throats.'

'But this time he seemed to have done it in a special way that takes someone a long time to bleed to death, and he was tied to a chair with his legs not touching the floor and was gagged. Does that sound like someone we know?'

'I wouldn't be surprised if Metin Denizci fits the frame'

'Exactly, but what I want to know is why was Chorley found in his flat? He was supposed to move to a new location. He was given a weeks' leave to do this.'

'He never showed up there guv, and when I checked with Perenco HR department, they told me that they had given his address to a man who phoned asking for him.'

'Why the hell did they give this out? They knew that he was being moved from the oilfield at Goathorn for his protection.'

'I did ask this and they said that whoever it was that phoned, sounded genuine, saying that he was a cousin of Bob's and that there had been a death in the family and they needed to give him the details. They said they sounded convincing.'

'I'm going to give that HR department a bloody good bollocking; they should have checked with us first.'

Anna suggested that it was too late now as the damage was done.

'That's all very well Anna, but we should have been checking up but because of someone's lack of common sense, another man who was actually very public spirited and a good chap, has lost his life to this bloody thug who is nothing but a sadistic killer. I mean to get this bastard, whatever it takes.'

'We will guv, we will.'

'I wish I had your confidence Anna.'

'There has to be a way of trapping him, I mean, he has to come back as we said earlier, and when he does we can be waiting. There will be some evidence; I'm absolutely sure that there will be some traces of his crimes somewhere and we'll find them.'

'As you say, he'll come back, so we have to be ready to know the moment he gets here. Any suggestions as to where he might come back to? At the moment we have absolutely no idea where he is or where he might bring the passengers to and drop them off.'

This was directed at the team who were all in the office.

Alice put forward a suggestion. 'If he's going to drop off illegals, the last place he would do this would be somewhere they might be seen, so maybe he would pick somewhere "out of the way" and if it were dark, they wouldn't be seen. Then he could come back here with no evidence.'

'Good thinking Alice, so where do you think he might choose to do this?' This was said with just a slight hint of sarcasm, but then he thought the better of this and said, 'I know you have a better knowledge of this area than the rest of us.'

Deciding to dismiss the irony, she said, 'Yes, I do know the area I had in mind, somewhere around Keyhaven or New Milton. That's where there the houses thin out. I'm sure we can check over the maps and find somewhere that might be suitable, somewhere out of the way and out of sight.'

'And somewhere with access for a vehicle or van perhaps,' ventured Anna.

'Precisely Anna because if they have a number of people, they'll want to get them away from the area and spread out as quickly as possible, so they'll need vehicle access.'

Tom looked pensive and no-one spoke, until he then said, 'Maybe there might be a way we could keep a check, at least on the boat.'

'Go on then Tom, out with it,' said Alex.

'Well, we need to keep a lookout for as much of the day as possible, don't we?'

'Yes, go on.'

'How about we ask the captains of the Sandbanks Ferry to keep a lookout? I mean they're always there aren't they, at least until the ferries stop running?'

'I think that's a brilliant idea Tom. As you say, they are but I don't know what time they stop at this time of year, but we can certainly find out. After that, well, I don't know at the moment, but I'm sure we can get coverage somehow overnight. I mean, we know that they operate in darkness, so we have to have a 24/7 watch.'

'Nice one Tom, good thinking,' said Anna. We just need to find someone else who is around all through the night who can keep watch. Any ideas anyone?'

Alice then had an idea. 'How about we install a "web-cam" in the same vicinity? I mean, the boat has to come through the Haven and it would be easy to cover that area with good picture quality, even at night with infra-red capability and low-light cameras. We could monitor this from here on the screens and we have staff who could monitor this round the night.'

'Now that's what I call thinking, Alice, brilliant. Just a slight problem, how do we install a web-cam, don't we need a router and all that stuff?'

'Yes, but there's sure to be a Wi-Fi hot-spot around or at least someone who has a router and we could use their router with access via their router code. It should be a doddle to find someone there who has this set-up.'

'How about the Haven Hotel,' said Anna, 'they're bound to have Wi-Fi; I'd say that's, and I hate the phrase, a "no-brainer" for sure.'

'I think you're right Anna; can you look into this and get it organised as soon as you can?'

'I'm on it guv.'

'In the meantime, I'd like you, Alice and Tom, to take a look at Bob Chorley's flat to see if there are any hints or clues to who might be the killer, although I do think we know already.'

'Guv, I've been talking with Jeffrey Boyd, you know, over at the Forensics Lab, and he has given me a bit of grounding in what to look for with DNA samples, you what sort of thing would provide DNA clues and stuff like that. Do you think I should follow his advice?'

'Do bears picnic in the woods Alice?'

This produced a smile and Tom said, 'nearly right guv.'

'One has to be polite, Tom.'

CHAPTER 53

On the way to the flat where Bob Chorley lived, Tom said, 'actually he lives, or lived, not far from Goodyear's house in Corfe Mullen. If it was him who topped Chorley, then it would've been easy for him to nip round the corner and do the deed and be back home for tea, wouldn't it?'

'Do you know Tom; sometimes you have quite a nasty mind?

'I know, but it's only black humour. I think it helps to take your mind off the harsh truth of life and death.'

'I suppose in that context, you have a point, but this poor man has lost his life and it shouldn't have happened if only people had carried out their instructions properly.'

'Do you mean the HR department at Perenco?'

'As they gave out the address without checking with us first, then yes.'

'But then, shouldn't we have checked?'

'Unfortunately, again yes Tom.'

They were quite soon at the address in Corfe Hills which was north of Broadstone. As they approached the door of the flat, they saw the crime scene tape which covered the door. 'Let's just hope that SOCO have not stripped out everything Tom,' said Alice.

'Actually Alice, I know they haven't been here yet; I checked this morning and they were so busy, they said they'd leave it until they had more time, probably later today.'

'Oh, that's good. Do we have all the necessary gear for inspection, so that we don't contaminate the area, you know the shoes and baggy suits and gloves and all that stuff?'

'We sure do; something else I checked earlier.'

'You're getting better Tom, there's hope for you yet.'

'Just because you've got a speccy boyfriend who's some sort of scientist, you've got all bossy.'

'Just for your information, he's not speccy, he's not my boyfriend and he is a very clever and good scientist. If you had a minute portion of the knowledge and ability that he has, then you'd be a thousand percent cleverer than you are, so put that in you pipe and smoke it.'

'Oo-er, take it easy Alice, I didn't mean it really. I know those forensic people are bloody good and they make our job a whole lot easier when they can find out details from such tiny bits of stuff, like telling us where something comes from that we can't even see.'

'Well, there you are then, we do our job and they do theirs, and between us, we keep crime down.'

'Hopefully,' said Tom.

They carefully removed the tape and with the keys which had been obtained from the letting agents of Bob's flat, they entered. Looking around, they firstly had a careful look to take in the layout of the rooms and the place where the body had been found. Everything was quite tidy and there was no evidence of a scuffle or fight; except that there was a chair standing by itself in the centre of what was obviously, the main room.

They were exceedingly careful not to move or mark anything which would compromise the SOCO examination.

Under the chair, was a large bloodstain which covered an area about the size of a medium-sized dinner-table.

'Bloody hell,' said Tom. 'Looks like he lost all his blood here.'

Alice then explained to Tom something that she had learned from her various meetings with her friend at the Scientific Support Department, usually known as "Forensics." 'From what I understand for the guys who found his body, it seems that his subclavian artery was cut. That would mean that he would simply pump all his blood out of that until there was nothing left to pump and his heart gave out.'

'What the hell is a "subclavian artery", I've never heard of that?'

'Jeffrey was telling me about this when I asked him about a cut to the throat. He says that this artery runs just above the shoulder under that deep muscle that runs from the neck to the shoulder. He said that if someone were cut here, although it is deep and hard to find between the clavicle and the first rib, it could take up to 60 minutes to bleed to death unless they had medical care.'

'That sounds really nasty, but if it's difficult to find, surely that must mean that whoever did it, knew how to do it.'

'That thought had occurred to me and again Jeffrey said that that sort of action would most probably be taught as a torture and killing method to military personnel.'

'Do you think that Goodyear or Denizci had this?'

'I don't know, but I wouldn't be in the least bit surprised.'

Whoever it is, they must be a really nasty bastard, that's for sure,' said Tom. 'I suppose that SOCO's will take whatever was used to bind him, back to the lab for analysis.'

Alice said, 'I'll get on to Jeffrey later to see what they can tell us. Let's take a look around to see if we can get some DNA from anything to show us who was here.'

They prowled around the room, but no matter how hard they looked, apart from a huge pool of blood, there was nothing they could see to give any further clues.

'No weapon then,' Tom observed.

Alice had brought a large magnifying glass with her to check small items.

Tom looked at this and with a smirk said, 'I see you've brought your special imaging enlarging apparatus along; excellent Watson,'

With that, Alice gave him a slap across his head.

'Oww. That hurt.'

'Serves you right for taking the piss, this is serious.'

'Sorry.'

She was looking as closely as she could at the chair and could actually see some fibres clinging to the back section, as well as some on the floor, soaking up the blood.

She had to reach over the bloodstain and had difficulty in getting close enough.

'Hold my hand Tom, please.'

'There's no time for this and this isn't the place to get all "touchy-feely,"' he said with a grin.

'Will you stop being a complete prat and help me. I can't reach the fibres I can see, without stepping into the blood pool, so if you can help me, I can lean right over.'

'Okay, only joking, sorry. Here, don't worry,' he said holding out his hand, 'I can take the strain.'

Now, Alice was quite self-conscious about her weight, and at Tom's phraseology, she gave him a very hard stare but decided to say nothing.

Tom reached out and Alice took a firm hold on his hand, wishing perhaps that she could crush it.

'Just don't you dare let go or we're both going to get a "you-know-what" from the guv.'

'Don't worry Alice, I've got you. You're safe with me.'

He took a firm grip on Alice's wrist and said, 'Just ball up your fist and it won't slip through my grip. If we just hold hands that might not be good enough.'

He's showing sense at last, she thought, and with that, she leaned as close to the back of the chair as possible.

'These don't look like rope fibres to me,' she said, looking very intently through the magnifying glass.

'That's supposing that rope was used, doesn't it?' ventured Tom.

'Yes, but these look like some kind of wool, you know like a jumper or something.'

'Now that would be interesting, that's for sure. I doubt the killer would have used knitting wool to tie him up.'

'Do you know Tom, sometimes your depth of knowledge and intuition really impress me.'

'I'm only joking.'

'I'm not so sure.'

Alice then produced a small polythene evidence bag and put the fibres in it. I'll take these to the Forensic department personally, I've got to see Jeffrey anyway, so he can take a look; they may give us some lead, who knows?'

'We don't for sure,' said Tom, 'but I expect that SOCO will get a load of good stuff as well.

Alice then decided that they weren't likely to find much else so she said, 'I don't think there's much more we can do here, so we'd better get back. I just hope we don't get it in the neck for taking forensic evidence.'

'I don't see why we should, I mean we are the investigating detectives aren't we, and we're just as able to find evidence as the others.'
'Okay then, I think you're right.'

Later that day, Alice was with her friend Jeffrey and she had given him the fibres which she had found close to where the body had been removed. They had become quite close and a firm relationship was developing. Alice had for too long been without a relationship and she had been becoming quite concerned about being "left on the shelf," but now she had changed into a much happier and fulfilled person. She had always been pleasant to work with but now this had been enhanced and everyone had noticed how much she had changed into an even better workmate. Nothing was too much trouble and she was much surer of herself.

Jeffrey had had a chance to take a quick look at the fibres under his very powerful microscope and he had confirmed that the fibres were indeed a type of wool. 'I would suggest that they were from some kind of jumper or cardigan. If you can find a similar garment and it turns out to have been worn by the suspect, then we would have some serious evidence linking that person to the crime. Almost incontrovertible I would say.'
This cheered Alice no end and she was fervently hoping that if their suspect actually owned a garment which matched the fibres, then they could almost be certain of a conviction.
She and Jeffrey had a very pleasant evening together, which made things even more acceptable.

The next morning, Alice was in the office before anyone and she was eager to pass on her findings to Alex.
It was Anna who was first in and as she walked into the main office, she spotted Alice who had just come back with a cup of coffee. 'That smells rather good to me Alice; very enticing.'
'Would you like a cup sarge?'
'I'd love one Alice. I hadn't thought about it until I caught the smell and now it's set my taste buds singing. That's kind of you, thanks.'
Anna went to her desk and as she was booting up her computer, Alice came back with a cup of Espresso, just how Anna liked it.
'That's great, thanks. I know that you and Tom went over to the flat where Bob Chorley's body was found, so what did you find, if anything?'
'As SOCO had not been there, we were very careful not to touch or move anything, but to be honest, it was pretty clear that there had been no violence or scuffle, you know, things like that.'
'Was it that obvious then, I mean no broken or smashed things round the place?'
'No, nothing like that, just a chair in the centre of the room, surrounded by a pool of blood.'
'Do you think he bled to death then, I mean if there was no scuffle, I presume that the chair meant that he was probably tied to it? If that's true, then the pool of blood could mean that he was either beaten in that position or cut or stabbed and left to bleed to death.'
'Well, I had a quick word with the chaps who first found the body and they were of that opinion as well, but they did say that he hadn't been obviously beaten, nothing that they could see anyway, but one side of his shirt was cut open and there were deep cuts into his shoulder. I called Jeffrey over at the Forensics and asked his advice on what that may have indicated. He said that it would point to his "subclavian artery" being cut and the amount of blood being on the floor, meaning that he had bled to death. He also said that it was a very brutal way of killing someone as it could take up to an hour to die in that way. It was a seemingly favourite way of killing for the military.'
Unknown to either Alice or Anna, Alex had come into the office behind them and had stood listening to most of the conversation. He coughed lightly and they both turned to see him standing there, with a stern look on his face. 'I'm sorry to sneak up, but I thought it would save time in having to repeat everything Alice, so I just listened; I hope you don't mind.'
'Not at all guv, it does save me having to go over everything again.'
'From what you've said, it would tie in with Goodyear having been in the military, something we've found out. We also know that he's a killer and has no compunction whatever in doing something like this. It would also point to him again as he knows, or has met, Bob Chorley and threatened him with drastic action if he passed on information. This

is precisely why we moved him to a secure location. Or so we thought! Why the hell didn't he get to the new address quicker?' There has to be a reason and I just hope that it wasn't something we did or didn't do. Anna, can you check on this as soon as you can please, I don't want to be caught out and I need to know.'

'Of course guv, as soon as I can.'

'Was there anything else Alice?'

'Yes, guv, I found a few strands of fibre which I could see weren't from rope, which he'd been tied with and the guys who found him took with them and gave to SOCO, so I put them in an evidence bag and took them to Jeffrey over at Forensics last night. He took a look at them for me and said straight away that they were from a woollen jumper or cardigan. He said, if we could find the person who was wearing this, then it was even possible not only to match this but to possibly get some DNA from it as well.'

'Fantastic Alice; that would be particularly damning evidence, for sure. All we have to do now is to catch Goodyear and Dimitriou and we could have closure on this sorry mess. Perhaps we could call at his address with a search warrant to see if he has any such clothes?'

'Shall I get a warrant authorised then guv?' said Anna.

'No, I think I'd better go to the Super again and explain the situation. I'm the responsible one and I'll just have to take the flak.'

Both Anna and Alice had similar thoughts of sympathy at this.

'While I'm there, I think it's a good idea to keep a check on Dobbs to see what she is up to at the moment. Alice, can you and Tom go over to her place first thing tomorrow and keep an eye on her so that we know what she might be going to do. Just don't lose sight of her if she tries to slip away somewhere; just keep me informed.'

'Okay guv, we'll be there.'

CHAPTER 54

Tom and Alice had arrived at Genny Dobbs' house at 8am and parked a little way from her address, in a position that they could keep a good view of when she might emerge.

'I wonder when she might come out, said Tom. I expect that she will sleep in if it's her day off.'

'If she's like most girls of her age, I'd think she'd be rather late, but we'll just have to sit it out and wait. You know what the guv said, we mustn't lose her on any account and he needs to be kept up to date with her movements.'

'Okay, so it means another load of waiting, but I have to say I've had enough of that for a while.'

'Never mind Tom; just think of it as healing time.'

'Yeah, s'pose you're right, but – hang on, that's her right now, look, coming out of the side door to her place.'

'You should know her Tom; very well as far as I'm aware. Let's just keep her in view.'

'Yes, well, I mean, yes, I do know her but I also owe her some trouble seeing as how she seems to have stitched me up when I got mugged. That just had to be Goodyear and she knows him, so it follows that it was him who did this to me.'

'I'm sure that's the way it happened Tom. You just have to put it down to experience and be more careful who you choose to chat up next time.'

Tom was looking at her wistfully, thinking about how good-looking she was and what a pity it was that things had turned out the way they had.

'You can say that again; hang on, she's going for a car, she's got keys in her hand.'

Genny Dobbs closed the gate to the entrance to the flats and walked over to one of the cars parked on the kerb. Tom recognised one she'd been in on one of their dates. It was VW Golf. 'That's hers.'

Genny Dobbs walked over to the car and as she opened the door she turned to look around. She looked one way and both Tom and Alice realised that she might see them and they both ducked down below their dashboard. After a few seconds, Tom said, you look Alice, she doesn't know you and if she sees you, it won't raise her suspicions.

Alice sat up and looked again. The exhaust from the Golf was emitted the usual starting cloud of emission and Alice said, 'It's okay, she's driving away.'

Tom started the engine and they moved off, following at a distance which would cause no concern for Dobbs, but would keep her in sight.

'I wonder where she's going?'

'I'm not a mind-reader but that's what we're here for Tom, no matter how long it takes. I mean, she could be going to the hairdressers or anywhere, we just have to wait and keep her in sight. Things are getting too important to lose her now.'

'You're right there Alice.'

Dobbs drove to a vehicle rental company in Hamworthy and parked. Tom and Alice drove into the car park and positioned their vehicle where they could keep a close eye on whoever came out of the office.

'Do you think she's going to hire another car?'

'It's a possibility; maybe she's being careful about being seen in her car.'

After a few minutes, Dobbs came out again and got back into her car. Driving off, Tom and Alice followed, again at a discreet distance. This time, Dobbs drove to a hairdressing salon in Lower Parkstone. As they parked, Tom said, 'Bollocks, this is going to take forever. What are we going to do for lunch if we have to sit here until she has all that hair tarted up?' Tom had often wondered how long it took her to keep it looking so good. The problem was that now, this beautiful girl who he'd thought was his girl-friend, had turned into the one who had set him up to keep the information flowing, not from her to the police, but the other way round. He had been very hurt to discover this fact, but it made him very determined to make her pay for the deception.

'Well, as she's only just gone in, and ignoring your choice of words, how about we wait for a few more minutes to make sure that she's not just making an appointment, and then we can nip round to a local burger place, there's bound to be one handy, and get something to keep us going?'

'Good idea Alice. Sorry about that. I thought you didn't eat that junk these days?'

'Needs must, Tom; sometimes, needs must.'

That's what they did and within around 10 minutes, they were back in place, watching the salon.

Having eaten their hastily obtained burgers, they were sitting patiently waiting for Dobbs to show again.

'That stuff smells disgusting Tom, the smell in the car is just too much. Do you mind opening the window to let some fresh air in?'

'Nope, 'course not,' he said opening the window.

They passed the next hour chatting about this and that, and the cases they had worked on, to pass the time.

Tom was shuffling around on his seat.

'What's up with you?' said Alice.

'I'm dying for a pee.'

You'll have to hang on then.'

'I can't.'

Well, you'll just have to do what they do in France then, won't you?'

'Oh, and what's that then?'

'The men just seem to stand on the side of the road and pee wherever they are. Disgusting I think, but that's what they do.'

'Yeah well, I don't suppose they do it in the middle of a town with houses and building all around.'

'Dunno; wouldn't surprise me though. Anyway there are some bushes just over there, maybe you could sneak behind those. I certainly don't want to see any dangly bits, thank you very much.'

Tom opened the car door and made a dash for the bushes.

At about two, Dobbs came out.

'Her hair does look good, doesn't it?' said Alice.

Mournfully, Tom said, 'Yes, she was a stunner until we discovered what she really is; just my luck.'

'Never mind, you'll soon find someone new Tom.'

'Maybe, but this time I'll sure as hell be a bloody sight more careful and do some checking.'

'Good idea.'

Dobbs returned to her car and drove off. This time she drove to a "gastro-pub" in Canford Cliffs.

As she parked in the car park, Tom and Alice had to wait until there was a suitable space so that they could sit and wait with a view of her car, but not in the car park as this would have been spotted and looked odd.'

'And we had to have that sodding burger and I think my stomach is rebelling Alice.'

'Oh, that's nice, thanks Tom; just what I didn't want to hear.'

'Yeah, well, sorry, but I may have to go in and use their loo.'

'Can't you hold on?'

'I'll do my best, but if I do, it's the only way as we can't leave here, she might get away and we'd lose her.'

'You're right, but just be very careful that she doesn't spot you.'

Tom looked around the car and spotted a cap on the back seat. 'I'll put this on; it might just change my appearance as she's never seen me with a hat on. Better than nothing I suppose.'

'Just be careful Tom.'

He opened the car door and looked around before closing it and walking across to the restaurant doors. As luck would have it, there was a vestibule with further double glass doors into the restaurant section and he was able to look into the area with the tables. He spotted Genny Dobbs very quickly and she was talking to another woman on her table. Tom had seen the sign and moved quickly across the vestibule to the door marked "gents."

Alice was glad to see Tom returning after a few minutes and he got back into the car.

'Better now?'

'Yes thanks. I wonder how long she's going to be in there nattering to her friend?'

'That's anyone's guess Tom.'

Alice put a call into their HQ and spoke to Anna.

'Hi Alice, anything happening? Where are you?'

'We're outside a gastro-pub in Canford Cliffs. She's been in there for some time but otherwise, apart from a hair appointment, nothing. Oh, except that she went first to a car rental office in Hamworthy. We don't know what she did there as we had to follow her everywhere she went.'

Anna had put the phone on loudspeaker so that Alex could hear.

He was not best pleased at this news. 'And you didn't think to tell us this Alice? We should know what she did there and what she rented, if anything.' He said this in a voice which spoke volumes to Alice and she immediately realised that he was not happy at all. She began to feel very hot as for once, she had not done the right thing.

'I don't know why we didn't think to pass this on guv, I'm so sorry.'

Alex knew that Alice was normally good at these things, so he was not too hard on her, but said, 'Maybe it's not too late as she obviously hasn't collected a car or whatever, seeing as you are with her, just hang on.'

He turned to Anna and said, can you get the address of this car place from Alice and either call them or even go over if you have to, but we need to know exactly what she did there.'

'Right guv.'

'Okay Alice, give Anna the address and we'll get them to give us what her business was there,' and went back to the work on his desk, shaking his head.

Anna took down the address of the car rental office and directly found this on her computer. She called the number and spoke to the receptionist.

'This is Detective Sergeant Jenkins from Bournemouth Police. We are making enquiries and a person whom we wish to contact to help with information, came into your premises this morning. She was about 25 years of age with long blonde hair. Do you remember her coming in fairly early?'

Actually, yes, I thought she was unusually attractive as we don't have many ladies hiring minibuses.'

'Is that what she booked?'

'Yes, but can I ask why you need to know?'

'As I said, we need to contact her for some information. Can you give me her name and contact details?'

'Doesn't this come under the "privacy" laws or something?'

Anna rather hardened her voice and sounded a little sterner. 'Oh, I don't think so, it is not exactly a private matter and it would make things a great deal easier and save a lot of our time, so if you don't mind, I'll ask you again for her details.'

'Of course, I understand. Her name is Maygood and her address is 11 Goodson Lane in Wareham. Her number is 01202 772934. She booked a 12 seater mini-bus to be collected late this afternoon.'

'That's great, thanks. Did she say exactly what time?'

'Only around 6 pm, she wouldn't be more exact, sorry.'

'No, that's fine; you've been very helpful, thank you.'

'Always pleased to help our local police.'

'That's good. We may have to wait for her to show up this evening, but please do not mention any of this enquiry to her as we would like to keep things as private as possible.'

'Of course, nothing will be passed on, you can be sure.'

'Good, and thanks again.'

Anna went into see Alex. 'She's booked a 12 seater mini-bus for later this evening. I have her address, but I'm sure that will be false, but we have a phone number. Perhaps I should check this in case that's kosher?'

'Hmm, mini-bus. Now that's interesting. Who would that be carrying I wonder?'

'It does seem to fit in with what we're thinking doesn't it guv?'

'It does, so yes, check the number; who knows, it might yield something.'

Anna did a phone number check on the computer and came up with quite a gem.

She almost ran to Alex's office. 'Guv - bingo!'

'What's that, a result?'

'Indeed, O great master. It's only Goodyear's number.'

'Yes!' shouted Alex. 'Now we're cooking on gas. Let's get a tail on her this evening and see where she goes with the mini-bus. If we're right, then she'd be going somewhere to pick up some passengers. Now I wonder where the hell that might be?'

'It'd have to be somewhere very "out of the way" where they wouldn't be spotted.'

'Yes, but where the hell that might be is anyone's guess. There must be a thousand places where it could be, around this part of the coast.'

Okay, I'll get the surveillance organised. Should we do the tailing or perhaps two cars and four pairs of eyes would be better?'

'Yes, we'll tail and to make sure she doesn't spot a tail, we'll have Tom and Alice do "swops" with us.'

'Didn't Alice have some ideas as to where the illegals might be landed?'

'Yes, I think she said that over towards either Keyhaven or Milford on Sea would be a possibility.

'I'll call Alice and let her know. She may as well come back as we have this information.'

'Right, and I'll get the camera at the Haven Hotel organised so that we'll know when "Predator" comes back in and we can have a reception party waiting this time, and no fuck-ups.'

Alice and Tom were grateful to receive their return call and made their way back to their station.

Meanwhile, Alex made arrangements for the camera at the Haven, tested, and confirmed the communications with their office was set-up and working, to make sure that everything was as ready as possible.

CHAPTER 55

"Predator" with Goodyear and Dimitriou on board had made a fast dash across the Channel following their lucky escape in Poole Harbour, when the RIB with the Dorset Marine Unit and the Armed Response team crashed into a craft while Goodyear and Dimitriou were alongside the Whaler containing the two bodies. Two days before, these had been found by the police in the large shed on Goathorn Peninsula, in a fairly advanced state of decomposition. Left there after being discovered by the police so that Goodyear and Dimitriou would be traced and caught, they had been collected by Goodyear and Dimitriou and moved to the "Boston Whaler," moored in the harbour. Following the abortive attempt to catch them collecting the bodies, they had made their escape.

'I'm bloody glad that we managed to get those two slimy bodies dumped Martin.'
'They were a bit whiffy weren't they?' said Goodyear.
'Whiffy; Christ, they were more than that. I thought they were going to dissolve and we'd need to get them in a bucket.'
'At least they're gone now and we can get on with what we have to do to get things back on track.'
'Oh, you mean pick up these blokes who come from Northern Cyprus?'
'Yes, they're paying a shed load of money to get over to the UK.'
'And they're paying us; well, you. Anyway, why do they have to come over this way, surely they can get over here by going through Italy and France?'
'You're so dumb. Of course they can get through Europe, but they can't use their passports as they are not recognised by the UK, so they can't get in through the usual channels. As they are all either professionals or highly skilled in some way, they can afford it rather than risk being caught at the ferry ports and they need to work where the pay and prospects are a great deal better than where they come from.'
'Okay, I get it now.'
'Well, it's about bloody time.'
'I know one thing Martin, and that's that I'm glad this boat has all the technical gizmos and stuff, 'cos belting across the water at the speed we're doing and with the Channel being full of ships, it'd be bloody dangerous wouldn't it?'
'More like suicidal, but we have radar which is good, so we know the course to take to miss any big boats.'
'Yeah, I can see from the screen that they show up really well, but if we can see them, can they see us?'
'They might, that's if their crew are watching their screens all the time, but I guess that they are more likely to be checking the cross-channel ferries, rather than a very fast moving target like us.'
'Yeah, well if they do see us, won't it make them ask questions, you know, what's a fast boat doing out here?'
'I think it more likely that if they do, they'll think it's some pleasure craft belting over to Frogland for a jolly.'
'But what I mean really is, if all these boats are being monitored by what I guess is the Coastguard and they can see all the boats that are in the Channel, how come we're not on the screen?'
'This is because, my dopey little friend, our AIS is not switched on.'
'AIS, what's that?'
'What is this, Question Time? AIS is the Automatic Identification System that all ships have so that they can be monitored and tracked, but as we don't want to be actually tracked, I have ours turned off, get it?'
'Oh, right, so they don't know where we are and they can't track us?'
'Fuck me, you are so quick,' he said with biting sarcasm. 'Now I know where your name comes from, "Dim" as in Dimitriou.' That brought a sour look. 'Anyway, never mind all this, we should be there pretty soon. Go down to the galley and make us a coffee; do something useful for a change.'
'Right'o, but can I ask one thing?'
'Go on then.'
'Will there be any trouble, you know, like last time when there was that fight and you topped one after he'd killed the other one?'

'Listen, providing that the money they owe is forthcoming and they behave themselves, then all will be sweet, but I don't need to tell you that I don't take kindly to being shafted.'

'I know that for sure Martin. By the way, there is one thing.'

'And that is?'

'Where exactly are we going then, to pick them up I mean?'

'Not that it's anything to do with you, but it's a place on the Cherbourg Peninsula called Pointe du Nez on the Ainse St Martin bay; any the wiser now?'

'Not really 'cos I'm not good at geography. As long as you know where it is, that's all that matters I suppose.'

'Well, luckily for you I do and you don't really need to know, but if it shuts you up, that's good. Now, for fuck's sake go and make that coffee will you?'

'Okay.' With that, Dimitriou scuttled down to the galley in the lower part of the boat actually beneath the helm position. He braced himself against the quite violent movement of the boat and managed to brew the coffee. "wedged" as he was between the two units which made up the galley space, so that he could actually make the two cups without spilling them all over himself. "This is bloody dangerous," he said to himself as he carefully poured the boiling liquid into the cups. "That would be all I need, to pour this over my you know what's." Being very careful he managed to fill them and after stowing the various items he'd used, he made his way back to the cockpit where Martin was intently watching the radar screen as he could see two or three vessels ahead of the course he was taking. Handing the cups over, Martin gave a grunt, which Dimitriou took to be thanks. "What happened to 'thanks' then," he thought. Then he realised what Martin was looking at so intently.

'Are those little arrows boats then Martin?'

'No, they're flying saucers. Of course they are, you little tit. We have maybe three large boats ahead of us and I'm going to take a detour just so that they don't see us; Hang on.' As he said this, he put the cup into a holder on the side of the instrument dashboard and put the helm over to make a long and sweeping turn to port. There was a noticeable 'G' force caused by the heeling of the boat as it turned. Dimitriou was taken by surprise by the movement causing him to spill some hot coffee, which fell on to his stomach area. He yelped in pain as the hot liquid very quickly soaked through his trousers.

'Fucking OUCH!' he yelled. 'That's burning my bollocks!' He skipped around, trying to alleviate the pain.

Martin took a quick look round at Dimitriou and laughed.

'It's all right for you,' he said grimacing, 'it's not your balls that are cooking.'

This caused even more laughter as Martin turned back to the screen to check progress and their position. 'You should take more care and watch what's going on around you. Just make sure that you take more trouble when we're loading these guys. It's going to be a little tricky as we have to use the slipway and you'll have to help them over the side.'

'Will they have luggage with them, you know, suitcases or rucsacs and stuff like that?'

'I expect they will, so you'll have to be ready to get all that on board quickly and stowed safely.'

'Can't we get close in to shore then?'

'Close enough but as they'll have to board back at the stern where it's lower, they'll have to get their feet wet. It won't please them, but it's just their tough luck.'

'Yeah, they'll dry out by the time we get back.'

'We should be coming into the bay very soon now, so go aft and make sure everything is ready and double check all the lashings so that we can get off the coast as quickly as possible, while I call my agent.'

'I guess that where we're picking them up, is quite "out of the way" then?'

'Yes, of course; it wouldn't be much good if 10 or so men were seen standing in a group, at night, in the middle of a deserted beach. Don't you think that would raise some sort of alarm?'

'Yeah, s'pose you're right, as always.' He moved aft to check on all the lashings and equipment which had been prepared for their "trip."

After another 15 minutes, Martin called out, 'Come back, we're here.'

Dimitriou moved back to the cockpit area. Martin said, 'Right, it's quite dark and I'm going in by GPS and radar, so very slowly. When we get to the slipway, I want you to go to the bow and as soon as I give the word, jump over and make sure that the bow is off to the port side of the slipway. Take the big fender with you and tuck it under the bow section. I don't want the concrete edge of the slipway to grind into the fibreglass hull. That would really not be a good idea, would it?' This was said accompanied by a glaring look at Dimitrou. The import of this last sentence was not lost.

'Right.'

The boat slowed and in the darkness the slipway became discernible. Also, a number of dark figures could be seen against the slightly lighter horizon above the edge of the bushes lining the edge of the beach area.

Very slowly, using the GPS tracking screen for positioning, the craft was guided toward the shore. The slipway become visible in the gloom and as the boat crept slowly to the shingle beach, he put the engines to reverse and gave a very brief burst of power to stop the boat completely alongside the concrete slipway.

'Now,' he shouted to Dimitriou, who jumped over the side onto the hard surface of the slipway. He immediately reached out, pushing the bow away from the concrete and quickly wedged a fender between the boat hull and the masonry.

'Okay, fender's wedged.'

This done, Martin put just a little forward thrust to keep the bow pushed against the fender, then said, 'Right; Get them on board as quickly as you can. Just tell them to throw their bags onto the deck and we'll sort them later as soon as we're away from here.'

All the men waiting had moved down the slipway and were jostling for position. Dimitriou said to them in harsh Turkish, 'Don't push, just wait your turn. Throw your bags on to the stern and then climb aboard. Use the rope which is hanging at the back of the covered section of the boat, to put your feet in so that you can climb up. Don't rush.'

He heard various comments in Turkish and moans about getting wet as the first men were knee deep in the water. Martin was at the controls, keeping the boat correctly aligned to the shore. He heard the comments from those in the water and leaned out of the wheelhouse, saying, 'Stop your whining and get on board. If you don't want to come, we'll just leave you here.'

This made them move a little faster and quite soon they were all aboard.

Martin told Dimitriou to take out the fender and get aboard himself.

When he was safely on board, Martin reversed the boat away from the shore. He could see the van which had brought the 10 men to the beach. He waved towards the driver, who was simply a vague black shape. The van then began to move back to the road and Martin turned back to Dimitriou and said, 'Before we get under way, ask them if they all have the money with them. Tell them, anyone who doesn't have the money agreed, will be thrown overboard.'

Dimitriou did not doubt this for one second. He went back to the men who were now inside the cabin area and were sitting on the seats. 'Do you have your money ready, the full amount that was agreed?' They all appeared to nod in agreement and there were a few murmured comments which were unintelligible, but which he took to be positive, by the tone. 'If anyone doesn't have the money, they will be thrown overboard. Those are the words of the skipper, not me.'

There were more comments at this, and there were a few more mumblings, but they all seemed accepting, even if they didn't really believe the words, just the sentiment and took it as being slightly humorous.

Dimitriou thought to himself, they might think that's funny, but I know the truth; Martin means it.

Dimitriou moved forward to the wheelhouse and said to Martin, 'They all say they have the money, but they weren't too chuffed at telling them they'd be thrown overboard if they didn't, but I think they took it as funny.'

'More fool them if they don't believe me,' and began to reverse the boat a little way and then moving forward, turned to the direction for the coast of England. 'Just go back and tell them to strap themselves in and then strap down all their gear. I don't want stuff floating around the channel which could be washed up and lead back to us somehow.'

'Right-o skipper.'

'You've got it right at last,' said Martin.

Going back to the men who were sitting in the very comfortable seats, "Freddie" Dimitriou heard comments about how luxurious they were and unusual for boats to have this type of seating.

'Now,' he said speaking in his native tongue, 'you are all in special seats fitted with safety harnesses against being thrown around, and they are fitted with pneumatic suspension to make things more comfortable. Put on your

seatbelts as we are going to be travelling at around 40 knots. That is very fast for a boat and can be quite rough when the waves get larger in the English Channel, so don't worry, you'll be safe no matter how rough it gets. If you feel sick, just shout out, but don't throw up inside the cabin – use the bags like in an aircraft; do you understand?'
No reaction except blank stares.

'DO YOU UNDERSTAND?'

'Yes,' they chorused. Freddie turned back and gave the 'thumbs up' to Martin, who pushed the throttles full ahead and the boat surged forward with incredible acceleration from the twin Yamaha diesel engines powering the stern jets. Quickly reaching above 35 knots, they were flying across the dark waters, guided by the GPS display above the wheel. The radar was giving very precise detail of all the large shipping which was making way along the channel as well as the cross-channel ferries operating from Cherbourg.

They were making excellent time and when there was a suitable moment with few ships ahead to worry about Martin called Dimitriou to the wheel. He said, 'Take the wheel and keep the boat heading exactly as it is on the compass at the moment. I'm going to get the money from these punters. They know the score don't they?'

'Yeah, I explained what would happen if they didn't have the cash, but I'm not sure they believed me.'

'We'll find out then,' and he moved back into the cabin and addressed the men. 'I want you to hand over the agreed price for your safe move to Britain. I will count each bundle, so make sure it is all there. Do you understand?'

He looked around the seated 12 men and they all were making movements to locate the money which had been agreed for their passage across the channel. One of the men asked where they would be landing in England.

'Not for you to worry about my friend; it will be somewhere very private and you will not be seen. There will be a vehicle waiting for you and this will take you to a pre-arranged place where you will be able to make your way to a destination of your choice.'

'But where will we go when we are in England?'

'That is entirely up to you. You will be taken to a train station or if you prefer, a coach station where you can make an onward journey. Where you go from there is your choice. All our agreement was is to take you safely across the Channel and then to a place to facilitate your onward journey to wherever you wish to go. If you have made arrangements in advance, this will be to your benefit. My concern will cease once we have landed you.'

There were a few exchanged looks, of which some seemed to look rather concerned. As he looked around, there was one man who seemed to look quite worried. Maybe he was just not happy about being on a boat, thought Martin, but he'd keep an eye on him anyway. The others were looking for their packets of money, giving it to Goodyear, albeit seemingly reluctantly. He came to the man who looked worried. Martin held out his hand for the money and the man looked very sad and said, 'I am very sorry, but I could not get the money for you, but I will have it sent on to you later. I have made arrangements for this.'

This made Martin extremely angry and he snarled, 'I said that the money should be with you as you came on board.

'But I will send it to you very soon.'

'That's not good enough. You know the rules, everything was explained. I'm not taking people for free.'

'What are you going to do; I promise that you will get your money.'

'I don't work on promises. Come with me, and with that he reached down and unbuckled the safety harness and roughly pulled the man to his feet, whilst pulling out a long thin knife from a scabbard under his jacket. The other men looked on with a growing fear. Martin pushed the man to the rear of the cabin and out on to the open rear deck. By now, all the men were craning their necks to see what was going on. As they exited the rear of the cabin, Martin turned back, saying 'This is what I do to people who try to cheat me, and he pushed the man to the stern rail and gave him a very sharp and forceful push. At the same time, with a single swift movement, the knife sliced the throat and the man bent backwards over the rail and was then given a further hard push. He disappeared into the twin powerful jet streams which produced in the region of 20,000 pounds of thrust and the body was instantly smashed by this incredible force and disappeared in the darkness. Without a sound, he was gone, left to drown in the middle of the Channel. Goodyear said to no-one in particular, 'Just a pity there are no sharks around.'

Moving back through the cabin, all the men looked at Martin with total disbelief. They were all holding out the packets of money.

'That's more like it. Are there any more of you who want a free ride?'

They all shook their heads in unison.

Martin took all the packets and said, 'I'll count these and if there's any missing, you now have a good idea what might happen to you.'

Several of the men muttered, "Bütün paranın orada olduğunu bulacaksınız, efendim," you will find all the money is there.

'We shall see,' said Martin and went forward to the wheelhouse where Freddie was concentrating hard on the screens and compass.

'I can't believe you just did that Martin,' said Freddie, although he was not totally surprised as three people had been killed already, so he knew exactly what Martin was capable of.

Trying to change the subject, he asked Martin, 'What's the score when we get back then?'

'Right, we are going to a place called Keyhaven. It's near Milford on Sea. We'll drop the "cargo" at a spot off the beaten track and should be clear of any traffic or parked vehicles as we'll be back in the dark. It's very awkward to get in but we have a GPS location and with our depth finder we can make a slow entrance as before as it's very shallow there, but enough room for us. There's a collection of rocks just on the coast and we can get close to them and do the same as in Cherbourg with the fender. They can jump off and the van will be waiting on the road just across the small bridge. They'll see it from the beach.

CHAPTER 56

With the webcam set up at the Haven Hotel on Sandbanks, everything was ready for the following of the van which Genny Dobbs was due to collect. The rental office was under surveillance via the CCTV cameras which covered that area of the trading estate where the office was located. Alex and Anna were to be in one car with Tom and Alice in the second. The intention was to follow the rented van to wherever "Predator" was presumed to be dropping the suspected illegal immigrants, probably collected from France. At that moment, this location was completely unknown, although it was suspected that it would be somewhere along the coast between Southampton and Poole. Only by following the van would they know the location.

Both teams were in the office and Alex said, 'When we know where she takes the van, we'll have to decide on our plan of action then. We don't know where or when at the moment, so we'll have to make some quick decisions once we know where she goes.'
Tom ventured, 'It will have to be somewhere quite out of the way, won't it? I mean, they won't want to have a number of bodies walking around a fairly populated area at night; that's bound to arouse suspicion isn't it?'
'Absolutely Tom; I'm thinking that somewhere along the coast as Alice has suggested, perhaps Milford way, as the access beyond that is very limited. She has to go where there is access for a van which won't arouse suspicion but won't look out of place. Does anyone have any ideas for a place like that?'
Alice said, 'I've been to the beach at New Milton, but it was quite some time ago. I seem to remember that we were staying at a caravan site along there. I know we walked along the beach where there was a road but beyond that part there was no road and it was only possible to walk along the shore.'
'Was there any access for a boat there Alice?'
'I really don't know. I only remember that we walked past a small lake or maybe it was large pond and came to a little bridge from the road. I think that beyond that there was a little, what you would call an "inlet" with a few small boats in.'
'That sounds a possible place to land some people out of sight Alice. Do you think "Predator" could go into this inlet out of sight of buildings?' Anna asked.
'I really don't know, although having seen the photos of "Predator," I somehow doubt it. All I can say is that is a place that I think could be suitable as it would be quite away from buildings or people, especially at night.'
'Thanks Alice,' said Alex, 'that does sound to be a possibility.'
There was a murmur and Alex said, 'Yes Anna?'
'I was thinking that perhaps if we looked at this area on Google Maps, we could check it out and other possible places which could be suitable, knowing the size of "Predator."'
'Damn good idea Anna. Do we know the draught needed for "Predator" Tom?'
'Not offhand guv, but I can find out quickly enough I think, but as it has stern drive jets, maybe it doesn't need too much water.'
'Good thinking Tom. The problem is that it makes it all the more difficult to pin down a possible landing place, but maybe the access road will be the deciding factor.'
'We have to have some idea of their approach possibilities. In the meantime, Alice, can you keep in touch with the CCTV operations room to make sure they understand the importance of letting us know the moment she collects the van?'
'Right-o guv.' She put the call through to the CCTV control room in Poole and passed on the message.
'Okay, listen up, I think we could be in for a bit of a "run-around" soon, so I suggest we all get some food and drink inside us before we get the signal. Who knows, we might be in for a long night, so I don't want any whinging about being hungry or thirsty as we have to keep tabs on this one and make no mistakes. We all know what happened last time. I try to forget it but it's something that haunts me, if I'm honest.'
'We all know guv,' said Anna. 'We're all on the ball, don't worry. This time, we'll get it right.'

'Thanks for that. I know we've had some set-backs already, but I think now that they think they've got away, I can't believe that Metin Denizci or "Martin" is the sort of person that will miss the chance of making money, whatever the circumstances. He's shown that by making his getaway when he must have known that he was being chased.'

'And he even managed to get the two bodies off the "Whaler," he must have thought that without them, we had no proof,' said Tom.

'He seems to have ignored the DNA evidence we have Tom,' ventured Anna.

Maybe he doesn't know we have any?'

'That's possible I suppose, but then perhaps he is so self-opinionated that he thinks he is bomb-proof.'

''Okay people, let's get fuelled up and be ready for the word from CCTV ops,' said Alex.

'Anna, words please before you go to the canteen or wherever,' said Alex. 'Come into my office please.'

She walked in and he motioned for her to close the door.

'If all goes well, we're going to be able to spend some private time together again; I'm rather looking forward to that.'

'Me too Alex,' she said. 'Do you think we'll be able to have another evening together soon?'

She was thinking that to be completely honest, she was having some rather disquieting thoughts about their future, but for now she put these thoughts to the back of her mind.

'I certainly hope so. I've been looking forward to some private time. I really need you and we've been just too busy lately. Especially after our last evening was brought to a rather abrupt ending.'

'I know; I think I feel the same; hopefully, this case will have a good ending soon.'

'Let's hope so. We've had a few setbacks, but I think it's going to come to a good conclusion soon; or at least it will, if we can catch these bastards in the act.'

'Do you think we can get them as they land the immigrants then Alex?'

'We could possibly get the blokes as they come ashore, but to stop the boat is going to be bloody difficult, if not impossible but once they drop them off and we get them, I'm sure that some of the blokes will give us a clue as to where they will take "Predator." 'If I'm right and they think we have no proof and they can just come back here, moor up and get away, then we can put on a reception for them. We should have a report of them coming back through the Haven, so we won't be caught out again.'

'We have enough evidence to get a conviction then?'

'We do. What with the DNA and other recorded finds together with the forensics, we've got them "bang to rights" I'd say.'

'Well yes, we have the bodies found in the shed on Goathorn which we then found on the "Whaler." Do you think they don't know that we found them?'

'I hope they don't. You see, I think that as they managed to get the two bodies off the "Whaler" before the Marine Unit got to them, they might think that they've removed the evidence, but again, there's going to be DNA traces everywhere on that boat. In fact, they'll probably try to get back to it and hose it all down to clean up the traces.'

'Yes, they can't be so completely dumb as to think there are no traces but I would think they'll do everything they can to get things cleaned up quickly.'

'If we can get this case to come to a satisfactory conclusion, then you and I are going to have some really quality time together; and that's a promise Anna.'

'Now that is something I am really looking forward to.' As she said this, Alex gently caressed the side of her face with the back of his hand. This sent a little quiver through her, although suddenly having to quell the memory of Fuller Masterson doing the same thing, and the feeling it gave her then.

They both took the opportunity to get a meal before the possible long night ahead. As they headed to the canteen, they were joined by Tom and Alice.

'What do think our chances are guv?' said Tom.

'Given that we have surveillance on the rental office and someone at the Haven, we should be able to follow the van that Dobbs collects to wherever the pickup point is going to be. I don't think we'll be able to make an arrest at that point as they are going to be on the water.'

'No, I don't suppose that would be easy guv,' said Alice. 'I mean, they could simply just go back off the coast and we'd not know where they went.'

'That just means that we have to time the event so that they don't see anything out of the ordinary until the very last moment.'

'But you said we had someone watching at the Haven guv, we'll know if they come back to Poole won't we?'

'Hopefully, yes and it's not a "someone" but a webcam and we'll have one of our back-up team sitting here watching the screen all the time, so we'll have instant knowledge. We have all we need to catch them, but I'm not going to be too cocky, just in case something happens that we haven't planned for.'

Anna put her head to one side as she said, 'What do you think that might be then guv?'

Alex gave a little smirk and said, 'If I knew what that was, I'd have planned for it wouldn't I?'

They all had a little snigger and Anna said, 'I asked for that didn't I? I mean, what do you think they might be able to do?'

'The only thing we don't really know is, do they have any guns. That could make things very messy as we know they're not going to stop at more killing if they're cornered.'

'That's true,' said Alice. 'By the way guv, I had a look at Google Maps, you know, in that place which I mentioned, and there's a place which I think could be suitable.'

'Good work Alice. Let me take a look after we've had a bite to eat and I can see what it looks like.'

All four were very keen to make this investigation end well, following the previous debacle.

Alex seemed a little apprehensive but positive and the others were eager to make good progress.

They were all a little subdued during their meal, each with their own thoughts. 'I'm not really feeling that hungry guv,' said Tom. 'I thought I was, but after all that time out on "Othniel" waiting for something to happen, I think my need for 'energy replacement' has taken a dive.'

'Just get the fuel on board Tom; it could be quite a long night. We don't know what time they expect to get back.'

'No problem for me guv,' said Alice.

As they were nearing the end of their meals, a DC came in and said, 'Message for DCI Vail.'

Alex looked up and motioned that the message was for him.

'Okay, we've had word from surveillance at the rental office over in Poole that the party you are interested in has just driven off in an12 seater white mini-van. They are following this and will report back as soon as they know the route being taken.'

'Great, thanks.'

'Okay people, let's go. The game is on.'

All four moved quickly.

'Right, you know what to do Alice and Tom. We pick up this van and switch and switch about during the tailing, so that she won't suspect that she's being followed. Is that clear?'

'Yes guv,' they said in unison.

'We'll keep in radio contact all the time and if either car gets blocked in by traffic, the other is to overtake and go ahead until we can get back to tailing her. Keep no more than two or three cars between you and the van, okay?'

'Sounds good guv let's go,' said Tom.

'Right, now as she's just leaving Poole, there is no real rush, just let's get into position and I'll let you know the route as soon as I can, and by the way, don't lose her or you'll be directing traffic for the foreseeable future.'

Both teams went down the staircase to the ground floor and got into their respective cars. Alex and Anna were in a suitably nondescript car and similarly, Tom and Alice.

CHAPTER 57

There was a radio call from the Poole surveillance team that the target van was heading towards Bournemouth along the A35 Commercial Road and was now approaching Ashley Cross.

'Okay, message received. Stay with them until you know the major road they are taking. We will take over after they get to Redlands Roundabout and then we'll know their intention.'

After a short while, another message came through.

"Poole surveillance to DCI Vail."

"Receiving, go ahead."

"Poole surveillance, target vehicle turned onto A35, repeat A35 towards Bournemouth."

"Poole surveillance, received, please continue to follow target to County Gates Gyratory and we will take over from there, once we know their final direction."

"Received; will do."

Alex turned to Anna and said,' Okay, you're the driver from now on. I'll tell Tom and Alice and we'll get to County Gates and wait there, to take over our rolling surveillance. Let's not lose them.'

'No way Alex.'

Alex opened his window and looked across to Tom and Alice. 'We'll pick the van up at County Gates. We can park up briefly in Lindsay road, just before the gyratory starts and wait for Poole surveillance lads to give us their approach accurately.'

'Okay guv,' said Tom. 'On our way,' and they drove off.

'We'll rendezvous with them there Anna.'

'Right, let's go.' Anna was secretly pleased that she was driving as she was a skilled driver, having passed her Advanced Driving Test and the ERDT course a couple of years previously. She loved driving and it was only the fact that her pay scale didn't run to a sportier car than her present Ford Fiesta, that she didn't have the Mazda MX3 which she would really like. She'd thoroughly enjoyed the ERDT or Emergency Response Driver Training course which gave her tremendous confidence.

'I know you like driving Anna, but please just keep our van in sight and don't lose them. Nothing fast, she's only driving a van, and I would assume that she'll be keeping to the speed limits and not attract the attention of speed cops.'

'No, I don't suppose she will. Don't worry, nothing fancy today Alex.'

'That's my girl,' he said with a friendly glance at her.

Both cars travelled along the A338 towards Poole and entered the County Gates Gyratory system where the A35 becomes the A338, arriving virtually at the same time. Again, both cars made the partial circuit of the one-way system and exited at Lindsay Road. Using their radios, Alex said, 'Alice, we'll make a "U" turn and park up so that we can both join up the one-way behind the van once we know it's on the A338. I don't think she'll be going through Westbourne as that would take her back into Bournemouth and we know she's going to somewhere along the coast.'

'Doing just that now guv.'

'Good, we just sit and wait for the word from surveillance.'

'Shouldn't be too long' said Anna.

'No I don't think so. I'm looking forward to a nice meal soon and I'll take you to a restaurant we haven't been to. One I've been checking out; you like Thai food don't you?'

'Love it.'

'Good. I was hoping you'd say that. It's a place not far from here actually, down near Ashley Cross. It's been there a good while, this little Thai restaurant. I know they've got a good reputation and it's not too far from your place, so maybe we could go back there afterwards.'

'That would be really nice and yes, of course we can go back to mine.'

'That's a deal then. I really like your flat as it always smells so deliciously feminine, well, it smells of you and that's what makes it so wonderful. It's just super sexy, like you.'

'I'll make sure there are some soft lights on when we get back.'

'You don't really think we need soft lights to get us in the mood,' he asked, raising his eyebrows, 'do you?'

'Not if last time was anything to go by Alex.'

'We were just a little passionate weren't we?'

'A little more than just a little, I'd say; something to look forward to.'

'I'll second that. Just a little.'

'Right, just you wait, you little minx.'

'Hmm.' Was her passion waning just a little?'

The radio burst into life. "Poole surveillance to DCI Vail."

"Go ahead."

"Target vehicle approaching County Gates. Are you in position?"

"Affirmative; vehicle registration please."

"Target vehicle registration is Papa 82 Charlie Mike Alpha. White Ford Transit 12 seat Mini-Bus – windows fitted."

"Received, understood, we'll take over now, thanks for your help."

"Good luck DCI Vail; Poole surveillance out."

Alex then put a call through to the marine unit. They were not too happy about the previous abortive and horribly expensive attempt at capturing "Predator" and its crew, but this time they had better warning.

Talking to Paul Rickson, the head of the Marine Section, he said, 'We have good information Paul, and we think they'll be going to land somewhere around New Milton. We've located what we think would be a suitable site which is away from traffic and buildings, but close to the coast. Can you liaise with the AR unit and be around that area at the times I will give you, I think we stand a very good chance of catching them as they unload. How does that stand with you guys?'

'Sorry to disappoint you old son, but we've been tasked elsewhere and it's completely impossible tonight, sorry. '

'Bollocks,' he said forcefully. 'Paul, I should have seen this coming but things have been moving so fast that we've not had time to make arrangements ahead. Actually, not to worry as I don't think we could have stopped the boat but we'll get anyone who is landed.'

'Sorry we can't be any help tonight.'

'Not to worry Paul, we've got other possibilities.'

'Okay, best of luck then.'

Turning back to Anna, he said, 'That's a bugger, a "no no" from Paul. Okay, the van'll be here at any moment.' He radioed this information to Tom and Alice, telling them to move off and as soon as they spot the van in question, to let him know and they will take up the following close behind. They waved their acknowledgement.

Tom moved off and as they entered the short section of the one-way system which joined the A35, Alice said, there it is; white van, reg P82CMA. That's the one.' Alice immediately radioed Alex. 'Got it guv. We're two cars behind it.' As they moved off he radioed, 'Okay Alice, we are another three cars behind you, so we have to stay on the Wessex Way until we get to the Bournemouth West Roundabout, then we'll be on the dual carriageway and things will be much easier.'

Alex was then about to radio their control to ask for a PNC check on the registration of that vehicle, but then thought the better of it, realising that it was from a rental company, so checking the registration was of no use.

With the van ahead, and Alice and Tom following close behind, they kept their distance.

Turning to Anna, he said, 'If she's on the A338, then she's either heading for Christchurch or beyond.'

'Don't you think Christchurch is unlikely, because wherever a boat might come ashore around there is going to be very visible?'

'Yes, you're right. Mind you, if she carries on the A338, that goes up to Ringwood, and that's way off a possible place, don't you think?'

'Absolutely; perhaps, if she goes through Christchurch, then she could be heading for New Milton or even that place that Alice told us about.'

'I think that's more than likely, so we'll have to wait and see where she goes at the junction with Castle Lane, you know, where the Royal Bournemouth Hospital is.'

With that, Alex passed on this possibility to Alice and Tom. After he'd shared his thoughts, he said, 'Okay, I think it's time we changed position, so you drop back a little and let us take over behind the van.'

'Will do guv,' Alice responded. They dropped back and Anna overtook them to take up station behind the van, which was travelling as expected, exactly at the speed limit.

After another few minutes, they approached the large roundabout at the junction with Castle Lane.

'Yes, she's signalling to exit the 338, so she must be going through Christchurch.'

Alex relayed this to Alice and Tom so that they could follow. 'I'll let you know when we need change over again.'

'Very good guv.'

Anna then said rather excitedly, 'Do you think we should have the backup team ready, now we have a good idea where they're going?'

'Did that earlier' He called the office for the pre-arranged squad to be assembled and get on the road towards the New Milton area. He told the station officer that they would be given the final destination as soon as this was apparent.

As the traffic was not heavy, it was probably a good idea to keep changing position or Dobbs might realise that the same vehicle had been following for some time. She was bound to be on her guard.

As expected, Dobbs took the exit and passed the Royal Bournemouth Hospital towards Christchurch. This was a dual carriageway section until the road narrowed up to the Iford Roundabout. As she approached this, she signalled a left turn.

'Tom, Alice, she's taking the exit onto the A35 through Christchurch as we expected, so there'll probably be no chance of overtaking until we get beyond that new system by the Travelodge just before the Christchurch By-pass, do you know it?'

'Yes guv; got that. We'll just stay behind you until we know for sure which route she'll take.'

'I reckon she'll take the by-pass and head toward New Milton; what do you think,' asked Anna.

'Seems reasonable as she can't keep going along the coast this way. If she'd been heading for somewhere near Southampton, she'd have stayed on the A338.'

'I'll confirm this to the lads in the van.' He passed on the confirmation to the backup van.

They were now on the Christchurch by-pass which was dual carriageway, so Alex told the other car to take over the follow.

When they got to the next roundabout, it became obvious that she was taking the Highcliffe direction.

Anna then suggested that by now, she may well have spotted the same car following her for some time.

'Yes, I think you're quite right Anna.' He then radioed to Tom. 'At the next roundabout we come to, we are going to go right round this, so that we exit on the same road, but If she's watching, she'll think we have turned off. We'll exit behind you and this should give us cover again.'

Alice confirmed this action.

At the next roundabout, Anna signalled and to all intents and purposes left the Highcliffe Road, but simply made a circuit and re-joined the road but behind Tom and Alice.

As the road, now the A337 was single carriageway, overtaking was not possible, so staying behind the white van was no problem.

The van continued on this road right through Highcliffe passing the Forest Arts Centre.

Coming up to the next roundabout, Alice radioed, 'Target vehicle turning right right right, on to the B3058.'

'Received Alice; If she stays on this road, it passes the Barton-on-Sea Golf Club doesn't it?'

'Yes guv; following.'

Anna then said, 'The road has changed to Park Lane, although it stays the B3058 and we're coming into Milford-on-Sea High Street.'

'Right; do you think she'll head for Lymington or somewhere nearer?'

'I'd suggest she's going to make for Keyhaven or somewhere like that as Lymington is very populated, especially near the water.'

'I think we should make a change,' said Alice. 'We can pull into that forecourt quickly and the sarge can overtake.'

Alice told the other car of their intention.

'Good idea, well done.'

Once again changing their positions, Anna was now ahead.

'And Keyhaven isn't very populated? I don't know this area too well.'

'I think Keyhaven is more likely.'

As Anna said this, the van ahead began signalling right. 'Yes, look, she's turning right into Keyhaven Road.'

Again, Alex radioed back; 'At the lights, target turning right right right, into Keyhaven Road.'

'Okay guv, we can see you, we're only two cars behind you.'

After turning right, the van travelled for about another half-mile and then began signalling right again.

'Target taking another turn right right right, into, hang on...' turning to Anna he asked, 'what road is this?'

'New Lane, guv.'

'Right right right, into New Lane.'

Tom said to Alice, 'I don't know why he has to say "right" three times, I mean, we can see him can't we?

Alice told him that she supposed the radio conversations were being monitored and recorded back at base and procedure has to be followed in case of any problems.'

'I suppose so,' said Tom, 'it just seems a bit over the top to me.'

After a fairly short time, they passed a large caravan site on their right, and after that, there was nothing; no buildings, just darkness.

Checking their GPS screen, Anna said, 'We're near the sea now, it's just over there behind the caravan park. It's very quiet here; maybe this is where she's going to stop.'

'Damn, yes, I think you're right; slow right down; so that we can see if she does stop.'

Anna slowed the car almost to a stop. The rear lights of the van were visible a little way ahead. As the road was straight at this point, it was easily spotted in the distance.

Alice came on the radio. 'Guv, this is the place where I found on the Google Map, you know where we thought it might be the likely place for "Predator" to land these blokes.'

'That's a big brownie point for you Alice.'

Anna then said, 'look, she's stopping. That's her brake lights and she's pulling over.'

'Okay, that's it, great. Do we have those binoculars with us?'

'We do guv; they're just behind your seat. Shall I turn off our lights?'

'Hell, yes.'

Alex reached back behind his seat and found the binocular case. He took them out and focussed on the van, which was discernible in the distance, although it was very dark by now.

'I'm glad we stopped when we did as it seems as though there is nowhere to park along this road without being obvious.'

'That could be a problem though guv, I mean, if the boat does come in and land some bodies, we're a long way off, aren't we?'

'Good point. I think if we get Tom and Alice to wait a while, and then drive past the van, to go further on and park up, we can approach from both sides when they come ashore.'

'That seems to be a cunning plan guv.'

'I thought so.' He then radioed to Alice. "DCI Vail to Alice."

"Receiving," came the reply.

"Alice, you and Tom, wait for about five minutes and then drive past the van, go along this road for about ¾ of a mile so that you're out of sight of the van, then do a 'U' turn and park up with the van in sight. Turn off your lights and I'll call you when it's time to get back.'

"Okay, but what if she sees us as we go past?"

"Hopefully she'll think you are a pair out for a bit of nooky."

This prompted a strange look from Tom.

'Okay guv, understood. Is that so we can get them from both sides then?'

'Exactly.'

See, she's quick, our Alice,' he said to Anna with a chuckle.

'So now we sit and wait to see if our predictions are right?'

'We do Anna. What can we do to while away the time I wonder.'

'I think you'd better just sit and wonder, 'cos if you do what I think you'd like to do, we'd miss everything as the windows would be all steamed up, wouldn't they?'

Glumly, he said, 'Hmm, I s'pose you're right. I'd better leave that for our night together which can't come soon enough for me.'

'Just make sure you don't then; too soon I mean.'

That occasioned a wry smile from Alex.

They settled for a covertly swift kiss and waited patiently.

CHAPTER 58

Alex then put a call in to the Bournemouth Police Control who were monitoring their radio transmissions.
"Control from DCI Vail - we are parked in New Lane, Milford-on-Sea. We have the target vehicle in view. We are waiting for the suspect boat to arrive with a possible number of illegal immigrants. The actual number is unknown, but the craft is known to have a capacity of 14. Therefore, as per our arrangements, can you please have the support vehicle, move to this location?' Pausing, he looked at Anna, who said, 'The Carrington Park Caravan Site."
He continued, "Park adjacent to the Carrington Park Caravan site, with no lights and to await my instructions by radio."
"Understood DCI Vail. Is there anything further?"
"Yes, for reference, can you look up this location on Google Maps and give me the GPS Location?"
"Give me two minutes DCI Vail." Shortly, the result came through. "The GPS Location at the junction of New Lane and Saltgrass Lane is 50.716504 – 1.576867. There is a small footbridge from the junction which leads onto the beach, but no vehicular access. The support vehicle will be in position in less than five minutes as they were on standby as arranged."
"Excellent, thanks Control."
"Control standing by - good luck."

*

Nearing the coastline of Britain, "Predator" was making a steady 35 knots in a sea which was not rough, but by no means slight. Accordingly, many of the men on board were feeling queasy and some had actually managed to stagger to the rear open deck and managed to lose whatever they had managed to eat, over the side. They had been warned by Dimitriou against leaving any mess on the boat and made to understand the consequences. In fact, they were in absolutely no doubt as to the veracity of these instructions, having witnessed what Martin Goodyear had done to the man who had not paid his passage. Accordingly, some of these men had moved to the stern and taken the appropriate steps to expel their food, downwind, albeit against the instructions not to leave their seats.
'Right, Freddie, we're getting near to Hurst Castle now and there are some pretty bad currents around here.'
'Why's that then?'
'Because dumbo, Hurst Castle, is the narrowest part of the Solent, so that when the tide runs either in or out, the turbulence caused can make some quite powerful whirlpools.'
'And will these whirlpools affect us then?'
'I really doubt it, but they may make the boat move a little strangely, so I want you to tell these muppets behind us, not to worry. Get it?'
'Got it.'
'Good. Now, we're going to have to get really close to the shore and I'm aiming for a pile of rocks which will give us something to hold up against. I want you to go over like you did on the slipway when we picked them up, and wedge the big fender under the bow. Place it so that we don't barge into the rocks and damage the hull, do you think you can actually do that without fucking it up?'
'Yes, of course I can.'
'You'd better, because if my hull is damaged, you have no idea how mad I can get.'
'Yes I do Martin.'

Using his GPS monitor mounted just below the weather-screen of the boat, Goodyear slowed the craft as he came towards the small mound of rocks which was about half a kilometre west along the shore from Hurst Castle.

'Right, we're here, so get that fender ready. Tell these muppets back in the cabin to stay in their seats with their seatbelts on, until I tell them to move. I don't want them to be running about trying to get off until I say, got that?'

'Yeah, got it.'

Goodyear slowed down to a virtual stop by using the reverse thrusters, bringing the craft to a standstill. Then he moved slowly ahead, gently to the shore where he could now just about make out the rocks. 'Tie that fender off to the bow cleat, in case we reverse and forget it. We can always pull it back on board later.'

Dimitriou was standing just back from the bow, ready to jump down on to the rocks with the fender. As the boat nosed in, he could also see the rocks and jumped down with the large fender. The bow was quite high, and he landed quite heavily, twisting his ankle badly on the rough rocks. He yelled out in pain and went down on to his knees. Goodyear looked out of the wheelhouse to see what the noise was about. 'What's up?' he called.

'I think I've broken my bloody ankle, that's what's up, on these sodding rocks.'

'Never mind that, just get that fender in place, or you'll have more than a twisted ankle.'

Although not broken, he had severely twisted his ankle and was in serious pain. Hobbling with the fender he managed to push it between the bow section of the boat and the rocks, which were very sharp in some places. He knew what might happen if the bow was pushed onto those and dreaded the consequences.

As an afterthought, Goodyear called to Dimitriou. 'Take the anchor up to the beach so that I don't have to stay at the engine controls to keep us on the shore.'

'I can't get back. I can't stand on my leg, it's too bloody painful,' he said.

'Oh, for fuck's sake,' was Goodyear's mumbled response.

'Okay, stay there, I'll release the anchor and pass it down to you, but don't take so long, we never know who might turn up here. I don't care if you have to crawl on your hands and knees, but get that anchor set.'

Goodyear went to the bow where the anchor was stowed and released the holding pin. After throwing the heavy anchor down to Dimitriou, he looked up at the shoreline and could see the ghostly shape of the white van. Just then he could just make out Genny Dobbs in the distance crossing the small bridge leading to the beach from the road where she'd parked the van.

She'd seen the boat in the gloom. Although it was a dark night, it was still possible to see the boat against the horizon, certainly enough to see them arriving. She waved to Goodyear and ran down the beach.

Good girl, he thought, just as arranged. He'd used a PAYG phone to call her advising the time of arrival accurately, thanks to the GPS. He'd also told her to destroy the SIM card and throw her phone away as soon as she could.

Meanwhile, Dimitriou had managed to drag the anchor part-way up the beach and bury the flukes as deeply as he could. He signalled to Goodyear which enabled him to put the engines into very gentle reverse to put strain to the anchor. This had the effect of keeping the boat stationary.

Goodyear then turned to the men in the cabin behind him and said, 'Okay, you can take off your seatbelts now and make your way to the rear of the boat, in the open deck, ready to go over. Take any luggage you have with you. Anything left will be thrown over the side later. Don't rush.'

'We are here, we have arrived?' They were all smiling and looking happy that they had finally got to their destination after a prolonged and usually arduous journey. Looking over the side of the boat, they realised that they would have to get wet; this did not go down too well. There was a murmuring of; 'We are going to get wet again, the water is quite deep here.'

'It's not deep and you'll soon dry out. At least you'll be on land and not in the middle of the sea – like someone else...'

This caused a few to exchange looks which were very expressive.

Goodyear told them in their own language, 'Anyway, yes you've arrived and there is a vehicle waiting to take you to the next phase of your journey. Where you go now is entirely up to you. You will be taken to a railway or coach station, whichever you decide. I would advise a railway station as this is more impersonal, but it's your choice. You were told to have British money ready, so if you haven't, you're going to have some problems, but my part of the arrangement is now fulfilled, so the sooner you are away from here the better. Go with this lady who is coming now.'

They clambered over the side of the boat, into water which was only knee deep. Several were moaning about this, but most decided that silence would be a better idea.

As Genny Dobbs approached the boat, she looked up at Goodyear. 'Hi Martin, it's good to see you.'

Goodyear then leaned down over the rail of the boat and kissed her on the forehead. 'Good girl, you made it on time. Were you followed?'

'No, I'm sure of it. I kept checking behind me and there were always different cars, some overtook and then turned off – I'm sure that no-one was tailing me, I mean why would they, it's only a hire van, pretty ordinary.'

'Okay, that's good. The sooner you get these guys on board, the sooner you can get them to a station.'

'Do they know which station they want to go to, I mean I can go to Christchurch, Bournemouth or Poole stations, they're all along the route back home.'

'I know Dimitriou had words with them about that on the way over, he'll have told them those three options and it's up to them now. Don't let them tell you otherwise. They'll have to tell you once they're in the van and on the way.'

'Just one thing Martin, do any one of them speak English, because I don't know any Turkish, do I?'

'Yes, I think a couple of them do, so they'll have to translate whatever they decide, and make them stick to it, okay?'

'I'll make sure they do, don't worry. I expect you want to get away as soon as you can, so will I see you back at home tomorrow?'

'Yes, we'll take Predator back to Cobbs Marina and moor up. I'll probably be home tomorrow afternoon.'

'That's great, I've missed you.'

'I've missed you too and with all that's happened before we got away to France, I'm knackered.'

'Why, what happened then?'

'The police chased us; well we think they were chasing us, but we got to the "Whaler" in time to unload the two "items" so now they would have no evidence even if they did contact us, so we are in the clear.'

'Are you sure there is no evidence?'

'There's nothing left, we've made sure of that. Just get these blokes off my hands, I've had enough.'

'Right, I'll get off then, see you later.'

 With that, she turned away and followed the men who were making their way up the beach.

Goodyear then shouted to Dimitriou to be ready to remove the large fender which was wedged under the bow, protecting it from the sharp rocks.

'Okay, ready when you are skipper.'

'Right, take out the fender, and then get back aboard.'

Goodyear then started the engines and Dimitriou pulled hard on the large fender. It pulled clear, and he let it drop, then ran back to the stern. 'Okay skipper, clear. I'm coming back aboard.'

As he was doing this, completely unknown to either him or Goodyear, there was a considerable wave heading towards them. Caused by the wash of a very large fully-laden tanker which had passed the Isle of Wight on its way to discharge the cargo of oil at the refinery terminal at Fawley. It had passed some time ago and in the dark it had not been noticed. The large wake from this craft caused by the displacement of some 50,000 tons had resulted in the wave now approaching "Predator."

At the moment Dimitriou had removed the fender, the wave, which had not crested, but rather was a "heap" of wave energy, pushed hard against the hull. As the boat was broadside to the oncoming wave, the full force of the energy pushed the boat hard against the rocks.

Goodyear felt the surge as the boat lifted and lurched sideways; he heard the splintering crack as the hull was forced against the rocks with a crunching sound as they broke through the fibreglass hull.

'What the FUCK was that?' he yelled.

Dimitriou was just climbing over the rail on the stern deck as the boat lurched. He fell backwards into the water and the boat swung sideways, on top of him, forcing him underwater, briefly pinning him down. Dimitriou, through his diving training, instinctively held his breath and remained as calm as he could.

The unexpected and unseen movement had taken Goodyear completely by surprise and he realised that some severe damage had been done. In the almost total darkness it would be almost impossible to see the damage.

As the boat swung back after the wave had thrown Dimitriou back overboard and driven him under the boat. He'd managed to struggle to the surface, coughing and spluttering, not knowing what had happened.

He'd heard Goodyear's shout and now was trying to clamber back on board once again with great difficulty and swearing. Being somewhat otherwise engaged underwater at the time, he'd not heard the sound of the damage, but as he moved back through the now empty cabin, he could hear Goodyear swearing loudly.

'What the hell happened skipper?' he asked.

'It was probably a wake wave from a large ship; I should have thought of that and checked the movements of shipping in the Channel.'

'What the hell is a "wake wave" when it's at home then?'

Not that it matters to you, you dummy, but it's when a large ship passes, it displaces a large amount of water causing a wave, just like the one that's just FUCKING HIT US! - Didn't you hear that bloody noise as the boat rocked? I think the bow has been breached; this is going to really fuck us up.

'No, I think I was under the boat, I nearly drowned.'

'Well, it didn't stop you bleating; and anyway, that bloody great fender should have been under the boat, to stop that happening.'

'Well, I'd just taken it out as you told me and thrown it back on board as the boat lurched.'

'I don't want excuses, you little shit, it's thanks to you we've now got this fucking problem.'

'That's not fair, it wasn't my fault, I just did what you told me,' he whined.

Goodyear realised that was exactly what had happened and it was an unlucky coincidence that the wave struck just a few seconds after the fender had been removed. He now had to quickly inspect the damage to see if the boat was taking in water.

CHAPTER 59

Alex was looking at the white van parked up and saw the girl open the drivers' door and get out. She walked over to the small bridge which gave access to the beach. As she got to the end of the bridge, he saw her wave. He swung the binoculars slightly to the right and could just make out the dark shape of "Predator" sitting, what would be, close to the beach.

'They've arrived,' he said to Anna and passed the binoculars to her.

She took a look and murmured her agreement as she saw Dobbs moving down to the beach and almost disappearing from view, but not quite.

'As soon as we can see more heads, that'll mean that the immigrants are here.'

"DCI Vail to support vehicle," he radioed.

"Come in DCI Vail."

"Follow me. I will close up to the rear of the white van up ahead at the point where the road turns sharp left, into Saltgrass Lane. We will make the arrest of the female and all the males. Keep close behind as we have to get all the illegals. No lights, repeat, no lights. Go on my signal."

"Understood. Moving now."

Alex had motioned to Anna to start the engine as he was saying this and then radioed to Tom and Alice.

'Vail to Tom.'

Alice answered, 'Yes guv?'

'Close up to the white van, it's here.'

'We heard you tell support, we're on our way guv.'

Tom also started the engine and put the car into gear, moving off to effectively block the road ahead of the white van.

'Don't use any lights; we don't want to spook them at this stage.'

'Okay guv.'

With all three vehicles closing up either side of the white van, the men, who were walking ahead of Dobbs, saw the white van but also two other cars and another dark blue van. As they were crossing the bridge, some turned to each other with questioning glances. Several said that they only expected one van, but maybe it was because they were going to different places, so there were different vehicles. They didn't know.

Alex radioed, "Go go go." The support team poured out of the dark van. Alex and Anna, together with Tom and Alice also joined the number of officers who were now surrounding the men.

They soon found out that everything was not right, realising that they were now in serious trouble.

A couple of them hurriedly put their rucsacs on their shoulders and tried to run. The basic problem for them was not only did they have no idea where to run to, but instantly, they were stopped by quite determined police officers.

Genny Dobbs, who had been the last over the bridge, saw this taking place ahead of her, and instantly realised that she had only one possible course of action. She turned about and ran back down the beach towards "Predator."

While the men had been tramping up the beach, Goodyear had jumped over the side of the craft to inspect the damage. With a torch, he could see a quite large hole in the bow, just about at the waterline, where the rocks had been forced into the fibreglass hull by the wave action.

Oh, that's just fucking great, he thought. Now we can't do any speed. Even at low speed we're going to be taking water. I'll have to make some sort of very temporary repair before we can move off.

Goodyear saw Genny running towards them.

'Police', she shouted.

'What, we've got problem here,' he said, not hearing her properly. 'We've got damage to the bow.'

'We'll have to go.'

'We can't go.'

'But we'll have to or they'll get us, there are loads of them!'

'Loads of what?'

'Police, like I said.'

'SHIT, SHIT, SHIT!' If I move now, we'll take in water and sink the fucking boat.'

'But you can't stay here, I mean, we'll be sitting ducks.'

Dimitriou, who had seen what was happening, shouted; 'Can't we just move down the coast out of sight and make some repairs? I mean they won't know where we've gone?'

Goodyear went silent for a short moment, thinking.

Turning to Dimitriou, he said, 'That's probably the most sensible thing I've ever heard you say. Get that anchor aboard and stowed. Genny, get aboard and get on to Google Maps; get a possible location as quickly as you can. Find somewhere close to here where we could beach without being near a road.'

She clambered aboard as Dimitriou pulled the anchor out of the sand and threw it up on to the deck and then hobbled back and climbed on board. Goodyear put the boat into reverse thrust and backed off the beach at full power, the engines roaring.

'Is the damage not that bad then skipper?'

'Not fucking bad,' he shouted, 'it's worse; this could sink us, so yes, it's as bloody bad as it can get, but going in reverse, the bow is not being pushed into the water.'

'Oh right, but if we go forward, that's going to be a problem then?'

'Of course it is you dickhead, but if we back off slowly, we could slip away in the darkness, they won't see us.' He had slowed their reverse progress as the darkness enveloped them, and then turned on the bilge pumps to full power to stem whatever water was being shipped in through the damage to the bow.

'Get everything that's heavy on to the stern deck and be bloody quick.'

'Right skipper.' He hobbled about, moving as much heavy gear to the stern section as he could find.

Genny Dobbs then called out, 'I've found somewhere; it's not too far.'

'Can we be seen from the road?'

'No, I shouldn't think so; it's below the cliffs at the Barton on Sea Golf Club. There's no road there, so we won't be seen.'

'Good girl; show me.'

They were quite some way off the beach by now, shielded by darkness. He put the engines into idle while he took a look at the computer screen.

'There,' she said, and pointed to the small cove just under the cliffs.

'Yes, there is a sandy patch there. We can beach her and I can get to the bow. Hopefully make some temporary repairs. If I can do that, we can get home without sinking.'

*

The police had heard the roar of the boat and could only just about make out the shape of "Predator" as she backed off the beach.

'She's getting away,' Anna called out.

'Let them go, we can't catch them, but we know where they'll be heading. As far as they know, we don't have any evidence and if we can't catch them actually on the beach, we still don't have anything solid in the way of evidence, just circumstantial. We'll sort things out back at Cobbs Quay, when they get there. I've asked the Marina Manager Roger Whitehorn to keep a lookout and let us know as soon as they arrive.'

In the meantime, most of the illegal men had been rounded up and put into the police van, with the help of the support officers. One man had made a run for it, but one of the support team just happened to be an athletic runner who was a sprint champion. The man running soon found out that he was completely outclassed in that department, and was very soon joining the others who would soon be on their way back to the Police headquarters for arrest and interrogation. Border Control were notified of their imminent arrival and they would be questioned very thoroughly about where they had come from and how they had managed to obtain a crossing, together with how much they had paid. Also, and what mainly interested the Bournemouth Police, was exactly how they had arranged their crossing and who their contacts were.

'I think we'll need an interpreter Anna,' Alex ventured as they moved over to talk to Tom and Alice.

'Thanks for your help you two. I think we made a good "pincer" movement there. We seem to have all of them. I don't think we even had a chance to stop the boat, so let them get back to Cobbs Quay and we can give them a good grilling there. I think we've done everything we set out to do here, so I suggest we go back to HQ and get something to eat and drink and we can get some sleep before we have to go to Cobbs to collect these two muppets.'

'How about the girl guv' asked Alice?

'Sorry, the girl, she's in the van with the others.'

'I don't think so guv. While those blokes were running around, I saw her going back over the bridge, running and waving at the boat.'

'Anna, can you check please, before they go?'

The van was just about to pull away, but Anna waved for them to stop. The driver opened his window and Anna said, 'Is the girl with you?'

'What girl sarge? We didn't see a girl; there're only blokes in here.'

'Oh shit. Never mind, thanks. I'll just check with DCI Vail that it's clear to go. There was a girl driving this rental van which was going to pick these men up, but you say she's not with you. Just hang on will you?'

'Will do sarge.'

Anna ran back over the bridge towards the shore. In the distance she could just make out Genny Dobbs clambering onto the boat with one of the two men pulling her up by the arms.

The boat backed off the beach and was quickly almost invisible in the darkness.

Anna walked back to Alex and said, 'No, as Alice said, she got back on to the boat and now it's gone.'

'Okay, we know where she'll be anyway. Just make sure that one of the plods can drive the rental van back and return it in the morning.'

*

"Predator" had reversed far enough to be out of sight of the coast in the darkness. Goodyear put the drive to "forward" and pushed the throttles ahead gently.

'Are we going to be alright?' asked Genny.

'I think so, if I don't push her too hard. Can you and Freddie go right aft and stand by the stern rail.'

'Why; it's cold out there?'

'Just do as I say will you?' He was in no mood to worry about how cold it was. 'I just want as much weight as possible to hold the bow up. If I go too fast, the boat will go on the plane and the bow will drop, so I want to keep her "on the hump," that'll keep our bow up and out of the water. The last thing I want is to ship any more water.'

'Okay, I see what you mean,' although "on the hump" and "on the plane" didn't mean a lot to her.

She turned and told Freddie to come with her to the stern rail, explaining why as they went.

Goodyear had pushed the speed to about 15 knots which kept the bow up at a steep angle, just before the boat levelled out to enable the planing speed, which is what he didn't want at all.

He could see on the GPS display, the point on the screen where he was going to beach the craft.

In a matter of about ten minutes, they were nearing the point for beaching, under the cliffs.

He could also see from the display that there were no roads anywhere near this section of the beach, so he was sure that they would go unseen.

He called back to Dimitriou, saying 'Come forward; get the anchor ready, I'm going to beach her slowly, just enough to put her bow where I can get to it. Jump over and I'll get Genny to throw the anchor down to you. Just make it secure enough to hold her steady. Got it?'

'Got it; how long will it take you do you reckon, you know, to patch the hole?'

'I've no fucking idea, since you ask; but I've got some stuff down below that should hold until we get back.'

'Okay skipper.'

'Genny, come here. I want you to stay here at the controls. I'll leave the engines running, but in neutral.' He was indicating some of the control levers. 'If I tell you to put these "ahead," I want you to gently push them forward; very gently; and then these two controls,' he said indicating the two throttle levers, 'very very slowly forward until I say stop. Do you understand this?'

'Yes Martin, I can see what you're trying to do, keep the bow against the beach so that you can work on it.'

'Good girl. I'm relying on you so that we don't actually sink on the way back.'

That comment made her slightly concerned, but she knew he was more than capable of looking after the boat.

The craft slowed as it approached the beach. The water was very shallow and about 5 metres off the line of the gently breaking waves, the bow grounded on the sand bringing the boat to a swift standstill, with a grating noise. "That's more of the hull damaged," he thought.

Dimitriou leaned over and looked at the bow section. It was not really clear of the water, so he shouted back to Goodyear, 'It's not up the beach enough I don't think.'

That's your normal problem, he thought, you don't think; but this time he was right.

'Bollocks.' I'll have back off and come in a little faster. He brusquely pushed Genny away from the helm position and said,'I'm just going to back off and come in again. We'll stop with quite a lurch, so don't go and fall off or we'll have broken bones as well as the boat.'

They both raised a hand in acknowledgement. Goodyear then set reverse thrust and the boat slid back off the sand and moved back some 50 metres. Then he put on forward drive and applied a burst of power. The boat responded by leaping forward and quickly drove onto the sand with a lurching "whump" and came to a sudden standstill. They were holding on to the substantial railings.

Dimitriou then jumped over the side and again landed quite badly on his sprained ankle, letting out a loud yell of pain.

'Quiet you stupid fucker! said Martin, if there's anyone up there walking their sodding dog, they're going to spot us and call the fucking police, and then we'll be in even more fucking shit than we're in now, thanks to you taking out that fender.'

'But you told me to take it out before the wave hit us.'

'Don't fucking argue,' he hissed, 'just bury the bloody anchor.'

He told Genny to throw the anchor down to Dimitriou.

She lifted the anchor and was very surprised at how heavy it was. It was just about all she could do to lift it, but she managed to move it to the bow and heave it over the rail.

Martin saw this and groaned. 'Oh you stupid bitch, you've thrown it over the top of the rail; the anchor chain should go under it.'

'How was I to know? I'm not a sailor and you didn't say, so don't go blaming me if you don't give good instructions.'

'Okay, okay, sorry. I'm just a little bit stressed at the moment, with the police not a million miles away and all those bloody Turkish Cypriots waiting to tell everything. At least they don't know my name or any details about us. Just get back to the helm as before.'

Dimitriou had moved the anchor up the beach a little and was burying it as deeply as he could.

Martin had gone below and located the materials he thought would make a good enough repair to keep the sea out until they could return to the Marina. Turning to Freddie, he said, 'Keep a good lookout at the cliff-top in case any old farts are out walking their dog.'

'What if they saw us then skipper?'

Goodyear reached into a locker and retrieved a large automatic 9mm pistol. Saying nothing, he said, 'Just tell me if you see anyone, okay?'

Dimitriou just looked dumbfounded for a moment, then said, 'Okay skipper. I just hope I don't see anyone. If we had to shoot him, or her; someone's bound to hear.'

'Look again dickhead,' said Goodyear, and held out the pistol. He reached back into the locker and pulled out a tube and began to screw this to the barrel. 'This is a suppressor, or to you, a silencer. It would only sound like a gentle cough, so just keep a good lookout, alright?'

'Oh, right, gotcha. Do you need a torch to see by skipper?'

'I suppose you'd like some loud music to make sure we're heard as well as seen do you?'

'Sorry skipper.'

'Right, just shut up and let me get on; just keep your eyes open.'

He climbed over the side and went along to the bow to inspect the damage.

At the bow, he then began to clean the broken and splintered area of fibreglass around the hole which had been punched through the hull when the boat was washed against the rocks.

He was working in the near darkness, uttering many curses at the damage to his lovely boat, although he had a small LED torch clenched in his teeth. Close-up he could see enough to make the area as watertight and secure as possible.

He realised that the boat was moving slightly, so he looked up and called, 'Genny, put one engine to forward and push the left-hand throttle lever gently forwards until I say stop.'

He heard the engine change note from idle to just a few revolutions and felt the boat push harder into the shoreline, putting sufficient pressure on the hull to stabilise it.

'Stop, that's okay. Just leave the settings as they are, don't move anything else unless I say.'

'Okay Martin.'

He continued working on the damaged bow with heavy-duty tape and patches. He was just about to tidy up so that there would be nothing left to show where they had been, when Dimitriou said in a loud whisper, 'I think there's someone up there!'

'Oh fuck. Are you sure?'

'I can't really see, but I thought I saw a silhouette moving just now.'

'Keep still, let's just see if you're right,' he said switching off the torch.

They both stood very still, looking at the cliff-top, which was about 30 feet high. They could make out the silhouette of one person and then they heard a voice.

"I say, are you all right, do you have a problem, shall I call the coastguard or something? I was just taking an early morning stroll with my dog and I can see that you've beached your craft. Not something you'd do without a very good reason, I should think. Is anyone hurt, can I help?"

Goodyear muttered under his breath, "No you can't, you silly old fucker, you can just shut up and piss off." Then he called out, 'No, everything is fine – had a little engine trouble, but it's sorted out now – nothing to worry about, thanks.'

"Oh, all right then, only I think I'll give the Coastguard a call just so that they know you're okay and your engine is working again. Better safe than sorry; I often see problems along the coast and they know me at the Coastguard office."

I'll bet they do, thought Martin, but I can't let him do this. He took the LED torch; he focussed this to give a long distance "spot" beam. He pulled out the pistol and aligning the small torch against the barrel, shone the beam on to the silhouette of the man on the cliff-top.

The spot illuminated the figure who was wearing a flat cap and a short jacket with light-coloured trousers.

The jacket appeared to be a beige colour which showed up under the light. This makes it easier, he thought as he took aim.

The man tried to shield his eyes from the beam with his hand. 'I say, steady old chap, that's blinding me.'

Good, thought Goodyear and without waiting, he pulled the trigger and the pistol gave the little "cough." The man clutched his chest and quietly fell back disappearing from view.

Dimitriou said, 'Christ, did we have to do that Martin?'

'Of course you prat. If he'd called the Coastguard, that's another body that knows where we are and the fewer of them the better, right?'

'Right.' Dimitriou had still not grown used to the fact that Goodyear was able to kill with no apparent concern.

'Good, I'm finished here, so get that anchor out and stow it back on board. Make sure that it's secure. If that goes over the side because you've fucked up again, you'll follow it.'

Dimitriou didn't need any more incentive.

Goodyear climbed back on board and took over from Genny.

When Dimitriou was on the bow stowing the anchor, he put the boat into reverse again and backed off the shore with a burst of power from the twin engines. This very nearly unbalanced Dimitriou and he had to grab the guard-rail with both hands to stop himself from going overboard. 'Fuckin' 'ell Martin, I nearly went over then, take it easy.'
'Shut up, you're still there aren't you?'
The sudden movement had occurred just as he was about to insert the pin which secured the shank of the anchor. Goodyear quickly turned the boat towards Christchurch Bay, throttled up and headed back towards Poole and Cobbs Quay Marina. This time, he was able to put the boat on the plane without too much concern over the damaged hull. Even so, he put the bilge pumps on to be sure.
'Did you do what I think you did Martin?' asked Genny.
'Yes; do you have a problem with that?'
'No, I'm sure you know what you're doing.' He didn't see the look on her face which would have shown her disdain and real feelings.
'I do, now shut up and let me concentrate on getting us back.'

*

As the boat carrying the three occupants made its way across Christchurch Bay, Alex and the team returned to their HQ at Bournemouth Police Station.
'As it's so late now, let's all get some sleep and I want a full review at 7.30 in the morning. Good work all of you, thanks. 'There's nothing more we can do
'Please make sure that the duty sergeant makes everyone aware of this meeting.'
'In the meantime, I just hope that we are correct in assuming that the boat will make its way back to Cobbs and we have officers waiting there, ready to arrest both Goodyear and Dimitriou.
We've got far too many bodies now, and we need to bring this to a conclusion.'

Thankfully, they all made their way home. As they were outside the building, Anna walked over to his car as Alex was about to get in. He stood and leaned against the open door. 'It's been a long day Anna.'
'It certainly has. I was about to ask you if you'd like to come over to mine tonight. We could do with some time together; I've really missed you for these last few days as we've been so busy.'
'That would be absolutely fantastic Anna, but if I'm honest, I'm so uptight about all this, that I really don't think I'd be good company. I'm sure you're also pretty stressed too.'
'Actually, yes I am, but I just thought it might be nice to simply have an evening together and try to relax.'
He looked around to be sure that no-one was close enough to hear their conversation.
'Anna, darling, do you honestly think that we could relax if I were to come over?' I'll tell you what would happen, my girl; we would be probably so exhausted if the other night were anything to go by, that we'd miss the morning briefing.'
Anna looked a little crestfallen, but said 'Maybe you're right Alex, but being in your company for so long, it's made me rather horny, to say the least.'
'Believe me, I'd like nothing better, but I want to give you my undivided attention and I'm sure you know that with all this hanging over us, that wouldn't happen.'
'I can't argue with that Alex, so I guess I'll have to wait.'
He reached for her hand and held it tenderly. 'I promise, we'll have a night to remember as soon as we can.'
'I remember all of them,' she said.

CHAPTER 60

The next morning, the whole team, which included all the DC's and assistants, assembled in the incident room, where the photographs of the bodies recovered from the shed at Goathorn, and subsequently seen on the "Boston Whaler" found moored in Poole Harbour near to the "Othniel" oyster farm, were up on the incident board. There were also the photographs of the original body found on the beach at Goathorn, together with the further body of Bob Chorley, who had been murdered at his flat.

'To put you all in the picture, with the help of Tom and Alice, last night we arrested the illegal immigrants landed from the boat called "Predator," at Milford on Sea.'

Turning toward Alice and Tom, he said, 'Right, first we'll interrogate these illegals we arrested, I've arranged for Turkish translators to be available. Tom and Alice, I want you to take half of them, and Anna and I will see to the others. I want as much information about where they were collected from, where they originate from and how they organised their trip. More importantly, who did they pay, how much and all the information you can get. Are you both okay with that?'
Tom and Alice both nodded their assent. Alex then addressed the whole room.
'For the benefit of all those who have been on the periphery of this investigation so far, I'll go through everything we have and the current state of play to bring you all up to speed.

'We now have a total of 4 bodies, all attributable to Metin Denizci, aka Martin Goodyear and his accomplice Furkan Dimitriou, aka "Fuckin Freddie."

The first body to be found is thought to be a friend, probably one "Gary"; surname unknown. This was the one found half-buried face down on the beach at Goathorn Point. He had been repeatedly stabbed and beaten. Further enquiries led to the large shed close to the jetty there, owned by Perenco and part leased to Goodyear, who purported to be a fisherman who took parties out to the English Channel on 2 or 3 day fishing trips. We suspect that he did not take fishing trips, but rather went over to France to collect illegal immigrants. The shed was investigated and two bodies were found, wrapped in polythene. We think that they were two illegals and possibly were killed during a fight on board, for some reason. One had also been killed in a similar way to that of the first victim. We decided to leave the bodies in situ to see if they were collected. They were; and we ascertained that they were removed from the shed and then placed on board a "Boston Whaler" which was then moored in Poole Harbour, close to the oyster farm building just off the shoreline of Brownsea Island. Tom had the unenviable task of waiting for hours, watching for the bodies to be recovered from this boat. I have to say here, that Tom was attacked at Cobbs Quay Marina whilst on duty, we think by Goodyear. He received injuries from which he is thankfully recovering.
We were expecting these corpses to be removed, but what happened then was most unfortunate. We had a team of armed response officers together with two Dorset Marine police in a fast boat. We traced their large boat called "Predator," and knew that they were heading for the "Whaler" to collect the bodies, but somehow there was a "balls up" and the RIB of the armed response team collided with a moored boat. Probably because they were going so bloody fast, they just didn't see it in the darkness. This gave "Predator" a chance to collect the bodies and make a very quick exit via the channel round the back of Brownsea Island called "Blood Alley Lake."

Subsequently, we had to take the route of presuming that they were going over to France to collect more individuals, or illegals, to bring back to the South Coast area, presumably on a prior arrangement. We also had to presume that the two bodies recovered from the "Whaler" would have been disposed of somewhere in the English Channel. We arranged for coverage of the Haven entrance to Poole Harbour, to be sure of their return. In the meantime, it was ascertained that a rental vehicle was collected and followed, to a part of Milton-on-Sea where our presumption was proved to be correct. We were able to arrest some 11 men who were landed at the point where we had set a trap. These individuals will shortly be interrogated and interviewed.

Unfortunately, due to the darkness, the boat was able to back off the beach, having been alerted by the driver of the rental van, one "Genny Dobbs." She apparently boarded the craft which disappeared into the night and we now know that it should have returned to Cobbs Quay Marina.'

The station duty officer came in and looked at Alex, passing a slip to him, Alex nodded his thanks. He read the note, held up his hand and was quiet for a moment. 'There has been a further development in that unfortunately, I have just received a report; the body of a man found early this morning with a single gunshot wound, on the top of the cliff overlooking the beach at the Barton-on-Sea golf course near New Milton. We are in the process of contacting his relative. Although he is not dead, we don't know his condition but we'll be informed as soon as this is known.'

There was a collective murmur at this news. Tom spoke up. 'Isn't that quite near to where we collected those immigrants, guv?'

'Yes, it was along the coast towards Christchurch.'

'That's a bit strange isn't it; I mean why would someone be shot out there at night?'

'That's a good question Tom, but at the moment, we have absolutely no idea.'

Alex looked over to Anna as he was saying this and she had an expression of intense surprise.

'As I say, this information has only just been passed to me and I will give more information as soon as I have it. Okay, that's all for now, so back to your allocated tasks. I need to know immediately, anything of relevance.'

After they'd all gone back to their desks, Alex motioned to Anna to come with him to his office, replacing his phone .

'This man who was shot, do we have any details at all, guv?'

'Only that he received a single gunshot wound to his chest. He was found lying on his back, as though he had been standing looking out to sea and the shot knocked him backwards. There was a dog with him which was found standing beside the body.'

'Who found him then?'

'Another dog-walker at about 6.30 a.m., he phoned it in immediately from his mobile.'

Anna looked a little pensive for a moment and then put forward a suggestion.

'Just a thought; we know the boat backed off the beach before we could get to it, but I'm sure I saw someone crouched down at the bow. I wonder now if there had been some damage to the boat and they were checking it.'

'I have to say that I didn't see that Anna, but yes, supposing you're right and there was some damage, maybe they had to do some repairs. If that's the case, then perhaps they had to stop somewhere and see to the damage. They couldn't or wouldn't stop where they landed the illegals to make any sort of repairs, or we would have made the arrests.'

'What I'm getting at is that maybe they stopped along the coast and that's when the man on the cliff-top saw them. We know that Goodyear is a murderer, so one more wouldn't bother him.'

'And if this man saw what they were doing, then perhaps they shot him to stop him reporting a sighting.'

'That would explain why an innocent man walking his dog is shot in a place where he would probably be the only person for miles.'

'Unless he was shot by someone else; but I can see your reasoning Anna. It would certainly be a possible scenario.'

'And if he was shot from down on the beach, that would account for him lying on his back. Surely forensics will establish the angle of the shot? Also, the time of this shooting might coincide with the movement of the boat.'

'Yes, they would. I want the area directly below where he was found to be thoroughly searched for anything which will prove the presence of a boat.'

'Do you think that there will be something if they were repairing the boat?'

'I do Anna. Will you call forensics and get a SOCO team down there pronto?'

'Will do.'

'In the meantime, I want to make sure that that boat "Predator" is gone over from stem to stern in the minutest detail. We have to establish the presence of bodies there so that we can tie it into the two taken from the "Whaler."

He called the Poole Police and arranged for a SOCO team to go directly to the boat.

Anna called the forensic team and gave them instructions regarding the man's body found on the cliff-top at the golf club. 'I need all the details you can give me about the time of death. This is particularly urgent as we need corroboration of the ToD to tie into the movements of the boat containing all the immigrants. I also need the angle that the bullet entered his body and the calibre of the bullet. Can you give us all this as urgently as possible please?' She was talking to Jeffrey Boyd, the head of forensics laboratory.

'I'll do my best sergeant, but we do have a lot on our plate at the moment, but you know I'll give you what I can, when I can.'

'Yes, and I appreciate that. Thanks Jeffrey.'

'Okay, right you are, and can you give my regards to Alice please?'

'Of course,' she said, ending the call.

She was heading to Alex's office and passed the desk that Alice was working at. 'Jeffrey sends his regards,' she said as she passed. Alice looked up and smiled her thanks.

Knocking on his office door, which was partly open, Alex saw her and motioned her in.

'What can I do for you Anna?'

'I wanted to ask whether they arrested our suspects, as you didn't mention it just now at the meeting.'

'Nobody else asked about it, either, did they?'

'I was just about to mention it and then you told us about the shooting on the cliff-top, and it went out of my head.'

'The truth is that they didn't show up at Cobbs as expected, so where the hell they are, we have no idea at the moment. I've just made a call to the Harbour Master over at Poole, your "admirer," you know, Fuller Masterson.' This made Anna quite uncomfortable as she knew she was going to blush. She did indeed find Fuller very attractive but again, she had to quash the feeling and put it out of her mind. I must keep focussed, she thought to her herself, and said, 'Oh stop it guv, you know there's nothing there.'

'Hmm, never mind that, I've asked him to get as many people as he can to search the area to look for these three and their boat. It must be somewhere as we have our webcam corroboration so we know it passed through the Haven at about 4 a.m., so they must be in the harbour somewhere, but Christ knows where at the moment.'

'Where do you think they might be hiding then guv?'

'Anna, if I had any idea I'd be out there myself, paddling across the harbour to catch these slimy bastards, instead of crapping myself, waiting for DCS James Gordon to give me a monumental bollocking for not collecting them.'

There was an incoming call. Alex picked up the phone saying, 'DCI Vail.'

'Hello Alex, this is Jeffrey from SSD. I've got a quick finding on the bullet to that unfortunate chap on the golf course.'

'Hi Jeffrey, that was quick, thanks. What do you have?'

'From the angle of the entry wound, we can definitely say that he was shot from the beach. It was a 9mm bullet and we have this as it did not exit the body. We'll be able to match it to others we have from previous bodies, but that will be checked later. Unfortunately, we don't have the definite time of the shooting yet but I would suggest that it seems very likely to be around the time you mentioned as a possibility.'

'That confirms what we thought, thanks Jeffrey,' said Alex, ending the call.

'So we can presume that he was shot by one of the three people on board "Predator," can we?' asked Anna.

'I think that's a definite. I think he, or she, come to that, must have had some sort of sight for the gun, or perhaps it was just a lucky shot.'

'I don't think it was the woman, I mean, how often do we get females who use a gun; not often do we?'

'You're quite right, but perhaps he had a laser sight. I've seen those used on handguns and they're very effective.'

'Not that it really matters how he managed to shoot this poor guy, does it guv, the fact remains that this poor innocent man was shot for no real reason. This man and I think it will be the same man, is a very sadistic killer who has no qualms about murdering anyone who gets in his way.'

'Unfortunately Anna, I think you've got it absolutely right.'

'All we have to do now is to find out where the hell they are hiding and where is that boat?'

CHAPTER 61

The Poole harbourmaster had called in many favours by asking various friends and contacts to scour the harbour and keep their eyes open for any signs of "Predator" or where it was being kept. It was expected back at Cobbs Quay after the illegal immigrants had been put on shore at Milford on Sea and had subsequently disappeared. So far, it had not been seen. Alex was running various possibilities around in his head he called a friend who was a sailor and knew Poole Harbour well, having lived in the area for most of his life, although they'd not been in touch for years.

'Hello Pete, Alex Vail here; how the devil are you these days?' He was talking to Peter Rist, a friend from way back in his school days.

'Bloody hell, Alex; now there's a voice from the past, I've not heard from you for absolutely ages.'

'I know, I'm not too good at keeping in touch these days. Work keeps me so busy and on top of that, I'm just lazy.'

'Not to worry, I've not been around for a while anyway, been doing a lot of sailing for the last few years. I'm very surprised that you've managed to get me after so long.'

Alex had done some searching on Google and Peter was listed on Wikipedia.

'I remember that you once said that you'd like to sail round the world, is that what you've done?'

'Actually, yes, I managed to get a "40 footer" and my wife and I have been visiting so many places around the world, and staying in some of them for quite a while. We've been doing that for that last 10 years.'

'Christ, is that how long it is since we last were in touch? I do remember you talking about the idea back then, so it must have been before you bought the boat, so maybe it was longer than that.'

'It must be, although we've been back for a couple of years now.'

'So I'm very lucky that I've managed to get in touch with you I think.'

'I don't know about lucky, but you obviously have something in mind. Are you still a policeman Alex? I know you were a DC I think, the last time we spoke.'

'Yes, still here, although I've made it to DCI now, with all the headaches and responsibility that goes with it, but I still love the job.'

'I tell you what Alex, why don't we get together one evening and we can really catch up on what we've both done with our lives? I'm sure you have quite a few gory stories to tell and we've certainly had some, what you might call "unusual" experiences in different places.'

'Hey, that would be really great and maybe I'd get a chance to meet your wife; you didn't have one back then did you?'

'No, and I know you were seeing someone yourself, did you marry her?'

'That's a bit of a long story and perhaps we could leave that for later as I have a favour to ask you.'

'Fire away, I just hope I can help.'

'Okay; I'm working on a case right now that requires some detailed knowledge of Poole Harbour. I know that you did a lot of boating in and around Poole back when, and I was wondering if you could shed some light on my dilemma at the moment.'

'I'll be glad to help if I can; what do you need to know?'

'That's good of you Peter. Well, we've been following a boat which has been bringing in illegal immigrants and to cut a long story short, we've lost it when it came back to Poole. What I need to know is where do you think it likely or even possible to hide a 36 foot, fast boat, somewhere in Poole Harbour?'

'Do you know that it has definitely come into the harbour?'

'We are pretty sure that it has, and we also know that it may have sustained some damage to the bow, so perhaps it has to be somewhere which would allow repairs to be made.'

'In that case, Alex, I'd say it was a "no-brainer."'

Alex then thought that this would have been something that he should have either known or at least seen the obvious which Peter was about to mention. 'Is this something that is going to make me look like an idiot then Pete?'

'No, of course not; if you're not a "boaty" type, which I don't think you really are, then perhaps it wouldn't be obvious.'

'Go on then, what would you do if you had to disappear?'

'The same as I would if I had a car in a similar situation, 'I'd take it straight into a garage or in this case, a boat shed which had either a dry-dock or a slipway. That way, it would be under cover and out of sight.'

'Of course!' I knew it was something I should have realised, he thought. 'Of course that makes sense. But surely, you'd have to know a business which had this sort of facility and be ready to take the boat immediately?'

'Was this boat usually moored in Poole Harbour?'

'Yes, up at Cobbs Quay Marina, but I know it hasn't gone back there.'

'Well, I would have thought that someone with a craft like that would know a number of companies who had that sort of facility.'

'I think that would certainly be the case and as this chap who runs the boat must know some pretty "questionable" people, then it is more than likely that he knew of someone who could take it in without too many questions being asked. I should have thought of this, I knew it. I don't suppose you know of any likely places then Peter?'

'Sorry Alex; as I said, I've not been back for long after some 10 years away, and as you'll realise, a lot of things have changed. I hardly recognised the surroundings of the harbour and for sure, Poole has changed a hell of a lot since I went.'

'Of course; but thanks a lot for your observation and advice. I'll follow up on this straight away and make some enquiries. Can we make arrangements to get together and we can maybe spend some time and catch up?'

'Absolutely; tell you what, I'll check with Maddy, that's my wife by the way, and I'll give you a call back to firm up a time and place, how's that?'

'Fantastic, I'll look forward to that with the greatest pleasure, thanks. Talk to you later.'

'Okay, and it's great to hear from you,' and after exchanging contact numbers, they ended the call.

'Anna!' Alex shouted. When she heard his shout, she realised that something had come up and she dashed into his office, leaving the door open.

'What's up guv?'

'Something I should bloody well have thought of. Where do you hide a bloody great boat so that no-one can see it?'

'If it was a car, I'd stick it in a garage and shut the door I suppose.'

'Ex-bloody-actly! You stick it in a boat shed and close the doors. I reckon that this boat is in the harbour but inside a boat shed. And one that has a slip-way so that they can do repairs.'

'Don't all these boat sheds have slip-ways then?'

'How the fuck should I know Anna, I know sod-all about boats.'

'But we know someone who does, don't we?'

'Who the hell is that then?'

'Old Jack, you know, Jack Sturney.'

'That old boatman who took us to and from Goathorn, of course! Good thinking Anna, he'd know most of the boatyards around the harbour I'll bet. Can you get on to your "lover-boy" Harbourmaster and ask him if we can speak to Jack?'

Anna instantly felt a blush coming on and quickly turning away, said, 'Right away guv,' as she left his office. She did think of questioning him over the remark, but thought that "letting sleeping dogs lie," was better.

Calling Fuller Masterson, the Poole Harbourmaster, she said 'Hello Fuller, this is Anna Jenkins, from...'

She didn't finish the sentence before he exclaimed, 'Anna, the delightful Anna, how nice to hear from you. What can I do for you?'

You know bloody well what you could do for me, she thought, but with an effort of will, put the thought to one side. 'I need to pick Jack Sturney's brain if that's possible.'

'I'm sure that Jack will be more than pleased that someone wants to pick his brain, Anna. As you've probably realised, he likes nothing better than to talk about his local knowledge. I take it that it is local knowledge that you want?'

'Yes; as you know we are still looking for the boat which we are sure came back to the harbour last night, but which has disappeared. We think it might have been taken into a boatyard or be hidden in a shed. We suspect that it suffered some damage to the hull and maybe it's been taken undercover and that's why we can't see it.'

'That would account for the fact that no-one has had sight of this boat – "Predator" I take it?'

'That's the one. Do you know of any place which might be a possibility?'

'I know most of the yards around the harbour, but I have to say that I don't know the owners too well and in any case they are mostly owned by people who don't actually work at the yard. They've too much money to be involved at that level and I mostly come into contact with them on an official level, to do with regulations and things of that nature. However, I would think that Jack would certainly know more about the local 'goings-on' and the more "questionable" aspects of the yards, so to speak.'

'That's the impression I got when we had the pleasure of his company, taking our little trips over to Goathorn.'

'He's a bit of a character, isn't he?'

'Actually, he's a lovely old chap, as long as he doesn't try to smile at you.'

'I know what you mean Anna; a bit of a shock when he does that. I'll get him to come in and perhaps you'd like to come over and you can interview him here.'

Anna was instantly caught between a 'rock and a hard place' in that she could hardly ask Jack to come over to Bournemouth and she knew full well that Fuller had probably said that so that she would come to Poole.

She hesitated slightly, and Fuller picked up on this, saying 'If you can, of course.'

He was such a nice man and Anna did have some private thoughts that she knew she shouldn't really have, given that she and Alex had a 'thing' going, but at the same time, Fuller did give her some stirrings in a place that she was sure Alex wouldn't have appreciated.

'Yes, of course, I can't ask the old chap to come all the way to Bournemouth, so I'll come over as soon as I can, if that's convenient?'

'You know you are always welcome to come whenever you want Anna,' he said.

Oh, there he goes again, she thought, just the leaving out of 'over' from the sentence, put the connotations which made her insides do a little flip. She knew damn well what his inference was, but she resisted the urge to come back with a remark which would add to her problem. 'Okay, see you quite soon then.'

'Not soon enough but 'bye for now.'

She ended the call and had to slip outside to cool down a little.

Having regained her composure, she quickly went back to Alex. 'I've arranged to see Jack Sturney, but Masterson would rather we see him over there if that's okay.' This was a little white lie, but Anna thought it was a better solution than to get into any conflict at this point.

'No problem Anna. You know what we need to find out, like who has a boat shed which could take a boat of that size and who might just be the sort of person who would not ask too many questions or be inquisitive, that sort of thing.'

'Got it guv; I'm sure that Jack would have a pretty good idea of someone who might be open to a little "encouragement," don't you think? Anyway, I did think that it would be better to see him face to face as maybe he wouldn't like to say anything which might incriminate someone in a phone call; you never know who might be listening.'

'Quite right and I'm sure the old bugger knows plenty of those people. Just get some names and places so that we can get some of our plods to do some quick checking. If anything looks really hot, just phone it back to me and I can get things moving here. Take one of the pool cars, not your own. I don't want any more expense than we already have. The last thing I need is for DCS Gordon to be breathing fire down my neck. He's been right on my back again today, demanding "finalisation."

Anna went straight down to the car pool and spoke to Philip Mason, the OC of the car pool. 'DCI Vail has asked me to go over to Poole Harbour to interview one of our contacts.'

'No problem sarge. Take that Corsa over there' He reached and took some keys from the board behind his desk.

'Are you sure that'll get me there and back then?'

'Cheeky young sergeant,' he said with a smile. 'I'll have you know that all our vehicles are in top condition.'

'I'm sure they are, but then you never know with a Corsa, do you?'

'Get on with you, or I'll have to have words with your governor.'

'Oh no - not that. He's an ogre when he's roused,' she said with a smile, thinking more of the word "aroused."

'Go on, get out,' and threw the keys to her.

She drove over to Poole and parked directly below the Harbourmasters office. Pushing open the doors to the reception area, she saw a pleasant faced woman of about fifty, wearing a smart white shirt with epaulettes which looked to be a uniform. Introducing herself, she said 'I'm here to see Jack Sturney. I believe that Mr Masterson has arranged for him to be here.'

'I think I saw Jack a few moments ago, he was talking to some of our staff over in the mess room. I'll just call Mr Masterson and tell him you're here. I'm sure he'll want to see you.' She said this with a very slight smile, the inference of which was not lost on Anna.

CHAPTER 62

Fuller Masterson appeared at the door from the foot of the stairs leading to his office. As soon as he set eyes on Anna, he broke into a wide smile. This caused an uninvited "stirring" deep in Anna. As lovely as this was, she didn't really want it to happen, but she felt herself being unable to resist the pleasure of seeing him.

'Anna, how really nice to see you.' She truly hoped that the receptionist had not overheard this but as she glanced toward the desk, she knew that although the words were not heard, the facial expressions were immediately tucked away for later gossip.

Anna looked back toward Fuller, moving a little further from the desk, turning her head so that she could not be seen, only by him. 'And it's really good to see you again Fuller.'

'It's been too long Anna, but now that you're here, you must allow me to offer you at the very least, a coffee. Do you have time for that?'

'Is Jack available for me to have a chat with him?'

'He will be as soon as he's back from a little errand which I had to send him on. He should be back in around half an hour or so I should think. I'm sorry if that's going to delay you.'

She had the very sneaking suspicion that he had been "sent" as soon as Fuller had known she was on her way.

'No, it shouldn't be a problem, although we are desperate to find this boat "Predator" and where it might be hidden. We think it could be somewhere within the confines of the harbour and Jack might be able to shed some light on this.'

'Well, he's certainly the man who would know. He's been around this harbour for most of his life and I'm sure if anyone knows a place where this boat could be hidden, he will.'

'Let's hope so, because now things are really coming to a head.'

'What's the latest situation regarding this saga then Anna, I don't know that state of play at the moment.'

'If we can have that coffee, I'll be glad to bring you up to speed.'

Holding the door open, he motioned for her to go ahead. 'You know where my office is don't you?' he said giving her a rather meaningful gaze.

'I do.'

'Please,' he said nodding toward the stairs. She walked up to the first floor ahead of him and she was about to enter his office, when he said, 'I'll tell you what, why don't we go to the observation room, it has a much better view over the harbour, and it's quieter and more private? My office is full of radio chatter and things like that.'

'Why not?' said Anna and they moved up to the next floor. Entering the room, it was evident that this room was kept for a quiet watch-keeping and as he'd said, a much better view was over the harbour and from this height, it was possible to see right across Brownsea Island and across to Evening Hill.

'Fuller, this is such a beautiful place isn't it? I mean, the views are spectacular.'

'I think the best views are as the sun sets. Sometimes, when the conditions are right it is so romantic and beautiful that it takes my breath away and I've seen it so many times.'

This insight into Fuller came as no real surprise to Anna as she realised that he was being quite open and not the usual official and sometimes quite stern, strong-looking man that she was coming to like more and more.

'Excuse me a moment,' he said and picked up a phone. 'Jane, would you be good enough to make me two coffees please, and put them on my desk, I'll pick them up, as I have a visitor; I hope you don't mind me asking.' A slight pause and then, 'Thank you Jane.'

'I'll pop down and pick them up in a moment; I'd rather like to have you to myself for even a short while, if you don't mind. Here we won't be disturbed.'

I'm disturbed already, thought Anna. 'Of course that will be really nice, just us.'

They stood looking at one another, saying nothing, for what seemed like ages. Finally breaking away, he said, 'Forgive me for staring, but you are just so attractive.'

She was trying not to blush at his direct gaze.

'Please excuse me for a moment, I'll just nip down and get the coffees.' He went down the stairs to the office below.

Anna, realising just how things were developing, had a sobering thought. I think I must make some enquiries into Mr Masterson because just how things had turned out with Tom and Genny Dobbs, made her particularly cautious. Just to be sure, she thought; it would do no harm to know a little more about him.

He returned, carefully bearing two cups of coffee with the aroma wafting before him.

'Thank you, that smells really enticing. Taking a sip she said in a mock "seafaring" accent, "and by golly it tastes good too."

That made him smile. Good humour too; another bonus.

'I really wish that we could have more time like this, but 'I'm sorry, I'm presuming far too much. I know you have Alex and you and he are an 'item' aren't you? Please excuse me.'

'Please don't worry Fuller; yes Alex and I have a sort of "arrangement," but it is not binding and to be honest, it is always a difficult situation in that as we work together, we have to be very careful not to let any of the other officers know that we have any sort of relationship. If they knew, at the very least, I would have to move to a different station. It does put quite a strain on things.'

'I'm sure it does; it can't be easy at all.' He was actually dying to ask where she might have to move to, which "different" station, but he was on thin ice here, as if he were honest, he would really like her to be free. He was more than interested in Anna. He thought she was a very bright person as well as being extremely attractive. Her figure was slim without being skinny and she was obviously quite athletic. This was something he really appreciated. Although he was very attracted to her and would really like to take things further, he was too much of a gentleman to push things. At the moment, he was just taking things slowly and getting to know her better. If things moved on, he would leave it up to her to make the moves or at least make it obvious. He was not going to risk anything just now, simply make his feelings subtly obvious.

'I feel really comfortable here in your presence Fuller, you make me feel rather "special."

'That makes me very happy and I'm so pleased that you are comfortable with me. I have to take a chance and, please forgive me if I've gone too far, tell you that I would really like to spend more time with you, away from work, if you know what I mean.'

'Yes, I do have the same thoughts, but as you know, I have this, let's say "connection" with Alex and although nothing is cast in stone, I do have to be very careful how I go about changing things, shall we say.'

'I completely understand Anna. Please just let things lie for now and I'll leave everything to you, as long as you are aware of my feelings. I simply don't want to complicate things any more than they are.'

Anna was looking at Fuller with an expression which he rightly took to be not only responsive but genuinely affectionate. This made him very happy.

'Enough of this Anna, you have work to do and much as I would like to keep you here, you need to speak with old Jack.'

'Oh yes, I should really. I think Alex will be expecting me to report back by now.'

'Let me see if Jack is back yet. I did tell him to come to the reception desk, so I'll just call down and check to see.'

As he was phoning down to the reception, Anna was standing at the big window, looking again over the harbour and taking in the incredible vista in the afternoon sun.

Fuller put the phone down and turning to Anna said, 'I'm afraid he's just walked in to reception, so I suppose you'd better go and have a word with him. I'll have to let you go.'

''Fraid so, I'm can't put this off, much as I'd like to Fuller, but as soon as I have a chance, I'll give you a call and maybe we can do something a little more private.'

'That would be fantastic Anna, but please don't do anything which will cause you problems'

'Don't worry; I think I know what I'm doing.'

'Very well, I look forward very much to our next meeting.'

She hesitated slightly and they stood looking at each other without saying anything, just letting their eyes do the communicating.

He held out his hand to her, and he lifted hers to his lips and gave a gentle kiss.

'Me too,' she said and with that, rather reluctantly went down the stairs to meet Jack.

The old seafarer was waiting, leaning against the counter. He was wearing a very old and very "weather worn" old jumper. It looked as though it had seen a great deal of sun and salt over the years, but it just seemed to be part of 'him.' When he saw Anna walking through the doors, he treated her to one of his "smiles," which were as Anna knew only too well, were unforgettable, to say the least. I don't think he's ever seen a dentist, she thought, and knowing the evil-smelling tobacco which he smoked during their varied trips across the harbour when they had to visit the earlier crime scenes, she wouldn't like to be the one to administer any treatment.

'Allo, missy, 'tis good to see 'ee agen. 'Tidn't like what we've set eyes on each other for quite a while now.'

'No Jack, it's good to see you again.' She actually quite liked the old chap and she'd found him to be an affable "ancient mariner" and had many stories to tell. She remembered one particular time when he recounted when he and his wife had taken a sailing boat along the coast, and how he missed her so much, now he was on his own.

'I do unnerstan' what you do need to know summat 'bout what a boat could be 'idden somewhere around the 'arbour. Be that roit?'

'Yes, Jack. A boat came back into the harbour very early this morning and now we can't locate it anywhere, although people have been searching for it. I think you know the craft, that "Redbay Stormforce 11."'

'Aye, I knows the one, she be that fast boat what do go out on them fishin' trips with, I think his name is Martin.'

'That's the one. What I need to know is, do you anywhere that such a boat could be hidden around the harbour somewhere, you know somewhere that it could be away from normal eyes?'

'Well, to tellee t'honest truth, I think that it would be right tricky, if not hardly possible, to hide 'em around the shores, 'cos she be quite long and being painted red, if my old memory serves me, she'd be right difficult to hide, 'specially as how she's drawing probable more than the shallow shoreline would allow, if you sees what I do mean.'

I think so, thought Anna. 'Yes Jack, so what would you suggest as the best way of keeping it out of sight? I mean, do you know of anywhere that it might be hidden. I'm asking you because you are probably the best person who knows this harbour so well.'

'That be right then missy. I do cert'n know this 'arbour well, as I be born and brought up in this area and been on the water hereabouts alls of my life, and I'm getting quite old now, as you can probable see like.'

That fact was completely beyond doubt – please just get to the point, she thought.

'So what I do think is that if'n I was lookin' to hide a boat like that, I'd probable like go to see a mate of my who does have a big boat shed. He used to do repairs on old wooden boats back in them years gone by, but these days, mostly boats are made of that fibryglassy stuff and he don't touch 'em. Too messy, he says, so he do only work on wooden boats, restoring them like. 'Avin' said that, he don't get much call for them and I do know that 'ee don't have any work on just now like. If'n I was to ask him, I do know what he could take a boat inside of the size of that there Redbay boat.'

Of course! If it was under cover in one of the numerous boat sheds in the harbour, that's why it's not been seen, but we should have realised that.

'Do you think that this "Martin" would know the owner of this shed then Jack?'

'Well, I'd say that was for cert'n sure. I'd think he do know the boatyards all about and if'n he was in a big hurry like, he'd probable run straight to 'im. 'S'posin' he do phone him with his mobile phone thingy, he could get the doors open and slip right inside real quick.'

'Do you know the name of the owner of this boat shed then Jack?'

'Well, 'co'rse I do, 'cos I do go down to the "Nelson" with him for a jar or two, quite reg'lar like.'

'The "Nelson"?'

'Aye, the "Lord Nelson," on Poole Quay, right next to where the old Poole Pottery used to be. 'Tis such as shame as how that's gone now.'

'And his name is?'

'Oh that be "Bert Jackson."'

Anna made a note of that. 'I suppose you don't happen to know his phone number or where he might be now?'

'I'm cert'n sure I don't know his phone number, but I do have it in my little book what I do keep at home, see my old memory b'aint what it used to be, so I do keep this little book so as I can put down them phone numbers when folks do give 'em to me, see, 'cos if'n I don't write 'em down, I do forget 'em, and then I can't call them, so I write it down in my little book when they do call me.'

Give me strength, thought Anna. Here he goes again with one of his monologues, just like the last time when he was telling us about his wife. She didn't like to cut him off, but time was pressing.

'Okay, Jack, thank you for this. I'll find his number, but perhaps you know where he might be right now, so that we can get in touch as it is very important.'

Jack looked at his watch and frowned. 'Well I'd think that he could very well be in the "Nelson" right now, but if'n he's got someone with their boat in his shed, then like as not he'll be there as well.'

'Jack, can you tell me where this boat shed is?'

'Well, co'rse I can my luvly, it be over on Brownsea Island.'

'Are you sure, I mean, I've been to Brownsea and I would have thought an island was not a good place to have a boat shed?'

'Ar well, see, when t'was builded, long time ago, most boats what did need repair, were wooden and I s'pose old Bert's dad and 'is dad 'afore 'im, would like to be away and quiet like, so'as they could get on and not be mithered by folks sort of droppin' in like.'

'Okay, I see. If you'll excuse me, I have to get this information to my office so that they can find Bert Jackson and pay him a visit.'

'Oh, right you are then. You go and see if'n you can find him. I s'pose you could telephone the "Nelson" to see if'n he be there, 'cos they do know him right well.'

'I'll do that, and thank you Jack for the information. It's been very nice to see you again.'

Jack treated Anna to another of his smiles. He then looked just a little inquisitive as he said, 'I suppose you might need another little trip over to Brownsea to see Bert, maybe?'

Anna realised that this was strong possibility. 'I'm sure that's possible Jack, but for now, I have to get back to my station, so I will ask Mr Masterson when we need you.'

'Right you are then, I'll be on my way; 'bye for now.'

CHAPTER 63

Anna had said a regretful goodbye to Fuller and called her office with the news that the possible location of "Predator" was in a boat shed on Brownsea Island.

'At last,' said Alex when she had passed on the information. 'Get his number, give him a call. He paused, – no, on second thoughts, don't. I don't want to warn him that we're coming. Just find out exactly where this boat shed is and we'll go there unannounced to see if "Predator" is actually there. Maybe it isn't, but it's our only lead so far. Did you tell Jack not to call this Bert bloke?'

Anna realised that she had been so wrapped up with Fuller that she hadn't followed through with the obvious points. She would have to put this right very quickly.

'Yes,' she lied, and realised that she would have to tell Jack not to contact this chap, but to also get Fuller to allow him to take her and Alex over to Brownsea more or less straight away. 'Shall I arrange for a boat to get us over to Brownsea then guv?'

'Yes, good idea. Just wait there and I'll be right over, just organise it. I don't think you'll be too worried with your fancy-man to look after you, although it might be better if we go some other way. Just ask Jack for now and have him standing by.

Anna felt an embarrassment which she was glad that Alex was not there to witness.

'Don't be silly, he's got loads of work to do, so I'll just have to talk to old Jack.'

'At least he'll keep you busy then.'

That made things a little easier for Anna, who, despite her best efforts, had blushed at the realisation that she was, in a way, two-timing Alex.

Ending the call, she ran out of the building and saw Jack in the distance, ambling towards the jetty where his little boat was moored.

'Jack, Jack,' she called loudly, avidly hoping that he was not deaf. The old man stopped and turned, putting a hand to his face, shielding it from the sun and looking back. He saw Anna running towards him.

'Hold hard there missy, why be you in such an 'urry then?' Is summat wrong?'

'No, but I should have asked you not to get in touch with Bert at the boat shed. We need to go over there quietly to see if this boat is actually there.'

'Oh, that be okay then, 'cos like I did tell ee, I don't have his telephone number, only in my little book what I do keep at 'ome like, so's I knows what I couldn't telephone 'im anyways, if'n you do see what I means.'

Two or three words would have done, thought Anna, but she said, 'Oh good, that's all right then. I'll just go back and see Mr Masterson to see if you will be available to take us over there.'

'Right-o then missy, I be ready to take you over there just as soon as you tell me that Mr Masterson has said it be okay for me to go.'

Anna simply couldn't take any more of Jacks effusive chatter, so she went back to the stairs up to Fullers' office. She could see him through the partition and she was about to enter, when he looked up and saw her. He smiled and moved over directly to the door. Opening this, he said, 'Twice in one day, I'm a lucky man.'

'Fuller, I've just spoken to the guv and he told me to stay here but to organise a boat to take us both to Brownsea, if that's possible.'

'But of course Anna, I know Jack is not wanted just at the moment, so that's fine, and there is a bonus as well.'

'A bonus?'

'Yes, of course, as you have to wait for your boss, I get to have you here for at least another three quarters of an hour.' He seemed very pleased at this possibility, and Anna was just as happy to stay here with Fuller. It meant that they could have a little more time to talk to each other in private. 'But don't you have work to do then, I mean there must be lots of things which you have to take care of, I mean you are the Harbourmaster for heaven's sake?'

'That is true, but there are times when all seems quiet and everything runs smoothly. Thankfully, this is one of those times and anyway, should anything turn up, my staff will call me. For now, I'm simply overseeing the harbour and keeping watch from the observation room, but to be honest, I'm happier observing you.'

This gave Anna a little warm stirring, somewhere deep down. She actually thought, but did not dare to say; "you're not too shabby either."

A call was made to the office and Jack had been asked to ready his boat for the trip across the harbour. Anna and Fuller were able to once again get to know each other better as the privacy afforded by this room was used to good effect, talking about this and that.

All too soon, there was a phone call and Anna quite rightly guessed that Alex had arrived. 'Your boss has arrived and he's downstairs in reception. I have to say that I've really appreciated our time today Anna and it's gone by all too quickly. I feel that I've been able to reach you a little more and I realise that I like you more and more. I hope you don't think I'm being too forward.'

'Not at all and I'm also more than pleased that we had this opportunity, although I really don't think that Alex is too pleased.'

I'm not happy that I may have come between you somehow; that is not my intention at all.'

'Yes, I realise that, but please don't think that way, because as I've said before, nothing is cast in stone and I am my own person. We'll just take things as they come, but I will be in touch again soon.'

'Now that makes me very happy. You best go and enjoy Jack's company.'

Anna was standing quite close to Fuller and she hesitated slightly. He moved very gently toward her and as he looked at her face, he had this incredible feeling as he looked slowly and deeply into her golden eyes, that he was looking right inside her head. He would long remember this feeling, as it gave him a real shock. He would later that day, think back and liken it to being "drawn in" to her mind.

Nothing was said for a few long moments, but then she moved her face close to his. He put his hand to her cheek and turned it, ran the back of his hand very gently across her cheek. She closed her eyes and they kissed. A slow, soft, gentle kiss, which sent a frisson through them both. She looked at him with a steady gaze as they moved apart, and opening the door, just said softly; 'Goodbye Fuller.' Her heart rate had climbed appreciably.

He said nothing, simply raising his hand as she opened the door and almost glided down the stairs.

Alex was waiting in reception and as Anna approached, he saw that her face was quite red. 'Was it warm up there then, looks like Masterson's been keeping you busy?'

This comment was accompanied by a look which Anna had not seen before. It seemed to be quite a hard look and not his usual pleasant visage, but then this was probably due to the predictable problems which the unsolved case had been building up.

His comment made Anna really blush with realisation. She just said, 'Yes, I was in the observation room at the top and they keep everything so hot in these offices. Quickly moving toward the main doors, she said, Jack's waiting for us, so we can go straight away.'

Without waiting, she held the door open and Alex followed her along the jetty to where Jack was sitting in the stern of his boat, wreathed in his usual cloud of evil-smelling smoke. As they approached, he hawked and spat toward the water, clearing his throat of what had to be the condensate of the tar-covered rope that he'd been smoking.

'I be waitin' for ee to come, so as I can take ee to Bert's boat-house, if'n you be ready.' The engine was gently chugging away.

'We be ready, I mean yes, we're ready Jack,' said Alex. This bloke is infectious, he thought.

'Right you are then, just you hop in and sit yourselfs down while I slip the moorings and we be on our way.'

Alex was thinking that Jack looked around ninety years old, but due to his weather-beaten face, could be a lot younger, it was hard to tell. However, he was still a sprightly mover as he quickly untied the bowline and freed the bow mooring and moved to the stern where he simply had a line from his boat, round a bollard and back to the boat. He sat in the stern, reached over and released the rope pulling it back on board. Putting the engine in drive, he pushed the throttle gently and the diesel gradually growled into a stronger beat and the boat picked up speed, and he sat with his left arm looped over the tiller.

'I really hope that this boat is there Anna, and not another wild goose chase. I'm bloody sick of things going pear-shaped. We've got the illegals and they're being questioned, or interrogated, whichever way you'd like to say it, by Tom and Alice and the other DC's back at the office. I don't know quite what that's going to tell us though'

'Surely we'll get to know the way they organise the trips across from France, I mean how they get in touch with Goodyear and how much they pay him?'

'That's one thing. At least we might get to estimate how much money he's been making from these trips, although we don't know how many he's made, so again, it's guesswork and no hard evidence. I'm just getting so pissed off with no results and no conclusion, not to mention DCS Gordon breathing down my neck.'

'I can understand that guv.'

'If the boat is in this boat-house, what about Goodyear, Dimitriou and the girl, surely they won't be there will they?'

'That would be just too much to hope for, so I've put a watch on both Goodyear and Dimitriou's houses and just hope that they turn up.'

'If they do turn up and we can arrest them, what do we charge them with, as we only have the bodies but nothing tying them to these two?'

'I think we do Anna. I'm sure that the forensics we got from not only the first body we got from Goathorn and then the two we found in the shed there, will tie into something on this boat, once we find it.'

'Yes, surely there will be something from the two bodies which they took off the "Whaler" next to the oyster farm. I mean, they took these two bodies, which must have been in quite a state by the time they took them from the shed and then left them in the "Whaler" for a couple of days. I can't believe that there will be no traces of them.'

'Let's just hope that we find this boat. I've started a wide search for both Goodyear and Dimitriou. It's a fair bet that they've made a run for it, so let's hope that our lads can turn something up while we chase about looking for this bloody boat.'

Shall I get on to the SSD tomorrow then guv?'

'Good idea. Let's just see what they can come up with.'

They were coming close to Brownsea Island and along the shoreline, showing just out of the trees bordering the coastal strip, was a large, what looked like a wooden, building. 'Is that the boathouse over there Jack?' asked Anna.

'Aye, that it be missy. Damn great shed though, big enough for many big old boats in their day. 'Tis bigger than it looks from here. It do go back aways into them trees look.'

As they drew closer, they could see that indeed, the shed was huge and went deeply into the woodland on the island which effectively screened it from most views.

CHAPTER 64

After taking more time than he expected to finish making the repairs to the bow, Goodyear had turned the boat towards Poole Harbour. The man whom he'd shot, was lying on his back on the grass. His dog was sitting next to him, ever faithful. He was not found until first light, when another dog-walker came across his body. Quickly making a 999 call on his mobile phone, he was informed that an ambulance would be there quickly. "I found this man lying close to the cliff-top," he'd said with a very incredulous voice, "I think he's been shot!" The operator asked him what condition the man was in. "Do you know, I didn't think to take a close look. He was very still and not moving. I suppose I assumed that he was dead.'

'If you are close to the body, could you take a close look and try to locate a pulse?'

'Of course; although I'm not sure where I should try to find a pulse.'

'On the side of the neck, just below the ear is probably the best place. Also tell me if he is bleeding or not.'

The dog-walker did as had been suggested and felt a slight pulse. 'Oh thank God he's still alive!' Looking down at his chest and taking a closer look, he could see that there was fresh blood oozing from the dark mark on his checked shirt which was obviously where the bullet had entered him.

'Yes, I think he's still bleeding. Should I do anything?'

'Try to place something over the wound to staunch the bleeding and make sure that the ambulance crew can find you. It seems as if you are not really near a road.'

'That's right, I'm on the golf course, but there is a sort of track along the cliff-top so perhaps the ambulance can get close.'

'Don't worry; we have your GPS co-ordinates for the ambulance crew. Just stay with the victim and do your best to keep the wound covered.'

'Okay, I'll do what I can.'

Rolling up a clean handkerchief and holding it to the bullet entry wound as hard as he could, he shortly heard the siren and then the flashing blue light as the ambulance appeared along the cliff-top. He stood up and waved his phone with the torch facility lit, waving it in the air to attract their attention. The ambulance driver flashed his headlights to acknowledge this.

'Oh thank heavens you're here. I do hope he'll survive.'

'Do you know this man?'

'No, but I have seen him a few times, walking his dog. Pointing, he said, that's the dog there; he's been sitting beside him all the time.'

We'll do our best and perhaps you'd wait until the police arrive so that they can get all the details.'

'Of course.'

***

Meanwhile, "Predator" was making way towards Poole Harbour, albeit at a reduced speed due to the damage to the bow.

'Are we going to make it Martin?' asked Dimitriou.

'I think so. Thanks to your stupidity, we can't get up any speed but we should be okay. Take over the helm while I make a phone call'

'Yeah, I can do that.'

'Just make sure that you don't increase the speed or you'll never walk again.'

Dimitriou knew that this was no idle joke; he'd seen Goodyear shoot someone in the knees before.

Goodyear made a call on his mobile.

A sleepy voice answered. 'Ello, who's that, callin' me at this ungodly hour?'

'Bert. It's Martin Goodyear. Sorry to wake you, but I need your help.'

'Oh it's you Martin; I was goin' to get up early anyway. What's your problem? You haven't buggered up that lovely boat of yours have you?'

'Just a spot of damage, but it needs fixing rather quickly and I happen to know that your shed is unoccupied at the moment, so could you take her up the slip and help me to get the repairs done?'

'You are in luck because I have a customer coming in later this week for some big repairs, so if'n you're quick, I suppose it'll be okay. When will you come in?'

'As soon as I can, is that okay with you? I reckon it could be round about an hour.'

'You be in some sort of trouble then, needing this so quick like?'

'Nothing for you to worry about Bert; just get me into the shed and everything will be good.'

'Okay then, I'll get the slip gear ready; get the winch running. She ain't been started for some while, and she do need some coaxing like. I'll have to fill up the fuel tank as it's been empty for quite a while.'

'Right, see you soon then.'

'Righty 'o.'

Ending the call, he went back to the helm. Genny then asked him, 'What about me?'

'Don't worry; we'll drop you off at the jetty on Brownsea Castle. You can get the ferry back to the Haven and get a taxi to get you home. I'll catch up with you later. Just take the money with you. It's in that bag over there. Pointing to a leather bag, he said, 'Just be bloody careful; there's a shed-load of cash there. Put it in the safe as soon as you get home. Don't talk to anyone and don't get involved, just get home as quickly as you can. I'll call you later.'

They were getting close to the entrance to Poole Harbour and there was a "wind over tide" swell running which made the boat pitch a little more than normal, especially as the boat had slowed down so they were "on the hump" and not planing as they had been after leaving the beach following the hasty repairs.

As they came into the section of the harbour entrance at the Haven, they entered the channel called "Training Bank" where the tidal current ran through the narrow section, scouring the sea-bed and keeping it clear of silt.

The swell increased considerably as the waves became steeper on the rising tide and the bow dipped quite suddenly, digging into the upwind side of a wave. This caused the boat speed to drop as though brakes were applied sharply. This caused the anchor, located in a "sleeve" on the bow, to be shunted forward. As Dimitriou had not actually inserted the holding pin in the shank, thanks to the sudden lurching of the boat when Goodyear had accelerated, the anchor flew forward over the bow. The anchor chain ran through a "hawse pipe" on the deck. As this chain was suddenly jerked up, it kinked and jammed after about two metres had run out. The consequence of this was that the heavy anchor was snagged to a stop, swinging and smashing through the hull, just below the waterline.

At the sound of the heavy thud and crunching noise, Goodyear yelled, 'what the hell was that!?' He throttled back quickly and put the drive to idle, taking the way off the craft. 'Have we hit something?'

Dimitriou went forward to investigate, quickly followed by Goodyear.

As soon as he saw that the anchor had disappeared, he guessed the worst.

Looking over the side he saw that the anchor fluke had smashed a large hole through the bow. Water would now be jetting into the boat and there would be no stopping it.

'FUCK, FUCK, FUCK! You stupid half-witted twat, you didn't put the pin in when I told you to stow the anchor. Now you're going to sink us. I'm going to make you sorry for this.'

Dimitriou knew exactly what Goodyear might be going to do.

'We have to beach her or we'll sink,' he yelled. As he put the engines into drive once more, he called to Genny, 'Find out what time the next high tide is.'

'Okay,' she replied. Quickly finding the tide times, she called out, 'it's a flood tide now, about half-way. What the hell has happened?'

'I'll tell you what's happened. This fucking moron didn't put the safety pin in the anchor and it's just been thrown over the side and it put a sodding great hole in our bow. If we don't beach her very quickly, we could sink.'

'What are you going to do Martin?' she said.

'Do you mean after I kill him? I'm going to run her on to the beach just after the Haven. We'll turn to port where there's very shallow water. That'll keep us from taking on too much until I've managed to get the anchor out and stuff something in the hole. We just have to get through Blood Alley to that boat shed on Brownsea and then we'll be okay I think.

Putting the bilge pumps to full power, he said to Dimitriou, 'Get right into the bow section and push the anchor out, then stuff something into the hole as tightly as you can. Then get back up here.'

'Okay, I'll do the best I can but it's going to be pitch dark in there.'

'So take a bloody torch you fucking idiot and make it good and tight or I'll stuff you in the hole, you useless piece of shit.'

Dimitriou struggled right into the forward part of the bow, through a small hatch to where the anchor chain and rope locker was. Propping the torch at an angle, he could just see the big fluke of the anchor protruding through the fibreglass hull. Water was gushing in and the section of the boat he was in was already more than half full. Looking around for something heavy to bang the metal out of the hole, he found a large metal shackle attached to some rope. 'I don't know what the hell that's for, he thought, but it should do the trick. He gave the fluke a heavy blow, but nothing moved. 'SHIT!' He tried again, this time swinging the shackle as hard as he possibly could. This time, the anchor was moved out a little. Again, he smashed the shackle onto the metal fluke. The shackle glanced off the anchor fluke, smashing his hand against the opposite side of the hull. In the time honoured fashion of "For every action there is a reaction," there were two results from these actions; one was that the anchor disappeared out of the hole, and the other was that he snapped three fingers of his left hand.

He let out an incredibly loud scream with pain, but managed with his other hand, to reach back through the hatch and grab a sleeping bag. He stuffed this into the hole as tightly as he could. The water slowed appreciably so he struggled back through the hatch and made his way back to the helm position.

Goodyear heard his yells of pain and said, 'Don't sound so happy, you don't know what's coming next.'

'I'm not fucking happy, I'm in pain, I've just broken all my fingers.'

'Serves you bloody well right, just shut up and get that anchor back on board or I'll break everything else. I've got to beach the boat now before we sink. And this time put the fucking pin in!'

Climbing back up to the deck, nursing his incredibly painful hand and moving to the bow, he somehow managed to drag the anchor back one-handed, although with great difficulty. He was silently saying to himself, do you know what, I'm bloody sick of this and I don't want to be here, I don't care how much he pays me.

Putting the engines into slow ahead, Goodyear gingerly motored about three hundred yards through the Haven and then turned to port just after the landing slip of the ferry, and into the lee of the Studland Peninsula where the water was shallow. Gently putting the boat onto the soft sand, he thought it was possible to wait for Bert to call back and tell him that the boat shed and slipway was ready. The incoming flood tide would help him to sneak through Blood Alley to the boat shed.

'How about me getting back home then?' asked Genny?

You can jump over here and walk back to the ferry slipway and wait for the first one. You can phone for a taxi from the other side. It'll save you getting back from Brownsea Castle.'

'Okay, but I don't know what time the first ferry is.'

'Just don't fucking whinge; I've got enough problems as it is.'

It had taken longer than planned to return, thanks to the damage limiting their speed. But Goodyear was sure that once the boat was inside the large shed, he could relax and not worry about them being found, at least for a while. The shed was not normally used, only very occasionally these days, so it would be way down the list of enquiries to be made by the police, who would undoubtedly be looking for them. They would effectively disappear, at least long enough for him to make escape plans. It was now the early hours of the morning.

***

Bert Jackson had gone into the large boat shed and over to the great winch, which was used to pull the cradle on the slipway where the incoming boat would be held. This cradle was a large flat carriage which ran on wheels up the rails on the sloping slipway, pulled by the powerful winch. The cradle had very strong beams rising vertically along each side. Along the base of the cradle, was a channel where the keel of the boat would be guided as it came into position. Once the boat was in the correct location, the craft would be supported by the vertical beams. When the boat was safely berthed in this way, the cradle with the boat secured, would be winched up the slipway.

He looked at the huge engine and gearbox which powered the large cable drum. The steel cable ran down to the cradle, round a large pulley fixed to the front, then back to the winch position, where the end of the cable was firmly anchored to the winch bed. By having this configuration, it was possible to move very heavy boats into the boat shed. It was actually capable of moving a craft of up to 50 tons, but "Predator" was only about 5 tons, so no problem for this winch. The more modern ones were usually powered by large electric motors, but when this shed was built, there was no electric power on Brownsea Island, so the big diesel engine was installed.

Bert was talking to himself as he inspected the engine. 'Now come on, me ol' beauty, I knows you've not had too much work these last years, but you can still pull this'n up, she be only a littl'un.' He checked the fuel tank and saw that it needed quite a lot of fuel. 'Mebbe 'tis enough to get you going my 'gel,' he said as he held the jerry-can to the funnel of the fuel tank. He swore as there was a "blow-back" up the funnel and an amount of diesel was splashed down on to the floor. 'Damned stuff stinks,' he muttered.

The engine area was not in a good state, suffering from some quite severe rusting in parts, and there was a lot of oil around the lower part of the winch workings. There was a huge gear wheel next to the winch drum containing the cable. This was driven by more gears taking drive from the engine and giving the drum the power necessary to haul the cradle with whatever boat was on there at the time. There were a number of levers on the engine and gearbox of the winch, which controlled the engine speed, the gearbox, the drum speed and drum brake. At least Bert knew these controls although they could be confusing to a modern boatyard worker. He just hoped that they still worked properly, as they'd not been used for a considerable time. To start the engine, there was a large flywheel which had to be cranked by hand. The flywheel had to reach a speed which enabled the pistons in the engine to compress the diesel fuel to the point of explosion and power to make the engine run. This was not easy and Bert was not a young man by any stretch of the imagination. 'I don't think I be able to turn that there flywheel but those two will have to do it when they gets here,' he muttered to himself.

Around the winch and along the side of the boat shed was a large accumulation of wood shavings and blocks of wood, left over from the last working on an old wooden craft which had been restored after many months of work. There was a lot of oil which had seeped from the gearbox of the winch and this had been soaked up by some of the shavings. I'll have to clean all this up sometime soon, he said to himself as he looked at all the detritus; Tis a disgrace. Looking around and saying to himself; I s'pose I'd better do it now or t'will be slippery. He found some rags and old sacking lying behind the winch, which he picked up. Walking over to the area around the winch, he wiped up as much of the oil and diesel spilt as he could and threw them into a heap over by the shed wall, onto a pile of wood shavings and old rags which had also soaked up some of the spillage.

What Bert had not seen was that at the bottom of the fuel tank, out of sight next to the gearbox, was a slow seepage of diesel. Not much, but it was slowly soaking into the wood shavings. Looking into the fuel tank, he cursed quietly to himself, damn and double damn, t'aint 'nuff to start 'er up. Damn good job I got some more out the back. He walked behind the winch and through a door to where some jerry cans were stored. Coming back he carried on filling the tank.

"Predator" was beached on the shallow section just behind the slipway for the ferry. Here the water was just deep enough to allow the boat to beach close to the Shell Bay side of the ferry slipway which made it possible for Genny to clamber over the side of the boat, helped by Goodyear.

'The water's cold,' she moaned.

'For Christ's sake stop moaning; that's all you have to worry about and I've got to get "Predator" out of sight or we're going to be found by the police and if they do, then you can kiss everything goodbye.'

Keeping quiet, she was not at all happy at the thought of having to wait for quite a while for the first ferry to arrive. She could see it berthed, dark and silent, at the Haven on the other side of the channel, but as it was hours before dawn, it was going to be a long wait. She was holding the leather bag containing a very large amount of money. She was thinking to herself that it was very clever of Martin to make sure that the illegals had all paid in Sterling. "He'd have a difficult job to get all types of different currencies changed at a bank, without raising suspicions, but that's what he's good at." She was also pretty sure that there would be some "goodies" for her when he got back and all these problems were sorted out, looking forward to some good times and good things too.

Although the bow was almost out of the water, there was still seepage into the hull, but the bilge pumps were keeping it at bay. Martin went below to check on the state of the hole. He managed to push the rolled–up sleeping bag a little further into the opening. Dimitriou was nursing his broken fingers but certainly not looking forward to Martin's rage when he finally managed to get the boat safely out of sight.

The tide was rising and the harbour was filling. There was a considerable current flowing through the Haven and Goodyear was hoping that this would help "Predator" to limp round through "Blood Alley" to the boat-shed.

'Get up here you useless piece of shit,' was the shouted command to Dimitriou.

This made him very nervous as he knew only too well what might be in store for him. Not wishing to antagonise Goodyear any more, he went forward to the helm position. He'd made a sort of bandage for his fingers and said, 'I need to see a doctor or go to the hospital to get these fixed.'

'I don't think that you need to worry much about your bloody fingers.'

This short sentence brought an ice-cold shiver through Dimitriou's body.

'We've got to move as soon as we hear from Bert.'

Moving to the winch, Bert once again tipped the can to the fuel tank, and once again there was a '"blow-back" which sent more diesel fuel spillage to the floor. 'Damn and bloody damn again,' he said.

Once more, he wiped up the spillage with old cloths and threw them onto the pile of previous rags.

Moving to the cable drum, he released the brake which was holding the cradle in place at the top of the slipway. Using the lever to control the descent of the cradle, he watched as it submerged below the water. When the carriage was at the appropriate depth to contain "Predator" in Bert's estimation, he pulled the brake lever and locked it in position.

He called Goodyear's number and the mobile phone on "Predator "trilled.

'Yes?'

'Tis Bert. We'm be ready for ee now, doors are open and the cradle is ready and waiting.'

'We've had a bit more of a delay, but we'll be there soon enough.'

'Okay, I be ready and waiting. Just keep between the upright posts and these will guide you. When you do feel her push up on the guide channel, just keep 'er running slow ahead 'til I gets a shackle on to your bow eye.'

'Understood Bert.'

"Predator" made slow progress in the early morning pre-sunrise gloom, but quite soon they were coming to the slipway of the boat-shed.

'Thank Christ I know this place,' said Goodyear. 'There it is, you could easily miss it in this light.'

Spotting the arms of the cradle protruding from the water, he manoeuvred the craft into the space between the arms and as the hull was positioned into the guide track underwater, he kept the engines pushing the craft onto the cradle. Bert appeared from the back of the shed and moved down to the waters' edge with a large shackle in his hand. He walked carefully up the steel framework of the cradle and as the bow was almost out of the water now, he was able to fasten the shackle to the bow eye on "Predator."

'Okay, you can shut off the engines now, she be fast,' called Bert.

'Right Bert, let's get her up and into the shed and then we can shut these doors.'

'Right you are then, I'll just go and start the winch but you do have to come up here and help me, 'cos I be too old to do this by meself.' There's going to come a time when I can't do this no more, he murmured to himself. Tis too damn heavy for me. I'm a wishin' I'd put in that electric start years ago, when I had the chance. Building up speed on that flywheel is the only way to start this ol' diesel.'

Goodyear jumped down from the bow and joined Bert and they walked back up the long slipway to the engine of the winch. Inserting a large handle which turned the big flywheel and making the necessary adjustments to the controls, he said, 'You turn that there handle and the quicker you turn 'em the sooner she'll start. Goodyear pushed the handle but found it extremely hard to move. The flywheel began to move a little. Bert said, you'm going to 'ave to turn that a sight quicker to get 'im goin'.'

'I'm pushing the fucking things as hard as I can; this is bloody impossible.'

Pushing harder, the flywheel moved a little quicker and Goodyear's face was becoming redder as he pushed as hard as he could, although it seemed too heavy to move.

Then Bert exclaimed, 'Damn and blast! – forgot to open the decompressor, no bloody wonder t'was so heavy.' He reached up and lifted a small lever at the top of the engine. 'This might be better,' he muttered, accompanied by a wry grin.

'You stupid old bugger,' said Goodyear and now he found the handle moved more easily. Putting all his weight behind the handle, it began to move more quickly, building up the speed of the flywheel which turned the crankshaft. When Bert judged the speed of the flywheel fast enough, he reached up and snapped the small lever shut which should have caused the engine to start. Only it didn't. It simply gave a "cough" and slowed to a very sudden stop.

'What the fuck happened Bert?'

'Are, t'was the compression what has to be overcome see, and we'm going to have to do that agin Martin, only a little faster this time.'

'You must be bloody joking Bert,' fighting for breath. He turned and shouted to Dimitriou. 'Get yourself down here NOW! Dimitriou ran up the slip to them and Goodyear said, you're heftier than me, turn this handle as fast as you can or your life won't be worth living.'

'But I've got broken fingers, I can't do this, he shouted, running as fast as he could.'

'You bloody can and you will. You don't need to hold it, just push with me and give it all your strength. We have to get this sodding winch working or we'll be sitting ducks, so shut up and get pushing.'

Taking hold of the handle with his good hand he began to push.

'Harder.'

'I'm pushing.'

'Push harder, damn you, just get it going faster.'

Again, when the flywheel had built up more speed, Bert snapped shut the decompressor valve. This time, there was a more definite sound and the engine began to give the characteristic "thump" as it built up speed. The speed of the thumping increased as the engine built up power.

Goodyear looked at Bert, who actually smiled. 'Do you know, I wasn't cert'in sure that 'ee would be a startin','

'It's a bloody good job it did, but can we now get my boat up the slip as quickly as you can?'

'Right you are Martin, I'll just take in the slack and she'll start to come up.'

He engaged the drum gear and released the brake lever. The drum began to move and as the cable became taught, the boat began to move slowly up the slipway. Goodyear ran back down and as soon as the boat had moved into the confines of the shed, he closed the big heavy doors with a sigh of relief, shutting out the very little early morning light.

Going back to where Bert and Dimitriou were standing, he said 'now we can relax a little and decide our next move. Can you give us a lift over to Poole Quay Bert?'

'Surely Martin, as soon as you want, but don't you want to do some repairs now?'

'I'll make a start and see how quickly I can get a suitable repair done, but I may have to go over to Poole to the chandlers for some stuff if I don't have enough.'

'Right you are then Martin.

CHAPTER 65

After Jack had told them of the boat shed on Brownsea Island, Alex had quickly found the telephone number of Bert Jackson, the owner. Trying this number gave no response, so once again, local knowledge supplied by Jack proved useful. Bert was found to have been in the bar of the Nelson Pub, but he'd been gone a good while ago. Where the hell is he then, he asked himself; maybe he's back at his shed.

Alex was on his way to the harbour marina where Jack was waiting with Anna, to take them over to the island.

Talking to Anna on his mobile he asked, 'Have we checked all the other possible boat sheds or buildings where this "Predator" could be hiding?'

'Yes guv, it's taken hours and checked all the ones that we considered large enough and this type of place is probably the only building which could take this boat, and is available, according to the different people I've spoken to. Tom and Alice as well as the other DC's have been asking all the possible owners, but no sightings so far, or at least no-one has said that they've seen it.'

'Then we need to get a look at this boathouse on Brownsea to see if "Predator" is there. It does seem to be the most likely place. Have there been any sightings of her as we know they were making their way back to Poole Harbour during darkness?'

'Nothing as yet guv, but I don't think our webcam at the Haven was being monitored all night.'

'Damn and blast. Someone was supposed to be checking this all night. We could have a result by now and we would have been notified if they'd come through the Haven at night.'

Anna actually felt sorry for the person who had been tasked with watching all the boat movements through the narrow channel for hours on end; but she had to agree with Alex that had someone been vigilant all night as they were supposed to do and not nipping off for a coffee or something, the boat they were desperately looking for may have been spotted. There was no excuse for not concentrating on this task and the person responsible would feel the full force of Alex's ire a little later on, that was for sure; but perhaps they'd not gone back through all the data yet.

'We have to assume that they've made it back and I think they will have got into that boat shed as quickly as they could. We have to raid the place as soon as possible, and with armed back-up I think Anna.'

'Do we have the authority to get into the boat shed guv?'

'Do you know, I really don't care at the moment? I just want to get in there and take a look. We've checked on most of the boat sheds around the harbour and this is probably the last one left. I had no idea that there was such a building on Brownsea.'

'I'm not surprised guv, I mean, who goes there except the tourists and I don't suppose that many even get to that part of the island.'

'That's as maybe, but now we know of its existence, we have to check it out. I know it's early, but the sooner the better.'

He called the AR team office and spoke with their team leader Paul Rickson and arranged for a party of officers with the appropriate equipment and transport to be ready with their RIB.

'I want the team ready and waterborne by 10am at the latest. Is that okay with you Paul?'

'No problem Alex, only I hope this time we don't balls it up by stuffing our boat into someone's yacht.'

'At least it'll be light this time.'

'It's the same outfit that we're looking for? Do you know if they're armed, I mean, do you know for sure?'

'Sorry Paul, no, but as they've killed at least 3 people so far and probably more, I think it's a fair bet that they'll be tooled up, don't you?'

'I think I'd go along with that. Anyway, our lads are all sorted and you can call the shots when we meet up at the location.'

'Okay, I've just texted you the position; you'll see that it's just on the corner by Ramshorn Lake. It's quite hidden by the trees.'

'Right you are then Alex, we'll keep in touch by radio once we're on the water.'

'We'll be going over from the Harbour Marina and meet you there.'

'Roger that Alex.'

Arriving at the Harbour Marina, he went straight to the quayside where Jack and Anna were waiting.

Alex turned to Anna. 'I have a feeling that this time we're going to get some closure to this epic.'

'Let's hope you're right, it's been taking us all over the place and we've been chasing our tails trying to find them. You'd think it would be easy in a place like the harbour, I mean, it's not that big but I suppose with them belting across the channel and then back again, together with the fact that we just don't have the manpower to cover all the places where they might be, it's not surprising that we kept losing them.'

'And all our bad luck, of which we've had more than our share. Maybe now they'll be cornered. My guess is that they've gone into hiding because they can't get away.'

'Why do you think they can't get away, I mean they've a very fast boat and they could make a dash under cover of night?'

'Yes, they could, but we do know that they've sustained damage to the boat and I think that because of this, they have to have repairs done and what better place than a boat-shed where they can not only hide out of sight but get repairs done so that they could make a dash for it to somewhere else when it's possible.'

'I see where you are going with this then guv. Let's just hope that they are where we think they are and we can have them cornered.'

'We'll soon find out Anna, and then maybe we can get things calmed down a little. We all need some quiet and private time don't we?'

Alex said this with a long look at Anna and she understood the meaning of his words very clearly. He wanted more time together. This wasn't altogether anathema to her, but now she had conflicting feelings which were clouding the water. Her recent time with Fuller had given her emotions a real kick and now she realised that her feelings for Alex were perhaps not what they were. Fuller was a completely different person; although Alex was a nice guy, and in most ways most pleasant company, there were disquieting points in that not only was he her boss which made things extremely difficult at work, and the separation of the two identities, but Fuller had an attraction which was different to anyone she had ever known in her adult life. There was a certain 'magical attraction' which he managed to extend to her when they were together. Yes, it was early days, but she had to accept that her innermost feelings could not be ignored.

She answered his question with a non-committal "mmm," and this made Alex's expression change to one of surprise. He said nothing, and turned away. They boarded Jack's boat and he quickly slipped the moorings and headed directly across the harbour towards Brownsea.

He was sitting looking ahead, and over his shoulder he said, can you fill Tom and Alice in on what is happening and what is going to happen?'

'Sure thing guv; the AR team are going to meet with us at the boat-shed location aren't they and we're going to effect an entry to see if "Predator" is there and maybe the two suspects as well?'

'I did see Dobbs being her being pulled onto the boat just before they made a run for it.'

'Damn, my thinking is all fouled up. 'Can you see what Tom and Alice have managed to get out of the illegals, if anything?'

'Okay guv,' and she turned away, grateful to be able to re-focus as she was now feeling quite unsettled as to what the future might hold between her and Alex, and for that matter, her and Fuller.

Making the call, she asked Alice what information she and Tom had gleaned from the illegals. Alice thought that one of their staff was actually from that area and had sought her out. It transpired that although she was Turkish, she had spent a number of years in Cyprus where the accents were slightly different and she could very usefully act as an interpreter as she was fluent in both. She was DC Sofya Aysun and she'd been living in the UK for some 12 years becoming a police officer 3 years ago. A very pleasant, attractive young woman with a gentle disposition, which actually belied a strength coming from her early years with a quite hard upbringing. She possessed a strong sense of purpose which was serving her well in her career.

Alice had spoken with Sofya at length and explained that everything she was to learn from the interviews with these men had to be completely secret and she was to discuss whatever she gained, with absolutely no-one. Alice made it clear that should anything "leak," then her career would cease. This warning was taken completely to heart by Sofya during the numerous interviews.

'So Alice, what are your findings from these illegals?'

'Well sarge, so far both Tom and I have had to use Sofya as you can imagine, although a couple of them actually spoke quite good English, so that made things a little easier.'

'Yes, yes, go on then, what are the results?'

'They all had made their way across from Northern Cyprus to Turkey and then across the continent to the French coast. She confirmed to me was why they just didn't come over to the UK in the normal way, but one of the first things I learned was that as they are from Northern Cyprus, their passports are not valid for entry to the UK, so they would be denied entry in the normal way. They are all skilled or educated to a high degree and this seemed to be their only way of getting entry and possibly a job suitable for their skills.

It had all been arranged that they would be collected from a specific point on the French coast at a predetermined time and date. They all had to be at the correct place or they'd miss the boat, so to speak.'

'Very droll Alice; so were there other trips like this or was this just a once-only pick-up?'

'From what we can gather, there would have been quite a number of previous runs, taking the same number of passengers each time. It does look like it was an "ongoing" and repeated run with possibly 50 or 60 passengers in total, but they can't give an accurate figure.'

'So how much did each one pay then, did they say?'

'Oh yes, they each paid anything up to £10,000, in cash and in Sterling, that was made clear.'

'Bloody hell Alice; ten grand each and 12 passengers each time!'

'I suppose that if Goodyear took that sort of money; what would that be, £120,000? – If that was in cash, he'd have a very difficult job in taking that to a bank without questions being asked.'

'Sure, 120,000 grand would certainly raise eyebrows wouldn't it?

'Well, I'd think so, but it depends on what Goodyear does to earn a living; if he in fact does have a real job. I suspect that he has other ways of depositing money and that's something else we have to find out. Maybe Miss Dobbs can help us with that, as she must have some idea of what he does and where he goes. I don't think he'll just "nip round to the bank" with that sort of cash, do you?'

'I'd suggest that he'll have some sort of account somewhere where there are no questions asked, don't you Anna?'

'Very, very possible Alice; anything else?'

She then said a quite "drawn-out" yeesss.' It seems that one of the illegals didn't bring the money with him that he should have and Goodyear dragged him out to the stern of the boat while they were crossing the channel and beat him with a steel bar. From what the others said, they could see him hitting him time and time again around the body. A couple of them said he'd made the man stand holding the rail at the stern and then smashed his arms with this bar. When he fell against the rail, then Goodyear cut his throat. The man screamed and then he was simply pushed over the rail and into the sea.'

'My God, another one. This makes 5 murders I think. Who knows how many more? This man is an animal. Okay Alice, thanks, I've heard enough. We have a reliable witness who can give us a cast-iron testimony to this I presume?'

'We do.'

'Then guard this guy with all the guarding you can put in place. He will be our star witness when this comes to trial.'

'Okay sarge, leave it to me and Tom. We'll get it sorted.'

'And will you thank Sofya for her efforts; I'm sure she's been a great help.'

'Will do sarge.'

CHAPTER 66

"Predator" had been hauled up the slip and secured in place, ready for work to start on repairing the damage to the bow. Goodyear took all the materials necessary for the replacing of the hull fibreglass and reinforcing the repair from the inside of the hull, setting them down on the concrete hard-standing in front of the boat.

Bert had seen Dimitriou holding his broken fingers and realised that he was in considerable pain. He said, 'We'd better take a look at them fingers my lad. Tell 'ee what, just you come along a' me lad an' we can get a bandage and some splints on them fingers. I don't think you can do much to help Martin there while he puts that new fibreglass into the hole. I don't suppose 'ee be too happy 'bout that, do 'ee?'

'You could say that Bert. I think he's going to kill me as soon as he has a chance.'

'Oh, don't you be so silly now, 'ee won't do nothin' like that.'

'You don't know him Bert, I've seen what he does to people and I'm not joking. If someone crosses him, he thinks nothing of either beating the shit out of them or cutting their throats, and he's got a gun as well. He's got the most appalling temper.'

'Don't you never mind, let's just get yon fingers splinted and bound up. I can see what Martin's got some problems and he don't want to be found and I'm not about to ask questions.'

Moving to the back of the shed he went through a door behind the winch engine. Dimitriou followed and looked back as he moved out of view, sneaking a look at Goodyear working on the hull. He inwardly shuddered at the thought of what might be in store for him and how he might escape. Then he realised – "shit, I'm on an island and there's nowhere to hide and how could I get back to the mainland? Maybe, I could hide on the island and steal a boat or something when I get the chance; but then if Martin does find me, I'm a dead man."

Just then, Goodyear called to Dimitriou.

'Where are you? Dimitriou, you lazy bastard, get back here.'

There was no answer, so Goodyear moved to the back of the shed. He saw the open door and shouted through, 'Dimitriou, where the hell are you?'

Bert called back, 'I just be a fixin' his hand, we'm be back in two ticks.' They walked on to Bert's house a little way behind the shed and hidden by the trees.

Goodyear walked back to the boat, mumbling as he went. "Fuckin' Freddie Furkan, I'll give him fixing his bloody fingers; I'll cut the fuckers off when I've finished with him. No, in fact, I don't need him anymore, I'll make sure that he becomes no problem at all, when the time is right."

Getting back to the job in hand, he was thinking that the police would be out looking for them and it wouldn't be too long before they came to look at this shed. He was actually trapped here for the time being, as to venture out on to the harbour, he could well be spotted by someone and that would close any chance he had of escape either with the boat or by other means. The boat was replaceable, but he had enormous sums of money in various accounts and it was more important that he was able to access them. To be caught by the police anywhere would put a stop to that. He was actually thinking, as soon as this job is finished, I'm out of here and well away to some other place until things quieten down. There's been too much going wrong lately, and with the last lot of immigrants caught, they're going to spill the beans about how they get picked up and all the details of landing places. No, it's time I got myself well out of the spotlight. Should I take Genny? He thought this over for a couple of seconds, then, No, I can get a new model anywhere. They're all the same, flash some money at them and they open up like a flower.

He carried on with the messy fibreglass repairs and Dimitriou came back with his hand splinted and bandaged, thanks to Bert. He was very "cagey" with Goodyear and he was silently telling himself to take great care to do whatever he was told, in case he found himself on the wrong end of Goodyear's temper, that was the last thing he needed right now. He was really thinking along the lines of making a break for it and taking his chances.

'It's about time you got your arse back here. Make yourself useful, if you can,' he said pointing to a large jar of resin, 'mix some of that resin over there and brush it into that matting. I've put some on the hole already and I have to go inside to put some material on the inside so that it forms a solid barrier. I'll try to push the parts which have been pushed inward, back to close the hole. When I do that, put the mat with the resin on, over the top and make sure it stays there until I come back out. Do you understand all that and can you do it right this time, or is that too difficult for your little brain?'

'Yes Martin.'

'Good, because you know bloody well what will happen if you fuck this up?'

'Yes Martin.'

He went back into the hull of the boat and pushed the damaged sections of the hull back as far into position as he could. Dimitriou did what he was told and although this gave a big patch of ugly fibreglass matting over the damaged area, he thought it would actually do the job effectively once the resin had set.

As Goodyear came back out of the confines of the hull, he said, 'We are going have to stay in here for the time being. We can't risk being out on the water or someone will spot us. Have you finished what I told you?'

'Yes, I think so. You'd better take a look. It seems okay to me.'

They walked back to the bow section to inspect the supposedly finished repair.

'What a fucking mess this is, but I suppose it'll have to do for now. At least it will be seaworthy for when we can get her back on the water and get away from here. Bert joined them and looked over the damaged section. 'What do you think Bert, will it do?'

'Well, Martin, I have to say that it's not the best looking repair job I've seen, but I s'pose t'will do the job for now. I'd say just don't push yon craft too hard, being that I knows you have a really fast boat here, but should you get into any sort of heavy sea, 'tis goin' to put one hell of a strain on that there patch.'

'I hear what you say Bert and I'll be careful. We are going to stay with the boat for now if that's okay with you. We need to keep out of sight of certain people, if you know what I mean?'

'I thinks I knows what you mean matey, and you can rely on me to keep myself to myself, meanin' I've seen and heard nothing.'

'Good man Bert, I knew I could rely on you and I won't leave you short on this for what you've done for me.'

'Just you keep yourselfs out of the way and things will surely calm down. I'm off to Poole Quay for to get some provisions and food and stuff, so I will see you lads later.'

'Okay Bert.'

Just near Brownsea Island, the Police in the form of Alex and Anna in Jack's boat met with the Marine Section RIB headed by Paul Rickson together with the AR team in their boat. As the craft came together, their commander John Sturton said 'We're all set here Alex, so when you're ready, you take the lead and we'll go along with you and give you backup.'

'Thanks John, I intend to approach quietly and take a look around the shed before we try to make an entry.'

'Right you are then.'

'I'd like us both to transfer to your boat and let Jack here get back as he's nothing to do with this investigation, is that okay with you?'

'No problem Alex, we'll just back off a little and slip over to that beach area just before we round the corner and we can transfer you both there.'

'Okay, let's do that.'

The two boats, Jack and the Marine Section with Paul Rickson simply beached and Anna and Alex simply jumped onto the beach and stood on the concrete sidewall, saying a big "thank you" to Jack and set him on his way. 'No doubt this'll keep him in many free pints in the "Nelson" when he recounts what's going on.'

'Good luck to him, that's what I say guv.'

The two RIBS's moved apart and with their engines on low power they moved toward the boat shed. The engines were just about audible in the very quiet part of the harbour.

But they could be heard by Goodyear and Dimitriou.

'Do you hear that?' said Dimitriou.

'Yes, it sounds like outboards and I'll bet that they are Police RIB's and they'll be looking for us. Unless they have a search warrant, they can't get in and Bert mentioned nothing about being asked if they can look over the shed, so we should be okay, but just in case, we'll keep ourselves hidden.

Just then, Bert came almost running back into the shed. 'I knows you are in here somewhere, an' I just seen two boats full of police and they be coming towards us here. Maybe you want to keep out of the way while they takes a look around. There be no winders so they can't see in and I can padlock the door good like and slip away afore they gets here.' With that, he locked the door and moved swiftly away to get to his boat which was moored in a little creek out of view of the police craft.

Goodyear and Dimitriou clambered aboard "Predator" and went to the area where they removed a hatch in the centre of the cabin. This gave access to a space below the deck level which was enough for them to make a relatively comfortable place to hide.

It was where most of the accessories and tackle that goes with a sea-going craft was stored but had sufficient space for them.

The hatch had a lock which was accessible from the underside. They had light from a fully charged battery lamp and Goodyear managed to make a rudimentary seal to the hatch lock. 'That's in case they come aboard and try to lift the hatch. They'll think it's just locked and hopefully won't look any further.'

'Are we going to have to stay her for long Martin?' asked Dimitriou.

'How the fuck should I know, but I'll tell you what, as soon as it's dark again, we're going to get right away from here and I'm going to make this boat disappear and I'm going to go somewhere a long way away until the heat dies down. I'm not going to give up this money-making enterprise just yet.'

'How about some food if we've got to stay here all day then?'

'You'll just have to forget about your stomach for the time being, so just stop bellyaching.'

'That's just the problem it's my belly that's aching as we've had no food for ages.'

'Do you know what; I think I'm going to kill you right now?'

That was precisely when Dimitriou didn't know his future. Was Goodyear joking or not?'

In the shed, up near the winch, the pile of oily rags which Bert had thrown onto the wood shavings was warming up considerably. This phenomenon was known as an "exothermic internal reaction" which in turn causes what is commonly termed as "Spontaneous Combustion." This process occurs when the temperature of such a material increases, without drawing heat from the surroundings, and ignition temperature is reached, much like a pile of new-mown grass cuttings will quickly heat up considerably. In this case, the wood shavings on which the oily rags had been dropped were very dry and extremely flammable. As there was plenty of air and therefore oxygen around this pile and no wind to waft away any heat build-up, this had been building up since Bert had dropped them many hours earlier, not to mention that the oily rags had been there for a considerable time, adding to the heat build-up.

The result of this was now that the wood shavings were beginning to smoulder. Also, some of the shavings had become soaked with oils and diesel from the leaking fuel tank on the winch engine, all of which fuelled the smouldering pile. The old building was completely made of timber and due to its age, was naturally very dry. As the pile actually caught fire, the back of the shed caught light and flames were beginning to gently spread up the walls of the shed. The more the fire took hold, the more it spread, and to add to the potential combustion, there was a shelf full of old tins of varnish and paint, together with all the other chemicals which accumulate in such a building. These in turn added a great deal to the increasing flames.

As the fire had started at the back of the shed, and the police were still on their craft, just off the shoreline, watching and deciding how to approach the shed, they were unaware of the flames. Furthermore, as the wood and shavings were very dry, there was very little smoke as would've been the case had the materials been damp. This meant that both Alex and Anna and the AR boat were at this time unaware of the fire.

'I think we should just take a look around the shed to see if there is a door apart from the big main ones on the slipway.'

'Okay guv, shall we take one side each and meet round the back maybe?' asked Anna.

'Good idea, I'll tell the AR boys to hang on until we know more rather than have them all stomping about.'

He looked over to the AR boat and said to Sturton, 'If you'd just like to hang on here while we do a quick "recce" to see if the boat is actually there, then we'll give you the word if I think it necessary to go in with force.'

'Okay Alex, it's your call. We'll just stand by.'

CHAPTER 67

Alex motioned to the helmsman at the controls to take them to the slipway so that they could jump out. As he manoeuvred the craft to the slipway side, there was a part of the concrete slope which allowed a craft to come close and tie up to a mooring bollard. This made it possible to exit their boat with ease. Anna was grateful that she didn't have to make any acrobatic moves in this direction as she had been dreading.

'I'll go this way,' said Alex, indicating the right side of the shed. If you see anything, don't make too much noise; if they are there, we don't want to let them know that we know. Just give me three taps on your Walkie-Talkie transmit button, and I'll know that you've found something. I'll do the same for you. If either of us finds anything important, just wait where you are and we can meet up. We'll then decide on how to play it.'

'Okay guv, got it.'

Alex moved off to the right side of the shed and Anna walked up the path to the left. There were no windows, so she tried looking through the wooden side of the building, but as the construction was similar to the way a "Carvel" boat was built, with the wooden planks overlapping, there was no way that she could see through.

Alex also found the same problem and they both moved toward the rear of the building, where Alex spotted the door, noting the large and closed padlock.

As he did so, he thought he could smell burning. Looking round, he then spotted the tongues of flame coming from the side of the building just behind where he'd just been walking. 'Oh, oh, that's not good news,' he muttered.

Inside the shed, both Goodyear and Dimitriou were unaware of the potential danger they were now in, as they could neither see nor smell the fire which was gaining a hold and moving to the side of the shed close to the craft in which they were hiding.

Some time prior to the arrival of "Predator," Bert had been doing some work on a boat in some very cold weather. As his shed was very large and therefore particularly cold, he'd hired some big space heaters to both keep warm while working and to allow paint and varnish to dry. To run these heaters, he'd installed two large Propane tanks with a special "twin" coupling unit which allowed the propane from the two tanks, standing side by side, to supply the heaters. One of these tanks had only been used for a relatively short while, as the weather had improved sufficiently, while the other was still full, with over a hundred pounds of liquid propane gas.

The fire had now begun to spread along one side of the shed. Alex could now see the fire had broken through the wooden planks and had really taken hold. He used his walkie-talkie to contact the AR boat. 'John, we have a fire in the building here at the back. Can you call it in please, I have to get Anna and get us out of here. We'll have to get some fire-fighters here as soon as possible as this building is all timber and will go up like a matchbox and Christ knows what that could do to the woodlands here.'

'Will do Alex, this could be really serious.' John Sturton then put a call through to the Dorset Fire and Rescue call centre to advise them of the situation.

"From Commander John Sturton of the AR team at Poole, we have a situation on Brownsea Island; a fire starting in a large timber boat-shed. This will become extremely serious very quickly, so I'll text you the GPS location to help."

"Thanks Commander, this will be passed to Fire Command. We'll also inform the Poole Harbourmaster of the situation and we already have your GPS location from your phone."

At this point, Anna was unaware of the situation as Alex had used the TETRA radio rather than the personal walkie-talkie function.

The boat shed walls had been built with a concrete base to the main timber construction. This formed a wall below the main wooden structure about four feet high. The reason for this was unclear; probably something to do with rot; but the effect was to keep the fire from going below that level.

Inside the shed, the fire had now taken hold of almost the whole of the side of the building and the flames were reaching almost up to the roof. The tins of varnish and paint on the shelves were now about to be ignited. The simple fact that these tins were adjacent to the two big tanks of Propane Gas was unknown to anyone outside the building. Bert had left the island some minutes before the police had arrived, so would not be able to inform anyone of the existence of the gas tanks.

The "twin" unit on the top of the two Propane tanks was still open, having not been turned off as it was "automatic"; to allow a switchover when one was empty. However, the hose leading to the heaters had deteriorated to the extent that it had been slowly leaking gas for a considerable time and virtually emptied one of them, leaving the second still full.

Propane was "heavier than air" and "Predator" was standing in the boat cradle in a "sunken" area of the slipway and below the concrete sidewall. Around the side of this area, these concrete walls were silently and effectively trapping the Propane gas from one of the leaking hoses. The gas had "pooled" in the sunken area, although previously, when the large doors to the shed had been opened, the gas which had accumulated had been blown away by the wind. Now that the doors had been shut for a few hours, the gas had now once again "pooled" and it was not being blown away and even though it smelled of "rotten eggs," Goodyear and Dimitriou were completely unaware, hiding as they were hiding deep inside "Predator."

Outside, Alex had run round to the other side of the building to meet Anna. 'We'd better get out of here Anna; I thought I could smell smoke, but couldn't see any. When I looked around, I could see the side of the building had flames coming out. I suppose that being so old and dry; it would burn far more quickly than smoulder. Let's go.'
The both began to move quickly back down the path on the side of the building which appeared safer.
 'Have you called this in Alex?' asked Anna.
'What do you think?' was the terse reply.
'Sorry, it was just a natural thing to ask I suppose,' she said, feeling rather hurt.
'That was the first thing I did. I've also asked that we tell your "Fuller" as well so he can get things moving with a fire boat – if they have one.'
Anna considered that this comment was said with just a touch of venom, which she found hurtful, but put the thought to one side thinking that the situation was to blame as they ran down the side path leading to the concrete quayside edge.
'I think there is a trained fire team here on Brownsea. Have they been alerted?'
'I don't know. I didn't even know they had one.'
That's one for you then Mr Clever Clogs, thought Anna. 'And in any case, Poole Harbour Commissioners will arrange for a fire team to be brought over to tackle the blaze.'
'Oh, so that's something else that your favourite Harbour Master's told you, I suppose,' said Alex.
He's done it again, thought Anna, considering the bitterness which was inferred.
'Actually, yes, while I was waiting for you to turn up for Jack to ferry us, I learned quite a lot about how the harbour works.'
'I'm sure you did,' was the heavily implied rejoinder from Alex.
Anna decided to say nothing to this, but kept her thoughts to herself, but these barbs were being stored in her mind.

They had almost returned to the front of the shed and approached the concrete wall, where the slipway entered the water. The Dorset Marine RIB was waiting with Paul Rickson at the helm, the engine ticking over. This is precisely when some tins of varnish which had caught fire fell down into the sunken area below "Predator," throwing out flames as they fell.

The accumulated Propane gas exploded.

The whole shed seemed to expand in a huge orange fireball ball as the walls were hurled outward in a flaming tracery of burning wood and the roof actually lifted and the doors blew outward.

The shock wave from the force of the explosion thumped them both so forcefully that it hurled them into the water, ahead of the fireball, actually saving them from being severely burned.

As they both surfaced, the AR boat team moved swiftly to them and Anna was unceremoniously hauled out of the water and on to the AR RIB. Alex was also quickly lifted onto the Dorset boat.

'You two were fucking lucky Alex,' said Rickson, if you'd been ten feet further back that complete wall would have fallen on the pair of you; as it is you've just got wet.'

'Yes, I suppose we are,' he said as he looked back at the boat shed, 'but that's not so lucky is it?' he said as "Predator" became visible in the inferno. That's the bloody boat we've been looking for.'

'You've found it, but I don't think it'll be going anywhere now, do you?' suggested Rickson.

The boat was now being engulfed in flames as the fireball had blasted a hole in the side of the hull and the resin in the fibreglass had caught fire.'

'At least we've found the damned thing, now all we have to do is to find the two bastards who brought it back. They could be anywhere by now.'

There was a shout from the AR team in the RIB, pointing to the boat, there they are!'

As they looked, there were two figures emerging from inside the boat. They were yelling and screaming as they were both engulfed in flames. As they jumped out of the burning hull, their clothes appeared to be melting on to their bodies. Dimitriou fell out on to the floor of the slipway. He tried to stand up, but fell over and was screaming with pain as his clothes were burning fiercely and his nylon jacket had stuck to his skin and this was roasting his flesh. He was followed by Goodyear, who was also burning, but he managed to stay on his feet. He began to run, with flames trailing behind him; but he had nowhere to run to. The main doors had blown down and had fallen against each other, so that the only water was at the bottom of the slipway, and just visible. His hair was on fire and his face was blistered as he stumbled towards the water. He was burning from head to foot; his nylon jacket melting to his body. In a last desperate move, he managed to throw himself into the shallow water just behind the main doors. He fell out of sight of the police in the boats, but the screams were only too audible.

'Oh my God,' shouted Anna. Can we get to them?'

'No, NO! Yelled Alex. We can't get close; we'll get burned alive, just like them. Stay where you are – they are beyond help.'

Anna had never experienced such a grotesque and horrible sight of a person actually burning as they moved; and that sight would probably never leave her. She was totally overwhelmed by the vision of whom or what once was Dimitriou, although she didn't know this. He was lying prostrate and burning to death and he had stopped screaming. He had breathed in fire and his lungs had burned from the inside, bringing death very swiftly.

Goodyear was in the water, with the flames now extinguished, but horribly burned. He was moaning but just lay there allowing the cooling water to bring some relief. At the moment, most of the nerve endings that would sense the pain had been cauterised and this meant that he did not feel much pain. The more severe and excruciating pain would come later. His problem was that no-one could either see him or knew he was there.

Meanwhile, the whole shed was now burning fiercely, the boat was also burning with the interior fittings well alight. There was the sound of engines coming towards the island. This was from the lifeboat from Poole Quay, which had a high pressure hose on board. There was also a team from Brownsea Island heading along internal roads towards the fire location.

As the fire teams arrived, the information was passed that a larger craft was on its way with heavy duty portable fire pumps from the Dorset Fire and Rescue service. They were being transported by a special craft designed to carry this sort of equipment and had been on standby quite close to Poole Quay. The whole building was ablaze now and in imminent danger of collapse.

One of the large main doors to the shed then collapsed into the water. It was then that Goodyear became visible, lying on his back in the shallow water at the point on the slipway where this met the water of the harbour.

'That's him,' shouted Alex, 'he's moving and still alive.'

Paul Rickson thought, "I don't suppose for much longer."

Anna was actually closest to Goodyear and could see the blackened portions of skin on his face which has peeled back and exposed the paler sub-cutaneous tissue. The most horrifying thing was that the lower part of his face seemed to have actually melted. She felt instantly nauseous and quickly turned away, hanging over the side of the RIB emptying her stomach contents into the water.

Alex and the other crew members had also seen the grotesque vision as he wallowed gently in the shallow water. There were various expletives and comments, such as 'That'll be painful,' and 'He's toast.' Such was the "black humour" which seems to be present in a proportion of the services which deal with highly unpleasant situations, usually involving death or serious injury.

'How about we try to get him out and into one of the boats then?' suggested Alex.

'I don't think we can do much for him, but we can try,' ventured John Sturton of the AR team. 'I've seen too many of these injuries, but there still might be a chance for the poor bugger. Let's give it a try.'

With that, he directed three more of his team of eight to the concrete edge and they jumped down to the slipway edge where Goodyear lay. They moved him as carefully as they could, but could see that he was extremely badly burned and his face was almost unrecognisable. His hair had gone, his eyelids seemed to be almost burned away and his eyes were staring but probably not seeing. The skin on his face had taken on the appearance of "melted wax" and what his body was like under the remains of the melted jacket could hardly be comprehended.

The charred and blackened body was put into the RIB and Sturton suggested that they take it back as swiftly as possible to Poole Quay, where there would be an ambulance waiting. The journey back would be made at full speed, which was about 40 knots and would take only a few minutes. Those minutes would be incredibly important to his possible survival.

'Okay John, quick as you can, we can keep things together here until the fire crews arrive and then we can back off. Please be aware that he is probably our main suspect and should be kept under guard at all times.

'Okay Alex, will do.'

Whilst the body was being loaded, Anna had moved back to the Marine Unit craft. 'Are you okay Anna?' asked Alex.

'I think so, but I never ever want to see a sight like that again, it was so horrible, I'll have nightmares for a long time I'm sure.'

'Maybe I will arrange some counselling for you when we get back Anna, would that be okay with you?'

'If you think I need it guv?' she said, 'I don't know if it would help.'

'That's what they are there for and I'd like to think that they can make things a little easier to accept.'

'I don't think I could ever accept that.'

'I know that a friend of mine who is a Fireman, says that when they get to a traffic accident, some of the sights are truly unimaginable, but that they do get used to it, and their training helps.

'But I've never been trained to look at something like that guv.'

'I do understand, so maybe counselling could help.'

'Maybe; I'll see how I feel later guv.'

A realisation made its presence felt in that she had used the term "guv" many times recently when she could well have used "Alex" and this thought had made her come to the conclusion that her feelings for him were not as deep as they once were. Perhaps this is serendipity, she thought, as her feelings for Fuller were becoming clearer as time was passing. Maybe the time has come to be more honest with Alex and to more open with how she felt now and all the pressures that existed. She had the feeling that her life had possibly been changed significantly and suddenly today, with the attendant complications. If she could come to terms with this terrible occurrence, maybe she would be a stronger person and more able to direct her life the way she wanted.

The Lifeboat arrived and the RIB moved away to let the powerful hose from the Lifeboat play on the fiercely burning remains of the boat shed. It did not really douse the flames, but the coxswain of the Lifeboat said their main purpose was to prevent the trees catching light and spreading to the woodland surrounding the boat-shed.

Not long after the arrival of the Lifeboat, a larger craft in the form of a fireboat specially fitted for fighting shipboard or shoreline fires came ploughing up the channel. They very quickly had their pumps running at full capacity and firemen moved onto the land with long hoses to tackle the blaze at source.

There was a shout; "Propane tanks!" At once, two hoses were placed in fixed positions and played onto the Propane cylinders, to keep them cool and prevent any chance of them becoming overheated with the obvious problems.

Although the Dorset Marine RIB still remained at the scene, the time came when Alex said, 'I think we've done all that we can here, so I suggest that we leave the clearing up and damping down to the Fire Service. The body recovered would not be identified until later in the mortuary where it would be taken.

Taking a last look at the still-burning hulk of "Predator," they went over to board the RIB.

CHAPTER 68

The fire team remained at the scene, whilst the two very damp Police officers boarded the Marine unit RIB. 'I could certainly do with getting into some dry clothes guv, I don't know about you.'

'Good idea; we need to get back to the station to see what the others have found out. We still haven't located this Genny Dobbs character.'

'I would suggest that if she's not here and probably be found dead if she were, then she would be making her way back to the house in Corfe Mullen.'

The charred second body recovered would be taken to the mortuary where it would be examined. The corpse had been loaded into the Marine section boat with as much dignity as was possible under the circumstances and placed in a "body bag," which was carried by the Marine Section as a matter of standard equipment.

'At least we won't have to sit and look at him on the way back,' said Anna quietly, and thankfully.

Alex then asked the OC of the fire team to check as soon as they could for another possible body. 'If you do find anything, can you let me know immediately as we have another suspect unaccounted for as yet.'

'Will do,' was the response.

'Do you have any idea what caused the fire?'

'Not as yet, but the Propane tanks would have made things a hundred times worse I imagine. As they were on the opposite side of the building, they didn't explode and from what I've seen at the moment, at least one was empty. One of my guys has told me that the taps were open and connected to a big space heater with some "iffy" looking tube. Possibly that was perished which suggests to me that there could have been a build-up of gas from a leaking tube and this pooled at the bottom of the slipway. Apparently, the fire began at the back of the shed, near the winch and worked its way down one side of the building. Once it was close enough to the pool of gas, it caused the explosion which blew out the side of the shed. Any more than this, I can't say at the moment. We'll have a Fire Investigation Officer here to go over everything forensically, and give you a report.'

'I'd appreciate that, thanks.'

'There's nothing more we can do here,' Alex said to the helmsman of the Marine section RIB, 'let's go,' which then turned and headed back to the quay at Poole.

They were halfway back to the quayside at Poole when Anna's phone had a call.

'Hello?'

It was from the Harbourmaster's office. "I have a call from Mr Masterson for you."

'Thank you.' Anna was instantly guarded and said, 'DS Jenkins, hello Mr Masterson.'

'Hi Anna, are you okay? I have heard all about the fire and I'm concerned that you were not hurt; were you close to the fire?'

'Apart from the guv and I being blown into the water by the explosion and now being very damp, I'm fine, thank you.'

'Good heavens, were you hurt?'

'No, we were both very lucky, as it seems it was the shockwave and not the fireball which pushed us into the water. One of the guys who were watching from the RIB said that had we been a few feet further back, we'd have been burned, so we are extremely lucky to just be wet.'

Fuller said, 'Oh my God; I'm so glad that you're not hurt, but you sound as though you cannot talk openly from the "Mr Masterson" bit, so I'll go and I hope you can get into some dry clothes. Perhaps I can call you tonight?'

'Thanks for your concern, but we are both okay. We're just going back to the quay and the Marine Section office. They've said they can give us some dry kit.'

'That's good. Will you pass on my good wishes to Alex? Tonight then, I can call you?'

'Yes, of course, thanks.'

Ending the call, she turned to Alex who was looking less than pleased. 'That was the Poole Harbourmaster who asked me to pass on his good wishes and that he was glad that we were not injured.'

Anna hoped that she had kept quiet the real inference of the call.

'I suppose he was just glad that the island hadn't gone up in smoke then.' It was more than evident that Fuller Masterson was not Alex's favourite person.

After being given some dry police kit, they were taken by a local police car back to the Harbour Marina to collect their respective cars.

Back at their headquarters, Alice and Tom were both at their computers, typing up reports. They stood up and welcomed them both.

'Hello guv, sarge, they chorused. Are you both okay?'

'Yes thanks,' replied Alex, 'apart from a dunking in the harbour, thankfully nothing even scorched.'

'We've had reports from the lads over at Poole about what happened. It seems as though you were both very lucky,' ventured Tom.

'Actually bloody lucky,' Anna responded, 'could've been a lot worse.'

'Tell us what happened then,' Alice said, all inquisitive, looking from one to the other.

'We'd gone over to the boat-shed with Old Jack and met the Marine Section on their RIB and we decided to take a quick look around the building, while they stayed on the boat. Anna was on one side and me on the other, just to see if there was a way in and apart from a locked door, there were no windows. I was just about to turn the corner of the building when I noticed some flames coming out of the bottom part of the shed wall.'

Tom then said, 'But if that building was wood, then you must have realised that it would go up like a box of matches '

'No shit Sherlock,' said Alice, instantly blushing at her invective.

'She's bloody right; the whole building is made of very old, very dry wood. I did think that it wasn't a good place to be and I alerted Anna and met her just as she came round to the corner. I said we'd better get out of there and we both ran down the side path back to the water. We were almost at the water and that was when the whole fucking place exploded and we were both blasted into the water.'

'Jesus Christ guv, you both could have been torched,' erupted Tom. 'We were given the version of what happened to you two by the Marine guys while you were driving back. They said that they saw the explosion and it was a sodding great fireball behind you which blew the whole side of the building off. What do you think caused the bang then guv?'

'The fire guys are pretty sure that it was a Propane build-up which had leaked from two tanks on the opposite side of the shed to where we were.'

'And they went up then?'

'No Tom, they didn't. According to the fire chief, the tanks had emptied through a faulty hose.'

'But wouldn't that just have been a big flame from the hose or something?'

'Again, no Tom; you obviously don't know about Propane. Apparently, it's heavier than air and as the Propane had leaked slowly down into the pit where the slipway and boat were, it gathered there.'

'So what caused the fire that led to the explosion then guv?' asked Alice.

'Very good point; don't know yet but the Forensic Fire Investigator will find out, I'm sure.'

'I'll bet Jeffrey will be interested in that information,' suggested Alice.

'Is that your boyfriend Jeffrey then Alice?'

'Shut up Tom,' she snapped, turning a gentle shade of pink.

'Just because your girlfriend turned out to be one of the main suspects,' said Anna, not unkindly.

'Oops, sorry sarge.'

'It's Alice you should be saying sorry to.'

'Yeah, right, sorry Alice.'

'Anyway, we're lucky,' Alex said firmly, 'so let's put it behind us and get on with trying to finish all this. We now have a destroyed boat, one dead suspect, one barely alive and very seriously burnt, and one who has apparently disappeared, unless you two have any details on her whereabouts.'

'I believe the one who died was pretty crisp guv?'

'Don't be so bloody ghoulish Tom. Do you think it funny to have to look at a badly charred corpse? Believe me, it was the most horrible sight I hope I never to see again,' was Anna's response to Tom's evil smirk. 'Do you know Tom, there are times when I could happily do something that would jeopardise my career?'

'And that's told you Tom, so stop making those sort of comments, especially as the survivor was also extremely badly burnt and barely alive. Believe me; I'm pretty sure that you could well have thrown up at the sight. It was not pretty.'

'Right, sorry guv.'

'So you should be; you can be an evil little git at times.' Tom felt suitably chastened at this response from his boss, which he was very surprised at. There must be something else that happened there, he thought to himself, but had the sense to keep quiet.

Alice then asked, 'Is the survivor going to live guv?'

Alex looked over at Anna, saying, 'I don't know but Anna has been on the phone to Poole hospital, where they took him.

She said 'the only news I have at the moment is that he has 3rd degree burns over 60% of his body. His nylon clothes actually melted on to his skin and that did a lot of the damage apart from the initial blast. He also inhaled fire, they think, which meant that his lungs probably burned from the inside. Also, his facial skin which was exposed has actually melted down on to his chest.'

'Oh my God,' said Alice, holding her hands to her face.

'That must look disgusting,' said Tom, laughing.

'TOM, will you stop it!' Anna snapped. 'I'm going to slap you in a minute. I still feel nauseous at the thought, never mind the sight.'

Alex then said, 'Right, that's enough, I want the reports from both of you on the interviews of the illegals which were landed at Keyhaven; now!'

Tom and Alice, muttered, 'Yes guv,' and hastily went back to their screens to finish their reports.

Just then, Alice turned back and said, 'Sorry guv, I should have said earlier, we've had a report that the woman, you know, Genny Dobbs, has been seen going back to the house in Corfe Mullen.'

'Christ, only now do you tell me?' When was this?'

'Just about half an hour ago guv.'

'Shit! I should have been informed immediately. How did we find out, was she under surveillance?'

'Apparently a neighbour phoned in, just being nosey I suppose, saying that she knew the police had been to the house recently and she was just doing her "Neighbourhood Watch" duty.'

'Thank Christ for nosey neighbours, just for a change; I just hope it's not too late. Right, get the local plod to go there immediately and make sure that she does not leave the house; that's if she's still there after this sodding delay.'

Alex was not in the best of moods, and this had made him even tetchier.

Both Alice and Tom had hurried back to carry out Alex's instructions.

Turning to Anna, he said, you've had enough excitement for one day I'd think, but before you do anything else, can you get on to the hospital for another update on the condition of the fire victim. We need to know who he is and who the dead man was; that's if he's able to talk.'

'Okay guv, I'll get right on to it.'

'Hey, Anna, just a minute.'

She was inwardly dreading what was coming.

'What's all this "guv" business, you don't call me Alex any more. Is there a problem that I'm not seeing?'

Instantly, Anna was on the defensive. She had been expecting this shift in their relationship and at this moment in time, she really didn't know quite how to respond to his question. 'No, it's nothing really, only that we are at work and I find it easier to call you guv without having to think about when and where I can call you anything else. Actually, to be quite honest, it's getting to me, I mean the splitting between us privately outside work and being here working with you so closely; I have to tell you that I'm feeling the strain.'

'Why haven't you said anything before now Anna? I'm now very worried about our relationship, I thought it was going well.'

As they were in his office, Anna moved swiftly and quietly pushed the door a little, in case they were overheard; although this was probably not likely, as both Tom and Alice were studying their screens, seemingly completely occupied.

This was not actually the case, as for some reason the acoustics in their office had a very odd similarity to the "whispering gallery" in St. Paul's Cathedral in London, where a person whispering against the wall at one side of the huge dome, could actually be heard clearly at the other side. Not quite the same, but the result of the similarity was that quite often, Alice had heard things said in Alex's office that she wasn't supposed to hear. This was the case now, as he and Anna spoke.

"I knew it," she thought to herself. "I knew there was something going on." However, she kept the knowledge to herself for now and maybe she could talk to Anna later on. She was not nosy, just being typically inquisitive, just as a detective should be. This was her vindication for hearing this conversation, and others. "Keeps me in the loop, anyway."

Tom had put a call in to the local station in Poole, which covered the Corfe Mullen area and asked them to immediately go to the address where Goodyear lived, to make sure that the girl had returned.

In fact, she'd managed to get back from Studland via the Sandbanks ferry. She'd been cold, hungry and miserable, waiting for the first ferry of the day, after being summarily shunted off "Predator" while Goodyear and Dimitriou made their way round to the boat shed. Then she'd had to wait for ages after phoning for a taxi to turn up. This had annoyed her intensely, as she'd thought the delay was completely unnecessary. However, when the taxi had arrived, the driver had told her that the delay was due to all the holidaymakers who wanted "shunting around," who couldn't be bothered to take a bus. Anyway, the result was that Genny Dobbs had taken quite a long time to get back to the house in Corfe Mullen, and was completely unaware that the house had been under observation for a considerable time. As soon as she was spotted getting out of the taxi, the report was made to the Police Station at Poole. This information was written on a message pad and the operator who wrote the message passed the slip to a PC asking that it be put on the desk of the duty sergeant. This was done, but as the duty officer was currently dealing with a very drunk and abusive holidaymaker who was shouting and swearing at him, the message was lying on the counter and the drunk had managed to vomit all over the desk, floor and two chairs, together with the message slip, before being hauled out and thrown into a cell to sober up. Only then did the duty sergeant manage to get someone to "mop up," clean the mess on the desk, including the message pad slip, and he was finally able to read the note that Genny Dobbs had been seen entering her house.

Now he knew that this was an important piece of information, but in true human nature fashion, did not want to appear incompetent, so phoned the message through to Bournemouth Central switchboard.

"I've a report just received that a "Genny Dobbs" has been seen entering her address in Corfe Mullen."

"What is the received time on the message?"

"That I can't tell you, because some drunken bastard, who has kept me busy for ages, has thrown up all over my desk and over this message as well; I can only just make out what I've just told you, but it can't have been long ago. That's all I can say, sorry."

"Okay, I'll pass it on to my DCI," the operator said, ending the call.

CHAPTER 69

The information which was to hand up to this point was passed on to the Poole Police and the two PC's were briefed on the current situation as they made their way quickly to the address in Henbury Park Road in Corfe Mullen. Knocking at the door of "Waypoint," there was no answer. However, to make sure that she had returned, the two PC's made a swift door to door check of the surrounding houses, but not actually close to "Waypoint." It was suspected that she had returned very recently and this fact was born out by a house a little further up the road who had seen her arriving in a taxi, early that morning, subsequently reporting it to the local police. She had not been seen leaving, so the two PC's split up and one went round to the back of the house, while the other waited at the front. This way, there would be no possible "quick escape."

At the rear of the house, there was a very stylish and opulent swimming pool, with a very futuristic stainless steel curving fountain which emptied into the water in a smooth flow. Obviously, money was no object with the owners of this property. That was the personal opinion of the PC. He checked around and looked in the many large windows, to no avail. However, as there was no sign of the woman they were there to arrest, he went back to the front of the house and his colleague. 'No sign of her at the back, but it's a big garden, but I couldn't see a way out. We'll have to contact the station and ask them what to do now. We can't break in as we don't have a warrant.'

'But we need to make an arrest; let's just break a window and get in, 'cos we know she's there,' was his colleague's suggestion.

'No way; don't be a bloody idiot. I was on a shout a while back and we did just that. The upshot was that without a warrant, the suspect made a claim and the force had to pay out absolute shed-loads of compensation and the sodding judge said that it was absolutely out of the question to force an entry without a warrant. I don't want to be up on a charge for illegal entry, thanks very much. No, we just wait here and maybe the station will get a warrant quickly.'

'I bleedin' well hope so,' said the second officer, 'as I don't fancy sitting here forever and a day until some pillock decides to get off his arse back at the station, so they'd better get their fingers out and get that bloody warrant up here pronto.'

'And that's your perceived wisdom is it?'

'Yep.'

'Well, as long as this bird doesn't try to fly, we should be okay then.'

'So we just sit here and wait then?'

'Well, matey, I'm going to do just that. I happen to like being a copper and don't fancy getting a large sized bollocking from the boss if we do it wrong and jeopardise my career into the bargain.'

'S'pose your right Phil,' offered his colleague, if a little reluctantly.

'You know it is, so shut up and be patient. Let's just keep our eyes open in case she tries to sneak out.'

Phil, the more intelligent of the two PC's phoned the station and passed on the information and the request for a swift warrant to be brought up to them as soon as possible.

'They reckon it won't take long as it's such a high priority case back at Bournemouth nick, so fingers crossed, we won't have long to wait and I won't have to listen to your moaning much longer.'

'Oh piss off. I don't moan.'

'What? You don't moan? You should bloody hear yourself sometimes. Moan bleeding moan; always whinging about something.'

'Well, that's me, innit?'

'You said it chum.'

'Yeah well, some partner you are. How about I nip off and get some snacks, you can keep watching?'

'Oh, that's a great idea. Just suppose someone else comes along, someone that she knows or is involved with this crime, whatever it is, and there's only one of us. They could be armed with something. That's a brilliant idea. You are really some kind of nut.'

'S'pose you're right; just a thought.'

They sat in brooding silence until Phil saw what he thought was a shadow of movement on the first floor.

'There's someone there, I just saw movement.'

'Where?'

'On the first floor; the third window on the right. I saw someone moving. Why don't you go and knock again, only much louder this time?'

'Something to do I suppose.' He went over to the main door and knocked very loudly on the door, as well as pushing the bell-push, holding it on for many seconds.'

There was still no answer, so he shouted through the letter flap at the side of the door. It was quite low, so he had to bend down to do this. "Bleedin' silly place for a letter box," he muttered, then shouted, 'Open up, this is the Police. We know you are there. If you don't open the door, we'll break it down.'

Phil heard this and said to himself, you stupid prick, these people know the law and they could report us for harassment, or possible unlawful breaking and entering.

This concern proved to be unnecessary as the door was opened and a blonde young woman appeared, holding the door and looking very nervous.

Phil was quickly with his colleague, who looked at him, motioning him to ask the questions.

They both displayed their warrants.

'Good afternoon Madame, we are from Poole Police and we need to ask you a few questions.'

'It's Miss, actually, and what questions?'

'Okay, Miss...?'

'Dobbs, Geraldine Dobbs, that's Genny with a 'G'.'

'Miss Dobbs, do you know the owner of this house, a Mr Martin Goodyear?'

'Yes, only his name is actually Metin Denitzi.'

'Thank you. Do you know if he the owner of a vessel named "Predator?"

'Yes, why?'

'Because a vessel of that name was severely damaged this morning in a fire following a blast at the boat-shed where the boat was being kept.'

She had turned very pale. 'Was anyone hurt?'

'I am sorry to say that one person was killed and another seriously burned.'

'Oh Christ, who was it, was it Martin? He was on the boat with Freddie.'

'At this time we don't know which of the two were killed and which one is now in Poole Hospital, under guard, Miss Dobbs. Can you please tell us who the second man on the boat was?'

'That would have been Freddie Furkan, or Furkan Dimitriou.'

After asking her to spell them, these names were duly noted by the second PC.

'We have to place you under arrest Miss Dobbs.'

'Me, why, I've done nothing wrong.'

'We don't know any further details except that we have to place you under arrest. You do not have to say anything, but it may harm your defence if you do not mention when questioned, something which you later rely on in Court. Anything you do say may be given in evidence.'

Genny had gone even paler as she began to realise that she was in serious trouble.

'Do you wish to say anything at this time?'

She thought quickly and instantly realised that she had been seen at the time the illegals were dropped off at Keyhaven. 'No.'

'Very well, if you could lock the house as we know there is no-one else in there, we have to handcuff you.'

She realised that she had the leather bag with all the money and it had to be put into the safe with all the other money which she knew was there. There was no way she could do this with a police officer present. But hang on, she thought, the safe was in the bedroom.

'May I just change my clothes if you're going to keep me?'

'Yes, but I will have to accompany you.'

'Yes, of course, that's okay.'

She led PC Phil through the house and upstairs. 'I have to go into my bedroom to change; can I have some privacy please?'

Phil thought for a moment and although he knew he should actually keep her in sight, he was too much of a gentleman to prevent this.

She went into the bedroom where the leather bag was lying on the bed. She'd not had chance to put this into the safe before she had seen the police car outside and had left it there. This was her chance.

'Thank you,' she said with a brilliant smile, and closed the door.

Phil had a momentary thought. "A smile like that and she's just been arrested. That doesn't make sense." He was very tempted to open the door to check on her, but once again, his knowledge of what could happen consequentially in court should he just "barge in." This made him hesitate.

Very soon, she emerged again dressed in jeans and a simple dark blue top. Then without the smile, she went down the wide staircase. Locking the main door behind her, she was handcuffed and taken by Phil to the police car.

They made their way back to the Police Station at Poole.

CHAPTER 70

Genny Dobbs was delivered to Poole Police station, by which time Alex and Anna had changed into dry clothes and although not to their taste, they were infinitely better than the wet and smelly things which had been bagged up and waiting for them. They'd returned to Bournemouth Headquarters where they had seen Alice and Tom. They'd also arranged for Genny Dobbs to be escorted back to their Headquarters and the car had followed on very quickly.

Eager to have more information about their experience, Alice said, 'Tom and I were saying that we couldn't imagine what that must have been like. Did you see the fireball?'
'No, it just blew behind us, so we just heard a great big "whump" and it was like being punched in the back by a soft and massive ball. The next thing we knew was that we were in the water.'
'But I believe you saw the chap who was burned?'
'Yes, and I never want to see that again. I was floundering about in the water which was thankfully quite shallow and as I looked back, they came stumbling out of the boat, both of them blazing. The one I saw first actually died on the spot. There was nothing that anyone could do. He just lay there screaming and burning. By the time anyone could get near him, he'd stopped. It was only when one of the doors fell down that we saw the one who's in hospital now. He was lying just in the shallow water; he was a terrible and grotesque sight.'
'I don't think I want a description thanks sarge, we're just thankful that you are both okay.'
'Thanks for that Alice, and believe me you don't want a description. Anyway, let's not dwell on that; just tell me what you and Tom have found out from the illegals, anything more?'
'Only that they are all from Northern Cyprus and I understand from Border Control that they are all going to be returned there as soon as they have been logged and processed. Oh, and another thing; one of the illegals was saying that Goodyear, or as he said, the Captain of the boat, had had an argument with one of the passengers. They went out to the deck at the rear of the boat and they saw Goodyear beating the man and then he seemed to slash something across his throat and then push him backwards into the sea at the back of the boat.'
'Oh my God, another one. This Goodyear is really a callous and murderous bastard, isn't he?'
'Apparently, from what they heard, this person had not brought the money for the fare with him as had been arranged and Goodyear lost his temper. They were asking if they might get their money back as their "contract" with Goodyear has not been fulfilled.'
'They've got a bloody cheek,' said Anna.
'I suppose they do have a point in law though sarge, don't they?'
'I'll have to take advice on that, but so far we don't know where the money is that they would have given to Goodyear when they came over. I can't see him not having taken the money just as soon as they were on the boat, can you?'
'That's a good point sarge. Maybe this Dobbs woman will know.'
'Do you know, I'm bloody sure that she does and that's just what we're going to ask her Alice? You and I will interview her in IR1, just give me 5 minutes and I'll meet you there.'
'Okay sarge. Do you want Tom to do anything particularly at the moment?'
'Yes, he can get on to Poole Hospital and check on the condition of the burn victim. Ask them when he is likely to be able to talk. If it is fairly soon, get him to report back to us immediately. It's imperative that we talk to him as soon as, in case he doesn't make it. From what I saw, I very much doubt that he will live long.'
'Okay, I'll go and tell Tom now.'

Tom, tasked with the visit to Poole Hospital, made his way to the ward where Goodyear was under guard. When he arrived, he showed his warrant card to the PC guarding the door and asked for the medic in charge of the burn victim. He was directed to Dr. Joseph Johnson.
'Dr. Johnson, I am DC Tom Peterson of Bournemouth Police.'
'Do you have some identification please?' asked the Doctor.

'Sorry, yes of course.' Tom once again produced his warrant card. 'I've been sent here to see if the burn patient Goodyear has come round yet, although I should imagine that he's still under sedation.'

'That is absolutely the case officer. That man is very seriously burned and he is at the moment, rather "touch and go" with regard to his chances of recovery. He has suffered more than 40 percent 3rd degree burns and the shock factor will keep him needing sedation for some time yet.'

'Has he had surgery or whatever is done for a burn victim? 'What will happen to him now; I mean will he stay here for treatment?'

'From what I've seen of him so far, once he's been stabilised, I'd imagine that he would be sent either to Odstock or Addenbrooks. He's in a very bad way. He's had an initial inspection and evaluation, but more than that I can't say at the moment. I understand that he is involved in an investigation which you are carrying out. Is that correct?'

'Yes, that's the case which is why we have a guard on the door. We have to speak to him as soon as possible, but I know that you are probably going to say that is not to happen, but we have to get some very important information before he goes anywhere, or maybe dies.'

'I understand officer, but until he comes out of his sedation and we can give him the appropriate drugs for what will be his incredible pain, we just have to wait and keep all his vital signs correct.'

'I understand, but can I ask that just as soon as he does, that you inform our office? Here is the number to contact.' Tom handed the doctor his card giving all the contact details.

'Very well, I will make sure that you are kept informed.'

'Thanks. I'll just have a word with our chap on guard here so that he is aware of the situation.'

'Just make sure that the patient is not disturbed in any way. His condition is extremely critical although I don't think he'll be going anywhere by himself.'

'Understood.' Tom then went to the guarding PC and told him the situation which existed and how important it was that any words that the patient might say should be taken down, however indistinct or inaudible they seemed.

'That's of course if he does wake up.'

'I believe he's in a very bad way; I'll bet that's bloody painful.'

'I'd think he'd be on so much sedation that he won't be feeling anything – until he wakes up that is.'

'I've always thought that being burned is probably one of the worst things that could happen. I hope I never have anything like that.'

'Me too mate; me too,' agreed Tom.

'He's not exactly going to run off is he; I mean why am I stuck here getting a square arse when he looks completely out of it?'

'No, but there could be some others who might like to have words with him; but just make sure that you stay here and keep him where he is.'

'Okay, but I'm going to be bored shitless.'

'You should have been stuck out on a building on stilts out in the harbour for 24 hours like I was; that's being bored let me tell you.'

Tom just walked away after firing that shot to the hapless PC.

*****

Back at Bournemouth Central Police Station, there was a call from the Dorset fire and Rescue Service in Poole which was handed to the desk sergeant. He knocked on the door of Alex's office.

'Yes Bob?'

'Guv, I've just got the report from the FIO in Poole.'

'FIO, what the hell is the FIO?'

'That's the Fire Investigation Officer guv,' said Bob, with just a hint of "one-upmanship" in his voice.

'Okay smartarse, that's one brownie point for you; so what have they got to say?'

'That the explosion was, as suspected, most likely caused by the build-up of Propane gas from a faulty and perished pipe leading to the space heaters. The gas "pooled" below the boat on the slipway area.'

'We know all this, but what else is there? Anything about how the fire started?'

'Yep; they reckon from the residue found near the winch and the engine, there were the remains of piles of oily rags.'

'Oily rags, what's that got to do with a fire?'

'Apparently, they say that oily rags which have been left for a considerable time, can spontaneously self-ignite.'

'So are they saying that the fire was not deliberately started, but all by itself then?'

'Seems that way, guv.'

'Well, bugger me, that's a new one. Normally it's some scrote who gets off on Arson. Well, at least we don't have to find the boatyard owner and charge him with attempted murder.'

'How's that then guv?'

'Well, if he'd started the fire deliberately, for some reason, then he would be in the frame for the attempted murder of the two men who he must have known were either in or on the boat.'

'No, it seems the fire was simply an accident. Mind you, I'd say that with dodgy hoses from the Propane tanks, it was an accident waiting to happen.'

'That's for sure. Thanks for passing this on Bob; back to your desk and do whatever you were doing.'

In IR1, Anna and Alice were sat opposite Genny Dobbs.

The tape recorder button was pressed and the sound of the 10 second buzzer invaded the room. When this stopped, Anna gave the date and time and said, 'Interview with Genevieve Dobbs. Present are Detective Sergeant Anna Jenkins and Detective Constable Alice Compton. Please can you state your full name and address?'

'Genevieve Dobbs, of "Waypoint," Henbury View Road, Corfe Mullen. Am I being arrested?'

'At this moment, you are not under full arrest, but we need to ask you a number of questions under caution, relating to the landing of a number of illegal immigrants at a point close to Keyhaven, sometime during the early hours of this morning, during which you were seen to be present, and your subsequent return to the address you have just given us.'

Genny was feeling very apprehensive as to how much they knew.

'Do you know a man named Martin Goodyear?'

'Yes, he is my boyfriend.'

'Is that his real name?'

'No, he is from Cyprus and his name is Metin Denitzi. He uses Martin Goodyear as his business name.'

'And do you live with him at the address in Corfe Mullen?'

'Yes, sometimes.'

'And does he own a boat named "Predator?"'

'Yes.'

'Are you aware that Mr Goodyear is in custody at this time?'

She felt an overwhelming sense of relief at this news. She knew that one person had been killed but she had no idea which of the two. She had no idea that the Police had actually found Goodyear and Freddie. She'd known that Martin was trying to take the boat into hiding and presumed that they had got the boat concealed somewhere. 'No, I had no idea,' she said desperately trying to keep her composure. Now the realisation of what she might say could compromise Goodyear was beginning to sink in.

'Where were you this morning?'

'At the ferry at Sandbanks.'

'Why were you at the ferry?'

'I was waiting for the first ferry, so that I could cross and get home.'

'Why were you at the ferry, presumably on the Studland side?'

Genny looked from Anna to Alice, unsure of what to say now and how much they knew and what they were getting at. She knew that she'd had all the money collected from the illegal immigrants, which she had managed to take back to "Waypoint," but she was sure that the police had no idea that she'd had this.

'I was going home. I'd been at a friend's house overnight and I wanted to get back as soon as possible.'

Alice then spoke. 'But we know that you were not at a friend's house because you were seen with the illegal immigrants when they landed. So what is the truth Genny?

Realising that they'd already said that she was seen on the beach at Keyhaven, she knew she had nowhere to hide and that they knew the times and where she must have gone and that she would have been on the boat and come back to Poole.

Deciding to tell the truth as much as she felt she could get away with, she said nothing for a while.

'Holding back will do you no good Genny,' said Anna. 'We know that you were on the boat which came back to Poole. What happened when you got back to Sandbanks, did they drop you off there while they went on to the boatyard to get their boat hidden?'

Genny paused again, trying to assemble her thoughts into something coherent and believable. 'They weren't going to hide the boat, just to get it repaired, because it had damage to the bow, or so Freddie said.'

'Freddie, being Furkan Dimitriou?'

'Yes.'

'Do you know where they were taking the boat?'

'No; when they dropped me at the ferry, Martin said to get home as soon as I could, and he'd see me there later.'

'And what were the necessary repairs to the boat?'

'There had been some damage to the bow.'

'And how had this damage occurred?'

'I think they said that when the boat was at the beach, the wake from a passing ship had caused a big wave and this pushed the boat against some concrete.'

'And was that the only damage?'

'No, apparently on the way back and nearly into Poole Harbour, the anchor fell out and smashed into the bow and Martin said the boat was going to sink.'

'And do you know where this place was that they were taking the boat?'

'No, only that it wasn't far from the ferry. They put the boat onto the beach and made me get over the side and I got wet and it was a long wait until the first ferry came.'

'So you won't be aware of what happened to the boat?'

'No, should I?'

'Genny, I have to tell you that the boat was taken into a boat shed on Brownsea Island and sometime later there was an explosion and fire. The boat shed was burnt down and the boat badly damaged.'

'But where are Martin and Freddie now then?'

Anna looked over to Alice and back to Genny. 'It has become apparent that both Goodyear and Dimitriou were hiding on the boat when the explosion occurred. Genny, I'm very sorry to have to tell you that Freddie was killed in the fire and Martin was badly burned. He is presently in Poole General Hospital, under police guard and is heavily sedated.'

Genny went very, very pale. 'Oh my God!' Why were they burned, I mean if the boat was in the shed, then they wouldn't have been on the boat, they would have been somewhere else, wouldn't they?' thinking that they would have tried to make a getaway.

'As we say, we have to presume that they were both hiding inside the boat whilst we were looking for them. The explosion was very close to the boat and subsequent investigation of the remains of the craft lead us to believe that they were both hiding under the floor of the main cabin, presumably so that they would not be seen if we were looking for them inside the shed. As soon as the explosion occurred, they would have tried to make their escape and Furkan was so badly burned that together with smoke and flame inhalation, he died very quickly.'

Genny had her head in her hands and tears were coursing down her cheeks. 'I can't believe it, Martin was so careful usually; he didn't take any chances normally.'

'I think this time, he had no time to do things with what you say would be his normal ways of doing things. The explosion was immediate, as was the fire.'

'Oh God, it must have been terrible.'

'It was Genny,' said Alice, DS Jenkins here, was there and saw the whole thing and was nearly badly injured herself. In fact, I believe it was Anna who helped pull Goodyear out of the water.'

'Christ, but you say he was in the water, surely he couldn't have been that bad?'

'Genny,' said Anna, 'I saw him fall out of the boat, covered in flames and although I didn't see him do it, he must have run down the slipway to the water's edge where he fell into the water. It wasn't until a door collapsed that we could see him. That was when I helped to drag him out with the help of the other police who were there.'

'Is he badly burned; I mean is he going to be all right?'

'Unfortunately, he is very seriously injured. We understand from the hospital that he has suffered 3rd degree burns to between 30% and 40% of his body. He has also suffered from smoke inhalation with possible toxic fumes from the burning materials on the boat.'

Genny could say nothing. She was completely lost. She was holding her head in her hands and was bent low on the chair. She looked up slowly, ashen faced and with tears streaming down her face. She looked between Anna and Alice. 'Is he going to die?'

'We don't know. All we can tell you is that he is under sedation in hospital and he will be transferred to another specialist burns hospital as soon as this is medically possible.'

Alice then said, 'We are sorry to be blunt at this time, but Mr Goodyear is involved in our investigation which relates to three and possibly more murders.'

Genny looked very shocked at this. 'No, that's not true, Martin wouldn't do anything like that, I mean, I know he has a temper but he couldn't murder anyone.'

Alice looked at Anna with a glance which suggested that neither believed that statement from Dobbs.

Continuing, Alice said, we have sufficient information to be sure that he has either murdered or been an accessory to the murder of an employee of the oil field site on Goathorn Peninsula, as well as the body of a man found on the beach near the oil site. Furthermore, an elderly man on the clifftop near Keyhaven was shot on the night that the illegal immigrants were landed. You were there Genny, so you must have seen this attempted murder take place. There could be others as well, so any information which you can possibly give us will help with your situation.'

Genny looked at both Alice and Anna with a quizzical look. 'My situation?'

'Yes,' said Anna, 'your situation is that you are an accomplice. By your association with both Goodyear and Dimitriou, you are deemed to be equally guilty of these crimes, and as such, liable for prosecution.'

Now the full force of her situation became clear to her.

Anna leaned toward Genny and spoke earnestly to her. 'Genny, you are not stupid and I'm sure that by now you are realising just what sort of trouble you are in, whether by design or by encouragement, and believe me, now is the time to tell us everything you know about what Martin Goodyear has been doing, and more importantly, how he makes his money. We know that he has, or had, a very expensive boat possibly two, and a very expensive house in Corfe Mullen. Do you think that you would be selling him out if you tell us these things, or does the fact that he may not survive his injuries, give you the motive to tell us everything.'

She looked ashen faced and said very quietly, 'If he survives, and I've told you everything, he'll make sure that I don't survive. Do you think he will survive?'

'From what we understand, it is most unlikely but he is in good hands and will receive the best care, but we have to be honest with you Genny, and say that his chances are in the opinion of the medical staff, less than 50%, so please be ready to understand that.'

Wiping a tear from her eye and tried to look stoic.

The interview was paused and Anna said, 'Will you excuse us for a moment Genny?'

They exited the room and in the corridor, had a conversation regarding the interview. 'What do you think of our Miss Dobbs then Alice?'

'Do you know, I began to believe her when we saw all the tears, it did look genuine, but later on when she admitted to the things we already knew, I am almost convinced that she is a very good actress.'

'I'm inclined to agree with you Alice, especially as Tom was taken in by her. She must be been prostituted by Goodyear to keep information regarding our investigation flowing from Tom being sucked in.'

'If that's the case, then she must be quite some devious person and we should keep tabs on her.'

'Absolutely Alice, I agree.'

CHAPTER 71

Anna had taken the view that they would now have to get a little firmer with Dobbs. They needed answers and quickly, in case Goodyear actually died without either answering questions or being able to give information. Resuming the interview, she said 'We have to assume that Goodyear had collected money from the illegal immigrants who, we believe, all come from Northern Turkey. Do you know what has happened to that money?' Genny looked startled by this question, looking straight at them, holding her gaze. 'No, I didn't know about any money.'

'Oh, come on Genny,' said Anna, 'you surely don't expect us to believe that you didn't know that Goodyear had collected money from these men from Turkey. Did you think that Goodyear was giving them a free ride?' Genny looked from Anna to Alice with a look which told them both that she was thinking hard about whether to tell the truth or to try to wriggle out of a situation to which she'd no idea how to handle. She had prepared an answer to this question and, as most trained interviewers seemed to know, when a person is asked a question to which they would most probably give a lie in response, their eyes initially look to the right before giving a reply.

This is exactly what Genny Dobbs did. She flicked a glance to the right, swallowed and then said, 'I didn't know what he did when he brought people over.'

'So what you have just said, leads us to believe that he has done this before?'

Again, Genny was like a rabbit caught in the headlights. She knew that she had said more than she should have and that Martin was going to be very, very mad when he found out that she had given away that he'd done this before. Then the thought hit her; perhaps he won't live and nothing needs to be said. She paused, saying nothing for a few moments, deep in her thoughts.

What she was actually thinking was that if he doesn't survive, then I know the account details and where he has the money stashed. I have the cash from the last trip and that would last me until I could sort out all the other details. Genny Dobbs was not as innocent as some people might think. Deep down she had been consorting with a man who had no scruples whatever and was just as dismissive of people as she feared. The only thing was that now, he was in a seriously bad state and is more than likely not to survive his severe injuries. She was having even more dark thoughts and her mind was racing.

'Is he on life support in hospital?'

'I would imagine that he is on all the support systems that are available Genny,' said Anna.

Genny's mind was running at great speed. What if his life support was turned off and he died, my troubles would be over?

She was not thinking coherently. She'd not thought things through by any means. 'But they think he has a chance of survival though?'

'That is possible, but I'm informed that he will have to be in hospital for a considerable time if he does.'

'How long do they think?'

'I've honestly no idea, but it won't be in weeks or maybe even months.'

'Oh God,' Genny said, and Alice was looking very hard at her as she said this. Alice's penchant for spotting mistakes or missing confirmation of intent or otherwise had surfaced, but she said nothing. She actually was unconvinced by Genny's facial expression and sound. There was something else in her tone and body language at this point.

Alice turned to Anna and said, 'Could I have a word guv?'

'Interview paused at – and spoke the time.'

They both went into the corridor and Anna asked, 'what is it Alice, your intuition again?'

'Yes guv, oh yes. I'm certain that when she was asking about the chances of Goodyear's survival, she was thinking more of his demise, if you get my meaning? And when you said it could be more than weeks or months, her reaction just didn't ring true at all.'

'Very interesting Alice; what do you actually think now?'

'Do you know, I actually think that she knows a damn sight more than she is letting on about finances and it really wouldn't surprise me if she knew exactly what the money situation was.'

'Alice, I know you have this reputation of getting to the root of things and I think I completely agree with you. Let's suppose that she does know about the money, perhaps she knows where Goodyear has put all what must be enormous sums of money. I would expect that most of it is hidden in offshore accounts and things like that.'

'If that's the case guv, then surely there will be other people who would be very interested in those accounts?'

'You can bet your sweet life on that Alice, I mean, there will be others who are involved in this illegal ferrying of skilled people, they would need to have things carefully organised for them I'd imagine and that would cost for sure. They went back into the interview room.

'Interview continued with Genevieve Dobbs at,' - and gave the time.

'We think that Mr Goodyear has made many trips to France, is that right Genny, he's done this before? I think that you realise by now, that we know a lot about what has been going on, but we need you to confirm this.'

'And if I don't?'

'Then I think you might realise also, as we have already told you, that you are linked to this investigation and are therefore involved in serious charges, such as accessory to murder, aiding and abetting assault, among other things.'

'Assault, I haven't assaulted anyone.'

'I think we have already covered that. Do you remember an assault on one of our Police Constables at Cobbs Quay Marina, where you work or worked?'

Genny remembered only too well the part she played in luring Tom to an assault, where he was quite badly injured, enticing him into a relationship at the behest of Martin. She remained silent.

'As I say Genny,' reiterated Anna, you are linked to this investigation and if you help us now, in every way you can, this will be in your favour when it comes to trial.'

At this point, Genny decided that the only way she could help herself was to tell all that she knew. Self-preservation, she thought. Martin always said look after number one, and she knew that he meant that if others had to suffer in the pursuit of looking after number one, then so be it. Surely he would understand that now, that she would have to look after herself first. Q.E.D. she thought, it's a no-brainer, if I tell all I know, maybe I can get away with this money. They still don't know where it is and if I don't say, they won't find it.

'Okay, I'll tell you. Yes, Martin has done this trip before, a number of times, although I don't know exactly how many.'

'And how much did each man pay Genny?' asked Alice.

'I don't know exactly, but I think it could be about £7,000 to £10,000.'

'Is that per person?'

'Yes.'

The two detectives looked at each other in surprise.

'So that could mean up to £140,000 per trip and we understand that the boat carried 12 passengers.'

'I was never allowed to know the full details, that's just my guess.'

Alice looked at Anna and blew a silent whistle. 'And he's done this trip how many times do you think?'

'I've no idea.'

'Come on Genny,' said Anna, 'You must have some idea.'

'Okay, if I think back it must be around 10 or 15 times.'

Alice looked shocked. 'Bloody hell, that's around; hang on, my maths is having a meltdown. Shit! - that's around two million pounds, sorry.'

Anna looked shocked as well. 'No wonder he had the boats and house like that – that's some return.'

'Right Genny, the $64,000 question, where is all this money?'

'I don't know.' In fact she did know and she knew about more which had come from the drugs trading element which hadn't been mentioned, yet.

'I suggest that you have a pretty good idea, I mean he must have bank accounts then?'

'Well, yes, I suppose so, but I don't know where they are. I know he has different accounts and some are not in this country.'

Alice then said, 'We'll have to do a forensic financial investigation on him. With this sort of money, he's bound to have offshore accounts and all that sort of thing. We'll have to track all this down.'

What Genny was not letting on was that she knew at least some of the account details and she was a joint signatory. Goodyear had organised this some time ago, "just in case," as he put it. Well now was that time, she thought. But there was no way that the police would get that out of her. She would have to play the "I'm upset at his condition," to the hilt now, or she would be left with nothing except the cash in the leather bag currently cosied up in the safe in Corfe Mullen.

'Genny, you seem to have overlooked the fact that you are involved in the murder of three people, possibly more. What can you tell us about this?'

Now was the time to really come clean about this because murder was infinitely more serious than bank accounts, she thought.

'I know that there was some trouble with a friend of his when he and Freddie had to do something on the beach at Goathorn, but I don't know exactly what.

Anna knew that this was the body found partly buried.

So are you saying that a friend of Goodyear's was killed and they tried to bury him on the beach?'

'Yes, I think so.'

'Do you know why he was killed?'

'No, only that there was a big argument, about what I've no idea, but Martin did say that "he had to be taken care of," so perhaps that was why he was killed.'

'The so-called friend was very badly beaten up and slashed with knives.'

'Martin has a very bad temper when someone does the wrong thing to him.'

Alice and Anna exchanged glances.

'If that's what he does to friends, who knows that he does to enemies,' suggested Alice.

'How about the bodies that were found in the shed at the Goathorn jetty?'

'I don't know anything about that.'

This time the body language seemed genuine.

'And then we have the oil company worker who was found dead at his flat. Was that the man who saw Martin and Freddie that night?'

'If you mean the night when they were on that beach, doing something and this man approached them?'

'Yes, that would be the one.'

'All I know is that I overheard Martin telling Freddie that someone called Bob something or other had to be silenced.'

'And by what you have just said, you knew that they were "on that beach, doing something," so do you know who did this silencing?'

'No.'

Alice then broke in. 'We saw only 11 men land at Keyhaven, but the boat held 12 passengers. Do you know if there were 11 or 12 on board?'

'I only know that I heard Martin and Freddie talking during the trip back to Poole, and I heard Martin saying that "the other bastard should have had the cash, he was warned; served him right."

'So we must presume that one of the passengers didn't make it to Keyhaven. We also have to presume that he was either left behind or killed during the passage from France.'

'I don't know; I suppose it's possible, knowing how Martin would react to something like that. I mean, he had a seriously bad temper and very quick. He was quite calm normally, but when something upset him, he could fly off the handle and become terrifying.'

'Did he ever hit you Genny?'

'He has once or twice, but he would always apologise later.'

Anna looked across at Alice, saying, I think we have covered everything here for now except,' and turning back to Genny, she calmly said, **'Genevieve Dobbs, I am arresting you in connection with the suspected murder of four, possibly more persons or persons unknown.**

'You do not have to say anything, but it may harm your defence if you do not mention when questioned, something which you later rely on in court. Anything you do say may be given in evidence.'

Genny Dobbs looked totally shocked. 'You said I wasn't under arrest.'

'You weren't when we started this interview, but having heard your responses, I now have to implement this arrest.'

You will be taken before magistrates in the morning for their decision on bail or arraignment.

She said, 'I've helped you all I can and now you arrest me. You said this would help me. It's not fair.'

'I'm afraid that murder is not fair, and we are complying with procedure. What you have told us, will be in your favour, but for now, we have to be sure that you do not disappear with the cash from the boat trip to Keyhaven.'

'I don't know anything about the cash from the trip with the immigrants,' she lied.

Genny knew that she was completely trapped. They know about the cash but not where it was. Maybe she would keep that as some sort of bargaining chip for later. Her main worry was the number of "friends" of Goodyear who would very soon hear of his situation. What they would do with the news, was anyone's guess, she thought, but she did have considerable doubts as to their "friendship" when they did find out.

The look in her eyes spoke volumes to Alice, who was acknowledged as a very observant and practiced interviewer. The quick movement of Genny's eyes from left to right, gave credence to the feeling which Alice had that she was lying and that she knew far more than she was admitting to.

Alice motioned to Anna to pause the recording. Anna said, 'for the benefit of the tape, this interview is being paused. The pause button was pressed and Anna said, please excuse us for a moment.'

Both the detectives went outside IR1 into the corridor again.

Alice then said, I'm sure she's lying about the cash from the last trip from France with the immigrants. If she's lying about that, then I would bet that she knows a lot more about the accounts and banking arrangements that Goodyear has.'

'Knowing your expertise with interviews Alice, I'm sure you're right. I think for now, we'll have to finish this and get some financial forensics digging done.'

Returning to IR1, the tape was re-started and Anna said, 'Interview with Genevieve Dobbs resumed,' giving the time, then, 'this interview is now terminated.'

Genny looked quite bewildered and said, 'Will you keep me here?'

'As a suspect of being an accessory to murder, that is the case.'

This caused a look of genuine concern on her face and she looked quite forlorn.

A constable was called and Genny Dobbs was taken to a cell, where she would dwell on her situation until the legal decision in the morning.

CHAPTER 72

At the hospital, the doctor had made a further examination and given the appropriate instructions to the nurse who was administering to Goodyear. He was still under sedation, but his vital signs were stable – for now.
Some of the more serious burns had been left uncovered, while treatment was prepared.
As with third degree burns, the nerve endings were effectively cauterised, thereby lessening pain and similarly the main veins and arteries had the blood flow restricted by the swelling and nerve compression leading to arterial flow being severely compromised. As a result, a life-support system was in place providing the necessary blood-flow and other vital constituents which kept him alive.

Given the condition of the patient, his prognosis was not good. Although sedated, it was necessary that he was conscious for several tests to be carried out prior to him being transported to a specialist burns hospital.

He was coming out of the sedation and this fact was mentioned by the nurse, to the doctor who was monitoring the patient.
The doctor, as was instructed, passed this fact on to the PC guarding the secure room where Goodyear was being kept. Accordingly, a message was passed to Bournemouth Central to the effect that the patient was coming out of sedation and should be able to talk reasonably soon.
Alex received this information with considerable relief. Maybe we can get some resolution to this bloody case, he thought. So many murders, people trafficking, bodies being moved and dumped, so much time being wasted in trying to catch all the perpetrators. Perhaps we can get some closure now, even though we only have one of the two main suspects still alive, and he probably won't make it.
He quickly called Anna and said that they were both going back to Poole Hospital to try to interview Goodyear.
On the way, he said to Anna, 'We'll try to get something coherent but I'm not holding out much hope.'
'Do you think we'll get a confession from him then guv?'
They were driving over to Poole Hospital and Anna was fighting her inner battle as she knew that there was something which had to be said.
'I don't know Anna; it would be something to bring this case to a close. Anyway, what's this "guv" bit again, I mean we're in the car and in private, so perhaps you can level with me and tell me exactly how you feel. Now that the case seems to be coming to a close, perhaps we can get some time together – if that's what you want?'
Anna was feeling very "put on the spot" and she had to swallow hard to gather her feelings on what she knew she had to say now.
'I don't know if this is the right time, but seeing as how you've brought the subject up, I have to tell you the truth. For some time, as I think I said a while back, I've been finding the mixture of work and private time to be a very difficult thing to come to terms with. I mean, trying to keep it quiet and knowing that if anyone found out or it came to the notice of the Chief Super, then we'd both be in the shit and my career could be finished or something just as bad, something like being moved to a different force. Believe me, this is something I really don't want. So, what I'm saying is that I think we should cool things off and we go our separate ways, keeping a working distance between us, which would make things a lot easier for me, although I don't know about you as you probably have a lot more to lose than I do.'
'And I suppose this has nothing to do with a certain Harbourmaster then?'
'I'll be completely honest with you Alex and say that I am interested in Fuller, as he is a really nice man and I find him attractive, in probably just the same way as you might find another girl attracts you. I haven't done anything about it yet, but I am going to. If that hurts you, then I am really sorry. I know we've had some good times and I don't regret them for a moment, but as I've said, the strain of keeping everything quiet has had a bad effect on me. I'm sure you can understand that. I'm not ready to settle down to a committed relationship and I am determined to keep my options open, if you can accept that.'

'I suppose I don't have much choice then, do I?' Alex said in a very strained voice. 'It's not what I want, as I'm sure you can understand, but I have to accept your feelings and I promise I'll do my best to accept what you say. But also understand that I won't stop trying to influence you as I really would like you to know that I'm in love with you.'

That was the first time Alex had actually said that, and it knocked the wind out of her sails somewhat.

Following a pause, she said, 'I hear what you say Alex and I'm very touched, but if I don't examine what is out there, I'll never settle and that would hurt whoever I choose to be with as they would never know if they were the only one and there might be others on the horizon. I have to be sure of myself. I just don't think that I'm ready to settle down at the moment; my career means too much to me and I am determined that nothing should jeopardise this; do you understand that Alex?'

'Yes, unfortunately, I do and I will say now that my feelings for you are undiminished, so you can take that thought with you when you see Mr Masterson; just keep that in your mind.'

All that needed to be said had been said, and they moved on to more pressing matters.

'We have a case to close Anna, so perhaps we should get some words from Goodyear while he can speak, if he can speak.'

The journey to Poole Hospital was, to say the least, rather icy, in that they said virtually nothing to each other, each having private thoughts about the way they would move on.

The strained silence simply seemed to make the journey longer, but eventually they arrived. Parking the car, but quite forgetting to take a parking ticket from the machine, they both hurried to the ward where Goodyear was being kept under guard.

Alex did suggest, as they approached the ward, that; 'A guard is probably a long way over the top, as he's going nowhere judging by the state of him the last time we saw him.'

'Quite honestly guv, I'm surprised that he's still alive, but who knows who else might want to see him?' The appalling memory of his injuries, were still very vivid in Anna's mind.

The guard checked their warrant cards as he was from the Poole section and both Anna and Alex were unknown to him. With a nod to the guard from Alex, they both pushed the door open.

Goodyear was lying on his back but hardly visible under the mass of tubes and wires surrounding him. His eyes were covered but his face was not. The sight was horrifying, to say the least. His hair was reduced to a blackened mess and his facial contours had changed into something intensely more grotesque than they had envisaged. The lower half of his face, from the nose down, had taken on the appearance of melted wax and literally drooped down almost to his chest. His upper body was covered with a translucent material which they presumed was a surgical covering to prevent any bacteria from settling on his ravaged skin. Through this, they could see the hideous results of the melted nylon jacket and what it had done.

'Poor bastard,' said Alex. 'You wouldn't wish this on anyone, would you?'

'Even though he has beaten and killed at least four people that we know of, I suppose that he deserves some sort of sympathy, although I have to admit, I'm finding it hard.'

A doctor was in attendance along with two nurses.

'Doctor, can he speak; I mean, is he aware and is he really conscious?'

'As aware as he's likely to be I would suggest, but as for conscious, yes he is although I would tell you that his prognosis is not good. He has suffered massive burns as you know and with this degree of damage, his vital organs are going into shutdown, despite what we can do. And there are secondary infections setting in, most probably from his lying in water which was probably not that clean. We are keeping him on life support at the moment.'

'We urgently need to speak to him, so how long do you think he will be rational doctor?'

'Very hard to say, but I would urge you to be quick. We need to keep a very strict check on him if he has any chance of recovery, or perhaps I should say survival.'

They moved to the bedside and with one each side of the prostrate body, she silently looked at Alex, the look in her eyes saying all.

Alex took in the covered eyes and he said, none too gently, 'Can you hear me?'

There was a muffled sort of grunt.

'Can you hear me?' he asked again.

This time, another grunt seemed to indicate agreement.

'Can you speak?'

'Mmmnno,' was the almost incoherently grunted reply.

'Okay, can you indicate either "yes" or "no"?'

'Mmm.'

Alex then decided that he would ask the most direct questions. 'Did you kill Bob Chorley?'

'Mmmmno.'

'Did you kill your friend "Gary," the body we found on Goathorn Peninsula beach?'

'Mmmno.'

Looking over to Anna, Alex said, I'm sure he's lying. I think he thinks that by denying this, he'll get away with all the killings.

'Okay, let me be brutally frank with you Goodyear, it is more than likely that you are going to die; in fact from what I've been told, you have only a ten percent chance of survival, and if even if you do, you're life's not going to be really worth living, so maybe you'd like to tell us everything now so that you don't have to take your lies to hell with you.'

Anna was stunned by the way Alex had driven the facts home. Does the man have no compassion, she thought, looking over at him with a twist to her lips that was something bordering on disgust?

Alex caught the look and stared back at Anna. Taking her aside slightly, he said very quietly, 'I imagine that he is a Muslim and don't they believe in Hell or something equally as bad?'

'But that was just brutal, telling him that he's going to die.'

'Yes, just as brutal as killing people.'

'But we don't know that he's killed, it's just supposition at the moment.'

'Hang on Anna; don't go all prim and proper on me. How about the poor old chap up on the cliff at Keyhaven, just walking his dog and he gets shot. We know for certain that it must have been Goodyear. As far as I'm concerned, anything that will make this bastard talk has got to be done.'

It was impossible to read any expression on the hideous face, but there was an indecipherable moan emanating from him.

'Okay, how about the missing passenger on your trip. We know that there were 12 on board and only 11 landed, so where is the missing one?'

'MMMmmmnnoonno.'

'Is that "don't know?"'

'Mmm.'

'You are a lying bastard. Of course you know. I'll bet you pushed the poor sod overboard, because he didn't pay up; is that it?'

'Mmmmm'

'This is getting us absolutely nowhere Anna. I know he can hear me alright, but I can't get a sensible word out of him, so I suggest we just leave him here to die and take all his wrongdoings with him to wherever he's going, which I'm sure is a particularly bad form of Hell.

Anna then leaned over close to Goodyear and said quietly, 'Do you know you are probably going to die?'

'Mmmm.'

'And do you think you will go to Hell?'

'Mmmmm.'

'Does that make you feel bad?'

'MMmmnnnnnmmmm, mmm nnnn mmmmm nnnnn.'

'That's the most sensible thing he's said,' Alex ventured. 'He probably was trying to say that he couldn't feel any worse. Serves him right. Let's go back and concentrate on the only one who can give us any information.'

The doctor returned and Alex said, 'It's completely impossible to get any sense out of him, all we get are mumbles, so we cannot get proper answers.'

'I'm not really surprised you know, as most of his lips are burned away and with his facial tissue so distorted, as you can see. I'm amazed that he can make any sort of noise.'

Anna turned to the doctor and asked, 'Would he be able to write anything?'

'I suppose so, as his hands, somehow did not suffer quite the same degree of burning and they are still relatively intact.'

Alex looked back to Anna with genuine respect as she had just suggested a way that they could get some proper information. 'That's really good thinking Anna; maybe we can get some answer after all. Would that tax him too much doctor?' not that Alex was genuinely concerned for the body lying there, just to give him an end to the case which had been falling apart despite all their efforts.

They moved away from the patient and the doctor gave his opinion, 'Providing you don't overstress him, although I think that might be difficult in his situation. We'll have to get transport arranged for Odstock where they might, just might, be able to help him. If anything changes radically, I'll make sure you are informed.'

'Thank you doctor. Do you think, if he survives, that he'll be able to talk again, I mean, so that we can understand what he's saying?'

'That, officer, is something that I cannot answer, although I have seen cases which have been severely burned, make some remarkable recoveries, but in this case, I have to say that I'm very doubtful about his chances of survival right now, but Addenbrooks and Odstock are probably the ones most able to help him and they do have some remarkable results.'

'If we can have some paper and a marker, perhaps we can just get a few answers now?'

'I'll get a nurse to arrange this, but don't overtax him as you can see, he is very weak.'

'Right; understood.'

The doctor left and had a word with a nurse outside the ward. Shortly, she returned with a notepad and a black marker pen.

Waiting for the nurse to exit the room, Alex bent over Goodyear and said to him, 'I'm going to ask you some questions again, and this time sunshine, I want the truth. But remember, I know most of the answers, but if you give me wrong ones, I will make you suffer more than you are now; do you understand my meaning, because you really don't have much going for you right now.'

'Mmmmm.'

'Are you sure?'

'MMMMmmm'

'Right, I'll ask you again; did you kill Bob Chorley?'

Goodyear's arm rose with the marker poised. Anna held the pad in a position that made it possible for Goodyear to write without being able to see. She said 'just put a 'Y' for yes and an 'X' for no.'

The scorched and blistered arm moved. The hand wrote 'Y'.

'Good, now we're cooking on gas – again,' said Alex.

Anna thought that this remark was completely unwarranted, but Alex seemed to think it was amusing, which did nothing for Anna's current feelings toward him.

'Next question, did you kill your friend Gary and try to bury his body on Goathorn?'

Again, the hand moved and wrote 'Y'

'Good boy, Goodyear, although not a good year for you I think.' Again, the smirk from Alex. This is so unlike you Alex, I think you're enjoying this, she was thinking. Perhaps this is the stress showing, what with the case and our situation.

'Now then, did you throw one of your passengers overboard on the way back from France?'

'X'.

Alex was more than sure that this was not true, and he gripped the burned arm quite strongly and Goodyear gave a deep-seated and higher pitched moan in response to the pain.

'You see, as I said, I know most of the answers and now you're give me lies. That won't do and I need the truth. I think that you are under the misapprehension that 'Taqiyya' is giving you clearance and some type of misguided protection under your religion to lie, but believe me, I don't give a shit about your religion; because the only religion I have is to get the truth and you are going to give me that, one way or another.'

Anna became seriously worried at the way this interrogation was progressing and she looked at Alex with an expression bordering of disgust.

'So, I'll ask you again; did you kill the missing passenger?'

There was a slight pause and then the marker moved. 'Y'.

'Good. Now we know that you also shot the chap on the cliff. Thankfully, we've been informed that he did not die and he has told us all about your working on the boat at the shore, so we have a very reliable witness, who makes you guilty, whatever else you've done. So you may as well tell us everything.'

'Mmmmmm.'

'By the way, I haven't told you, but your mate "Fuckin Freddie" died in the blaze and guess what, your lovely boat is a melted and burned-out hulk, so you won't be doing any more trips to France.'

'MMmnnnn.'

'I thought you'd say that.'

Anna didn't dare to look at Alex.

'Now for the burning question.' Alex paused and tried to suppress the smirk, without success. 'Where is all the money which you must have stashed away, heaven knows where?'

The arm raised and Anna held the pad while the marker moved slowly, to spell out, '?'

Alex was losing patience now and squeezed the arm holding the marker again. This time harder. Again, the muffled scream of pain.

'Alex, stop!' she shouted, looking at the door and wishing the nurse would come in.

'He knows where the money is and he's going to tell me.'

'Of course he knows, but he won't be able to tell us things like account numbers and details, but I'm sure that Genny Dobbs can tell us a lot.'

'Does Genny know? This question was back to Goodyear.

'N' was the mark on the pad.

'Alex, that's enough now.'

'One more question. Does anyone else know about your accounts and other details?'

'Y'.

'Who?'

The marker moved and once again on the pad, 'M'.

'Who is 'M'?

'Mmmmmnnn nnnn nnn mmmm.'

'That's crap, I've not a clue what that means. 'Does Genny know these other people?'

'Y'.

'Right, that's it. She's the one with the information we need.'

Anna pulled Alex a little away from the bed and said, 'I expect that only Goodyear can authorise any withdrawal and stuff like that and he would know the access codes and passwords.'

'Maybe, but he's in no position to give that sort of information?'

'I suppose not. I think we should go now.'

'Yes, you're right. Can you call the nurse back in please Anna?'

She went out to the corridor to find the nurse. While she was gone, Alex bent down to Goodyear and said quietly into his ear, 'You'd be surprised at what I could do to you and your pain level, so just don't piss me about, as I can be probably as nasty as you, so just don't go and do a runner, will you?'

The nurse came back and checked the tubes and lines and all the equipment which linked his life support to the monitors which gave all his vital signs.

The trip back to their station was equally as icy as the first and they only discussed the next moves to try to make sense of the litany of apparent disasters and the lack of finality to the case.

Anna was still in a kind of shock at the apparently vicious treatment Alex had meted out to Goodyear, especially one so appallingly injured.

Alex was moaning about the lack of funding and resources which had led to the missing of vital sightings of the craft at various points in the investigation, and not being able to supply the necessary police presence when needed; was the main topic. The only positive thing which was said referred to the continued questioning of Genny Dobbs and her possible and very probable knowledge of the account details pertaining to the money which Goodyear obviously had made and more than likely, stashed away in offshore accounts. The only person who could further their investigation now, was Dobbs.

CHAPTER 73

With Genny in custody, she was now the main focus of the investigation. There was a briefing taking place in the main CID office at Bournemouth Police Headquarters, with all the staff and assistants present who were working on the case.

'For the benefit of those who weren't here for the previous briefing, I'll go over the entire course of this investigation. I will give you a resumé so that we all know where things could and should have been different. If anyone can spot where things might have been done better, please let me know.

Firstly, a body was found on Goathorn Peninsula, partly buried. This was subsequently found to be possibly a friend of our main suspect, Martin Goodyear, whose real name has been found to be Metin Denitzi. He was originally from Cyprus and has been living in the UK for many years. Apparently, his command of English was very good, to the point where he sounded virtually the same as a local man. This is probably why he changed his name to Martin, to enable him to live the lifestyle which his activities made possible. But I'm digressing; the first body was found by two National Trust Beach Wardens on a routine check of the coastline. It was discovered that while the attempt to bury the body was being made, the two men were seen and approached by an employee of the oil-producing site run by Perenco. During questioning, he admitted that he had seen the two men and had been given money to "keep quiet." He was subsequently killed at his flat, being left to bleed slowly to death. This was before he moved to a safe house which he should have done; why we don't know at the moment. The first body from the beach on Goathorn was identified by his clothing and a shop assistant who recognised him as a friend of her abusing husband, a one Furkan Dimitriou from Northern Cyprus. His nickname was "Fucking Freddie."'

This brought a snigger from some of the support staff.

'All very well to find this funny, but let's face it, to have so many deaths is no laughing matter. It should be said that the partly buried body was very severely beaten and there were deep cuts on his body which were attributed to a large knife or blade. This indicated a very angry killer. Why he was killed, we shall never know. The friend of Dimitriou was identified as our main suspect by this shop assistant who said that both Dimitriou and Goodyear used to go on, what she knew as "fishing trips" for days at a time. We now know that these were not fishing trips but trips to France to bring back numbers of illegal immigrants from Northern Cyprus.'

There was a hand held up by one of the DC's. 'Yes John?' said Alex.

'Guv, why Northern Cyprus particularly?'

'Good point John; passports from there are not valid in the UK and these immigrants were therefore strictly speaking illegal, although they were usually very skilled people, be they practical or academic. They paid a very high price for being brought to the UK, as I will cover a little later.'

'To continue; It was initially thought that these immigrants were being brought over to work on oil pipeline installations around Swanage, but this proved to be a false lead. It was found that Goodyear and Dimitriou went on these so-called fishing trips on a very fast sea-going craft called "Predator." This boat could carry up to 12 passengers at high speed and was fitted with extra fuel tanks to enable a two-way trip to France under cover of darkness. This boat was moored at Cobbs Quay and DS Peterson was tasked with trying to get information on this craft. He formed shall we say 'an association' with a staff member at the Marina, in an effort to get information on this craft and its movements. At one point, Tom was fixing a tracking device to the boat when he was attacked and quite badly beaten. It transpired that his 'associate' was actually an informer who was the girlfriend of Goodyear.'

This brought a number of sly looks toward Tom from other DC's which made him very uncomfortable.

'It was her that gave the information to who we assume was Goodyear or perhaps it was Dimitriou as he does have a history of violence, although we will perhaps never know the truth now that he is dead. Tom did manage to fix the tracker, which for some reason failed quickly. We managed to trace the boat from Cobbs Marina to a hiding position in the Arne River, where we managed to get a further tracking device fixed by a scuba diver. However, all these trackers failed to give us the information we really needed except to prove that the boat went to France and subsequently returned with 12 illegal immigrants who had paid up to 10,000 pounds sterling for the trip. Whatever else they had paid to get from their homes in Northern Cyprus, we have yet to find out. They are currently being questioned by our team. We now know that although 12 men were on the trip, only 11 were landed at a point near Keyhaven where we were waiting for them after following Goodyear's girlfriend Genevieve Dobbs in a hired people carrier. After they were apprehended and brought back here to be questioned, the boat which we understand had suffered some damage to the bow, moved along the coast and beached at a point close to the Barton Golf Course. This is where a man, who had seen them working on the boat, was seen and shot by one of the people left on the boat. We also know that there was Goodyear, Dimitriou and Dobbs on the boat which made its way back to Poole Harbour. Dobbs was left at the ferry terminal to wait for the first ferry in order to make her way back to her house where she was subsequently arrested and is currently in custody. The boat with both Goodyear and Dimitriou on board then moved to a boathouse on Brownsea Island and was concealed there. They hid, we think under the floor of the boat's cabin, while we were investigating this boat shed following enquiries made regarding the possible hiding places for such a craft.

DS Anna Jenkins and myself were checking round this building when what has been confirmed by the FIO as a build-up of Propane Gas, exploded.'

'FIO guv?' asked a voice from the back of the room.

'Fire Investigation Officer, June. They checked on the cause of the fire and found that it was due to a leaky hose to a propane space heater, and this gas had pooled under and around the boat. Spontaneous combustion of some oily rags actually caused the gas to explode. This explosion blew the whole side of the building off and caused a big hole in the side of the boat. DS Jenkins and I were close to the explosion outside the building.'

'I believe you were both blown into the water guv?' asked another DC.

'That's right; we were very lucky to be here and uninjured. Anyway, the fireball caused both Dimitriou and Goodyear to be enveloped in fire and Dimitriou actually died very quickly from the flames and smoke inhalation, while Goodyear managed to stumble out and fell into the shallow water at the base of the slipway. DS Jenkins actually found him as one of the large doors collapsed and managed to get him to one of the police boats in attendance. He is currently in hospital suffering very serious and life threatening injuries.'

'If he's the only one left guv, what happens if he dies, all this chasing around has been for nothing?'

This came from DC Peter Goodrich who, like all the team, had been following the various twists and turns of the investigation all along.

'Good of you to point that out DC Goodrich,' said Alex with biting irony. 'Actually, and unfortunately, you are right. Although we do have one other avenue of investigation and that is Genevieve Dobbs and she is going to get some severe interrogation regarding the financial situation of Goodyear. I think I can honestly say that all our endeavours have come to nothing really unless Goodyear lives and is able to give us the information in order to obtain some degree of restitution. I have to say that this looks unlikely. For me, the most important lesson we have learned is that the restriction of funds and resources that have been foisted upon the police force have resulted once again in missed opportunities and the ability to mount suitable surveillance with reduced manpower which would have caught these murderers before the act in most cases.'

Anna looked across at Alex and then said, 'I think I speak for DCI Vail to thank all of you for the hard and resolute work you have all done. It is such a shame that we could not have a firm conclusion to this case, but as soon as we have any definite results, we will let you know. In the meantime, can you please all resume your normal duties?'

It just left Tom and Alice, Anna and Alex to interview Genny Dobbs for financial intelligence as to the whereabouts of Goodyear's money, if that were possible. The web of "offshore accounts" and twisted financial "boltholes" that he had used, would take a considerable time to unravel.

CHAPTER 74

Genny Dobbs had used the time she spent locked up in a cell at Bournemouth Police Station to consider her options. One evening, when Goodyear had been away on one of his 'trips' she had gone into his computer and, risking his deadly wrath, were he to have found out, she'd copied his offshore account details. He had also, and very unusually for him she thought, made a list of all the pass-codes on a flash drive which he'd secreted in a special compartment of his desk. She had once watched him through a partly opened door as he had secreted this flash drive, so she knew where to look. Armed with the account numbers, the pass-codes, and her legitimate authorisation to access certain other codes, she could soon be an extremely rich young lady.

Realising that these "friends" would very soon be contacting her and asking all sorts of questions which she certainly had no intention of answering, she resolved to take action as soon as she possibly could.

The next morning, she was to appear in the Magistrates Court to face the charges which had been outlined by Alex the previous day.

In the court, she stood in the dock and the Magistrates Clerk asked, 'Is your name Geraldine Dobbs?'

'Yes'.

'And do you live at a house called "Wayfarer" in Henbury Park Road, Corfe Mullen?'

'Yes'.

'And do you live with a man called Metin Denitzi, also known as Martin Goodyear?'

She was going to answer "sometimes," but thought the better of it.

'Yes.'

'Miss Geraldine Dobbs, you are charged with being an accessory to several counts of murder and to the illegal transportation of citizens of another country. How do you plead?'

'But I had nothing to do with any of this.'

'Please answer the question; do you plead guilty or not guilty?'

She felt trapped but held on to the knowledge that she would take whatever action was necessary and she could not weaken.

'Not guilty.'

The leading Magistrate then conferred with her colleagues and turned back to address Genny.

'These are serious accusations which we understand appertain to other suspects, who are unable to attend court. In the meantime, you will be bailed to appear at a time that you will be advised of, after the police have concluded their investigations and prepared the documentation prior to trial. You will be bailed in the sum of £10,000.'

Genny actually gulped at the sum she had to find. It was almost all she had, but it was possible as there was the money in the safe and after her plan had worked, then she would be free and with the sort of money that could take her anywhere.

She left the court-room, feeling absolutely convinced that she could do what she intended. Going back to the house in Corfe Mullen, she immediately found the flash drive, inserted this into the computer and brought up the pass-code details of all the off-shore accounts that Goodyear held.

Outwardly, Genny seemed to be somewhat of a "dumb blonde" but she was actually a very hard person, as her subterfuge with Detective Tom showed, and she had absolutely no compunction at all in doing what she was now embarking on, since her future life depended on her actions.

She called up the various accounts and entered these with the pass-codes.

However, there was a problem. It appeared that a signed authorisation was necessary for some of these accounts and only Goodyear had this authority.

Well, they won't be much good to him now, will they, she thought. Still, there must be a way around this. Contacting the various banks and institutions where these accounts were held, she variously explained by emails, the situation regarding Goodyear and also using her limited authority to transfer what was enormous amounts of currency to a new private account. She also had the foresight to delete these emailed questions immediately so as to leave no incriminating copies.

The authority which Goodyear had given her previously had stood in good stead and there were not too many problems, but there was still an enormous amount of money still to be obtained.

She did think that one way round this problem was to go to the hospital to see him and get him to give her the authority; if he would agree to that – he had to.

The result of long hours through the night, of comprehensive communications and transfers, was that Genny Dobbs had now become an extremely rich young lady, with a new name and new accounts but she wanted more; a lot more.

Shortly, there was a phone call from a "friend" of Goodyear who asked questions about his condition and where he was, details of that nature. Was he expected to recover?

Genny was quite unnerved by the tone of this phone call and she decided to take the course of action she had been considering, as soon as possible. In haste, she went to the hospital to see Goodyear who was expected to be transferred to Odstock Hospital near Salisbury within four days or so. In the meantime, he would remain on the ward under intensive care and life support.

When she arrived, she found out that the police guard had been removed. She was told that it was considered that Goodyear was unlikely to try to escape and the Poole Police were understaffed as it was, and couldn't spare the PC. She went into the private room where the patient was surrounded by all the paraphernalia of medical equipment. Genny was about to approach Goodyear, when she heard footsteps in the corridor. Aware of what she was about to do, she moved to the door and saw through the window two men she had never seen before, approaching. Seeing their faces, she saw expressions of confusion and then anger. That'll be his "friends" no doubt, she realised. She moved away from the door and quickly hid behind a mobile screen to one side of the room.

The door opened and the unknown men entered. They looked at Goodyear, taking in his bandaged eyes and saw the hideously contused mouth. One of the men was tall and immaculately dressed with an air of "quality" about him. His hair was white and he wore a small goatee beard.

This man took a long look at Goodyear and said, 'This is a fucking waste of time; he can't even speak. He's buggered and won't last long but we need those access codes.'

'Yeah and how're we going to do that then? He can't speak so he can't give us those codes, even if he knew them off by heart, and I don't suppose he does, so we're fucked,' ventured the other man.

'Maybe not, he's got that woman he lives with; that Dobbs girl. She's very attractive as you can be sure with Martin,; she'll know something.'

'Yeah, I know the one you mean. She's a looker all right; I wouldn't mind giving her something to think about,' he said with a lascivious grin.

'You're only saying that because you know that Martin is lying there scorched to fuck and he can't do anything about it, but if he knew, he'd cut your balls off and stuff them down your throat; and that's before slitting it open.'

'I know you've said that he's a sadistic and vicious bastard, but he's no threat now, is he?'

'So we go and see his woman tomorrow then, maybe we can make her give us some details, she's bound to know something.'

'Yeah, let's do it.'

'I think she'll know something and whatever she knows, she will tell us, I mean she WILL tell us.'

'I know what you mean boss, 'cos if she don't tell, she'll probably suddenly lose her good looks, knowing you.'

'That is your department isn't it?'

As they left the room, Genny took a cautious look to see if they had actually gone and saw the doors closing after them along the corridor.

She'd heard everything and she quickly realised that she would be in serious danger unless she did something at once. In fact, the taller of the two gave her the impression that although he was so well dressed compared to the second man, he had an air of real menace.

Actually, what she had just heard had made her very scared indeed.

She moved back to Goodyear....

Leaning close to him, she said quietly, 'I know you can hear me, so you must give me authority to transfer funds or I suspect that those two, especially Mason, who reminds me of a snake, will do anything to get their hands on your money. I know you gave me limited access and I've transferred that, but I need written authority from you for the bigger funds or they'll steal the lot. If you let me do this, I can keep it all safe. Do you understand? If you do, just raise one finger to say "Yes."

Goodyear raised a finger slowly.

'I knew you would trust me Martin. I've prepared something and you can sign it. With this, I can fax it to the appropriate people to prove that I have your authority.

She delved into her bag and withdrew the pre-prepared paper, reading it to Goodyear.

'This, as you can hear, gives me the authority to transfer funds from accounts in the name of Metin Denitzi, to an account which I will open, in your name or maybe a different one. If you sign this now, I can move funds before anyone can get their hands on anything. That Mason made it more than obvious that they would come back and do anything to you to make you tell them what they wanted to know and I'm sure you know what that would mean. Do you know this man called Mason?'

A finger was raised again.

'And is he a friend?'

The finger rose and then moved from side to side quite aggressively.

'I thought so, so if you can sign this, I can get everything I need to do, and do it quickly.'

Goodyear could not see her expression.

She held the paper onto the firmer pad and put a pen in Goodyear's hand. Positioning it in the appropriate place on the paper, she said, okay, sign.

He did, slowly and fairly legibly.

She had also taken the trouble to video this action on her iPhone, as a precaution.

She then went to the door, and as she reached for the handle, it opened almost hitting her in the face, which gave her a start, thinking that the two men had come back.

But it was a nurse who came in and said, 'I'm sorry but I have to check on the patient, I won't be a moment. Please don't be too long as he is very tired and needs to be kept calm or it could risk complications.'

'I understand,' Genny acknowledged.

The nurse took readings and made notes on the board at the foot of the bed. Finishing, she turned and said to her, 'I realise that this man is your partner and you must be very worried about him, but he is receiving the best of care and we are doing all we can to keep him stable, but I must warn you that his condition is liable to change so we need to be very vigilant.'

'I do understand and thank you; you are doing a wonderful job.'

'You must be very worried about him.'

'Yes, I am,' she said, although maybe not as worried as I should be, perhaps?

The nurse left the room saying, don't be too long will you?'

'I won't, I was just about to go anyway,' she lied. 'I'll come back and see him again later.'

About to go back to Goodyear's side, she heard footsteps and realised that this was not a nurse wearing soft shoes. Realising that the two men had returned, she moved back behind the screen where she'd hidden before.

Entering the room, the shorter man said, 'Do you think he'll agree to write down something then Mr Mason, I mean his hands didn't look that bad, did they?'

'Do you know, I don't think he's in a position to refuse, do you?'

'He could say no, but I don't think you'll take that will you?'

'You know me, as you said.'

'That was good idea of yours, to make him write something down boss.'

She could just see enough through a very small gap in the screen edge to see the tall man who she had heard the second man call Mason, leaning over and speaking to Goodyear. There was a writing pad and marker pen on the table beside the patient and Mason held Goodyear's arm and made him take the pen. Holding the pad, Goodyear began to write, slowly and obviously painfully, the words, "FUCK OFF."

The man referred to as "Mason" smiled an evil smile and said very quietly, 'Martin that was not very polite of you.'

As he said this he took the marker pen and ran the back end of this fiercely down Goodyear's arm which was uncovered but had gauze over some of the blistered parts. The pain which this must have caused could only be gauged by the deep scream which he emitted.

'Shall we try again, old chap, I don't think you'd like that would you?'

'Nnnooo.....' was the moaned response.

'Well then, I think it would be best if you just gave me the information which I need and we can leave you in peace, and you can live or die, whatever you want.

This time, the marker pen rose and began to make a mark on the pad.

"GD flash". This was barely legible.

'What the hell is that supposed to mean?'

The pen rose again. "FL desk".

Mason looked at this, turning it in his hand, thinking. Then he said, 'Do you know, I think GD could be Genny Dobbs and "FL" could mean a flash drive. It then follows that "FL desk" could mean that it's where he keeps codes safe and secret, in a desk.'

'How the hell did you work that out Mr Mason?'

'Because that's who and where I am and you are where you are; and that's where I'd keep my details safe just as I know Martin would; he'd be just as careful.'

'But does that mean that his girl, what's her name, Genny something, does she know about it?'

'If she doesn't, I would be very surprised as most women would take a sneaky look around when he was away.'

'Does your wife do that Mr Mason?'

'She did and that's why she's long gone.'

'Where did she go then?'

'That's none of your business; let's just say that she is somewhere else.'

He knew Mason well enough to let things end there.

'So we go to see the girl then?'

'We do,' he said slowly, 'we do; first thing tomorrow.'

They both left the room and walked down the corridor.

A nurse, a little further down the corridor had looked up, seeing the two men as they left the room.

Moving back to the door, she opened it slightly and looked down the empty corridor.

Going back to Goodyear she saw the pad and what he'd written. She felt a cold shiver run through her realising that these two "friends" were nothing of the sort. Realising that they would more than likely be paying her a visit, she knew then that Goodyear could not be allowed to say anything more and that she had to take whatever steps she could to improve her situation.

She had to use the authority to transfer the remaining funds to new accounts to keep them from being found.

She moved round to the far side of the bed. All the life-support tubes were linked to the monitors and she looked carefully at those she thought would do what she wanted. She'd searched on the web to understand which sort of life-support systems would be used in his case.

Pulling apart a tubular connection below the level of the bed, she saw a change in the monitor read-out. Feeling no compunction whatever, she moved close to him and spoke quietly; 'Goodbye, and good riddance, you nasty, sadistic, evil, murdering bastard. Now I can get away, as far as possible and become someone else and out of your clutches and influence.'

Goodyear began to make noises as though he were trying to speak, but his lips were so burned that no sound he uttered made any sense, just moans, unintelligible moans. Which stopped and the monitors began to subside. Reaching down she pulled out the electrical plugs which supplied power to the breathing equipment and alarms as well as the line feeding the pain-killing morphine to his system.

Taking a very quick look back at the writhing body, she opened the door a fraction and peered out of the room, looking both ways along the corridor, making sure that she was not seen.

She made her way home as quickly as she could, going through the events. She thought that because the nurse had checked the patient whilst she was there and then seeing the two men leave; there was every chance that the blame would cling to them.

CHAPTER 75

Back at the Office, Alex was speaking to his team in the main office.

'Right, listen up. We have the situation that Goodyear is in Poole hospital and is expected to be transferred to Odstock Hospital near Salisbury in the next few days and Dimitriou is dead.'

'How is the old man who was shot over at Barton then guv?' asked Alice.

'Thankfully, he is recovering well as the bullet apparently only grazed his collarbone. We have the bullet and I'm sure that we'll recover the gun when forensics has given the remains of the boat the "once-over."'

'Now, thanks to the situation over at Brownsea and the explosion, we have only two suspects and although Dobbs is not the murderer she is in the frame as an accessory. If Goodyear or Metin Denitzi to give him his real name manages to survive, however long that takes, we will have to have a concrete case with all the details and forensics in place for a conviction even if it is post-mortem. However, we need to get Dobbs back in for an interview to get as much information regarding the bank accounts and financial holdings as possible. She is currently on bail and her hearing has been delayed for two or three days, so we have to dig as much as possible to get details quickly. We have to build the best case we can to make an effort to finalise this fiasco.'

'We've not had much luck have we guv?' said Tom, 'especially as both trackers didn't work properly.'

'You can say that again Tom and thanks for reminding me. Once again we've had the lack of personnel and available people to keep more detailed watches, with the results which you all know by now.'

Just then, the main doors opened and a uniformed constable looked over to Alex. 'Yes, what is it?'

'Sorry to interrupt, but I think you'll want to hear this. There's been a phone call from Poole Hospital.'

'Okay, just hang on people, I'll be right back.' Going out of the room to the constable, Alex said 'What's happened?'

'It's your suspect, Poole station told us that they took the guarding officer away this morning because they were short staffed.'

'Oh shit, not another "we haven't got anyone" excuse?'

'Yes, it seems like that, but they said could you call them back, as it's quite urgent and there's something else but I don't know what.'

'Right, thanks, can you get them on the line and put it through to my office; as quickly as you can?'

'Yes, right away.'

Alex went back into the main room and the look on his face gave them all a clue that he wasn't happy.

'That was Poole Station telling me that they took the guard away this morning, and without telling us.'

'That's bloody marvellous, I mean they could have mentioned it couldn't they guv?' said Anna.

'Damn right, but I have to call them back as there's something else I believe. Don't go away people, just give me a minute.'

Alex went to his office where the phone was ringing. He picked up the call and said, 'DCI Vail is that Poole Station?'

'Yes chief, we have some news about your suspect; you know the one who's a bit crisp.'

'Nicely put, but go on.'

'Well, he's dead.'

'Oh shit; but then we did expect that but maybe not quite so soon. What was it, cardiac arrest or something like that?'

'No chief, someone pulled his life support tubes out and the staff couldn't save him.'

Alex was instantly incandescent with rage. 'Bloody hell; who did that then, and why the HELL do you think that we had a guard placed and you load of plods took him away and now our main suspect is dead? What sort of fucking outfit are you that did that without telling me, for Christ's sake!? Another bloody murder, I don't sodding believe this.'

'Sorry chief, not my decision but as far as I know there were two blokes who came to visit your suspect, and from what we can find out from the staff there, it was not long after they'd gone that matey had his last gasp.'

'Then whose fucking decision was it to take the guard back?'

'It was our DCI Trevor Johnson chief.'

'And this DCI Johnson didn't have the courtesy to let me know, I can't believe the stupidity.'

'Shall I tell him what you said chief?'

'No, just leave that to me. When I've cooled down a little, I think I'll have a chat with DCI "clever Trevor" Johnson.'
Alex realised instantly that he shouldn't have said that.

'Right you are chief.'

Alex was fuming. 'I am not "Chief," I am DCI Vail, or "sir" to you; is that clear?'

'Yes sir, sorry.'

'Do you know anything about these two visitors?'

'Personally, nothing, but I'm sure that DCI Johnson can fill you in.'

I'd like to fill him in, thought Alex. 'Right, can you put me through to him then?'

'Sorry, I can't transfer you but I can give you his number.'

'Oh, for fuck's sake; go on then.' The number was passed on and Alex put through a call.

'DCI Johnson, yes?' was the response from his call.

'This is DCI Vail from Bournemouth.'

'I thought you might call; is it about the suspect you have in Poole Hospital?'

'Good guess, and before you say any more, do you know that the patient had two visitors not long after the guard was removed contrary to our request and without this information being passed on to us?'

'It was a procedural move as we are so short staffed.'

'And no-one thought to inform us?'

There was a hesitation on Johnson's part before he said, 'I think there was an instruction to let you know, but maybe this was either lost or not carried out.'

'Fucking Bullshit!' said Alex. 'Not good enough; that was incompetence. To give such an off-hand and half-assed reply is not going to be ignored or treated lightly. Do you realise that because the guard was removed, it seems that these two male visitors, who called after the guard was removed, appear to have removed the power supply to the patient's life-support and he subsequently died?'

'It seems that way, yes.'

'And you think that by just saying "it was procedural," you can absolve yourselves?'

'I don't know what else I can say, to be honest.'

'Well, for one thing, these two are going to be treated as murder suspects, so I suggest that you get looking for them and in the meantime, I want a complete description from the staff who actually saw these two and any other visitors the patient may have had.'

'Okay, I'll get on to that.'

'Good, and my report will go to the Chief Superintendent.' Saying no more, he slammed the phone down.

Johnsons' manner really irritated Alex to the point that he was fuming as he went back to his team, muttering to himself. Of all the bloody incompetent, offhand, self-satisfied pricks, he's not going to hear the last of this.
Alex had only thought this and not said it out loud. What he did say to his team was 'My understanding is that two male visitors entered the patient's room and it appears that they removed the life-support equipment which led to his rapid death. The alarms which should have alerted the staff were disconnected as well, and by the time a nurse came in, he had died. So now we are left with only one suspect and this case is now descending into a pit of fuck-ups. All we can hope for is that Genny Dobbs can lead us to the money stashed away by Goodyear.'

'Why was the guard removed then guv?' asked Alice.

'The lame excuse I got from Poole was that it was "procedural" due to the "lack of manpower."'

'Well, we can't argue with that can we guv?' said Anna, 'given that we've had the same problems.'

'The difference is Anna, that we would have informed the other station what was going on and made them aware of the situation. As it is, either their system is at fault or one of their staff is incompetent, I don't know which, but I know that I'm not going to let that rest, as it's effectively bollocksed our case even though it was shaky. Now we only have the girl, so I suggest that we get round there as soon as we can and politely ask her in for another interview, don't you think?'

Genny had gone back as quickly as possible to her house. She had the signed authorisation for the final transfers from the various hedge funds and investments together with all the holdings and accounts which Goodyear had set-up over a period of around 3 years. The amounts involved came as a huge shock to Genny, in that although she had known the sums to be big, she really hadn't known how big and now she was simply stunned when she did some adding up.

She went through all the entering of account numbers, codes and passwords that she had copied from the flash drive which she had found and quickly managed to fax the relevant authority document to enable the transfer of the funds to the new accounts which she set up; in her name now.

Isn't it strange, she thought to herself, just how quickly she had put Martin Goodyear or Metin Denitzi, whatever he liked to call himself, almost out of her mind and the fact that she had hastened his death or actually killed him, bothered her not one bit. She only saw it as saving him from an extremely long recovery and life-changing operations, not to mention the hideous scarring. This made her feel that she had actually done him a favour, although she didn't give much time to that thought. Actually realising that her quick thinking by waiting until the two men had left, swiftly hiding whilst no-one was approaching; removing the life-support tubes and power supply as quickly as possible and then not waiting for any result, but exiting the room before any nurse saw her leave had provided an excellent opportunity. In fact, she was congratulating herself on the fact that she had been seen and spoken with the nurse when she first went in to see Martin, then hidden out of sight as the two men entered the room. She had no idea who they were, but apparently they must have known Martin and realising that they were definitely not going to be happy that Martin was likely to die without giving his financial details away, she thought that they were to be avoided at any cost. By saying goodbye to the nurse, this had given her a fantastic alibi, because when questions were asked about Martin's death, the nurse would say that when she'd checked him, as she had done just before Genny had left the room, everything was in order and she'd seen the two men go back in.

As she sat at her computer, quietly wondering what she might take as her next move and where she might go to get away and hide, use the new passport which Martin had obtained for themselves as a precaution and go somewhere a long way from where she was now, a thought then struck her. Who were these two men and the one named Mason, who had seemed to be the leader and the more educated and intelligent of the two, who was he and where did he fit in to Martin's scams?' The more she thought about them, the more worried she became. To her this Mason man was infinitely more sinister than the other one who had seemed a little short on the intellectual front. No, Mason was definitely the one to worry about. He had seemed to be very sure of himself and in control. He showed no emotion when he realised the terrible state that Martin was in and had shown no outward signs of any sort of compassion, in fact quite prepared to cause more pain and suffering to a man who must be experiencing incredible horrors. This man was more of a snake than a rabbit.

As she was finishing the transfers and deleting everything which might be revealed should there be a forensic examination of this computer, she heard the doorbell sound.

That's probably the police again, she thought. They're going to be hounding me now.

She was confident that she had covered her tracks and her final act had been to completely destroy the flash drive unit which had contained all the codes for the transfers. She had faxed the signed documents to the appropriate institutions and these had all gone through correctly and she had shredded the faxed documents. She was quite au fait with the computer, so everything had worked well and gone smoothly. She actually gave a small "thanks" to Martin for having a high-speed internet connection which made things much easier and faster.

Finishing what she thought was a thorough cleansing of the computer; she had just closed it down when the doorbell had sounded, so she made her way downstairs to answer the door to the police.

CHAPTER 76

Going down the stairs, she saw through the engraved and frosted glass panel in the main door, two figures, obviously male.

She was about to open the door to what she presumed were two police officers, when she suddenly thought, don't police wear hats? These two men had no hats on, except one had what appeared to be a baseball cap. Police don't wear baseball caps do they; well only special types and these would have been local constables, and they should have ordinary caps on? She became suddenly very worried and stood back from the door. She knew she couldn't be seen from outside, so she retreated further back and waited. The bell sounded again.

Silence.

Then a third time and now a voice shouted, 'Genny Dobbs, we know you're in there, open the door.'

Now she knew that they weren't police and recognising the voice as one of the two that she had seen at the hospital, she began to think about how to get away.

There was a way at the back of the house, through a disguised door in the garden. She ran up the stairs to her room, quickly gathered her bag with a change of clothes and her necessary documents which she had prepared earlier on the expectation of a need to make a quick exit. Running down the stairs, she headed for the back of the house and intended to go through to the large garden at the rear.

She was at the bottom of the stairs in the main hallway when the front door glass shattered with an incredible crash and the man with the baseball cap almost fell through the remaining shards of glass, slicing his arm in the process.'

Come here you fucking bitch,' he yelled, holding his arm and letting out a string of swearwords as Genny ran for the large glass doors leading to the garden. She turned and looked back to see this man wearing a baseball cap running toward her, with blood streaming down his arm. As she looked back to the glass doors, she was terrified to see the other man she recognised as "Mason" standing there. He was holding a large rock and he called, 'Open this door or I'll break it.'

Genny had nowhere to run. She was trapped. "Baseball cap" had now reached her and grabbed both her arms. His arm was dripping blood on to the white carpet. A thought struck her, 'That'll annoy Martin'. She wasn't thinking clearly; terror had gripped her throat. Mason said again, 'Open this door or you are going to be extremely sorry.'

His tone and courteous manner only served to heighten her feeling of impending trouble.

"Baseball cap" held on to her arm with a vice-like grip and dragged her to the window where he pulled the latch holding the huge sliding glass doors shut. Mason then pulled one open and stepped inside.

'Now Genny, you don't know who we are, but let me tell you that we are friends of Martin and he owes me a great deal of money. We know that you know where this money is and we need to have access to the accounts.'

'I don't know anything; I'm only his girlfriend, why would I know where his money is?'

'I'm afraid that I don't believe you.'

Baseball was bleeding heavily and the blood was pooling on the tiled floor now. 'I'm fuckin' bleedin' to death 'ere,' he moaned,' she must've summink to wrap this up.'

'To keep things amicable, do you have a bandage or something to keep this little creep from dying right here Genny?'

She thought that by getting the first-aid kit from the bathroom might help the situation, although quite how, she didn't quite know, but said, 'I'll just get the kit, there're some bandages there.'

'Good, that'll keep him quiet for a while, but I think he's really quite annoyed now, so do be careful of him. He has a very nasty temper and he can be very violent.'

'Go with her and sort yourself out,' Mason said to "Baseball cap," 'but don't let her out of your sight.'

They went to find the first-aid kit and returned to the ground floor where Mason was sitting in a very expensive 'Barcelona' leather chair which had chromed steel legs at the sides. He was now smoking a cigar and looked completely at ease. This did nothing to make Genny feel easier, in fact in simply added to her tightened feeling of danger.

Her breathing had become very difficult. 'Who are you and what do you want?'

'Before I tell you, perhaps you could just put some sort of bandage to his arm. This will go some way to preventing him from doing you some very unfortunate things to you.'

She wrapped the bandaging round the wound in the arm, but the blood still seeped through.

'It's still bleedin', baseball cap moaned.

'Just shut up, it will stop in good time, just be patient for once in your life, you little worm.'

"Baseball Cap" did that, not wanting to anger Mason any more

'As I said, we are friends of Martin and we have just seen him in Poole Hospital. He's in rather a bad way isn't he?'

'Yes, but I've never heard him mention you before; are you really friends or are you more his enemies, breaking in like this?'

'Let us just say that Martin owes us a quite substantial amount of money and we would rather like it remitted to us, or me I should say.'

'How do I know this because he's never mentioned anything about this to me?'

'That, my dear girl, is by the by; please believe me when I say that I intend to have this money returned to me, with interest I may add, very quickly, or there will be repercussions.'

'What do you mean; I know nothing about his financial affairs.'

'Come come, my dear, I happen to know that Martin has given you some authority to handle his affairs should this become necessary, and I think we both know that this time has arrived, don't we?'

'Martin is going to recover, they are taking him to Odstock Hospital tomorrow I believe and he will get treatment and he will eventually be back.'

'Unfortunately, from what we understand, he is very unlikely to recover and therefore we are asking; no demanding; that you arrange for a certain sum to be transferred to an account, the details of which I will supply you with.'

'But I can't do this and in any case, I'd have to get Martin's permission, and even if I could do this, I won't, I mean I can't.' She was so nervous that the words were tumbling out. This Mason was so icy calm that it made her more terrified than ever. He was speaking as though he were a snake facing her, with poisoned fangs waiting.

'Oh, I think you will young lady. I have ways of ensuring that you do what I want. Should you refuse, then I will have to resort to other methods of persuasion than politeness.'

Knowing Martin's predilection for "methods of persuasion" which he had employed from time to time, she was now actually shaking with fear. She was telling herself that she couldn't do what they wanted because she had covered her tracks and destroyed the means by which she could do anything. She was desperately trying to convince herself that she could make Mason believe that she was unable to do what he wanted, without success.

'I can't help you, as I don't know how to move any money and anyway Martin wouldn't let me do this; he's always very secretive about his money and I don't even know where he keeps it.'

'Shall we start with his safe?' I know he has one, so please just open this as I also happen to know that he has just completed a "delivery" which was paid for up front, and as you returned before he did, I am sure that he would have given you the proceeds of this venture, which you would, of course, have put in the safe.'

Genny was amazed at just what this man actually knew about Martin's movements. Perhaps he was involved in the organisation of the illegals?

'I don't know where the safe is,' she said.

'Come now Genny, may I call you Genny? Perhaps you should know that Martin told me quite recently that he'd had this safe installed and that he had made sure that you knew not only the whereabouts but the code as well. One has to presume that you would need to access this for time to time for him to continue his business when perhaps he was not in the vicinity; would that be a fair presumption?'

She didn't know what to say to this as he obviously had so much information that all she could do was to say nothing. She just looked at him.

'I'll take that as affirmative then,' as his voice hardened, 'so shall we just stop fucking about and you open the safe, there's a good girl.'

She had the feeling that to try to stall him any longer would result in something rather unpleasant, so she said, 'Okay, yes I do know it, but it is upstairs.' She was desperately hoping that this would assuage him.

'Let's go together, shall we?'

Mason turned to "Baseball cap" and said, 'Wait here, and for pity's sake, stop dripping that blood everywhere, you are making a mess.'

'S'not my fault, this is still bleedin'.'

'I've always said that you were a little bleeder,' said Mason with a hint of a smile that was more than slightly venomous.

'Ha bloody ha,' said "Baseball cap," I could bleed to death and you wouldn't care anyway.'

'How right you are, my little ray of sunshine.'

'Yeah, well, who would do your dirty work then, eh? It's a dead cert that you won't and if it weren't for me there would be a lot of people who would be after you. As it is, they've been taken care of so'as you can sleep easy like.'

'I suppose that as you so eloquently put that small piece of information, you are absolved from doing as you are told. Never forget my faithful servant, who actually pays you to enable your debauched lifestyle. Should that be removed, I do wonder if you could actually find gainful employment of any kind, or just perhaps you might find that the people you have 'convinced' in some way or other, would be rather eager to mete out a similar rendering to you.'

'Yeah, well, I'm still bleeding and I need to go to hospital don' I?'

'Possibly, but do remember just one small thing, we have been there quite recently and they will remember your ratty little face, so perhaps you might think again should the police be making simple enquiries.'

'Oh, well, yeah, maybe you're right.'

'I think you will find that I usually am, so just wait here and do what you can to stop yourself leaking all over the floor, there's a good chap.'

Turning to Genny, he said, 'My apologies for this little excuse for a sub-human, but he does have his uses and maybe I should tell you now that he has a particular bent towards hurting people; and when he is annoyed, he takes even greater pleasure in hurting them more.'

Genny knew that the well-dressed and suave mans' name was Mason, but he'd not referred to "Baseball cap" by any name so far, not that she wanted to know.

Once again this was said in a very smooth, gentle and controlled manner, which made her skin crawl as she realised more than ever that there was going to be no way out of this situation. Whilst the exchange between Mason and "Baseball cap" had been taking place, she had be furiously thinking of making a run for it. However, she had looked out of the smashed front door and she could see that there was a large SUV parked across the drive, effectively blocking her car. So that was out of the question and she was running out of options.

'She we go to the safe?'

She turned and walked up the stairs, repeatedly looking behind as she climbed up.

'Don't worry Genny, I'm right behind you.

Going into the master bedroom, Mason looked around him and taking in the decor and furniture, he said, 'I must say that whoever decorated this room has taste; it's quite attractive, was it you or Martin?'

'Me.'

'Then I must congratulate you on your expertise. Let's just hope that you are as good with figures when it comes to transferring a rather large sum of money to my account; which is something you are about to do very shortly Genny.'

Her mind in turmoil, she looked the very dark and foreboding framed print by Pierre Soulage covering the safe. Pulling this back from the wall exposed a touch-screen panel. She entered the code and there was an audible click from the safe and the door moved slightly open. Mason said very quietly, 'Thank you Genny, perhaps you could just stand back now.'

With that, Mason thrust his hand inside the safe and brought out the leather satchel containing the money from the recent French trip. Genny didn't know how much was in the bag as she hadn't touched it since pushing it in, but she had taken a rough guess for fourteen; but now that one man had disappeared she thought, thirteen times what she estimated they had paid for the trip; around £10,000 each. What she didn't know was that they'd paid £14,000 each, which made somewhere in the region of £180,000. She realised that even at £130,000, no wonder Mason wanted this, but he seemed to be saying that he wanted more; just how much more?

He was standing and looking around the room. Spotting a door to one side, he asked, 'what is through there?'

'Just a dressing room.'

'I think I'll just check, if you don't mind.'

Her mind was racing now. This was Martin's office and his computer was on the desk. Mason opened the door and looked inside. He looked back at Genny with a very hard stare. His soft manner had abruptly disappeared and he simply gave her a very cold, hard look. Then he said, 'The time for lies is up Genny. If you give me any more information which I find to be false, you will suffer; I hope you believe me.'

She really tried not to believe him, but as she was debating with herself as to whether he was bluffing or not, he called down to the floor below. 'Get up here, now.'

This time, there was nothing soft or gentle about his voice. Footsteps came running up the staircase, which was made of beautiful dark hardwood. Feet sounded on this and there was no doubt that "Baseball cap" was running quickly, as he had been told. This man obviously did what he was told even though he was treated by Mason as a half-wit. No doubt this was his "enforcer" much as Freddie Furkan had been. He appeared at the top of the stairs and Mason looked at him, saying, 'Hold on to her, and do NOT let her go. I think this silly girl might make some kind of break for freedom, before I have finished what I came for. That is not going to happen.'

With that, "Baseball cap" took hold of both of Genny's arms, pulling both of them and twisting them both into a "half-nelson" hold. This made her cry out in pain.

'Now then young lady, I see that Martin's computer, and I must assume that this is his computer, is switched on. Can I assume from this that you have been doing something on this machine just before we arrived?'

Answering his own question, he said, 'I think that is a given, isn't it?'

'So, let me suggest that you have been doing some financial work, would that be an accurate guess?'

Again, Genny said nothing.

'Right again, methinks; give the man a prize. Now, let me guess, would you have been transferring money from one account to another, or something of that nature?'

She simply gave a gentle nod and he gave a beaming smile, showing a beautiful set of white teeth, which in her eyes were as sinister as those of a shark.

'Okay, now we have the main thread, it think it time for you to give me the account details and all the bank details, so that I may place the transactions in the correct places, don't you?'

Everything was going wrong now and she had absolutely no idea as to how she was going to stop something more serious happening. Realising that they had not seen her at Goodyear's bedside and therefore not seen her leave, she said, hesitatingly, 'I can't give you any details because I couldn't get anything from Martin at the hospital when I saw him before. As you must know, he couldn't speak so he couldn't tell me anything about the accounts.'

Mason looked at her with a steady gaze, which seemed to her like a predator staring at its prey. 'I presume that we both know you have a flash drive containing all the details and I would presume that you have already used this. This indicates to me that you have managed to transfer large sums of money to a new account.'

Her silence was palpable which served to reinforce his presumption.

'Therefore, I would like you to give me this piece of hardware, so that I may make some alterations, do you understand me?'

'That won't be possible, because I have destroyed it,' she said with a slight hint of pleasure.

'Then, you will now go to the computer and do exactly as I tell you and we can leave you alone.'

She already had the feeling that he would say this and he was going to take everything away from her. He'd already taken the leather bag with the cash and now he wanted everything else.

'I can't do that,' she said, with a bravado which she did not feel.

'Genny, you can, and you will. All you have to do is to make transfers to accounts which I will provide the details of, and we can finish our business here.'

She had used her silence to good effect, saying 'I've only transferred a small amount as I need authorisation from Martin to change anything else.'

Mason took this and was quiet for a moment as he realised that this was in fact quite probable.

'If this is true, then we will go back to the hospital and get Martin to give me that authorisation. He can sign something can't he?'

'But he won't, he'll not give up his money easily.' She held on to the thought that Martin would be in no position to do anything now, but this did not stop what was about to happen.

She was still being held by "Baseball cap" although as she had not tried to move, the pain had subsided slightly.

'I think I have something which will make him change his mind.' He looked over to "Baseball cap" and said, 'find something to tie her to a chair and make it so that she cannot move, and you know how to tie her legs, don't you?'
"Baseball cap" looked back at Mason and leered. 'Yes boss, I understand all right; I know exactly what you want.'
Genny could not see "Baseball cap's" face, but his words chilled her.
He dragged her to the leather "Barcelona" designer armchair which had chrome steel legs and a reclined back.
'Sit there and don't move.'
She actually thought of trying to make a run for it, but as she looked at Mason, a small pistol had appeared in his hand.
'I really don't like using these things,' he said, but if I have to, if you try to move, I will simply shoot you in your kneecap; I think that will make things more difficult.'
This was said again in a voice which was not aggressive, not rough, but gentle and held appalling menace.
She sat still, mesmerized by the gun in his hand. It was not long before "Baseball cap" came back with some nylon cording which he had found in a utility room cupboard.
He tied her very securely round her shoulders and upper body to the back of the chair. Her arms were tied carefully but thoroughly to the steel arms on the side of the chair.
He then pulled out a knife whilst he threatened her; he roughly cut open her jeans, pulling the legs off. He then tied her legs to each of the steel chair legs. With horror she realised what the intention was, but did think that it might be somehow possible to move, should the occasion arise, although currently she had absolutely no idea how.
When she was safely secured, Mason put the gun away and said, 'Now I can go back to the hospital and convince Martin that he should give me the necessary authority.'
'He won't do it,' said Genny with more bravado than she felt.
Mason simply looked at her, said nothing, but pulled a Smartphone from his pocket, touched the screen and pointed it at her. He said, 'As you can see, Genny is in a very vulnerable position. I think you know that the little rat with the "Baseball cap" that you see standing behind her, is more than happy to do help me do something which will encourage her to comply with my requests, and that she is in a position which makes this eminently possible.'
He turned off the phone, and returned it to his pocket.
Genny now realised why her legs were tied and the thought revolted her.
'Right,' Mason said to "Baseball cap," 'I'm going back to the hospital. Make sure she doesn't try anything. You know what to do to stop her. Is your mobile phone working properly?'
'Yes boss.'
'Good. I'll call you with instructions.'
'Yes boss.'

CHAPTER 77

Mason drove back to the hospital, to find police cars outside. Maybe they are there for another reason, he thought. He walked in and climbed the stairs to the floor where Denitzi was kept.

There were a couple of people standing talking to a nurse and doctor. They looked very much like police to him. What do they want? He wondered.

As he approached the ward, the two people looked in his direction and broke off their conversation with the two medical staff, who turned away and began talking to each other quietly.

'Excuse me; are you here to see the patient who was in this room?'

'As a matter of fact, yes; is there a problem?'

'May we ask who you are?'

'I am just a friend of Mr Goodyear.'

'Then I'm sorry to tell you that Mr Goodyear has died of his injuries.'

'Oh dear, that is a pity, but I know that he was in a serious condition and it was to be expected.'

The two people were in fact, Alex and Anna, who had gone to the hospital in response to the news that Goodyear had been killed by "a person or persons unknown" at the moment and they were talking to the nursing staff who had been in contact with Goodyear up to the time he was found dead.

Anna was thinking hard and she realised that this man who had come to "visit" Goodyear must have been well known to him and therefore needed some careful checking.

'Can I ask your name please?' she said.

Mason then responded with his most pleasant and cultured voice, 'Do you know, I don't think that is any concern of yours. May I ask you the same question, as at the moment I have no idea who you are?'

Holding out her warrant card; 'I am DS Jenkins of Bournemouth Police and this is DCI Vail. We are making enquiries into his death.'

'But surely, he died of his injuries as you have just told me? As you are making enquiries, this tells me that the cause of his death is not quite clear, would that be a fair assumption?'

'I cannot discuss this with you sir, if you'll excuse us,' said Alex.

'Of course,' said Mason in his best suave manner, turning away and walking back down the corridor to his car.

Now he was cursing to himself. Swiftly realising that if Goodyear had been deliberately killed, rather than just dying, as was the case made obvious by the police presence, then who could have done this? I should have asked if he'd had any other visitors, but I guess that there would be only one, and he knew who that was.

He was really mad now that it was impossible to get the authorisation necessary and he was rapidly losing his usual coolness. As he approached his car, he called "Baseball cap" on the phone.

'Hello,' said "Baseball cap," 'who's this?'

'Who do you think it is, you stupid pillock? Somebody's only gone and topped Goodyear and fucked my chances of getting my hands on the funds.' All trace of his affected upper class accent had disappeared. 'I want you to give that bird a good slapping but leave her ready for when I get back. I'm going to give her something she won't forget.'

"Baseball cap" knew exactly what Mason had in his mind for Genny.

Following the departure of the man who didn't or wouldn't give his name, Alex asked Anna to get the CCTV footage of the relevant times that day, so that they could see who else had visited Goodyear.

Resuming the conversation with the two medics, Alex asked if either of them had seen anyone that day, prior to finding Goodyear following his demise.

The nurse answered the question. 'I saw Mr Goodyear's girlfriend; well I think it was his girlfriend, perhaps it could have been his wife, but she came in earlier and I spoke with her as I was checking on Mr Goodyear.'

'And was he in good condition when you checked?'

'As well as someone in his condition could be expected, yes.'

'And then what did you do?' asked Anna.

'I entered the appropriate notes on his chart and then asked the woman not to be too long with him.'

'Did you see her leave?'

'Yes, I think I saw her come out of the room very soon after I'd been there; she seemed quite upset and probably affected by seeing someone who was close, in that condition.'

'And did anyone else visit him.'

'Yes, there were two men who came almost as soon as she had gone.'

'And had you seen these men before?'

'No, never.'

Could you describe them for me?'

One was quite short and stocky and wore a "Baseball cap" and the other was much taller and was very well dressed in a suit. He had very fair hair and wore a small goatee beard.'

This caused Anna to look sharply at Alex. 'We've just seen him!'

'Did you speak to him?'

'No, I only saw them as they left the room.'

'Did you have alarms to alert you?'

'No, I just found him dead. '

'When was this?'

'Very soon after the two men had left actually.'

Anna then asked, 'How did Mr Goodyear actually die, can you be specific?'

The doctor took over to answer this question. 'He had breathing assistance as well as morphine drip to alleviate some of the pain. At some point, the morphine drip was disconnected at a point below the level of the bed and this was apparently unnoticed until after his death. This would not have caused the actual death but the removal of the electrical plug to the breathing unit effectively cancelled everything, including the operation of the unit and the monitor.'

'So what set off the alarms then?'

'There were no alarms as the electrical plugs had been removed.'

'His heart rate rose rapidly, due to the failure of the morphine supply. As this rises beyond an acceptable level, an alarm should sound. 'Unfortunately they didn't and by the time we attended him, his heart just couldn't take the strain.'

Anna then asked if there was any CCTV coverage of the ward.

'Not of the ward but all the corridors are covered.'

Alex looked to Anna and had the visual agreement. 'Could we have copies of the footage covering the visit by both the woman and the two men please, as soon as possible?'

The doctor said, 'of course, I'll get this organised.'

'Thank you, I think that's all for the time being. We'll be back in touch later.'

Alex and Anna walked quickly back to their car. 'Are you thinking what I'm thinking Alex?' she asked.

'If you're thinking that one of these two men actually pulled his plugs, then yes, that's exactly what I'm thinking, and if that's the one we've just seen then we know where he will be going don't we?'

'And if they know; sorry, knew Goodyear, then they'll probably know where he lived and let's guess where Dobbs has gone.'

Alex called the office and updated them on the situation on their way back to the car.

'Should we get some bodies there to assist, guv?' asked Alice.

'I think, under the circumstances that might be a very good idea Alice. Can you call Poole and ask for some very urgent armed backup. We know that it's a strong possibility that there could be some trouble at Goodyear's address and it won't hurt to have some muscle up there in case things go belly up. We'll be there in about six minutes and please tell them to make a silent approach.'

'Will do guv, leave it to me.'

'Thanks Alice, but make it very quick and very urgent please.'

They got to the unmarked police car and Anna noticed a yellow packet tucked under the windscreen wiper. 'I don't believe this,' she said passing it to Alex. 'A bloody parking fine; we've only been here a few minutes and they do this. And it's an £80 fine!

'Well, they can stuff that,' said Alex. Just let them try to make that stick as we're on legitimate police business.'

'They seem to get away with sheer robbery these days, that's what we get for privatisation of the NHS services; I mean charging for people who are probably visiting relatives and friends who are in hospital and would rather not be there, and then they get a bloody fine.'

'Calm down Anna, they know the rules when they park here.'

'That's not the point though, is it, I mean it's just profiteering, as though the NHS doesn't get absolute shed loads of money from the government and so much of it is squandered on overpaid managers and people who actually do nothing to help the people who have to be there, and yet the nurses get crap wages and have to work their arses off.'

'Take it easy Anna, you'll blow a fuse.'

'Well, it's just not right that these bloated fat-cats get so much and make everyone else do the work.'

'I do support your thinking on this, but we have our work to do, so let's go!'

Anna was driving and she exited the car park rather faster than she should have, putting the "blues and two" on as she did so.

She drove very quickly and made their way from Poole Hospital, up through Broadstone.

The trip from the hospital to Corfe Mullen did not take long.

'We're almost there, so I think we'll make a silent approach,' said Alex as he reached down to switch off the sirens.

At "Waypoint" the scenario had been unfolding. Mason had returned and "Baseball cap" had done what he had been instructed and given Genny a generous amount of slapping and pummelling. She had cried and screamed as she had been hit repeatedly.

'What are you doing to me, why are you treating me like this?' she had pleaded.

'Because Mr Mason, as you know, likes things done his way and I'm just doing what I'm told. Believe me, I know what he can do and he might seem very gentle to you, but he can be extremely brutal when he thinks he has good reason.

'What does he want from me, I can't help him.'

'He obviously thinks you can, and I'm sure that he'll do whatever it takes to give him something which he likes; and I don't just mean money.'

This made Genny squirm inside.

As she had said this, Mason had returned and came running up the stairs. 'Right, now let's make this little bitch do what I want.'

He then looked at her with a withering gaze which had absolute menace. He took off his jacket and slowly removed his tie. Carefully hanging these over the back of another armchair, he turned to "Baseball cap" and said, 'When I've finished, you can take over if she hasn't acceded to my wishes.' At this "Baseball cap" gave an evil grin of expectation.

'Now let's just see what she will agree too.' He then began to unbuckle his belt and it was at this point that Genny realised the full reason why she had been tied to the chair in the way she had. Mason gestured toward "Baseball cap" and pointed to her legs. He knew what to do and was 'Before that, do the necessary and push her forward, while I get myself in the mood?'

"Baseball cap" then went round to stand in front of Genny, kneeling down and reaching behind her knees pulled her legs forward, making her slope more than before. He then roughly tore her panties off her body, violently, literally ripping them off.

With her vagina exposed now, she felt so desperately vulnerable and dreaded what was about to happen.

"Baseball cap" was literally salivating as he thought what he might do after Mason had finished. He had taken out his mobile phone and was videoing the scene in front of him.

Genny was thinking that all the gentle suavity that had seemed so palpably dangerous had now been proven to be the case and now the true malevolency was becoming clear.

Mason had now stripped after carefully putting his clothes over the chair and was standing naked in front of her, gently massaging his penis which was becoming erect. He only wore a smile which was more of a sneer. 'Now, Genny, you are going to agree to make those transfers to my account, aren't you?'

'I can't,' she said, 'I've told you I destroyed the flash drive.'

'You may have destroyed that, but you have transferred all his assets I would think. Am I right?'

She said nothing, not knowing how to extricate herself, because he seemed to know exactly what she'd done. Her silence, told him everything he wanted to know.

'You see, I am way ahead of you my dear, and before we go back to the computer for you to carry out my instructions, I will do to you,' and he said this slowly, 'what I am sure you have just done to Martin.'

With what was now a very erect penis, he moved toward her. She was sitting in the designer chair at an angle now which made her pubis very accessible to him. In any other scenario, she might have found this type of sex to be acceptable, but to be raped against her will, by a man she did not know and the thought of the other one doing the same thing, without any finesse whatever, made her feel repulsion, added to which she had the definite feeling that what he was about to do, would not be gentle.

He approached her and holding his erect penis in one hand, and the pistol in the other, he approached her.

'Now just let me do something which I will enjoy enormously, but which I, for some reason, doubt you will.'

He held his penis and with his other hand gently stroked the muzzle of the pistol down the lips of her vagina. It made him feel good but completely reviled her. She gave a shudder and tried to writhe out of the way, to no avail.

His face changed and his smile became a snarl as he seemed about to force the gun into her.

"Baseball cap" was watching with a leering smile and he knew just how vicious his boss would be, knowing that he would show no mercy and would be very violent.

Mason looked over to "Baseball cap" and licked his lips in a vicious parody.

This caused him to shout, 'Go on boss, give it to her.'

There was a noise from downstairs, which made "Baseball cap" look up but it appeared not to have alerted Mason, who was about to thrust the pistol and then himself into her.

'What was that?' said "Baseball cap."

'Shut up, you little bastard, don't interrupt me.'

'There was a noise boss, downstairs.'

'I said, don't fucking interrupt me.'

***

The police had arrived, and in force. Anna and Alex had arrived literally seconds before the back-up team from Poole Police Station pulled up in their van. Seeing the broken glass in the front door, they instantly realised that something was in progress. They quietly stepped through the broken door, entered the building and quickly looked around the open plan rooms. Seeing nothing and no-one, they both looked up the large open staircase. Nodding to each other, Alex looked back at the five armed police who had entered just behind them. They very swiftly checked the downstairs rooms and then, signalling their silence and gesturing for them to follow him, Alex and Anna mounted the stairs as quietly as they could.

The scene which greeted them caused Anna to draw a very quick breath and she had to stop herself from making an exclamation.

"Baseball cap," standing behind Genny, saw the two figures appear at the top of the stairs and just looked dumbstruck for a moment. He tried to say something, but for some reason, nothing came out, save for a groan. This Mason took for a sound of pleasure from "Baseball cap," and simply said, 'I told you to be quiet,' you little shit.

But then; 'BOSS, POLICE!' he shouted.

Now this did cause Mason to take notice and he stopped his intended thrust just at the point of entering Genny. Turning round to look, it has to be said that his erect penis returned to flaccidity rather quickly. He saw both Alex and Anna, together with five police with guns held at the ready, looking at his nakedness. There were a number of grins under the helmets of the armed squad and Anna also had the impossible task of keeping her face straight.

Alex then said, with a very officially straight face, 'We would ask you to accompany us to the station at Bournemouth, where we will take down a statement from you; although there appears to be nothing else to be taken down.'

This brought a muted cheer and guffaws from almost everybody and even Alex broke into a smile, except maybe "Baseball cap."

Anna turned to Alex and said, 'Alex, I am so glad that we arrived just in time to save what I suspect could have been a very nasty and vicious rape.'

'Me too Anna; me too.'

CHAPTER 78 Epilogue.

Gerald Mason, since the police had now ascertained his name, was summarily taken to the police car, simply covered with a blanket, although protesting loudly with his usually "polished" accent strangely absent. "Baseball cap" was also bundled into the car, giving vent to his anger and protesting his innocence all the time, to the point where the police driver shouted over his shoulder, 'Will you shut the fuck up!?' This did not work that well, but he was a little less vociferous while they drove back to Bournemouth Police Station, for them to be separately interviewed.

As the scene which had presented itself to Anna and Alex as they entered the upstairs room in the house in Corfe Mullen, one of the AR team had a body camera as standard procedure and the whole scene was captured in clear detail. This made the prosecution of his intended rape far easier. "Baseball cap," was also finally named as one Albert Noggins; faced a lesser charge of aiding and abetting attempted rape, except that he was also accused of being an accessory to murder. This he vehemently denied although how Dobbs came to be tied to the chair in the way she was, he found exceedingly hard to wriggle out of, saying that Mason had tied her, but no-one in the jury believed that.

The ongoing enquiries during the time that he and Noggins were in custody quickly revealed that Mason was deeply involved with the onward transportation of the illegal immigrants whom Goodyear or Denitzi as he was correctly referred to in court, had brought over from France in his boat. Mason had been responsible for the arrangements of their onward travel and their insertion into the fabric of the United Kingdom. He had also somehow arranged for the issuance of Social Security numbers for them. This allowed their entry to the Social system and gave them access to funds and accommodation, and allowed them to enter the country with no records, save that he also arranged for fake passports to be made. With the co-operation of Europol, this was a whole new area for the police to investigate and they were able to find some useful contacts for deeper checking. Further enquiries were ongoing as his financial situation was throwing up doubts and intrigue faster and faster.

When Genny Dobbs was questioned over the series of events on the day that Goodyear was found dead in his ward, she said repeatedly that he was in a reasonably good condition when she visited him and when she left, he was no more than agitated at not being able to say anything because of his facial disfiguration due to the burning. This was confirmed by the nurse who had taken the vital signs. When asked if she had seen the two visiting men, she had answered that she had not seen them at all; when in fact she'd seen them whilst hiding inside the room and seeing them return to the bedside. She had, as well as disconnecting his morphine supply tube, removed the electrical plug supplying power to the breathing support and alarm systems, and slipped out of the room. Although this had no immediate effect on him, the heart rate alarm would alert the nursing staff very quickly. However, this meant that when Mason had coerced Goodyear into writing the "GD" and "FL desk" on a pad, which subsequently he'd had taken with him, they were unaware that he was about to die very shortly. Dobbs had watched their final exit from the hospital from her concealed position.

In court, under examination, she said that she'd not seen the men arrive. Examination of the CCTV showed that she had arrived before them and actually left after them. However, as the nurse had given evidence that Goodyear had been checked and his vital signs entered whilst Dobbs was still there, this caused much confusion; especially as she had reiterated that Goodyear was fine when she left. She claimed that it must have been the two unknown men who had killed Goodyear. When asked why she had apparently left after the two visitors had gone, and not before them, she said that after going into the toilet just along the corridor from the room in which Goodyear had been, she must have come out after the two men had left.
The cameras which would have shown this happening were actually facing the opposite way, only showing the two men leaving. It also showed Mason coming back shortly after and going back into the private room, then exiting a few minutes later. It then showed Genny walking along the corridor toward the exit after Mason had gone, without re-entering the room.

The jury decided at trial, that Mason was the one who had removed the life support from Goodyear and the morphine drip, the two things combining which led to his death. They were both convicted of murder and accessory to such, after much shouting from "Baseball Cap" that he was innocent. Mason also vainly attempted to protest his innocence, but the evidence provided had convinced the jury otherwise.

However stringently denying this, Mason was convicted of attempted rape and the murder of Goodyear with Nobbins as an accessory. The attempted rape was further proven by the short video clip found on his mobile phone shortly after his arrest.

Genny was bailed to appear at a further hearing after the Police had investigated further into her financial affairs. Due to the fact that she had opened new accounts in a different name and therefore her newly acquired extreme wealth was not evident, she appeared to be simply a girlfriend of Denitzi, not married to him or connected in any other way.

Her employment at Cobbs Quay Marina was completely legitimate and she had been working there for a number of years, subsequently meeting Denitzi and becoming embroiled in his activities. However, when this took place, she had no idea of his real activities. This was to come later and thanks to him giving her many gifts and such things, she had been taken in, and she was in thrall to him, even though she had good reason to be afraid of him. It wasn't until later in their relationship that she found out just what he really was like and how brutal he could be.

Back at the headquarters of Bournemouth Police, Alex and Anna were in a final meeting together with their team. Together with Alice and Tom were the other various support members of their group.

Alex said, 'I have to say that although we have a conclusion to this complicated case, the real murderer has escaped justice in the usual sense, except that he died in an unusual way. He can never be held to account for the lives he took. Dimitriou paid the ultimate penalty as well, so again we had no one to be apprehended. It seems that no-one else was indicated in this extended fiasco.'

'Why do you say it was a fiasco guv?' asked Alice.

'Because we should have been able to arrest them far earlier and we once again have been let down by various occurrences where we could and should have had more manpower.'

'Another case of not enough bodies then,' suggested Tom, 'but it wasn't our fault that the AR boys lost the plot and ploughed into that Boston Whaler near "Othniel," was it.'

'No Tom, but we should offer our thanks for your efforts over there; you must have been bored to a standstill, waiting all that time.'

'I don't know about standstill guv, I couldn't move much anyway, could I?'

'Not after your mugging by who we know was Goodyear.'

'Do you know what pisses me off most guv?'

'Go on then, Tom.'

'Well, the fact that we know Genny Dobbs was the one who gave Goodyear all the details and she had me in a honey trap, but now she's got away almost scot free.'

'Not yet Tom,' said Anna, don't forget she has to appear before the magistrates again once we've finished our examination of her finances.'

Genny, as we now know, had transferred most if not all of Goodyear's money to new and re-named accounts. Only she knew the details and whereabouts of this money as Mason and Noggins were safely behind bars.

Also unknown to the police was the fact that some time previously, Goodyear had arranged with Mason to provide both himself and Genny Dobbs with new passports. His had been burned in the boat fire, but Genny's had been safely kept in a safety deposit box. She now made her moves which been thought out during her time on remand.

People have always underestimated me, she thought. Now is the time to get everything right. Her new but fake passport was in the name of GENEVIEVE DUBOIS. With many of her clothes and possessions bearing the initials GD, this was to save a good deal of questions. She was to be apparently of French origin, hence the name of Dubois.

She very quickly made reservations for flights under her new name and in person at a travel agents' where she was not known.

'Do you think we should keep Dobbs under surveillance guv?' asked Anna.
'That might be an idea, certainly. Do we have enough staff to keep a 24/7 watch on her?'
'I don't think we can do that, but we can certainly try to arrange some sort of coverage, surely?'
'I'll look into some full-time coverage and get back to you Anna. If it is okay, then perhaps you can see to it they don't fuck things up again?'
'Of course, I'll see to that side of things once you have clearance. I guess you'll have to use Poole station to provide the manpower.'
'Very unfortunately, yes. They can keep tabs on her tonight and I think that tomorrow, we can just ask her very nicely to accompany one of our friendly DC's back here for some more interviews. That will save us from having to take even more risks.
'Okay guv, whatever.'
She arranged the coverage with the Poole Police station for overnight surveillance.

She was about to leave his office, when he said quietly, 'before you go Anna, could you just close the door; I need a word?'
Closing the door, she had an idea that what was about to happen, and it was not going to be particularly pleasant.
'Anna, I've been thinking about what you said the other day, about not wanting to settle down. I have to accept that things are very difficult for us being together at work but as I said before, I will not change my mind and just have to accept that you will find other men. All I can hope for is that you come to realise that I am the one for you; I'll always be here Anna – I love you.'

She felt tears welling up in her eyes and she just looked at him and said 'Alex…' but the following words stuck in her throat. She could say nothing but gave a very small smile, turned, opened the door and went out, closing it gently behind her. Nothing more to be said. She had made up her mind to make some time to see Fuller Masterson, but not before she had done a little "investigating."

*

Genny Dobbs, now to be known as "Genevieve Dubois" together with all her new financial details and minimal luggage, was not at home when a DC from Poole Police arrived to take her to Bournemouth Police station for further interviews.

When Alex asked DCI Trevor Johnson why she had not been seen leaving the house, as she was due to be under surveillance, he received the answer that 'There was not enough manpower keep her watched 24/7. She was watched until midnight.'

Alex blew his top. 'For fuck's sake! You've done it again; let us down by not doing what we asked. This time I'm going to report you to DCS James Gordon. So you don't know where she is then?'
'Nope, she's probably legged it by now.' This was said in a very "unconcerned" way, which further angered Alex.
He did indeed send a very strongly-worded report to DCS James Gordon, leaving nothing out. This did go some way to appeasing Gordon although Alex still got a severe dressing-down, no matter how much he pushed the points about lack of staff and equipment.

She had certainly "legged" it - looking out of the aircraft window, tightly clutching her handbag containing a new flash drive with all the relevant information, she was a very, very wealthy young lady, about to start a new life.

Genny with a 'G' had disappeared and holding her passport in the name of Genevieve Dubois, she was going to have a life-changing new beginning as a new person, in a new place where no-knew her or her past – she hoped.

Also perhaps taking a new direction, Anna was determined to spend some time with Fuller Masterson.
 Who knows where that might take her.

END.

Printed in Great Britain
by Amazon